HIS CURVY STRANGER

A SMALL TOWN CURVY GIRL ROMANCE

BOOK BOYFRIENDS WANTED
BOOK 14

MARY E THOMPSON

His Curvy Stranger

Book Boyfriends Wanted, book 14

Copyright © 2023 Mary E Thompson

Cover Copyright © 2022 Mary E Thompson

Cover Photo from depositphotos, Copyright © -Robbie-

Cover background from depositphotos, Copyright © tomert (lights) and Milanares (blue)

Cover watercolor stripe from depositphotos, Copyright © ronedale

Published by BluEyed Press, All Rights Reserved

Ebook ISBN: 978-1-953879-59-2

Print ISBN: 978-1-953879-60-8

Audiobook ISBN: 978-1-953879-61-5

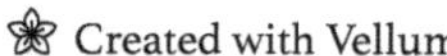 Created with Vellum

BOOK BOYFRIENDS WANTED

There's someone new in town, and MacKellar Cove has had a little trouble welcoming her in. But that's okay. Small town living is all about nosy neighbors, new friends, and falling in love with your new home. And maybe a new man, too.

Thanks for visiting! Grab a drink, a slice of cake, and get to know your next book boyfriend and book bestie! Never miss a thing when you sign up for Mary's newsletter.

Romancing the Curves comes with subscriber exclusive freebies, sneak peeks, and a first look at everything Mary has to offer. Be the first to know about new releases and sales and all the curves ahead!

SUBSCRIBE NOW AT MARYETHOMPSON.COM

Happy reading!

For the ones who drew the short straw... That you know someone is out there cheering for you to show everyone exactly how badly they underestimated you.

1

HALEY

I waved to my last client of the day and pocketed the extra large tip she gave me. It was nice to feel appreciated. Especially by a woman who was not all that friendly to me when I moved to town nine months ago.

Small-town living was supposed to be fun and easy with people who looked out for each other and welcomed you in. Unless you were the other woman in a marriage that blew up on your arrival.

Some people were willing to listen to my side of things. Others... not so much.

"Where's Debby?" a voice said from behind me.

I hadn't even heard the door open. I spun, the broom in my hand like a weapon to fend off the woman standing just inside the salon. Her pursed lips and seventies feathered hairstyle were bad enough, but the way she clutched her purse like she expected me to steal it and the daggers that shot from her eyes when she cast her glance through me made my spine stiffen and my eyes water.

Not that I'd let her see that.

"Debby's already gone for the day. She must not have

realized you had an appointment," I said, pouring on the sweetness and adding a forced smile that probably showed too much teeth and definitely hurt my jaw.

Madeline huffed like it was a personal aggression that Debby wasn't there. "I don't have an appointment, but I have an event tonight. I thought she'd be here. I've been a customer most of my life, and if I can't count on her to be available when I need her, why am I so loyal?"

I pressed my lips together before a nasty retort spilled out. Loyalty didn't mean complete control of another person's schedule, but clearly Madeline didn't agree with that. "I would be happy to help you."

The sneer started with her back going ramrod straight. She turned to face me, meeting my gaze for the first time since she walked in. Her brown eyes widened for half a second before they narrowed and assessed me.

My jeans were comfortable and fashionable, and my top hugged my ample curves in a way I thought was flattering when I chose it. My hair was tied up in a ponytail that hung between my shoulder blades, out of my way and off my neck for long days on my feet in a shop that was far too warm for me and all my curves.

I thought I looked good when I walked out the door that morning. But the disdainful, dismissive look in Madeline's eyes said I was frumpy at best and disgusting to a woman like her.

Feathered hair aside, of course.

"No. I'd rather not have you get your hands on me. Might infect my marriage like you did poor Valentina's."

And there it was. The truth of my life since relocating to MacKellar Cove. I was a homewrecker. And Madeline was one of the many who had zero intention of every letting me forget it.

The desire to defend my actions burned inside me, but she was a client. My boss's client. It didn't matter that there wasn't another salon around for thirty miles, Madeline was the type of person who would poison the town, and Debby, against me and make my life an even worse living hell.

"I'd be happy to schedule an appointment for you with Debby," I said, shoving down the pain and reaching deep for kindness.

"I already have an appointment scheduled for next week." Madeline huffed her way to the door and shoved it wide open, not bothering with another word. She slid her sunglasses into place and hiked her handbag up onto her shoulder, then held her head up high and sauntered off.

I was not going to cry.

I was not going to cry.

I took a deep breath and let it out slowly, walking to the door and flipping the lock before anyone else came in.

Dammit.

Every time Madeline came in, she made comments about me. Quietly, and only to Debby, but she still made them. I wasn't sure if she thought she was quiet enough that I couldn't hear her or if she knew I could, but it never mattered. I knew what she thought of me, and I knew my boss did little to defend me. Even though Debby heard the whole story.

I needed to get out of my head and stop worrying about what these people thought of me. I had met some pretty great people since I moved to MacKellar Cove, including Valentina. I wasn't sure I'd say we were friends, but we didn't hate each other. I carried a truckload of guilt for sleeping with her husband, but even though I never knew he was married. I never even suspected he was.

Which only added more guilt and shame, but it was the truth.

A ding brought my attention to my phone instead of the spiral I was sliding down like a kid on a playground. I shook my head and half expected a social media notification or something equally mundane, but this made me smile.

HANDYNOTHANDSY

I can't wait to see your smile in person. Are we still on for tomorrow night?

My heart fluttered. Damn. Actually fluttered. It had been almost three months since we started chatting. At first, I was not willing to talk to another man. Being the other woman was painful. Not just finding out I was his side-piece, but ending a relationship I thought was going somewhere. I uprooted my entire existence. I moved to a new town. I changed jobs and left behind friends and planned a future with a man who had no intention of being with me long term.

And I had to choke down all that pain because I wasn't his wife. I was the woman he cheated with. She'd been married to him for decades, so her pain and heartbreak took priority over mine.

I didn't resent her for it. I resented him. He was the one who screwed us both, and screwed us both over. He was the one to blame for everything, even though I shouldered most of the blame. He skipped town as soon as I showed up. Never reached out. Never spoke to me again. Divorced Valentina and pretended I didn't exist.

Not that I wanted contact with him. Nope. Cheating was a clean, sharp line for me. A line he made me cross. I hated him for it, almost as much as I hated myself.

Trying again was hard. I didn't trust myself anymore. I

didn't trust men, either, but before Dawson the cheater, I trusted myself. I thought I had good instincts about people. After, I knew that wasn't the case.

Which was why it took me so long to agree to meet HandyNotHandsy. His name made me laugh, and the understanding that he respected women made me think maybe he could be trusted. Maybe not. Maybe it was a ploy. But dammit, I wanted him to be a good guy.

SINGLEMENWANTED

Looking forward to tomorrow.

I debated saying more, but I hit send and closed the app. Getting to know the details about another person happened over time. Warning him no one in town liked me would only put the brakes on whatever things could be before they even got started.

It was time to move on. To let go of my mistake and forgive myself.

Or at least to try.

I finished cleaning the salon and went out the back door. Light snow was drifting to the ground, accumulating in small mounds a few inches deep. I was grateful I'd driven that morning. February usually meant lots of snow, but the last few days had been surprisingly mild. I only lived a few minutes from the salon, but walking home in a foot of snow that fell during my workday was not fun.

Ask me how I knew.

I grabbed my handbag from the seat beside me and headed inside, ready for my sweats and a large glass of wine. I yanked open the heavy door to my building and stepped inside just as a gust of wind caught the door and flung it open. I grabbed it, tugging against the wind to close the door, sighing when it slammed shut.

"Rough out there?"

I spun and found my first friend in town. Sofia Frank was the maintenance manager for the building I lived in. She was sweet and welcoming and had become a good friend since I got to MacKellar Cove.

"All of a sudden, it seems to be."

"Yay for me," Sofia said, changing places with me in the hall as she walked toward the door I just fought to get inside. "I have to grab a flapper for the toilet in four-b, but do you want to grab dinner tonight?"

I adored Sofia, but there were days when I really wanted to be alone. I'd never known another person to understand that the way she did, which only made us better friends. "I think I need a night alone. Madeline came in right as I was about to close looking for Debby."

"Who was already gone since it's Thursday and Debby leaves early on Thursdays."

"Yep, but Madeline didn't care. I offered to help, but—"

"She made you feel like crap," Sofia finished for me.

I sighed and nodded. Sofia had lived in MacKellar Cove long enough to understand the inner-workings of the town. She helped me navigate it all, including warning me about some of the women I'd meet working at the salon.

When I signed my contract with Debby to rent the chair for a year, it came with a client list from the previous stylist. Theresa retired a few months before I arrived, and her former clients were being mostly handled by the three part-time stylists at Teased by Debby. A few of them had been absorbed onto Debby and Chelsea's, the other full-time stylist, client list, but most were squeezed in when they could get appointments. When I started, those clients were directed toward me.

Not all of them were thrilled with the option. Sofia

helped me to ease the tensions with them and make sure they knew I wasn't in town to steal everyone's husband. Or anyone's.

"I'm sorry, Haley. Shit. I thought this would all be over by now."

I shook my head. "It'll never be over for some people. But there's nothing I can do about that. I'm just going to enjoy a very large glass of wine and watch a movie that makes me believe love exists before my date tomorrow night."

"Date? What? You didn't tell me that!" Her grin was as big as mine.

"I'm trying not to get my hopes up, but we've been talking for a while. He seems nice."

"Okay, then lunch Saturday? You can tell me all about your date."

I nodded. "Sounds good. It's my one Saturday off this month."

"I'm on call, but I'm always on call. I—" Her phone vibrated and sang, drawing her attention. "Hang on. I need to answer this." She tapped the screen to answer the call. "This is Sofia."

I heard the frantic voice from where I stood. The person on the other end of the line definitely needed help, and needed it now.

"I'll be right there," Sofia said. "Give me ten minutes, maybe less."

More frantic shouting had Sofia checking her watch and shaking her head. "I understand. But if you've turned off the water, it'll be okay. I am not ignoring what you need, but I'm—"

She closed her eyes as the shouting ramped up.

I tapped Sofia's shoulder. She lifted her gaze to me and

raised her eyebrows. "I can pick up what you need from the hardware store if it'll help."

She tilted her head like she thought I was joking. She pulled the phone away from her ear and tapped the mute button before asking, "Are you sure?"

I nodded. "Just text me what you need. Whatever that is sounds urgent."

She groaned. "Mrs. Watson's dishwasher leaked all over her kitchen. And the cycle never finished, so it's still full of dirty water and dishes."

I wrinkled my nose. "That sounds like a mess."

"Yeah, it is." She held up a finger and tapped to unmute the phone. "I'll be right there, Mrs. Watson. I'm heading your way right now."

Whatever the reply was didn't reach my ears, but Sofia hung up.

"Are you sure you don't mind? The store is closing in ten minutes. I only need the flapper, but the toilet in four-b has been leaking for a week, so I promised Mr. Maxwell I'd fix it first thing in the morning."

"I got it. Not a problem. I'll leave the bag on your door so you have it for the morning."

Sofia blew me a kiss and hurried toward the stairs. "Thank you. I owe you. Lunch Saturday is on me."

"You don't have to do that."

She shook her head. "And you don't have to help me out, but you are. Thank you, Haley. So much. I'll see you Saturday. I hope your night gets better."

"Thank, Sofia. You, too!"

Her mirthless laughter followed her up the stairs.

I'd never been to Al's Hardware before, but I knew where it was. I'd driven by it a few times, but living in an apartment and having zero maintenance skills meant I didn't do anything even remotely requiring a trip to a hardware store.

I parked on the street out front and hurried to the door, getting there just as the guy inside was getting ready to flip the open sign to closed.

"Wait, please. I only need one thing. I promise I'll be quick. I know exactly where to go."

The guy raised one dirty blond eyebrow and gave me a look that said he definitely did not believe me.

"Okay, fine. I have no idea where to go. But I really do need only one thing."

"Is this one of those I only need one thing, but it's really a collection of things that's going to mean I'm open an hour later than I planned?"

The smile he gave me softened the words, even though the words were delivered in a teasing tone. A deep, rich, smooth, teasing tone that had all my long-neglected parts quivering.

Going without sex for months was definitely not good for me.

"Well, I'm happy to take my time if you're looking for an excuse to keep me here that long."

He chuckled, his hand coming up to rub his beard. The scratchy sound vibrated along my nerves and sent more shivers through me.

I hadn't been so drawn to a man since the day I met Dawson. I was a sucker for a man who was funny and sweet with a side of sexy thrown in. Dawson capitalized on the sweet when he changed my flat tire, then added sexy with his bulging muscles and asking me out for a drink.

This guy was funny. Charming and sexy and so very tempting.

"I think I'd be a fool if I passed up a chance to spend

more time with a beautiful woman. Especially one who knows how to talk her way into the store as I'm about to close up for the night." He stepped back to let me into the store, the door closing softly behind us.

I grinned, looking up at him from under my lashes in a way I knew was tempting and sexy. "I wonder what else I could talk you into."

"What exactly did you have in mind?"

I shrugged. No man had hit on me since I moved to town. Sure, the men I knew were either clients, married to clients, or in committed relationships with the women I'd started to call my friends, but still. This man in front of me was like water in a desert. He probably wasn't real, but I was willing to use my last bit of energy to throw myself his way.

"One night," I said, willing myself to hold on to the bold-ness I felt slipping through my fingers like sand. "No names. No future plans. Just one night."

He crossed his thick arms and leaned back against the counter, eyeing me. His gaze trailed down my body, snag-ging and skipping before returning to meet mine.

He arched an eyebrow. "One night?"

I nodded.

"Why no names?"

"We don't know each other. We clearly don't travel in the same circles. I'm not looking for anything serious."

"Why don't we know each other?"

I shrugged. "Does it matter?"

"Are you involved with someone? Married or engaged?" His gaze went to my bare left hand.

"No. I've never been either, and I don't have a boyfriend or girlfriend. You?"

"Same."

"So?"

He studied me for another long moment. "Any other conditions?"

I thought about his question, then nodded. "Two. One, you sell me a flapper for a toilet, whatever that is."

He chuckled. "I can do that. And the second?"

"We go to your place. I'll be gone by morning."

He eased away from the counter and uncrossed his arms. He extended one hand to me, waiting until I slid my hand against his before he said, "Deal."

2

KNOX

I WATCHED HER OUT OF THE CORNER OF MY EYE WHILE WE walked the aisles of the store. She looked vaguely familiar, but I knew for a fact she'd never been into Al's Hardware before. She did not look like the type of woman who would be getting her hands dirty, and I definitely would have remembered her if she'd ever set foot in my store.

I stopped in front of the toilet flappers, wondering if she was going to actually buy one or not. Of all the things to need, this had to be the least sexy. A woman in a tool belt? Hell yes. A woman who knew how to use those tools? Oh yeah. But fixing a toilet was the least desirable task for most homeowners and maintenance workers.

"Is there a difference between them?" she asked.

She was actually studying them. Guess she was there to buy one.

"No. It's a pretty standard part. I'd go with this one just because it's universal, unless you have a specific brand you need."

She shook her head, that long ponytail curling over one shoulder with the move. I couldn't wait to wrap my hand around it and find out if it was as soft and silky as it looked. "I don't think so. This should be fine."

There was something she wasn't saying. Something that made me think she wasn't shopping for herself. I was probably playing with fire by asking, but I had to know... "Are you sure you're single?"

She blanched, fumbling the flapper and nearly dropping it. She clutched it to her chest and leveled me with a glare. "I'm pretty sure I would know if I were involved with someone."

"You don't seem to know what you're buying. If you were here to get this for yourself, you probably wouldn't be unsure about it."

She shook her head. "I'm helping out a friend. She couldn't get here before you closed, and I said I'd run over."

I nodded. That made more sense. "Got it."

"I don't cheat." The vitriol in her voice told me there was more to the story than she was letting on. But she said no names, and no tomorrow, so I didn't have the right to push for more. As long as I wasn't going to get a jealous significant other banging on my door.

"Good."

I gave her a bag for the flapper and waved off her offer to pay. She had cash, but it felt awkward to accept money from a woman right before I slept with her.

"I really hope the sex is worth more than the five dollars this thing would cost me."

I snorted a shocked laugh. "I was just thinking it felt sleazy to accept payment from you."

"And like I said, I hope you're better than five dollars and a free toilet flapper."

I stalked around the edge of the counter, keeping my gaze locked on her face. I loved a woman who could hold her own in a conversation, in bed, and in the world around her. This one already proved two out of three, and I was ready to show her the way to my bed.

I didn't stop when I got around to her side of the counter. It was hard enough to keep my hands off her from the moment she forced her way into the store. Now that her business was done, it was time for pleasure.

I grabbed her ponytail and tugged, her lips parting with surprise just in time for my mouth to seal over them. I pressed my tongue inside, getting a moan from her at the first slide of my tongue against hers.

She didn't stand there and take it, though. Hell no. This woman was an active participant, and she kissed me right back. Her tongue dueled with mine. Her hands slid up my chest until she reached my neck. She didn't stop there and dragged her fingernails into my beard.

Damn. I didn't know that could feel so fucking good.

I groaned and pressed my body against hers, letting her know just how much I wanted her. She pressed right back.

My greedy side wanted to lift her onto the counter and have her right there, but I wanted to see her in my bed. Even if it was just for one night, I needed that memory.

I pulled away from her, grabbed the bag she'd dropped to the floor, and took her hand. She didn't resist or question me, just hurried in those fuck-me boots after me toward the back of the store.

I flipped the switched to turn off all the lights up front, then unlocked the door between the store and my apartment. Then I had her back in my arms.

She spun us and pressed me against the door. I smirked at the force of her, throwing her weight around and getting what she wanted.

And thank God, what she wanted was my dick in her hand.

"Fuck," I hissed when she wrapped her fingers around me. She hadn't even bothered to unzip my jeans. Not that I was complaining.

She stroked me in short, impatient jerks, her movements restricted. I unzipped my jeans and shoved them down my hips until my cock sprung free.

I saw fucking stars when she squeezed and pumped her hand along the entire length of my erection.

"Marry me," I teased her.

She laughed, like I hoped she would.

I pulled her lips back to mine and kissed her like I had nothing to lose. Because I didn't. Our chemistry was off the damn charts, but that was all. One night. Let off some steam. Move on.

As we kissed, I moved her toward my bedroom. My place was small, one bedroom with one bathroom, a kitchen that barely counted, and a living room big enough for a couch and a TV. I loved it, though, because I put my hands on every inch of the place and made it my own.

I didn't bother with lights when we got to the bedroom, opting for the soft glow of the rising moon to highlight her. I reached for her jacket, then lifted her shirt, getting my hands on her bare skin for the first time. It was soft and smooth and warm. Her full breasts heaved over the edge of her green lace bra. I bent down, erasing the six inches between us, and licked the upper swell of her breast.

Her hands went into my hair and held me in place as she lifted her breasts and pressed herself against my mouth. I tugged the cup down and captured her nipple, biting lightly before I licked it.

"Oh, God, yes," she moaned.

I loved a woman who wasn't afraid to tell me what she liked, and this one was already getting vocal.

I nudged the bra straps off her shoulders and released both breasts, alternating between them until she was panting and hanging on the edge of an orgasm. Fucking hell, she was stunning.

"Please," she whispered.

My hands went to her jeans, unbuttoning and unzipping as quickly as I could. Her hands brushed mine aside, shoving her jeans and panties down while I moved my hand between her thighs.

She was wet and warm and ready for me, her hips jerking with the first brush of my fingers. I couldn't go slow, and I couldn't give her time to adjust. I needed to feel her come around my fingers.

I plunged two inside her, dragging my thumb over her clit, and she let go. Her shout was full of praise and demands for more. Her channel tightened around my fingers as she coated my hand and her body begged for more.

My cock pulsed, needing to get in on the action, but I wasn't ready to stop just yet. I pressed a third finger into her and pumped them in and out quickly. Her jeans kept her from spreading her thighs wider, and the restriction seemed to send her over the edge faster.

She whimpered and hung off me like her bones had turned to liquid. I held her with one arm, careful not to touch her nice clothes with the hand that had been inside her. I walked her to the bed and wiped my hand on my jeans before letting them fall at my feet. I put my hands on her jeans, meeting her gaze for approval.

"You just made me come twice. I think modesty has gone out the window here."

I laughed with her and eased her jeans and panties down her legs. I stopped when I reached her boots, untied those and tossed all of it to the floor. When I looked back at her, she'd discarded her bra and was beautifully naked on my bed.

"Damn," I whispered.

Her gaze slid down to my cock. "Same."

I chuckled. I never thought of myself as all that impressive, but I'd also never whipped it out and compared myself to other men. Besides, the size of another man's dick never mattered to me. All that mattered was if the woman I was sliding into was happy with my performance. So far, I hadn't had any complaints.

She eased herself up the bed to lie on the pillows while I dug into my nightstand for a condom. I made a mental note that I had five more in there, but I didn't take them out. I didn't want to be too presumptuous, although I was not opposed to using a few more before she hightailed it out of my place and disappeared into the night.

I crawled onto the bed over her, settling myself between her widespread thighs. She smiled at me, a connection between strangers who were sharing something special.

I held myself still with one hand and pressed into her. She let out a moan, her body resisting me as it tried to pull me in. Back and forth, push and pull, we moved together until I sank all the way into her and our bodies rested against each other.

"How in the hell did it feel so good before you even really did anything?" she whispered.

I swallowed back my own need to let go and nodded. "I was wondering the same thing."

"I'm not sure I'm going to survive the night if this is how good it is already."

"Then I guess we better get started so I have time to call you an ambulance."

She chuckled and squeezed her pelvic muscles.

I groaned, the tightening around my dick making me see stars.

"It sounds like I'm not the only one who's going to need medical assistance."

"Death by orgasm. I'm willing to risk it."

She slid her hands up my chest and met my gaze. "Me, too."

I eased back and slowly pushed into her. We stared at each other, watching the other for cues as we slowly built up the tension and passion between us. Her eyes fluttered closed and her lips parted in a silent moan, and I thrust a little harder into her.

She lifted her thighs and brought her knees up alongside my hips, widening her entrance so I slid deeper into her. We both moaned, and I went faster.

Sweat trickled down my spine and beaded on my forehead. Droplets appeared between her breasts. We both held back, resisting the pull toward the edge, wanting the moment to last.

"Please," she whispered. That one word again, her waving the white flag and needing to fall.

I slammed in harder, changing the angle just enough that her core clenched tight and her body flushed red. I watched her breasts rock with my movements, and I couldn't stop myself from pounding into her, losing my mind as I lost my battle to stay in control.

She cried out and moaned, her body tightening just before she let go. I swore as I followed her, just a few seconds later, unable to stop the racing need to come with her.

She reached up for me, her fingers once more going to my beard. The gentle tug of her fingertips and the scrape of her nails sent a tingle down my spine that had my cock twitching and hardening again before it even had a chance to fully soften.

I collapsed onto her, my muscles shaking and my body wrung out. She wrapped her legs around me and held me to her, neither of us speaking for a few minutes as we fought to catch our breath.

My breathing finally slowed, and I rolled off her. I had to get rid of the condom, but before I did, I wanted to look into her eyes and make sure she was good.

She forced her brown eyes open and smiled. "Hey."

"Hey. Are you okay?"

"Better than I've been in months."

I smiled and nodded once, then went to the bathroom. I trashed the condom and washed my hands. She hadn't moved from her spot on the bed, but her gaze followed me.

"You're welcome to the bathroom, and whatever else you need."

"Bathroom first. Then I think I need more of you."

My cock twitched, hearing the praise and ready to accept his prize.

She grinned. "Glad to see you're on board."

"Absolutely."

I WANTED to know more about her, but I fought the urge to ask. We agreed to one night, so I kept my mouth shut. Maybe someone would know who she was and I could run into her somewhere. Although, my guess was she didn't live in MacKellar Cove. If she did, I would know who she was.

While she was in the bathroom, I grabbed bottles of water. We chugged them, then went for round two. I couldn't remember the last time I'd been reluctant to let a woman out of my bed. I enjoyed sex, but I had gotten sick of sex without a connection. Even without knowing anything about this woman, I felt the connection.

Sometime after round three, we laid in the dark, panting and lazily touching each other. She whispered, "I'm glad I met you."

"Me, too," I told her.

She curled up against me, her body warm against my side. I wrapped an arm around her and let the lazy patterns she drew on my stomach lull me to sleep.

My alarm blared to life, scaring me upright in search of my phone. I found it on my nightstand and turned off my alarm, but I already knew she was gone.

The sheets were cold, and there was no trace of her except the three condoms in the trash and the second empty bottle of water on my nightstand.

She lived up to her end of the deal. I couldn't help but wish she hadn't.

I stomped around my apartment, grouchy and pissed off, as I got ready for my day. When I walked into the store, I found a five-dollar bill on the counter with a note.

Definitely worth a hell of a lot more than this.

I smiled and pocketed the note, then unlocked the front door and started my day.

3

HALEY

The lease on my entry table mocked me. Who knew something inanimate could do such a thing? But it did. It sat there and stared at me, judging and demanding.

I only had three months left on my lease. Less than that to decide if I was staying or leaving.

But I had no clue what I wanted to do.

I moved to MacKellar Cove with such hope and excitement. It all crashed and burned the second Valentina opened the door and I realized my boyfriend wasn't who I thought he was. At all. At that point, I had no choice. I'd signed a one-year lease on my apartment and a one-year lease on the chair I rented in the salon. Getting out of both would have cost more than I had available.

I'd checked. In that lease. Daily, for months. Just in case it had changed. Even after I gave up on leaving town immediately, I left the lease on the table, a reminder that I was temporary in MacKellar Cove.

But in three months, I could be free. Find a new town that didn't know me as a homewrecker. That didn't judge me for something I never knew.

Leaving meant starting over again. Not just finding a new place to live and work, but finding new friends.

My eyes watered at the thought. Dammit. I expected to meet new people, but I never expected to be welcomed in like I was. Especially by my ex-boyfriend's wife. Ex-wife now. Valentina never let anyone say anything about me. She defended me from the beginning. Said we were both victims of Dawson's lies.

I'd never be able to repay her kindness. She didn't have to do that. But it showed me the kind of people who called MacKellar Cove home.

Well, some of them. Madeline and some of the other ladies at the salon clearly didn't agree with Valentina and blamed me for everything.

Which was part of why I hadn't been able to decide what I wanted to do. I had two months to either sign a new lease or let Sofia know I was moving out.

The lease reminded me constantly. Like a timer ticking down to the end of my life in MacKellar Cove.

I groaned and tossed my keys on top of the lease. I needed a few more hours of sleep, and a few more weeks of ignoring it, before I could make a rational decision. That and to not smell like sex with a gorgeous stranger. He was enough to tempt me into staying, but sex with a stranger was what got me to where I was. I couldn't let it influence anymore of my choices.

After a few hours of sleep and a very large cup of coffee, I felt more like myself. I considered going out and getting something to eat, but I didn't want to risk running into someone who would burst my bubble. I had my first in person date in a few hours. With HandyNotHandsy from Book Boyfriends Wanted. I was going to ride my post-sex high to the date and get to know a man who made me laugh and reminded me I was desirable.

I took a long shower and scrubbed every inch of myself. Not that my date was going to get up close and personal with me, but I didn't want to walk in smelling like another man. Or feeling his very talented hands on my skin.

When I got out, my phone dinged with a new alert.

HANDYNOTHANDSY

Only a few more hours until we meet in person. Hopefully I get to see that smile.

My lips curled up at his words. He made me laugh more than any man I'd ever had contact with. If I wasn't wounded from Dawson, I probably would have met this guy a while ago, but I was afraid.

No. I was chickenshit. I worried he'd judge me like others did. That he'd take one look at me and walk away because I was responsible for another man cheating on his wife.

SINGLEMENWANTED

Maybe you already have. I keep wondering if we know each other.

HNH

Small town life. We might. But I'm happy we met here. I feel like I already know you.

SMW

Same.

HNH

Hopefully that's a good thing.

SMW

It is.

HNH

Good. Then before I screw this all up, I'm going to tell you I'll be at a booth wearing a black shirt and jeans. I'll have a daisy on the table for you.

SMW

Daisies are my favorite!

HNH

I know. You told me once. I'll see you tonight.

I sighed and clutched my phone to my chest. No one had ever brought me flowers before. It was small, and it was a way for me to find him, so I tried not to let it go to my head, but it convinced me I'd made the right choice meeting him. I really didn't think men like him existed.

Two hours later, I was dressed in jeans and a flirty orange top. My hair was curled and fell in loose waves over my shoulders. I grabbed my sparkly black handbag and headed for O'Kelley's.

I was not a regular at the local bar, but the owner was married to a friend of mine. Hudson and Anna were both married before they got together, and definitely people I assumed would not be friendly toward me. Anna followed Valentina's lead and agreed with her that when someone cheats, they're the one who broke a promise. I got the feeling she was speaking from experience, although not experience with Hudson.

Hudson was one of the nicest people I'd ever met. He was a bit gruff and not overly friendly, but he was a good man. And knowing he was there when I was meeting HandyNotHandsy made me feel more comfortable because he would keep an eye on things.

I glanced around the bar and spotted a man in a booth.

He was faced away from me, but I could see his black sleeve and jeans. The clear giveaway was the orange Gerbera daisy on the edge of the table. An orange that perfectly matched the top I wore.

What were the odds of that?

My pulse skipped, and my heart fluttered. My lips curled into a smile as I walked toward him. Strong forearms covered in dark blond hair were the next thing I saw of him. I was a sucker for forearms. His shirt was pulled tight across his biceps. He reached for a glass of clear liquid and brought it to his lips as I stepped around the edge of the booth.

"Oh, shit," I breathed, my smile slipping from my face.

He looked up at me, eyes wide, and pulled his glass away, dumping some on himself in the process. "No way."

I dropped onto the other side of the booth and looked at the man whose apartment I snuck out of that morning. "Well, at least we know we have chemistry."

He wiped at his wet shirt and looked up at me. He held my gaze for a minute, studying me.

I tried not to squirm. He never made it seem like he knew me the night before, but that didn't mean he didn't. I resisted the urge to ask him why he was staring at me.

Then he extended his hand. "I'm Knox Randall. Also known as HandyNotHandsy. I'm assuming you're Single-MenWanted."

I sucked in a shaky breath and nodded, slipping my hand into his. I was beyond appreciative of him for using his screen name as an introduction and confirming mine without making it weird. "I am. Also known as Haley Jordan."

Knox held my hand for a minute, neither of us pulling back, even when it should have been awkward. His lips slowly lifted into a grin, and he shook his head before releasing his grip on me.

I couldn't breathe. The man was seriously killer when he smiled.

"I think you're the last person I expected to show up here tonight."

I nodded to the flower. "It appears you were at least somewhat expecting me."

He dropped his gaze to my shirt and chuckled. "Great minds?"

I smiled. "Great minds."

He leaned back in his seat. "Not even close to what I imagined."

My body flushed with embarrassed heat. My smile fell. I crossed my ankles to stop myself from fleeing. "Excuse me?"

"Your smile," he said. "It's so much better than I thought it would be. Because you're sitting here."

My lungs expanded. Tears stung the backs of my eyes. I nibbled on my lower lip. He was just as tempting in person as he was during all our chats. And knowing how good we were in bed made resisting him almost impossible.

"I need to bring up the elephant in the room. I like you. I really enjoyed chatting with you for the last few months. I'm so happy we're here. And last night..." He shook his head. "Last night was amazing. But I know that's not why we're here tonight. I don't want you to worry that I'm going to try to get you back to my place."

I wasn't sure if I should be disappointed or not. I was a little of both. Not because I thought it was smart, but because I knew it was good. And I'd been missing good for a long time.

"Do you want a drink?" Knox asked when I didn't say anything.

"Um, yeah. Hudson will make something good."

Knox made a move to stand, but I grabbed his hand. He looked back at me with eyebrows raised in question.

"Thank you."

He smiled at me and winked, then went to the bar to get me a drink from Hudson.

I drew a deep breath as soon as he stepped away from the booth. I put both hands to my lips and exhaled slowly. I still wasn't sure if he knew who I was, that I was the woman who ended Valentina's relationship, but he was acting like he didn't. Did that mean I had to tell him?

Probably.

Dammit.

I didn't know if he knew Valentina, but I knew enough about McKellar Cove to know pretty much everyone did. And Knox was clearly a local, so if I didn't tell him, someone else would.

Knox came back a minute later with a blue drink topped with an orange. He set it in front of me and said, "Hudson thought this would be good. I told him not much alcohol because I didn't want you uncomfortable and I wasn't sure if you were driving."

I took a sip. It was delicious. And it either didn't have alcohol or it was expertly blended to be incredibly dangerous. Both were very possible with Hudson. I turned to the bar and found him watching me. I lifted the drink and nodded my thanks. He returned my nod, then went back to what he was doing.

"Are you two friends?"

I wondered if his sharp tone was jealousy or curiosity. "I know Anna. I've met Hudson a few times through her, but we're not really close."

"He's a good guy."

I nodded. I didn't really want to talk about other people all night. Especially married people. Our conversations were always deeper. Private. About what we wanted from life and what we regretted about our pasts. I'd never confessed my biggest regret, because it would tell him exactly who I was, but I'd hinted at it.

"I'm sorry this is weird. I suck at dating. Which is why I'm thirty-eight and still single."

I chuckled. "I'm no better. I'm thirty and the last relationship I had was—" Crap. I grabbed my drink and chugged it, praying it was full of alcohol and I could blame that for confessing my not-so-secret shame to him after five damn minutes.

He leaned in and raised an eyebrow.

It shouldn't be a sexy look, but with the added quirk of his lips and the slight smile, I wanted to tell him everything about me. About not being close to my parents and feeling like I was unwanted. About falling into one relationship after another to feel like someone actually cared about me. About sleeping with a married man for nine months and not knowing because I was so desperate for attention, I never saw the signs.

"The last relationship you had was what? We never talked about exes."

"Isn't that the last thing you're supposed to talk about on a first date?"

"Probably, but this doesn't feel like a first date to me."

"I thought we weren't counting last night."

He exhaled a laugh. "I wasn't talking about that. We didn't do much getting to know each other. I meant the months of conversations. I feel like I know you. Even though I just found out your name."

I sighed heavily. "If you know Hudson, and you're from

here, which I know both are true, then I know you know who I am. It's okay."

He tilted his head to the side and scanned my face. His eyes narrowed, and he tilted his head the other way. He was good at making me think he didn't know my story. "Before last night, I don't remember meeting you. I feel like an ass saying that. I'm sorry I don't remember."

"We've never met, but you've probably heard of me."

"Are you famous?" He chuckled. "Come on. Tell me. Clearly, I'm no good at guessing."

I sighed and leaned forward. He did the same, bringing us a few inches apart. I smelled minty toothpaste on his breath and a hint of some kind of alcohol. I closed my eyes so I didn't have to see the look in his when I told him the truth. "My last relationship lasted nine months. I moved here last spring because my boyfriend lived here. Except I didn't know he lived here with his wife and two teenage daughters."

He didn't say anything for a long moment. Long enough that I wondered if he left and I was sitting there like an idiot with my eyes closed.

I finally pried them open. Knox was still there. He was still leaning toward me.

He reached across the table, palm up. I stared at his hand, wondering why it was there. He waved his fingers, like he wanted me to put my hand in his.

Hesitantly, I did.

He wrapped his hand around my wrist and stroked his thumb over my skipping pulse. "I didn't realize that was you. I'm sorry you went through that."

I inhaled a shaky breath. The words were so simple, but dammit, they were nice to hear. I rolled my lips in and nodded, swallowing over the emotional lump in my throat.

"You were all alone in a new town, and knowing the way some of these people are, you weren't treated well, were you?"

"Sometimes," I whispered. "But Valentina is amazing. She defended me from day one."

Knox chuckled and nodded. "Sounds like her. She's a pretty spectacular woman."

"She is. I will never be able to apologize enough to her for what I did."

"Why do you owe her an apology? You didn't do anything wrong. Unless he told you he was married and you still kept seeing him. Hell, even that, you weren't the one who vowed to be faithful to her for the rest of your life. I'd never say I'm okay with cheating, but if I were married, I'd blame my wife for an affair, not the man she cheated on me with."

I chuckled softly. "You are not like most people."

"I think I'll take that as a compliment." He lifted his drink with the hand not holding my wrist. He stopped before he brought it to his mouth. "Wait. That's why your screen name is SingleMenWanted, isn't it?"

I nodded. "Yep. I'm not interested in dating anymore married men. You said you're not married."

Knox shook his head. "Not now, never have been. No serious relationships for a while. I was seeing someone about a year ago, but we didn't want the same things."

"Which means?"

"Which means I want a wife and a family, and she wanted sex."

"And you couldn't have both?"

He laughed. "Ideally, yes, I'd want both. But she wasn't interested in getting married or having kids. Now or anytime soon."

The word family meant a lot to me. For a long time, it was a word used to instill guilt on me. My parents would tell me we had to do something because of family. It was a dirty word. A punishing word.

My best friend in middle school came from a big family. When I grumbled about the obligations of families, she said it wasn't like that for her. She loved spending time with her cousins and siblings. They were some of her closest friends. She would do anything for them.

Even my parents wouldn't do anything for me. Hearing those words made me realize I was missing something for the first time in my life.

It only got worse as I got older. Family was something I always wanted. It was my Holy Grail. But I was no treasure hunter, and I was definitely not fortunate enough to luck into something like that.

"Since we're breaking the rules, I'm going to ask... Do you want a family?"

I looked up into his blue-green eyes. The crinkles around the edges were charming. The hope in his gaze was honest and real. The way he continued to stroke my wrist was comforting.

It was our first date. The first time I'd sat across from a man since I moved to town. I debated downplaying how I felt. Making a joke or blowing off the question.

But as I stared at him, the only thing I could do was whisper the truth. "More than anything."

4

KNOX

HER WHISPERED WORDS WERE PART CONFESSION, PART REGRET. There was more there than she was saying, but she wasn't lying to me.

She was a stranger. A beautiful, curvy, enticing stranger, but still a stranger. We'd slept together, and we'd talked for months, but there were truths we'd never shared. Big truths. I had no idea she was the woman who showed up at Valentina's house last spring. And she didn't know that I wasn't just a guy who worked behind the counter of the town's one and only hardware store.

"Okay, so heavy topics out of the way, how's your pool shot?" I asked, hoping to see that smile I'd been dreaming about for months.

She looked up at me from under those lashes, a tentative smile lifting the edges of her lips. "Pool?"

I nodded toward the tables on the other side of the bar. "Friendly game?"

She raised one dark eyebrow as a smirk lit her gaze. "Friendly? Does that mean you won't get upset when I wipe the floor with you?"

I chuckled and leaned back, a little shocked at her declaration and more than a little happy she wasn't willing to back down so easily. "I didn't promise that. I'm hoping you won't pout when I destroy you."

"Bring it on." She lifted her brows in challenge and narrowed her eyes. When I slid out of the booth, she took my offered hand and let me help her up. Not that she needed the help, but it was good to feel the spark that was between us the night before.

One-night stand Haley might not have been interested in anything long term, but Book Boyfriends Wanted Single-Men Wanted Haley was.

We grabbed our drinks, and she picked up the flower that was so close to the bright color of her shirt I was amazed, and we headed toward the tables. No one paid us any attention, for which I was happy. Not that I was ashamed of being there with her, just that I wanted her to myself for a little while.

One table was open in the back, and we claimed it as ours, setting her flower on the long rail and our drinks on a high-top table nearby. I racked the balls while she selected a cue stick from the rack on the wall.

I removed the triangle and nodded for her to break. She grinned, and damn if the look didn't go straight to my dick. Confidence lit her eyes and determination drew her focus. She lined up the cue ball and steadied her stick before taking her first shot.

The crack of the cue ball hitting the racked balls was loud and effective. Solids and stripes flew across the table, one of each dropping into a pocket before her triumphant smile lifted her lips.

"Well, damn. I might be screwed," I said.

She laughed, lining up for her next shot. She stood

behind the solid blue number two, tapping gently before it rolled into the pocket.

"I'm solids." Her smile was intoxicating. Just like I knew it would be but so much more.

I was a sucker for a woman who knew what she could do. Haley had been through hell the last few months, but she was still standing there, destroying me as she sunk one shot after another.

She moved around the table like she owned the damn thing, ignoring everything else in the noisy space. She was focused, and she was talented.

She finally missed a shot, and I had a turn to show her what I could do. I made three shots, during which she nodded appreciatively and moved out of my way in anticipation of where I was going to go. I missed the fourth in a row, and she winked at me, telling me before she even stepped forward she was going to win before I had another chance.

And she did. Gracefully. Without gloating or celebration.

"Good game," she said, offering her hand to shake.

"Great game. Where'd you learn to play?"

She shrugged. "Cosmetology school, mostly."

"Yeah?" We both pulled balls from the pockets and rolled them across the table to rack them for another game.

"There was a table in the basement of the community space where I went to church."

"Your church had a pool table?"

She nodded. "The cosmetology school was near a local college, so they had a safe place for students to hang out. One of the things we had was a pool table. There were also darts, ping-pong, and foosball, but I was never much good at any of those. Pool was my game."

"That sounds like a fun place to spend some time. Where did you go to school?"

"In Indiana. Not far from Chicago."

"Where are you from?"

"Kansas City."

"How in the world did you end up here?"

She looked up at me with a question in her gaze. Asked and answered.

"I mean, this part of the country. You grew up in Kansas City, went to school outside Chicago. Is that where you lived before here?"

She shook her head and avoided my gaze for a minute. She focused on the table and nodded in question to break again.

Watching her play was fun, so I nodded for her to go ahead.

She bent over, her front of her shirt drooping and giving me a view of the tan bra covering her breasts. Her breasts swayed with her movement, and fuck me, I was finding it harder and harder to resist her. Again.

I had no intention of sleeping with her on our first date. I wasn't going to break the promise I made to myself. But it wasn't easy when I knew how good it would be.

She was as good in bed as she was at running a pool table. Which she was in the process of doing again.

I chuckled when she sank another ball with a trick shot few people could ever pull off. "Wow."

She looked up at me with delight in her eyes as she leaned over the table and lined up her next shot.

I stepped back, doing everything possible not to distract her. I wanted to, but we agreed it would be a friendly game, and I wasn't going to play dirty. That wasn't my style.

She called her shot and dropped the eight-ball into the side pocket, winning before I took even one shot.

"I think I might need to find something you're less dominating at, so we can actually play together."

"We are playing together." She smirked at me.

I laughed. "If you count me holding up the wall while you clear the table playing together, then I guess."

She laughed, but her cheeks reddened like she was embarrassed. "You can break this time."

I shook my head. "That's not how you play. Winner breaks. And I'll know if you tank a shot."

"But you just said—"

"I was teasing, Haley. It's fun to watch you."

The smile slid from her face, replaced by a tightness that hadn't been there all night.

I moved closer to her, not touching her, but close enough that our conversation was more private than public. "I didn't mean anything by that. You're talented, and you're having fun. We all need to have fun in our lives."

"It's fine. I get it." She stepped away from me and lined up. She shanked her shot, barely hitting the target ball. The cue ball rolled to the side and hit the rail, resting a few inches away. Nothing went in.

I leaned my cue stick against the side rail and walked toward Haley. She was still behind the head rail, not looking at me. Her gaze was focused solely on the table.

"I apologize for what I said," I whispered, not touching her but getting close. "I am having a really good night, and I don't want to ruin it by saying something stupid. I'm really sorry."

She forced a smile and glanced at me long enough for me to see the wariness in her gaze. "It's fine. There's no way for you to have known Dawson used to say that to me."

"Say what?"

"It's fun to watch you."

"Watch you do what?" I asked, even though I was sure I knew the answer.

She shrugged. "Anything. Everything. He'd pick me up at the salon and watch me cut hair. He would stare at me during dinner. Watching movies, anything. I would catch him just staring at me. At the time, I thought it was sweet. I told myself it was because he was falling in love with me. But everything with him was a lie."

"Dammit. I'm sorry, Haley. I... I don't know what to say."

She smiled and shrugged again, trying to dismiss her emotions. "It's fine. It's my thing. I just..."

"Do you still love him?"

"How do you know I loved him?"

Now it was my turn to shrug. "Not a lot of people would relocate for someone they only liked a little."

She drew in a breath and let it out slowly. She grabbed the chalk and rubbed it over the end of her stick. Buying time. "I'm not sure I know what love actually feels like. Yeah, I thought I loved him. I thought he loved me. But he was playing me."

"Unfortunately, that doesn't mean how you felt was wrong. You can be in love with someone who doesn't feel the same way. Ask Brantley."

"The one Valentina's with?"

I nodded. "He's been in love with her forever. Since they were in high school. Even through her dating Dawson and marrying him and having two kids with him, Brantley still loved her. He never thought he'd get a chance with her, and he never wished divorce on her, but he loved her anyway."

"Wow. That's... I've never had anyone who felt that way about me."

"Besides family, of course. But yeah, me neither."

She pressed her lips into another smile. One that didn't feel real. "You said you were never married."

I shook my head and gave her the out she clearly needed. "Nope. Never even close. I had a few serious relationships, but none that ever felt like Brantley and Valentina, or anyone else I know."

"It kind of sucks, doesn't it?"

I nodded. "Yeah, but I'm not ready to give up just yet. How about you?"

She looked up at me. Her brown eyes sparkled with the reflection of the neon lights around us. She looked vulnerable and beautiful.

I ached to know what she was thinking, but I didn't press for anything. Not for answers, and not for more. She'd been torn apart by MacKellar Cove, but she didn't run away. She didn't hide. She was out here, at the locals bar, on a date with me.

She was so much stronger than she realized.

"No, I'm not ready to give up yet either," she finally whispered.

I smiled. "Good. Then I'm going to finally beat you in pool, and we're going to get something to eat, and then I'm going to regretfully say good night and try to make it seem like I'm a good guy."

She exhaled a laugh. "You are a good guy, Knox."

I took her hand and lifted it to my lips, pressing a gentle kiss on the back. I winked at her and said, "I'm trying to be. But it's tough to keep my hands to myself when I know how good you feel."

Her eyes dilated with her sharp inhale.

I let go of her hand and lined up my shot, focusing on the game before I went back on my promise and dragged her out of the bar.

WAKING up in my bed alone was not a new thing. It was my normal. I'd been doing it my whole life. But it still sucked.

Especially after my date with Haley.

We talked and laughed and shared dinner after she beat me a third time. For all my talk, as soon as I missed a shot, she stepped in and ran the table. Again.

When the date ended, I walked her to her car and kissed her on the cheek. I wanted to kiss her, to claim her, but I liked her. The woman I wanted to take out on a date was not the woman I wanted to screw senseless the other night at my shop. One was lust, the other was companionship. To find out they were the same woman kept me bouncing back and forth with desire and decency. But damn, did I want to say screw it to all the above.

Saturdays were always busy in the store, so I dragged myself out of my lonely bed and into the shower. I dressed quickly, making a mental note to trim my beard later, then fixed a quick cup of coffee and hoped I'd have time to eat before anyone walked into the store.

Almost as soon as I unlocked the front door, someone walked in. For the next hour, it was busy as the weekend warriors started their days. It always surprised me people got up as early as they did on the weekends, but they came to me and bought things, so I wasn't going to complain. Much.

I found a minute to eat a granola bar and finish my cold cup of coffee when the store was quiet. As the morning rush died down, I braced myself for the regulars who would show up before long.

The first one in was Tony. He was always looking for something to organize his garage. Nothing was ever quite right, and half the time he left without making a purchase. But that wasn't why he was there.

The second one through the door was Dick. He used to be a brick mason, but he retired a decade earlier when his back started to give him trouble. He preferred being around people who liked to get their hands dirty, so he hung around.

And last was Wayne. He was the ringleader. The one who sparked the conversation. And the ridicule. As much as I loved Wayne, my gut twisted whenever he walked in. Especially when he walked in with a look on his face that said he had something juicy to share.

"Morning, gentlemen," Wayne said. He eased himself onto the stool on the other side of the counter.

"Morning," Tony and Dick said together.

The three of them could have been brothers, but they weren't. Weathered, tan, wrinkled skin was from years of working outside. All had brown eyes and, once upon a time, had brown hair. Tony was the youngest, getting close to seventy, and completely bald. Dick was the oldest and approaching seventy-five, with more hair than the other two. Wayne was in between them in age and hair loss, but as the loudest, he was in charge.

"I heard Genevieve and Teddy are having another baby," Wayne declared with all the bravado of a man who had the inside scoop.

Except that scoop came out a month ago. Not that I was going to tell Wayne that.

"Oh, yeah?" Tony asked. "Where'd you hear that?"

"Saw them the other day." Wayne liked to be the one who shared town news. Half the time it was wrong, and the other half the time everyone already knew about it.

When Valentina and Dawson broke up, Wayne said she

tossed all his things into the street when he wasn't home. I told him that wasn't what I heard, and he lit into me. I've learned not to correct him when he's wrong.

"Good for them," Dick said. "Kids should be having kids. Keep the town going."

"Unlike this one," Wayne said, hitching his thumb toward me. "When are you going to find you a nice woman and knock her up, Knox?"

I shook my head and ignored the question. It wasn't any of their business, but it also stung a bit. All three of them were married with kids in school by the time they were my age. Thirty-eight was still plenty young enough for me to have kids, but they were happy to remind me it wasn't how they did it.

"Leave the boy alone," Tony said.

Wayne chuckled. "Knox knows I'm just picking. Don't you?"

"Yep," I said, knowing it was the only answer I was allowed to give.

Tony, Dick, and Wayne had been customers forever. It didn't matter how much they bugged me, they were staples of the store as much as I was. Every Saturday morning and Wednesday evening, they would saunter in and hold court, sharing gossip and offering advice to customers. I had to suck it up and deal with it, usually offering whispered apologies to the annoyed customers. The three men were friends with my father, and they'd run right to him if I said so much as boo to any of them.

So, I kept my mouth shut and took whatever they dished out, and prayed the customers would keep coming back.

"Knox learned we're always right when he tried to change things after he took over. Damn near lost the store right out from under him. Thinking he could flip a switch and stop supplying the town with the things we all need. He came back around, though. Finally listened to us. Been smart enough to do it ever since." Wayne chuckled and slapped his hand on the counter like he told the best joke ever.

I just forced my expected smile and let him take the win. Because as much as I hated it, he wasn't wrong. I did try to change things. I did almost lose the store my dad built from the ground up. And I did turn everything around and put it all back the way it'd been before.

Just because I hated the twice weekly reminder that I fucked up didn't mean I could argue against it. He was right, and I was wrong. And if I wanted to keep the store open, I had to put aside my dreams and goals and keep stocking the things the people of MacKellar Cove bought on a regular basis.

Like toilet flappers.

5

HALEY

"How early did you get up to leave the toilet flapper on my door the other night?" Sofia asked as she added guacamole to her grilled chicken soft taco.

We bonded over our love of tacos, and whenever we went out to eat, we seemed to end up at Just Tacos. The food was delicious, and no one ever gave me a side-eye.

"What do you mean?" I asked.

"I stayed up late hoping to catch you. I felt bad for sending you on an errand, especially when you weren't back by the time I was done with Mrs. Watson's dishwasher. I crashed on the couch watching a movie, but the part still wasn't on my door. I planned to run to Al's Hardware early the next morning, but when I walked out my door, the bag was there."

"Oh, um, I, uh..." Crap. I never thought she'd notice, so I never came up with an excuse.

Sofia looked up at me with a question in her gaze. "Whoa. What happened? Why are your cheeks bright red?"

I glanced between Sofia and my taco and chose the lesser of two evils. The taco. I took a big bite, trying not to laugh when she gave me a look that said she knew exactly what I was doing.

Stalling.

Sofia set her taco on her plate and watched me chew. Slowly. If I was slow enough, I could come up with an explanation that didn't involve telling her I slept with the guy who sold me the part and then ended up on a date with him the next night.

Although I wasn't sure there was an explanation I could get through without confessing the whole thing.

And besides that, Sofia had never judged me. I wasn't sure why I was having a hard time telling her the whole story now. She wouldn't care.

I finally finished chewing my massive bite and took a sip of my water. Sofia kept watching me, her hands patiently crossed in front of her. When I set my drink down, she raised one blonde eyebrow and sighed.

"I'm sorry."

"Um, what?"

She shook her head. "Knox is usually so nice. I never would have thought he would say anything about you being there so close to closing. I never should have sent you. I'll talk to him next time I go in there. I can't believe he was anything but helpful to you."

I gawked at her, half wondering if I should roll with the excuse she was giving me or if I should tell her the truth. But I couldn't do that to Knox, or to Sofia. Neither deserved to be lied to, and I, of all people, believed in the truth.

"I slept with Knox when I went to get the part. And it was really, really good, and I felt like... I don't know. But then he was my date last night, and we had fun and he's really sweet, and he's funny, and he's so good-looking, and I—"

"Whoa, wait, what?" Sofia said, each word increasing in volume and shock. "You slept with..." She cut herself off and glanced around, dropping her voice before she hissed, "Knox?"

I buried my face in my hands and nodded. "I did. When I rushed in there, he was about to close, and I talked my way in, and he was funny and we flirted, and oh, my God. Do you have a thing for him? He said he's single, but I never even thought, but the way you're talking about him—"

"No," Sofia declared. "No. I have no interest in Knox. We've never been anything more than friends. I promise you. I'm just... surprised. He's nice, but I've never seen a flirtatious side to him."

"Really?"

Sofia nodded and picked up her taco. She took a contemplative bite and chewed slowly, as though the gooey, cheesy goodness would give her clarity.

"Knox is nice, and a lot of people speak only well of him."

"A lot of people?" I asked, sensing a story.

Sofia shrugged. "The ones who say anything else are usually just picking at old wounds, from what I can tell. No one has ever said he's anything other than an amazing man."

I tore off the edge of my napkin and rolled the paper in my fingers. Nervous habit to keep my hands busy. And to distract my mind.

I didn't want to find out Knox had some dark secret. But I also didn't want to learn who he was from a third party. Sure, learning Dawson was married would have been nice before I uprooted my entire existence, but that didn't mean I wanted to know everything about Knox before we even went on a second date.

"As far as I know, Knox is single. He's good friends with Brantley, so you can ask Valentina at book club tomorrow. Sebastian and Ian seem to be friends with him, too. I can't think of any serious relationships I've heard about him being in, especially lately. But you know I keep to myself a lot."

I tore the napkin into smaller and smaller pieces. I chewed on my lip. I wanted to ask her more, but I didn't.

"If you want me to ask around, I will. But I think Knox is a good man."

"Sleeping with him was a whim. I had the date lined up, and I was anxious and I worried I'd show up at O'Kelley's and the guy I was meeting would recognize me and laugh his way out. Knox made me feel desirable. He made me feel good. And we agreed it was one night. I didn't even know his name until our date."

"You didn't know his name?"

I shook my head. "I wanted it to be anonymous. I feel like everyone knows who I am, and I didn't recognize him, but I knew the look in his eyes. A look that said he was attracted to me. I needed to feel good. I just needed a win."

"And there's nothing wrong with that," Sofia defended. "I didn't mean to make you feel like I thought you shouldn't have slept with him."

"You didn't. I just feel like everything I do is wrong these days. After Dawson... I don't trust myself."

"Well, you need to start. Dawson was to blame. He lied to you."

"I never asked if he was married."

"Because you shouldn't have to! It was on him to say no when you met and to tell you he was married. You didn't go into things assuming he was and ignore it."

"What if I did?"

"Did you?" Sofia asked, her voice low and serious.

"No. I mean, I don't think so. I never suspected he was, but shouldn't I have picked up on the signs? Shouldn't I have known?"

Sofia put her hand on my arm and waited until I lifted my gaze to hers to speak. "You did nothing wrong. You met a man, he flirted with you and you flirted back, and you started a relationship. He had an excuse for every single question."

"I know, but—"

"No. Don't do that to yourself. When we first met, you were so excited to be here. You even told me he traveled a lot for work. You said you wanted to be near his home base so you could spend more time together. If you'd even suspected he was married, you wouldn't have moved here."

I sighed. "You're right, but—"

"Haley, you can talk yourself in circles and wonder if you missed the signs. The truth is you weren't looking for signs. He never wore a wedding ring, he never talked about his wife or kids, he never gave you any reason to believe he was lying to you about anything. You have got to stop blaming yourself."

I listened to her words and tried to let them sink in. "Okay."

She arched an eyebrow. "Okay? As in, you're actually going to do what I said?"

"I'm going to try."

"Wow. Okay, good." Sofia took another bite of her taco, then set it down and smirked. "So, now that we got that out of the way, just how good was really, really good sex with Knox?"

"Sofia!"

"What? I'm not getting any, so I have to hear all about it from my friends. Spill."

I tried not to smile, but just thinking about it had my lips lifting in joy. "You have no idea how good really, really good sex is."

Sofia snorted. "You're right. I don't. Maybe one day."

"I really like him, Sof. More than I expected."

She smiled. "That's not a bad thing. Now tell me everything, and don't leave out a single detail about the sex or the date."

I laughed, then did exactly as she asked. It was nice to be able to share something good with her for once.

I WAS GETTING ready for work Monday morning when I got an alert from Book Boyfriends Wanted. I ignored it, not wanting the distraction when I was already running a bit late, but curiosity got the better of me and I picked up my phone as I pointed the hair dryer at my head.

HANDYNOTHANDSY

Were you able to get your toilet fixed?

I put the hair dryer down and stared at my phone. Wow. I definitely got my signals crossed with his if that was the first thing he asked me after a one-night stand and a really good date.

My fingers hovered over the keyboard as I debated how to reply. Before I typed anything, another message came in.

HNH

Please ignore me. That was example number 437 why I'm still single.

I laughed to myself. It was comforting to know he was awkward, since that was how I felt.

SINGLEMENWANTED

I'm just hoping it means you were looking for a way to reach out and didn't know what to say.

HNH

Yes, I was. Bringing up your toilet was a really bad idea that sounded good right up until I hit send and saw it in writing.

SMW

I get it. If it makes you feel better, it wasn't for my toilet.

HNH

Oh. So that was just an excuse to get into the store?

SMW

Nope. I was helping out a friend. Sofia said she knows you.

HNH

Uh, yeah. I didn't know you were friends.

SMW

I live in her building. She's awesome.

HNH

She is.

But I don't have a thing for her. I didn't mean to sound like I do. I really suck at this.

SMW

You were good the other night

OMG. I meant at our date! I'm going to crawl back into my hole and never come out.

HNH

LOL! Glad to see I'm not the only one who
doesn't always say the right thing.

SMW

Definitely not.

HNH

Good. I just wanted to say good morning.
And I hope you have a good day.

SMW

Good morning. I hope you have a good
day, too.

HNH

Thanks.

Might you want to go out again?

SMW

Yes.

HNH

Phew. I didn't scare you off yet.

SMW

Not yet.

HNH

I'll take it. How's Wednesday night?

SMW

Wednesday night is perfect.

HNH

Perfect.

I smiled at my phone like an idiot until I glanced at the
time. "Crap." I was running late before, and now I was really
running late.

I dried my hair the best I could and added some product

to tame the rogue waves. It refused to cooperate, so I pulled it all back into a ponytail and tied it up. I tugged a few pieces free so it looked planned and put together, then lightly curled the ends so they would be wavy and not frizzy.

I rushed out the door, makeup bag in hand, and hurried to my car. Work was close enough to walk, but it would save me a few minutes to drive, and I needed those few minutes.

Teased by Debby wasn't open yet, but it would be very soon. We were expected to look the part when the doors opened, even if we didn't have clients first thing.

Debby raised her brows at me but didn't say a word when I rushed in. She was the only one with an early appointment, which meant I would stay in the back until I was presentable. Debby walked out of the back, passing Chelsea on her way through the curtain.

"Hey," Chelsea said. "How are you?"

I looked up at her from the mirror I was staring into, eyeliner in my hand and not on my eye.

"Whoa. What happened?"

"Running late," I muttered. "Debby's pissed."

"Debby was pissed when she got here. Said something about Madeline manipulating her way into an earlier appointment and messing with her whole schedule."

I rolled my eyes. "Madeline was here Thursday night looking for Debby."

Chelsea froze. "When you were here alone?"

I nodded.

Chelsea sucked in a breath. "Shit, Haley, I'm so sorry. How horrible was she?"

"No more horrible than usual. But she said she had an appointment for this week."

Chelsea watched me in the mirror as I added mascara to my eyeliner. "She has a standing Wednesday evening appointment, but she decided she wanted to come in today. Debby told her she had another appointment scheduled, and Madeline figured out who had that appointment and convinced her to switch days."

"Seriously?"

Chelsea nodded. "Yep. Didn't matter that Rebecca's appointment was for a cut and style only and Madeline wants a cut and color with a style. Madeline gets what she wants."

"Oh, boy. And me walking in here late and not show ready didn't make Debby's day any better."

Chelsea waved her hand and rolled her eyes. "Debby will be fine once Madeline is done."

"Why does she put up with her?"

"When you're the only one in town, you have to deal with it. Debby knows if she refuses, it'll mean other people will leave with Madeline."

"No one likes her. Why would they follow her?"

"Because everyone wants the approval of the queen bee. Even fifty years out of high school."

I sighed. "I think that gene skipped me. Or maybe after wanting approval from my parents my whole life and never getting it, I've given up on caring what others think."

Chelsea gasped. "That's so sad."

I shrugged. "It's just reality. My parents were pretty worthless as parents, but they never hurt me. Just didn't really care that I existed. I know it could have been so much worse for me."

"Yeah, but that's not what parenting is supposed to be like. Family is important."

"Are you close to your family?" I asked her. We'd worked together for months, but I didn't know much about Chelsea outside work.

"Mostly. I see my parents all the time. I have a cousin I used to be really close to as kids. We drifted apart for a while, but the last few years we've been closer again. Actually, I think you know Elise, right?"

"Elise is your cousin?" I blurted.

Chelsea nodded. "We're a year and a half apart. Our moms are sisters."

"No shit. Elise is hilarious." I stopped myself from sharing some of the more haunting things Elise said during book club, in case Chelsea didn't know about Elise's abusive ex.

"She is. And she's been through a lot. I was really happy she found Colin. He's such a good man. She deserves someone like him."

"She does. And so do you."

Chelsea chuckled. "Well, meeting a man while working in a beauty salon is not really that easy."

"Are you on that dating app? Book Boyfriends Wanted?"

Chelsea wrinkled her nose. "I haven't tried it yet. Everyone talks about it like it's magical."

"Magical?"

Chelsea nodded. "Yeah. Elise met Colin there. Blake and Ian, Hudson and Anna, Finley and Trent. All of them. They never told you?"

I shook my head and thought back over the last few months. I knew there was some mention of the app, but not the magical aspect of it. "Didn't Karissa make it?"

"Yep. She calls it the Magic of Mom. Her mom died a few years ago, but she was really good at putting people together. Karissa made the app after Ms. Georgia died, almost like a tribute I guess."

"Wow. That's... a little scary."

Chelsea laughed with me. "Right? I think it's pretty awesome, but definitely a little odd. Are you on the app?"

I thought back to my conversation with Knox that morning and the explosive chemistry between us and wondered if the magic was real.

"Haley?"

I looked up at her and smiled. "Yeah, I am."

Chelsea grinned. "I know that look. You met someone, didn't you? On the app. And he's amazing. Damn. Maybe I should join it. You've been so against relationships, but you found someone who makes you smile like you won the lottery."

"We only had one date."

"And it looks like it was a very good one if that blush on your cheeks is anything to go by."

I tried not to smile but couldn't help it. "It was only one date."

"Well, hopefully there's another one soon. And hopefully he's a good one. You deserve a good guy, too."

"Thanks, Chels. So do you."

She gave me a sassy look and cocked her hip out. "Hell, yes, I do."

I laughed at her just as we heard Madeline's demanding voice from the other side of the curtain. Our gazes locked, and we laughed when we both fell silent, hoping to avoid detection by the older woman.

We laughed again, clapping our hands over our mouths.

Maybe I did want approval. But not from the queen bee. From the people who mattered in my life. Chelsea, Sofia, and maybe Knox.

But the one who mattered more than all of them was me. And that was never going to change.

6

KNOX

ONE WEEK AFTER I MET HALEY, I WALKED INTO O'KELLEY'S for guys' night. I'd skipped the week before when she showed up at Al's Hardware and I decided to spend the night with a curvy, sexy stranger instead of a bunch of guys.

But I was going to pay for it. No doubt they would talk, especially when they found out we'd had a second date already. They were almost as bad as Tony, Dick, and Wayne. Gossips, all of them.

"Hey," I said, taking a seat next to Colin. I'd gotten to know Colin over the last few years since he'd taken over his grandmother's maple farm. He was smart and knew his way around a toolbox, and he was a regular customer.

"Hey. Glad you made it," Colin said without any hint of teasing. Of all the guys, he was the one I expected to let me off the hook. He was a good man, and he knew what it was like to be the one everyone in town was talking about.

I nodded and thanked Hudson when he slid a beer in front of me.

Hudson didn't say anything either, just moved down the line pouring drinks.

I waited for the commentary. Missing guys' night. Dating the one woman in town every man seemed to want to avoid. I was sure somewhere in there, I'd hear about how I was an idiot for trying to change Al's Hardware when I took over years ago. Might as well throw all my indiscretions at me at once.

But as the conversation picked up, no one said a thing.

I wasn't sure if that was good or bad.

"Hey, Knox," Derek Bailey said. Derek owned Stone Auto Repair and had done more than a little work on my old truck.

"Good to see you, Derek." I shook hands with him. Derek didn't make it out during the week often because he was a single dad. I stuck my foot in my mouth a few months ago when I said something to him about it, and I knew I'd never live it down.

"You, too. I need to pick your brain for a minute. I know this isn't the best place for shop talk, but—"

"All good, man. What's up?" I'd gotten used to people asking me all kinds of things all over town since I took over for my dad. I'd make a note of whatever Derek needed in my phone and order the part or tool or whatever the next day.

"I need some new storage for my workshop. I've been trying to find something online, but none of it feels quite right. I'm thinking I might need to go custom."

"Oh, yeah, sure. What are you looking to do?" I was more than a little flattered he was asking, and definitely excited to tackle the job.

"I figured with everyone who comes in and out of Al's Hardware, you might know someone who could build me something."

"Uh, sure."

"Yeah? I know your customers might not want you

sharing their information with me, but if you know someone who might be interested, I'd really appreciate you sending them my way." Derek looked hopeful as he dashed my hopes to the ground.

"You should hire Knox," Xavier said from Derek's other side. "He's talented as fuck."

Derek looked between us, her gaze drawn tight in confusion. "What do you mean? What does he mean? I didn't know you did custom work."

"He made the sign at MacKellar Theater. Damn good job," Xavier said. "He also did the sign outside Al's Hardware. I asked him who made it to see if I could hire them to make one for me, but I didn't know Knox was the one who did it."

"Really?" Derek had a different look in his eyes when he turned back to me. Approval maybe? Admiration?

"It was no big deal," I said, blowing off the praise Xavier heaped on me. I knew better than to spout off about my goals to anyone. Last time I did that, it blew up in my face.

"It wasn't no big deal," Xavier argued. "You're talented. And you could really make some money if you wanted to do custom work. I know you love the store, so I don't push, but don't sell yourself short. You're skilled. Truly."

"Would you be interested in the storage units I'm talking about?" Derek asked. "You can say no. It'll be a big project."

I didn't have to think about it. Interested? Fuck yes. But could I make it happen? That was the big question.

"Just say yes," Brantley said from a few seats away.

I glared at him, but he ignored me and focused on Derek.

"Knox'll do it. He loves this shit. When I was remodeling my house, every room, he had ideas. He's got an eye for this stuff, and a ridiculous talent for it. I think if he could make a go of it and find someone to run the store, he'd do it full time." Brantley nodded at me as if I asked him to say what he did.

I wasn't sure what to say. It was more than a little unnerving Brantley and Xavier were able to see through to what I wanted to do. And that they were supportive of it.

"How about you come by the shop in the next week and we can talk through the details? I can show you the space and tell you what we need and go from there. Does that work for you?" Derek asked.

I nodded. "Absolutely. Thanks for the opportunity."

"If you're half as good as they're making it sound like you are, it'll be well worth it for me. I didn't realize you liked getting your hands dirty," Derek teased, showing me his grease stained fingernails.

I chuckled with him. "It's all about balancing what I want with what the town needs."

"You mean the old men give you shit for wanting something other than what they're used to," Derek said with far too much insight.

I shrugged, like it didn't bother me or wasn't the whole story, but Derek seemed to be able to see right through me.

"Let me guess... Tony, Dick, and Wayne?"

I wasn't quick enough to mask my surprise.

Derek laughed again. "Yeah. They made sure I knew changing things wasn't an option when Mr. Stone retired and I took over. Made sure they all brought their vehicles in on the same day and reiterated that I was the only shop around for miles and people needed a place to get their cars worked on that wouldn't cost a small fortune or cater to brands no one around here drove." Derek shook his head. "I didn't intend to change things, but if I had, they'd have had to deal with it."

"Until you lost business and almost went under," I confessed.

Derek shrugged. "There are risks with everything. But doing something that makes you miserable sucks."

"I'm not miserable," I argued.

Derek looked at me closely. "Maybe not, but you don't look like you love selling parts, either. You'd rather be the one using those tools."

I nodded reluctantly, admitting more than I ever had to the group of men around me.

"Everyone thought I was nuts when I started my business," Ian said. "I always loved working on old wooden boats, but to become good enough at it that I could make a living was far beyond everyone's belief."

"Except yours," Ramsey said.

Ian nodded. "It wasn't easy, but it's a whole lot better than working for someone else and feeling like I wasn't doing what I wanted to be doing with my life."

"What would you do with the hardware store?" Sebastian asked. He was another regular customer who maintained a lighthouse not far from MacKellar Cove in the middle of the St. Lawrence River.

"I'd hire someone to run it, like Brantley said," I said without hesitation.

"You've actually thought about this," Brantley said, sounding surprised that he was right.

I met his gaze and nodded. "I know the hardware store is important to the town. Wayne, Tony, and Dick aside, it does good business. There are a lot of people that count on it every week. It's necessary. But it's not what I want to do for my entire life. But I don't know anyone who could handle it. Who would be willing to take over the whole thing and keep it running for me?"

The others nodded, understanding the dilemma.

"I'll listen out for anyone who might be interested," Xavier said.

"Yeah," the others agreed, nodding.

I looked down the line at the men I didn't know well, but men who were all looking to help each other out. They didn't have to find me someone who could run the store while I made a go at my dreams, but they were willing to.

And that was cool as hell.

THE OTHERS FADED one by one until I was the last one at O'Kelley's. Hudson worked until closing on Thursday nights from what I could remember, but the rest of them went home to their wives, girlfriends, or kids.

There was a part of me that was grateful no one said anything about Haley, but I couldn't help wonder if there was a reason for it.

"Can I ask you something?" I asked Hudson when he came over to check on me.

He nodded and leaned against the bar. "What's on your mind?"

"Why didn't you rat me out for being here with Haley last weekend?"

Hudson looked at me and scowled. He rolled his lips in, and he looked like he might reach across the bar and deck me. "Why were you with her?"

I shifted on my stool and wondered if asking him was a bad idea. "We were on a date."

"Did you ask her, or did she ask you?"

"We met on Book Boyfriends Wanted. We've been talking for a few months. Finally agreed to meet in person."

"Did you know who she was before then?"

Heat rushed to my cheeks as I debated my answer. The thought of how we met the night before was enough for me to claim that yes, yes, I knew her before our date. But the truth was much more complicated than that.

Hudson shook his head before I answered. "Haley's been through shit. But none of it was her fault. Anna's close to Valentina, and I've been married twice, so trust me when I wanted to judge the woman off the bat. But Dawson isn't me. And the fact that he cheated at all is proof of that because it wouldn't have mattered what a woman ever did, I'd never fuck someone other than my wife."

The venom in his voice was not what I expected.

"Haley didn't go after him. She didn't target him. People around here... She's not the one who created the mess. Dawson was the only one who knew he was married. Haley got wrapped up in his lies, and she's been paying for it." Hudson shook his head like he felt sorry for her.

"I don't blame Haley."

"Then what's with the look? Did you target her so you could make her feel like shit?"

"What? No. Why would I do that? Is that really who you think I am?" I was more than a little offended.

"Honestly, I have no idea. What I do know is that when a woman comes in here alone, I pay attention. Finley used to meet her dates here. I would get so damn mad at her, but I realized it was a good thing. If I knew Finley, or any of the other women, were meeting random people somewhere else, I'd flip out. As for Haley, I didn't know you two were on a first date, but you didn't show up together, and she looked around when she walked in like she didn't know who she was looking for. I paid attention. But I don't know what you're doing with her."

Hudson had no right. He wasn't her protector. Her keeper. He was just the guy who owned the bar. He already had a wife. And kids. And everything he wanted. Why was he the self-appointed guardian of single women in MacKellar Cove?

"Haley and I have been talking for months. Not that it's any of your fucking business, but we met the night before we were here, but we didn't know who the other was. We never exchanged names, so we didn't have any way of knowing each other. When she sat down across from me, I was surprised, but not in a bad way."

"You don't owe me an explanation," Hudson said, trying to dismiss me.

"It sure as hell feels like I do. Are you a friend of hers? She said she thought you were a nice guy, but you have a wife."

Hudson raised his eyebrows and stared hard at me for a long minute.

Yeah, I was being an asshole. I couldn't explain why, but I also couldn't stop the attitude I was giving him.

"You like her." He wasn't asking.

I nodded once.

Hudson lowered his brows and leaned on the bar between us. "I don't know Haley well, but I know how this town can be. I can only imagine the bullshit that's been spewed in her direction for Dawson's fuckup. I've heard some of it and stopped it, but I know it still happens. I'm going to be protective of any woman who comes into my bar because I own this place, and if someone gets hurt while they're here, I'm responsible. So, you can get pissed off all you want, but until you're going to share with the others that you're with Haley, and you're fucking proud to call her yours and to be called hers, then I'm going to watch out for her."

"It's too soon for that," I mumbled.

"Fine, then back the fuck off me and get your shit straight. I don't care if you marry her or move on. All I know is you're not going to add to her trauma. She's been through enough, and she deserves better."

"Yeah, she does. And I'm not going to cause her more harm. I didn't know who she was until we talked when we were here. But I like her. I enjoy talking to her. And the sex—"

I clamped my mouth shut when Hudson's brows jumped high again. "You slept with her?"

I sighed and nodded.

"Not my business, as long as you were a gentleman."

"It was before our date. When we met the night before."

Hudson stared at me, piecing it all together, then shook his head and chuckled. "You know what? I'm too old to get wrapped up in all of this. Haley's sweet. She's one of the book club women. If any of them find out you fucked with her, they'll gut you and you'll never have a date in MacKellar Cove again."

"I didn't," I growled.

"Good. Then we're good."

I nodded, and Hudson moved to walk away, then stopped.

"For what it's worth, I think you two might be good together. Anna and I didn't have the easiest start. She hated me for a long time. You're further ahead with Haley than I was when Anna and I started seeing each other."

"Yeah?"

He nodded. "Yeah. And thanks for setting the record straight about things with her. For all the things I love about MacKellar Cove, there are some people who aren't going to give Haley a chance no matter what. Even with Brantley and

Valentina racing toward a future, people still think Valentina and Dawson are going to work it out."

"For Brantley's sake, I hope that's not going to happen."

Hudson chuckled and shook his head. "Agreed, but also, definitely not gonna happen. Those two are solid."

I nodded.

Hudson got called by a customer at the other end of the bar, so he moved away, but not before giving me a smile that might have been approving of my involvement with Haley.

But what he said wasn't wrong. None of the guys brought up Haley, but neither did I. I was too chickenshit about whatever they were going to say to start the conversation.

If I wanted her in my life, I needed to tell my friends about her.

Maybe I'd start with Brantley. After all, Haley showing up was what led to Brantley finally getting a chance to show Valentina how much he loved her.

All I knew was I wanted to keep seeing Haley and see where things went between us. Maybe it would fizzle and end. Or maybe she'd be the woman I'd been waiting for most of my life.

Or maybe she'd just be a good friend one day. No matter what, I liked her enough to find out.

7

HALEY

I knew the knock on my door was Sofia. I wasn't paying attention to the time and was trapped. She'd see my car and know I was home, so even if I pretended not to be there, she'd come back in and drag me to book club.

Usually I ran an errand thirty minutes before she would be leaving so I could say I wasn't home and couldn't go with her. I loved that she always wanted me to go, but I knew the others were only tolerating me because Sofia was amazing and they liked her.

Me? I wasn't really their friend, but they were all too nice to ask me not to come back.

"Come on, Haley, I know you're home," Sofia called from the other side of the door.

I sighed and let her in. "I'm not dressed."

"You're also not gone. Not paying attention to the time tonight?" She smirked at me.

My cheeks heated as I struggled to explain my standard behavior as if it wasn't intentional. "I have no idea what you're talking about."

"Sure you don't," Sofia said in a patronizing tone.

I growled. "You should go without me. I'm not ready to go out."

"If you think I'm going to walk away and trust you to show up, you haven't been paying attention. I thought you liked going to book club." The hurt in her eyes made me feel like crap.

"I do. I just feel like I'm not really supposed to be there."

Sofia's blonde brows shot high, her eyes widening. "Did someone say something?"

I shook my head before she finished asking. "It's not them. I just... I don't know."

"Yes, you do. You are still letting Dawson take things from you. Valentina moved on with her life and is married to Brantley now. She spent twenty-five years with Dawson. You were only with him nine months."

"Yeah, I know. I'm so ridiculous. I should just move on already," I said sarcastically, rolling my eyes as I walked away.

"Whoa. What was that?" Sofia asked.

"Nothing. I'm just not in a great mood. You should go. I'd only ruin the night."

"Nope." Sofia grabbed my arm and tried to pull me toward the door. "You're coming."

I tugged my arm from her and shook my head. "No. Sofia, I'm fine. I don't want to go."

She studied me carefully, her gaze taking in all of me from my messy ponytail to my comfortable tee and sweats. It wasn't my usual look. I made every effort to always look like I could do anything from watch a movie to go to a nice dinner, but at the moment, I was wallowing hard and not ready to do anything else.

"What's really going on, Haley?"

I pulled my bottom lip between my teeth and crossed my arms. "Nothing."

"Liar."

"You can't say that. You don't know."

"I know I mentioned Valentina, and you lost it on me. I know you've been seeing Knox and instead of the stars that were in your eyes a week ago, you're acting like things are over. You're not the person I've gotten to know. So talk to me." She sat on my couch and settled in, like she was happy to skip book club.

"You have to go."

"Either I stay here and you tell me what's going on or you go to book club with me." Sofia raised a brow in challenge.

I really didn't want to go to book club, but none of them would notice something was off with me. They wouldn't pry or try to get me to talk. It was by far the safer option. As long as I could keep my mood in check.

"Fine, I'll go. But then you leave me alone."

She held up her hands in defense and watched me as I backed out of the room to change.

I tossed my clothes into the hamper and yanked open my closet door. I grabbed a pair of jeans and a sweater that was so soft and cozy it felt like pajamas but looked good enough to go out in. I tore the band out of my hand, ignoring the tug when I pulled out a few strands of hair. I ran a brush through my hair and fluffed it to make it somewhat presentable, then I added some mascara and lip gloss and decided it was going to have to do.

I took a deep breath and tried to stop the frustration I felt. It wasn't because of Sofia, and I knew that even as I took it out on her. It wasn't fair.

"I'm sorry," I said as I walked out of my room. She was standing near the door, waiting for me.

"You have every right to be upset with me for throwing Valentina in your face. It wasn't right."

I shook my head. "It's fine. I know you're right. I'm just off today. I shouldn't have taken it out on you."

She looked closely at me for a second, but she didn't push. "I wish I could look as good as you do in twice the time you just did that." She gestured to her worn jeans and sweatshirt. "I always feel like I'm so frumpy."

"Your job requires you to wear things that don't matter if they're destroyed in Mrs. Watson's dishwasher. I'd never get a client if I wasn't put together all the time. To be honest, it's kind of exhausting, but I chose my career."

"True. And I chose mine. I love what I do. Even if I don't always feel like I make a good impression on people."

I wrapped my arm around her shoulders and led her away from my apartment. "You make an excellent impression on people. And anyone who isn't willing to see past what you wear to who you are underneath doesn't deserve to know you."

She smiled. "Thanks, Haley. Same for you, you know. If someone can't see your talent and judges you by your appearance, they're not worth your time."

I chuckled but didn't say anything. Most people didn't understand. I was the person women went to to look and feel good. I could ruin their day with a bad cut or style, or I could make their night with a great one. And if they walked into the salon and I looked like I could barely pull myself together, they wouldn't trust me to be the one who made them feel amazing.

Sofia and I decided to drive, even though it was a nice night. It was dark on the early side, and she was always anxious about walking anywhere at night. I'd never asked her about it, just went with it and figured if she wanted to tell me, she would.

Finley was letting Piper and Zoey in when we arrived. They all waited for us, hugging Sofia warmly before giving me much cooler hugs with forced smiles and empty joy that I'd joined Sofia.

Yay. Book club.

I took my seat and let them all talk around me, eating the cake Karissa made and melting into the background as much as possible. I thought I was going to get away with it, too, but Sofia ratted me out.

"Haley didn't want to come," Sofia said. "She needs some cheering up."

"No, I don't. I'm fine," I protested before they started in on me. They were all kind and wonderful people, but I wasn't in the mood for them to make me feel worse when they tried to convince me they really wanted me there, even though they didn't.

"What's going on?" Anna asked. "Is it Knox?"

"How do you know about Knox?" I blurted before I could think about it.

"Whoa, you and Knox are together?" Valentina asked. She grinned and nodded. "I can see that. He's a good friend of Brantley's and a really good man."

"Sebastian thinks very highly of Knox. He must not know. He didn't say anything to me," Zoey said. "Tell me everything."

"There's nothing to tell. We went out on two dates. That's it." I didn't want to admit I hadn't heard from him since our second date. Not even after I sent him a message saying I had a good time.

"Are you going to see him again?" Blake asked. I'd

spoken to Blake a few times when I went to eat at Cracked, but I still didn't know her well.

"I don't think so," I admitted.

"What? Why not? You were so excited after your date a week ago," Sofia said.

"And I don't think it's going to work out," I told her, shrugging like it was no big deal.

"I don't believe that," Sofia argued. "Is that why you're in a mood and didn't want to come today?"

I shrugged, not wanting to admit all of it. Between Knox not replying, work being busy yesterday but not so busy I didn't overhear someone making a comment about me, and then feeling like the third wheel in a group of friends, I was just tired. And a little bit done.

I'd started to think about sticking around MacKellar Cove, but every time I thought it might work out, something else kicked me and made me doubt everything. Just like after I met Valentina, my instincts were off. I was off.

"I know you don't know us well, but you can trust us," Valentina said. "You and I are bonded in a truly messed up way, but I know none of it was your fault. I apologize if I ever made you feel as though you had something to do with it."

"You didn't. It's not you. I'm just..." I looked around at all of them staring at me and couldn't decide if they were waiting for me to make a fool of myself or if they actually cared. "I should go."

"Sit your ass down," Elise said as soon as I lifted myself from my chair. She glared at me until I lowered to the seat again. "Say it."

I shrugged. "Say what?"

"Whatever it is that's in your head right now. You're holding back. You want to say something, but you're not sure if you should. Just say it." Elise leaned forward, elbows on her knees, and looked at me.

I'd never noticed how similar she and Chelsea looked until that moment. I should have picked up on it before, but neither mentioned it. Now, looking at her made me feel like I was looking at my friend.

"I don't belong here. Sofia brought me the first time because she thought it would help, but all I've done is create division and make everyone uncomfortable. You're all sitting here waiting for me to say something stupid or do some-thing stupid. And I'm waiting for you to all tell me exactly what you think of me. I usually avoid Sofia on Sunday evenings so I don't have to come, but I wasn't watching the clock today. So, I'm sorry I ruined everyone's night. I'll just go."

"I said sit your ass down," Elise growled when I stood again.

I sighed and looked at her. "Why? I know when I'm not wanted somewhere."

"Then you're an idiot because I promise you, this group doesn't invite people who aren't wanted. Yeah, your situation is fucked up. So was mine. So was Valentina's. So was Laura's. So many of us have shitty stories that brought us here. We've all needed each other at one time or another. We don't know you well, Haley. But we want to. We want to know the woman beneath the flash and style. We want to know what we can do to show you we're serious when we say we're your friends." Elise stood and put her hands on my arms, holding me in place. "Chelsea's talked about you a lot over the last few months. She knows the real you. I know I'd like that woman, if I got to know her, too."

"Chelsea's great."

Elise nodded. "Hell, yeah, she is. Hard not to be when she's related to me."

I snorted as everyone around us laughed.

"I've had enough fucked up failures in my life to even think about celebrating when someone else is going through something that sucks. If I had to guess, you've dealt with a lot of pain and trust issues over the last few months because of Dawson, but you haven't felt like you could talk about it because of Valentina."

I risked a glance at Valentina. All she did was smile sadly at me. "Is that true?"

I shrugged.

"Shit, Haley. Neither of us were spared Dawson's crap. I'm sorry you didn't feel comfortable talking about it."

"It's fine."

"No, it's fucking not," Elise argued. "I'm not saying Valentina should feel guilty. You were both broken by a man who lied to you. Trust me, I know how it feels. But you've let Valentina deal with her pain and shoved your own down. I know how that goes, too. But if it's creating problems with Knox, then talk to us. And if it's something else, talk to us. I don't care what it is, just talk to us."

I looked to all the other women surrounding Elise. They weren't smirking or sneering. They met my gaze with one of concern and care. Like they actually wanted me to be okay.

And dammit, that did me in.

"I've never been close to my parents. They weren't warm or nurturing. They pretty much ignored me as soon as I was old enough to microwave my own dinner. They were never mean or abusive, just not interested in having a kid. As soon as I could, I left. Went to cosmetology school and moved on with my life. But I never really knew what it was like to have someone who was looking after me."

A few of them nodded as if they understood. Elise let go of my arms and took a step back to sit again. I followed suit and returned to my seat.

"I have a tendency to jump into a relationship with both feet. To convince myself that this one is the right one and we're meant to be and it'll last forever."

"So you won't be alone," Sofia whispered.

I nodded. "Exactly. With Dawson, I told myself..." I glanced at Valentina, but she just smiled kindly at me. "I told myself his work kept him busy, but that he loved me but he was just busy. I thought moving here was right. We'd been seeing each other for months. I was sure I finally followed the right cues and didn't jump too fast. Obviously, I was wrong again."

The others chuckled with me.

"Knox and I talked for months on Book Boyfriends Wanted. He made me laugh, and he seemed nice and when he asked if I wanted to meet up, I was looking forward to it. The night before our first date, I went to Al's Hardware for Sofia and met him, but neither of us knew who the other was. He flirted with me. It was the first time since I moved here that a man looked at me with desire instead of disdain. It was... so damn nice. And before my date the next night, I wanted to feel desired. No names, no future contact, just one night together. He was just as eager as I was."

"Well, most of them think with their dicks, so yeah," Elise said, winking at me.

"True, and I didn't mind that. He looked shocked when I showed up for our date, but it was good. We had fun. He was exactly who he seemed in our chats."

"But..." Sofia prompted me.

"But nothing. Our date was really good, and he messaged me a few days later and asked me out again.

Wednesday night, we went to dinner. Just dinner. We talked and got to know a little more about each other, but he didn't kiss me either night. Just a kiss on the cheek. Then he said goodnight and walked away."

"And you think that means he doesn't like you?" Elise asked.

I shrugged. "I don't know. You just said men think with their dicks. If he is, why isn't he even kissing me? And for that matter, he hasn't reached out since then, even though I said I had a good time. I think he's not interested. But dammit, I really thought after months of talking, it would be different. That he wouldn't run as soon as he found out who I was."

"But he didn't. You went out on a second date," Blake said.

"And then nothing," I whined. I drew a breath and let it out slowly. "I don't know how to be patient. Like I said, I jump. And two dates and one night together, plus him not walking away as soon as he realized who I was, especially in this town, made me think maybe there was something there."

"Don't let this town get to you," Elise said. "I know that's easy to say, but the people who care that you were the one Dawson was cheating with are the same ones who think Valentina is going to ditch Brantley and get back together with Dawson."

"Never going to happen," Valentina growled. She shook her head and shivered.

I smiled at her. She was strong. She took a situation that would have made most people want to hide and turned it into a future that's so much better for her.

"It's just hard when someone calls me a homewrecker," I confessed.

They all made noises of frustration and anger, but it was Valentina who leaned forward.

"My marriage ending was not your fault. If Dawson hadn't been sleeping with you, he would have been sleeping with someone else. He might have been anyway. If I hear someone saying that to you, I promise you, I will set them straight. The reality was I wasn't happy. Goldie and Anna know this, but I didn't like airing my dirty laundry, so I pretended everything was fine, even though it hadn't been for years. Dawson never should have cheated. There's never an excuse for it. But neither of us were invested in our marriage. I tried to be what I thought he wanted, but I hadn't been happy in a long time. Not like I am now. You showing up at my house was the best thing that could have happened to me. I wasn't thrilled about it, but my anger was never at you. I'm sorry you've felt the anger of others, though. Others who have no right or knowledge of what was going on."

"Thank you," I whispered.

"And for fuck's sake, can we stop blaming the woman for the man not being able to keep it in his pants?" Elise said. "I mean, really? He's swinging his dick everywhere, and it's the single woman's fault for hopping on? Fuck that. Own your sexuality, but he needs to own his. I'm with Valentina. I'll knock down anyone who says anything to you."

"Mind hanging out at Teased by Debby on Saturdays?" I teased.

They all turned to me with varying degrees of anger in their eyes.

"Seriously?" Elise asked, her voice dark and dangerous. "They say shit at your work?"

I shrugged.

"Fuck that. I'll be there on Saturday. Who's with me?" Elise asked.

Every hand went up.

I chuckled and tried not to cry. Dammit, I was happy I went to book club. And that I was wrong about the women sitting in the room with me.

I just hoped I was wrong about Knox and maybe we still had a chance.

8

———

AFTER HOW ENCOURAGING AND SUPPORTIVE VALENTINA WAS at book club, I decided to stop into Cove Bakery on my way to work Tuesday. I heard amazing things about her talents for months, but I was too afraid to go in and see her. But I wanted some sugar, and Cove Bakery was too tempting to keep resisting.

The pink and white striped awning was welcoming and joyful before I even stepped inside. When I did, the place was busy but not packed and only a few people looked up at me, smiling before returning to their treats and conversation.

"Welcome to Cove Bakery," the woman behind the counter said. "How are you today?"

"I'm good, thank you," I told her. "How are you?"

She chuckled. "Can't complain when I get to talk to people and enjoy the fruits of Valentina's labor."

"I can understand that. It's why I'm here."

"I'm Harriett. I don't think we've met."

I shook my head. "No. It's the first time I've been in. I'm Haley."

Her eyes widened for half a second before her smile tightened. "Oh. It's nice to meet you."

I smiled back at her. After the way Valentina seemed to defend me at book club, I didn't expect one of her coworkers to have such a negative reaction to me showing up, but maybe I read into what she said and I was wrong about her.

"Um, what do you recommend?"

"Oh, uh, well, if you like chocolate, the chocolate croissants are divine. If you're a caramel fan, we have some spectacular brownies. And we have some more savory options, too. But most people are here for the sweets."

"I'm definitely here for the sweets."

"Then I highly recommend the croissants or a muffin. They're all delicious."

I scanned the case and decided to indulge, especially if this was the only time I'd step foot in Cove Bakery. "I'll try both. Chocolate croissant and a caramel banana muffin. Ooh, and I think I'll try one of those brownies, too. And a water, please."

Harriett smiled and got up from her stool. "To go?"

I choked back the disappointment and shook my head. "For here. Although I know I won't finish it all while I'm here. Can I get a bag?"

"Of course," Harriett said. She was pleasant and kind, but she did not want me there.

She handed over a bottle of water, an empty plate, and a bag with all my treats inside. She accepted my card and said to enjoy, but I knew she just wanted to get me out of there.

I sat at a table with my back against the wall. No one paid any attention to me while I unpacked my chocolate croissant and took a bite. I groaned. Damn. Valentina was a wizard.

"Homewrecker," I heard from a few feet away. Not

directed at me, but part of a conversation whispered about me.

The first tears stung my eyes. Dammit.

I looked over at Harriett and saw her whispering to another woman at the counter. The other woman scowled in my direction. Harriett glanced at the door that led to the kitchen, then back to me.

She nodded to the other woman, then slid off her stool. She waddled toward the kitchen, checking I hadn't moved before she pushed her way into the kitchen, the door swinging closed behind her.

The woman at the counter glared at me.

I forced myself not to cower, but it wasn't easy to sit there and take it from them. Most people in town ignored me. Only a few had ever said anything to me. But sitting there, in Valentina's bakery, I knew I shouldn't have come.

"Haley!" Valentina exclaimed from behind me.

I turned to face her, forcing myself to smile.

She walked over to me and hugged me before pulling out the other chair at my table. "I'm so glad you came in. Why didn't you tell me you were coming?"

I glanced around the bakery, seeing every single person watching us. "Um, I figured I'd try it after what you said the other day."

"About you not being to blame for my marriage to Dawson ending?" she said loudly, clearly for the benefit of the others. "God, no. My cheating ex-husband is the only one to blame for lying to both of us. You did nothing wrong except fall for the wrong guy, which is what I did, too. I'm glad Dawson's lies are out in the open so we can both move on with our lives and be happy. God knows I'm happier with Brantley than I was with Dawson."

I swallowed my unease and smiled gratefully at her. "Thank you. This is delicious."

"The chocolate croissants are dangerous. I could eat a whole tray of them. If I ever bake them at home, I barely get to pull them out of the oven before Brantley and the girls are grabbing them."

I glanced around and realized the number of people watching us had dropped off dramatically. "Thank you," I whispered.

Valentina winked at me. "How's the muffin? That's a new one. Karissa samples new items for me, and she was a big fan of that."

"It's amazing."

"Good. Karissa practically forced me to put it on the menu. She and McJenna love it. Do you know McJenna? Xavier's daughter? She and my oldest are good friends."

I shook my head. "I don't know a lot of people in town."

"We need to change that. There's not a ton going on this time of year, but as it gets closer to spring, and definitely through summer, there's a lot. Did you go to any of the events last year?"

I shook my head. "I was busy with work."

"You have to get out more this summer. Come with us to stuff. Knox usually joins us since he and Brantley are good friends," Valentina said without a hint of irony. She grinned, letting me know she knew what she was saying but that the rest of them wouldn't pick up on it.

"I'll think about it," I told her. I still hadn't heard from Knox, and making plans to double date with Valentina and Brantley wasn't a good idea if Knox was avoiding me.

"I hope you join us."

"Me, too."

"I need to get back to the kitchen and take some

blondies out of the oven, but it was good to see you. Let me know when you're coming in again and I'll make you something special." She stood and hugged me again, then turned to Harriett at the counter. "Harriett, Haley is a good friend. Make sure to let me know whenever she comes in. She's going to come back soon, right, Haley?"

I chuckled at her announcement and nodded. "I definitely will."

"Excellent. Bye, Haley! See you Sunday at book club!"

I smiled and waved at Valentina's retreating form. She was amazing. Most people wouldn't welcome their husband's girlfriend to town, let alone stand up for her when others got catty about the situation, but Valentina was definitely not most people. She was special.

I finished my croissant and half of my muffin, packing up the rest for later with my brownie. I drained the last of my water and carried the empty bottle to the counter to be recycled.

"I'm sorry about the way I treated you," Harriett said when I handed over the bottle.

"It's okay."

She shook her head. "No, it isn't. I thought I was protecting Valentina. I was worried about her coming out here and seeing you, but when I told her you were here, she was so excited to see you."

"She's really wonderful. She's been so kind to me."

"That's who she is. She said from the beginning that she blamed Dawson for things ending, but I didn't know you two were friends."

"I've tried to keep to myself, mostly."

Harriett shook her head. "Please don't. You are always welcome here."

"Thanks. I know not everyone feels the same."

"Don't worry about Annabeth." Harriett shook her head. "I love her, but she'll never agree with divorce, no matter the situation."

"I understand." I didn't, but I wasn't going to argue. Not all marriages worked, and what happened in a marriage was between the two people who made the vows. No one else should have a say in whether a marriage lasted or not. It wasn't anyone's business.

And even though I had a part in Valentina and Dawson's marriage ending, I didn't get a say. When I learned Dawson was married, I blocked his number and deleted him from my phone. It didn't matter if he wanted to keep seeing me, I didn't trust him, and I didn't want to be with anyone I couldn't trust.

I said goodbye to Harriett and promised to come back soon, then left to go to work.

I put my handbag in the back and was about to walk out front when Chelsea burst through the curtain. "Did you go to Cove Bakery this morning?"

"Yes, why?" I asked cautiously.

"Madeline just came in to talk to Debby and was telling her about it. Said you went in there like you owned the place and got an attitude with Harriett, then demanded to see Valentina. She said Valentina was kind and sweet to you as you told her the food was not as good as everyone says. She said you threw away your food and told everyone you're never coming back."

"What? None of that happened? Why would she say that?"

"Because she's a hateful bitch. What actually happened?"

I sighed. "Valentina was really sweet at book club Sunday, so I decided to go to Cove Bakery today. When I told

Harriett my name, she got all weird, then someone named Annabeth came in and said something about me being a homewrecker. Harriett told Valentina I was there, and Valentina came out to say hi. She was amazing. She announced to everyone that we were friends and that Harriett should always tell her when I arrive and that she was happy to see me and never once blamed me for her marriage ending."

"Sounds more likely than what Madeline just spouted."

"And I did not throw away anything. I would have bought the whole damn case if I could have eaten it all. Everything was so good," I groaned.

"I know. I love it there. Ugh. I'm sorry Madeline is telling one more lie about you."

"I take it she's friends with Annabeth?"

"Yep. I think they might be sisters, actually."

I rolled my eyes and groaned. "Of course they are."

"Don't worry about it. Debby tsked and made noncommittal noises until Madeline happily trounced away, having spread her evil for the day."

"You know, I was almost looking forward to today. I had an amazing, sweet breakfast, I talked to a friend, and I was going to spend all day working with another friend. But now these hateful women just ruin everything."

"It's what they want," Chelsea said. "You can't let them get to you."

"It sounds so easy to do," I said sarcastically.

Chelsea laughed. "I know. But Madeline isn't likely to come back since she already came by, so at least there's that to look forward to."

I folded my hands in front of me in prayer. "Please, God, let that be true."

Chelsea laughed again, then looped her arm through

mine. "Come on. Let's go get to work and forget all about people who want to bring us down."

"Yes, please." I let Chelsea pull me out into the salon and get to work.

MY DAY ENDED up going better than I expected. I got three new clients, one walk in and two who'd scheduled appointments with me. All three gushed how much they loved their new looks when they left and gave me huge tips.

And then I got home and had a lengthy message from Knox.

HANDYNOTHANDSY

You probably don't want to hear from me anymore, but I wanted to apologize for not being in touch. I had a rough week at work, but that's no excuse. The big thing was my dad ended up in the hospital. He's okay now, just a minor scare Friday morning, but everything snowballed and I was working longer hours than usual. This is the first day I've been able to stop for more than a minute or two, and I wanted to reach out. I really am sorry, and I hope you're willing to let me apologize in person one day.

His story would be easy enough to check, and I was sure he knew that. But that wasn't why I believed him. He said he was sorry. In my experience, people didn't say that, especially men, unless they were trying to get me into bed or really meant it.

Knox had already gotten me into bed, so I was leaning toward he really meant it.

I couldn't stop the smile that lifted my lips. I checked the time and realized he should be closing the hardware store in less than an hour, unless he closed early. But if I could time it right, I could surprise him with dinner and maybe spend some time together.

Before I second guessed my decision, I went back to my car and pulled out of the lot. I drove to Will Work For Burgers and ordered two cheeseburgers, two large orders of fries, and two bottled drinks. I checked the time as I got back in my car and crossed my fingers that I'd make it.

The lights were still on when I parked in front of Al's Hardware. I grabbed the bag of food and the drinks and headed for the door, smiling when the store was quiet.

"We're about to close. Can I help you find anything?" Knox called out.

I couldn't see him, but I followed his voice toward the front of the store. "I found what I'm looking for," I said when I finally laid eyes on him.

He looked exhausted. His hair was disheveled and curling over his collar. His beard looked like it could use a trim. And his eyes were red and weary. But he smiled when he saw me. "Hey. What are you doing here?"

I held up the bag and said, "I got your message. I was hoping you'd be interested in dinner."

"Yeah?"

I nodded. "Yeah."

"Dinner would be excellent. Give me a second to lock up and we can head back to my apartment. If that's okay with you?"

"Absolutely."

He gave me a relieved smile. He walked by me, squeezing my arm as he passed, and locked the front door. He turned to me and asked, "Where did you park?"

"Out front. Is that okay?"

"Yeah. Um, you can move your car around the back if you want. You don't have to, but then you won't have to go all the way around. Never mind. It's not a big deal."

"Knox, I can move my car or I can walk. Either way is fine."

He took a deep breath. "I'm sorry. I'm just still all over the place, and I'm really fucking happy to see you. I was sure you were never going to talk to me again."

I walked over to him and smiled. "I've had a few people jumping to conclusions about me over the last few months. I figured the least I owed you was a chance to explain. And I got the feeling you were telling me the truth, so there was no reason for me to get mad. Family comes first."

He sighed again and nodded. "Thanks. That... Thank you."

"Should I move my car?"

He nodded. "Yeah. It'll just be easier when you leave. God knows these crazy people will probably see me walking you out and try to buy something."

I laughed with him and tried to ignore the doubt lingering in the back of my mind that said he was trying to hide that I was spending time with him. Moving my car so it was closer to his apartment made sense. It had nothing to do with my car being parked on the street in front of his shop and the wagging tongues of our town.

"Where should I park?" I asked.

He opened the front door and stepped outside with me. "See that driveway at the end of the building?"

I nodded.

"Go through there. There's a lot, but give me a minute to open my door so you know which door to park near."

"Is your truck back there?"

He chuckled. "Duh. Yeah, you can just park next to it.

Sorry. Wait until I open the door to get out of your car, though. I don't want you standing outside in the cold."

I nodded, feeling oddly touched he was worried. He wasn't trying to hide me. I was being ridiculous.

I drove slowly into the lot behind the hardware store and parked next to his truck. A minute later, he opened the door that led into his apartment and walked out to meet me.

"Can I hug you?" he asked when I got out of the car.

I nodded and stepped into him, enjoying the way he relaxed against me more than I expected. He leaned on me for a minute, letting me take some of the stress and anxiety he'd been dealing with for almost a week.

"I'm really happy you're here. I never expected you to show up, but damn, am I glad you did."

"I figured we can all use someone to talk to sometimes, and dinner we don't have to think about ahead of time. If you've been working and spending time with your dad, I figured you probably hadn't been to the grocery store. It's just burgers, but I was hoping it would be a nice surprise."

"Definitely," he whispered into my neck. "Thank you, Haley."

"You're welcome, Knox."

We stood there until the cold air sank in and I shivered. Knox took a step back. "Shit. I told you not to get out of your car so you wouldn't be out in the cold, then I kept you out here. I'm sorry. Let's go inside."

I nodded and followed him into his apartment, telling myself I was only there to be a friend. We were not going to end up in his bed again.

Probably.

9

———————

KNOX

I GROANED AND LEANED BACK IN MY SEAT, RUBBING MY stomach. "That was delicious," I told Haley. "Thank you."

"You're welcome. I'm glad your dad is doing better."

I nodded. When Dad called me and said he didn't feel well, then slurred his words, I freaked out. For all the shit Tony, Dick, and Wayne gave me, I was thankful they were there. They didn't hesitate to take over the store so I could get to Dad right away.

"Me, too. And I'm grateful you were willing to forgive me for ignoring you for days."

She shook her head and smiled. "Nothing to forgive. I get it."

"Are you close to your family?"

Her smile faltered. "Um, no. I'm really not."

"Really? I would have thought you were after what you said. That family is important."

She shifted next to me on the couch. The movie we started when we sat down to dinner was half over and we were still sitting a few feet apart, but her shift seemed to push her even farther away. "Family is important. But I've never really felt like I had one. My parents were always sort of distant, and I don't have any siblings."

"Wow. That sucks. I don't have siblings either, but I'm really close to my dad."

"What about your mom?"

I didn't like talking about my mom. Not because she wasn't great, but because it hurt. "My mom died when I was two. Got sick and ended up in the hospital. They couldn't figure out what was going on, and eventually, she just died."

"Holy shit. That's insane."

I nodded. "It was. It destroyed my dad. He was so mad at the doctors. I think that's part of why he didn't go to the doctor earlier last week when he wasn't feeling well. He doesn't trust them."

"That's hard. But I can understand him feeling that way. It's hard to put your faith in people who've let you down in the past."

"It is. I don't remember my mom, but there are some guys who hang around the store who've told me a little of what my dad was like before Mom died."

"Yeah?"

I smiled, thinking about some of the stories they'd shared. "He adored my mom. Worshipped her. She was his world. He said they talked about having more kids, but she died before they had a chance."

"I'm so sorry."

"Thanks. I wish I had memories of them before she died."

Haley nodded thoughtfully. "My parents aren't like that. They were never affectionate with me, and they aren't with each other either. There were times I wondered why they even had me."

I hated that for her. I couldn't imagine feeling like I

wasn't wanted. My dad never once made me feel that way, even though I knew there were a lot of things he wished my mom had been around for when I was growing up. "You said you're from Kansas City, but you never told me how you ended up here. Where did you live before moving to MacKellar Cove?"

"After cosmetology school, I stayed in the Chicago area for a few years. Then I started moving east. Cleveland. Buffalo. Syracuse. I never felt settled. When I decided to come here, I thought I was creating a family for myself."

"With Dawson. Damn." I hesitated, wondering how much I could or should pry.

"Go ahead and ask me," she said softly.

I met her gaze and smiled sheepishly, wondering how much she hated that people were curious. "How did you meet?"

"I had a flat tire, and he offered to help me change it. We talked while he was working, and I liked it. I liked him. I never knew he was married. Never even suspected it."

"I know."

Her head snapped up, her brown eyes fixed on me. "You do?"

I nodded. "Of course. You said it before, and I believe you. I don't know you all that well, but I feel like I know you. Like, I can tell the kind of person you are. I don't see you as someone who would get involved with someone who was already in a relationship."

"I wish others understood that," she whispered.

"Not everyone is interested in the truth," I told her, thinking of Dick, Wayne, and Tony. As much as I thought they were decent guys, they also weren't overly concerned with the truth. They liked to tell their stories, whether they were full of truth or not.

"I've definitely learned that. Working at a salon isn't always easy."

"But you like it?"

Her smile was quick and genuine. "I love it. It was something I could learn quickly and make money without having to spend a ton to get a degree or anything. I've kept up with my training, but it's affordable compared to some options. It allowed me to be independent as soon as I turned eighteen."

"Get away from your parents," I said.

She nodded. "I talk to them once or twice a year, catch up and wish them well, but I don't visit often. I think it's been three or four years since I saw them."

"Wow. That's hard for me to wrap my head around. Hell, I just moved in here a few years ago. I never bothered to move out of my dad's house. There was no reason to."

"It's nice you're close to him. You said he used to own the hardware store?"

"Yep. He loved it. He only retired because he found the long hours were getting to him."

"It was probably easier for him to know you were willing to step in and keep it going."

My cheeks warmed at the implication. That my dad left the place in good hands. That I wouldn't change it or do anything different. That I wouldn't fuck the whole thing up the second I got my hands on it and almost tank my dad's business.

"Yeah," I said noncommittally.

Her smile slipped at my tone, but she forced it back in place. "I should probably go. I just wanted to bring you dinner."

"Yeah, I'm pretty worn out. But I really appreciate the food. And the company."

She smiled up at me as we both stood. We were close, close enough that I caught the scent of her shampoo.

"I'm trying to be good here," I told her.

She gazed up at me. "Why?"

I swayed closer to her, wanting to lose myself in her like I did the night we met. "Because I don't want to take advantage of you. I don't want to be that guy who drags you off to bed after I've had a tough week."

"I don't need you to be," she whispered.

I closed my eyes and inhaled her. I wanted nothing more than to forget the outside world and focus only on her. But if I did that, I was treating her like any other woman. She was more than that to me.

She was months of talks and weeks of smiles. She was moments and sweetness and the potential for so much more than a night or two.

"I like you, Haley. I know we've only had three dates, if you count tonight, but I like you. And I don't want to fuck it up. Even though we were already together once, I want to make sure we're both in the right space when we're together again."

She smiled up at me and lifted slowly onto her toes, giving me time to back away.

I had no intention of backing away.

Her hands slid up my chest as slowly as her lips moved toward mine. I waited, letting her lead. When she pulled on my neck for me to close the distance between us, I didn't hesitate to do so.

Her kiss was sweet and tentative, like she was trying it out. The memories of the night we spent together slammed through me. I wanted her, bad, but I knew it wasn't a good idea. For either of us.

Her tongue brushed my lips, and I groaned as I opened

for her. She teased the tip of her tongue against mine, still shy and cautious with her kiss. I wasn't in a hurry to have her walk away, or in a hurry to move things along. Kissing her was perfect.

We stood in front of my couch forever, making out like kids who didn't know how to take things to the next step. My hands stayed on her hips, hers around my neck, and neither of us tried for anything more.

It was exactly what I needed. Which made me feel like an asshole to be taking from her, but she offered. She initiated the kiss. She made it so much better than I would have.

She eased back slightly and lowered herself down to flat feet. She was six inches or more shorter than me and she tucked right under my chin like she was made to be right there.

Her arms went around my waist and held me close, her head on my chest. Neither of us said anything, just held on to each other.

"I should go. I know you need to be up early tomorrow." She pulled back, not meeting my gaze.

"Hey," I said, catching her before she stepped away.

She looked up at me, a question in her eyes.

"Thank you. For being here."

She smiled. "You're welcome."

I walked her outside, waiting until she pulled around the corner before I went back in. It was a much better night than I expected. All thanks to Haley.

THE NEXT MORNING started out quietly, but by mid-morning, the store was busy. Word was finally getting around town that Dad ended up in the hospital and people were coming in to ask how he was doing. The extra traffic kept me from standing around and thinking about all the things I wasn't doing with my life.

Dad's health scare was a bit of a wake up call for me. More than I thought about until Haley left the night before. Sure, it scared the hell out of me, but after talking to Haley, it made me think about all the things I'd given up in my life. Things I'd always planned to do and hoped to do.

Like the changes to the store.

Things finally hit a lull just before lunch, but I knew another rush would come in when people were on a break from whatever job they were doing. Either stopping to grab a tool or part when they were out to lunch, or picking up something on their lunch break. When a woman with a bright smile wearing overalls and a bright yellow tee came in, my first thought was that she was lost.

"Morning. Can I help you?" I asked.

"I hope so. Are you Knox?"

I straightened, wondering how a woman I'd never laid eyes on knew my name. "I am. Have we met?"

She laughed. "No, no. Sorry. I just moved to town. I'm Daisy Lincoln."

"Lincoln Toys?" I asked as I shook her offered hand.

"Yeah! That's me. Wow. I didn't know anyone had heard of it."

"Small town."

She laughed again. "True, true. That's why I moved here. A friend of mine from college lives here. She said it's a beautiful place. Every time she posted pictures online, I was jealous and wanted to be here."

"And now you are."

"Now I am. To be honest, it's a little overwhelming, though. Natalie, my college friend, she's been a big help, but there's just so much to think through. She's the one who told me about you."

"Natalie Edwards?" I asked.

Daisy laughed. "That's the one. She said she comes here to get a lot of the supplies for the games and projects she plans for the kids to do during summer camp. She recommended I come in to see if you had what I am looking for to get my register situation all set up."

"I didn't realize you were that close to ready to open." When Tony mentioned the toy store that was supposed to be near his house, I figured he was off by a few months.

"Oh, I'm not. Not for about four months. I'm planning the grand opening for early summer, right after school lets out. Natalie is going to help me. She introduced me to Goldie at the tourism department. Everyone here is just so wonderful."

"It's a good place to live."

"So far, I'm enjoying it a lot. Once I get the toy store up and running, I think I'll settle in. For now, I'm pretty much nonstop."

"Well, what can I do for your register to help you move that along?"

Daisy talked with her hands as she described the piece of furniture she was planning to use for the register area. The size of it was enough that she could fit everything she needed, but it wasn't overly conducive to point-of-sale product displays. Which was what she was trying to figure out.

"I like what you have," she said, looking at the simple shelving my dad set up forever ago.

"It works. It's not overly attractive, but my customers don't care much about appearance. Yours might be a little more particular."

"True," she said, studying the shelves carefully. "I'm also trying to decide what little things I'm going to want to put at the front of the store."

"I go for low cost, impulse stuff. Things people might stick in their pocket or handbag, but also the tools everyone needs and usually forgets to grab when they're walking around the store." I pointed to the multitools that were a big seller.

"So smart. It's one of the many things I feel like I'm in over my head with."

"What made you decide to open a toy store?" I asked, always wondering what inspired a person.

"Because it's fun," she said with a loud laugh. "I mean, who doesn't want to play all day? I am definitely focused on kids and the toys they will like, but I'm also going to include options for adults."

"Really? Adult toys?" I asked, realizing how dirty it sounded as soon as the words were out of my mouth.

She laughed again, slapping her hand on the counter. "Not those kinds of toys. Not in the same store."

"Future plans," I teased her.

She threw her head back and laughed. "I'm not sure I'd be able to do that without my cheeks flaming and being embarrassed to talk to customers. Especially in a small town. I don't want to know what kind of toys the couples around here are bringing into the bedroom."

"There are definitely lines I'm not interested in crossing. Especially knowing some of the locals."

She chuckled. "Understood. Hey, do you mind if I take a few pictures of this?"

"Not at all," I told her, stepping out of the way of her shot.

She snapped a few pictures, changing angles and

getting closer to see certain things. Then she turned and looked at the rest of the store. "I need to get so many things. I need all the shelving for the toys. I can't decide if I want custom shelves or if I want the standard metal shelves so many stores use. I fell in love with the register and couldn't walk away from it, even though I knew it wasn't perfect."

"I get how that is."

"I do need a few things before I leave you to the rest of your day, though."

"Sounds good. Anything you need help finding?" I asked as another customer walked in.

Daisy shook her head and waved off my offer. "I'm going to wander and get a feel for everything, if that's okay. I'll find what I'm looking for as I go."

"Sounds good. Let me know if you need any help," I told her.

"I will. Thanks, Knox."

I turned to the customer and pointed him in the direction to find what he was looking for, then said hello to Teddy. He worked on a local construction crew but was always stopping in to pick up things for projects at home. He and his wife, Genevieve, had a beautiful fixer upper that Teddy only had time to bandage together between his work schedule and their growing family.

"Hey, Knox."

"How're Genevieve and the baby?"

Teddy looked exhausted. Like he could barely keep his head up, but when I asked about his family, he grinned like he'd just won the lottery. "All good. Michael turned one in January, and she's due in July with the second baby."

"Wow. That's great."

Teddy nodded. "It is, but man, it's busy. I love Gen, and I

love Michael, but the time she was off work when she had him was stressful. I'm not sure I'm ready for a second kid."

"Not really sure you have a choice. It's coming whether you're ready or not."

He shrugged. "I know. It's just... I'm not around enough to help her out. If I had a more regular schedule, I think everything would be easier."

"I can understand that," I said, even though I didn't. I'd only ever needed to worry about myself and Dad. No kids. No wife.

One day.

"We'll figure it out. We did last time, and Michael wasn't planned. Sorry for unloading on you."

"No worries."

He swiped his card and grabbed his bag before hurrying out the door with a wave.

Daisy dumped an armload of things onto the belt with a laugh. "Hardware stores are like catnip to me. When I walk around, they always spark new ideas. I have a feeling I'll be back very soon."

I laughed with her and scanned the items. "What are you going to do with this?" I held up a collection of hooks of varying sizes and shapes.

Daisy laughed. She laughed more than just about anyone I'd ever met. "That's what I actually came in here for. I needed something for all the little things I have. Some I'm going to use to organize cables and things like that, but some are going to be for things I need to have at hand, like clipboards and item lists."

"Smart." I finished scanning everything, then waited for her to swipe her card. I debated offering to help her get the toy store set up, but I didn't want her to think I was hitting on her.

"Thanks. I can't wait to get all this pulled together. And thanks for letting me check out your register. I think once I wrap my head around that piece, I'll feel better about the rest of the store."

"It sounds like it sets the tone."

She nodded. "It really does. That's what I love about it. I hope I can find other things that work with it." She grabbed her bags. "I just have to keep looking and trust that the right thing will come along. Great meeting you, Knox!"

"You, too, Daisy."

I waved as she walked out and kicked myself for not telling her I could build her whatever she needed. But I was just the guy who owned the hardware store. I should be introducing her to Teddy. He was the professional.

But I really wanted the job. If I could get out of my own way.

10

____

I CHECKED THE TIME AS I RUSHED TO MY TRUCK. I WAS LATE closing because a customer came in at the last minute, then took forever to figure out what they needed. My dad drilled it into me never to rush a customer, so I patiently waited until they were done, then rang up their ten-dollar purchase and flipped the sign to closed.

I sent Derek a quick text that I was running late but on my way. I pocketed my phone before he replied, hoping he wasn't too upset when I made it to Stone Auto Repair.

His parking lot was mostly empty when I arrived, and a customer walked out the front door, holding the door for me to go in. I thanked the woman, and hurried to grab it so she didn't have to wait.

"We don't have time for a walk-in," Derek called out when I stepped foot inside. He grinned and came closer, shaking my hand. "Thanks for coming."

"Not a problem. Sorry I got held up."

Derek waved off my concern. "It happens. I get that. Ready to take a look?"

I nodded. Derek led the way into the shop area, past the

Employees Only sign on the door. The sound of tools and the clanging of work echoed through the space. It was quiet compared to how it would be if the shop was full. Only two guys were left, that I could see.

Derek whistled loudly, getting the noise to stop. "Knox is here," he called out.

I wasn't sure why he was announcing my presence until six guys approached us, each shaking my hand and apologizing for getting me dirty.

I dismissed their concern and said, "Nice to meet you all."

They nodded and murmured the same, then all turned to Derek.

"I know what I want, but I wanted them to talk you through what they need. None of this is customer facing, so appearance isn't an overly big deal. Function is far more significant than appeal." Derek gestured to his crew, who all nodded.

"I can understand that. Is this going to be parts storage, tools, what are we talking?"

"A little bit of everything. We want to replace these old shelves. The metal is strong, but the wire shelves mean shit falls through and stuff falls off the back all the damn time. We like being able to see where everything is and the easy access, but the bad outweighs the good."

I walked over to what they had and started thinking about options. The shelving was standard industrial style shelving. Sturdy and big, with varying heights to accommodate different sized tools and parts, but I understood what he was saying. The cord for one tool hung through the open metal shelf and rested on top of another tool. Parts were scattered on all the shelves, not organized and overflowing the bins they were supposed to be in.

"Okay, so what works about what you have?" I asked, letting my gaze scan all of them. If Derek valued their opinions, I was going to do the same.

One guy stepped forward, approaching me in front of the shelves. "I like that the spaces are big. I have thick hands, and if the shelves are just barely tall enough, I smash my knuckles when I pick something up." He demonstrated what he meant, grabbing an impact wrench from one of the shorter shelves and showing me how much space he had between the top and his hand.

"That makes a lot of sense," I told him. "Are there any shelves that don't have the right amount of space?"

He stepped back and looked at the different shelves. He shook his head after a minute. "I don't think so. But there are some with one big tool and a bunch of smaller ones, so I think we can reorganize and make things fit better."

"I'm going to ask about organizing in a second, but yeah, I was wondering the same," I told him. "What else is working well?"

They all shared a few things they liked, mostly that they could see what was there and it was easy to find things, the space fit what they had, and there wasn't anything they wished wasn't up there.

But there were a lot of negatives, too. Nothing was organized. The tools were never put back in the same place. And the big one was that tools and parts were jumbled together instead of separated and sorted.

"You have a set of tools at each station, right?" I asked.

Derek stepped forward. "We do. The tools that are pretty much used on every car, every time are at each station. We have them at hand's reach to save time and effort. These are only the things we use for bigger projects or more specialized projects, plus backups in case what's at a station breaks or isn't charged or something. Some of these we use once a year, some once a month. Some we use more regularly, but not daily. The parts are usually about the same, but the parts we only use once a year or once a month, we don't keep on hand. Almost all of this is stuff we'll use this week. Or could use this week."

"That's good to know. Tell me how your stations are set up. Does everyone work on all the stations?"

All the guys nodded.

"Okay, and is every station equipped to do the same jobs?"

"Yes," Derek said. "They're all set up the same way. Are you asking if we can reorganize so one station works on one thing and another station does something else? Like station one is for oil changes, two is for tire work, something like that?"

I shook my head before he finished talking. "No. I don't want you to have to change things. I'm just trying to figure out how it works. I was asking because if you operated like that, then things like an impact wrench or extra jacks could go closer to the station that operated on those parts. If everyone does everything, then parts and tools can go anywhere on these shelves."

"Yeah. I mean, there are some tools they use more than others, and they can show you which ones they reach for most often, but all the stations will access all the items."

"How do you feel about labels? If I make a space for each item?"

"Are you saying like a cubby specifically for that tool?" the guy with the big hands asked.

I nodded. "I could. If it's not something that would work, that's okay."

He looked at the others and nodded. "I think it might be good."

"What about pulldown bins for the top shelves?"

"You can do that?" another guy asked.

I nodded. "If it's something that would help, sure."

We talked through more ideas and other options, and the wheels started turning in my mind. My fingers itched to draw up everything we talked about.

When the guys shared all their thoughts, Derek and I walked back to his office and sat down. "What do you think?" he asked.

"I have a ton of ideas. I think this is going to be a lot of fun."

"Yeah? You think you can do it?"

"I do. I'm looking forward to it."

"Let's talk price," Derek said.

"Let me work on some options first. I'll get prices for what it would take for each of them, and we can go from there. Does that work for you?"

Derek nodded. "Perfect. Thanks for doing this. I know you said it's no big deal, but it is to me. The way you spoke to them and really listened, but also offered your own thoughts was great. I know they appreciated it, too."

"The people who use the items every day need to be able to use them."

Derek smiled. "I couldn't agree more. Thanks, man. See you tomorrow?"

I stood and nodded. "I'll be there. Does Monday work for me to bring back some options?"

"Yeah, definitely. Same time?"

"Yep. Thanks, Derek."

We shook hands, then I made my way back outside to my truck. I let my mind wander as I replayed the conversation. The notes and pictures I took on my phone would help me come up with the right options for them. But for the budget's sake, I would offer Derek two or three options.

It had been a while since I was so excited about a project like that. One I couldn't wait to dig my hands into and get done. I just hoped Derek liked what I came up with.

I WAS SO WRAPPED up in the designs I was creating that night I missed a message from Haley on Book Boyfriends Wanted. When I finally came up for air and saw it, I wasn't sure if it was too late to message her back but hoped not.

SINGLEMENWANTED

How is your dad doing?

HANDYNOTHANDSY

Better. Thanks. He's fighting the doctor on what he's supposed to do, but he's arguing less each day.

I started to put my phone away and figure out a very late dinner when it dinged with another message.

SMW

It'll be an adjustment, but he'll figure out what's right for him.

HNH

I hope so. Until then, he's going to make me a little crazy.

SMW

I imagine that's what most parents do.

HNH

Payback for all the years I made him crazy.

SMW

LOL! I can see that. What was the craziest
thing you did as a teenager?

HNH

I snuck out constantly. Almost every
weekend when I was in high school. A
bunch of us would wander around town and
pretend like we were cool. The craziest thing
I ever did, though… I stole my dad's truck
when I was a senior.

SMW

Uh oh. I sense there's more to it than just
stealing the car.

HNH

Yeah. It was bad. I got pulled over and
tossed in jail. The cop was a friend of my
dad's and called him. Dad left me there
overnight, and I had to pay to get his truck
out of the impound lot.

SMW

Oh, no. That's not good. I would have
thought they'd let you go since your dad
knew him.

HNH

LOL! He told them not to. They weren't
going to impound the truck, but he told
them to, and he told them to make sure to
throw every charge possible at me.

SMW

I imagine it sucked as a teenager, but it
sounds like he is a great father.

HNH

He is. It was a hard lesson to learn, but I
needed to learn it. He brings it up every so
often.

SMW

Life is all about lessons. And rubbing it in when someone does something dumb.

HNH

He'd agree with you.

SMW

LOL!

HNH

I'm surprised you're still up. What time do you work tomorrow?

SMW

I'm off tomorrow. I work Friday and Saturday, though.

HNH

Do you work on Sunday?

SMW

Nope. The shop is closed on Sundays. Gives everyone a guaranteed day off work every week.

HNH

Want to get together Saturday night? I open Sunday, but it's a shorter day.

SMW

I'd love to.

HNH

Good. Can I pick you up?

SMW

That would be nice.

HNH

Excellent. I hate to get off with you now, but I need to be up early tomorrow and still haven't had dinner. But I'm looking forward to Saturday.

SMW

Me, too. Have a good night.

HNH

Good night, Haley.

I finished my quick dinner and got myself ready for bed. I laid down with a smile on my face, more than a little anxious for my date Saturday night.

SINCE HALEY WAS FAIRLY new to town, I decided to give her an in-depth tour of MacKellar Cove. I had the route all planned out and was really excited about it. And then I second guessed myself.

Did she really care? If she wanted to know all about the town, maybe she already did everything I'd planned. Plus, it was barely March. Was it too cold to be walking around town?

I decided to roll with it and leave it up to her if she wanted to tour the town or do something like dinner and a movie instead.

I parked on the street in front of her apartment building and grabbed the flowers I'd picked up for her. I buzzed her apartment and waited for the door to unlock so I could go in.

She was waiting for me in the hallway when I got to her floor. Her eyes brightened, and she grinned when she saw the flowers in my hand. "Are those for me?"

I nodded. "They were bright and fun and beautiful and reminded me of you. I hope that's okay."

She pressed her lips together and nodded. "No one's ever bought me flowers before."

"No one?" She'd dated Dawson for almost a year, and she mentioned others she'd been involved with before.

She shook her head and led the way inside. "Except the one you gave me on our first date. I don't even own a vase."

I followed her, shaking my head and making a mental note to show her how much she deserved to be treated well. Even if things didn't work out for us, she needed to know she was special.

"I can use a pitcher, right?" she asked, searching her cabinets for something to put the flowers in.

"Absolutely. Do you have scissors? I can cut the ends for you."

"You need to do that?"

I almost laughed at the innocent vulnerability in her eyes. She looked up at me like she had no idea what to do. It hit me that she didn't.

"Yeah. If you snip the ends of the stems, it opens them up so they can drink the water. You can also put a penny in the water and that's supposed to help, too, but I've never tried it."

"Do you buy a lot of flowers?"

The way she asked made me think she was asking about more than flowers. "No, I don't. I've bought flowers for other women I've dated, yes, but not all the time. The orange Gerbera daisy I got you when we met was the first time I'd bought flowers for anyone in a while."

"I didn't mean to—"

"You can ask me anything, Haley. I don't want you to feel like I'm keeping things from you."

"I... Thank you."

I smiled at her and held up the freshly snipped flowers. She took them, our hands brushing. Her cheeks pinked as she focused on putting the flowers into the pitcher and arranging them just right.

When she looked up at me, I said, "You're welcome, Haley."

She held my gaze for a long moment, the air growing thick with desire. Again, I wanted to be respectful of her, especially after finding out she'd never gotten flowers from anyone.

"Should we go?"

"Yeah. Am I dressed okay? You didn't mention where we were going."

I looked at her jeans and sweater. A tank peeked out from underneath. She wore boots and had a handbag that she carried across her body. "You're perfect."

"Good. So, where are we going?"

"Well, that's up to you, actually. My first thought was a tour of MacKellar Cove. I thought it might be fun for you to see some things you might not have seen and to hear some of the crazy stories about the town. But then I wasn't sure if you would actually want to do that. So, if you don't—"

"I do," she blurted, her cheeks pinking with her declaration. "That sounds really fun. I didn't know much about the town when I moved here, and I haven't decided if I'm staying beyond my one-year lease, but I think it would be interesting to learn more about the town."

I filed that bit of information away and made a mental note to find out when her year was up. "A tour of the town it is, then. Walk or drive?"

"What do you think would be better?"

"If you're up for a walk, we can go a few more places."

She smiled. "A walk sounds like a lot of fun."

"Good. Then let's go. I thought we could grab dinner

while we're out, too. There's a new pizza place. If you like pizza."

"I love pizza."

"Okay, we're set. A walking tour of all the colorful history of MacKellar Cove, pizza for dinner, and time together."

She looked up at me and smiled.

Before I could think twice, I leaned down and pressed my lips to hers. She paused for a second before she opened her lips under mine and snaked her tongue out to wrap around mine.

My hands went to her hips, pulling her closer. Her hands eased around my waist, holding on to me. I angled my head and deepened the kiss, hardening when she moaned against my lips.

Her little noises brought me right back to the night we spent together and how much fun we had. Even though I didn't know her name and thought I'd never see her again, it still ranked up top for best sex. And kissing her in her kitchen, the scent of fresh flowers in the air around us and the promise of a great date ahead of us, I knew when we flipped the switch and crossed back over that line, it was going to be even better.

HALEY

I STARED OUT OVER THE WATER AT THE MACKELLAR ESTATE while Knox told me the stories he'd heard over the years about the family who founded the town, and the feud between them and the other family that originally settled in the area.

"So, Catherine Park is named for Trent MacKellar's mom?" I asked.

Knox nodded. "Yep. She wanted a place for the entire town to come together and enjoy each other's company. Supposedly, it was really important to her. Her husband donated the land to the town with the stipulation it was only ever used for a park and for town events. No private citizen could ever buy the property for their own personal use."

"What about weddings or events like that? Can it be used for that?" I asked.

Knox nodded. "A few people have gotten married there over the years. There aren't a lot of places in town that are big enough for an event, so most people who get married do it farther away."

I turned to look back at the park. Even with the furniture

packed up for the winter and the cold wind whipping off the cove water, it was stunning. The oversized gazebo welcomed people to MacKellar Cove and invited guests to stay for a while. I could see a wedding there. Bride and groom central, guests spilling down the gentle hills that led away from the gazebo. Catherine Park was in the center of town, a place where everyone was drawn multiple times a year to spend time together.

It made the place feel like home, even though I wasn't sure if I would ever call it my home.

"Should we keep walking?" Knox asked after a few minutes.

I nodded. We'd already seen the south side of town, starting at MacKellar Cove Inn and working our way through that end of town. He showed me the historical buildings that were used for different things than originally intended, like the old fish market that was converted into a restaurant and an old church that was now a private residence. We ate dinner at Pete's Pizza, a new place not far from O'Kelley's with a charismatic owner who insisted on meeting every customer and remembered your names.

We moved away from the water and onto the streets for the tour heading north of Catherine Park. "That house right there," Knox said, pointing to a small white house with blue shutters and a basketball hoop above the garage, "is where I grew up. My dad still lives there."

"Really?" I asked.

He nodded. "I'm a couple of years younger than Trent, but my parents moved here not too long after the town was founded. There were families here, and houses were starting to pop up in the area. Everyone went to school a little south of here in Alexandria Bay. This section of town, close to Catherine Park, was the first section built. The homes are all relatively small. Originally, all of this was part of the MacKellar Estate."

"Wow. All of it?" I looked at the homes that lined the road all the way to Catherine Park.

"Yep. The MacKellars owned the property where their estate currently sits, and all of it around the cove to a little south of O'Kelley's. Trent's grandparents, from what I've heard, wanted to keep all that land for the family to build generational homes and control the cove, but his mom thought it would be nice to have other people in the area. They ended up holding on to the waterfront property and selling off the land that was a little farther inland, developing it for other families."

"I'm glad they did that."

"Yeah, a lot of people are. It's funny to think it hasn't been that long since the town really grew. I've never lived anywhere else, but MacKellar Cove hasn't been here for much longer than that."

I looked around the street, noting the faint smile on Knox's face as we walked. Memories flashed in his eyes, a good childhood and a lifetime of happiness.

A part of me was jealous of that. Jealous that I'd never experienced the simple joy and pleasure of being somewhere that I felt like I completely belonged. I'd hoped for that when I moved to MacKellar Cove. That I'd be welcomed in by the locals and feel like I was meant to be there.

Instead, it was the opposite. There were some who didn't care if I stayed or not, but it was the vocal minority who made my life hell. If it weren't for them, I was starting to think I'd try to make MacKellar Cove my home. But I wasn't sure I was strong enough to defend myself and my actions forever.

"How was work today?" Knox asked as we moved to the end of the block.

I chuckled when I thought back to book club showing up at Teased by Debby.

"That sounds good," Knox said, a smile lighting up his face.

"There's this one client of my boss's. Do you know Debby?"

Knox nodded. "Everyone knows Debby."

"True. She has this one client who hates me. Well, she has a few, but this one came in today. She talks about me as if I'm not there, barely addresses me at all. She's never once asked for my side of the story. She doesn't care. She believed I destroyed Valentina and Dawson's marriage."

"Who is she?" he asked, his voice tight.

I shook my head. "It doesn't matter."

"It matters to me. She has no right to make you feel like you did anything wrong."

"Well, she got put in her place a little today," I confessed.

"By whom?"

"I was talking about her at book club on Sunday, and Elise and some of the others said they were going to show up at the salon and show this client that they were on my side. They all know her, I guess, so she was kind and talkative to them when they arrived, but one by one they made it clear they were there to see me and were friends with me, and the woman grew more uncomfortable by the minute."

Knox chuckled with me, reaching out to take my hand. "That's brilliant."

"It wasn't my idea, but I'm very grateful to them for coming to my rescue. I'm not sure it'll keep her from making comments in the future, but it was nice to not have to deal with her for once."

"That's the good and bad about this town. About most small towns, I imagine. The people here protect each other. The problem comes when there are different interpretations of what that protection looks like."

"I get it. Valentina is well-liked and respected. Her boss almost kicked me out when I went into the bakery the other day."

"Harriett? She's the sweetest person ever. I'm surprised she was like that."

I shook my head before he could get more upset. "She was protecting Valentina. She didn't realize we got along. She went to the back and told Valentina not to come out because I was there, and Valentina came out, hugged me, and sat with me, then announced to everyone there that we were friends and for Harriett to let her know whenever I showed up at the bakery."

"She's good people," Knox said, nodding to himself.

"She is. I hate that I had any hand in ending her marriage."

"That's not on you," Knox said firmly. "Dawson was the one who made those vows, and he was the only one who knew he was violating them."

"I know, but—"

Knox stopped in the middle of the sidewalk and turned me to face him. He cupped my jaw in both his hands, his warmth seeping into my cheeks. He brushed his thumbs over my skin and waited until I met his gaze to speak. "Valentina is better off without Dawson in her life. I know divorce is tough, and I know you feel guilty, but I'm guessing Valentina never blamed you, right?"

I nodded.

"Then don't blame yourself. Dawson is the one who holds all the blame."

"But I showed up—"

"And if you hadn't, Valentina wouldn't have known her husband was cheating on her. She would still be married to a man who didn't deserve her. A man who doesn't deserve you either, or you accepting blame for his actions."

I nodded, knowing he was right. I hated that I kept going back and forth about Dawson and my part in the end of his marriage. If I'd never moved to MacKellar Cove, they might still be together, but Valentina herself told me that wasn't a better option. She was happier with Brantley, and she deserved to be happy.

I needed to let go of my guilt and move on.

"Want to know the history of this place?" Knox asked, nodding his head toward a two-story house that looked drastically out of place compared to the other homes next to it.

"It's a totally different design than the others. Brick instead of siding, two floors, and a huge yard. I definitely want to know the history."

He grinned and wrapped his arm around my shoulder. "This was the original elementary school."

"What?"

He laughed. "Crazy, isn't it? The current elementary school was built to be the junior high and high school. There weren't a lot of kids who would be zoned for the district when it was built, so they built this school, right at the end of the first residential street, so it was easier for young kids to walk to school. The idea was to bus in the older kids, but for the elementary school to only be the kids from right here in town."

"That's not a bad idea."

Knox shook his head. "It wasn't, but it only lasted a few years. The town grew, and the district grew, and they built the other schools to be able to accommodate the other students. This house was sold to a large family with five kids."

"Do they still live there?" I asked.

"No. They moved a long time ago. Another family lives there now. From what I understand, they're trying to get the house on the historical registry, but it's a process, and the house isn't really that old."

"No harm in trying, though," I said.

Knox smiled. "No harm at all."

WE KEPT WALKING, touring the residential section north of Catherine Park before we looped around and ended up back at my apartment. I invited Knox inside, although I didn't have much to offer him.

"Want to watch a movie?" he asked, nodding to the small TV I bought a few weeks after I moved to town.

"Sure. Do you want a drink?"

"Water would be great. I did a lot of talking."

"Thank you for telling me all about MacKellar Cove. It makes me want to stick around here for longer."

"You mentioned that before. When do you have to decide?"

I handed over his glass of water and sat down next to him. "My lease is up at the end of May."

Knox shifted on the couch, bringing one knee up between us on the cushion. "Where would you go?"

I shrugged. "Somewhere people don't think of me as a homewrecker."

Knox shook his head. "I hate that people have made you feel that way."

"It's okay. I mean, it's hard, but I know not everyone here hates me."

"I definitely don't hate you, Haley," Knox whispered. His voice deepened. His eyes met mine and held. He leaned closer, setting his water on the coffee table before bringing his hands up to cup my jaw. His palms were cool from the glass, but they felt good on my skin. "Can I kiss you?"

I nodded. I was tired of pretending I didn't want things between us to move ahead. I liked Knox. I liked talking to him and being around him, and I really enjoyed sex with him.

I knew he could influence me to stay. That if I let him, he would be the deciding factor. Maybe if I was involved with him, the people in town who didn't like me would see I'm not so bad. But I didn't want to put Knox in the middle of all of that.

"Stop worrying, Haley," he whispered, his face an inch from mine.

"I'm sorry."

He smiled. "Don't be sorry. Just be here with me right now. I don't want to kiss you if you're not interested and in the moment with me."

I sucked in a breath and pushed away all thoughts except how much I wanted his lips on mine. My gaze darted to his lips, and I licked my own.

He finally closed the gap between us. His beard tickled my cheeks, grounding me. I'd never been involved with a man who kept a full beard, but I liked it. It was softer than I expected under my fingertips.

Knox licked against my lips, silently asking for entry. I sighed as I opened for him, feeling like everything was right in my world for the first time in far too long.

He lowered one hand from my jaw to trail over my neck.

I shivered at the touch, but he kept going, sliding his hand across my shoulder and down to my hand where he wrapped our fingers together and held on to me. I was sweet and intimate and oh, damn...

He used our joined hands to lift mine above my head and ease me to lie down on the couch. He covered my body with his, not breaking our kiss as he positioned himself between my thighs.

He didn't grind himself against me, but I felt the hardness of him, anyway. We laid on the couch, kissing without a thought for what would come next. I knew I wanted him, but I also knew he wanted to take things slowly.

"Tell me to stop, Haley."

"I don't want you to stop," I confessed.

"This isn't the same as last time for me," he whispered against my neck. "This isn't a quick fuck without names and no contact tomorrow. Are you okay with that?"

"Yes."

He pulled back from kissing my neck and looked at me. His blue-green gaze skipped over my face before settling on my eyes again. "I know last time was different. It was impulse, and we made no promises. I don't want you to think I'm interested in that again. I like you, Haley. I want to keep seeing you. If you say no right now, I still want to keep seeing you. No matter what happens tonight, if you're interested, I want to keep seeing you."

"I want that, too."

He smiled, a small smile that held something back. "Are you going to stay in town?"

"What?"

"I want you to stay. I know that's not fair of me to ask, but I want you to stay. I at least want you to think about it. To seriously consider staying here. I know you love it, and

I hope you'll let the town show you how amazing it can be."

I looked up at this man, a man who could make me fall in love with not only the town but with him, too. Knox was everything Dawson wasn't. He was sweet and caring. He wanted to go slow with me because he wanted me to know he respected me. He was willing to walk around town holding my hand and saying hello to people. He was a good man.

My track record sucked. I moved too fast and fell too hard. Starting something with Knox when I might not be staying wasn't exactly fair to either of us, but I couldn't resist him. And after seeing MacKellar Cove through his eyes, I couldn't resist the town either.

I wanted this place to be my home. I wanted to stay there. I wanted to meet Knox's dad and build my clientele. I wanted to keep the friendships I'd developed. I wanted a home for the first time.

"I want to stay here," I admitted.

He grinned and opened his mouth to say something, but I stopped him before he could.

"But I can't stay because of you. Or anyone else. I don't mean that in a bad way, just that I moved here because of a guy. I've made most of my moves because of men. To be near one, to find one, to get away from one. I have let others rule my life forever. And I need to do what's best for me. So, yes, I am seriously considering sticking around MacKellar Cove, but I can't do it for you. It has to be the right choice for me."

Knox's smile widened. "Thank you. That... fuck, I want you even more after hearing you say that."

"Yeah?"

He wiggled his hips, letting me feel his length.

I moaned.

"Oh yeah," he said. Then he closed the distance between us and kissed me until I was panting for him and clawing the clothes off his back.

"Please, Knox. Don't hold back."

He grinned. "With pleasure."

12

———

KNOX PUSHED HIMSELF OFF ME AND REACHED BEHIND HIM, grabbing the neck of his shirt and yanking it off with one efficient move.

It was not fair how hot that was. The man was just taking off his shirt, but I swore I had a mini-orgasm just from the effortlessly sexy move.

"What?" he asked, a tentative smile lifting one side of his delectable mouth.

I shook my head. "You make the smallest things ridiculously sexy."

He cocked an eyebrow. "Taking off my shirt is sexy?"

I lifted my hands to his warm skin and nodded. "I mean, yes, definitely, but not just because it means I get my hands on you."

"Am I going to get my hands on you?"

I nodded and pulled him down on top of me again. "In a minute."

He chuckled as our lips met again. He eased mine open with his tongue, his weight sinking onto me and pressing me into the couch.

I lifted my knees and eased my heels up his calves. He supported himself on one elbow while he used his other hand to lift the edge of my shirt, giving him minuscule and frustrating access to my bare waist.

I wanted more. I needed more. We'd gone from getting to know each other and playing it safe to *get naked now* in about five-point-two seconds. And I was on board.

I spread my hands wide on his back, touching as much of his body at once as I could. I wrapped my leg around his hip and held on. We hadn't crossed any new lines. We could still walk away and go back to where we were. But I didn't want to. I wanted this man. I wanted him in my bed.

"Bedroom," I whispered, barely breaking our kiss to hiss the needy word.

Knox ignored me, kissing his way down my neck. He licked my collarbone and left open-mouthed kisses up and down my neck. He rocked gently against me, his erection rubbing my clit through our jeans and sending my heart rate skipping faster and faster.

"Knox," I moaned, halfway to an orgasm and even closer to falling for the man.

"If I'm not holding back, neither are you," he growled against my ear. "Let go, Haley."

He shifted, his pace kicking up as he claimed my mouth again. I whimpered, unable to hold back or stop the slow climb and sudden drop of my orgasm, sending me into a mini state of bliss that was so good and so not enough.

"Bedroom," he demanded, his lips against my ear.

The word skated down my spine and settled in my soaked panties.

Knox moved to climb off me, my limp, post-orgasmic body wrapped around him. I tried to extract myself from him, but he stood with me hanging off him like a spider monkey. One large hand went to my ass, holding me right where he wanted me, as he stalked to the one and only bedroom in my apartment.

Knox flipped the switch and flooded my bedroom with light. I ached to turn it off, knowing the harsh apartment lighting did nothing to flatter me, but Knox didn't give me time before he stomped across the room to my bed.

He eased me from his body, leaning over me as he lowered me to the mattress. "You want me to stop, you tell me, Haley. Okay?"

I nodded, nibbling my lip to keep from saying the words lingering on my tongue.

"What?" he asked, his gaze drifting around my face as though it was giving him clues to my thoughts. "What are you thinking?"

I shook my head, still unwilling to share my thoughts.

"Haley, if you don't want this, please tell me. I'd never forgive myself if—"

"I want you so badly I can barely breathe," I whispered on an exhale.

"Well, damn if that's not the same thing I was thinking, beautiful."

We shared a secret smile before he kissed the tip of my nose.

"Let's see if we can finally get you out of these clothes so I can get my hands on you."

I chuckled until the lust-soaked look in his eyes took my breath away. Jesus, the man was potent. I knew it the night we met, when I couldn't resist his easy charm and sexy laugh, and I was reminded of it every single time we spoke since.

But seeing it, the plain need in his eyes, made me want to say *fuck it, I'm staying* and not even consider another option.

I couldn't. Even as he stripped my clothes from my body and set about worshipping every single one of my inches, I knew I couldn't. For the first time in my life, I had to make a choice for myself. Not for a man.

Even if he was finally the kind of man I should be choosing.

"Where'd you go, beautiful?" he asked, his lips trailing up the inside of my calf.

"Just thinking about how perfect you are."

He raised one blond eyebrow. "Oh, really? You don't seem all too happy about that."

I breathed a laugh. "It would be really easy for me to fall for you, Knox."

He inhaled sharply, taking all the air from the room with him.

I laid there, my entire body heating with an embarrassing flush at what I just admitted to him.

I tried to pull my foot out of his grip, but the move seemed to snap him out of whatever trance my words put him into. His gaze slid up my body and locked on my eyes. "And that would be a bad thing?"

His question more than surprised me. "Considering my track record, it's a scary thought."

He kissed my calf, then my knee, working his way toward my inner thighs, without another word. When he rested my leg on the bed, he looked up at me. "I don't know where this is going, Haley. I wish I could tell you I do, but even if I did, I'd still want you to get to wherever we're going on your own. I'm not going to say I won't be a manipulative asshole and try to convince you to stay, but I will tell you you're not the only one who sees how easy it would be for this to become so much more than it is right now."

My lungs filled to bursting at his confession, delivered without breaking eye-contact. Letting me see all the emotions on his face and in his heated gaze.

"Now, can I get back to making you scream? Because if I give you enough orgasms that you can't get out of bed, then I can convince you not to leave MacKellar Cove."

I laughed softly, trying not to fall for his sweet and dirty words.

"Was that a yes? Because I really want to know you're here with me, Haley."

"I'm here, Knox."

"Good. Are you ready to scream for me, beautiful?"

He didn't give me a chance to answer before he muscled my thighs farther apart and speared his tongue into my channel.

"Oh, God," I moaned.

Knox hummed his approval and swirled his tongue around, tasting me thoroughly before withdrawing his tongue and slowly exploring the skin between my thick thighs. He unfolded all my folds and took his time making his way to my clit. Even when he made it there, he didn't stay long, frustrating me with his dismissive swipes and far-too-quick flicks.

I shifted my hips, trying to get him where I wanted him, but he didn't hurry up or move to where I was directing him. I was about to tell him to get on with it when he prodded my entrance with one thick finger, sliding it in and spinning it around before retreating to collect another digit.

"That feels good," I whispered.

He groaned in agreement and pumped his fingers in and out of me at the same lazy, unhurried pace he'd set on my couch.

"Knox," I whimpered. "Please."

At my hushed plea, he growled and used his free hand to push my thighs wider. With more room for his shoulders, he crawled closer to me, burying his face between my legs and wrapping his lips around my clit. His relentless attack had me wheezing for breath and desperate for release.

My nails dug into his scalp, my lust driving me to insanity as he curled his fingers deep inside me and sent my body flying, flinging, crashing over the edge.

I screamed, the orgasm like a fist in my hair, insistent and impossible to ignore. I flailed and moaned, wave after wave dragging me deeper as Knox continued to deliver his version of manipulation and send me back for another orgasm before the first had fully let me up for air.

"Knox. Oh, fuck. Yes!" I moaned long and loud, my thighs trembling as my core pulsed with my orgasms.

"Fuck me, you're beautiful," he growled. He lunged for me, his hand still buried between my thighs. He kissed me, the scent and flavor of my orgasm coating his lips and beard as he devoured me.

He pumped his hand fast and faster, dragging his fingers out of me to swipe them over my clit before thrusting them back inside. His thumb took over for his mouth on my clit, and he kissed me until another orgasm slammed into me like a freight train on a runaway track.

I broke our kiss with a scream. I thrashed through the intensity, my body out of control. Every muscle twitched, every cell on fire. And when Knox dragged his hand from inside me, I whimpered at the loss even as I knew he wasn't done.

A foil packet tore, the sound a buzz in the background as my pulse pounded in my ears to the tune of my orgasm.

"Haley," Knox whispered.

I pried my eyes open and looked at the stunning man kneeling between my thighs.

"Hey, beautiful. Still with me?"

"God, yes," I moaned, not willing to stop. I was worn out, tingling in all my good parts, and would be sore as fuck in the morning, but there was no way in hell I was done with him.

He lined himself up with my entrance, his gaze flickering from me to where he was going. My core thrummed in anticipation. He sank in, one inch at a time, watching me the entire time.

"Knox," I moaned, dragging my calf against his back and urging him forward.

"Fuck, beautiful, I want to last. I'm not going to if you rush me."

"I told you I didn't want you to hold back."

The look in his eyes was what long baths, vibrators, and soundproof walls were made for. Feral and intoxicating, my core flooded half a second before he let loose and plunged deep into me.

"Yes," I moaned, the feel of him fully seated inside me enough to send my eyes rolling to the back. I reached for him blindly, needing to touch him.

"Are you sure about this, Haley?" His gravelly voice was pained, like he was still holding back and teetering on the edge of his ability to control it.

I opened my eyes and met his gaze. "Fuck me, Knox."

A switch flicked in his eyes. A switch that said this man was one of many layers. Sweet, kind, and gentle when he wanted to be. Passionate, demanding, and dangerous when he wanted to be.

I loved both. And all the other pieces of him I was going to discover.

Knox retreated, just far enough to give himself space to slam back inside me. He brought our joined hands above my head, and he leaned over me, staring into my eyes as he pounded into me.

Beads of sweat popped up on his forehead. His cheeks turned red from his efforts. His breath panted from him in time with the way he fucked me.

I was mesmerized by him. He was gorgeous. Powerful and sexy and focused on me so intently that I couldn't look away. I didn't want to miss even one second of watching Knox as he fucked me harder and harder, his desire and demand blending to fuel us both.

"Come for me, beautiful. Let me feel you."

The orgasm I was too distracted by Knox to anticipate snuck up on me. At his growled demand, my body leapt to do as he asked and the first ripples of my orgasm pulsed around his hard length.

"Yes, beautiful. There you go." He hooked my knee over his forearm and spread my thighs wider, sinking deeper for a few strokes. Enough to hit just the right spot deep inside me that sent my orgasm to the surface and my sanity out the fucking window.

"Knox!" I grabbed him, needing the steadiness of him to carry me through the whirlwind I was in the middle of.

"Yes, Haley. Fuck." He growled and grunted, following me into the whirlwind.

His erection pulsed inside me, the force of his orgasm making both of us tremble with aftershocks.

Knox's arm shook for a few seconds before he gave in and collapsed on top of me, rolling us instantly so I was sprawled on top of his body instead of smushed beneath him.

Not that I would have minded.

I laid my head on his chest, listening to his racing heartbeat, and smiled.

His fingers trailed up and down my spine, lulling me and my spent body to doze as our hearts slowed and our bodies cooled.

"I need to get rid of the condom, Haley," he whispered, five minutes or five hours later.

I groaned and let him roll me over onto the mattress.

He chuckled and kissed the side of my head before walking across my room to my bathroom, his beautiful, naked body on full display for me.

He didn't close the door all the way, leaving it cracked in a wholly domesticated move that sent emotion straight to my throat. Dawson never did that. He always closed the door and took his phone with him. Knox's phone was definitely not with him in the bathroom.

He opened the door and caught me staring at him as he made his way back to my bed. "You're awake?"

I nodded, scooting over to make room for him on the bed before I realized he probably wanted to leave.

He laid down next to me, snuggling up against me and kissing my neck. "You are amazing."

I laughed softly. "I could say the same to you."

He nuzzled against my jaw, his beard tickling my cheek. He laid one heavy arm over my body and pulled me as close to him as possible.

"What are you doing?" I asked with a laugh.

"Well, I need twenty minutes or so before I can sink into you again, but I wanted to be as close as possible. Unless you want me to go."

"No!" I blurted.

He laughed with me. "Good." The one word was a whisper against my hair. A promise.

He tucked me against him and laid there for a few minutes, his hands lazily stroking my naked body.

It was new for me. He wasn't counting the minutes or making his next plans. He wasn't running out the door or hiding being with me. He was just laying there, enjoying time together.

"African safari or beach bungalow?" he asked.

"What?"

"If you could pick, would you rather go on an African safari or chill out in a beach bungalow?"

"Are those my only choices?" I wrinkled my nose. I'd never considered either before.

Knox laughed, his chest jolting at the sudden sound that burst from him. "Obviously not, but I'm curious. I'd go on an African safari. I always thought it would be really cool to see all those animals in their natural environment. Watch them playing and wandering and exploring."

"I'm not a fan of zoos," I admitted.

Knox shook his head. "This would be nothing like a zoo. At a zoo, they're the ones who aren't supposed to be there. We bring these animals in and expect them to perform for us, but it's not their natural state. A safari would mean seeing them where they belong."

"You sound really excited about this."

He shrugged and relaxed. "I haven't traveled much. The guys at the store tell me I should get out more. Of course, they also tell me I should be open longer hours so they can shop whenever they feel like it."

"That's not fair to you. You need to have a life, too."

Knox grunted something unintelligible.

I drew a deep breath and considered my words. "I've never been on a vacation. My parents... I was never a priority, and family vacations weren't something we did when I was growing up. Since I left home, I've been working. I don't take time off to get away or relax, so I've never thought about either of those options, or any other options, because I've never been on vacation."

Knox was silent after my rushed confession. I wanted to look up at him and see the shocked and horrified expression I was sure was on his face, but I couldn't bear to do so.

"Aren't we a pair? Dad always kept the store open, so I never went on vacations either. Holidays were spent at home because all my family lived here. When I went to college, I had a few friends who would drag me along on weekend trips, but that was the most of it."

I exhaled a laugh. "We're both pretty pathetic."

He stilled beneath me, then shifted. I turned to look at him and saw the horrified look on his face and the delight in his eyes. "Oh, no. You don't get to say that." His face broke into a grin right before he dug his fingers into my sides.

I burst out laughing at the aggressive tickling, squealing when he crawled on top of me and pinned me down.

"Knox! Oh, my God! Stop!" I laughed and wheezed.

He didn't stop. "Never! I'm the tickle champion!"

I laughed harder, trying to reach out to tickle him back, but every time I did, he'd find a new place on me to tickle and I'd have to block him. "I can't breathe."

He laughed with me, his laughter booming and encompassing. His eyes pinched at the sides, laugh lines folding into his face and making him that much more attractive to me.

"Maybe I should give you mouth-to-mouth," he volunteered.

I nodded. "I think I need you to."

He lowered his weight onto me, getting in one last squeal as he tickled my sides, then sealed his lips over mine and gave me mouth-to-mouth until I was panting for an entirely different reason.

13

KNOX

A FEW WEEKS AFTER MY WALKING TOUR DATE WITH HALEY, I was still thinking about the night we spent together. I couldn't remember the last time I had so much fun with another person, let alone a woman I was dating.

We'd spent a lot of time together over the weeks. We worked a lot, which limited our available time, but when we were free, we were together.

My friends still hadn't mentioned it, and I still hadn't said anything. Hudson gave me a look every week when I walked into guys' night, but I never found the words to tell them I was involved with public enemy number one.

So I did what I always did when I didn't know what to do. I worked my ass off. And I went to see my dad.

"Hey, Dad," I called out as I let myself into his house.

"What are you doing here?" he asked, looking up from his recliner in front of the TV. "I didn't know you were coming over tonight."

"I haven't seen you in a few days. I wanted to check on you."

His bushy gray eyebrow popped up over one brown eye. He rolled them both, not falling for my line. "What's wrong?"

I laughed to myself and took a seat on the couch across from him. The plaid brown and orange couch was out of fashion when I was a teenager, but Dad never bothered to replace it. He said he and my mom picked it out together when they first got married. He'd considered having it refurbished, but every place he talked to said they would have to remove the fabric, so Dad refused.

"Can't I just stop by to see you?" I asked.

He snorted. "You were here for dinner three days ago. And you'll be back in a few days. If you're here now, something happened. Let's have it."

I shook my head and stared at the game show he was watching on TV. I muttered the answer to myself a few seconds before the contestant figured out the puzzle.

Dad laughed. "You always had a knack for things like that. Smarter than hell. Got that from your mother."

"Yeah?" He didn't talk about her often, especially not anymore. "If you knew how things would end, would you have changed anything?"

His eyes grew serious, and his face fell. He shook his head, even though the movement was full of sorrow. "I loved your mother. She was everything to me. I didn't have enough time with her, but having any time with the people you love is better than none. There were times I wondered if it would have been better if we never got involved, but..." He rubbed his chest like the thought pained him physically. "I can't imagine a life without her being in it. Even if it was only for a few years."

"Do you think you would have done things differently if she'd lived?"

"What kind of things?"

I shrugged. "The store. Working the hours you did. Anything."

Dad thought about my question for a while, then slowly shook his head. "I don't know, son. I tried my best to give you a good life. To raise you to be a good man. If your mother was around, I know things would have been different. There were days it hurt to think about her. Days I wanted to stay at work until I was too exhausted to function so I didn't have to come home and know she wasn't there. There are still times when grief hits me so hard that I lose my breath. But I can't say what I would have done over the last thirty-six years if she'd been here for it."

I nodded, thinking about his words. I never felt like I was missing something as a kid. Sure, I wished I had a mom, but I loved my dad. He was always there for me, and he made sure to get involved with the things I did. Having him around wasn't a replacement for my mom, but he made sure I knew he was there.

"What's going on with your lady friend? You getting serious?"

I'd mentioned Haley on one of my visits, but I never told him her name. I wasn't sure I was ready for my dad to start in on any accusations. "I really like her, Dad. I have a lot of fun with her."

"Fun is only part of it. You have to think with something other than your penis, son."

"Jesus, Dad."

"Don't you swear at me. And don't you be disrespecting a woman. Your mother wasn't perfect, and neither am I, but I always treated her like she was my queen. Because she was. I'd have done anything for your mother. We had fun together. Hell, that's why you exist, but life is about more than just that."

I groaned. It didn't matter how old I was, I did not want to think about my parents having sex. "I know, Dad. And that wasn't the kind of fun I was talking about. She's funny and kind, and I enjoy spending time with her."

"But there's no chemistry?"

"Oh, no, there's chemistry. I just meant that wasn't what I was talking about."

"Okay, so what's the problem?"

"She might not be staying here."

"She's not from here?"

I shook my head. "She moved here last year, and she's trying to decide if she wants to stick around or not."

"Well, convince her to stay."

"I can't, Dad. She... She has her reasons for needing to choose on her own."

Dad was quiet for a long few minutes. I clasped my hands together, resting my elbows on my knees. I focused on the show, answering two more puzzles before my dad spoke again.

"Is this your way of telling me you're leaving town?"

"What? No. Why do you think that?"

"Because you're acting like you're in love with this woman. And if she's not sticking around, I'm guessing you're not either."

I shook my head as he spoke, his words like a blow. I wasn't in love with Haley. I knew I could fall for her, but I wasn't there yet. But I also knew her possibly moving was part of it.

MacKellar Cove was a part of me. It was my home. It was the only place I'd lived besides the time I spent away at college. I knew I wanted to raise a family there, to build a life there. Even if I didn't want that life to be everything it was at the moment, I wanted my life to be in MacKellar Cove.

I'd dated other women who left. Who said they loved MacKellar Cove, but got sick of the small town life and the lack of amenities and left. Many tried to convince me to go with them, but all of them failed. I had no interest in leaving my hometown.

"I'm not in love with Haley. And I'm not leaving."

Dad narrowed his eyes at me, giving me the look he used whenever I did something stupid in high school. The look that always had me rushing to confess before the punishment got worse. I learned that lesson the hard way.

But this time, there was nothing to confess, so I met his gaze evenly and waited him out.

He finally blew out a breath and shook his head. "Fine. Then why are you asking me all of this? If you're not in love with this woman, and you're not leaving town, and you're not unhappy at the store, then what's going on?"

I thought back to the way I spent my day. The store was closed so I could have a day off. And I spent the day working on things I wanted to do. Like the shelves for Stone Auto Repair. I was almost finished with their custom shelving units. I'd white-washed the wood earlier that day and when it was dry, I was going to add three or four coats of lacquer to make sure the shelves were waterproof. I didn't want the guys to worry about getting things dirty, because they would, and I didn't want the grease and other stains to soak in and make things harder to keep clean. From what I'd seen, Derek ran a tight shop, one that was damn near spotless, even though they were clearly working with dirty tools and cars all the time.

"Nothing's going on," I told my dad, hoping he'd believe the lie.

He stared at me again, the same look, and this time I knew I had to confess.

"Fine. I've been taking on custom projects on the side. Doing things for people in town. And I enjoy it."

"Okay. So why all this talk about the woman?"

"I... I don't know. I guess it's just been on my mind lately. I wonder if I'm enough for her."

Dad laughed softly. "Let me tell you that one right now, son. No. You're not. You're never enough for the woman you love. Because you're always going to put her on a pedestal. You're always going to see her as someone who deserves more than you. If she's the right one for you, she's going to see you the same. She's going to think she'll never be good enough for you. Because when we love another person, truly love them, we want the best for them. And we know our own faults. We know the things we fucked up along the way. We know all the skeletons in our closets, and we believe the person we love is going to find out those secrets and run screaming. But if it's right, she's going to help you unpack that closet and get rid of all that stuff that's weighing you down. And she's going to let you help her do the same."

I leaned back on the couch and wondered at the wisdom of my father's words. For years, I'd wanted to change the store and do my own thing. To get my hands dirty and bring things to life. After my initial failure, I never took the jump to do it full time, but over the last few years, I'd been testing the waters. I loved it.

But then I met Haley. I still loved working with my hands, but I never shared that with her. I'd hidden away the project I was working on for Derek, even hiding it when she came over so she wouldn't see it and judge me.

The way I hid my relationship with her from my friends so they wouldn't judge me.

I'd spent most of my life, my adult life, hiding the things I cared about because I was afraid of the opinions of others.

"You should tell this Haley what you're thinking. If you care about her, you should let her know."

I nodded slowly, knowing Dad was right. Just because I wasn't in love with Haley didn't mean I didn't care about her. I'd made time for her in my life, and I wanted to make more time for her. I knew she had a tough decision to make, but I also knew she was leaning toward staying.

And I wasn't afraid to help her make that final decision.

I SNAPPED a few photos of the finished shelves and covered them back up before work the next morning. Brantley was going to come by at the end of the day and help me deliver them to Stone Auto Repair, but first I had to open the store and get through a long day.

It was Wednesday, which meant Dick, Wayne, and Tony would be there in the afternoon. They didn't know anything about the shelves, and I was going to need to close early in order to deliver them before Derek closed for the day, so I was likely going to have to kick the men out. It was not going to be fun.

I was halfway through my day before I was able to take a break and grab a drink of water and something to eat. I knew to be quick, but I also knew if anyone came in, it would be fine.

The store was still quiet when I walked back in a few minutes later, which was good, but I could tell someone was there. "Can I help you?" I asked when I found the man on aisle three. I didn't know his name, but he was in there a lot. I was fairly certain he worked with Teddy on David's crew, but I wasn't positive.

"Last time I was in here, I swore I spotted a dovetail jig. Do you have one?"

My neck burned as I shook my head. I'd taken the one he was talking about. I paid for it, at cost, but it'd been sitting on the shelf for a year and no one had ever said anything about it. I wanted to try it out for some of the pullout drawers on Derek's project, and on a project I was doing for myself. "I did, but it's, uh, not here anymore."

"Dammit," he said. "I've been saving up for that, keeping my eye on it. It was a really good one, and I didn't want to have to pay for shipping if I ordered it online."

"I get it. I can get another one in here in a few days."

The guy groaned and shook his head slowly. "I guess I don't really have a choice. The big stores would take just as long."

"Sorry about that, man. I'm Knox, by the way. I know I've seen you in here a bunch."

"Yeah. Andre."

"Nice to meet you. Let's go check out what you're looking for and see how quickly we can get it in."

Andre nodded and followed me up front to the register. I pulled up the system I used to submit orders and searched for the jig I had in the back in my workshop.

"Shit," I mumbled. I looked up at Andre. "It's on backorder."

Andre exhaled on a huff and stared up at the ceiling. "Of course it is. I'm finally ready to get it, and it's impossible."

"Can't get what?" Dick asked, choosing that moment to walk into the store. Tony was on his heels.

Andre looked at the men, frustrating clear in his gaze.

He could have been their grandson, probably no older than twenty-five, and not content with having to wait. "I came in here to get a dovetail jig, but it's been sold."

"Sold? Who in town would need one of those?" Tony asked.

"Got me," Dick said. "I didn't even know Knox had one of 'em in stock."

"It's my own fault," Andre said. "I was waiting until I had the cash to pay for it, and now I have a project I need it for this weekend."

"If I had one I'd let you use it, but my wife doesn't let me keep tools anymore," Tony said, shaking his head like it was the worst possible thing to happen to him.

"Annabeth did you a favor," Wayne said, walking in and joining the conversation as if he'd been there the whole time. "If she hadn't taken away all your tools, you would have cut off a finger. Or your pecker."

"It wasn't that close," Tony grumbled.

There was a story there, but I wasn't sure I wanted to hear it.

"What tools are we talking about? Besides you two," Wayne asked, hitching his thumb at his friends. He focused on Andre.

"I was looking for a dovetail jig. Knox said it was sold since the last time I was in here," Andre lamented.

My ears burned. My neck itched. If I offered to let him use mine, I'd have to admit I was the one who bought it. Under any other circumstances, it wouldn't matter, but with Wayne, Tony, and Dick sitting there, I would have to answer for it.

"I don't have one of those," Wayne said. "You?" he asked Tony.

Tony shook his head. "Not even sure what it's for. Knox, what's it for?"

"It's used to create dovetail joints, which are stronger, for things like drawers. Anything at a right angle, really, but usually drawers," I explained.

"What are you building, Andre?" Dick asked.

"My wife's pregnant. First baby. I told her I'd built a changing table for the baby, but work's been so busy I haven't had the time. She's due in a few weeks, so I need to get it done now."

Fuck. I couldn't keep quiet anymore. He wasn't just an impatient jerk who thought he was entitled to have something immediately. He was a man trying to take care of his family.

"You can use mine," I told him. "It's the one that was in the shop. I've already used it, so it's not new, but you can borrow it for as long as you need it."

"You don't have to do that," Andre said.

I shook my head. "It's all good. I was using it for a project, and I've finished what I was doing. I can be without it for a while."

"Are you sure?" Andre asked.

I nodded. "Yeah. Definitely. If you want to follow me, I can grab it for you."

Andre smiled for the first time since I saw him. He eagerly followed me, thanking me the whole time. He promised to return the jig in perfect condition, and waved to the other men as he raced to the door, like he was afraid I'd change my mind and make him pay for it, or just snatch it out of his hands.

Other customers had come in while I was with Andre, but Dick took care of them, working the register like he'd been doing it forever. He finished the last customer in line, then moved back to his seat.

They all looked at me expectantly.

"What?" I asked. I should have known better.

"What the hell project were you working on that you needed a dovetail jig?" Wayne demanded.

Shit.

14

The grown ass man I was pretty sure I was wanted to tell him to fuck off. That it wasn't his business what I did with my time. But my father's voice was in my head, reminding me to be respectful of my elders and to be considerate of customers.

Dammit.

"I was working on a project for Stone Auto Repair," I admitted. I mentally crossed my fingers they wouldn't push for more, but even as I thought it, I knew there was no way in hell they'd let it drop.

"A project? You turning this place back into that stupid custom thing you tried before? Where you thought you could make a living building things and cutting all of us off from the suppliers?" Dick asked. He laughed, elbowing the other two, who joined in his laughter.

I seethed. Yes, I failed. Yes, I fucked up. Yes, I almost lost the store. But dammit, I tried something. I followed my passion and tried a new idea. It wasn't my fault that idea wasn't embraced by my community. That my small town couldn't see me as anything other than Al's son and wasn't willing to let me get my hands dirty.

"The store isn't changing," I forced out through my gritted teeth. I'd learned my lesson. I knew I couldn't make a go at custom work full time. There wasn't enough of it in MacKellar Cove, and it wouldn't support me. The store needed to stay open. It was needed in town, even if the people who spent the most time there were no longer actual customers.

"Well, that's good. You need to keep things the way they are. People around here don't like change," Wayne said.

I nodded, grateful when a customer came in and needed help finding something. By the time we made it back to the register, Tony, Dick, and Wayne had moved on to another topic of conversation.

Customers came and went for the rest of the afternoon. As it got closer to when Brantley was supposed to arrive, I checked the clock and wondered if the trio were ever going to leave.

"I need to close up soon," I told them, keeping my voice light to avoid a confrontation.

Wayne looked at his phone and scowled. "We still have an hour. If I go home too early, Madeline will put me to work."

"Isn't she at Debby's tonight? I thought she always got her hair done on Wednesday nights," Dick said.

"Yeah, but when she gets home, she starts dinner. If I'm home before her, she asks why I didn't start anything," Wayne said, as if the suggestion was entirely laughable.

"Why don't you?" I asked him.

The three of them turned to me like I'd lost my damn mind. They looked at each other, then turned back to me with matching expressions of shame, shaking their heads in unison.

"That's a woman's job," Wayne said. "I went to work and earned the money so she could stay home with the kids. We agreed to it when we got married. She said it was what she wanted, so don't get all high and mighty on me. She suggested she stay home. Now, all these years later, she's trying to change the game. Telling me I should help her out around the house."

"You could," I said, digging my grave deeper. I knew they were going to give me shit, but I didn't agree with one person being expected to do everything around the house. My dad taught me that when I was a teenager. I resented it at the time, but he was right. I lived there, too. I made the mess, too. So I needed to be responsible for cleaning up, too. As an adult, it was still how I thought things should be.

Wayne shook his head. "We can't go back and have her get a job, so why should I have to change?"

"Because you live there," I said, standing my ground.

"And she takes care of things. I'm not a housewife," Wayne growled.

"Yeah, but imagine how nice you'd look in an apron," Brantley said. He walked in without any of us noticing and clearly heard Wayne's last comment.

Wayne spun on him, scowling before he saw who it was. His face transformed, and he chuckled, shaking his head. "Should'a known you'd say something like that. How're your parents, Brantley?"

"Doing well. How are things here? Besides picturing Wayne in an apron." Brantley clapped Wayne on the shoulder and laughed.

Wayne rolled his eyes and shook his head. He was

always more agreeable with Brantley around, although I'd never figured out why.

"Good, Coach. You got a good team this year?" Tony asked.

Brantley nodded. "First practices look pretty promising. Got a couple kids with scholarships already locked up, so keeping them healthy is always a priority."

"True, true," Dick said. "I tell you, when I was the coach, it was a full-time job just to keep those boys in line. I couldn't have done it if I had to grade papers and make lesson plans and all that, too."

Dick was a gym teacher once upon a time, and he coached baseball, basketball, and football. From what I remembered, Brantley never coached with him, but they obviously had a bond.

"I've made it work. I was also single for a long time." Brantley shrugged, like that made the difference.

The three men didn't comment on Brantley's status or ask anything about Valentina. I was a little surprised by it, but I couldn't put too much thought into it before Brantley asked if I was ready to go.

"Go where? Store isn't closed yet," Wayne barked.

Brantley looked at me, then back to the others. "Knox has to deliver shelves to Stone Auto Repair." Brantley turned back to me. "I thought you were closing up early so we could get there before Derek has to close."

I nodded. "I am. I need to. All right, it's time for you guys to pack it in and head out."

The three of them glared at me.

"I thought that was a joke. First, you use that jig thing off the shelf and poor Andre can't build a table for his baby because you were playing at craftsman again, and now you're closing early." Wayne shook his head like I was his greatest disappointment.

Brantley gawked at us, eyes wide, mouth hung open. Clearly the men had never spoken to him the way they did me.

"I didn't realize I needed to approve my work schedule with you guys. I also didn't realize I needed to pass any purchase decisions or work choices through you."

"You said you weren't changing things," Tony argued.

"And I'm not."

"You're closing the store early. That's a change," Dick said.

"It's one day. And it's less than an hour. And we have to go." I crossed my arms over my chest. I knew better than to try to touch any of the men to get them moving, but I wasn't going to miss out on getting paid for a job I worked my ass to finish because these three were stubborn assholes who thought they ruled me.

"Why don't you all come by practice tomorrow and have a look at the team for me," Brantley suggested. He circled around the backs of the men and clapped Wayne and Dick on the shoulders. "I'll love to get some outside eyes on how things are going, but only people I can trust."

Wayne smiled at him. "That would be good, son. We'd be happy to help you out. I have been hearing good things about that Mitchell kid. Said he could be a real contender. Only a sophomore, too."

"We should check out the JV team, too," Dick said.

The four of them moved toward the doors as one, Brantley guiding the older men from the store as though it was their choice.

"JV is where your players will be coming from," Dick said. "We'll let you know what we think of those kids. See if there's any you should keep an eye out for. Maybe pull up if you need a player."

"That's a great idea," Brantley said. He rubbed his jaw thoughtfully. "I don't get a chance to check them out since they're practicing and playing when my team is. Having people to give me an inside perspective would be real helpful."

The door swung behind the men, cutting off the rest of the conversation, and I finally exhaled. Brantley was a master. I wasn't entirely sure how he did it, but he handled the three of them like it was nothing. Sacrificing himself in the process.

I would never want those three judging me and critiquing what I was doing, but Brantley volunteered so they would back off me.

I closed out the register and made sure the rest of the store was empty. Brantley came back in a few minutes later, grabbing the keys I left on the counter and locking the front door before following me to the workshop out back.

"Are they always like that with you?" Brantley asked, handing over my keys.

I snorted. "Usually worse."

"Damn. I had no idea. What's up their asses?"

"Do you remember when I changed everything? Tried to set this place up for higher end jobs and custom work?"

Brantley nodded.

"Almost went under, and the three of them made sure I never forgot that I fucked up."

"That's not right."

I shrugged. "It's how they see it. When I mentioned I made these shelves, they about went nuts. Said I couldn't change everything again."

"It's your shop. You can do whatever you want."

I shook my head. "I have a customer base I need to serve. I've accepted that. I'd love to do more work like this, but there isn't enough around here. And people need a hardware store. I can't do both."

"What about hiring someone to run the store? You said that's what you wanted to do."

"That would be ideal, yeah. Shorter hours for me and time to do work like this, but I don't know anyone who would want that job."

"There's gotta be someone. Because you are stupid talented." Brantley ran his hands along the shelves I'd made. He whistled and shook his head. "I should have had you make cabinets for me."

I chuckled, knowing he was just saying that. "You couldn't have handled that kind of time without a kitchen."

Brantley didn't take his gaze off the shelves. "No, but if I'd known you could do this, I would have waited to tear shit up until you had something done. This is amazing."

"Thanks." My cheeks heated at the awed praise in his voice.

"I mean it. You really could make a living doing this."

I shook my head. "Nah. Not enough to do around here. But I'm good. I'll take these projects here and there, if I can get them, and it's enough to keep me going."

Brantley raised a questioning eyebrow at me, but I didn't give him the chance to say whatever it was he was going to say.

"Let's get these loaded up so we can get them over to Derek."

Brantley nodded.

We carried each piece out to the moving truck I'd rented. They fit inside perfectly, and we strapped them down so they wouldn't shift and damage each other on the quick drive across town.

The lot was mostly empty when we made it to Stone Auto Repair. One bay was open, so I backed the truck up in front of it, knowing Derek left it up for us. Before I'd put the truck in park, Derek was waiting.

"Evening," he said, shaking my hand.

"Good evening. You ready for me?"

Derek nodded. "We are. Got the old stuff moved out today. I got a few guys here to help if you need it."

Brantley rolled up the back of the truck and pulled out the ramp, positioning it for us to walk up and down. "There's five in here, so help would be good."

I nodded, meeting Derek's gaze.

"Sounds good." Derek whistled, and three guys came out from a door to the side. "Grab an end."

Brantley climbed into the truck and lifted the end of the one on top. One of Derek's guys grabbed the other end, and they walked the shelf out of the truck, giving Derek his first look at what I'd created.

Derek whistled low in the back of his throat. "Holy shit, dude. That's stunning."

"Thanks, man."

Derek looked into the truck at the other pieces, running his hand over the end of one. "I'm gonna feel like we can't get these dirty. This is not a clean place."

I launched into the design for the shelves, detailing the way I'd finished them so they wouldn't absorb stains and would be easy to clean.

"You really thought of everything, didn't you?" Derek asked.

I nodded. "I tried."

Derek and I grabbed one shelf and moved it inside. All

of us worked together, moving the shelves in before deciding where his crew wanted them positioned. I'd included mounting hardware on the back so the shelves wouldn't be at risk for tipping over, and I had brackets to anchor them together.

With all of us working together, the shelves were secured to the walls quickly. Derek stepped back and shook his head as he admired the work I'd done.

"That's one hell of an upgrade," a voice said from behind us as we were looking at the shelves.

Derek turned and grinned. "Omar. I agree. Sorry no one was out front when you arrived."

Mayor Omar Knight waved off Derek's apology. "Nothing to worry about, Derek. I can understand why you were all here. Where did you get these from?"

Derek hooked his thumb toward me. "Knox made them."

Mayor Knight regarded me with a raised eyebrow and an approving smile. "Impressive work. Do you do a lot of custom work?"

I shook my head. "No, sir. I own Al's Hardware. This is just a side hobby for me."

"It's his passion," Brantley said. "He loves doing it, but people need the hardware store, so Knox keeps it running. His dad is Al."

"Family legacy," Mayor Knight said. "I understand that all too well."

I wasn't sure what he was referring to since I didn't know the man well, but I wasn't going to question the mayor. About anything.

Derek ushered him back to the front, where I assumed he had a vehicle to pick up. The guys started loading up the shelves with all their tools and parts, talking and deciding where they wanted to put things.

Brantley and I stepped back and admired the work I'd done. I was proud of it. It was a big job, but one I could tell would be right for the job it was intended to do. One of the guys grabbed a shelf and realized it pulled out and laughed. I heard him say how convenient it was going to be.

"This is amazing." Brantley clapped me on the back. "You really are talented, Knox."

"Thanks, Bee."

"Sorry about that," Derek said, joining us again. He handed me an envelope. "The rest of your payment. Thanks again for doing this. I know Xavier sort of talked you into it, but it's better than I could have imagined."

"Thanks. It was a lot of fun for me to do."

"Good. Hey, do you guys think anyone would mind if Omar came out to guys' night sometime?"

Brantley and I exchanged a glance and shrugged.

"I don't go every week," I told him. "I'm fairly new to the invite list, but they've always seemed pretty welcoming."

"Same. I doubt anyone would be upset about it. Why?"

"Omar doesn't really have people he hangs around with. He's single, and he's in charge of basically everyone in town, so he keeps to himself, but he's a really nice guy. I think he'd get along with the group, but I make it about once a month, if that. I don't want to be that guy everyone talks about because he crossed a line," Derek said.

I shook my head. "Can't see that happening. Doesn't Patrick work for him? It would be another person Mayor Knight knows."

"See if he's interested and bring him. I'm sure it'll be fine," Brantley said.

Derek nodded. He opened his mouth to say something

else, but a crash drew our attention. His guys were standing next to the shelves with a box of parts at their feet.

"I should help them get things set up. We want to be ready to go tomorrow morning without missing a beat. But thanks again. I really appreciate it."

Brantley and I nodded and headed toward the door. We closed up the truck and got in the front. Brantley nodded to the envelope Derek had given me.

"Let's grab something to eat. You're paying."

I laughed and shook my head, but agreed. I owed him for helping me out, after all. Probably more than dinner once he had Tony, Dick, and Wayne weighing in on his team.

I didn't envy Brantley, but I was definitely grateful.

15

HALEY

I leaned back in the chair and closed my eyes. It was one of life's simple pleasures to have someone else wash my hair. As a stylist, I washed dozens of people's hair every week, but getting the same treatment wasn't something I indulged in often.

But Chelsea insisted. She'd been after me for months to let her cut my hair, and I finally agreed. Only because she said she'd let me cut her hair, too.

"Water okay?" Chelsea asked as she soaked my hair.

"Perfect," I told her, sinking into the relaxation of the moment.

Chelsea was quiet as she washed my hair, using her nails to scrub my scalp and work up the suds to a comfortable clean. She rinsed my hair, then smoothed conditioner over my hair. After another rinse, she wrapped my hair in a towel and sat me up.

"You sure you trust me?" she asked, meeting my gaze in the mirror in front of her station.

I exhaled slowly, the question throwing me off. "Are you telling me I shouldn't?"

Chelsea laughed and shook her head. "Not at all. But I know trusting isn't easy for you."

"Ain't that the truth," Sofia muttered from her seat next to me. I'd just finished cutting her hair, and she helped Chelsea talk me into a new style. One I hadn't chosen. One they were keeping from me.

"I have never had anyone trustworthy in my life. It's not easy to let my guard down when no one else I've ever known has been decent enough to me that I could try. I mean, look at my track record."

They exchanged a glance behind me, one I caught in the mirror, one that said they pitied me. Dammit. I hated that.

"That's why you need a new cut," Chelsea said, squeezing the water from my hair.

Admittedly, it was too long for me. I had been keeping up with trimming the ends, but the overall style was outgrown and less than ideal.

"Don't go short," I said. "A trim."

"A good trim," Sofia said. "Like you talked me into."

Sofia's blonde hair looked good on her. She argued that she never did anything and had to keep it out of her face for work, so she never bothered doing anything with it. I talked her into a trim that added layers and framed her face, while still being long enough that she could tie it up in a ponytail and not have to worry about it.

"You keep touching your hair, so we know you like it," Chelsea said.

Sofia stopped caressing her lightened locks and blushed. "It feels so different."

"That's because it is. But different is good," Chelsea said.

Sofia smiled. "Sometimes."

I rolled my eyes at them, then focused on Chelsea in the mirror. She sectioned off my hair, twisting the top up onto my head and securing it with a clip. She grabbed her scissors and looked up, finding me watching her.

"Nope. We're not doing that." Chelsea spun my chair so I couldn't watch her in the mirror.

"Hey! Why did you do that?"

"Because you're going to judge and critique, and I'm going to lose my mind. I'll show you when I'm done."

"What if I don't like it?"

Chelsea stepped in front of me and met my gaze evenly. "Haley, I'm your friend. I want you to look good because I want everyone who sits in my chair to look good and feel good. I promise you, I'm not going to give you a crappy cut. But I know you're going to freak out over every single piece I cut. Like Sofia did."

"Hey! I resemble that remark."

I snorted.

"Please, trust me," Chelsea said.

I finally nodded, and she moved behind me again, leaving me without a view of my head as she worked her magic on my hair.

I hoped.

"Sofia, you have to distract me," I told my friend.

"I talked to my dad the other day," Sofia said.

"You did? I thought you weren't in touch." Sofia didn't share much about her family, but I knew her mom died when she was a teenager and she moved in with her dad. She made it sound like they weren't close and she left as soon as she could.

"He calls every so often," Sofia said. "He said he wants to visit."

"Here?"

Sofia nodded, picking up the ends of her hair and examining them. "I told him I'd have to think about it."

"When's the last time you saw him?" Chelsea asked.

Sofia shrugged. "A few years."

"Wow. I can't imagine going that long without seeing my parents. I have dinner with them every week," Chelsea said.

"Not everyone has a family that's close like yours," I told her.

"I know. I think I'm lucky."

"You are. I was close to my mom. It was just the two of us, and she was awesome. When she died, I felt like I was on my own. Piper was the first person I met who made me feel like I wasn't alone," Sofia said.

"Piper has a way of making everyone feel comfortable," I said. "I bet that makes running the Inn that much easier for her."

Sofia chuckled. "There are days she says she doesn't know why she bought MacKellar Cove Inn, but she always remembers when new guests arrive."

"I can relate to that," Chelsea said. "This job can get repetitive, but it's fun to talk to people and see the reaction when someone gets a cut that they love and makes them feel good."

"That's why I do it, too," I admitted. "Being curvy, I've always struggled with my appearance and feeling good. I know a lot of my clients feel the same. When I'm able to make someone feel good, it makes a huge difference. It makes me smile for days."

"That's why I opened this place," Debby said from to my left. She'd been in the back doing paperwork, but I didn't realize she was able to hear our conversation.

"And why you're still successful," Chelsea said, smiling at our boss.

"It helps that I'm the only salon in town," Debby said.

She studied what Chelsea was doing to my hair and smiled. "It's going to be a good look on her."

"Thanks," Chelsea said. "I won't let her see, which is making her a little crazy."

"Or a lot," Sofia said with a laugh.

I growled at them.

Debby met my gaze. "You're going to be happy with Chelsea's work. It's a very flattering cut for you. Still long enough that you look like you, but fresher. I've never been very good at giving my clients new styles."

I wanted to glance at Chelsea, but I kept my gaze firmly locked on Debby. "If they don't want a change, it's hard to force it on people."

Debby shrugged. "Maybe. But it's also harder for me to see what new styles would look good on someone. I never would have done what Chelsea's doing, but I can see that it's going to look great on you."

"Thank you," Chelsea said. We'd talked many times about Debby's older hair styles, but we'd never admit to our boss that we thought she needed a refresh, or that her skills could benefit from the same. We both really liked and respected Debby.

"I'm going to head out. Will you ladies lock up for me?"

"Of course," Chelsea and I said together.

"Have a good night," Chelsea said.

"You ladies do the same," Debby said, waving before she disappeared behind the curtain in the back.

We were all quiet for a few minutes. Chelsea continued to cut my hair, and Sofia and I were lost in our own thoughts.

Debby seemed strangely introspective. It was a little unnerving. She was an institution in town, from what I knew. Everyone had heard of Debby, and at least half the population in MacKellar Cove were regulars at the salon.

The way she spoke sounded like a woman who was on her way out, not one who was coming back to work the next day.

"Was that weird to you guys?" Sofia asked a few minutes later.

I nodded, which made Chelsea grab my head and still my movements. "Sorry."

"That was almost bad," Chelsea mumbled. "And yes. That was weird. I wonder if something's going on."

"The rumor mill hasn't said anything," Sofia said. "She just sounded like she was ready to retire."

"That's kind of what I thought, too."

Chelsea mumbled her agreement, then picked up the hair dryer. She was done. It wouldn't be long before I could get a look at my new cut.

We were all quiet while Chelsea dried my hair. When she finished, she insisted on styling it for me. I chewed on the inside of my lip the entire time. Too anxious to speak.

What if I hated what she did?

What if it was bad?

What if—

Chelsea spun me around and all my fears vanished.

"Wow." I leaned forward in the chair, getting closer to the mirror as I inspected her work. It was stunning. I was stunning. She'd added a lot of layers, but they worked with my long waves. She gave me a ton of texture and body, both of which were amplified by the soft curls she added to my style.

"Is it okay?" she asked.

I met her gaze in the mirror. Her hands were clasped in front of her, worry etching her face.

"It's amazing. I look so damn good."

Chelsea exhaled a sigh of relief.

"You always looked damn good," Sofia said. "Chelsea just helped you to show that off."

I laughed with the two of them and looked around the salon. It was starting to get dark outside, but inside, the three of us made our own little group. I'd never counted on other people in my entire life, but in the last year, I'd counted on these two women for everything from friendship to work to a shoulder to cry on when I discovered Dawson was married.

I told myself I'd never trusted people, but I'd trusted Sofia and Chelsea. I knew they were people I didn't want to not have in my life.

And if I was being honest, Knox was becoming one of those people, too.

I got out of the chair and turned to hug Chelsea. "Thank you. So much. It's amazing, and I really appreciate you cutting my hair and being my friend."

Chelsea laughed and hugged me back. "Being your friend is easy. And helping you feel like the person I see inside is absolutely my pleasure."

"Hey, I helped. I was moral support," Sofia said, jumping up to join our hug.

We all laughed.

I nodded. "Absolutely, Sofia. I would have left MacKellar Cove a long time ago if it weren't for you two. Thank you for being my friends."

"That goes both ways, girl," Chelsea said.

Sofia nodded. "What she said."

I turned to Chelsea. "Now I cut your hair?"

Chelsea shook her head. "Not tonight. I'm starving. Anyone up for pizza?"

"I thought you were going to let me cut your hair."

"I will. Next week. Trust me, I'm ready for it. But tonight, we need pizza and wine and you need to tell us what's going on with Knox."

"Ooh, yes, I want to know what's going on with Knox, too," Sofia said.

I tried to argue with them, but just hearing his name made me smile. "Fine. If I must."

They traded a smile. "Oh, you must. Everyone to my apartment," Sofia said.

Chelsea and I locked up the salon, then we all drove over to Sofia's and my building. Chelsea parked in a visitor spot and met Sofia and I at the door. We all went to Sofia's apartment, where we ordered pizza and opened a bottle of wine before settling on her couch.

"Okay, spill," Sofia said. "How are things with Knox?"

I shook my head, laughing at her impatience. We'd barely sat down before she asked the question. "Things are good."

"Good? That's all you're going to give us?" Chelsea asked.

I laughed. "What do you want me to tell you?"

"How's the sex?" Chelsea asked.

Sofia raised an eyebrow and shrugged before nodding. "I was wondering, too."

"You guys are bad. But the sex is not."

"Yeah?"

I nodded. "This is weird. I've never talked to anyone about sex before."

"Wait, ever? Like ever? You've never had friends you could talk to about sex? You know what sex is, right?" Chelsea asked.

"Oh, my God. You're crazy. Yes, I know what sex is. But

I've never had close friends. I always felt like they were judging me, so I kept my distance from other women."

"We're not judging you," Sofia said. "We're just living through you since I know I'm not having any sex. You?"

Chelsea shook her head. "Same. Is he good to you? Makes sure you're enjoying yourself? He seems like the kind of guy who'd be aware of that kind of thing."

"He is," I admitted before I could think about it.

They grinned widely. "Good."

"What does he think about you sticking around?" Sofia asked.

"You're staying?" Chelsea screeched. "Yay! You never told me you'd decided."

I shook my head. "I haven't decided. I think Sofia meant about my choices."

"I did. Sorry," Sofia said.

"Knox said he wants me to stay, but he understands that I can't decide for him. It has to be the right choice for me."

"And the fact that he knows that and isn't pushing you tells me he's a good guy," Sofia said.

I nodded. "I agree. But I've been here ten months, and there are still people who want me gone."

"Forget about them," Chelsea said. "They don't matter."

I breathed a laugh. "If only it were that easy. I might not be overly concerned with what random people say, but it's tough to not let it get to me."

"I thought it was better after we all came to the salon a few weeks ago?" Sofia asked.

I nodded. "It was. It is. But what happens when those people find out I'm dating Knox?"

"Knox isn't married. Never has been. What can they possibly say about you dating him?" Chelsea asked.

I shrugged. "I don't know. I'm sure the people who want me to leave will find something to say."

A knock on the door interrupted any other arguments from Sofia or Chelsea. We settled back on the couch with pizza and wine and found a movie to play in the background while my friends tried again to convince me to stay in MacKellar Cove.

"Where would you go if you left?" Sofia asked.

I laughed. "I have never once thought about where I would want to live. I've always gone wherever my newest boyfriend lived, or where my old one didn't."

"Where was the place you liked the most?" Chelsea asked.

"Here," I admitted.

"Then stay!" they said together.

"I'm leaning that way. I'll think about it."

"I think that's the best we can expect," Sofia said with a smirk. "But that doesn't mean we're giving up on convincing you."

"Definitely not giving up," Chelsea agreed.

I smiled at them and picked up my slice of pizza. It was different to have friends. Good, but different.

When I got back to my apartment that night, comfortably warm and fuzzy after time with my friends and maybe one too many glasses of wine, I decided to send Knox a message.

Chelsea and Sofia bugged me all night about staying in MacKellar Cove, but the one thing I couldn't answer was what Knox would say if I stayed. I didn't want him to think I was staying for him, because I wasn't, and I needed to know he would be okay with me staying if that was what I decided.

SINGLEMENWANTED

If I stay, and things don't work out between us, what will happen?

HANDYNOTHANDSY

First, why do you think things won't work out?

SMW

My track record.

HNH

Every single person on the planet could say the same. Until you meet the right one, your track record sucks.

SMW

Sure, but does everyone have the same luck as me?

HNH

Okay, fine. Maybe not. But I'm not like Dawson.

As for your question, hopefully we can be friends.

SMW

You want to be friends?

HNH

Um, no. But if what I want to be doesn't work out, then yeah, I think friends is good.

SMW

Oh. Um, okay.

HNH

I'm saying I like you, Haley. A lot. And I want you to stay in town. And I want to keep seeing you. And I want to be more than friends with you.

SMW

Me, too. All of the same.

HNH

LOL. I was hoping so. Are we still on for dinner tomorrow night?

SMW

Yes.

HNH

Good. I'll see you then, beautiful. Have a good night.

SMW

You too.

I clutched the phone to my chest and smiled. More than friends sounded really damn good. But friends was good, too. As a back up. One I really hoped I didn't need because I wanted to be more than friends with Knox.

For a very long time.

16

―――――

KNOX PICKED ME UP AT SIX WITH A KISS THAT LEFT ME breathless and a bouquet that made my eyes tear up. "More flowers?" I asked.

He shrugged. "I figured the ones I got you a few weeks ago were gone, and you needed some new ones."

I took the bouquet and brought them to my nose. I turned to retrieve the pitcher I'd used last time, Knox behind me, when he cleared his throat.

"I, um, also got this."

I stopped and spun to face him, gasping when he held up a simple vase. It was tall enough for the flowers he brought, but not so tall it wouldn't fit shorter blooms. It was crystal clear glass with vertical lines on it that added movement to the glass.

"You got me a vase?"

He nodded and moved to set the vase next to the sink. "I noticed you didn't have one last time I brought flowers. I hope it's okay."

I nodded as I walked over to him, lifting up on my toes to

kiss him. "Thank you," I whispered, one arm around his neck, the other clutching the flowers.

His hands rested on my hips. "You're welcome, Haley."

We stood there for a long moment, debating skipping dinner and going straight to the bedroom. Or maybe that was just me.

I dropped back down and busied myself with cutting the flowers and arranging them in the new vase while I tried to calm my racing hormones.

I really liked Knox. More than I felt like I should. Things were good between us. Easy. I didn't feel like I had to pretend to be someone else, something I did with almost every other boyfriend. And I wasn't sure what that meant, but at the moment, I wasn't looking too closely at it.

"Your haircut looks really nice," he said, breaking through my thoughts.

I fluffed the edges of it, loving the light feel of it. "Thanks. Chelsea talked me into letting her have her way."

"She did excellent. You look different, but the same. Still beautiful."

My cheeks warmed with his appreciative look, and I debated skipping dinner again.

I focused on the flowers and ignored the pull I felt toward Knox, knowing building a relationship on sex alone was what brought me to MacKellar Cove, and I didn't want that again.

With the flowers set, we left for dinner. Knox held my hand on the short drive south to Alexandria Bay. He parked in front of a brightly colored restaurant with lights strung up over the sidewalk to the front door. Music filtered out of the building, a soft, sensual song that was definitely being played live.

"What is this place?" I asked, taking Knox's hand on the sidewalk.

"The Bay Place. I thought it would be fun. They have great food and live music every night. The musicians are all local, so they play a lot of covers and some of their own music. I've been here a few times."

I glanced up at him, trying to decide if he was telling me this was where he brought dates or if there was another reason he'd been there. Before I asked, I decided it didn't matter. He was there with me. And the place sounded like fun.

"Sounds good," I said after a minute.

Knox relaxed next to me, then led the way inside.

It was brighter than I expected from the outside. A stage was in the middle of the restaurant with open space around it for people to dance. Tables filled in the rest of the restaurant in a ring so you could see the musician from every seat in the place.

Knox told the hostess there were two of us, and she led us to a table on the upper ring of tables. I was surprised to find we could speak to each other without shouting.

The hostess handed us menus, then left us alone to look them over. I looked everywhere but the menu, taking in the restaurant and the fun atmosphere of the place.

"How did you find this place?" I asked Knox.

"My ex used to play here," he said, wincing slightly when he admitted that.

My brows winged up. "You brought me to your ex-girlfriend's job?"

"She doesn't play here anymore. Hasn't for years. I haven't been here since we broke up."

"But you did break up?" I whispered.

He reached across the table and took my hand, waiting

until I looked up at him to speak. "The only person I'm involved with is you, Haley. The only person I want to be involved with is you."

I nodded, feeling like an ass for questioning him. He'd never given me a reason to think he was anything but honest with me.

"From what I remember, all the food is excellent. The music is fun. I'm hoping I can talk you into a dance at some point, too."

His thumb stroked across my wrist, lighting me up for no reason other than he was touching me.

I nodded, knowing I couldn't form words as long as he was touching me.

We turned to our menus and ordered dinner and drinks when the server came over. Once he walked away, I turned to listen to the music.

It was beautiful, and a little haunting. About a man who was living with regrets about his life, the biggest being leaving behind a woman he loved once upon a time.

"Well, that's not depressing," Knox said.

"But it's real," I replied. "It's sad, but you can feel his pain."

"Why doesn't he go back to her?"

"It's not always that easy."

Knox studied me carefully for a minute. "Can I ask about Dawson?"

I inhaled a sharp breath and nodded. Hiding it wouldn't change anything. "What do you want to know?"

"How did things end?"

That wasn't the question I expected. Everyone seemed to know how it ended. "Um, I showed up at his house when he was having dinner with Valentina and their daughters, and Goldie and her son."

"Yeah, I know that, but after. What did he say?"

I sipped my water. "I haven't spoken to him."

"What?"

"We never talked again. Valentina threw him out, he spent the first night with Brantley, and he left town. He's never once reached out."

"Are you kidding me?"

I shook my head.

"Shit. I thought he was an asshole before, but that's low. You didn't do anything wrong. He did."

"That's not how he sees it, I guess. He blamed me. If I hadn't shown up, everything would have been fine."

"Nothing about that situation was fine. It's not okay that you're taking all the blame."

I shrugged, wishing he would change the subject. Dawson was my least favorite topic of conversation.

"What would you do if he called you?"

"Like now?"

"Yeah. It's been months, but what if he wanted to get back together?"

"I blocked him, so I wouldn't know if he reached out, but I'm done with him. He might have been cheating on his wife with me, but as far as I'm concerned, he was cheating on me with her. He never said the words, but I thought he was in love with me. I thought we were building toward a life together, and instead, he never had any intention of us being more than we were. He lied to me, and he manipulated me, and he used me. I have no interest in getting back together with him, or ever seeing him again at all."

I sat back in my seat and fought the tears building in my eyes. I hated Dawson. Of all my exes, he was the one who hurt me the most. I thought I finally picked a good one. I fell for him, hard. But he was the worst of them.

"I'm sorry, Haley," Knox whispered, taking my hand.

I fought him, tugging back for a second, but Knox didn't let go.

"I didn't mean to upset you about Dawson. I heard some of what happened from others, but I wanted to hear about it from you."

I swiped the tears from the edges of my lashes and avoided his gaze. "I believed all his lies. I had no idea who he really was. And I feel like an idiot for uprooting my entire life to move here to be closer to him. I just... I regret ever getting involved with him."

"I'm happy you did," Knox whispered. "It brought you to MacKellar Cove. It brought you into my life. I know that's selfish, and you went through hell to get here, but I'm happy we met."

"I am, too," I admitted. "It would have been nice to meet without the heartbreak and the entire town hating me, though."

Knox chuckled. "I don't think they all hate you."

I glowered at him, and he laughed again.

"Fine, they all hate you. But that's their loss. They have no idea what they're missing out on."

I smiled. "Can we talk about something other than how much everyone hates me?"

He laughed again. "Sure. Why don't you tell me about work?"

I wrinkled my nose, and he laughed again.

"Not a good subject?"

"No, work is fine. But if I don't stay in town, then I'll be looking for a new place to work and live."

"I built a storage unit," Knox blurted.

The sudden subject change threw me for a second, and I

gawked at him. "Um, cool. I'm guessing. Was it a good thing?"

He nodded, exhaling a laugh. "Yeah. Sorry I just threw that at you. I... Have you always known you wanted to be a hairdresser?"

I shrugged, unsure why he told me about the storage unit, then immediately changed the subject. "Yes and no. It was easy to earn money when I was going through training, so I jumped into it without considering a lot of options. With the way my family was, I wanted to be on my own as soon as possible."

"But you're happy with it?"

"Yeah, I guess. I like knowing when someone gets out of my chair, they feel good. They stand a little straighter and smile a little wider and toss their hair a bit more. It makes me feel good that I was able to do something like that for another person."

Knox smiled at me for a minute, then leaned across the table and kissed me sweetly. Closed lips, and over too soon, but it brought a smile to my lips.

"You're a good person, Haley. Most people choose their job because they have an elevated sense of self. But you do it because you make people feel good. To give back."

I shrugged, feeling like he was seeing a piece of me I hadn't shared before. Not that he was wrong, but I didn't accept praise well.

"I want to do custom design and construction work," he blurted, the words tripping over each other as he forced them out.

"You want to... Like building houses?"

He shook his head. "The shelves I built were for Stone Auto Repair. For their tools and parts in the shop for the employees. Derek asked me about finding something or who could build something, and Xavier offered my help."

"Xavier?"

"Xavier Hogan. He runs MacKellar Theater. Married to Karissa, who designed the app."

"Oh! Okay, I'm with you now. I didn't realize you were friends."

"I made the sign at the theater."

"You did? That's amazing."

Knox nodded thoughtfully. "I tried to change my dad's store into a place where I could do that. I almost lost it all."

"I find that hard to believe."

He shook his head. "It's true. I changed everything. The town wasn't interested in what I had to offer. I was practically laughed out of town. I changed it all back."

"But you hate it." It wasn't a question. I could see the pain in his face and the rounded hunch of his shoulders. It wasn't like when he talked about building the shelves.

Knox nodded slowly. "I wish I loved it like you love what you do. That I was excited to walk into the hardware store every morning."

"Then quit."

Knox laughed mirthlessly. "I can't quit. My dad built that store. He made it what it is. He loves it."

"Okay, then change the hours. Open half as long and spend the other half of your day doing custom work. Hire someone to run the store. Do something. Life's too damn short to be miserable. Trust me. I've spent most of my life searching for something that I haven't found yet. I hate it. I don't want to keep chasing a dream that might not exist."

"What dream is that?"

"Love," I confessed, meeting his gaze. "I want to know what it feels like to have someone love me. To know I'm safe with another person. To know there's someone out there who's wondering how my day is and thinking about me and hoping I'm smiling. Someone who will stand up for me to all the people who think I'm so horrible for sleeping with a man who never told me he was married. Someone who wants me in his life as much as I want to be in his." I shook my head. "It sounds so small and silly, but I've never had that."

Knox reached across the table for my hand. "It's not silly. And it's definitely not small. I know my dad loves me, and that's been a huge thing for me. I haven't had that one woman in my life who's the same as my mom was for him, but I'm looking for that, too."

I smiled at him, drawing a shaky breath. I hadn't meant to confess my thoughts to him, but he asked and I couldn't keep the words inside.

The server brought our food over, forcing us to let go of each other to make room for the plates. He walked away again once he made sure we had everything we needed.

"I meant what I said last night about wanting to be more than friends, Haley, but I also think the best relationships are with people who are friends, too. I look at Brantley and Valentina and everything they went through to get to where they are. I have no doubt it was hard for him to be patient and wonder if he'd ever get a chance to tell her how he felt, but they were friends for a very long time. It made them becoming more than friends a lot easier."

"What are you saying, Knox?"

He smiled. "I'm saying I like you, Haley. And I'm saying I'm happy we can talk. That you're willing to have conversations with me. And to not have conversations with me."

My cheeks warmed at his lust-fueled look. He wasn't the

only one feeling the desire swirling around us. Or the joy at finding someone I could talk to about real things.

Dawson only wanted to talk about superficial things. He never shared details about his life or much about what he wanted from life. He always said he liked his job, but that it was just a job and he didn't want to talk about it. He didn't talk about anything. He asked me questions and made me feel special instead of opening up himself.

Sitting across from Knox as we ate dinner and listened to music, the differences between the two men were even more apparent. Knox nodded his head along to the music. He offered me a bite of his dinner, wanting to share the experience. He smiled and talked and made me feel like I was important to him, even though we were still getting to know each other.

When we finished dinner, Knox asked me to dance. A slow song came on, and he stood and offered me his hand. As he led me to the dance floor, I felt the eyes of others on us, appreciating the man I was lucky enough to dance with.

Knox pulled me in close, one hand possessively low on my back, the other holding my hand in his close to our bodies. His beard tickled my cheek as we swayed together, letting the music guide us.

Knox's fingers flexed against my back, pulling me tighter to him until I felt his arousal growing against my belly.

"Sorry," he whispered.

I smiled at him. "Unless you're apologizing because you're thinking about someone else, you don't need to worry about me."

He leaned down until his lips brushed my ear. "Definitely not thinking about anyone but you. Having you in my arms has that effect on me."

"I feel the same," I confessed.

Knox pulled back far enough to catch my gaze and slowly closed the distance between us. His lips touched mine like a live wire, sparking and spinning and lighting me up inside and out.

I gasped against his lips, giving him an opening that he took full advantage of. We shuffled our feet as we kissed like we'd never done it before, making out like we needed each other to survive.

And I realized Knox Randall just might be the man I'd wanted to find. He might be the man who made me feel safe and loved and cherished. With his hard body at my front and his possessive hand at my back, there was nowhere in the world I'd rather be than right there in his arms.

17

———————

WE STAYED ON THE DANCE FLOOR UNTIL THE MUSICIAN TOOK A break. Knox led me back to our table, where he paid the bill, then dragged me out of the restaurant.

Not that I was fighting him.

He opened my door for me, waiting for me to get in, then closed it and hurried around to the other side. He cranked up the truck and blasted the air conditioning, even though late March was still cool.

"Where to, Haley?"

I met his hungry gaze. I wasn't ready for the night to be over. His place meant no neighbors, but mine meant we wouldn't be forced to spend the night together. Since he picked me up, I didn't have a car at his store, so either he'd have to drive me home, or I'd have to stay the night.

"Your place," I whispered.

He held my gaze a minute longer, then nodded and took off. He stayed exactly at the speed limit until he made it out of town and onto the highway, then pushed it as high as he could go without risking a ticket.

Neither of us spoke on the drive back to his place. His

hand gripped my thigh, his fingers digging into my jeans and making me wish I'd worn a skirt.

I wanted his hands on my skin. His body on mine. His tongue in my mouth. I was so wet I was sure I'd leave a mark on the seat. It was almost embarrassing how badly I wanted him.

Until I caught the look in his eyes and knew I wasn't the only one feeling that way.

Knox slammed the truck into park so fast the gears squawked at him. He flipped the key and yanked it out, his seatbelt already off and his door open by the time the key was free of the ignition.

I fought to unbuckle my seatbelt, my hands shaking. Knox was there, opening my door and freeing me, then lifting me from the truck into his arms.

His erection was solid between us, as ready as I was for whatever was coming next.

Oh, who was I kidding? I knew exactly what was coming next. Us.

Knox took two tries to get his door unlocked and us inside. As soon as we were, and the door was locked again, we were tearing at each other's clothes.

One boot went one direction, the other opposite. His shoes were toed off at the door, left for us to trip over on the way out. My hands went to his jeans as he worked on my jacket.

Items were tossed and scattered on our path to the bedroom. We weren't willing to slow down or take our time. It felt like something shifted between us. Something changed. I didn't know what it was, but there was something new.

Knox pressed me against the wall just inside the door to his bedroom, the cold drywall making me yelp. He ducked his head and licked my throat, his hands warming me up on their path down my body.

"I need you, Haley."

"Me, too."

He dropped to his knees in front of me and nudged my thighs wider, dragging his hand up between them. He pushed one finger inside. He kissed my belly and looked up at me.

"You're so beautiful."

I opened my mouth to reply, but nothing came out.

He added another finger and rubbed his thumb over my clit.

"You're so wet, Haley. Were you thinking about this on the drive back here? I was. I couldn't wait to get my hands on you."

I nodded.

"Good."

My knees trembled as my orgasm started to make itself known.

"Let go for me, beautiful. Let me hear you. Please, Haley. I was hoping you'd want to come here so I could make you scream for me. Will you, Haley?"

"Knox," I groaned.

"Louder, beautiful."

"Fuck. Knox." I moaned.

His fingers moved faster, his thumb teasing me.

"Can't stand," I grunted, my concentration going to keep myself upright instead of letting go.

"I've got you, beautiful. Lean on me."

His free hand went to the center of my chest, holding me upright as a wave of pleasure washed over me and nearly sent me to the floor.

"There you go, beautiful."

He added a third finger, and my body splintered, breaking apart as I came with a shout.

"Yes, beautiful. So damn good." Knox murmured encouraging words to me, praising me as he continued to stroke my body. "Let's go to the bed. I need your next one to be on my face."

I gasped as he withdrew his fingers from inside me.

"Don't worry. I'm not leaving you without a few more of those."

I exhaled a laugh, my knees shaky as he helped me across the room to his bed. He eased me down on the edge of the bed, my legs hanging over the end. He positioned himself between my thighs and wasted no time settling his shoulders between my thighs.

Those three fingers went back inside me in one stroke, and he encouraged my legs over his shoulders. His mouth closed over my clit, and holding back wasn't an option.

I let go, shouting and coming and so beyond blissed out that I was sure I was flying.

The mile high club had nothing on Knox Randall. I didn't need a plane to get there with that man.

Before I came back down to earth, Knox had a condom on and was positioned in front of me. As soon as my eyes opened, he surged into me, stretching my body and filling me up and making my eyes roll back in my head.

"Knox," I gasped.

"So good, Haley. So fucking good." His words were forced out through a clenched jaw.

"Yes."

I watched him as he eased back. His pace was slow, steady, like he was trying to hold back from losing it. I loved seeing the way his face twisted like it was hard to resist his impulse.

"Knox," I whispered.

His eyes flickered open and landed on me. His pace faltered, his body reacting to what he saw instead of his mind convincing him what he knew.

"I can't resist you, Haley."

"Who said you had to?"

"I don't want to hurt you."

"Then don't hurt me. Make me come again, Knox."

Determination lit his gaze, and he slammed hard into me. He stood upright, looking down to where he slid into me. The hard slap of our bodies together was erotic and sexy and the best feeling in the world.

He lowered his hand between us and brushed a finger over my clit. After the other orgasms I'd had, it was sensitive and tender. Adding in the feel of him inside me, and I almost came from just one touch.

"Do you like that?" he asked.

"Yes," I moaned. "More."

He rubbed over my clit, the gentle touch counter to the pounding of his dick inside me. The two together were enough to twist and turn my body and my brain into spinning out of control.

"Knox! Oh, fuck, Knox. Yes!" My entire body ignited as I came hard, my legs locking around him and holding him deep inside me while I came all over him.

"Fuck, Haley," he grunted, fighting against my legs to stroke a few more times before he was right there with me, shouting and coming and collapsing on top of me.

There was no way he was comfortable, but he didn't make a move to get off me immediately. I held on to him, my body shaking and my heart clenching painfully as I accepted that things had definitely changed between me and Knox.

I'd fallen in love with him.

I wasn't surprised, but I knew it meant it was the beginning of the end. If I loved him, I'd find a way to fuck it up.

And that was the last thing I wanted to do.

KNOX MOVED a few minutes after my private declaration. I avoided his gaze when he helped me up and thanked him when he told me to use the bathroom first.

I needed to be normal around him. He couldn't know how I felt. I had to keep it quiet. Knox wasn't likely to run for the hills, but in my experience, men didn't love being told someone was in love with them. Especially if they weren't in the same place.

While he was in the bathroom, I retraced our steps and collected my clothes. I had my panties and bra on when he walked out of the bedroom and found me, one foot in my jeans.

"Are you leaving?" Knox hadn't bothered to grab any of his clothes and was still gloriously naked.

I avoided looking at him, putting all my energy into pulling my jeans on. "Um, yeah. I figured it was the best. We've never spent the night together before. I didn't want you to have to get up in the middle of the night to drive me home, and this might be a quiet town, but I'd still rather not walk."

"Yeah, you're not walking home from here. But I feel like something's wrong. Did I hurt you?"

"What? No. Of course not."

"Then why are you trying to run out of here like I did?"

I focused on a spot over his shoulder, close enough that I

could see his face but not direct eye contact. "I just thought you'd want to take me home."

He shook his head and moved into my line of view, not allowing me to avoid meeting his gaze. His bright blue-green eyes were compassionate and understanding. Not at all what I expected when I was trying to get the hell out of his apartment.

"Haley, what did I do?"

"You didn't do anything. I promise."

"Then why are you running away?"

"Because I'm... falling in love with you."

His eyes narrowed. "And that means you have to leave?"

"It means I'm going to screw all of this up. It's what I always do. I fall in love, then I think it means we're in the same place, then I tell him, and it's over. So, I figured I'd get out of here so I didn't have to stand in front of you when you tell me you're not feeling the same."

He took my hands, ignoring the shirt I clutched in one, and smiled at me. "And what if I am feeling the same?"

"What?"

"I told you I don't want to be friends, Haley. I have my own shit. I want kids. I want a family. I want a woman who's going to fit into my life. Who thinks this crazy town is the place she wants to live for the next few decades. I want someone who's not going to turn up her nose at what I do, and encourage me to do what I want to do. I want someone easy to talk to and funny and kind. And if she happens to be gorgeous and we have chemistry that damn near terrifies me, I'm good with that, too."

"Yeah?"

He nodded. "Yeah, Haley."

I tugged my shirt over my head and said, "Well, I hope you find her."

He laughed and wrapped me in his arms, lifting me off the floor and carrying me back to the bedroom. "I found her. And I'm not driving you home just yet. Your tactic was enough for me to recover, and I'm ready to see if there are other ways I can make you scream my name."

"Knox," I moaned as he lifted my shirt and trailed his fingertips down the center of my belly.

"Haley, I'm falling, too. I don't know if we're going to be together in a year, but I want to be together right now. I want to be together next week and next month, and as of now, I want to be together next year. If you decide MacKellar Cove isn't the place for you..." He shook his head. "This is my home. I'm not leaving. And I can ply you with orgasms and hope you decide you want to stay, but I also understand if you decide you can't."

"Knox."

He shook his head. "You don't have to say anything else, Haley. I know it's a big decision. And as much as I'm happy Dawson brought you here, I do get why he might also run you off. I hope he doesn't, but I won't force you to choose me."

"I have to choose me," I whispered.

"I know. I've already made that choice for myself, and it means staying here. It means running my dad's store and putting aside my dreams. But you've made me see there are options. You have a beautiful heart, Haley. And a beautiful body. One I'm more than ready to sink into again, if you're willing."

I threw my arms around his neck and leaned into him. "I'm definitely willing."

"Good. And this time, you're not holding back."

"Who said I was holding back?"

"We're on the same page, beautiful. We have been from

the beginning. From that first night when you knocked my socks off and snuck out in the middle of the night. I woke up pissed because you were gone, even though you told me you would be. I hadn't had a night like that in a very long time."

"Neither had I."

"Then we agree? No sneaking out. No holding back. And no more nights apart."

"No more nights apart?" I asked.

Knox shook his head slowly. "I want to spend as much time with you as possible. If you leave, I want to know I did everything I could to convince you to stay. If you stay, I want to know we're going to work. So, if it's a date night, I want us together. I know you need time with your friends, and I have nights I see mine. But I don't want you worrying about walking home in the middle of the night after I fall asleep. I want you right there in the morning."

I smiled. "I think I can handle that."

"Good. Can you handle a few more orgasms?"

"I think I can handle that, too."

"Good, because I'm about ready to explode."

"I think I can help with that," I whispered, dropping to my knees in front of him.

"Haley," he groaned as I leaned forward and wrapped my lips around him.

He was salty, a little tangy, and smelled like sex. It was an intoxicating combination that had my body readying for him.

I licked the underside of his erection, making him groan. I sucked him back in, deep, and he jerked against me, hitting the back of my throat.

"Fuck. I'm sorry."

He tried to pull back, but I held onto his thighs and kept him in place, using my teeth to show him I meant it.

"Jesus, you look like a fantasy come to life," he whispered. "Look at me, Haley."

I lifted my gaze to his. His blue-green eyes were nearly black with desire, blazing into mine. He stood before me completely naked, where I was on my knees and fully clothed.

It was sexy as fuck.

"I'm going to spend the rest of the night making you scream my name. I hope you don't have to talk to anyone tomorrow, because you're going to be hoarse. And sore. You're going to remember I was inside you all night."

I moaned my approval, soaking my already drenched panties.

"You like that, don't you?"

I nodded, licking my way up his cock.

"Oh, fuck, Haley. Can I put my hands in your hair?"

I nodded, barely moving before he was smoothing my hair back from my face and plunging his hands into the strands.

"Watching my dick disappear into your mouth is so fucking beautiful. Almost as beautiful as watching it disappear into your pussy. Fucking hell, Haley."

He thrust into my mouth, his hips not stopping like they did the first time.

I dragged my nails down his thighs. He tightened his hold on my hair. He cupped my jaw tenderly, lifting my gaze to his as his jaw clenched and his cock throbbed.

"Haley," he grunted. "Haley, I'm there, beautiful."

He tried to pull me back, but I didn't budge, letting him come in my mouth with a curse and a thrust that sent him to my throat and tears to my eyes.

He pulled me back just enough to ease up on my gag reflex. He apologized until I was able to swallow and stand.

"That was perfect," I assured him. "I might need to borrow some shorts when I go home tomorrow because I think my jeans are soaked through."

His brows jumped high. "It turned you on that much to give me a blowjob?"

I nodded. "And to see how much you enjoyed it."

He kissed me hard on the lips, holding me close to his naked body. "I'll happily suffer for you any time in the future."

I laughed with him. "Such a hero."

He grinned. "As long as I get to return the favor, because you're not the only one who finds that a major turn-on."

"I think I can suffer through the same," I whispered against his lips. "Anything for the good of others."

"Better not be any others," Knox growled as he cupped my ass and carried me the short distance to his mattress.

Then he took off all the clothes I'd just put on and found out just how wet he'd made me.

18

KNOX

I LOCKED UP THE STORE AND POCKETED MY KEYS. I DEBATED walking to O'Kelley's, but it was a bit of a walk, and even though it was a nice day, walking home after dark would be chilly.

I rolled down the windows and sang along to the music. It was a good day. A good week. I couldn't get Haley off my mind. I was starting to think she was actually going to stick around. She still had two months before her lease was up, but every night we spent together, she seemed more and more reluctant to leave.

Which made me endlessly happy.

I found a spot right in front of O'Kelley's and pulled over next to the curb. Xavier was walking down the street when I got out, so I waited for him to reach me before going inside together.

"Knox!" Xavier said when he saw me standing next to my truck. "How are you?"

"Hey, X. I'm good. How's the family?"

"Good. Really good. J is starting to think about colleges and figuring out where she might want to go."

I chuckled and opened the door to O'Kelley's for Xavier to walk in ahead of me. "I bet that's a ton of fun."

Xavier winced. "I adore my kid, and I love my wife, but when the two of them start arguing about college, I just want to run and hide."

"Really? Karissa always seems so balanced to me. I can't imagine her getting upset."

"When J starts talking about going far away for college, Rissa goes a little crazy. She doesn't want McJenna too far."

"Ah, I can understand that. A little bit of mama bear."

"Who's a mama bear?" Ian asked, catching the last bit of our conversation as we approached the bar.

"Karissa," Xavier said. "J is looking at college options and has mentioned California and Hawaii as options."

"Because of the weather," Rowan said with a shiver. "How the fuck is it still cold here in the spring? It's almost April and there's still snow on the ground!"

"Quit bitching, Arizona boy," James said, elbowing Rowan.

"Ow," Rowan groaned. "I'm just saying there are places on earth that aren't cold enough to snap my dick off if I take a piss outside in April."

"I could arrest you for that," James said. "Public indecency is a very serious crime."

"I was there when you arrested that one guy," Rowan said. "Trust me, I'm not looking to get cuffed when my dick is hanging out. Unless Willow is the one putting the cuffs on."

James rolled his eyes at Rowan's smirk. Everyone else chuckled and nodded their agreement. James and Rowan spent too many hours together as police officers, and with a town as quiet as MacKellar Cove, it was obvious they had a fair amount of downtime. Downtime that usually led to one of them irritating the other.

"Anyway," Ian said, returning his focus to Xavier. "Why is it a problem that J wants to go out west?"

"Rissa wants her to stay close to home," Xavier said. "I think she's taken to the whole mom thing and worries J is going to run off and never come back."

"I can't see her doing that," Trent said. "That kid adores Karissa."

Xavier nodded. "I keep telling her that, but she's worried. Since she's not McJenna's mom, Karissa thinks J sees her as just a replacement."

"Man, that's tough," I said. "My dad never dated after my mom died, but I know no one could have ever replaced her. I think it's just a different relationship. Especially since you said J and her mom don't know each other."

"Not even a little. J wouldn't recognize her if she walked into our house. Not that she ever would." Xavier nodded to Hudson in thanks for the beer Hudson slid in front of him.

"College is tough, man," Hudson said. "Joey decided to stay in New York and play baseball, but even though he won't be too far, Anna is freaking out about him not being under the same roof as us."

"I think that's how Karissa feels, too. But since she's only been in J's life a few years, she doesn't know how to handle it," Xavier said.

"I don't think anyone knows how to handle it," Hudson said.

Xavier nodded. "Probably true. I can't really say I'm doing any better."

"I'm not looking forward to all of that," Ian said. "At this point, we're anxious about preschool."

"Maddox just turned one," Ramsey said. "How in the world are you worried about preschool?"

Ian shrugged. "It'll be the first time he's not with one of us or family. We know it'll be important, and we want him to go, but it's not easy. Especially since we'll have a new toddler by then."

"Whoa, wait, what? Blake's pregnant again?" James shouted.

Ian grinned widely and nodded. "She is. Finally into the second trimester, and she approved me sharing the news with everyone."

"Congratulations," Hudson said, reaching across to shake Ian's hand.

Everyone else said the same, wishing Ian and Blake the best.

"How did you keep it a secret?" Rowan asked.

Ian shrugged. "Our families knew. Blake was anxious, though. She had a few concerns early on, but the doctors have assured us all is good. We're really excited."

"When is she due?" Xavier asked.

"October 1," Ian said.

"That's a few weeks before Melody's birthday," Ramsey said. "I didn't realize it was that close."

"You knew?" James asked.

Ramsey shrugged.

James gawked at Ian. "You told him and not me?"

"I knew, too," Trent said with a wink for James.

"You're married to his sister. I understand that one. I've known him almost as long as Ramsey," James argued.

"Almost being the key," Ramsey said.

James rolled his eyes and pouted that he wasn't told before everyone else.

"Well, I have a secret, too. If you guys are up for me sharing," I said.

They all leaned closer.

"I've been seeing Haley Jordan," I said.

Hudson smirked.

James waved his hand like he already knew. The others behaved much the same.

"We all knew that forever ago," Rowan said.

"You did?" I asked.

"Dude. Small town. Everyone knows everything. Especially when you take her on a date walking all over town. How many people do you think told us about it that week?" James asked, nodding to Rowan for confirmation.

Rowan nodded. "A lot."

"Seriously? Everyone knew? Why didn't you say anything?" I asked.

"Why didn't you?" Ian asked. "I mean, it's cool with me if you want to keep your relationship secret. Blake didn't want everyone knowing when we were first together. It was fun sneaking around for a little while, but after a bit it was exhausting. I wanted to tell everyone we were together, but she wasn't ready. It put a strain on us."

"You didn't even tell me," Brantley said.

I looked at him, then at the others. "Hudson knew. He—"

"Don't bring me into this. You didn't confess to me. I knew because you brought her here for a date and we talked a month ago about you not being an ass to her. You were the one who said you weren't ready to tell everyone else." Hudson glared at me.

"You're right. He's right. I didn't know where things were going with her. I didn't know how everyone felt about her, and—"

"She's one of my favorite people ever," Brantley said. "If she'd never moved her, I wouldn't have Valentina."

The other guys chuckled and nodded their agreement.

"Haley isn't the bad guy in that story," Xavier said. "Dawson was the one who cheated. And I know some people in town aren't fans of Haley, but that's not me."

"Not me," the others all chorused.

"So, we're back to you and why you didn't want to tell us," Brantley said.

"We had a one-night stand. She came by the store to get something for Sofia, and we hit it off. Promised each other no names, no contact. The next night, we met here for our first date. We were paired on Book Boyfriends Wanted and had been talking for months but never exchanged names, so neither of us knew who the other was the night before," I explained, staring at the bar top while I spit out the whole story.

No one said anything, leaving me to wonder what they were thinking in the silence surrounding our group. I finally looked up and saw them all smiling with varying degrees of astonishment and amusement.

"What?" I asked.

"You hooked up?" Rowan asked.

"After you'd been talking for months," James continued.

"And had a date the next night?" Ian said.

"Because you met on Book Boyfriends Wanted," Xavier confirmed.

"Yeah."

They all snorted and laughed, shaking their heads.

"What?"

"You never should have doubted things would work out," Xavier said.

"Why not?"

"The app has magic," Ian told me. "The magic of Ms. Georgia. Rissa built it in honor of her mom, and she believes her mom is working her magic from heaven, pairing up the people in town who are meant for each other."

"I don't know about that," I said.

"Valentina and I were paired on the app," Brantley said.

"Melody and I were, too, when we were separated," Ramsey said.

"Trinity," James said with a nod.

"All of us," Hudson told me. "Every single one of us who's not single met our better halves on that app. If you and Haley were paired there, and you're still seeing each other after all the other crap, you're done. She's it."

"She might not be sticking around," I blurted. It was the one thing that held me back from falling for her. I knew I was already on the way, maybe already in love with her, but if she left, I wouldn't go with her. MacKellar Cove was home.

"You can go with her," Xavier suggested. "The rest of the world isn't all that bad."

I shook my head. "I'm like Karissa. This is where I belong. I don't want to live anywhere else. I never have. My dad's still here, and my store, and everything. I love it here. I want to be here."

"Even if she's not here?" Ramsey asked.

I drew a breath and nodded. It was painful to admit, but I'd given up my dream career to stay in MacKellar Cove. It was home. I wanted to be with Haley, but I also wanted to stay here.

"Then, I guess you have to convince her to stay," Hudson said.

"And what if I can't?"

They all suddenly looked too busy.

"Are you really willing to give her up to stay here?" Xavier asked.

"Would you have done things differently?" I asked him. "Would you have moved here for Karissa if you could go back? Change your whole life? You wouldn't have had McJenna, wouldn't have met Trent, wouldn't have lived all the experiences you lived. Would you do it?"

Xavier inhaled fully, his chest rising with indecision. He thought about my question, then shook his head. "No. Because in the end, I have both my daughter and my wife. I can't choose between them. But you wouldn't be giving up a child. You might be giving up a future, though."

"If we're really meant to be, she'll decide she wants to be here. If not, then I'll move on," I told them.

"Then I guess we all need to hope she stays because you're a miserable bastard when you're single," Brantley said.

I flipped him off and sipped my beer. The others laughed and moved on with the conversation.

I let it happen around me and hoped I wouldn't have to find out what it would be like to be single after Haley. I wanted her in my life. For good.

WALKING into a salon was something I'd never done before in my life. I had no idea what to expect, but complete silence at my presence was not it.

"Can I help you?" Debby asked. I knew she was the owner. Aside from having her name on the sign outside, Haley had mentioned her. She was an institution, and supposedly, she'd been friends with my mother.

"Is Haley here?" I asked.

The other women in the salon exchanged looks and whispers. There were four women in chairs, getting their hair cut or styled, two under dome looking things that I had no idea what they were for, and five stylists. The place was busy.

But there was no Haley.

I was sure she said she was working all day.

"Haley is with a client right now. Perhaps we can schedule an appointment for you," Debby said in a placating voice. One that told me she neither knew about our relationship nor appreciated me stopping in. Debby took my elbow and guided me toward the desk near the front door.

"Knox," Haley gasped, appearing from somewhere.

Debby let go of me and looked me up and down. "Knox? Are you Eleanor's boy?"

I tried to focus on Debby, but my attention kept going back to Haley. She looked delightfully disheveled at my appearance there. Her hair was tied up off her neck, a sheen of sweat coating her skin. Her cheeks went pink when she saw me, and she nibbled on her lip.

I tore my gaze from her and nodded at Debby. "Yes, ma'am."

"Oh, my. I don't know why I didn't recognize you before. You have your mother's eyes. How is your father doing?"

I stole another glance at Haley and found her staring at me, a small bowl in her hand with what looked like a basting brush in it. "He's doing well. Had a bit of a scare a few weeks ago and is fighting me on taking care of himself, but he's good. Thank you for asking."

"It's been far too long since we've seen him. I'll have my Harold give him a call and invite him over for dinner sometime soon. You should join us."

"Thank you, ma'am. That would be wonderful." I smiled at her.

"You know you can call me Debby, Knox," she whispered conspiratorially.

"Yes, ma'am," I replied, knowing I never would. She was my mother's friend, and just because I didn't remember my mother didn't mean I'd forgotten the manners my father drilled into me.

"Well, I can see I'm not the woman you're here for. Be good to her, Knox. She deserves a man like you in her life. Better than that no good scoundrel she moved here for. Glad he's out of her life," Debby said so quietly no one else could hear.

I nodded. "I agree, ma'am."

Debby winked at me and patted my arm before she walked away. She took the bowl from Haley and said something to her that had her eyes widening and her lips curling up into a grin.

I stayed at the front, away from the other women for fear I might break something or knock something over, and waited while Haley moved across the room toward me. When she reached my side, she nodded toward the door. "We can step outside if that's okay."

I nodded and opened the door for her, letting her precede me. Before the door closed all the way, I heard the excited squeals of the women inside.

I glanced back, but it looked like a normal salon, as if I knew what normal looked like.

"Are you okay?" Haley asked a minute later. Her arms were crossed over her chest, and she looked up at me like she was waiting for bad news.

I nodded. "I just wanted to see you."

"You did?" she gasped.

I exhaled a laugh. "I guess I haven't been doing a very good job of showing you how much I like you if you're surprised by that."

"No, I... you... No one's ever stopped by my job to see me before. Dawson would pick me up for dates, but I always knew he was coming."

I mentally kicked myself for not coming by sooner. All the things most women expected were big deals to Haley. Firsts she should have experienced long ago. If I was going to convince her to stay, and show her I wanted her to stay, I needed to up my game.

"Well, I should have before now. I was thinking about you, and I didn't want to wait until tomorrow night to see you." I glanced inside, finding everyone staring at us. I chuckled. "Are they going to freak out if I kiss you?"

She nibbled her lip. "I might."

I took a step back and frowned. "Oh. I'm sorry. I didn't mean to make you uncomfortable."

She smiled and stepped toward me. "It's not that, Knox. We've been on dates, we've gone out, but coming to my work and kissing me in front of all those women is sort of like putting a sign out in Catherine Park that we're dating."

I stepped closer to her and grinned. "Should I do that, too?"

Before she could move away from me, I wrapped my arms around her and pulled her in close. I nuzzled against her neck and kissed her racing pulse.

"Think this will convince them?" I whispered, our lips a breath apart.

Then I erased the distance between us and claimed her lips.

She sighed heavily, a happy, content sound that sent a jolt right to my dick. God, I wanted her. I wanted everyone to know I wanted her. I wanted her to be mine, and I didn't care who knew it.

I probed her mouth with my tongue, mindful of how quickly I was losing my ability to slow down, and tasted her thoroughly.

She hung on, not withdrawing or fighting me at all. She threw herself into our kiss with the same eagerness she always did. An eagerness that reminded me of the way she looked on her knees in front of me, fully clothed and making me come.

"What time are you done tonight?" I whispered against her lips.

"We close at seven."

"Can I talk you into a late dinner?"

She nodded. "I won't argue with that."

"Good. Should I come by here and pick you up, or do you need to go home first?"

"I have my car here, so I will need to go home."

"Or you could give me your keys and I can take it home for you, then be back here at seven."

She pulled back and stared up at me. Worry creased the space between her brows.

"No? You don't have to."

She shook her head. "I've never given anyone my keys, and I've never had anyone else's keys. You're really testing me here, Knox."

"No test, beautiful. Just want to spend as much time with you as possible."

She inhaled a breath and nodded. "Okay. Give me a minute and I'll bring my keys back."

I kissed her once more, a quick kiss that still sparked inside me. "I'm not going anywhere."

She hesitated a second, then hurried inside. She rushed

through the salon, ignoring the obvious questions being thrown at her. She disappeared behind the curtain, then came back a minute later with her keys in her hand. She burst outside and held them out to me.

I wrapped my hand around the keys, then pulled her to me. I kissed her once more, then stepped back and winked. "I'll be back by seven. See you then."

"Bye," she whispered.

I waited until she went into the salon, then walked away twirling her keys around my finger.

19

―――――――

After I dropped Haley's car off at her apartment, I walked back to where I'd parked my truck and sat in it. I could see into the salon, and like a creeper, I watched her work.

The light in her eyes and the joy on her face mesmerized me. She was beautiful, and it was easy to see how much she loved what she did.

The longer I watched her, the more convinced I was that I wanted the same thing. Not just Haley, but a job that made me feel the way hers made her feel. She could have a good day just by doing something she enjoyed. What was better than that?

When the last customers left, Haley and the others started to clean the salon. She laughed with one of her coworkers, Chelsea I thought, and Haley double checked that she'd cleaned everything up. Debby approached her after a few minutes and said something to Haley. Something that had her gaze lifting and colliding with mine. Her lips lifted into a smile as Debby kept talking.

Haley protested, but Debby shook her head and nudged Haley toward the curtain in the back. Haley smiled and finally moved to the back on her own. A minute later, she walked out front with her handbag over her shoulder and a jacket on. She waved to the others as she walked through the salon toward the front door.

I got out of my truck and met her on the sidewalk with a quick kiss. "I wasn't trying to rush you out. I was happy to wait."

"Debby insisted. She said you'd been out here since you came by earlier."

"I took your car back to your apartment," I defended.

She exhaled a laugh. "Then you came back here and sat in your truck?"

I shrugged. "I was enjoying watching you work. You looked like you were having a lot of fun."

"I was," Haley admitted as I opened the truck door for her to get in.

I closed the door, then walked around to climb in behind the wheel. "It's nice to see a smile on your face."

"Thank you. I really like it here."

"Good." I paused, debating my next words. "I really like you here."

She smiled at me, holding my gaze for a long minute. "So, what are we doing tonight?"

I shifted the truck into drive and pulled away from the curb. "I was thinking we could pick something up somewhere. If you're okay with that. I have to open the store tomorrow morning."

"That works for me."

"Are you sure?"

She nodded. "Yeah. I'm pretty drained after being on my

feet all day, so dinner at home sounds good. I was trying to decide what I was going to do tonight, but you saved me from deciding."

"Happy to help."

We agreed on subs for dinner and went to Subs Plus to order. It was busy inside, and I didn't hesitate to wrap my arm around Haley and keep her close when we waited our turn. We talked about the options, and she snuggled against my side.

I paid for our subs, insisting that it was my idea and I wanted to pay, and she carried the bag of sandwiches and chips while I grabbed our drinks. The drive to her apartment was quick, then we were carrying everything inside.

"There were a lot of people staring at us," Haley whispered when we settled on her couch.

"When?"

"At Subs Plus. I think they were surprised to see us together."

Dammit. One more thing I should have paid attention to. I hadn't exactly been hiding my relationship with Haley, but I also hadn't been flaunting it. What I told the guys the night before was true. I was holding back until I knew what she was going to do. But I didn't want to any longer.

"I told all my friends about us last night," I said.

Haley stopped with her drink halfway to her mouth. She slowly set it down and looked at me. "Excuse me?"

I nodded. "They all said they knew."

"But not until last night? We've been seeing each other for almost two months."

I took a seat next to her on the couch and grabbed her hands. "I should have told them all when we first started seeing each other. I don't really have a reason I didn't. I'm not ashamed of us being together. I haven't been great at showing you that, but—"

"We go to dinner in other towns. We do things where a lot of people aren't. Aside from our first date at O'Kelley's, we haven't been anywhere that a lot of people would see us until tonight, and that was just to pick up food."

"I think everyone in there tonight knew we didn't just happen to be standing next to each other."

"No, but it doesn't mean they're okay with us being together. I'm hated by half the town. People want me to leave. And you're loved. Everyone who comes into the salon tells me how wonderful you are."

"Why would they be talking to you about me?" I asked, realizing the guys were right and everyone in town knew about us, even if no one had said much of anything.

"I don't know. It's a salon. Women talk about men. All the time."

"But why specifically me?"

"I... I don't know."

"Because they know, Haley. If they're saying something to you about me, it's because they know we're together and they're trying to tell you they approve."

"No. They haven't said that. They've just said you're a nice guy or you are always friendly and kind. Stuff like that."

"Are they telling you or Chelsea or Debby or someone else?"

"Me," she admitted. She chewed on her lip for a long moment while I waited for her to accept what I was telling her. "They do know. And they haven't run me out of town yet."

"I think more people like you than you're willing to admit. Working in a salon means people get to see you.

They figure out who you are. It's like me working at the store. They know me."

"The part of you that you show. They don't know that you really want to be doing something else."

I nodded, her words hitting me dead on. "You're right. And it's time I stopped fighting that. I'm going to do what you suggested and reduce the hours the store is open so I can focus on custom projects. And if things go well, or I find someone who's willing to work the store, I'll look at other options."

She beamed brightly at me. "Really?"

"Yeah. Watching you today... I want to feel that kind of joy when I go to work. I feel it when I'm doing a custom project. I want it more often. I know it'll take me a while to find jobs that'll make money, but it's time I start moving in that direction."

"I'm really happy for you, Knox."

I leaned over and kissed her. "I wouldn't have done it without you."

She smiled. "Good."

"I've been trying to hold back from getting too serious with you," I blurted.

"Um, okay?"

"I don't want to leave MacKellar Cove. My dad's here, my friends are here, my job is here. Even if I'm going to be changing things and want to do something different, I don't want to leave. I know that's selfish, and I know I should be open to moving, but—"

"You don't have to explain it to me," Haley whispered.

"I didn't talk to my friends about us because telling them meant we were serious. It meant I was hoping things would work out. I want it to work, but I know you have to decide what's best for you. I was naïve enough to think everyone didn't already know about us, and that not saying anything would mean you wouldn't be pressured by anyone to stick around for my sake. I want you to stay, Haley. I've made that clear. I hate being an asshole and telling you if you don't, we're over, but I've never wanted to live anywhere else."

"I know. And I understand. I've never had a home. A place where I felt like I belonged. MacKellar Cove is the closest I've ever had to that, and I'm leaning toward staying, but..."

"It has to be your choice. I know that. Even though I really want to use all my powers of persuasion to convince you."

She laughed at my dancing eyebrows and teasing tone. She leaned closed and cupped my jaw. "Thank you, Knox."

"Are we okay? I mean, are you okay with me taking this long to talk to my friends about us?"

She shrugged. "I understand it. And I'm sorry I've made you feel like I'm leading you on."

I shook my head before she finished talking. "Never, Haley. I promise you."

She smiled. "Okay, good."

"I'm proud to be seeing you, Haley. So damn proud."

She nodded, the look in her eyes happier than when I first confessed.

We turned on the TV and dug into our dinner. The subs were delicious, and the company was even better. Haley started fading at one point, and I asked her if she wanted me to leave.

"Not at all," she whispered. She wrapped her arms around my neck and pulled me down for a kiss. "But I am tired. I think it might be a good idea for me to go to bed."

"Okay."

She stood and pulled her shirt off, tossing it at me. I caught it and grinned just in time to see her reach back and unclasp her bra.

I groaned and caught on, rising from the couch in time to catch up to her at the door to her bedroom. I cupped her breasts and teased her nipples.

She moaned and pressed her back against me. She worked the button and zipper on her pants and shoved them down her hips with her panties, leaving her completely naked in front of me.

When she spun in my arms and made a move to drop to her knees, I stopped her. "I need to be inside you tonight," I whispered in a rough voice. I was more than ready for her.

She backed up to her bed, opening the nightstand to retrieve a condom while I yanked my clothes off. She rolled the condom down my length, then laid back on her bed.

I crawled over her, positioning myself between her thighs. She held my gaze while I pushed into her, one inch at a time until we both sighed with pleasure.

"I'm really happy you wanted to see me tonight," she whispered.

"I want to see you every night," I told her.

Her lips lifted in a sad smile that made me wonder if she thought I was lying.

"I mean that, Haley. I love spending time with you. I know you have to decide if you want to be here, but I want you to stay. I'm not ready for us to be over."

"Neither am I," she whispered.

It wasn't a confession or an agreement to stay, but it was the best I'd gotten from her so far. And as we raced each other to orgasm and breathed each other's names, I knew it was better than anything else she could have said.

I EASED out of Haley's bed, hating that I had to leave her. I kissed her gently, enough to wake her up so I could tell her I had to open the store. She mumbled something that sounded like bye, then rolled over and went right back to sleep.

I let myself out of her apartment, closing the door softly to avoid waking anyone up.

"Good morning," a voice said from right behind me.

I nearly jumped out of my skin. Sofia was right there, and I hadn't seen her until she scared the crap out of me. "Morning, Sofia. How are you?"

She raised an eyebrow. "I'm good. How are you?"

"Good."

She smirked at me and nodded to Haley's door. "I'm hoping you sneaking out early in the morning means things are going well."

I nodded, unable to keep the smile from lifting my lips. "Yes, things are going well."

"Have you convinced her to stay here yet?"

I shook my head. "I know she wants to decide for herself."

"That doesn't mean we can't give her some really good reasons why sticking around would be a great idea."

I chuckled. "True."

"Are you helping with that?"

"Yes, Sofia. I'm trying."

"Good." She sized me up carefully. "I feel like I should have thought to introduce you before. I'm really no good at connecting people. I don't have that ability."

I laughed. "Neither do I. And I think we needed to meet

when we did. I'm not sure she would have been ready for anything if we'd met sooner."

"Probably true. I'm glad you've been good to her. She really likes you."

"The feeling is mutual," I confessed.

Sofia's smile widened. She nodded. "Good. Have a good day, Knox." She walked past me.

"You, too, Sofia."

She waved right before she turned a corner and disappeared.

I followed her down the hall, then turned the other way and headed out. But I was happy I ran into her. And even happier she said what she did about Haley. I definitely liked her a lot.

The rest of my morning was good. The store was busy, but not so busy I couldn't think about the best hours to be open and when I could close up so I could do custom work.

Once I found some.

I was at the counter creating a schedule based on the busiest times of day when Teddy walked in looking like he was about to fall asleep standing there.

"You doing okay?" I asked him.

He nodded. "Yeah. One of the guys I work with asked if I could return this to you." Teddy held up the dovetail jig Andre borrowed the week before.

"Andre. Yeah. Did he finish the changing table?"

Teddy nodded. "He did. Just in time, too. His wife had the baby on Monday. He's going to be off for a few weeks and asked me to bring this back. Had it all week. Sorry, man."

I shook my head. "No worries. You doing okay?"

Teddy laughed mirthlessly. "Michael is having trouble sleeping through the night lately. Genevieve thinks he might be getting some new teeth in. All I know is a crying toddler and long workdays are not good for my sanity. Not to mention I'm trying to get the other bedroom ready for the new baby."

"Oh, man. That's a lot going on at once."

Teddy nodded. "It is. I need to go grab a few things for the room. It's pretty much gutted, so I'm starting from scratch."

"Let me know if you need any help," I told him as he walked away.

"Will do."

I watched him until he turned down the lighting aisle. It had been years since I'd seen the house they bought, but I could still picture how it was before. Four bedrooms, if my memory served, and two-and-a-half bathrooms. Two stories. Two-car garage and a shed out back. But a lot of work for one person. Maybe Teddy needed someone to help him out?

I'd ask when he came back to the register.

"Good morning," a woman said.

I looked up and smiled. "Daisy Lincoln. Back again?"

She laughed. "I am. How are you, Knox?"

"I'm great. What are you looking for today? Did you ever figure out your point of sale display?"

"Unfortunately, no. That's why I'm here. I've been online looking at store setups and think I've found something I like, but I'm afraid it'll have to be custom. I was wondering if you know any local people who might have time to take on a small project."

My fingers itched to take on the task myself. But before I leapt in, I needed to know what I was getting into. "Do you have pictures of what you're thinking about?"

Daisy nodded as she pulled her phone from the back pocket of her jeans. She unlocked it and swiped a few times before turning it around and handing it over. "I really like this. It doesn't have to be exact, but the open style is appealing to me. Bins and baskets will add appeal instead of just the boxes toys come in. I've looked at a lot of things from shoe displays, because they're angled like this, to bookshelves, and nothing is just right."

"Wood or metal?"

Daisy shrugged. "Either, honestly. I think both could look good if done well enough."

"I could build this in wood, if you're okay with that." I handed her back the phone and registered the surprise on her face.

"You could do this?"

"I haven't built anything exactly like that, but I know I could. I've done some custom work around town, and I'm looking to start doing more. If you're willing to let me use the work to show off what I can do, I'd be willing to do it at cost."

"I couldn't do that. Your time is valuable. I'm more than happy to pay your going rate."

"Is that your way of saying I've got the job?"

Daisy clasped her hands and grinned. "Yes, definitely. Thank you. I would love that." She dug into another pocket and retrieved a card. "Give me a call when you want to stop by the store and take a look. You can get all the measurements you need and we can figure out the details."

I took her card and nodded. "I'll give you a call Monday, if that works for you."

"Absolutely. Thanks so much, Knox. I'm excited now."

"So am I."

Daisy breezed out of the store like she was floating. She was a ball of sunshine. Working with her was going to be a whirlwind.

"I wish I had a little bit of her energy," Teddy said, setting a basket on the counter in front of me.

I snorted. "Right?" I pulled his items from the basket and scanned them one by one.

"You're looking to get into custom work?" he asked when I scanned the last thing.

"I am. I was going to ask if you need any help with the nursery."

Teddy breathed a laugh. "Probably. I'll have to remember you offered. If I can remember I was in here. What are you going to do with the store? Are you closing up?"

I shook my head. "No. Definitely not. I made that mistake before. I'll probably change the hours it's open, though. Give me some time to do custom jobs. It's what I really enjoy and want to do."

"That's really cool. It's nice to have that flexibility." Teddy looked around the store. "I'm glad you won't be closing up shop. I feel like I'm in here every week."

I chuckled. "You probably know this place as well as I do."

Teddy nodded. The look in his eyes made me keep talking.

"What I really want is to hire someone to run the store full time so I can do more custom jobs. Once I have a client base and can afford to do that, it's definitely what I'd prefer."

"Really?" Teddy asked, his gaze snapping to mine.

"Yeah. It would mean keeping the store open more. I'd probably still work here some. I'm a bit limited on the hours right now because I'm the only one who works here. I have a few stock guys that come in part time, but if I had someone here full time to run the place, it'd be better. One day. I hope."

Teddy nodded thoughtfully.

I told him the total, and he swiped his card, then carried his stuff out, looking around the store on his way.

I wondered if I piqued his interest. Something to think about.

20

HALEY

"WHAT ARE YOU DOING NEXT WEEKEND?" KNOX ASKED Saturday night.

We were having a quiet evening in at my apartment after he worked all day. He offered to go out in town, but I told him I would cook. Maybe he wasn't the only one content to keep our relationship between us.

I wasn't a pro in the kitchen, but I liked cooking sometimes. Especially if I had some help in the form of a sexy hardware store owner who nibbled on the veggies as fast as I could chop them.

"I'll probably still be cutting veggies for dinner next weekend," I teased him. "Why?"

"There's that Easter celebration next Saturday. Egg hunt for the kids and a carnival and food for families."

"Yeah, Debby was talking about it this week. She closed the salon since it'll be a busy day."

"Are you going with Sofia?"

I stopped cutting mushrooms and looked up at him. "I wasn't planning to go at all. It's for families. I don't have one of those."

He rubbed the back of his neck and blushed. "Um, well, I was sort of hoping you would want to go with me."

"Why?"

"Because it's a town event."

I set my knife down. "Okay. And?"

He sighed. "Because I want to go with you. I want to show you off. I want everyone to know we're together."

"You do?" I breathed. It was a change from just twenty-four hours earlier. His offer of dinner out had felt forced, but this felt... sincere.

He nodded and moved toward me. He tucked a loose strand of hair behind my ear, his fingers lingering on my neck. "Yes, I do. I said I wouldn't push, and I won't, but I want you to stay here. I want you to see this place the way I see it. I want you to love it as much as I do. Part of that is having this town see you with me. Showing them you're not the villain."

"Yeah?"

He kissed me softly, nodding as he pulled back. "Yeah."

"Okay, then. I'll go with you."

"You will?"

I chuckled. "Did you think I was going to say no after all that?"

"Well, I wasn't sure."

I lifted onto my toes to kiss him. "I'd love to. Thank you."

He grinned and stole a mushroom from the cutting board, popping it into his mouth.

"Hey! I was going to use that."

"You can cut more," he teased.

I picked up my knife and waved it at him. "We need it for dinner!"

Knox laughed. He helped me get things ready, only stealing a few more things, then joined me in cooking. We talked about normal things, like how his work day was and what life was like growing up in MacKellar Cove, as we cooked.

Once the food was ready, we sat at the small table in my kitchen and ate dinner together.

"This is really good," Knox said, shoveling food into his mouth.

"Are you even tasting it?"

He rolled his eyes playfully. "Yes. And it's delicious."

"Well, thank you."

He helped me clean up the kitchen when we finished dinner, then we curled up on the couch, watching a movie. When the movie was over, Knox distracted me with kisses and touches until we were both naked and panting and ignoring everything except each other.

I TREATED myself to coffee the next morning. Knox left early, kissing me gently while I was still mostly asleep. He'd worn me out, and I was not at all disappointed or feeling guilty about my urge to sleep in. But once I was up, coffee was first on the agenda.

Cove Bakery was busy, and Valentina wasn't there, but Harriett smiled warmly at me and said it was good to see me again.

I found a seat near the window and sipped my coffee while I watched the people walking down the street. Families held hands, swinging toddlers who delighted with laughter I could feel. Couples walked arm-in-arm. Everyone was enjoying the warm early spring day, soaking in the sunshine before an expected few days of rain.

"Have you gotten Knox to ask you out again?" a woman said, drawing my attention.

I wondered if she was talking to me, but as I turned, I realized she was talking to her friend. A friend who looked years younger than me, perfect and perky, with an impeccable curvy body that would have been right at home on the cover of a magazine intended to tempt and tease straight men.

The woman wrinkled her tiny nose and shook her head, her strawberry blonde hair cascading over her shoulders with the move. "Not yet. I keep texting him, but he always says he's busy."

"He does work a lot. Maybe you should go into the hardware store."

The strawberry blonde one looked like her friend suggested something truly heinous. "Why would I go in there, Mickie?"

"Because you want him back, Ivy. How long has it been since you were together?"

Ivy sighed. "Too long."

"I heard he was seeing someone new," Mickie said in a hushed tone.

The two of them looked around, checking to see if anyone was listening to their conversation.

I sipped my coffee, pretending to be wholly engrossed in my breakfast instead of their conversation.

"Everyone knows Knox is mine. No one would go after him."

"I think it's that woman who moved here to be with Dawson."

"Seriously?" Ivy asked, her laugh obvious in her voice. "Then I have nothing to worry about."

"I'm sure she's nowhere near as gorgeous as you are. I

heard she's really overweight," Mickie added.

Ivy snorted. "I guess Knox needed to go slumming before he came back to me and settled down."

"I don't know why people do that. Especially when he has you waiting for him."

"Knox will figure it out soon. I just need to make sure he knows I'm still available," Ivy said.

"What if he still doesn't come back to you?"

"Then I'll seduce him," Ivy snapped. "It's not like he can resist me. He never has before. He knows I'll do *anything* he wants."

Mickie grinned, her eyes wide and approving. "You're so lucky you found him and fell for him. The single men in this town are not the greatest."

"Except Knox," Ivy was quick to say.

"Well, yeah, but I'd never go for Knox."

"You better not. He's mine."

"I know, Ivy. I'd never even think about it."

Ivy glared at her friend for a long moment. She smiled, the look not meeting her eyes before she shrugged and pretended the whole idea was laughable. "He'd never go for you, anyway. We need to find someone who would. You might need to do more yoga. And start running. It's too bad Valentina snapped Brantley Pierce up. It would have been so much fun for us to be with both of them."

Mickie smiled tightly. "Yep, definitely."

Ivy finished her coffee and stood. "Let's go by the store and see if we can see Knox."

"I thought you didn't want to go to his store."

"When did I say that? I need to go see him." Ivy threw away her cup, heading toward the door without waiting for Mickie to finish her croissant or coffee. "Let's go, Mickie."

Mickie scrambled to collect her stuff, shoving the last

bite of her croissant into her mouth and carrying her coffee to the door.

Ivy scowled at her and turned up her nose. "Gross." She walked out, letting the door swing and almost hit Mickie.

If I wasn't so stunned, I might have felt sorry for Mickie. Instead, I was trying to figure out why in the world Knox was dating me and not ideal Ivy.

I WAS STILL in my head when I made it to book club that night. I wasn't fighting Sofia on attending anymore, but after overhearing Ivy and Mickie, I wasn't sure I was good company for the others.

I declined a slice of cake, Ivy and Mickie's words about Knox slumming with me still rattling in my head.

Sofia looked at me as the others talked, her face pinched with worry. I wanted to reassure her that everything was fine, but I wasn't entirely sure that was the case.

Ivy was thin and beautiful with curves that had most men drooling. She didn't give me the best impression of her personality, but the conversation I overheard was one of stress and pain over breaking up with the man she seemed to love.

Was I coming between another couple? Knox told me he was single, and everyone in town said he was single, so I didn't think he was cheating on her or anyone else, but I still couldn't shake the thought that Ivy was right and Knox was just biding his time with me.

"Do you have a size you want to be? Your goal size?" I blurted, needing to know I wasn't the only one who was always looking to lose weight. I hated when insecurities popped up, but dammit, they always did.

"Yep."

"Of course."

"Hell yes."

"I do," Elise said when the others had agreed. "The size I am right now."

My eyebrows winged up. Not because Elise wasn't gorgeous, because she was, but because she wasn't thin, or perky, or any of the things society told us we should be. She was curvy like me with too much junk in the trunk and wide hips. I saw her as stunning, but I couldn't turn that around for myself.

"You don't want to change what you look like?" Finley asked.

Elise shook her head. "Nope. I used to, but not anymore."

"What changed?" Blake asked. "The baby weight was killing me before I found out I was pregnant again. I know it'll be even worse after the second one."

"Colin changed," Elise said. "I went through the depths of hell with Andy. He constantly told me I wasn't good enough. Before him, I didn't think much about my appearance, even though I could have definitely lost some weight. But when I was with him, nothing was right. He always said I was fat, I was lazy, I needed to change what I looked like to attract him."

"Fucking asshole," Willow muttered.

"Exactly," Elise said. "He beat me down with his words, then he beat me with his hands. But if his words could take away my confidence and make me feel worthless, Colin's words could bring it all back."

"Wow," I whispered, feeling what she said in the depths of me.

"I hated myself when I left Andy. I believed all the things

he told me. I thought I was worthless and ugly and not good enough for someone to love. It led me to destructive behaviors like sleeping with anyone I could and not taking care of my body. For a long time, I didn't care if I lived or died. I was getting better before I met Colin, but I still believed I was unworthy, so when we started talking, I pushed back. Hard."

"That's what I'm doing right now," I admitted.

"We all do that," Blake said.

"So, how did you get past it?" I asked Elise.

"He pushed harder." She shrugged like it was no big deal. "Colin refused to give up on me, on us. He knew there were big things I needed to deal with, but he saw who I was beneath all that. The person I thought was long gone and never coming back. He stuck around. He told me I was beautiful. He let me see myself through his eyes. It was hard. I had more than a few emotional breakdowns, but he was there for all of it."

"I'm so happy you found him," Laura said, reaching out to squeeze Elise's hand.

"I am, too. It's very possible I'd be dead if I hadn't met him because the darkness threatened to pull me back in a lot. The unworthiness. But Colin just kept pushing. Asked why if I could believe Andy's words, why couldn't I believe his?"

"Damn," I said.

Elise nodded. "Yep. That was the one that got me, too. When he said that, it was like a balloon popped inside me. All that evil had a light shone on it. Colin's love was like a bomb inside, obliterating all the darkness Andy left behind."

"That's a seriously twisted analogy," Blake said.

Elise shrugged. "Best way I can describe it. Once he said that, I started to see pieces of me that I'd buried. I let myself out again. It wasn't overnight that I changed, but it was overnight that I was willing to try."

"It's really hard to be willing to try. To give someone else that control," I confessed.

"Colin doesn't have that control. He never did. And he never wanted to. He tells me how he sees me. He tells me why he loves me. He never tells me I'm good enough or not good enough. He just loves every piece of me, good and bad, and lets me see that all those pieces he loves are worthy of being loved. I had to go a step beyond and start to love those pieces myself. It's a journey, and there are still things I struggle with, but my body?" Elise stood and wiggled her hips. She spun in a circle and waved her hands over her curves. "My body is hot as fuck. And no one is going to tell me that's not the case. And if they do? Fuck them because I love my body and so does the man I share a bed with every night. Those opinions are the only ones that matter."

Everyone else cheered for Elise.

I wanted her confidence. Her self-assurance. Her kick-ass attitude. I felt it hovering there, waiting to come out, but I was scared. I used to be that woman. Before Dawson, I didn't think twice about what others thought of me. But he twisted something in me. Something that didn't exist before. I felt guilty for ruining a marriage, breaking up a family. I was a classic homewrecker, even though I didn't set out to be.

I knew what people thought about me and said about me. If I was thin and drool-worthy, men wouldn't judge me. Wouldn't hesitate to date me. But I had curves. I had a booty. I had a big laugh and a loud mouth at times. And in a small town like MacKellar Cove, most people didn't want to be the man who dared to get serious with the woman who ruined someone else's marriage.

Except Knox.

Knox wasn't afraid of my reputation. He was willing to listen to my side of things, and believed me when I said I had no idea Dawson was married until I met Valentina. Knox was gorgeous, smart, kind, and he'd never think twice about cheating on someone. He was the better man in every way. So why would he want Dawson's leftovers?

Especially when he could have Ivy without any other marks against her.

"Is everything okay?" Sofia finally asked.

I looked at her and shook my head. "I don't really know. I overheard a conversation today that really shook me up."

"What conversation?" Elise asked.

"Two women at Cove Bakery. One of them was talking about getting back together with Knox," I said, hoping they would know who I was talking about so I didn't have to explain the whole situation. Not that I knew what the situation was.

"Ivy," Blake said. She rolled her eyes. "She thinks Knox is in love with her and is telling everyone in town they're about to get back together."

"She's delusional," Zoey said. "Sebastian said Knox has only been talking about you lately. He hasn't said anything about Ivy in months."

"Brantley said the same," Valentina added. "Knox is not like Dawson."

"I know," I admitted. "But why in the world would he want me instead of Ivy? She's stunning."

"And she's a bitch," Elise said.

"What she said," Piper added.

"I don't like to say things about others, but I can't argue with them," Sofia said. "Ivy and Knox went out a year or so ago. I think it was casual, but Knox isn't the kind of guy who dates more than one woman at a time. Ivy didn't take it well when Knox tried to back off things. I don't know her well, but I've seen her arguing with Olive at Island Designs about prices and lecturing servers at Cracked about her food. She's kind of a miserable person."

"She cursed me out once for bringing her sourdough toast instead of wheat. She asked for sourdough toast, but she insisted the customer is always right and demanded I fix it," Blake said.

"Seriously?" Finley asked. "She bought a bunch of books once and returned them a week later, creases in the spines so she clearly read them and told me she DNFd all of them and I needed to give her a full refund."

"Wow," I breathed. "She sounds like a peach."

"Being skinny isn't everything," Elise said. "Knox is a smart man. He's with you because he knows you're so much better than Ivy. He adores you. And he's smart enough to know that more curves just means more curves. Thick thighs save lives."

"That's what Ian says!" Blake said with a laugh.

"It's so damn true. Do you know how many times my thighs loving up on each other has saved my phone from falling in the toilet?" Elise asked.

"Mine too!" Willow said. "There's nothing wrong with thick thighs and flabby bellies and a booty that won't quit. And finding a man who agrees means finding one who appreciates what really matters."

"Yes. A really good fuck," Elise said.

We all collapsed into giggles.

But damn if I didn't feel better hearing them all talk about Ivy. I wasn't going to hate on another woman, but if she was horrible, I also wasn't going to defend her. And I sure as hell wasn't going to push Knox into her arms.

That choice was up to him. And as far as I could tell, he'd made his choice.

Me.

21

———————

Knox gripped my hand and led me into the foray of people in Catherine Park. It was overwhelming. People turned to look at me, to sneer, then saw our linked hands and narrowed their eyes in confusion.

I thought that was good, but I wasn't entirely sure.

"Do you want to get something to eat?" Knox asked.

I nodded, unable to say much of anything for fear it would be overheard and misinterpreted. I was a disaster.

"Just relax," Knox whispered, his lips brushing my ear.

I shivered at the feel of him pressed against my side. I didn't want to be so unsure of myself that I relied on a man to make me feel safe, but dammit, he did. He was right there, protecting me and guarding me from anyone who dared to look at me sideways. He glared back at a few people when he thought I wasn't paying attention, and he kept one hand on me the entire time we were there.

"Grilled cheese or pierogi?"

I looked up at him in confusion. "I have to pick one?"

Knox laughed loudly, drawing the attention of everyone

close to us. "Good point. Want to share both, or do you want your own?"

"It depends on how much of mine you're going to eat."

He grinned, then surprised me when he leaned down and laid a quick, hard kiss to my lips. He lingered for a minute when he pulled back, our joined hands wrapped around my back and his other hand stroking my cheek. "I guess we're getting two of each."

I smiled at him. Shit, I loved him. I didn't want to admit it, even to myself, but I did. I really loved him. I'd been trying to decide if I was going to stay in MacKellar Cove before I fell for him, but the more time we spent together, the more I wanted to stay so I could be with him.

He made it clear he felt the same, but he hadn't said those words yet. Not that I had, but damn, it would be nice to not be the first one to say them for once.

Or the only one.

We waited in line together, getting grilled cheese first. We wandered around, watching the kids play games while we devoured our grilled cheese sandwiches. Knox got one with cheddar, mozzarella, and turkey, which I argued wasn't a true grilled cheese because it had meat. He said the same about mine since it was a mac-n-cheese grilled cheese with the pasta dish coated in gooey cheddar cheese, layered with more cheddar slices and almost falling apart.

"But it's so good," I moaned, offering him a bite.

He leaned forward and took a bite right next to mine. He chewed slowly, a surprised smile on his face. "Okay, I agree. That's delicious. But you have to try mine, too."

I took a small bite of his sandwich and agreed. The two cheeses were definitely the star of the sandwich with their melted yumminess, but the turkey had the right amount of spice and texture to give the sandwich a little more oomph. "Wow. That's good, too."

Knox nodded, taking another bite of his. "I don't think I've had anything bad from them."

"Knox!" someone called out, drawing his attention from me.

We both turned, spotting Ivy waving at him from a few feet away.

His shoulders tensed, and he stepped in front of me, blocking me from her.

"I didn't know you were going to be here, baby. How are you?" Ivy threw her arms around him, nearly smacking me in the face in the process.

I sidestepped her, standing next to Knox.

With his sandwich in his hand, he could only use one hand to push her back, which wasn't extremely effective.

I watched, feeling both jealous and sorry for her. The pinched look on his face said he was uncomfortable, but the way he avoided my gaze made me wonder if I was reading the situation correctly.

"Ivy, this is my girlfriend, Haley," Knox said, still fighting to extract Ivy's iron grip on him.

Ivy relaxed a bit, enough to turn her head and spot me. She gave me a tight smile and a sneer, then turned her attention back to Knox. "I never heard back from you. I sent you, like, a dozen texts in the last week."

"I've been busy," Knox said. It wasn't a brush-off, or a declaration that he wasn't interested.

"Well, you're here now. Did you come to see me paint? I'm on a break for a minute, but you should come watch me." She grabbed his arm and pulled him toward the face-painting booth. "These kids are so adorable. We'll have kids like this one day."

"No, we won't, Ivy. I told you a while ago we were over." Knox stood his ground, refusing to go with her.

"We can talk about that later. Call me, okay?" Ivy let go of his hand and danced away like he hadn't just told her things were done.

He exhaled roughly, rolling his neck before turning to me. He winced when he caught my expression.

"She's gorgeous," were the first words out of my mouth. Damn my insecurities. I couldn't say she was a little psycho or she was definitely crossing a line, both of which were true. Nope, all I could think was how stunning she was and how insane it was that he was with me and not her.

"You're gorgeous," he said as an answer. "She's my ex, and we haven't been together in a long time. Since a while before you and I started talking on the app. I promise you, Haley. There's nothing there."

I drew a breath and nodded. "I know."

"You do?"

"You're not Dawson. For one thing, everyone in town would have told me if you were involved with someone else, but more importantly, you told me. I trust you."

"You do?"

I nodded, the feeling strange inside me. Even though I thought she was a better fit for Knox physically, given how beautiful they both were, I knew he wasn't lying to me about being involved with her.

"I don't know if I'll ever understand why a man would want to be with me instead of her, but I trust that you're telling me the truth."

Knox shook his head and smiled. He set his grilled cheese basket down on a table near us and pulled me against him. "I'm with you because you're kind and you're smart. You make me laugh. You captured me before we ever met with your sass and wit. And when I met you? It took everything in me to resist you as long as I did because I knew you were everything I've ever wanted in a woman. You see flaws when you look in the mirror, but I see perfection when I look at you. I see a woman who makes me happy and who makes me imagine a future. I don't want Ivy, or anyone else. I want you, Haley. Only you."

Breathless didn't even come close. Tears stung my eyes. My heart felt too full. I wanted to blurt out those words I ached to say, but I wasn't ready yet. Not until I knew he felt the same.

"I only want you, too," I whispered against his lips.

"Thank fuck for that," he groaned, pulling me in for a kiss that was borderline inappropriate for a public family event.

When we finally came up for air, Knox grabbed his grilled cheese basket and my hand and led me into the crowd once more, and away from the face-painting booth.

"ICE CREAM?" Knox asked. He'd been feeding me constantly all day, and I was fairly sure I was going to pop, but everything was too good to resist.

"Yes, please," I said, tilting my head back for a kiss.

Knox obliged, then followed Ian, Ramsey, Sebastian, and Derek, who I'd just met, to get ice cream for the rest of us.

"You two look very happy," Zoey said, reaching out to touch my arm.

I nodded, watching Knox laugh at something Ian said. "It's going well."

"That's good to hear," Blake said. "I saw Ivy accost him

earlier. You were a lot nicer than I'd have been. I wanted to rip her hands off him, and Knox isn't my man."

I laughed. "It was tempting, don't get me wrong. It was sort of like walking into Dawson's house and seeing him with his family, but different. Knox would never cheat on me."

"Definitely not," Melody said. "He's one of the good ones."

I nodded again. "He really is. I don't know how I finally picked a good one, but I'm happy I did."

The others exchanged a smile. "The Magic of Ms. Georgia," Blake said.

"Who?"

Blake pointed to a mural on the side of a large building overlooking the square. I'd noticed it before, but I didn't know it was an actual person.

"Ms. Georgia was Karissa's mom. She worked at Cracked with me forever, which is on the other side of that wall. The owner, Earl, asked me to do that mural after Ms. Georgia died so she was always there looking over our town," Blake explained.

"Wow. What a tribute. I wish I'd known her," I said, looking up into the smiling face of a woman who looked like Karissa, now that I knew it was her mom. "She looks really kind."

"She was the best. She's the reason I met Rissa, since we weren't in school at the same time. She connected people. She knew when you needed someone, and who you needed. She always saw the good in others, and she was always willing to go above and beyond for anyone. She's missed around here," Blake said, a wistful note in her voice.

"But she's the reason for Book Boyfriends Wanted," Melody continued. "Karissa wanted to honor her mother and built the app to connect people the way her mom did. She calls the connections the Magic of Mom since it always seemed as though Ms. Georgia magically paired people."

"Like she's still doing it, still pairing people," I said, remembering Chelsea's reference to it from a while ago.

"Exactly," Zoey said. "Not every connection on there is the right one, but once you get to a certain point, it becomes pretty obvious that you're trapped by the magic. That's how Sebastian and I got back together."

"Ramsey and me, too," Melody said.

"And Ian and me. I think we were the first ones paired on Book Boyfriends Wanted, but Ms. Georgia was working on us long before then," Blake said.

"Really?"

They all nodded.

"You look like you're falling for Knox. And he looks like he feels the same. The magic is working on you two. If you want it to," Melody said.

"I can resist it?" I asked.

"I tried," Zoey confessed. "I'd hurt Sebastian when I left years ago. I wanted better for him than me, but love is funny."

"I think we all resisted at one point or another. Ms. Georgia never believed in forcing people together. She believed in putting people in situations where they would bring themselves together. But if Knox isn't right for you, you can walk away," Blake said.

They all looked at me like I was going to get up and run off.

"I've made a lot of mistakes with men. I want this to be right. I want it to be for the right reasons," I confessed.

"The only reason to be with someone is love," Melody said. "Do you love Knox?"

I looked at where he stood with the other guys, talking and laughing with them. He glanced over at me, as if he could sense me watching him. He winked and smiled at me, only turning away when Ian said something that Knox responded to.

"Yep, she loves him," Zoey said.

I exhaled a laugh, not admitting it, but not denying it either.

"He's definitely a good one, Haley. You deserve it," Melody said. "If you weren't with Knox, I'd probably try to set you up with Derek. I don't have the same magic, though."

"Derek seems like a really nice guy," Blake said.

"He is. I know Jude's been playing with Cameron a lot, and Ramsey and Derek have become closer friends over the last few years. He's a great dad, but I think he's a little lonely being single. It would be nice to introduce him to someone," Melody said.

"I agree," Zoey added. "Jude and Cameron are the best of friends, so we see Derek a lot. We need to start thinking about someone he'd be good with. Someone amazing." Cameron was her son.

"What about Sofia?" I suggested.

Zoey shook her head. "They've met. They get along, but there was no spark."

"Amber's best friend's parents just got divorced," Melody said. "I've been thinking about setting Derek up with Casey, but I'm not sure she's ready for a new relationship."

"Divorce is tough," Zoey said. "I wasn't ready to move on even when I did."

"Do you regret it?" Melody asked.

"God, no. I'm thrilled. I'm just saying I don't think you're ever ready. It's sort of like having kids. You just close your eyes and pray you don't mess up too badly."

The other moms laughed and nodded.

I watched the kids running around, playing and laughing and having fun. I wanted that. I wanted a family and a future and forever with someone.

Knox appeared in front of me, ice cream in his hand. He raised an eyebrow, as though to ask if I was okay.

I nodded and accepted the dish from him. "Thank you."

"You're welcome." He sat behind me on the blanket he'd brought for us and wrapped his body around mine.

The day could not have been better.

WE WALKED BACK to my apartment after the day's events, holding hands and laughing about the families at the celebration.

"I think Jude and Cameron are going to be sick for days," Knox said. "I don't know how they ate as much as they did."

"I don't know how I did either! Everything was so good, though."

"It really was. Whenever there's a festival or event or anything, I always go because the food is always amazing."

"And everyone loves you," I teased.

He was hugged by no less than thirty women of all ages, and shook hands with half the men in town. "I've been here my whole life. Between wanting to know how my dad is doing and wanting to say hi, I'm a well-liked guy."

"I understand why," I said.

He stopped in the middle of the sidewalk and kissed me gently, lingering against my lips like we had all the time in the world, and all the privacy we could want. "You're well liked, too. Anyone who doesn't know that yet will once they meet you."

"I don't need everyone to like me," I admitted. "I've spent a lot of my life wanting to be liked, but I've learned since I've been here that it only matters when it's people I like."

"Really?"

"You don't agree?"

He shook his head. "I do. Absolutely. It's not always easy to remember that, but I agree."

I nodded and unlocked the door to my building. Knox followed me inside without asking if he should, comfortable enough to know I wanted him there. "When I came here, I wanted Dawson to tell me he was in love with me. I was convinced he was, and moving here was going to open up the options for us. Sofia and Chelsea, even Debby and Valentina and the others at book club, all showed me that worrying about the opinions of people I don't know or like is a waste of time."

"It's important to have people in your life like that."

"It is. They helped me when I overheard Ivy telling her friend she was going to get back together with you."

"She did what?" he barked.

I smiled up at him and let us into my apartment. "I don't think she knew who I was, but she really pushed all my buttons. Talking about getting back together with you and how I'm overweight—"

He swept me up from behind, his hands possessive on my body. "You're perfect," he growled against my ear. "You are not overweight, and you have nothing to worry about. I don't want Ivy. I haven't wanted her since I realized we wanted different things in life."

"Like what?" I asked, hating how breathless my voice sounded.

"I want a family, and she doesn't. I want to settle down."

"She told her friend she was waiting for you to realize you wanted to settle down with her."

He shook his head and spun me in his arms. His blue-green eyes were serious as he searched my face. "She never wanted to settle down, but it's more than all of that. We had fun together. But it was never serious for me. I never talked to her about anything. I never felt like I could. Before you, I've never dated someone I felt like I could have a real conversation with. Someone I wanted to share my life with."

"Thank you."

"You're different, Haley. Everything is different with you. Ivy and I were over long before you and I met. I promise you."

"I know."

He held my cheeks and studied my face carefully. "I'm really happy we were paired together on that app. You mean a lot to me, Haley. More than you know."

My breath caught in my throat, but he didn't say those three words. But for the first time in my life, I felt them. I felt them in his touch, in the way he kissed me, and when he led me to my room and made me crazy, I knew he was showing me how he felt.

And I returned the unspoken words, showing him he wasn't the only one falling hard and fast in love.

22

───────

KNOX DIDN'T OPEN THE HARDWARE STORE ON SUNDAY, SO WE spent the day in bed. I'd never done that with a man before. Alone, sure. Watching movies and getting over a broken heart. But with a man who spent all day telling me how beautiful I was and how happy he was to be there with me? That was new.

I debated skipping book club that night, but Knox encouraged me to go. He said he needed to check on the store and finalize his proposal for the project he was working on for the new toy store before his meeting with the owner the next day. I was really happy for him, and I was excited to see how it would turn out.

Because I'd also decided I was sticking around.

I wasn't telling Knox yet, but I knew it was what I wanted. Even if things didn't work out for us, there were a lot of reasons why I wanted to stay in MacKellar Cove. But I did hope he would be one of the reasons long term.

Book club was a small crowd because of the Easter celebration. Between the traffic that made parking tough near

Finley's store and the activities going on, only seven of us made it to book club.

"It sounds like things are going well with Knox still," Valentina said with a knowing smile.

"Really well," I said.

"We're all so happy for you," Trinity said. "From what James has told me, Knox is a really good man."

I nodded. "I'm definitely a fan of his."

"And she handled Ivy like a pro yesterday," Zoey told the others. "Didn't let her ruffle any feathers."

"That was a challenge, but Knox made it very clear to both of us that he was choosing me."

"I feel bad for Ivy," Piper said. "She used to come into O'Kelley's a lot when I worked there. She was always trying to go home with Hudson, but he was never interested. She hooked up with anyone who would give her the time of day."

"There are tons of women like that, and if they enjoy it, more power to them," Trinity said.

"Oh, I agree," Piper said, "but with her, I think it was always because she had no one in her life. She got really drunk one night and told me she didn't have anyone who actually cared about her. Her parents are gone, she said, and her friends aren't really good friends. I told her she should come hang out with Sofia and I sometime, and she gushed about how excited she was to have people who cared."

"Did you guys get together?" Trinity asked.

Piper shook her head. "Nope. Next time I saw her, I asked her about it, and she pretended she didn't remember. She avoided me after that. I guess she thought I wouldn't actually try to be nice to her and then freaked out when I was."

"That or she didn't want your pity," Valentina said. "It's

not always easy to show your true self to someone and trust that they aren't going to throw it in your face later."

"I agree," Piper said. "It was just weird. Shortly after that, she started seeing someone a little more consistently, then she latched on to Knox. I think she regrets letting Knox go."

"She definitely made it seem that way," Zoey said. "But that doesn't make it Haley's fault."

"God, no. Absolutely not. If Ivy and Knox were supposed to be together, Knox wouldn't be gaga over Haley," Piper said with a wink.

"He's not gaga over me," I argued.

"Yeah, he totally is," Sofia said, not backing me up at all. "I saw him leaving her apartment a week ago, and he was sneaking out all quiet like he didn't want to wake her up."

"When was this?" I asked. Neither of them ever mentioned it.

"Last weekend. I asked him if he'd convinced you to stay yet. He said he was working on it." Sofia grinned.

"Well, he isn't the only thing that convinced me. All of you did, too," I admitted.

"What? You're staying?" Sofia blurted. "Really?"

I nodded. "I decided this weekend. I love it here. Knox and I might not last forever, but I want to be here. Dawson doesn't get to have the whole town."

"Dawson isn't even here anymore," Valentina said. "But I'm really happy to hear you will be."

"Are you sure?" I asked her. Of everyone in town, her opinion was the one I was most worried about. Not because I thought she would say or do anything to turn people against me, but because I wanted to make sure I wasn't causing her any pain.

Valentina smiled warmly at me and nodded. "I never blamed you. The people who did were misguided in their protection of me. Brantley has dealt with some of the same crap as you. They think he swooped in and took advantage of my pain, but Dawson is out of my life for good. If you wanted to be with him, I might warn you off that idea, but Knox is nothing like Dawson."

"No, he's not," I agreed.

"Dawson did a number on both of us. I don't want you to suffer for his actions, Haley. I really don't. I think this town is a great place to be. I love it here. And I'm glad you do, too." Valentina was far kinder than I felt like I deserved, but I was grateful as hell for her.

"So, when do we celebrate you staying?" Sofia asked.

"Well, first I have to make sure I can sign a new lease."

"Done," Sofia and Piper, who owned the building I lived in, said at the same time. They both laughed and nodded.

"I'm going to talk to Debby tomorrow. I haven't said anything to her about staying or leaving, but my chair lease was only for one year."

"I'm sure she'll be thrilled to have you stick around," Trinity said.

I nodded. "I sure hope so. And then we can celebrate."

"I'm going to hold you to that," Sofia said.

I grinned. I was definitely making the right decision to stay.

I was feeling sure of everything until I woke up to a text from Debby the next morning asking me to be in early. I'd never gotten a text like that from her. Anxious wasn't even the half of it. I was downright terrified.

I hurried through my morning routine, knowing I didn't have enough time if I was going to make it to work early. I grabbed a granola bar on my way out the door, hoping I'd have a chance to run out during my lunch break because, like usual, I didn't pack a lunch ahead of time.

When I got to Teased By Debby, Chelsea was in the back, chewing on her nail. "What are you doing here early?" she hissed.

"Debby sent me a text and asked me to be here before my shift. Did you get the same?"

Chelsea nodded and showed me her phone, the message identical to mine. "What do you think she wants to talk to us about?"

I shrugged. "I have no idea. I figured she was going to fire me or something, but there's no way she'd fire you."

"I'm not firing either of you," Debby said from right behind me.

I screamed and jumped, glaring at Chelsea for not warning me that Debby was right there.

"Good morning, Debby," Chelsea said in a far too chipper voice for so early in the morning when we might be in trouble.

"Morning," I grumbled, still uneasy even after Debby's weak assurance.

"Morning, ladies. Thank you both for coming in early. I wanted to have a chance to speak to you two before any customers came in and before anyone else was here. Should we sit?" Debby gestured to the salon, the only place with seating.

Chelsea and I exchanged a worried glance and trudged to the chairs we would soon have clients in. We spun to face Debby, neither of us speaking.

"You two are the best stylists here. I know you've been restricted by some of the clientele we have and their desired style, but I've seen your talents, and so do most clients."

"Thank you," we mumbled together.

Debby chuckled. "You two act like you're in trouble."

"Aren't we?" Chelsea asked.

Debby shook her head. "Quite the opposite, actually. You may or may not have noticed, but I've been slowing down lately. Taking more time off. Handing off clients to the rest of you. I'm ready to retire."

"What?" I gasped.

"You're so young," Chelsea said diplomatically.

Debby was not young. Not that she had one foot in the grave, but young was not a word I'd use to describe her. It didn't surprise me she was talking about retirement. What did surprise me was she was talking to us about it.

"I'm nowhere near young anymore, but thank you. What I am is ready to slow down. My kids all have kids and I want to be around to help them. I was given this salon when my kids all went to school and I was looking for something to keep me busy. Now, I want to do the same for you two."

Chelsea and I stared at each other. I had no doubt the confusion on her face matched mine.

"We don't have kids," Chelsea said.

Debby laughed again. "I know. Poor choice of phrasing on my part. What I meant was, I'd like to give you two this salon."

"Give it to us?" Chelsea blurted.

I was speechless, so I was happy Chelsea knew how to form words.

Debby nodded, looking between us. "You can say no, of course, but this salon has been paid for. The property is owned by whoever owns the business. There are taxes to pay, but you also get to make all the decisions. Hours, schedules, how many stylists and who they should be. I do hope you'll keep a space for the ladies here right now, if they choose to stay, but all the decisions will be yours. Both of you, if you want."

"Why?" I spat, finally finding my voice and coming across as an ungrateful bitch. "Sorry, I mean why me?"

"Why not you?" Debby asked. She tilted her head, looking like she genuinely didn't understand why I was asking.

"Half of your clients can't stand me. Half the town can't stand me. I've been here a little less than a year. You barely know me. I mean, I just—"

"You're smart and creative and kind. You've handled everything thrown at you like a boss, and never once lost your shit on the hateful people who made comments about you. I wish I had half your cool. Which makes me wonder why in the hell you'd choose me," Chelsea said, addressing her last sentence to Debby.

"That's why. For both of you. Haley, you've been an excellent addition to this place, and to this town. I know things didn't go the way you'd hoped when you moved here, but I hope you want to stay and will run this place with Chelsea. The two of you make a great team, which Chelsea just proved. And Chelsea, how could I not want you to take over? You've worked here tirelessly for years, never once complaining, even as you gently encouraged me to update things. You've been both a cheerleader and a resource for me more times than I can count. And since none of my kids have any interest in the salon, and I'd never give the place to someone who wanted to turn it into something else, I really am hoping you two will do this."

Chelsea and I looked at each other. Smiles lifted both of our lips, but before we could say anything, someone walked into the back.

"Think about it," Debby said. "If you can stay after work,

we'll talk. If you need more time, that's okay, too. But thank you for at least thinking about it."

Rose, one of the part-time stylists, came out from the back curtain and stopped when she saw the three of us. "I didn't realize we needed to be here early."

Debby dismissed her concern. "No need. We were just chatting. I love this top."

Rose grinned and gushed about the top she was wearing, falling right into Debby's distraction.

Chelsea and I exchanged a glance and a grin. The idea of being in charge was overwhelming and exciting. My guess was Chelsea was feeling the same, but more excited than anxious.

Our first clients arrived before I had a chance to ask Chelsea what she was thinking, and the day was a whirlwind after that.

As I cut and styled and colored hair, I thought about how things would change if Chelsea and I were in charge. There were four part-time stylists at Teased by Debby. Chelsea and I were the only two who worked full time, which made me wonder if that factored into Debby's decision, but she easily could have handed everything over to Chelsea alone and I wouldn't have thought twice about it.

I kept an eye on Debby and what she did all day, realizing she really had taken a step back. She had less than half as many appointments as Chelsea and I did, and fewer than Rose, too. Debby spent her time chatting with everyone who walked in and commenting on the new cuts and styles people were getting.

By the time the day ended, I was on board with taking over. I was excited about the chance to do something like that, and I was looking forward to it with Chelsea.

"I'm in," I told Debby. "Thank you for trusting me."

"Absolutely, honey. I'm happy you're open to it. And you, Chelsea?"

"I'm in, too. I think it's going to be great."

"Excellent. Thank you both so much. You two can talk and decide what you want to do about the employees, but please let me know. I'll do everything I can to make the transition smooth. I'm hoping to have everything done in the next month or two, if that works for both of you. Ramsey Holland will take care of all the paperwork," Debby said.

Chelsea and I exchanged a look, and I knew we were going to be excellent partners because I could read her expression.

"We want to keep everyone who wants to stay," Chelsea said for us. "And we are open to whatever timeline works for you. We're really excited, Debby. Thank you."

Debby looked between us, and we both nodded. "Well, that sounds good. I'm assuming you'll want to choose a new name. You can talk to Ramsey about that, but I'll have him move forward with everything. Now, you two go out and enjoy your evening. I'm sure you have people you want to tell."

We both hugged Debby, then hugged each other. We agreed to meet on our day off to discuss everything, including a new name.

I got in my car and squealed with excitement. Debby was right. I did have someone I wanted to tell.

Knox.

I drove across town to the hardware store, unable to contain my smile or my excitement. I wasn't sure how Knox would take the news, but I was hopeful he'd be just as excited as I was that I would be staying in MacKellar Cove.

I schooled my expression, not wanting to give everything away before I had a chance to tell him my news. The store was still open, so I expected to wait to talk to him, maybe even until the store was closed.

I was not expecting to hear my name as soon as I walked in the door.

"What were you thinking getting involved with that Haley woman?" someone said.

I didn't recognize the voice, but it wasn't Knox speaking. The next one wasn't either.

"Yeah, that's almost as bad as changing the store. You gonna bring all that frou-frou stuff back?"

My heart broke for Knox. The men talking had to be his longtime customers, the ones who made him second guess what he wanted to do.

"Haley is worse," a third voice said. "She ruined a marriage. You can't go back on that. Changing the store is a pain in the ass, but breaking up a marriage is inexcusable. Why would you be with a woman like that?"

"Agreed," the first voice chimed in. "That woman has no place in this town. All she's done is make a mess of things that she had no business being a part of."

I stood there, frozen, waiting for Knox to defend his choice to be with me. Waiting for him to defend me. I wasn't sure how long I stood there, but as tears started to run down my cheeks, I knew it was long enough.

He didn't say a word. He just let these men talk about me.

"Excuse me," a woman said from behind me.

I moved to the side to let her pass, but she stopped me.

"Are you okay?"

I shook my head. "Not really, no."

Then I turned and left. My heart broke as I walked to my car and climbed in, driving away from Knox. For good.

23

KNOX

I RANG UP THE CUSTOMER IN FRONT OF ME WHILE TONY, DICK, and Wayne ripped into me about Haley. My hands clenched into fists, and my jaw cracked with rage.

How fucking dare they?

As soon as the customer collected his bag, I turned on Tony, Dick, and Wayne.

"You don't know what you're talking about," I seethed.

"So she didn't ruin a marriage?" Wayne challenged me.

"No, she didn't. Dawson ruined his marriage by fucking someone other than his wife. The woman who didn't know her boyfriend was married is not to blame. And besides that, Valentina is better off with Brantley than a cheating asshole like Dawson."

"Ending a marriage is never okay," Tony said, shaking his head like a divorce was equal to murder.

"Definitely not," Dick said. "In our day, you worked things out. You kept your problems in the house. You didn't get divorced."

"And you think it would be better for that family? If Valentina looked the other way? If she didn't get bothered by Dawson sticking his dick where it didn't belong?" I barked.

"A woman should know how to keep a man happy," Wayne huffed.

"Fuck no," I growled. "Do not put that on her. Valentina doesn't deserve it. No woman does. It takes two people to make a relationship work, and if one of them is a waste of fucking space, the other one shouldn't be required to sit back and accept blame for it. Dawson has seen his daughters exactly once since the divorce. Do you think that's acceptable?"

"I heard Brantley won't let him," Tony said.

I closed my eyes so I didn't punch the man. "Are you really that fucking stupid? You really think the man who was fucking around on his wife is such a dedicated father that he's reached out to his kids, and their new stepdad, who's a teacher and who loves them like his own, is going to refuse to let them get together? What is wrong with you?"

Tony opened and closed his mouth like a fish, unsure of how to respond. Dick and Wayne gawked at me like I'd grown an extra head.

Nope, just a set of balls. I was fucking done letting the three of them come into my store and tear down everyone in town. They showed up on a Monday, a day they didn't normally come in, so they could tear into me about taking the job with Daisy. Then they ripped into me about other work and how I was going to ruin the store. Next, they moved on to talking about other people in town and how Finley's bookstore was telling women they should want sex and demand it from their husbands. Karissa's app was teaching 'young people' to abandon relationships because there was always someone else waiting.

Then they started on Haley. Tony mentioned he heard

we were at the Easter celebration over the weekend. When Dick and Wayne didn't know who Haley was, Tony was happy to fill them in.

And they went nuts.

Accusing me of being part of the problem, saying I was wrong for getting involved with her.

I couldn't take it. Who I dated had nothing to do with them, and their backward ways of thinking the woman was the only one responsible for keeping a relationship together was why men like Dawson cheated. They could hide behind the viewpoint that Valentina didn't do what she was supposed to do, so Dawson strayed to find his happiness.

Fuck. That.

"You don't get to talk to us that way," Wayne bellowed. "We're your elders."

"And you're being disrespectful and mean. This is my store, and I don't want you here if you're going to act like men can say and do whatever they want without consequence. Dawson got what he deserved, except for the blame. He should be the one shouldering it, not Valentina and not Haley. But until you can see that, I don't want you in here spewing your garbage."

The three of them looked at me like I was a disappointment, then stalked out of the store with mumbled words and scowls.

I shook my head, watching them go, until they stepped to the side and revealed Daisy standing near the door.

Crap.

"I apologize for all of that," I said as she approached me.

She glanced behind her, waiting until the door closed to address me. "I don't know everything they were talking about, but I have to admit, it makes me a little hesitant to work with you after the way you spoke to them."

I drew a breath and nodded. "I was unprofessional, and I'm sorry. It was... They pushed some buttons. Big ones. Those three were regular customers when my dad ran this place. When he retired, they kept coming, but they use the store as a place to gossip about people in town, and tell me all the things I'm doing wrong."

"Gossip isn't the most flattering thing in the world." Daisy's lips thinned, like she knew firsthand how disastrous it could be when you were the victim of false rumors. It was the first time I'd seen her without a smile.

I jumped on it. "The woman I've been seeing moved here almost a year ago to be closer to her boyfriend. When she got here, she discovered he was married."

Daisy gasped.

"She had no idea. It blindsided her. The wife didn't know about the affair, and when Haley showed up at their house, Valentina threw Dawson out. Some of the people in town blame Haley, not Dawson. Those three are some of the ones who blame her."

"And you were trying to set them straight."

I exhaled roughly. "When it first happened, I ignored their comments. Usually, the things they say are only half true. I heard the story from a friend, the man who is now married to Valentina. I didn't give Haley much thought. I never blamed her, but I knew Valentina was better off with Brantley."

"Sounds like a happy ending for them," Daisy said.

"It is. They're really good together. Valentina said her marriage to Dawson was declining for a long time before Haley showed up. She never blamed Haley. But I can't stand here and let those guys attack Haley, or say Valentina didn't do something and that's why Dawson cheated."

"There's never an excuse for cheating," Daisy said. For a

normally bright and cheerful person, she was downright scary when she was serious.

"Agreed."

Daisy drew a breath and released it slowly. "Thank you for explaining it to me. I don't love that you swore at them, but I do understand standing up for the woman you love. It's good to see you're that kind of man."

"Haley is a good person. She's been debating staying in town, and people saying things like that are why she hasn't committed yet."

"Can I ask you something, Knox?"

"Of course."

"What does Haley look like?"

I pulled out my phone and unlocked it, swiping to find a picture I'd taken of us over the weekend. She was sitting in front of me, laughing at something Ian said. She was so beautiful. I smiled at the picture before spinning my phone around to show Daisy. "This is her."

Daisy pursed her lips. "I was afraid of that. She was here."

I looked at the door, but no one was there.

"When I walked in, she was standing at the door. I think she heard what they said about her."

"No." My gut dropped to my feet.

Daisy nodded. "I'm sorry. She left in tears. She looked really upset."

I closed my eyes and sighed. If she heard them, did she hear me defending her, or did she leave before that?

"She left before you said anything," Daisy said, answering the question I hadn't asked.

"Which means she thinks I let them trash her and didn't defend her."

Daisy chewed her lip and nodded. "Yeah."

"I'm sorry. I know this is horribly unprofessional, but I have to go talk to her. I need to explain."

Daisy nodded and moved toward the door with me. "I understand. I wouldn't feel right continuing with our meeting knowing someone was hurt who shouldn't be."

"Thank you, Daisy. That means a lot. And I promise, I will make this up to you. I have all the designs and budgets ready. We can review them whenever you want."

We made it to the door when Teddy walked in.

Daisy stopped short, barely avoiding colliding with Teddy.

"I'm so sorry," Teddy said. "Are you okay?"

Daisy nodded. "All good. Knox, we'll talk soon."

Daisy left, one obstacle out of the way before I could rush after Haley. "Sorry, Teddy, but I'm on my way out. Is there something you need right now, or can you come back in the morning?"

"I can come back, but I can also stay and run the store for you. A trial run," Teddy said.

That stopped me short. "What?"

"You said you were thinking of hiring someone to run the store. I want that job. If you were serious."

"I am. I'm very serious. I... I need to go, but yeah, if you want to stay here and keep the place open for another hour or so until I get back..." I dug the keys out of my pocket and unhooked the ones for the store. "This is everything. I have spares in my apartment, so you can hang on to these until the next time you come in."

Teddy nodded. "Thanks, Knox. I really hope this works out for both of us."

"Me, too," I told him as I ran out the door, fighting a smile. First, I needed to find Haley, then I'd figure out how to make things work with Teddy and the store.

Haley wasn't answering her phone or her door. Teased by Debby was closed, and Sofia didn't know where Haley was, but she did have more than a few choice words for me when I admitted I messed up.

But dammit, I needed to explain. I did defend her, I just did it after she'd left, broken and forsaken. I felt like an asshole, but it wasn't like I agreed with Tony, Dick, and Wayne.

I drove around town, looking for Haley's car, but I didn't spot it anywhere. As it started to get dark, I found myself pulling into my dad's driveway.

"You sure screwed the pooch tonight, didn't you?" my dad asked when I walked inside.

"Yeah, I did. Wait, how do you know?"

"Wayne called me as soon as he got home. Lit me up about my disrespectful son tearing him a new one."

I rolled my eyes. "Wayne can kiss my ass."

"Don't you come into my house and speak that way to me," Dad growled.

"Sorry, Dad, but he was being a jerk. Did he tell you what I said that was supposedly so disrespectful?"

Dad smirked. "Said he told you getting involved with Haley was a bad idea because she's a homewrecker."

"He doesn't even see that Dawson was the one who wrecked his home. Haley was innocent in that whole thing. Her only crime was falling for a guy who didn't deserve it."

"I agree," Dad said. "And I told Wayne that."

"You did?"

"Hell, yeah, I did. Wayne and Tony are going to defend Dick until the day they die, but he was known for screwing around on his first wife, when she was alive."

"What?" I blurted.

Dad nodded. "You were a little young to have noticed any of it, but when they were younger, Dick was always picking up his newly graduated students. Always waited until they were legal, but it was well known he had one or two in mind for when they turned eighteen."

"You're kidding me, right?" I asked, feeling like my entire childhood had been a trick.

Dad shook his head. "Dick's first wife, Marjorie, she was a good woman. Kind and patient, and she never said a bad word about Dick. She did everything to try to make him happy and keep him from straying, but nothing worked. He would complain about how plain she was, how boring their life was. She walked out one day. He was at work, and she just packed all her stuff and left him. Crashed her car not too far away and died before anyone found her."

"Why don't I remember this?"

"You were young. I think you were in school, but maybe not. But it wasn't like you knew the wives of those guys."

"I can't believe he cheated on his wife and blamed her for it. That's what those guys were doing today. Trying to say Valentina was why Dawson cheated."

"I know. And I think they believed it. I wouldn't be surprised to learn Wayne and Tony were unfaithful to Madeline and Annabeth, too. It was almost expected when we were younger."

"Did you cheat on Mom?"

Dad looked me dead in the eye and said, "No. Not once. I adored your mother. I know people cheat even when they say they love their partner, but it wasn't how I was built. Once I met your mother, I was done. Couldn't even think about another woman."

I nodded, grateful my father wasn't one of those men,

but also hating that Tony, Wayne, and Dick ran off the woman I loved.

"I love her, Dad," I whispered.

"I know, son. Go tell her."

I shook my head. "She overheard what Tony, Dick, and Wayne said."

Dad leaned back in his chair, eyes wide. "Well, shit. That's a load you stepped into. Is that why you lit into them?"

I shook my head again. "I didn't know she was there until after they left. A customer walked in while I was telling Tony, Dick, and Wayne what I thought about their opinions. She mentioned Haley heard what they said."

"And I'm guessing she's not answering your calls or texts?"

"Nope."

"So what the hell are you doing sitting here with me?"

"I don't know where she is! I went to her apartment, her job, asked her friend. Her phone goes right to voicemail. Texts aren't getting delivered."

"Do you know she's safe?"

I shrugged. "No. I... I drove around to see if I could find her car and couldn't find her car. I don't even know where she'd be if she's not home. She doesn't have a ton of friends."

"Start calling them. Now. Call anyone you can reach out to and tell them you just need to know she's okay."

I nodded, pulling out my phone and calling Brantley first. Even though I knew Haley wouldn't be at his house, there was a chance Valentina would have heard something.

"Long story short, Haley's pissed at me for good reason, and she's gone dark on me. I need to know she's safe," I told Brantley when he answered the phone.

"Hang on."

He muted the phone, leaving me to listen to the sound of my own breathing for several long minutes.

"Vee just sent a text to everyone at book club. When she—" He broke off, leaving me hanging and desperate for him to finish his sentence. "She's good. With a friend and safe. But she doesn't want to talk to you."

"Thank God," I breathed. "Okay, thank you. If she's willing to listen, I want to talk to her, but I'm just happy she's okay."

"Listen," Brantley said, his voice quieter, clearly no longer in the same room as Valentina. "I don't know what happened, but it might be a good idea to give her a night. I'll find out what I can about where she is and where she'll be for a few days."

I exhaled, hating that I needed to rely on someone else to get me information, but it was better than nothing. "Okay, thanks, Brantley. I owe you."

"Nah, man. I know you'd do the same. We'll get your woman back."

"I hope so."

"Don't stress." Brantley offered a few more placating responses, then hung up to have dinner with his family.

"She's safe," I told my dad. "She's with a friend."

"Good. Now you can figure out what you're going to do. Because you need to do something that'll show her, and everyone else in town, how much she means to you."

"Agreed."

I ate dinner with Dad, then headed home, feeling dejected and disappointed. In myself. I understood Haley being pissed at me. She had every right to be. And if I couldn't fix things with her, it was all my fault.

I forgot until I let myself into my apartment that Teddy had been the one to close the store that night. I went through everything quickly, noting that he left me notes about the customers who came in after I'd left, and made sure all the receipts and the register were in order.

One hour and I was ready to hire Teddy.

The next morning I was up early, having barely slept anyway, and opened the store. I was more than a little surprised when Tony, Dick, and Wayne were the first ones through the door.

"Morning," I said cautiously.

"We came to apologize," Wayne said. "Your dad had a few things to say last night."

I nodded, struggling to meet their gazes.

"It appears he had a few things to say to you, too," Dick said. "You know about my past, and about my first wife."

I nodded and crossed my arms. I felt like I'd been caught listening to the adult conversation, but I'd been brought into it. And I was a damn adult.

"We can say it was a different time," Tony started, "but the reality is we were horrible husbands. Annabeth knew I was running around on her, and she threatened to leave. I got it together, but I've never been able to get past the regret I felt for what I did."

"Same with Madeline," Wayne said. "I know she hasn't been all that friendly to Haley at Debby's. She's made comments that I know were really directed at me. She never called me on my cheating, but she knew."

"I think the women of your generation," Dick said, "don't take the same shit. They have options. Our wives... they didn't. I'm not proud of who I was, or of what it did to my family."

I wasn't really sure what to say to them. I couldn't tell them it was okay, because it wasn't. But holding a grudge wasn't my style, either. "Haley heard what you guys said last night."

"What?" Wayne barked. "She wasn't here."

I nodded. "She was. I didn't know it until you left, but she heard you guys tell me to stay away from her."

"Well, shit. We need to go talk to—" Tony said.

"No," I interrupted him. "I need to talk to her. She's not upset with you. She hates that there are people here who think she's not good enough for our precious town, but she's angry with me for not defending her."

"But you did," Dick said.

"After she'd left, apparently. Which means I have some groveling to do."

"Flowers," Tony suggested.

"Jewelry," Wayne said.

"Be honest with her," Dick told me. "Tell her how you feel about her. Make sure she knows she matters to you. If it'll help, we'll apologize, too."

"I'm sure that'll be good at some point. For now, I just want to see her and hope she'll talk to me."

"I can watch the store," Teddy said from the door. "If you want."

I smiled at him and nodded to him. "Gentlemen, Teddy here is going to be managing the store for me. I'm going to be working on a big project for Daisy Lincoln, and Teddy is going to be working here full time. We haven't figured out the details, but I expect the three of you to treat him like family. Better than family."

The three of them looked appropriately chagrined and

nodded. They knew Teddy, of course, and were all happy to get the inside scoop on Genevieve's pregnancy.

"Thanks, Teddy," I told him as I changed places with him. "I owe you. And I will make it work for you."

He grinned. "I know. That's why I want this job. It'll be better for my family, and I know you'll be an excellent boss."

"Thanks, man."

We shook hands and for the second time in as many days, I left the store under his care while I went off to win back the woman I loved.

24

HALEY

I STILL COULDN'T BELIEVE I'D DONE IT AGAIN. I'D FALLEN FOR a guy who pretended to be someone he wasn't. Every damn time, I thought I knew who I was getting involved with, and every damn time, I was wrong.

But none hurt quite this much. Because none mattered quite this much. Dawson, and every man before him, had been men I wanted to love. Men I thought I loved. Men I was hoping to fall in love with because it would have meant I wasn't alone.

None of them were Knox. None of them was close to how I felt about him.

When I showed up at Dawson's house, I was shocked. Hurt, sure, but surprised. I had no clue, and I felt stupid for trusting him. For believing he could have been the one.

This time... This time I just felt numb. Like after an injury where your body protects you from the pain by making the whole area numb. Except all of me felt numb. Because all of me hurt.

I'd cried into the pillows on Chelsea's couch all night. I couldn't go back to my place. He would have shown up, and he would have tried to explain. I would have forgiven him, because I love him, and I would have just gone on being a fool.

I wasn't going to be a fool anymore.

A knock on Chelsea's door had every cell in my body on alert. Did Knox find me? How did he know where I was? I certainly wasn't the most clever person in the world, but was MacKellar Cove really so small that he knew where Chelsea lived?

"Sofia brought you some clothes," Chelsea said as she walked past the couch to open her door for Sofia.

"Hey," Sofia said softly. She couldn't see me from the door, and I didn't sit up to show my face. "Is she okay?"

"Are you okay?" Chelsea asked, ratting me out as being able to hear Sofia.

"No," I grunted. I was going to lean into my misery because it was all I had. At least this time when I got my heart broken, I didn't destroy someone else in the process.

The door closed, and Sofia moved across the room toward me. She sat at my feet, where I refused to move them, and gave me a look of pure pity. "What did he do?"

"I don't want to talk about it," I mumbled.

"She hasn't figured out yet that everyone in town is going to know what happened by lunchtime, and if she wants to tell her side of the story, she needs to start talking," Chelsea said.

I glared at her, wondering why I went to her. She wasn't sympathetic. Just annoyed with me.

"Unfortunately, Chelsea's right. Knox called me last night. He knows he fucked up. He reached out to Brantley to make sure you were safe, and Valentina sent out a group text to find you." Sofia looked up at Chelsea. "I'm assuming Elise reached out to you and that's how she knew Haley was still alive."

Chelsea confirmed with a nod.

Sofia focused on me again. "Everyone in book club knows something happened, but no one knows what yet. You let the rumor mill take over with Dawson. Tell us what happened, and we can put it out there so you aren't the one who's hated again."

"What's the point? Everyone loves Knox. He's perfect and he's kind and he's..." My lips wobbled and my voice shook. Dammit.

"What did he do?" Chelsea asked calmly. She'd asked more than once after I showed up at her door, but I refused to tell her. I was hurt, and I was upset, but I didn't want people to go after him.

I looked at my friends and drew a breath. I closed my eyes and saw it again. "There were three men in the store yesterday. I went there to tell Knox we were going to run Teased by Debby. I was so excited to share my news with him. But when I walked in, they were asking him why he was involved with me and saying he shouldn't be."

"Bunch of assholes. Don't listen to them," Sofia said.

"I agree. Don't let them ruin things. What did Knox say?" Chelsea asked.

And that right there. That was the kicker. I opened my eyes and looked at my friends. "Nothing."

They flinched. A quick jump backward like I'd slapped them. Eyes widened and faces paled. They traded a look that was a mix of disbelief and horror.

"He said nothing?" Chelsea asked.

I shook my head. "I was standing there for a few minutes. They were obviously talking to him, but he didn't say a thing."

"Did you see him? Maybe he wasn't paying attention," Sofia said.

"I didn't see him, but there's no way he couldn't hear them. They were not shy about their opinions. Shouting for the entire store to hear. Knox could have been in the back and heard those guys."

"Shit," Sofia whispered.

"What an asshole," Chelsea mumbled.

"That's why I didn't want to tell you," I confessed. "I knew you'd say that."

Chelsea gave me a look that said she would say it again. "What word would you use?"

I shrugged. "I'm hurt. A lot. But I still love him. I can't just stop loving him."

"You don't have to. I'll hate him for you. He should have defended you. He knows what you've been through since you moved here. He shouldn't let anyone talk about you like that."

I shrugged. "It doesn't matter. He did, and I can't pretend it's okay."

"Can I be the selfish bitch?" Chelsea asked.

I nodded.

"Are you still going to stay in town? Run the salon with me?"

I drew a breath and let it out with a nod. "It's going to be hard to see him, but I lived here for months without meeting him. I'll just avoid all the places he would be. He's not a client, and I have no reason to go to the hardware store. Eventually, it'll get easier. But I love it here. I decided I wanted to stay because I love this town. I can't let him take that from me. I've done that too many times."

"Are you sure it's over?" Sofia asked.

I exhaled a laugh. "I wish that weren't the case, but I

can't be with him if he won't defend me. I thought he was before yesterday. He spent all day Saturday introducing me to people at the celebration. And now... I haven't been able to come up with an explanation."

"What if he has one?" Chelsea asked.

I shrugged. "I'm sure eventually I'll be willing to listen, but I don't know."

"I'm sorry this happened, Haley. I really thought you two were perfect for each other," Sofia said.

I nodded sadly. "So did I."

I LEFT my phone off for the rest of the morning. Chelsea snuck me out of her apartment, but if Knox was going to show up anywhere, it was at the salon. We parked in the back and hurried inside. Without a Knox sighting.

I wasn't sure if I was happy or disappointed.

An hour into my day, a dozen Gerbera daisies showed up with a note.

> *I wish you heard what I said to them. I promise you, I did not ignore their comments.*
> *~Knox*

My throat tightened. Could I have been wrong?

Debby's first client of the day said his name when Debby was styling her hair. I froze, eavesdropping shamelessly.

"Knox ripped into Tony, Dick, and Wayne. Not that I blame him. They were being downright awful. Everyone knows those three used to run around, and that's why they were saying all that. Their wives stayed with them, turned the other way. They were just like Dawson, and maybe they finally feel guilty."

Debby met my gaze in the mirror with a kind smile.

I nearly cut two inches off my third client's hair, without meaning to. Chelsea stopped me and suggested I take a break.

The back was quiet, and it gave me a chance to think. Until Debby strolled back there with a letter in her hand. "This was just dropped off for you."

"What is it?" I asked.

She flipped it over and revealed the seal. "I don't make it a habit of getting that involved in other people's business, but if I had to guess, he's trying to say he's sorry."

"Do you believe what she said? About what he did?"

Debby sat next to me and put her hand over mine. "Madeline is a piece of work, but I've always put up with her because I know she takes out her pain on others. She hated you on principle because you were the other woman. It didn't matter to her that you never knew, it was still the reality. She was here late one night and told me she admired how you'd stuck around, even though people weren't nice to you. I encouraged her to change, but she couldn't. She couldn't separate you from the women her husband cheated with. I'm not sure she ever will. But those are her issues."

I studied the letter and the neat, curvy scrawl of my name across the front.

"Gretchen, who was just here, she's Madeline's cousin. I don't think she has any idea who you are. She's heard things from Madeline, but she makes her own decisions. And her gossip is usually right. If she said Knox defended you, I believe it."

I swallowed roughly, feeling like I was being pulling in two different directions. On one side, I knew what I heard.

But on the other, I could have left before Knox said something.

The big question was if it was enough.

Debby walked out, leaving me alone with the letter. I turned it over a few times, debating reading it.

In the end, I couldn't resist.

Haley,

I'm so sorry about what you overheard yesterday. I didn't know you were there. Not that it would have changed the way they spoke about you.

I have no excuse for not saying anything as soon as they started spewing their crap. The only thing I can say is I was talking to a customer, which was their opening. They knew I wouldn't ignore the person in front of me. They were smart.

But as soon as I was done, I told them to go to hell and to leave the store. I told them they weren't welcome back unless they apologized. If you don't believe me, ask Daisy Lincoln. She said you can call her. She was the woman who walked in behind you and told me you were there. She almost fired me for the things I said to Tony, Dick, and Wayne, but it wouldn't matter to me if she did. All that matters is that you believe me, and that you know I never intended for you to be hurt.

Love,

Knox

He almost lost a job because of me. And he said he didn't care.

But was he just saying it?

I tried to push the questions away and went back to work. Lunch showed up for the entire salon, including customers, with plenty of cookies for dessert so we could enjoy them all day. More flowers arrived after lunch. And then a woman walked in.

"Daisy Lincoln," I breathed.

She smiled when she saw me and approached. "I wanted to see how you're doing today."

I exhaled a mirthless laugh. "I'm great."

She grinned, her eyes kind and her smile genuine. "I know you don't know me, but I was worried about you when you left Al's yesterday."

"I'll be okay."

Daisy shook her head and took in my appearance. "You definitely look like a woman who is not going to let anything stop you. I think we could be good friends."

I laughed, surprised by her words. "I think I should say thank you for that."

"You might regret it. I've been told I can be a handful. And I'm far too chipper most of the time."

"I'd rather be like that than feel the way I'm feeling."

She smiled and grabbed my hand. "I had a feeling that might be the case. Knox reached out to me this morning. Asked if he could give you my number. I asked around and found out you worked here and wanted to stop in and see you."

"Was it true? What he said in the letter?" I blurted.

Her brows went sky high. "Well, I don't know anything about a letter, so I can't say."

"Oh. He said you heard him telling those guys off after I left. That you threatened not to work with him."

"Oh, yeah. All of that's true. He was mean. I make toys, and I can't have negative energy around me. It messes with my entire mood, and I make toys for crying out loud. I basically live to have fun. When I heard the things he said to them, I thought he was all wrong for the job."

"And now?"

She shrugged and chuckled. "He explained. He told me a little about you, and why they were saying what they said, and why he lit into them. I told him I understood him defending the woman he loves."

"He doesn't love me," I breathed, the words painful to push out.

Daisy laughed. "Oh, honey, he does. So much. When I told him you were there, he looked like he was going to collapse. We were supposed to have a meeting last night, and he cancelled on the spot to find you. I'm guessing he never did if you're still upset."

"No, he wouldn't cancel. He was so excited to work with you."

"Nothing matters if the person you love is upset with you."

"He... I..." I took a breath and looked at the stranger in front of me. I didn't know her, but she was kind yesterday in the moment when I wanted to collapse. She was back now, not judging, but helping.

She could be lying, but why?

"Knox is a good man, and from the look of the truck outside, he's your man," Daisy said.

"What? What truck?"

Everyone in the salon stopped what they were doing and moved toward the windows. The gasps and laughter had me hesitating.

"Haley, you have to see this," Chelsea said, waving me over.

I moved through the crowd like I was in wet cement. Daisy walked with me, her hand encouraging and a little pushy on my back.

The group of women parted as I reached them, smiles and admiration in their gazes. I'd never seen so many looks of approval directed at me.

When I reached the window, I gasped, just like they'd all done. Knox's truck was parked across the street. It was covered in spray paint. Yellow, orange, pink, blue. All with declarations of love. For me.

My heart belongs to Haley Jordan

Haley Jordan is beautiful

I love Haley Jordan

Without thinking, I opened the door, walking across the street to see the truck up close. It was definitely Knox's truck. I walked around it, reading the things he'd painted onto his truck on all sides.

"He's got it bad," a man said as they walked by.

"How come you never did something like that for me?" a woman replied.

I covered my mouth and let the tears fall.

"If that's not a declaration, I don't know what is," Chelsea said, joining me on the sidewalk. "I think you might need to forgive him."

I nodded, my eyes locked on the truck.

"It's him."

"He's here."

The voices around me brought me out of my stupor and I realized Knox was standing a few feet away from me.

"Knox," I gasped.

"Hi, beautiful. I know I don't deserve your forgiveness for what I did, but I wanted you to know how I feel. I figured if you won't answer my calls or texts, I'd make sure you knew."

"You're crazy," I said, shaking my head.

He nodded. "Crazy for you, Haley. I'm so sorry for not saying something to those guys sooner, and I'm so sorry you heard their nasty words. I will never let anyone ever say anything like that about you. Not for one second. I will stop whatever I am doing and put an end to it, and I will defend you to anyone who even thinks about saying something negative about you. You don't deserve it, and I don't deserve you, but—"

"I love you," I blurted, needing to say the words to him.

"You do? Why?"

I breathed a laugh. "Because you make me laugh. And you make me happy. You make me forget about my mistakes and trust that any I make in the future will be okay because you'll be there for me. You make me believe in myself and know that running my own business is something I can actually do. You are the only person I want to share things with and the first person I want to see in the morning. I can't imagine you not being in my life, Knox."

He stepped closer, tucking my hair behind my ear. "I don't ever want to not be in your life, Haley. I know I have to make everything up to you, but I promise you, I will never hurt you on purpose, Haley."

I nodded. "I know. I should have known that yesterday. I should have stuck around and given you a chance to explain."

"No, I understand why you ran. Why you doubted me."

"You're not Dawson," I whispered so low that only Knox heard me. Only Knox knew what my words really meant.

He inhaled quick and sharp, the movement of his chest bringing his body into contact with mine. He shook his head. "No, beautiful, I'm not. And I'm never going to treat you the way he did. I love you, Haley. So much it hurts to not have you in my arms already."

"Then what are you waiting for?" I asked.

He didn't wait another second. Knox sealed his lips over mine to the delight of our audience, who made it well known they approved.

I let myself get lost in the man I loved, the man who loved me, and kissed him back with everything I had.

Knox pulled back far too soon, kissing me gently before asking what time I was done with work.

"Dinner?" he whispered against my lips.

"Yes."

"Forever?"

"Yes."

"Good. I love you, Haley."

"I love you, Knox."

He smiled, slow to let me go as I turned to follow the others back to the salon.

I turned when I got to the door. Knox was standing next to his truck. He tipped his head back and shouted, "I love Haley Jordan!"

I laughed and shook my head. He winked at me, but I stepped forward.

I leaned my head back and shouted, "I love Knox Randall!"

Knox laughed loudly. "That's my woman."

I waved at him and let Chelsea pull me back into the salon with a swoon.

"You are one lucky woman," Chelsea said.

And for once, everyone in the room agreed. It was nice to be the lucky one.

EPILOGUE
SOFIA

I TWISTED MY HAIR BACK AND WRAPPED THE RUBBER BAND around it to secure my ponytail. The thin wispy pieces I let Haley talk me into weeks ago snuck out of the tie and tickled my nose. I blew them away with a frustrated huff of air.

I don't know what I was thinking changing my look. It didn't matter that I'd grown sick of my reflection in the mirror, it was economical. I didn't do fancy or pulled together in my job. As evidence by my current task.

I locked the door behind me, closing in the disaster of an apartment. Renovating it was supposed to be something I had time to do, but instead, a short-term rental request came through. Piper approved it, after checking with me. She was my best friend, but she was also technically my boss. I wasn't going to tell her no. Even though it meant rearranging a few things and getting the apartment back to habitable in a week instead of being able to finish gutting the place over the summer.

I hurried toward the exit, knowing I was pushing it to make it to Al's Hardware before Knox closed for the day. I was just about to the door when it opened in front of me, and Haley walked in.

"Hey," she said, her voice bright and happy, just like she'd been since she and Knox had gotten together, except for that short disaster of a day where they broke up. But she was back to being happy.

"Hey."

"Where are you headed in a hurry?"

"I need to get to Al's. And as always, I'm running late."

"I'll go with you. I'll distract Knox while you take your time."

"You don't have to do that," I protested.

"Sofia, I want to. I feel like I haven't seen you. I was going to ask if you wanted to get together tonight for dinner."

I did a quick calculation in my mind about how little free time I had between now and next week when the new tenant moved in and shook my head.

Before I could turn down Haley's offer, she spoke again. "You have to eat, Sofia. You're working yourself to death with this place."

I sighed and knew she was right. It had been two days since Piper said the new tenant was coming, and I'd barely slept. If I wasn't careful, I was going to start losing weight, too. Not that I couldn't stand to drop a few pounds, but I was comfortable with my body. Anyone who didn't like it could kiss my ass. And I had plenty for all of them to kiss.

"Okay. Dinner sounds good." As long as she didn't push me to talk because that wasn't an option.

I wasn't okay. I knew I wasn't okay, but I couldn't bring myself to tell anyone about it. Not even Piper knew what was really going on. I threw myself into getting the apartment ready so I didn't have to think about the disaster my life was going to be in a few weeks.

My dad was coming for a visit.

I hadn't seen my dad in years. We weren't close, and he was never the one who reached out. Which meant he was either dying or he was in some program with a bunch of steps and needed to make amends for something. The list of possibilities was long, but chances were good he would do what he always did and issue a blanket apology for not being a very good parent and think that was good enough.

It never was.

But he was the only parent I had left, so I let it slide. I let him get away with being a shitty parent because it was better than a dead parent.

I rubbed my chest at the thought of my mother. She'd once been my best friend, and it didn't matter that I was thirty-nine and she'd been gone more than half my life, I missed my mom.

Haley talked about her day on the drive to the hardware store. I wasn't sure if she knew I wasn't in the mood to talk or if she was just being Haley, but I let my mind wander while she told me about her clients and the town drama I'd missed while I was buried in the building I maintained.

I loved my job. It allowed me to work with my hands and to help people. Something else my mom taught me. She worked hard, usually two jobs at once, and was never afraid to jump in and do anything. She taught herself how to fix and replace toilets, how to install shower heads, how to do basic plumbing since plumbers were so expensive. She was a powerhouse, and she taught me not to ever stand back and let a man do something I could do myself.

There was only one man I ever ignored that rule for, but I couldn't think about him.

Haley parked in front of Al's Hardware and got out with a skip in her step and a smile.

Knox was at the door, getting ready to flip the sign to closed, when he spotted us. He still flipped the sign, but he opened the door to let us in.

"To what do I owe this pleasure?" Knox asked.

Haley went up on her toes to kiss him soundly on the lips. She pulled back, keeping her arms around his neck, and said, "Sofia needed to get something, and I said I'd come distract you so she could take her time."

Knox's brows went up, and he smirked. "Is that so? I seem to remember Sofia needing something another time and you coming alone."

I tried not to gag as I remembered what Haley had told me about their first night together. I was happy they found each other, but I didn't really want to witness them recapping sex, or acting on it.

I stepped around them and spotted Teddy at the register and veered off to say hi to him. "I didn't know you were here tonight. How's Genevieve?"

Genevieve was one of the sweetest people I'd ever met. Karissa said Xavier said Genevieve was having a tougher pregnancy this time around. The look on Teddy's face confirmed it.

"Seven weeks to go, but she's probably going to be on bedrest soon. The doctor said she's running herself ragged and if she doesn't slow down, he's going to force her to do it."

"She is not going to like that."

Teddy chuckled. "She already doesn't. Has talked about finding a new doctor who won't tell her what to do."

"Ouch."

Teddy rubbed a hand over his beard and shook his head. He looked like he'd aged a decade in the last few months. Gray strands wove through his beard and took over at his temples. His eyes looked vacant and haunted. He was exhausted. "The doctor keeps telling her it's for the good of the baby, but she insists she knows how to have a baby. She was working all the way through her first pregnancy, and everyone said the second one is easier, so she thinks she can do more this time around."

"Ah, man. I'm sorry it's been so rough. If there's anything I can do to help you guys out, let me know."

Teddy nodded. "I will. Thanks, Sofia. Is there anything you need today? Something I can help you find?"

I shook my head. "I'm good. I'm sure Knox won't mind if you head out. I know my way around this place, and he's not going anywhere as long as Haley's waiting for me."

Teddy chuckled. "Smart move."

I smirked. "It was her idea."

"Even better. Good to see you, Sofia."

"You, too, Teddy. Hi to Genevieve and Michael."

Teddy waved and hung his apron on the hook behind the counter. He moved toward Knox and Haley while I dove deeper into the store.

Before I knew someone would be moving in, I'd gutted the bathroom in the one-bedroom unit, so my priority was getting it back to functional. I'd spent the last two days fixing the shower plumbing, which had been leaking without my knowledge. The tub was in good shape, so I was leaving that in place, but I wanted to do tile on the shower wall and the floor. I didn't have time to order anything, so I was looking through the options in stock.

I selected a tile and took a picture of the tag on the end of the shelf, then moved to the other things I needed for the project. Grout, backerboard, and mortar. The bathroom was small, so I didn't need a lot of any of them, but all were heavy and more than I could get in my SUV.

I grabbed a wax seal for when I re-installed the toilet, a new faucet for the tub and shower, and made a mental note to come back and look at the sink base cabinets. I had a pedestal sink I could use if I needed to, but I'd prefer to put in a base with storage since it was the only bathroom in the unit.

Haley and Knox were still snuggling and whispering when I made it back to the front. Knox pulled away and smiled at me. "Did you find everything you need?"

I nodded and unloaded the things I'd grabbed. "I need some stuff delivered if you have time to do that tomorrow. If not, I'll figure out how to make it work."

Knox flashed a worried glance at Haley, who simply raised her brows as if to say, *I told you so.*

"I'm right here, guys," I snapped.

"Sorry. I just... Are you okay, Sofia?" Knox asked with far more concern than I expected.

I drew a breath and forced a smile, lying through my teeth. "I'm just stressing about this rental. I started tearing things out and have to get it put together quickly instead of having all summer to really do it right."

"Ouch. That's tough. Do you need any help?"

I shook my head. Working on the apartment was the time I worked through my emotions. I couldn't have Knox there if I was going to lose my shit and end up in tears. Not that I was going to tell him that.

"I'm working in the bathroom, and it's a pretty tiny space. Maybe in the winter when I can do the kitchen, I'll take you up on that."

"Sounds good. I'll be happy to help."

"Thanks, Knox."

He finished ringing up the purchases and put me on the schedule for deliveries the next day. He said he'd bring everything over himself, so I gave him the apartment number and arranged a time to be there with him.

Haley kissed him again and promised she'd call him later. She giggled as she followed me out of the store and got back into my SUV.

"You can hang out with him tonight if you want," I suggested, avoiding her gaze.

"I'm having dinner with you. And you're going to tell me what's really going on. You've never been like this in the year I've known you, and I'm worried. Plus, I miss my friend. It's been weeks since we've gotten together."

"You've been spending a lot of time with Knox," I said without thinking.

Haley nodded, scrunching up her face. "I know, and it's made me a shitty friend. Between him and learning everything about taking over Teased by Debby, I haven't been around. But I'm here now, and I really want to know what's going on. Are you okay?"

I looked at her, then looked out the front window and sighed. "My dad is coming to visit in a few weeks."

"That's awesome! I know you're not close, but it's good he's making an effort. Isn't it?"

I shook my head. "No, it's not. Because my dad isn't just my dad. He's... My dad is Jensen Carmack."

Haley gasped and grabbed my arm. "The rock star?"

I nodded, my gut swirling with anxiety. "Yep."

"I didn't know you were famous. That is so cool."

My gut tightened. Cool. I thought that when I first joined that world, but by the time I'd fled it, I knew the truth.

That world was one I never wanted any part in. Ever again.

THANK **you** for reading Haley and Knox's story! I was really inspired by Haley and wanted her to find her happily ever after. I adored the two of them together, and I hope you felt the same!

The next book in the series is Sofia and Trey's story. Sofia's rock star father is coming to town for a visit. A father she's never been close to. When she flees from her apartment one night, she runs right into the new tenant in her building. Trey is charming and sweet and interested in Sofia. She can't resist him, even though she knows he's not sticking around. Or maybe because she knows he's not sticking around. But Sofia's not the only one with a secret. Preorder His Curvy Muse now!

WANT MORE from Haley and Knox? Haley has everything she's always wanted, except a family. But that's all about to change! Bonus epilogue is only available to subscribers. Sign up now!

AMBER HAS BEEN TRYING to straighten out her life since she lost her scholarship and left college. Just when she thinks she might have it back on track, Caleb walks in and throws her off all over again. Check out Playing By The Rules today.

ABOUT THE AUTHOR

USA TODAY Bestselling Author Mary E Thompson spent most of her childhood wishing she had a few less curves. She hid in the pages of books because her favorite characters never cared what size her clothes were. Now, neither does Mary, and she writes stories that celebrate women like her. Real women who have curves, chase dreams, and find love, because we should all be happy, no matter our dress size.

Mary spends her non-writing time with her husband and two kids, watching too much TV, cheering for her hometown football team (Go Bills!), and hiding chocolate from her family.

Visit https://MaryEThompson.com/ to sign up for Mary's newsletter, **Romancing the Curves**. Subscribers get free ebooks and other fun stuff, like exclusive, members only content and giveaways, plus are the first to know about new releases and sales!

BEN STEMPTON'S BOY

A Novel

By Ron Yates

Acknowledgements

I am very grateful to my friend and former colleague Cathy Smith, who, before her retirement, was the best high school media specialist in the state of Georgia. Besides providing much inspiration through her work ethic as I struggled with this material, she was also gracious enough to read an early, unwieldy draft and offer constructive feedback. Cathy continues to provide encouragement and support to many who strive in a variety of endeavors to realize their dreams.

Thanks also to the current and former faculty and staff of the Queens University of Charlotte MFA program. Fred Leebron, Michael Kobre, Melissa Bashor, Pinckney Benedict, Daniel Mueller, Ashley Warlick, Elizabeth Strout, and Naeem Murr helped me realize how much I had to learn and showed me multiple ways to proceed. Their dedication to writing and teaching has helped countless aspiring authors find their voice and their way to publication.

I'd also like to thank the Queens alumni who were with me in the program, about a decade ago now. I remember you all and appreciate your constructive comments and encouragement. I congratulate you on your accomplishments thus far and look forward to celebrating your continued success.

Thanks to the team at UP, a kick-ass press, for their professionalism and willingness to publish this decidedly untrendy novel.

Finally, thanks to my wife Carol for her support during the stressful time of editing, proofreading, and promoting. She helps me in myriad ways.

Contents

Part I—The Orphan and the Old Man

Chapter 1

There was still plenty of heat in the late afternoon sun, and the asphalt was releasing what it had stored during the day. The hitchhiker, a boy on the verge of manhood, was near the limit of his endurance. His shoulders burned and ached like salt-packed gashes where the straps of the backpack pressed. He had been carrying it for over a week. This day marked the collapse of his plans, but a stubborn sprig of faith remained, a belief that, if he kept on walking, something good would happen eventually.

Sticking out his thumb had become a formality. Dozens of cars had passed him by since he left the nursing home that morning. His journey had gone well up to that point, but the news that there was nothing there for him—that his great uncle had passed away—was an unexpected blow. There was no back-up plan, and now he couldn't even get a ride. He would have to stop soon. Maybe he could find a barn or shack to rest in. Perhaps tomorrow would present new opportunities. Thinking this way, he didn't notice the drone of the approaching vehicle until it was quite close. An unmuffled engine had been pulling hard, but the sound suddenly changed when the truck crested the hill. The throttle closed, and the engine popped and cackled, straining to hold its burden back rather than pull it forward. The boy turned and raised his thumb.

The truck, loaded with pulpwood, slowed as it passed, but overcoming its inertia on the downhill stretch was a big task. It finally lumbered to a halt, brakes smoking, a football field's length past the boy. Its engine idled roughly, exhaling fumes from underneath, as the boy, struggling under the weight of his backpack, stumbled towards it.

He wriggled free of the strapped burden, opened the door, and set the bag on the floorboard before climbing in. Breathing heavily, he pushed his wet, ropy hair out of his face and looked at the driver, an old man, white-whiskered, unkempt, whose pale blue eyes were scrutinizing him.

The man said, "Where you going?"

"Back toward the main highway, I guess."

The truck, stacked high with green pine, strained and growled as they began to roll. The man spat brown tobacco juice out his side window as the boy fidgeted on the tattered seat, sticky with pine rosin.

"Where you from boy, up north somewhere?"

"Yessir, Pittsburgh. I've lived all my life there."

"Well, what the hell you doing here with no place to go? Don't you have no folks?"

Something in the old man's voice told the boy that he already knew the answer. He turned away from the pale eyes. "No sir, I don't. I lived in an orphanage as a kid, but it closed in '66, when I was twelve. Then there were foster homes. I turned eighteen back in April—officially out of the system. The family I was with, they wanted me to stay . . . but things got weird." He stopped, feeling the need to breathe, to fill the vacuum with air before the memories had a chance to form.

"You didn't answer my question," drawled the old man. "I asked you what you were doing here in Georgia."

Another deep breath and some effort yielded a reply: "I came here to look for my only living relative, Uncle Oscar Prather, but I just missed him. He died in the Stone Bottoms nursing home on the Fourth of July. Eighty-six years old. They told me he was a good man, though. Did you know him?"

The man spat again and double-clutched the truck into third gear, wrestling it onto a dusty, red dirt road. "Nope, can't say that I did, but chances are he's more pleasant dead than he was living. That's the way with most folks around here anyway, just plain meaner'n hell. Have to be to reach old age in these parts."

"I don't know what to do now. I had a plan a few weeks ago, but now it's all shot. I guess I'll look for work."

The old man turned his head, examining him as a surgeon would a tumor. "I'll bet you can't do shit, boy. It's different here from in the cities. People here work for what they eat."

What could he say to that? He stared ahead at a web-shaped crack in the windshield. Light from the summer sun was being refracted in the lines of cracked glass. Yes, it was different here from the city, Pittsburgh. Jack and Emma, his last foster parents, lived in a decent neighborhood, but he couldn't stay there any longer, couldn't look at them after what they'd done, what he'd let them do.

He was only half listening when the old man began speaking again in a thoughtful voice: "I had a nigger used to help me load my truck, but he got carted off to the county farm for cutting another nigger. Don't know where his wife and younguns went, but they left owing three months' rent. Can't complain, though. Buena was a good worker, so long as he stayed outta the whiskey. His shack's just standing empty. It ain't earning no rent, and I ain't got nobody to help me."

Through the roar inside the truck, the glare in the windshield, and his struggling with the past, the boy tried to make sense of what he'd just heard. The old man's words, shocking enough at face value, were made frightening by the manner in which he spoke them: matter-of-factly, as if these were commonplace circumstances. He wondered what he'd gotten himself into, a heavy dread settling into his groin. He studied the door handle and the ground passing by beneath his window.

He should have jumped sooner from that other situation. He'd seen it coming in the way Emma looked at him. She would lean in close at the breakfast table and run her fingers through his hair, right in front of Jack. And they had had lots of teenage boys at their house before him. He could have stopped what was happening, but he had not been strong then. Now he was in an old truck with a person he didn't know. He looked back at the man's face, which he found benign under the whiskers, stained brown around the mouth, and he realized it was his turn to speak. "So, will you hire someone to replace the guy who left?"

The old man glanced at him as he wrestled the steering, avoiding potholes in the road. "I lost my son a few years back. He thought he could do better in the city than stay where he was raised and help his pa. I'm getting too old to keep this truck loaded by myself, and if it don't get loaded, my wife and me don't eat. I'm stepping out of my normal way here, but you got an honest face. I don't see much harm in you." He paused to spit, then continued, gruff impatience back in his voice. "There's Buena's old shack you could stay in, and I could provide your food and maybe a little spending money."

"Wait a minute. Let me get this straight. You want me to work for you?"

"That's right, boy. You said you needed a job. I got one for you."

"Well, what do you do? I don't know anything about trucks."

"Damn boy! Hauling pulpwood don't call for no education, just a strong back and being able to stand the heat. I reckon you'll do awright."

"I, I don't know." He looked again at the cracked windshield. "Other than some part-time stuff, I've never really had a job."

"Well, you won't have much of one if you take my offer, but at least you'd be supporting yourself. That's better'n some folks do."

He shifted roughly into fourth gear, and the truck growled and lurched toward a speed that seemed excessive, producing a whirling wake of dust and exhaust fumes. The boy looked down at the floorboard and his tattered shoes. "Sure. Why not? I don't have much to lose."

"That's for damn sure."

They continued in silence for some distance, the old man gripping the wheel, staring straight ahead except when he spat out the window. The boy watched the countryside as it sped by, a tattered braided rug covered with a fine red dust that choked the colors and frayed the edges. A dull roar from the engine throbbed inside the cab, and waves of heat seeped in through the firewall. Images flashed intermittently into his mind of Emma's bedroom: her body under soft light; Jack, naked, watching from a chair on the other side of the room. He shook his head and blinked, glanced at the old man. Drops of sweat traced lines in the dust on his weathered face.

A few houses were scattered along the road—unpainted, tin-roofed shanties, warped and etched by years of sun and rain. The boy knew about the sharecropper system, having studied it in school, but most of these shacks stood empty except for the hay that was stored in them, visible through gaping glassless windows and open doorways.

Occasionally, they passed a shack that was still occupied. He saw rawboned black children, nearly naked, playing in hard-packed yards. Hound dogs and chickens. A sagging mother hanging out her laundry. At last the old man turned the truck into the packed clay yard of a shack that appeared to be waiting for its occupants, its front door standing open.

The house leaned toward the evening sun like a plant starved for light. Two ancient oaks stood in front. In their shade a handful of chickens gossiped among pebbles, but they scattered, cackling and running in circles, as the truck approached. A child's swimming pool, about five feet in diameter, sat half deflated in the sandy spot beside the house. The twin vinyl rings held within their blue circle enough murky water to cover the plastic bottom. The brightness of the plaything and its suggestion of children and laughter stood out against the surrounding muted colors. The boy was caught in a moment of wonder—*where are they now?*—as he opened the passenger door.

The engine's growl continued to reverberate inside his head as he stepped down. From a rafter hung a potted plant whose withered tendrils retained a hint of green. His surveying eyes caught movement in the shadows underneath the porch. He kneeled and looked under to find what he thought he'd heard and seen before his eyes adjusted. Again, the unmistakable whimper; then the wagging of tails and the anxious quivering of little bodies. "Puppies!"

"Oh hell, just some hound pups Buena and them left behind. Probably starving to death. Ought to put them out of their misery, but I guess they'll be some company to you while you're here by yourself—them and the chickens."

The boy reached under and dragged one out into the light. Fleas were working under the thin hair of the bloated little belly, and the pup's eyes were matted. It squirmed, wagged, and licked his hand.

"Put that thing down and come on up here," the old man ordered. "I want you to see your new house."

The steps looked unsafe, but the boy followed him inside. The sun had dropped low over the hills behind the shack, and it was dark inside. The old man flipped a switch on the wall, and a bulb hanging from the ceiling responded, pushing the shadows back.

The boy looked around at the sudden closeness of the walls, unnaturally lighted by the glaring bulb, and felt queasy.

"Well, this is it," the man said. "There's a bed and a stove and refrigerator in the back room. The well's out on the back porch." Recognizing the boy's confusion, he added, "Oh, it's got an electric pump. You won't have to draw your own water. This ain't the frontier days, but it ain't the Holiday Inn neither. If you use too much, you'll run it dry and burn up the pump motor, especially this time of year. Think of the place like it was your'n, and I'll be back in a little while with something for you to eat."

While he waited, the boy saw what there was to see: two large rooms with bare wooden walls and ceilings and crumbling rock fireplaces. He found the smell of the place soothing, as if the pine planks had absorbed the essence of life over the years. The odors triggered the desire to belong, a gentle persistent tug.

He knew he didn't have to stay, but he was confused. His vitality and zeal for travel were used up. He walked back out to the lopsided porch, sat, and studied the two oak trees in the yard. One of them was gnarled and twisted halfway up like a giant, dirty licorice stick. The other oak was taller and straight. The shadows of the trees grew, stretching along the ground beyond the shadow of the house, which reached across the yard almost to the dirt road in front. Crickets and tree frogs began their nightly chorus. He ran his hand over the smooth porch step as the shadows merged and darkness surrounded him. The simple animal hunger of the pups beneath him, evident in their feeble whimpering, reached through the floorboards, reminding him of the gnawing emptiness within his own belly.

He guessed the old man would probably do what he'd said and bring food. Listening to the night sounds, he convinced himself that he should try to trust him, and the faith he found proved not to be misplaced. Before long his belly was filled. The old man even brought a few scraps for the pups.

★★★

He was roused at daybreak by the urging of a raspy voice: "Come on, now. Gotta get started before it gets too hot." The man had let himself in, and he carried a sack filled with buttered biscuits and a thermos of black coffee. He rushed the boy through morning necessities and prodded him into the truck—"Come on, you can finish eating on the way"—and to the woods for his first taste of "real work." By nine o'clock, they were wet with sweat under a wrathful sun.

It was the boy's job to load the truck while the old man cut, running the snarling, chip-spitting saw as if it were a part of himself. The boy stumbled, awkwardly dragging the green tops out of the way. Sometimes he tripped over the pulpwood "sticks" themselves, which lay in five-foot lengths, zigzagged all over the ground like Union troops who died as testaments to the old man's dexterity.

The boy carried them on his shoulder one at a time to the truck, where he stacked them across the frame, between two upright standards made from four-inch channel iron. The more he stacked, the harder his work became as the top of the stack got higher. The old man, after watching him struggle to lift an eight-inch diameter log above his head, told him to get just the smaller ones and they would use the loader to hoist the big sticks onto the stack.

The loader consisted of a free-swinging boom attached to the top of the standards with a long, unwinding cable that could be hooked around the heavier logs. A slow, grinding winch, driven by the truck's fuming engine, would tighten the cable, swinging the boom around to face the log as it was dragged through the leaves, honeysuckle vines and briars, and to lift it from the ground when it reached the side of the truck. With the cable around its middle, the log would be hoisted slowly to the top of the stack. Muscle power was then required to swing the boom and its burden around so the log could be dropped into place. A pair of levers attached to the top of the iron standards controlled the cable. Mastering the operation of this device required strength, balance, and dexterity in measures far exceeding what the boy thought he possessed.

They stopped working at noon, and he stretched out in the shade, propping his head against the trunk of a poplar tree. The old man brought out lunch in a brown paper sack. They shared their meal without speaking, waving their hands to shoo the buzzing flies.

The old man asked, "Well, how do you like it?"

"It's different. I mean pretty good. I don't think I've ever had a tomato and onion sandwich before."

"I ain't talking about the damn sandwich! I already knew you Yankees don't know how to eat. I was talking about your job, the work, the deal we made."

The boy scratched his head, looked at the fresh blisters forming on his palms. "I haven't thought about it much."

"There ain't no need to think about it. You work, and you're given food and shelter. That takes care of the basics simple as that. Time comes in a man's life when he gets to wondering, though. Did you know that, boy? All men get to wondering sooner or later."

"Wondering about what?"

"It won't do no good for me to try to 'splain it. You'll find out when the Lord wills it. You ain't in no way bound by this agreement, you know. You can leave whenever you like, if you don't think you can cut the mustard."

He met the old man's gaze. "I guess I can cut it, for a while. Until I figure out something else to do."

"Good." The old man swigged some iced tea from a tinfoil wrapped Mason jar. "We about got a load here. Might as well drive it to the yard." With effort he stood and gathered the remains and containers of lunch. Then he pointed to the still-warm saw. "Let's go. If we hurry, we can get back in time for another load this evening."

The truck emerged from the woods fully loaded once again just as the sun was setting. The day was over at last, and there wasn't much to talk about. The old man drove the ponderous rig slowly back toward the shack. He stopped in the shadow of the trees and left the engine idling. Over the noise he said, "You'll get used to it." The boy dropped stiffly from the cab and limped toward the porch.

The days that followed seemed identical, as if God were snipping them off his reel of unspooling time. The old man, normally stiff and slow, was fluid in the woods, an intricate, well-oiled machine. The boy had to struggle to keep up, but his body soon adapted. The old man, true to his word, attended to his basic needs, providing breakfast and lunch each day as well as a big covered-dish dinner every night: fresh vegetables such as corn, squash, or beans cooked in butter, with fried pork or chicken and cornbread. There was always sweet iced tea to drink, and by the end of the second week he had gained some weight.

During the third week the old man began to linger each night to tell stories and drink corn whiskey. The boy occasionally took a sip of the clear, oily stuff. "It'll put lead in your pencil," said the old man as he told of the loves, battles, and poker games of his youth.

Many of his stories contained local characters, all larger than life, who had accomplished tremendous feats long before the boy's arrival to the area. Big Ot Brown was a recurring hero. For years he'd operated a general store in the community, and he was known and respected as an honest man who didn't have much to say. Ot had given up farming on the advice of his doctor to get some rest for his back, which had grown tired of supporting over three hundred pounds. Though tired, Ot's back was still capable of great feats of strength, and his usually gentle nature could take surprising turns at the accumulated aggravations of life.

On a busy Saturday morning some years back, Ot's temper was provoked by a black man who came in the store still drunk from the night before, needing cigarettes and money for more whiskey. Ot reminded him, as the man swayed at the counter in front of several women customers, that he already owed over $100 and he didn't need any more whiskey. "Get on home, Leon," he said. "Sleep it off and come back when you're sober." Leon grumbled an obscenity before stumbling out through the screen door. Ot's customers noticed his clenched jaw as he took their money and sacked their purchases.

Leon returned to the store a couple of hours later. This time Ot met him at the door. "I told you to get home and I meant it! I don't want to see you no more till you're sober." Ot placed his massive bulk in front of the screened entrance, feet squarely planted. Leon stood on the porch facing him, swaying silently and blinking his bloodshot eyes. Then he turned, grumbled another obscenity, and staggered back to his car.

Leon visited Ot's store briefly one more time that day. When Ot saw that he had come back and was again mounting the porch steps, he strode out from behind the counter and grabbed a wooden bottle crate off the stack against the wall. He moved surprisingly fast toward the door as Leon was coming through it. Ot's big hand had a firm grip on the crate's handle as he swung it in a wide arc, level with Leon's chest. The force of the blow lifted Leon and propelled him back through the screen door with enough momentum to carry him past the porch and gas pumps. He landed limply with a slight bounce, face up, on the rough blacktop road.

Big Ot tossed the busted crate back onto the stack and resumed his position behind the counter, ready to get back to business. A couple of old farmers were resting on the porch when Leon went flying past them. They decided they'd better check on him, lying still in the road, but they did so quietly, not wanting to get Ot upset again. To their surprise, the men found Leon dead.

"Ot hit him so hard with that crate, he knocked the life clean out of him," the old man said. He explained that Leon's people didn't make much of a fuss since he had been in the wrong, and everybody knew what a good man Ot was. "Since then," the old man concluded, "ain't no nigger, nor white man neither, come in Ot Brown's store drunk."

This and other stories the old man told fascinated and horrified the boy. He thought of his life so far as being without depth, a two-dimensional existence. Here he'd found a different reality where he could live deep and suck out all the marrow. People and events in this world were thick, solid, and hard to understand, but he intended to learn. Names, facts, and quotes he'd studied in school, like Thoreau, took on a new vitality, as if to say, "See, we knew you would need us some day. Your life has started at last! How do you like it so far?"

He wasn't sure, so he listened to the old man, who could really talk, especially after some whiskey. He'd bump his knees together and wave his arms in the air, laughing at his own cleverness; then, as if a switch had been flipped, his wrinkled face would become stern, his tone low and serious. Time would pass until his voice became hoarse and his tongue thickened. Then he would rise and shuffle out, stooped and tired. He always mumbled something at the door that could have been "Good night." It was understood they would meet again at daybreak.

★★★

Another week passed before the old man invited the boy into his home. On that evening he drove his Ford Galaxie up to the front of the shack at the usual time, but instead of carrying the supper plate, he honked the horn. "Come on," he said to the boy, standing puzzled on the porch. "You're gonna eat with me and the wife at my house tonight."

He explained that his wife had become upset when she found out the new "hand" was a white boy. She'd assumed she was preparing the supper plates for a poor black man. She called it "disgraceful" to have a white person stuck off in that old shack by himself, "treating him worse than a nigger, like he was some kind of prisoner," and insisted that from now on the boy would eat at the same table with them.

"I never felt like a prisoner," the boy offered. "I know I can leave whenever I want." His voice betrayed his true feelings: at times he did feel helpless to control his own future, his comings and goings. Since meeting the old man, he felt that his will was being sucked out of him. There had been a purpose before, to find a connection with his real family. When he finally tracked down his uncle, though—great uncle, really, on his mother's side—he was too late. He'd mustered the courage to direct his life this far away from Pittsburgh, but now he felt like a lost dog dragging a broken leash.

The old man's house was larger than he'd expected. It was a modest old "home place" at best, except when compared to the boy's shack; in that light it became a mansion. It stood straight and proud in its shady, well-kept yard, painted and shingle-roofed to protect it from the elements. The white paint covering the clapboard walls was peeling, but its presence expressed a modicum of pride.

The woman of the house met them at the front door, wiping her hands on her apron. She reached through her embarrassment to grasp his hand. "I'm so pleased to finally meet you. I'm Bea Stempton."

"I'm happy to meet you too. Randy Walls—from Pittsburgh."

"Well come in, Randy. Supper's almost ready. You can relax in the den with Papa while I set the table. I think the Braves are on tonight. You do like lemon in your tea, don't you?"

"Uh . . . yes, lemon's fine." He stood motionless in the center of the living room, awash in the sights, smells, and textures of a real home: curtains, doilies on the armchairs, end tables topped with *Guideposts* magazines, potted plants, bric-à-brac shelves, framed photographs of relatives. He regained himself and followed the old man—Mr. Stempton—into the adjoining den, the comfortable room, where the TV flickered warmly.

The scene didn't seem right and would have been unimaginable before. The old man in the woods deftly running the saw, driving the overloaded truck over the roughest of back roads, shifting gears without even using the clutch, drinking whiskey in the shack and telling of past adventures—could this well-scrubbed man reclined in front of the TV be the same person?

"Hurry up, Bea," Mr. Stempton called out. "Me and Randy's hungry. We put in a hard day today—got two loads out."

Then Randy realized he did live this way, comfortably and decently, but never talking about it or sharing any of this life with him. The old man had shown him only what he had wanted him to see: the straining, grumbling bowels of life.

He swallowed a hard knot that remained in his gut as they sat at the supper table, passing around the squash, butter peas, fried okra, and pork chops. Mrs. Stempton asked about his past, and he politely offered up his standard replies: the auto accident that claimed his parents when he was three; the aunt and uncle who divorced, leaving him with nowhere to go but St. Jude Home for Boys; being passed over by couples wanting to adopt because he wasn't a baby anymore; the strictness of the nuns; being shuffled through a series of foster homes; and, finally, how grateful he was that things had turned out as well as they had.

"You mean you're a Catholic?" asked Mrs. Stempton.

"Well, I guess—I mean I was trained to be, but I really don't know what I am anymore."

"Why, the nearest Catholic church is nearly 30 miles from here, on the other side of Aaronville. We all belong to Living Waters Baptist Church, over the hill yonder. I get tired of going by myself, though. It's just me and Papa now, and he ain't never took much to sitting in church. You're more than welcome to go with me this Sunday, but I wouldn't want to confuse you too much, since you ain't sure what you are. We probably do things a lot different—"

"I know what you are!" interrupted the old man with his mouth full of okra.

The woman and the boy looked up.

"I know what you are," he repeated. "You're a damn good hand at hauling pulpwood. The best I had in a long time, even better'n Buena, and that's a fact." He looked at his wife then the boy, nodding at each to affirm the statement before returning to his meal.

The boy felt his face flush with embarrassment and pride. He looked at his plate and dabbled in the squash. "Well, I guess I've had a good teacher," he mumbled. With this, he felt the knot of resentment in his stomach loosen, allowing the small of his back to relax.

Mrs. Stempton resumed her theme. "Anyway," she said, "you're welcome to go to church with me anytime you feel like it. I'd be glad to have you, and I'm sure the congregation would too."

"It won't hurt him none to stay out of church for one more week, Bea. I've got different plans for him this weekend. I think he's earned a holiday, and I intend for him to have one."

Randy stared at him for a second, then back at his plate. The stomach knot retightened at the sound of praise that before would have been welcome. He wondered how the old man could think flattery would make him feel better, after he'd been exiled in a shack and kept like a farm animal. I wouldn't be here now, he thought, if it weren't for his wife. . ..

His mind skipped back to the orphanage years when so many nice couples had showered him with affection and almost adopted him only to change their minds and explain what a fine boy he was in order to assuage their guilt. His admiration for these people ebbed away in proportion to the amount of patronizing praise they left him with.

"I think it's time to reward you for your fine behavior," the old man said through another mouthful of okra. "Here," he belched, reaching across the table. "I want you to go out and have some fun." He tossed a fifty-dollar bill and a set of keys almost into the boy's plate, then settled back and resumed eating as if that were all.

Randy wondered if he was serious. Could he really leave? Is that what this meant? Yes! He could leave in the old man's Ford and with his money. This was an opportunity to escape, but why had he offered it? Maybe he wanted to be rid of him. "What do you mean?" he asked. "I don't know where to go or what to do around here. I don't know anybody but you and the guys at the pulpwood yard, and I don't even know their names. You do all the talking." He paused to take a breath and to press his fork tines into the yellow squash. "I don't know anything about fun. All I've learned about this place is work."

"I know, I know, and it ain't natural. A boy your age needs to get out and blow off a little steam."

Mrs. Stempton looked from her husband to Randy and back with an incredulous expression. The old man acknowledged her. "We'll talk more about it afterwhile."

Mrs. Stempton didn't reply but began to clear the table. When she was in the kitchen running dishwater and rattling things, the old man revealed more of his plan: "There's a hot spot in town called the Billy Goat Bar. I hear they got some cute little waitresses. If you get into trouble, call me. Just make sure you're back here by Saturday evening. Bea'll need the car for church Sunday morning."

Chapter 2

The town of Prathersville was fourteen miles away in the opposite direction from Stone Bottoms, where they went to sell the pulpwood. The boy left that evening and drove with the radio off. He clenched the steering wheel intermittently until his knuckles turned white then opened his palms to look at the calluses. He looked at his fingernails too, and once or twice at his hair in the rearview mirror. He'd spent twenty minutes before leaving the shack worrying over the part and trying to get the front just right so that it covered his forehead and curved away just above his eyebrows. The sides also: he liked to completely cover the ears, then sweep the hair back without any flip-ups. He wasn't nearly so particular on workdays, but this was different.

He found the night spot where the old man said it would be. Inside was an old-fashioned wooden bar extending nearly the length of the room, with a darkened coat of varnish remaining only in spots that weren't rubbed against by arms, elbows, and stomachs. Behind the bar were beer taps, a mirror, and shelves filled with dusty bottles. Randy took a stool next to a white-haired man whose arms encircled a longneck bottle and a glass ashtray that held a smoldering cigarette. Along the wall to Randy's right the glaring lights of a juke box and pinball machine beckoned.

There was a red door at the end of the bar to his left. It swung suddenly toward him, set into motion by a young waitress passing through, carrying a tray of empty bottles and wet napkins. The bartender said something to her as he loaded a new tray with fresh beers and what looked like sandwiches and chips in little plastic baskets. She carried the orders back the way she'd come, passing in front of Randy before disappearing through the swinging red door.

The bartender, wiping his hands on a towel, acknowledged Randy with a nod. "What can I get for you?" His thinning hair was touched with gray and parted in the middle over his round face and bulging eyes. His shirt, high-collared and boldly striped, was stretched over his belly and tucked into flared jeans.

Randy said, "I'll have a beer."

The man pulled a mug of foaming draft and set it down. "Fifty cents."

Randy fished his wallet from his back pocket and handed over a dollar. The bartender said, "'preciate it," and turned back to his duties. Randy took a sip, his attention drawn back to that red door and the girl who'd passed through it. He only half heard the white-haired man sitting next to him. The old guy was saying something about how times had changed, how there used to be only colored folks on the other side of that door. Then he started talking about the drought and how his garden had just about dried up.

The girl came through again, singing with the jukebox, her movements matching its rhythms. Carrying empty trays, bottles, mugs, and baskets, she glanced at the men sitting along the bar. She was about Randy's age, blond, and she wore tight jeans. Her T-shirt was emblazoned with "Billy Goat Bar" on both sides over the cartoonish portrait of an old bull goat with an unkempt beard, reprobate grin, winking eye, and long curved horns. She also wore dark glasses although the room wasn't brightly lit.

Randy looked up and smiled. He thought she saw and acknowledged him with her eyes, but he couldn't be sure because of her glasses.

He sipped his beer and watched as people began to pass through the swinging door. Most were about his age, laughing in their groups and pairs. He imagined the room on the other side filling up with young people, all knowing each other and having fun.

The man next to him said, "You never been here before, have you? Young people don't usually sit in here with us old timers. We're too tired for the kind of action that goes on back yonder."

Randy turned and looked at the gray-stubbled face for the first time. "What does go on back there?"

"Why don't you go and find out?" The man winked a yellowish-brown eye and laughed, showing his bottom teeth, black at the gums. "I think that little waitress has got her eye on you."

She slid through the door again, sideways, carrying a tray. This time she seemed to look straight at him and smile.

"See, I told you!" said the man.

Randy watched her working carefully with the bartender to arrange a full tray for balance, then disappear again. Snatches of laughter and conversation wafted through before the door swung shut. He made up his mind, stood, and finished off his beer.

It was much louder and darker on the other side, except over by the pool table in the center of the room, where two couples holding sticks were clowning around, their laughter rising above the balls' clacking. People near the back wall were leaning against a rustic counter as they talked and drank, their location providing an opportunistic view. Plain booths of rough wood were placed around three walls; a few tables were spread throughout. There was a small dance floor in one corner, but no one seemed interested.

Randy blinked and looked around for a moment before he found the only unoccupied booth and sat down. He felt conspicuous sitting there by himself, and long moments passed before the waitress came to take his order.

"What can I get for you?" she asked, leaning close and speaking loudly enough to be heard over the noise. "You look kinda hungry."

"Uh, well, yeah . . . I am. Bring me a reuben, please."

"A *what?*"

"A reuben. You know, corned beef and sauerkraut on rye."

"Honey," she answered, not quite laughing, "we ain't got nothing like that, but I could get Mac to fix you a cheeseburger basket. They're real good."

"Yeah—okay—that sounds fine. And bring me a beer too, please."

"Sure. Hey, where you from anyway?"

Randy looked away. "It's a long story."

"Well, I'd like to hear it sometime." She smiled as she turned to go.

He felt his heart pounding. The girl was pretty and seemed really interested, even if he had been weird, ordering a stupid reuben. He was in Prathersville, Georgia, not Pittsburgh.

He ate his greasy burger and fries and drank more beer. He watched the other young people and compared himself to them. Even though the room was crowded and growing louder, no one joined him at his booth. No one seemed to notice him, except the waitress with dark glasses. Each time she passed, she would smile and ask, "You okay, hon? Can I bring you something else?"

Randy watched her as she worked, smiling, taking orders, and moving gracefully among the customers. Once, she stopped to talk to a tall, muscular guy with sandy hair and black boots. The conversation went beyond small talk; their expressions were lingering and earnest. Not wanting to stare, he looked away, wondering about their lives and how intertwined they must be. When he looked again, the tall guy was gone. After a minute, the girl was back to ask if he was okay.

She brought fresh beers as needed and kept the booth tidy. Once, when she leaned over to wipe the table and pick up an empty mug, he smelled her hair and perfume. When she came back the next time, he tried to talk, but his words were like peanut butter in his mouth. She smiled and uttered syllables Randy couldn't make out over the laughter and music.

When he got up to go to the restroom, he discovered he couldn't walk normally, but he found a kind of balance inside what felt like a bubble with wavy Plexiglas walls. The people he walked past were on the outside, the beer having removed them so that their glances didn't matter. He'd become confident, a foreigner no more.

The evening wore on as he drank there in his booth, a tiny island. He observed the others as they began to leave in groups and pairs. The rowdy stragglers maintained the noise level. Somebody turned up the jukebox. Movement and raucous laughter increased as couples flailed about, hunching and grinding on the tiny dance floor.

A vision materialized: the waitress sitting across from him lighting a cigarette. She leaned her face close to his and spoke over the noise, releasing smoke with her words. "Hope you don't mind if I join you. I can take a break now that it's almost closing time."

He smiled and stammered, "Sh—sure, great. Maybe you'll have a beer with me."

"That would be nice, but I'm still technically on duty and it's after last call, so I can't serve any more beer. Besides, I think you've had about enough." She tilted her head, smiled, then looked directly at him. "I'm ready to listen to that story about where you're from and what you're doing here."

Randy began awkwardly: "Well, I . . . I really don't know what I'm doing here, but I can tell you where I'm from."

"I must admit, I've been curious as hell ever since you ordered that weird sandwich. I mean, I'm wondering how does a nice-looking guy from up north somewhere end up here at the Billy Goat Bar in Prathersville, Georgia? Oh, I'm Stacy, by the way."

Randy, rambling, cleared up most of the mystery as the girl listened. Talking to her became easier as the customers thinned out. Words were flowing but he couldn't see their effect. Talking through Stacy's dark glasses became so frustrating that he finally asked her to take them off.

"Oh, why not," she answered. "Everybody's 'bout gone anyway. You see, I had a little accident."

She removed the glasses and shook back her honey-colored hair, revealing the purple flesh around her eye, which flashed like a beacon from inside the dark circle. "Awful, ain't it?" she said.

Her blue eyes were surprising. The injury seemed to make them softer, lovelier. "Yeah—I mean, that must have hurt. What happened?"

"It's a long story."

"I'd like to hear it."

"Maybe sometime, but now I've got to get back to work. Got some cleaning up to do."

"Okay, sure. I guess I need to pay my check and get out of here myself."

Stacy slid out of the booth. Randy stood up, clumsy and disoriented, fumbling in his back pocket. When he dropped his wallet, she bent to pick it up. "Here. Look, are you gonna be awright? I don't think you need to be driving. Where you going anyway?"

"I don't know . . . I mean, I haven't decided, but I'll be fine."

He swayed as he talked. She studied him for a moment then put her hand on his shoulder.

"You sit right here," she said, pushing him back down. "Let me finish up and I'll give you a ride over to my place. I got a couch you can sleep on, but you'll have to leave early in the morning. Ty works the third shift and he'll be coming over soon as he gets off."

Stacy's apartment was across town, not very far. They rode in her beat-up old Valiant while she fiddled with the radio and talked. Randy tried to control his feelings. He listened quietly as she told of her zany friends, musical preferences, and relationship with Ty.

"He's really a great guy," she explained. "He's just got this bad temper sometimes, especially when he drinks, and he's jealous as hell."

She told about her family, revealing that her one brother was homosexual. "He moved to Atlanta. Him and Daddy didn't get along—he couldn't believe Timmy was that way, tried to make him tough, make a man out of him. Finally, Daddy got to where he couldn't stand the sight of him. One day, Timmy just sort of disappeared. I still hear from him sometimes, though."

Randy reflected for a moment. "Having a parent who doesn't want you must be worse than not having one at all."

"You know, I never thought about it that way, but I guess you're right."

Then, after a few more turns, they were at her apartment, one side of an old house that had been converted into a duplex. As Stacy was getting out of the car, she said, "Wait, it's kinda dark out here. Let me help you inside."

The next thing Randy remembered was waking up to the sound of her voice: "Hey handsome, wake up. We've gotta get you outta here. Ty'll be here in a few minutes."

When he opened his eyes, her hand was gently nudging his shoulder. Her smell brought everything back as he raised himself on the frayed sofa and tried to focus. A sheet, wrapped tightly around him, made him feel like a mummy. Stacy wore socks and a baggy sleep shirt that came down to her knees. She was smiling in the brightly lit room, and Randy blinked her face into focus.

"Hi," she said, "how's your head?"

"Feels like it's full of foam rubber."

"Ha! I know that feeling. You'll probably be okay after you get some breakfast." She paused, dropping into a more serious tone: "Listen, I've got to take a shower before Ty gets here. Becky can run you back over to your car on her way to work. She's my roommate, you'll like her. Oh, your shoes, billfold, and everything are right here on the table."

Randy noticed the sound of water running in another part of the apartment, then a toilet flushing.

"You can have the bathroom next, when Becky comes out. And there's coffee in the kitchen. She'll find a cup you can take with you. I hate to be in such a rush and all, but you understand. Ty's just so jealous about *everything*, and he might make a big deal out of this."

"Sure, I understand."

"I enjoyed it, our talking and all."

"Yeah, I did too."

Her eyes met his. "I'm sure our paths will cross again."

"I hope so," Randy replied before looking away.

He got himself dressed while Stacy scurried about in the background. Then the other girl was out of the bathroom. She was tall and dark-haired, freshly scrubbed and dressed for her day. "You about ready?" she asked. "I'm gonna be late if we don't hurry."

They didn't talk much as they rode back to the parking lot where he'd left the Ford. She was preoccupied with her face in the mirror and getting to work. Randy's mind was struggling to sort out the events of last night. When she dropped him off his head was pounding. His agenda now was very short, dictated by the need for food. He'd feel better after a good breakfast. Then he could take one step at a time until he figured out what to do. He steered the Ford through the old downtown section of Prathersville and happened upon Maggie's Café among the storefronts. The sign said "Open" and he could see they were busy.

He ordered eggs, bacon, grits, buttered biscuits, and coffee. His problems were made difficult by too many options. His feelings for Stacy—and for the old man too—were stifling and intertwined, like kudzu around a young pine. Leaving would be best. Something of what he'd been before might be saved if he could get away now.

He thought of going back to Pittsburgh, a polluted world that had never afforded him happiness—only loneliness, frustration, and shame—a place from which he'd been eager to escape. But at least things there were familiar. The old man's Ford and the remaining dollars in his pocket would take him back. He could find a job in a warehouse or something. Pulpwood, snarling chain saws, Stacy and her jealous boyfriend, the old man and his puzzling ways—along with flea-bitten hounds, lopsided shacks, and everything else of this place—could be left in the dust. But in Pittsburgh he would need a place to stay. . . No! Resisting the attraction of that worn path, he pulled his mind back to the present and ate vigorously.

His hearty breakfast was quickly consumed, without the development of a plan. Of course, there were other places to go, an entire country—Louisiana, Texas, California, Washington, and all the stops in between. He could work a while at one, then move on, making friends and seducing women along the way. There are girls prettier than Stacy in every town, he told himself, and jobs a lot better than dragging pine tops and stacking pulpwood. But, in the middle of his fantasy Stacy's face intruded, along with the thought of getting a real apartment with furniture and a television. His efforts at reconciliation worsened his head pain.

The Ford was waiting for him in the morning sun. It could be his home for a while. But he knew the gas money would soon run out, and he couldn't live in a stolen car. He would be arrested. Besides, stealing was wrong, especially from people like Mrs. Stempton. She needed the car for church and groceries, and she was a sweet, decent lady who'd invited him into her home. Would the old man ever have treated him as anything but a hired hand had it not been for her insistence?

While part of Randy wanted to reject him, another part wanted to stay and try to pass his tests—to live up to the expectations the way a son strives to please his father. This was a test now of his loyalty and integrity, and, as from the beginning, the old man made all the rules.

I don't have to play his games, Randy thought. I'm a free agent and I don't owe him anything. I've worked hard for what little I got—just food, an old shack to sleep in, and a little money. Besides, I had to listen to his boring stories all the time. That ought to be worth something. He owes me respect instead of treating me like a slave.

He started the car and jabbed the accelerator, making the engine race noisily. He didn't like being split this way, and he blamed the old man for his condition. If he'd not climbed into the truck with him that day, there was no telling where he might be. But then he realized he would never have met Stacy without the old man. He wished he could talk to her now, in the sunlight.

A troublesome thought surfaced: he wasn't sure if he could find her apartment again. He'd been so preoccupied earlier when that other girl drove him to his car that he hadn't noticed the turns. Maybe he could retrace his steps. He needed to know where she lived, even though he couldn't go there now because of that jealous boyfriend. The thought of them in bed prompted a prickly feeling at the back of his neck.

Soon he was on the side streets in the general vicinity. He passed the chain-link fence encircling the dilapidated factory, which looked more like a red-bricked prison than a place of employment. The sign out front was colorful, though, brightly proclaiming Jupiter Mills as "Georgia's largest independent supplier of yarn for the textile industry." The surrounding side streets were arranged in neat blocks in three directions, with a larger avenue in front.

Randy negotiated the streets looking for something familiar. The modest frame houses were similar: aging but well kept. There was something about the place that reminded him of Allentown, his Pittsburgh neighborhood, although the architecture was different and the lots more spacious. Then he saw the faded red pick-up on blocks in a cluttered yard. He'd noticed it before because its front end was the same as the old man's truck. He was on the right street.

At the next block he took a left on instinct. The third house on the right was the one. Larger than the others, it had been converted into two apartments with separate drives. Stacy's old Valiant sat in front, covered with dew. A big motorcycle leaned on its stand next to the car.

Randy trembled from his concern for her: *This Ty character is dangerous. What if he hurts her again?*

He stopped the car and hesitated, tense and staring. Then a young woman appeared from behind the house with a toddler walking beside, holding her hand. She stared back at him, a stranger sitting there looking at her apartment. She picked up the child and held him on her hip, never breaking her gaze.

Randy finally recognized the look of concern on the young mother's face. He jerked the car back in gear and pulled away, gassing the engine excessively. *She must think I'm crazy, or a burglar. I shouldn't be here. I barely know the girl. Besides, her boyfriend might be crazy enough to shoot me. Or hurt Stacy even worse if I go sticking my nose into their business.*

Driving out of the mill village he gripped the wheel hard, looked at his sinewy forearms, and imagined a confrontation between himself and Ty. He decided he could handle him, and would if he had to. If he ever saw either of them again.

There it was, another facet of the unforeseeable future. One step at a time, he told himself as he rode aimlessly through the small-town streets, an activity that provided at least the illusion of freedom. The nagging thought that the old man expected him back that evening persisted, but he had hours to kill. Might as well enjoy them. And he may not go back at all. He needed to entertain all possibilities.

He passed a Tastee-Freez restaurant and several convenience stores a few blocks out from the center of town. Then he noticed a sign that read, "Prathersville Public Library," in front of an empty parking lot and modern brick building with boxwoods planted in front. He convinced himself that an hour or two of reading would be relaxing and could possibly provide insight. He might find a book by that guy he'd studied in school, Thoreau, who wanted "to live deep and suck out all the marrow of life."

The librarian greeted him with a quick smile before resuming her cataloging duties. There seemed to be only one other person there, an older man, neatly dressed in an Oxford shirt and pressed khakis, browsing the magazine racks. Randy explored the nonfiction shelves until he found Thoreau's book, *Walden*. The life of spartan simplicity described in "Why I Went to the Woods" was similar to his own existence, but he didn't share Thoreau's enthusiasm for it. Inside Randy was a yearning that involved others: love, companionship, belonging.

As the morning slipped by, his interests shifted from American literature to geography, people, entertainment, science, and world events. He indulged himself for several hours until the awareness of time passing pushed him back outside into the midday heat.

The old Ford felt familiar now. He liked the way it started right up with a throaty rumble, making him feel part of something larger, more powerful. He drove back toward the middle of town, through traffic that had picked up considerably, with the sense that the inevitable moment of commitment was just around the corner.

Chapter 3

He wondered who they could be after, as the blue lights flashing behind him drew near. The patrol car kept coming, accelerating right up to the rear of the Ford, close enough for Randy to make out the officers' scowling faces in the rearview mirror. Then they blasted the siren. When he tried to pull over, he hit the brakes too hard, causing the police car to bump his rear. After the screech of tires and the jolt, everything was still except for the whirling lights. He pushed the gear selector to park and loosened his grip on the wheel.

Glancing in the mirror, he saw one officer using the radio and the one on the driver's side getting out and unbuttoning his holster. He stood there for a moment, then reached back inside the car and brought out a bullhorn. The amplified voice assaulted Randy: "Get out of the car and put your hands in the air!"

He must be talking to someone else. After all, they were nearly close enough for conversation; no need to shout. But there was no one else, and Randy knew he must obey the booming voice. He slowly stepped out and turned to face the uniformed men.

Another amplified command: "Hold it right there. Put your hands up where I can see them." He stared at Randy, tossed the bullhorn back inside the car, and approached with measured steps. He looked him over, walking behind, then back to face him. He looked around inside the car. Then, with an expression of mock amazement, he stared directly into his face. "What the hell's the matter with you boy? Are you drunk or on dope? When you see blue lights, you're s'pozed to pull over, right then!"

"Oh no sir, I was just riding and looking for a place to eat lunch. I guess I wasn't paying attention," Randy replied, his voice quavering.

"When you operate a motor vehicle on my streets, you'd better pay attention one hundred percent! I think maybe you just didn't want to stop 'cause you're hiding something. Where you from anyway? Let's see some ID."

"Can I put my arms down?"

"Yeah, go ahead. You ain't toting nothing but a billfold and maybe a pocketknife. I can tell that already."

Randy handed the man his license. The officer studied it for a moment. "Now you walk right around here to the back of the car," motioning with his large head, dark and greasy as a pot roast. "Turn around and lean forward with your hands on the trunk. Go on, I don't want to put the cuffs on you. Don't you move till I tell you to. You got that?"

Randy said, "Yessir." He heard the officer walking back toward the patrol car, and he could hear the radio squawking over the traffic noise. He knew they were checking his license and the registration of the Ford and realized there might be a problem, but he remembered the old man's words before he left: "If you get into trouble call me. . . ."

Minutes dragged by before he heard the doors of the patrol car open and shut and steps approaching from behind. A tingling in his spine prompted him to rise and turn. The response was immediate: "Hold it right there," the large-headed officer barked. "Turn yo'self back around!" Randy obeyed; then both men were against him, pushing him onto the trunk and pulling his arms back behind him.

"It looks like I'm gonna have to use these after all," grunted the officer as he snapped the cuffs around Randy's wrists. "It seems that besides prowling around the mill village and scaring the women, you also a damn car thief. Ain't no telling what all you been up to on your way down here from Pittsburgh. But your little spree's about over boy—you know that? We fixing to put a stop to your business. C'mon here, get in the back of that police car. We going to City Hall."

The men's efforts were uncoordinated as they pulled him upright. "Can I have a chance to explain?" Randy asked, struggling for balance.

"Yeah," said the other officer, who was shorter than the first one and not much older than Randy. "But not now. Let's go."

He pushed Randy into the back seat. The other man got behind the wheel and began talking into the radio in what seemed like another language made up of grunts and barks. Randy's head was pounding. He couldn't understand the gibberish over the roaring inside his skull. He took a few deep breaths to control his voice. "I want to make a phone call. You will allow me that, won't you?"

The tall officer replied, "You just hush up now, boy. We'll be asking the questions from now on."

Randy continued taking deep breaths. His surroundings dissolved into a blur until they arrived in the middle of the old downtown section. The three-story brick building was crumbling at its edges. Ornate with columns, vaulted windows, and domes atop each corner, it seemed out of place with its modest surroundings. Looking up, Randy saw, at the top of the domed clock tower, a tarnished bronze statue of Blind Justice holding her scales.

They marched him through the oak-paneled front entrance and down a long, marble-floored corridor. At an intersecting hall, the men guided him through a door marked, "Police Department." They pushed him down onto a metal folding chair where he sat while the officers laughed and talked behind a high counter. There was a woman back there too, the radio operator. Randy saw her just before he sat down, and he could also make out another man's voice. He wondered if all that talk was about him. Surely, they would soon decide it was all a mistake.

Other policemen came and went while he sat in that hard chair with his hands cuffed behind him. One stood looking at him for a moment before disappearing through a different door. Randy's wrists, arms, and back ached.

Another policeman, who wore his uniform in a more casual way with less hardware around his waist, came around the corner. His hair was black and wavy, graying at the sides, and combed straight back. He was older and heavier than the officers who'd arrested him. Randy noticed his name tag: Capt. Bidwell. This new officer smiled pleasantly. "Hello young man. Let's you and me go have a little talk." He helped Randy up from the chair, then removed the handcuffs. "I don't guess we'll be needing these."

He led Randy into a sparsely furnished room. "We'll have more privacy in here," he said, pointing to a chair as he positioned himself on the opposite side of the table. He switched on a glaring lamp. "Now, why don't you tell me what you're doing in Prathersville, prowling around that neighborhood, and why you're driving a car registered to Mr. Ben Stempton?"

"Mr. Stempton loaned me his car," Randy began, blinking. "I work for him, and he sent me into town to have some fun. If I could just call him, we could straighten this out."

"Well, son, there's a slight problem with that. We've been trying to call him since the officers radioed in the tag number, to ask him if his car was missing, but we haven't been able to get an answer. Maybe we'll try again later. Right now, I'd be interested in knowing how you got hooked up with this Mr. Stempton in the first place, you coming from Pittsburgh and all. Y'all related or something?"

Randy recounted his story. He told about the orphanage and foster families, coming to Georgia to look for his uncle, meeting the old man and moving into the vacant shack, helping the old man with cutting and hauling pulpwood, and finally the "holiday" he'd been given with spending money and the loan of the car. He even mentioned meeting a girl the night before and used this as an excuse for his odd behavior in the mill village. "She gave me her address," Randy explained, "and since I'm not familiar with this town, I was just trying to find her place, in case I ever wanted to come back and visit. I didn't mean to scare anyone or cause any harm."

The policeman listened with what seemed to be mock interest at first, but as the telling progressed, he leaned forward with furrowed brow. After a while, he began resting his head against the fingertips of one hand then the other, alternating elbows on the table as he listened and stared. This silent scrutiny continued after Randy finished talking.

Finally, he sat erect, slapped both palms on the table and stood up. "That's a damn good story, boy. I'm tempted to believe it, really tempted. It's too farfetched to be made up, but then again, you could be more clever than I'm giving you credit for. You see, most people, when they lie, try too hard to make their story seem believable. Fact is, ain't nothing in real life very realistic. Everything that's real is really kinda strange, and that's what your story is, boy—strange. Either it's got to be true or you're an exceptional liar. I'm gonna think about it while we keep trying to contact Mr. Stempton. Maybe we'll make a call up to Family Services in Pittsburgh. We're gonna check this out real good. In the meantime, though, we got this slight problem of what to do with you. I wouldn't want to tempt you with the notion of trying to slip out of here, so I guess I'd better put you downstairs till we can find out something. C'mon—we'll have to go back to the front counter for our registration procedure, then we'll escort you down to our guest rooms."

★★★

The slamming shut of the iron door made Randy feel small and alone. Before bringing him down, they stripped him of his few belongings, even his belt. "Wouldn't want you getting depressed and trying to harm yourself," was the explanation given, although he hadn't asked. To question these people seemed unthinkable. It had been that way in the orphanage: obedience was required and expected. Challenging the nuns' authority brought swift and unpleasant consequences. Randy tried not to think about the possible consequences of disobeying the Prathersville Police Department. The officers carried those nightsticks for a reason, and he felt sure they'd welcome a chance to use them, especially that large-headed one who'd shouted through the bullhorn.

Randy's imagination tormented him as he waited, pacing in that tiny cell. Images came to him of southern chain gangs and shotgun-toting guards who encouraged their prisoners to escape so they could shoot them and bury them in the swamp. He wondered if they had really tried to call the old man. Then a new fear: would the old man even come to his aid? Maybe this was all part of some set-up conceived to reduce him to even lower levels of slavery and degradation. How did this happen? How did he manage to end up in a stinking jail without doing anything wrong?

Time dragged on. His frustration turned into anger as minutes became hours. Pent-up emotions prompted him to grab his cell door and rattle it hard. A gruff response came unexpectedly, a strange voice that rang out from another cell across from him: "Hey, cut out the racket! I'm trying to get some rest over here."

Randy, startled, turned to locate the voice. The jail consisted of two rows of three cells, facing each other across a corridor wide enough to accommodate the opening of the doors. The other "guest" was across from him, on his left at the other end. He hadn't noticed the man over there lying on his bunk because of the angle and the obstructing rows of bars. Now he felt embarrassed, as if he'd been discovered doing something childish or private. He finally managed to answer, "I'm sorry. I didn't know anyone else was in here."

"It's okay kid, don't worry about it. I just hate to see you get all worked up when it don't do no good." The man spoke without lifting himself from his bunk. The iron bars gave the voice a ring. "They can use that against you, you know, acting crazy like that. They ain't gon' let you out till they good and ready, and if you act like a young buck, it only makes it worse." The man lifted himself, then swung his legs over the side. He walked across his cell as far as he could toward Randy, put his face between the bars and began to speak in a hoarse whisper: "They can see and hear everything you do in here, boy. They watching us right now. Look up above you, right in the middle of the hallway there."

Randy glanced upward. The hallway between the cells was without overhead bars, open all the way to the old wooden ceiling. Puzzled, he looked back at the man and saw his whiskered face clearly for the first time. The expression was earnest. "Right there, about middle ways—straight up so's they can look all around. It ain't real obvious. You see it?"

"Uh, yeah, I think I do now." Really, all he saw was an old porcelain light fixture, a forgotten appendage, bulbless and painted over with many layers of paint.

"Yep, they can see into every nook and cranny of this jail anytime they want. They can hear us too, but I don't care. They've already done all they can to me. I just want to warn you before it's too late, before you do something that'll sneak up from behind and kick out your props." With this, the man turned and went back to his bunk. Randy watched him for a moment then looked up at the ceiling again. There was nothing there but that fixture, smooth and painted over like the boards it was attached to.

He sat down on the edge of his bunk and rubbed his pounding head as it filled with questions: *What happened to that guy? What did he do to end up here? Most likely nothing. He was probably minding his own business, like I was, and they arrested him, locked him up, and he's been here so long he's lost his mind. That's what'll happen to me, or I'll starve to death sitting here and they'll find me about a week later and throw me in the swamp and that'll be the end of it, my life over with nothing to show for it and nobody to even care or remember me.*

He'd not eaten since breakfast, and his stomach churned as if it were trying to digest itself. A burning, metallic bile rose in his throat, causing him to swallow over and over. When he got up and walked to the toilet to spit, he almost regurgitated. His body shuddered as he clamped his jaw shut. He overcame the urge and turned away from the toilet to glance up again at the bare light fixture. He didn't want anyone to see him vomit, and, even though he knew there were no hidden cameras or microphones there, he was glad he'd held it down.

He refreshed himself at the lavatory by splashing his face and drinking a little water, but there was still nothing to do but think. He alternately paced and sat on the edge of the bunk. When he tried to lie down, he had to raise himself after a minute because of the burning in his stomach and throat. He tried to ignore the incoherent mutterings from the other cell. He discovered a comfortable way to sit on the bunk with his back against the wall and his legs extended. He was just beginning to relax when he heard a door open and footsteps on the stairway.

A husky young woman came into view carrying a box. She had short, sandy hair and was dressed in slacks and shirt like the policemen but without a gun or badge. "Got y'all a little something to eat here," she declared as she put the box down in front of Randy's cell. She brought out a sweaty paper cup. "Iced tea," she said handing it through the bars. "And I don't know what this is, but it smells good." She slid a paper plate covered with tin foil under the door, then picked up the box again.

As she was about to proceed Randy said, "Thanks . . . I mean, wait. Could you tell me if they've found out anything yet—about me, I mean—and when I might get out of here?"

"We're real short-handed this evening, and nobody told me anything. I just help out with the radio and paperwork and stuff."

"But they were supposed to be trying to contact Mr. Stempton— that's the man I work for—and that was hours ago, and I didn't even do anything—"

"I don't know about that, and I'm not supposed to be talking to you. Why don't you just eat your supper and relax. I'll try to send one of the guys down later, if we have time." She finished speaking as she walked away, carrying her box toward the last cell where the other man was rising from his bunk.

Randy bit the inside of his lip while he watched their exchange. The man said something to the woman about that food making him chase his tail. "Is that right," she replied as she quickly slid his plate under the door then moved away with her empty box.

As she approached Randy's cell, he said, "Please help me. I need to get back tonight. They're expecting me, and Mrs. Stempton needs her car for church in the morning."

She only paused for a second, but her face softened. "I'll do what I can. Now eat your supper."

Randy found encouragement in these words. He felt sure he would soon be on his way. He only hoped that Mrs. Stempton wouldn't be too disappointed in him. Surely she would realize that it was all a misunderstanding and these Prathersville cops were an incompetent bunch. He unwrapped his supper plate and dug into the pinto beans, cornbread, and fried potatoes. Feeling better, he sat back to await his release.

Nothing happened, though, except the glacial grating of empty time. He was deep into the night and his pacing when the man in the other cell began to laugh out loud. "That girl's gon' get you out, ain't she boy? She's up there right now talking to people and working on your behalf, ain't she?" Then the laughter returned, high and hysterical, like a zoo full of monkeys.

Randy replied loudly, "I'll be out of here before you. I'll betcha that!"

The man laughed even harder, then abruptly stopped. "Sure you will, but that ain't saying much cause I ain't gon' never get out. I been in here so long, I done turned into this place. I am the jail and this jail is me. That's why it don't bother me none being in here, no more'n it bothers an old oak tree to stand in one place all the time." His words came in a monotonic rush as he pressed against the bars. "The tree is, and I am. Can you understand that, boy? When you understand that, then you'll know something, and they won't be able to get to you. See, that girl they sent down is part of your punishment, to get your hopes up so you'll be disappointed and weaker later on. Don't nothing go unpunished in here. You're even punished for your thoughts." His eyes had grown large in their black sockets. He narrowed them, lifting his whiskered cheeks into a grotesque grin. "You 'member dat." He nodded quickly to punctuate this imperative before turning his back and walking to the other side of his cell.

"Yeah right, I'll try to remember that," Randy answered before throwing himself back on his bunk.

After a while a rising tide of fatigue began to lap at the underside of his consciousness. Anxiety was slowly submerged as the edges of his thoughts were washed over and blurred. Just before dawn, he went completely under and slept that way until a fatherly voice came to him from a distance. "You need to wake up now, son," said the heavy-set policeman, Captain Bidwell. "We need to have another little talk."

Randy jerked himself upright, rubbing his eyes and blinking. He glanced right and left, then back at the officer. "Can I get out now?" he asked.

"Yes, but we've got something to discuss before you leave, and you'll want to get your things. I'll be waiting for you at the top of the stairs, in the room on the right."

He left Randy alone, with the cell door open, to get himself organized and presentable. It didn't take long to splash himself and do what he could with the limited facilities, and, as he stepped out of the cell, he was exhilarated at the sight of blue sky through the window at the end of the corridor. Then the man in the other cell spoke: "So, you think you can leave that easy, do you?"

"Yeah, I'm pretty sure I can."

"Well, don't you let nothing knock your props out, and be careful what you say to that old man up there. He's full of the devil."

"Okay—I mean yes sir, I will. I'll remember everything you told me, and I appreciate all the good advice. You take care now." As he started up the stairs, the man's laughter followed him, becoming hysterical like before, but when Randy passed through the door at the top, he couldn't hear it anymore.

The policeman ushered him into the sparsely furnished room of the previous interview. "Come on in, son, and have a seat. This won't take but a minute."

As Randy sat down, he noticed his belt, billfold, change, the car keys, and the Tree Brand pocketknife the old man had given him neatly laid out on the table top. Puzzled by the need for this second interview, he looked expectantly at Captain Bidwell.

The man's voice was that of a patient parent: "First, let me apologize, for keeping you so long. The night-shift boys don't always follow through with things and we were two men short and that new girl on the radio don't know her ass from a hole in the ground. Anyway, I'm sorry you had to stay in there all night. You didn't deserve it."

"So, you were finally able to contact Mr. Stempton?"

"Well . . . no." The man looked directly into Randy's eyes, then down at his meaty hands, fingers interlocked on the tabletop. He opened his hands, took a breath. "You see, there's been an accident. Mr. Stempton's dead."

Randy felt blood draining from his face and his body growing heavier in its lower portions. He gripped the edge of the table.

"It was one of those freaky things," the policeman explained, "that should never have happened. He was in the woods yesterday morning loading his truck. He was trying to hook the loader cable around a big log and the winch must have got knocked into gear or maybe the cable slipped, and he was trying to rehook it while it was still in gear—that's the way they figure it, anyway—and somehow that cable got wrapped around him and just kept on winding in. It cut him practically in two, right through the middle."

Randy looked down at his white knuckles and shook his head. The man continued: "I'm really sorry. You see, that's why we ended up keeping you so long. We couldn't get an answer at the Stempton place. By the time we started calling, the sheriff had done come and got Mrs. Stempton and took her to identify the body. Then she had to take care of the arrangements. Nobody on the evening shift remembered to keep trying the number like I told 'em to. I meant to check with Sheriff Tucker over there myself, but when I got off duty I got sidetracked, I guess."

"I was supposed to have the car back last night," Randy answered. "Mrs. Stempton needed it for church. They were expecting me."

"I know, son. She told me all about it this morning over the phone. She's a mighty sweet lady, and she spoke highly of you. Said Mr. Stempton was always bragging about you and how proud he was that you come along and took an interest in helping him. She'll need you now, to help her through this time of grief. And she did mention the car and having it back this afternoon for the funeral. I believe she'll want you there with the family."

Randy placed his arms on the table. His hands trembled. He started to speak, stopped, then started again. "I guess I don't like funerals. I've never really been to one, except my parents', and I don't remember it. I'm afraid I won't know what to do or say."

"You'll know when you get there. It'll all come natural. Funerals are hard things, all right, but they can be joyous times too when families are brought closer together. You'd better get your things and go on now. They'll be expecting you."

Walking through the door of the city hall building into the bright morning sunlight was like entering a different world. Everything was changed, and he felt a new kind of dread. The old man had placed a responsibility on his shoulders much heavier than the pulpwood logs he'd grown accustomed to carrying. Still, he wasn't really obligated. They weren't even that close, and he had never been treated like family. But when he thought about the policeman's words, Randy knew that getting the car back was the least he could do.

He drove back to Maggie's Café to get his bearings. Sipping coffee, his next step became apparent. He had to go back to the shack. All his things were there, and he desperately needed a bath. There was no need to think beyond this, and he was tired of thinking anyway.

He tried to focus on the immediate need, but his mind had become a three-ring circus. Images of the old man working, talking, and then being cut in two with the loader cable kept him from enjoying his bacon and eggs. He tried to imagine how it might have happened. Then, between bites, Stacy popped into his mind, bringing a painful longing. Her smile was dominant for a while and snatches of their conversation reverberated until the image of her boyfriend Ty, surly and jealous, came to the forefront. Other thoughts and pictures came and did their tricks: the jail and the paranoid man in the other cell, Mrs. Stempton crying, the fatherly policeman whose image melted into the large-headed one shouting through that bullhorn . . . then Randy realized his plate was empty. The sounds of a busy café returned—the clinking of silverware, laughter, the hum of a dozen conversations. He paid his bill and made his way outside into the sunlight, back to the old man's Ford.

As he rolled along the highway toward the shack, the familiarity of the scenery—parched pastures, grazing cows, weathered barns and farmhouses—allowed the circus of thoughts to return. His eyes felt scoured from within when he finally steered the Ford into the bare yard and parked beneath the oak trees. When he glanced up at the porch, dappled in shade, he blinked and rubbed his eyes to make out what he thought he saw there: the still image of a man in front of the door.

The figure didn't move as Randy watched from the car, but after a moment it swayed and turned as if to face him. It became startlingly apparent that there was no head atop the straight shoulders, and there was something wrong with the body as well. Randy stared, horrified, for another moment before he recognized the true nature of the specter: a suit of clothes was hanging from a rafter, and as it swayed in the breeze, he saw what appeared to be a sheet of paper attached to the lapel.

When he stepped out of the car the hound pups, fat and sleek, greeted him playfully, bumping and wriggling against his shins and pulling on his pants and shoelaces. "Go on, dogs," Randy implored, pushing them out of the way with feet that shuffled across the bare yard. As he mounted the steps, the suit caught the breeze again and turned to offer the note. Blue-inked words, painstakingly formed in a wavering cursive:

Randy, these clothes belonged to our son but he never wore them. I think they'll fit you about right. I thought you might need something to wear to the funeral which will be at 4 this afternoon. We need you to drive the family car and I want you to be a pallbearer.

Yours in Christ,
Bea Stempton

Chapter 4

The scene at the Stempton home place was not what he expected. There were people everywhere. Men were standing around outside talking in small groups, and the front porch was full of ladies fanning themselves with cardboard fans. As soon as he parked the Ford and got out, he felt that everyone's eyes were on him. The ill-fitting navy-blue suit, with sleeves and pants that were too short, added to his embarrassment. He was surprised to see so many people talking and laughing. He'd imagined a few old people sitting quietly with folded hands, whispering, praying, or singing hymns, but these people were chatting, telling stories, and even joking.

As Randy walked past them, tugging at his sleeves, the men acknowledged him by nodding their heads or saying, "Howdy." The hearse was parked next to the house, headed out. It also seemed to watch as he approached the front porch steps, its chrome grill a confident grin. A lady got up from her chair and walked toward him. She hugged him tightly. "Come here to me, young man. The last time I seen you, I was changing your diaper."

When she stopped squeezing, he answered, "My name's Randy. You must have me confused with someone else."

She held him at arm's length. "Oh my, I'm sorry. I thought you was Timmy Stempton, come home from Atlanta to his daddy's funeral, but I don't reckon he's got here yet. Whose boy are you?"

"I'm not from around here. I've been working for Mr. Stempton the last month or so."

"Oh yes, of course. I heard Bea mention you just now. I know she'll be proud that you're here. She's inside the parlor with the casket. Poor soul, she's been right by his side since last night when they brought him in."

The mood was different inside. Folding chairs were placed in every spot possible, and the occupants sat quietly or talked softly, nodding their heads in sympathy. A group of five or six stood near the casket, massive in the center of the room. As Randy tried to find an inconspicuous place to stand, he recognized Mrs. Stempton from the back. She stood looking into it, occasionally reaching inside with stroking movements. A sobbing young woman pressed to her side led her away, stooped and shuffling, to two empty chairs in the corner. When they turned, Randy caught a glimpse of something familiar. The young woman wore sunglasses even though the room wasn't brightly lit, and by her hair, cheekbones, and mouth he recognized her as Stacy, the girl from the bar.

The shock immobilized him. He stood for several moments before an elderly gentleman approached him and shook his hand. "Hello young man. How are you on this sad day?"

"I'm okay, I guess. How are you?"

"Oh, I'm fine. When you get to be my age, these things become routine. I probably average about two funerals a week now, but this one is especially sad since it came so sudden. I thought you was Ben's son, but I see now that you're not."

"No. I just work for him—"

"That's right, I remember Bea mentioning you, what a fine boy you were and how you were to be a pallbearer and drive the family car today. You'd better go on over and let her know you're here. She's been expecting you."

Randy looked to the corner of the room at the two women he knew there, and they noticed him at the same time. Their smiles were sad, warm, and eerily similar. Mrs. Stempton stood first, opening her arms to Randy. Then Stacy was up at her side. Randy walked toward them. "I knew you wouldn't let us down," Mrs. Stempton said in his ear as she hugged him tightly.

Stacy said, "Oh Randy, I knew it was you when Momma told me about the young man from up north who was working for Daddy. I'm glad you're here. I knew I'd see you again, but I didn't think it'd be like this."

Warmth permeated his body as if the afternoon sun had settled in his belly. His skin was already hot and sticky from the late summer heat, but now his bones began to thaw and loosen in a marvelous way.

When they had finished hugging, Stacy found another chair and Randy sat down between the women. In their mutual amazement they talked about Mr. Stempton and what a fine, hardworking man he'd been. When Stacy mentioned her brother Timmy, Mrs. Stempton said, "I don't think I'll be able to forgive him if he don't show up at his daddy's funeral."

Then everyone stopped talking and turned at once to look at a compact man in a dark suit who entered the room decisively. His manner bespoke refinement among rubes: "I need to see the pallbearers, please. All pallbearers meet with me in the kitchen." He turned and left the room, walking briskly down the hall toward the rear of the house.

Mrs. Stempton patted Randy's knee. "That's you, son, you'd better go on back. It's almost time now."

The funeral director sounded as if he were reading from a script as he gave instructions and pinned a white carnation to each man's lapel. Randy recognized one of the men from the pulpwood yard as someone the old man often talked and joked with. They acknowledged each other with a nod. The pallbearers followed the compact man back into the parlor and took their places on either side of the casket.

Randy, positioned at the head, glanced down at the old man's face. It looked like a wax figure he'd seen in a museum once, with an expression about the mouth that was completely foreign. Then the director and a young assistant, fat and pimply-faced, came to close the lid. Randy stepped back to give them room. When it was fastened securely, the director turned, cleared his throat, and addressed all who could hear:

"Would everyone please rise. We are now ready to take the body of Mr. Stempton to its final resting place. After the coffin is placed inside the hearse, the immediate family will lead the procession, which will follow the deceased to the Living Waters Cemetery for the graveside service."

Then the man stepped back, turned to face the pallbearers, and nodded as a signal for them to begin their task. Randy, when he took hold of the handle, was surprised at the weight of the thing. The men lifted and shuffled awkwardly to turn the casket and get it out of the room. Everyone was standing back out of the way, except for Mrs. Stempton and Stacy, who were still seated, hugging, and trying to comfort each other.

Randy and the men crossed the porch and front steps and loaded their burden into the back of the hearse. They stood there awaiting further instructions; then Randy realized he knew what to do. He went to the old man's Ford, started it, and brought it around to the front of the house and waited with engine idling. It occurred to him that he should be standing when Mrs. Stempton came out and he should open the door for her and Stacy.

Mrs. Stempton leaned on her daughter as they crossed the porch. Another lady, older than Mrs. Stempton, walked with them, and the people who had been chatting hushed themselves and stood as if in the presence of saints. Randy went around to the passenger side and opened the rear door. Mrs. Stempton and the lady got in the back while Stacy waited. He experienced a moment of puzzlement before he thought to open the front door for her.

When everyone was seated, the ladies began telling Randy what to do. The one he didn't know said, "Back the car around that way—just don't run into the flower bed—then pull out right behind that hearse. We don't want nobody to get between us."

Randy glanced at Stacy who said with an indulgent half-smile, "This is Aunt Ruth, my daddy's sister. Aunt Ruth, Randy Walls, from Pittsburgh."

"I know who he is. Your momma's already told me all about him. Randy, I'm pleased to meet you, and I'm proud that you could be here for us today. I only wish . . . well, it don't do no good to fret over it."

"Pleased to meet you," Randy replied, backing the car around as she had instructed. Then he drove out the gravel drive and onto the dirt road in front of the house, pulling up behind the hearse, which was moving very slowly in a futile attempt to keep the dust down.

It was hot in the car and having the windows down circulated hot, dusty air. "I wish this car was air conditioned," Aunt Ruth said. "I told Ben when he bought it to get one with air conditioning, but he was stubborn about things like that. Said the purpose of an automobile was to get you from place to place, not keep you cool. He never was much concerned with being comfortable, bless his heart."

"Daddy always thought that having too many luxuries spoiled people and made 'em soft. He didn't have much use for anybody who couldn't put in a good day's work outside in the heat."

"I know, I know. He was a hard man in many ways, but I'm convinced of the love in his heart. He always wanted what was best for his children."

The conversation continued, mainly between Stacy and her aunt, about the old man and how he had been. Mrs. Stempton occasionally sobbed or said, "Yes, yes."

Then Stacy said, "Turn your lights on, Randy," as they came to the end of the dirt road and were turning onto the blacktop.

Randy replied, "Oh," as he pulled out the knob. The road was straight and uphill for about a half mile. In his rearview he could see the fifteen or twenty cars that followed with their lights on. As they crested the rise, a great distance unfurled before him: an expanse of mottled green, brown, and red farmland between them and the green line of trees on the horizon. The sky above, threatening a thunderstorm, provided dark contrast. This panorama seemed patterned, like pieces of a puzzle, except the edges were imprecise, frayed and smudged.

He could see the church jutting out from a little rise just ahead, its steeple piercing the black cloud that was forming. The white, clapboard-sided structure, twice as long as it was wide, spoke of a different era. The main roof was high and steep. A smaller roof with the same pitch extended over the front porch. Randy noticed the stained-glass windows along the side as they followed the gravel drive to the sloping grounds behind the building.

A blue canvas canopy imprinted in white with the name *J. Dougherty and Son* was erected on poles over the freshly dug grave. When the hearse pulled over and stopped near the grave, Randy did the same. Not knowing what to do next, he sat there with the family while the other cars filed in and parked. Aunt Ruth tried to comfort

Mrs. Stempton, who'd begun sobbing again. "Come on, dear," she said, "we'd better go sit down now. The people are starting to gather."

This was a cue for Randy to get out and open the door for the ladies. In his haste, he stumbled. The older ladies stepped out and shuffled toward the grave. Stacy didn't wait but opened and shut the door herself. She placed her hand on his shoulder. "You'd better go on over to that hearse and wait for the other pallbearers. I expect y'all will be carrying Daddy out pretty soon." The dark glasses covering her eyes could not hide the tremble in her voice.

He joined the other men with flowers in their lapels, and they assumed their burden under the compact man's watchful direction. Randy wondered if that man was J. Dougherty or his son, but the thought quickly left as the sloping terrain required his full attention. He stumbled through a panicky moment as they approached the canopy. A metal apparatus, threatening in appearance, was positioned over the grave, but as they approached it an understanding of its purpose and how to release his share of the burden came to him.

Afterwards he took his place with the other men, just inside the canopy across the grave from the seated family members. He and Stacy exchanged glances over the coffin. She showed the hint of a sad smile, and he was proud of her courage. He noticed the empty chair beside her and the sobs of her mother and thought for an instant of going to them, but he knew it wouldn't be right. Beyond the small crowd that surrounded the canopy, he could see the big Honda parked in the driveway with Ty propped against it in his boots and jeans. Randy stared for a moment; then the preacher started speaking.

He was a large, barrel-shaped man with a bald head and sweaty brow. His voice echoed the thunder which rumbled in the distance. He talked at length, mostly about how the old man's "abiding faith in our Lord and Savior Jesus Christ" had assured him a place in the "Kingdom of Heaven." Once he raised his Bible with one hand, made a fist with the other, and shouted out, "O death, where is thy sting? O grave where is thy victory? Thank you, Jesus! Thank you, Jesus!"

Randy had never heard such preaching, and he was startled when several people answered loudly, "Amen!" He understood that the words were meant to comfort the grieving family. He looked at Mrs. Stempton and saw she'd stopped crying and was sitting erect.

The preacher's cadence rose and fell. In the low points, he wiped his brow with a rumpled handkerchief as if to punctuate an important point. Randy's eyes shifted, focusing briefly on individual details: the coffin; Stacy; the faces gathered outside the canopy; Ty, still propped against the motorcycle. As the preacher came to a brow-wiping pause, a lone crow cawed from somewhere in the darkening sky.

Randy, mind wandering, fingered the car keys inside his pocket. When the preacher waved his handkerchief at the expanse and read from Psalms—"I will lift up mine eyes unto the hills, from whence cometh my help"—Randy was thinking about the old man, wondering how in the world he could have let himself get cut in two like that.

Part II—Ty and Stacy

Chapter 5

Ty Ragsdale's motorcycle pumped each exhaust note into the surrounding atmosphere through four straight pipes. As he left the cemetery, he had the decency to idle out the gravel drive to the blacktop. He was the first to leave. Friends and family were mingling and hugging around the grave, but that stuff wasn't for Ty. He had done enough by showing up. Now it was time to move, to get away from death. Stacy would understand because she knew how he was and loved him no matter what. He'd made her love his toughness, and he was confident of the bond his hardness had forged. He thought about loving her roughly later that evening—Sunday evenings were supposed to be their time—but he realized she may not be able to get away from all those people.

His third-shift job required him to report at 11:00 p.m., leaving him the intervening hours to be free. He was rested and full of energy, having gone to bed early the night before. He wanted to be with his girl now, to release energy and passion and mold her to his desire.

He couldn't help but think of those funeral people as encroachers, especially the stranger in the blue suit. The image of him driving the family car and carrying the casket burrowed its way to the forefront of Ty's thoughts as he eased the Honda off the church grounds onto the paved road. He'd noticed him in the bar Friday night, and now he was standing under the canopy with the family. Ty also noticed Stacy looking at this stranger. She'd been attentive to him in the bar also, even though she gave no indication of knowing him as an old family friend or cousin. These thoughts produced the vague sense that something wasn't right. Turning onto the blacktop road, he twisted the throttle back as far as it would go, wicking up the power between his legs, as his left hand and foot worked in synchronization, snatching the mechanical beast through its gears to a landscape-blurring speed. The four pipes hammered out their staccato notes in rising pitch. He knew the people heard, could not help but hear, the bellowed message: "Don't get in my way or mess with what's mine!"

Soon the funeral was far behind and his peripheral vision was narrowed by the Honda's velocity. All that remained was the narrow strip of twisting pavement in front, treacherous with its curves and dips, requiring all his concentration. He could outrun anything on these curvy back roads. He handled the turns with such aggression that trails of sparks chased him around as the foot pegs of the steeply leaned machine were ground into the pavement.

He sometimes rode this way with Stacy on the seat behind him. He had taught her to trust him, giving her weight over and becoming neutral in the turns, an extension of his own body. She would clamp herself against him, thighs squeezing, chest pressed against his back. Her presence was hot and tense, but as far as handling the machine was concerned, he couldn't tell she was there.

Still, there was a special freedom he enjoyed without her. Now, after slowing to a moderate speed, Ty was leaning the bike from side to side, weaving along a straight stretch of road from one shoulder all the way to the other in an undulating rhythm. He wouldn't do this with her on board. She wouldn't understand. He didn't understand either, but he didn't question himself. He hated explaining or defending his actions to anybody, especially teachers, when he was in school, or his bosses at work. He had not finished high school for this reason, even though he had little trouble with the studies and was gifted in sports.

Whenever Ty remembered high school and why he'd quit, he always felt justified. That cocky little Coach Thompson deserved to be pushed into the wall that day when he'd gotten in his face about not doing the history project. A class presentation about World War II based on a personal interview with someone who'd been involved was a stupid assignment, and the skinny coach was stupid to expect him to go around interviewing old people. That war didn't matter. There was a new war now to worry about. The coach should have recognized that Ty was his own man with his own agenda centered around his job, the Ford coupe he'd fixed up, and girls—how to use them and move from one to the next.

The qualities that made Ty so appealing to the opposite sex were difficult to isolate. He embodied a mysterious blending of elements:

a hint of danger in his bearing, fine muscular definition, an infrequent smile that was challenging to provoke, and opaque brown eyes. And there was also his confidence, bolstered by the cumulative effect of his romantic conquests, that enabled him to continue talking with the boys about football or car engines when girls like Dawn Shumake or Natalie Price—objects of sexual fantasy for the other guys—flirted openly, practically offering themselves for his pleasure.

He first experienced this sexual power at age thirteen when Florene Otwell invited him to her home for a cold drink and a fried pie after he changed a flat tire for her on the side of Taylor's Gin Road. It was a blistering July afternoon, and Florene, damp and disheveled, had grown frustrated from struggling with the grimy jack and lug wrench. Ty had been riding his bicycle to his cousin Toby's house, which was only a short hike away from their favorite fishing spot: Dorsey Weaver's farm pond, a secluded place that often produced a stringer full of fat shellcrackers. He was on his way there to fish or maybe throw a baseball around with his cousin, who was his own age and full of the same kind of energy, just not quite as strong or sure of himself.

Ty's physical development was impressive: young muscles bulged under his tight jeans and sweat-dampened tee-shirt. He didn't hesitate in taking on the task of changing the tire, and he handled the jack and lug wrench with ease while Florene watched.

As he was tightening the last lug nut, the wrench slipped, misdirecting his applied strength. His right hand ground into the crunchy asphalt at the road's edge, scraping skin away from two middle knuckles. Florene winced.

"Shit!" said Ty as he held the injured hand with the other and pranced about in pain. "That hurt like hell!"

"Let me look at it," Florene said.

She took his hand in both of hers and carefully wiped away the grit with a Kleenex tissue. "It's not too bad, but we better put something on it. Let's go to my house. I can take care of it, and you can have something cold to drink and a homemade fried peach pie." She smiled and looked into his eyes.

The offer of a cold drink and fried pie was more appealing than having his hand doctored. He was always getting nicked, bruised, or scraped without benefit of medical attention, and the injuries took care of themselves. After the initial pain, business as usual. Since his mom left three years ago, he'd had few opportunities to enjoy homemade pie, or anything homemade for that matter. He and his dad ate mainly out of cans or occasionally at the truck stop.

There was no reason for not accepting. He didn't have a set time for arriving at his cousin's, and this was something new. As she held his hand to examine the knuckles, he breathed in the flowery fragrance of her hair. Florene's position before him in a pink tank top offered a deep view of plump breasts, damp from the heat, pressed together and restrained by the elastic of her bra, the top of which was visible beneath the plunging neckline. Flesh pressed and rose against fabric toward Ty as he held up the bloody knuckles for this woman to inspect and daub. Her speaking didn't break the spell. It took him several seconds to answer. "Yeah, that'd be great. I love peach pie."

As they loaded his bike into the trunk, Florene nervously glanced up and down the road. Once underway, she tried to make small talk. "You might know my son. I'd guess he's about your age. Name's Danny, Danny Otwell. I'm Florene by the way. What did you say your name was?"

"Ty Ragsdale. We—my daddy and me—live in town, in the mill village. That's why I don't know nobody that goes to Aaron County schools, except for my cousin Toby. He might know your boy."

"I'll bet he does. I'll mention that name to Danny when he gets home. He's gone off to summer camp. Won't be back for another week." She looked from Ty's face back to the road. "Seems like he's always got someplace to go now that he's older. Leaves his momma alone a lot. And his daddy—Tom, that's my husband's name—he's gone all the time, has to stay on the road. Travels all over the Southeast. It's a good job, though. He makes good money. Sells electrical stuff to supply houses. What does your daddy do?"

Ty looked out the window. "Construction work mostly. He's a real good carpenter, but sometimes there ain't no work. He can fix cars too, and different things. He does lots of different things."

Inside her home Florene was solicitous. "Come on," she said. "Let's go back to the bathroom and clean up that hand."

The bathroom was the fanciest one Ty had ever seen. The lavatory, tub, and toilet were a harvest gold color, and the floor was covered with ceramic tiles in a blue and gold pattern. On the top of the toilet tank, an extra roll of paper was covered in a blue and gold knit bonnet, encircled by a garland of tiny green leaves made of silk. The walls were adorned with framed pictures of gentlemen on horseback jumping over hedges. There was also a glass shelf with ceramic doves, an angel and a candle. Scented soaps in flower shapes—pink, red, and yellow—were heaped into a green bowl shaped like a fig leaf. Blue towels, perfectly folded, hung from glass rods with brass rosette ends, and the heavy fragrance of a woman's scented lotions, shampoos, and creams hung in the air.

She held his hand over the sink and poured on the hydrogen peroxide. As it sizzled, she asked, "Does it hurt?"

"Naa."

She patted the hand dry with a washcloth, applied Mercurochrome and a band-aid, stretching the strip gently across the knuckles and rubbing down the adhesive.

"There. That ought to do it. How does it feel?"

"Fine." Ty lifted his eyes to meet hers. She squeezed his hand gently and rubbed the back of it with her thumb.

"Let's go get you that cold glass of milk and fried pie."

After he'd eaten three of the pies and drunk a large glass of milk, she nervously began clearing the table.

"Well," she said, "I guess you need to be heading along your way, and I've got some chores to tend to."

Ty didn't move in his chair but looked at her face, meeting her eyes for a second before dropping his gaze to her bosom. His voice cracked slightly as he spoke: "I'll leave if you want me to, but maybe there's something else I could help you with."

She hesitated with her hand on the milk jug. Ty watched her chest rise and fall twice before she turned to walk to the fridge with the milk. When she turned back her face was flushed. She said softly, "I mean, you don't have to go. I just thought you might rather be out playing ball or something with your friends instead of inside here with . . . just me."

When she reached to gather up the saucer and napkin, he leaned closer in, allowing the side of his face to brush against the pink fabric of her top. She didn't pull away but turned toward him, and Ty shifted in his chair. Then her hand found the back of his neck and pressed with gently rubbing fingers into the stubble, skin, and ligaments. Their position was awkward, and Ty didn't know what to do next.

Florene dropped the saucer back on the table and swung her leg over his lap, straddling him in the chair. He put his face between her breasts. Both of her hands were behind his head now, rubbing his ears and neck, and pressing him into the tight fabric.

He wasn't hampered by shyness. His awkwardness was due only to inexperience, so he needed but little coaching. Florene had fanned the flames of his longing, kindled by pictures he'd seen in magazines and stories he'd heard at the pool hall, and now this freshly fueled energy animated him as he struggled for its release. She pulled him out of the chair and led him to her bedroom where they struggled together, this boy whose mother had left and this mother with a young son of her own and a husband who was absent, locked into each other and transformed into something—sticky, aching—much larger than the middle-class home whose walls could not contain the surging power of denied love and raging hormones. At last the energy was spent and they became who they were before, awkward and unsure, but profoundly changed.

Minutes passed before they spoke. Reassembly was done in silence. Then Florene smiled a mother's smile and smoothed his close-cropped hair. "This has to stay our little secret," she said. "That way we can do it again. If you don't see my husband's Chevy wagon under the carport, it's okay to stop. If Danny's here, he'll never suspect. We can just talk or maybe you could have some more pies and milk and we could say you're gonna do some work for me—yard work or painting in the back. I do need some work done. Maybe you could stop again, and we could talk about it."

Ty was ready to go. "Sure," he said, hurriedly tying his sneakers. It was late enough in the afternoon for the fish to be biting. He was eager to sit back in the shade and catch a few and think about what had just happened. Of course, Toby would never believe it, and it would be best not to tell him. But the boys talked about sex every day, sharing their fantasies and discussing the men's pool hall stories. Not sharing this would be difficult. Soon he was on his way—a thirteen-year-old boy going fishing with his cousin or to throw a baseball around and talk about whatever came to mind. Knowledge that he would never be the same swelled as he pumped the bicycle toward a childhood that was vanishing, receding into the fog that had claimed his momma, erased the man his daddy used to be, and sooner or later made everything disappear.

Chapter 6

Ty started working for Dorsey Weaver the same summer he met Florene, after he and Toby stopped by his place one afternoon in August. The boys carried their fishing poles, but Ty had other interests: he wanted to know if Dorsey could provide some paying work. They'd done chores for him before, such as helping old Sally Boone—grizzled and eerily silent in tattered overalls—load a stack of cast-off tires onto the truck. Once they helped clean some junk out of the loft to make more room for hay. Dorsey usually paid off in ice-cold Royal Crown colas from the drink box in the weathered building that served as both barn and shop, where his junkyard customers gathered. Sometimes he compensated the boys by letting them fish for free, a considerable privilege since he charged everyone else a dollar.

Dorsey, Sally, and a big black teenager they called Stinkum were busy trying to break the bead on a flat rear tractor tire when the boys approached and leaned their poles in the corner beneath the dusty hanging fan belts.

"What are y'all up to?" Dorsey bellowed, turning away from his work.

"We were going fishing, Ty replied, "but we thought y'all might need some help today."

"Hell, there's always more work around here than any six men can do, but I don't reckon you boys would be much good to me just yet."

Toby was turning to go back out the way he'd come in when Ty replied, "I guess I can do about anything y'all can, that is if somebody takes the time to show me."

"If I had time to show you, I might as well do it myself. Y'all go on down to the pond now so we can get something done."

"Let's go, Ty," Toby said.

"You go ahead. I'll be there afterwhile," Ty said to his cousin before speaking to Dorsey. "What about that pile of old starters and generators there. What y'all gon' do with them? You need me to load them on the truck or something?"

Dorsey paused thoughtfully. "Naw, that's Sally's job. He's got to get all the copper out so we can sell it now that the price is right. He's had to let it go, though, till we can get this damn tire fixed and he can finish bush-hoggin'."

Sally and Stinkum, who'd continued struggling with the tire, made sudden progress in forcing it to yield to their irons and hammers. "That's it!" Dorsey said. "Me and you can get it the rest of the way now, Stinkum, if you'll put some more soap around the bead. Sally, take this boy over there and show him how to get them starters apart. We need to get that copper out before the price drops."

Ty sat down on an overturned milk crate across from the grease and manure-smeared old man with tobacco-stained whiskers. Sally, using a few hand tools and fewer words, showed the boy what to do. Ty finished the day much later, driving the tractor with the newly-patched rear tire. Sally taught him how to weave the brush mower in and out of the pines and hardwoods at the pasture's edge in order to cut the saplings, vines, and briars that encroached on the cleared land.

Dorsey also sold recap tires, and Ty became proficient at mounting them, after being taught initially by Stinkum, the resident expert. Their method relied more on technique than equipment. Besides the manually operated bead-breaker, they used only hammers, irons, and skill. Ty got to where he could mount a set of tires in about half an hour, but he never reached the ultimate goal, despite his best efforts, of becoming as fast as Stinkum, who was four years older, bigger, and stronger.

By this time, Ty was enjoying attention from females, but the growing need for the approval of men and older boys sometimes drove him to do stupid things. One breezy Saturday afternoon in August they were working in Dorsey's hay field, trying to get the bales to the barn. Dorsey relied on the hired help to do the heavy work of loading the blocks of scratchy dried grass onto the flatbed truck that he drove gingerly through the rows and over the terraces. Ty, Sally Boone, and Toby were heaving bales that day, but Stinkum had the most demanding job of all, stacking them on the moving truck. This had to be done in a weight-bearing, interlocking way to keep the bales from tumbling to the ground. Stinkum had learned the techniques over the course of several hay seasons, and he took pride in his ability to get the hay to the barn without it falling off. Along with balance and patience, his job required endurance to keep up with the others who unrelentingly lifted the bales, one after another, onto the truck for him to place.

Stinkum's position grew precarious as the stacks got higher, and the placing of the bales had to be done ever more carefully. Dorsey grew impatient with having to stop the truck while the others waited before lifting their bales. At last, his voice boomed from inside the cab: "Hey Ty! What are y'all doing standing around while Stinkum does all the work? Get up there and help him so we can get to the barn sometime today."

Ty took this as a compliment, being singled out for special service. Obviously Dorsey was grooming him for new responsibilities. He climbed onto the truck, ready to show what he could do.

Stinkum said, "You stay there on the back where the stacks is lower. Lift 'em up here to me so's I can stack 'em right."

Ty looked to see if the others had heard Stinkum giving him orders. He took the spot and did as the older boy told him, but when Stinkum began to struggle near the front with getting a bale placed just so, Ty decided to expand his role. He took a bale from Toby and began to climb up the stacks to where Stinkum worked with his back turned. Moving with the heavy load on top of the stacked bales was harder than he'd anticipated, and he could feel Toby and Sally watching from the ground.

He saw a spot for the bale to go, just to the left of Stinkum. To push it up there would require better footing, so with effort he carried it up one more layer. He was behind the other boy now, and he only needed to make a lifting turn to get it into position. With both hands gripping the cords, Ty lifted the bale and, turning his torso, swung it toward Stinkum and the slot where he wanted it to go. At that moment the rolling truck lurched over a terrace, amplifying his motion. The bale struck Stinkum squarely in the back, causing him to release the weight his arms had been supporting. Ty's bale tumbled down to the next layer as the truck's lurch reverberated throughout. The tumbling was sudden, and before they had any chance at correction, the boys, along with eighty bales of hay, were on the ground in a pile that resembled the dumping out of a child's toy box.

The truck stopped. Ty, trapped inside that horrible moment, struggled frantically to get out from under the pressure and cruel scratching of the hay. They got to their feet at about the same time. Stinkum surveyed his wasted work with an incredulous expression. He turned to face Ty. In a voice loud enough for the others to hear he said, "You stupid son 'bitch. I told you to stay at the back of the truck. Now look what you done caused!"

Ty's response spewed out as the caustic distillation of injured pride: "You go to hell. I ain't got to take orders from no nigger."

A guttural "Uunhh" came from Stinkum as he erased the distance between them and, with the full force of his momentum, pushed Ty in the chest with both arms, sending the younger boy backwards over a bale. Ty, knocked breathless, reclined there for a few seconds with his feet resting on top of the bale as if it were a large ottoman. Then he began struggling for breath, pushing and kicking, scrambling to regain his footing before the others.

He launched himself into a frenzied attack, awkward and flailing. He blew snot from his nostrils like a crazed bull, and his eyes were large and strange. He was met by a knotted brown forearm coming up hard from underneath, stopping his mad charge and sending him once again backwards to the ground. The discharge from his nostrils turned red.

His movements were no longer frantic but slow, as if he were drugged. He rolled to his side and pulled his legs up to a fetal position. From there, he slowly managed a hands and knees posture while Stinkum watched over him, poised with fists clenched.

Ty crawled slowly away toward Dorsey. Blood thickly dripped from his nose into the grass and loose hay. Dorsey dropped to one knee, reached around his shoulder, and put a faded handkerchief to his face. Sally took a reluctant step toward Stinkum as if he might try to restrain him if the need arose. Toby stood by, stupefied.

Dorsey helped the injured boy to his feet as the others turned away. Stinkum looked at the ground and kicked at a clump of grass. Dorsey, with his arm around Ty's shoulders, walked him the few steps to the front of the truck where he talked in low tones and wiped his face with the handkerchief after wetting it with cold water. The others couldn't see Ty's shoulders shaking or the tenderness in Dorsey's face and hands. Not knowing what else to do, they began lifting the bales back onto the truck. Stinkum climbed up to his place, and soon it was over with nothing remaining but the cracked, sprouting seed of bitterness between Ty's shoulder blades. Silently, he helped with the re-stacking.

Chapter 7

Ty continued working after school started, a few hours each afternoon and all day on Saturday. He saved what money he could, although more and more was required for meeting their basic needs as his father slipped further into self-pity and the numbing effects of alcohol. Ty's money and other treasures were not safe around this man who often managed to find the hidden tin box, pop the lid, and take what he wanted for a night's drinking. Ty learned about paying bills and how to be devious about what money was left. More than once he took beatings for not coming forth with the $20 bill that would buy an evening's oblivion.

He worked hard, growing taller as his duties at Dorsey's increased. When Stinkum was called to the army, the second summer after the hay bales had tumbled, Ty was promoted to chief hay stacker. And there was another significant event to mark this season: the putting away of his bicycle in favor of an old car he had fixed up the previous winter.

It was a '54 Ford coupe, V8 with straight shift and overdrive. Ty had first spotted it in the junkyard during one of his early fishing adventures with Toby, about the time he started working for Dorsey. It looked as if it didn't belong there with the other rusty hulks. "Look at this old Ford!" he said to his cousin. "I bet I could get this baby running again."

"Yeah sure," Toby replied as he tried to raise the trunk lid.

Ty approached Dorsey that afternoon about the car. The booming response was, "Aw hell, that thing's got two burnt valves and a worn-out clutch. It was barely able to pull itself up the driveway when that fella drove it in here and left it. I was gonna fix it for him, but when I told him how much it was gon' cost, he said to hold off for a while. That was about two—oh, hell—three years ago. I ain't heard from him since. I finally dragged it off to the pasture with the rest of the junk to get it out of the way."

"I sure would like to have that car and fix it up myself," Ty said.

"It would take a lot of work to get that old thing in shape again."

"But it could be fixed, couldn't it?"

"Son, I reckon 'bout anything can be fixed if you put enough time, effort, and money into it. Question is, would you be able to invest what it takes, and would it be worth it if you did?"

"Well sure, I mean yessir. I can stick with something and work really hard when I get my mind made up."

"Well, we'll see."

Ty took that as yes. He began to make plans for the car, and a glorified image of it, powerful and shiny, formed in his mind. He held onto this vision throughout that summer and the following fall and winter. When the next summer rolled around, he began to worry Dorsey again about getting started on the project.

"You don't let go of nothing, do you boy?" Dorsey said one afternoon after they'd fixed the fence on the lower side of the pasture. "When we get done with the haying this time, we'll see about moving it into that empty stall on the back side of the barn. But listen now, I ain't paying you to work on that damned old car. You'll have to do that on your time, when we're caught up on other things." His voice boomed out from a large wooden box as he replaced the hammer, staples, and pry bar, rattling the loose boards and hinges. "I guess I could give you the car. . . ." He straightened, looked up at the dusty fan belts hanging from the rafters. "Let me back up a minute. I've been storing that thing all this time. Aw hell, I'll let you have it for $35. That's about what it'd bring as scrap. And I might help you a little with it, if I have time."

"Really?" Ty exclaimed. "And it'll be mine?"

The day finally came. They hooked the wrecker to the Ford and dragged it out of the briars and to the shop, as Dorsey had promised. The coupe's rotten tires remained re-inflated long enough for them to roll the forlorn hulk into the back stall where it would remain for many months before rolling out again under its own power, having benefited from hours of knuckle-busting effort. Dorsey directed Ty's work, usually from his cane-backed chair beside the wood heater.

Discouragement set in during late January when the disassembled engine was strewn across the grimy workbench and the transmission lay on the dirt floor. The amount of effort required to remove the parts and make necessary repairs was far greater than Ty had anticipated. His hands, cut and raw, hurt from handling cold steel and exposure to mineral spirits. Scraping off the grime and old gasket material was the worst part, along with fighting the rusted bolts that resisted removal to the point of shearing off, producing even greater difficulties and more pain. But Ty held tenaciously to his vision.

The engine was finally brought to life in early May, just days before Ty's fifteenth birthday. Dorsey's involvement was heightened during this phase of the project, and he reflected Ty's adolescent excitement as he helped with the various settings and adjustments. He sold Ty a new battery off the rack at a discount price, on credit against his next two paydays. The engine was tight and stiff with new, unseated parts and at first resisted the starter's spinning. Dorsey loosened a bolt, twisted the distributor a tad to the left, then boomed from under the hood, "Try it now!"

It hit sporadically a few times with powerful, angry reports. Dorsey made more adjustments and tightened a leaking fuel line.

Ty, inside the car, was like an expectant father. He cringed and held his breath as Dorsey called out, "Try it now!"

This time the engine came to life with a vibrant roar and revved smoothly as Dorsey worked the throttle linkage by hand. Ty marveled as it settled into a smooth idle.

Dorsey stepped out from under the hood beaming. "Sounds good, don't she? You done a fine job, boy."

"I, I . . . well, I guess I did. Is it awright? Is everything working like it's supposed to? When can I drive it?"

Dorsey smiled patiently. "She ought to run in for a few minutes, then we can check everything out real good. Let's take a break. I'll buy the RC's!"

With the car running, the problem arose of what to do with it. His dad had expressed disapproval of Ty's wasting money on an old car that "ain't never gon' be worth a shit." But he didn't know how extensive the repairs had been. Purchasing new engine parts, clutch, brakes, mufflers, tires, and a long list of miscellaneous items and shop supplies had depleted Ty's savings, and his take-home pay had been slashed to nearly nothing since almost all his time at Dorsey's was spent working off the clock. Ty worried over how his dad might respond if he brought the coupe home in its fresh vitality and parked it in the driveway beside the threadbare Falcon station wagon, their "family car" since before his mother left.

Ty's ace in the hole was the fact that even during the long winter of the project, he'd continued to pitch in a little, helping out with groceries and paying bills. There was another source of income that no one, not even Toby, knew about. Ty managed to make time to visit Florene about once a week. Her appreciation extended beyond fried pies and milk, and, after learning more about his situation at home, she was glad to slip him a twenty each time he stopped by.

When she first offered the money, he didn't want to take it. "Naa, I don't think that would be right. I like coming here and you always treat me real good. You don't need to give me money."

"I'm giving you this because I want to. Don't you need it? Don't you have bills to pay? I wouldn't feel right if I couldn't help out in some way, after what you do for me. You make me feel . . . well, you know. Let me do this for you. I've got a little money put away that Tom don't know about. It's the least I can do."

Thinking about trying to explain at home why he had no money after spending all those hours at Dorsey's made it easier for Ty to take the proffered bill. It was money that was already spent, and having it allowed him to buy parts for the coupe and avoid the heavy blows of his father. Reaching to accept the payment was painful, as if a part of him were being torn away, but the money bandaged the wound. The vision he carried of the coupe—powerful, with the ability to transport and transform—sustained him and justified the pain.

Ty knew from the first time he drove the car that they would become inseparable. Its grease had gotten into his blood as the blood from his hands had alloyed itself with the coupe's metal heart. The power of the engine magnified his personal power, making him much more of a man. Driving over back roads, giddy with excitement, he fantasized the admiration he would receive from Stinkum, Toby, the guys at school, and girls.

When this amplified Ty wheeled into the driveway, his dad was sitting on the front porch drinking a beer. He wiped his mouth on a soiled sleeve and tossed back his long, oily hair. "What you got there, boy?" he asked, stepping off the porch. He walked toward his son with an admiring grin.

"This is my car," Ty said, getting out. "It's what I've been working on all this time out at Dorsey's, and I paid for it with my own money."

"I see. Well, that's great. I'm proud of you. Let me take a good look here. Yeah, that's all right." He reached in through the window and worked the steering wheel back and forth. "She run good?"

"Yeah, runs great."

"I like them new tires. Guess they set you back some, huh? I sure would like to have new tires for the old Falcon there, but I just ain't got the money, what with paying bills and trying to keep food on the table."

"They're just cheap recaps. Dorsey let me have 'em at a discount."

"Uh huh, well, still a whole lot better than what's on my car. Mine's about slick as an onion. I could hear you coming up the road. Sounded real good. Got new glasspacks on there?"

"Yeah."

"'Yeah?' Ain't I taught you better'n that? You forget who you're talking to?"

"I mean, yessir."

"That's better. You know, it seems that you got a lot nicer vehicle than your old man." He stepped to the front of the car and raised the hood as he spoke. "Looka there: new plug wires, belts, hoses. And new gaskets everywhere. Y'all rebuild that whole motor?"

"Yessir."

"Damn! That's a fine thing, ain't it?" He slammed the hood. "Here I am, barely making ends meet, driving a beat-up old clunker, and my boy—who ain't even got a driver's license—rides around in this fine little coupe with new everything! Who you think you are, boy? You done forgot who the daddy is around here?"

"No sir, but—"

"They ain't no buts to it! This coupe's gonna be our car. I'll just sell the Falcon for whatever it'll bring and drive a decent car for a change. You'll get to drive it some, maybe. I'll take you to school in the mornings on my way to work. Yeah, that'll do. I believe I'll take her for a spin right now. Hop in on the other side if you wanna go."

Ty clenched his jaw as he shook his head and stepped between his father and the driver's door.

"I said get in on the other side or step out of the way. I'm gon' try out my new car."

Ty stood his ground. Having his back against the side of the coupe steadied him. "It's my car, Daddy," he said, "and I ain't gon' let you take it."

"You'll do what I say, you little shit!"

Ty anticipated the blow and blocked it. When the enraged adult moved in to grab him, Ty's knee snapped up, seemingly of its own volition. His father doubled over, leaning against him. Ty pushed with both arms, the car at his back magnifying his strength, and sent the man sprawling to the ground where he balled up like a roly-poly bug.

While the father writhed and moaned in agony, Ty scrambled into the coupe, started it, and backed out the driveway. His father was rising by the time he made it to the road and wheeled around in the right direction. He snatched the gear lever down into low and, in his haste, let the clutch out too quickly, stalling the engine. His daddy was on his knees now, shaking his fist and cursing. The starter strained to spin the engine. Ty's father made it to his feet and began to wobble, one hand cupped at his crotch, toward the road and his son in the stalled Ford.

Ty patted the gas pedal as he tried to start the engine. It coughed, sputtered, and ran erratically, belching black balls of smoke out the twin exhaust pipes. He got it to rev, finally, and with the engine clearing and his enraged father only a few steps away, he brought his foot up off the clutch, abruptly engaging the drive train. The rear end of the coupe squatted like a pouncing cat. Tires squealed and smoked. Ty was off, launched into uncharted territory, leaving thick fumes and his dismayed father behind.

His mind dropped into a state of numbness while his heart continued to pound. The landscape surrounding the familiar road became strange and foreboding. Florene's house, with her husband's station wagon parked in the driveway, offered no sanctuary. He could go out to Toby's and try to forget that anything had happened, but his father would likely come looking for him there. But at least he could get something to drink and hang out with his cousin for a little while. There was a chance his father wouldn't come, that he would just go off and get drunk.

Toby's admiring response to the coupe was encouraging. He wanted to go riding in the car, but Ty suggested throwing the baseball around instead since the gas gauge was nearing empty. "We'll do plenty of riding," he promised, "when I get some gas money. Let's just play pitch for a while."

Toby replied, "Sure," and the boys idled away the afternoon. Ty didn't leave when evening approached but stayed for supper and lingered afterward until Toby's mom suggested he spend the night.

"Why don't you call your daddy and let him know where you are," she said.

Ty agreed, knowing his father wouldn't be there. He let it ring a few times with his finger ready to press secretly the button just in case, then hung up. "It's okay. Dad's gone out, but I'm sure he wouldn't mind."

Ty knew he had to go home sooner or later. Filled with dread, He stopped at Big Ot's store for gas before heading back to the mill village. It was Friday evening. With any luck, his daddy would be gone for a weekend of drinking, gambling, and carousing. Otherwise. … He didn't want to think about what might happen. He had never stood up to him before.

When he got to the house, it was empty and smelled of stale beer and cigarettes. He dumped the ash trays, took out the trash, and washed the dishes. He found some bologna in the fridge for his supper and, after eating, got himself cleaned up. He rested apprehensively, not quite comfortable in the belief that his father would be away all night. He did some of his homework, reread an old

Hot Rod magazine, and watched TV. In his bed he tossed and turned on musty sheets, rising on his elbows each time he heard a car pass.

Sleep finally wiped over the dread, holding his eyes shut like a dark hand, and the night flowed by like a deep river. Then, he was wide awake, raised by the fully formed thought of getting to work early so he could have the afternoon off. It didn't take him long to get ready, knowing that the coupe was waiting to transport him.

He spent the next two days working, fishing, and goofing around without seeing his father. When they finally met on Monday evening after school and work, the man was prostrate on the tattered couch, too hungover to address his son's defiance. He only asked him to fetch some Goody powders from the bathroom cabinet and a glass of tomato juice to wash it down. There was no juice, so Ty obliged by going to the store to get some. He nursed his father with the remedies and a cool washcloth over the eyes, as he'd done many times. After he'd recovered, the father said nothing about taking the car or the confrontation. His silence acknowledged a fundamentally changed relationship. From that day on Ty came and went as he pleased.

Chapter 8

When fall came Ty was anxious to return to school to put the car on display. The dramatic effect of the glass-packed mufflers was complemented by this time with a new candy-apple-red paint job and a set of chrome-reversed wheels. Kids gathered around him that first day in the parking lot—guys to look at the engine and discuss the flawlessness of the paint, and girls who wanted to be noticed. They played the radio, laughed, and smoked with Ty, who sat quietly in the driver's seat, relishing the attention. When the bell rang to start the day, he lingered through the rest of his cigarette then sauntered at the end of the procession, victorious as Caesar, into the building where he remained untouched by the authority of the instructors and impervious to their lessons.

His grades dipped sharply after he started driving, much to the dismay of teachers who wanted to help him rise above his circumstances. He lingered with one foot inside the schoolhouse door, knowing what the teachers said was true: dropping out was for losers. They tried to pull him back in, but much of their instruction seemed irrelevant now. The admiration he received from his classmates held sway for a while. He knew the girls outside weren't so pretty and the guys not so easily impressed, but his newfound mobility and hormonal urges were pulling him, against his better judgment, into a coarser world that smelled of cigarette smoke, grease, and stale beer.

His insulated high school life grew blurry as it dissolved around the edges. What remained vanished abruptly when he blew up at Coach Thompson and pushed him into the wall that day. Coach had been riding Ty hard since the previous fall, when he tried to get him to come out for football. He'd seen Ty goofing around on the practice field with the other guys and recognized his natural abilities. Coach hated to see talent go to waste, but Ty wasn't buying. Even though he loved the rough contact, he didn't have time for all that practicing. Making money and being free were more important than lining up and doing dumb drills every day. Resentment grew throughout the year and almost reached the flashpoint when Coach tried to embarrass him into joining the team.

This incident occurred in the spring, when the coaches called an assembly in the cafeteria. They were trying to build next year's squad by persuading as many boys as possible to come out for spring training. Coach Thompson delivered a speech about pride in oneself, school, and country. "School spirit should run deep in your souls, like your pride in being American. Hearing the National Anthem ought to give you goose bumps, and so should the Panther fight song. There are people out there dodging the draft, leaving this great country they were born in, so they won't have to go to Vietnam and fight. Those people aren't men: they're queers, hippie cowards, and sissies.

"There are people out there saying we ought to close this place down, consolidate with the county because we can't even put together a decent football team anymore. I don't believe that's true. I believe there's still plenty of fight left in the Prathersville Panthers. Are we willing to stand up for our school, our heritage? Or are we a bunch of draft dodgers like those queers going to Canada? You can show what you're made of by being a Panther and putting on the pads, or you can run from life's battles and live on the sidelines with Ty Ragsdale and all the others who squat to tee-tee."

An explosion of laughter followed. Coach Thompson stood on the small stage smiling and nodding as he looked out into the boys' faces. His searching eyes found Ty, and they glared at each other for several seconds while the laughter subsided. Ty's emotions slipped like slick tires on a muddy road. His brain tried to register what had just happened. Dawning comprehension brought heat to his cheeks and tightened his neck muscles. He felt an arm around his shoulders and turned to look into the grinning face of one of his buddies. The boy said, "Coach Thompson's just messin' with you, man. Don't worry about it."

So he let it go. The laughter subsided, the boys went back to class, and by the next day no one seemed to remember the comment, except Ty. He mentioned it to Toby when they were fishing a few days later: "That pissed me off, what Coach Thompson said."

"What?" Toby asked, puzzled.

"At the assembly. About me being one of the sissies on the sidelines who has to squat to pee."

"Hah! Yeah, that was kind of funny!"

"*Funny?*"

"Well, yeah. He was just joking. I mean everybody knows you ain't no sissy."

"He still didn't have no right saying that about me. It pissed me off."

"Don't worry about it. He was trying to make you mad enough to come out for the team, that's all. He knows how good you can play."

"Well, he 'bout made me mad enough to whip his ass. I just might do it too, if he keeps messing with me."

"Man, you take things too serious. Just forget about it, or you'll get kicked out of school."

Ty tried to follow his cousin's advice by pushing the incident back into the dark closet in his mind with the memories of his parent's fights, the slapping sounds, the wailing and the cursing, and his own pain at having his drunk father's quick hand against his ear. There were many memories in that closet, but his daily routines did not require his going there.

Sometimes, though, stressful situations arose that caused the closet door to fly open, releasing a rush of foul-smelling tormentors that flapped dark wings and altered his perceptions. Ty's behavior at these times could be unpredictable and illogical, like his mad bull-like charging at Stinkum that time in the hay field. Unpleasant consequences followed the blind reactions, but he couldn't always keep the closet door shut. Anger flung reason aside again during the winter of his junior year, when Coach Thompson resumed his tactics of scorn and ridicule.

That American history project, just before Christmas, brought out the worst in everyone. Coach wasn't getting much participation from the students, so he singled out Ty as the object of his indignation. They were about one week into the World War II unit. Coach had worked hard to build student interest by bringing in relics—GI helmets, disarmed grenades, and samurai swords. He'd shown films containing actual footage of the various campaigns: destroyers at sea bristling with big guns and trim, cocky sailors; bombing missions showing the sky filled with droning planes, flak, and bombs falling like hateful metallic rain; and the amphibious troop carriers hitting the beach and spilling their cargo of courageous, weapon-toting Americans.

The students were mildly interested at first, but when he assigned the project, moans went up from around the room. It would involve work: writing, documenting sources, and—worst of all—sitting down and talking to adults for extended periods. Coach Thompson warned them that he would be checking their progress at regular intervals. They would have to produce a list of sources and a thesis statement, then a formal outline and a rough draft. As Coach explained the steps and requirements, Ty sketched in his notebook a side view of the coupe with much bigger tires and flames coming out of exposed header pipes. This was his last class and he was ready for a cigarette, to get outside and haul ass over to Ot Brown's store for a cold drink and cheese crackers, then to Dorsey's for two or three hours of work, applying his energy to something useful and real. When the bell rang, he was the first out of the room. He didn't hear Coach say that the source list, outline, and thesis were due in two days.

When the time came, Coach called the students up individually to check their work. They had little to show. Ty had even less—nothing. He sauntered up to the front desk, shrugged, grinned a little. Coach Thompson's response was immediate. "What the hell do you think this is," he exclaimed, "some kind of free lunch program? Do I look like Santa Claus or LBJ? I got news for you: that Great Society crap don't apply to my classroom. You got to work for what you get here. This ain't where you pick up the government cheese! But I guess I ought to expect that from you—looking for a handout, I mean. That's what you're used to, ain't it, Ragsdale? Letting other people do the sweating for you."

"I ain't expecting nothing from nobody. I forgot to do the assignment, that's all." Ty could feel the eyes of the other students boring into him, anticipating some response, something out of the ordinary. He rose from the straight-back chair hoping to avoid further conflict by returning to his desk, but Coach rose with him.

"*Forgot!* How could you forget the most important assignment of the semester? Truth is you just don't give a damn—about my class, this school, or your country!" Coach stepped toward Ty and began poking him in the chest with his finger. "The whole concept of sacrifice for the common good escapes you, don't it boy? I got news for you: the center of the universe—"

The poking finger pushed the closet door in Ty's mind fully open, allowing the fluttering filth to spew into the narrow space between him and Coach's contorted mouth, bringing a stench and the taste of rusty iron. His verbal response was a loud, high "Shut up!" as his caged energy exploded through shoulders, arms, and hands against Coach Thompson's bony chest, propelling him backwards into the chalkboard. The small of his back struck the chalk tray and his head cracked against the board. Coach's knees buckled and he slumped to the floor. Ty strode out of the room.

The students sat in shocked silence for several seconds while Coach Thompson recovered. He finally regained a standing position, then rubbed his head and looked around the room. "Where's that son of a bitch?" he asked nobody in particular. "He's going to jail for this."

He went to the doorway to look up and down the hall, rubbing his head. He didn't see Ty, but soon everyone heard him in the coupe heading out from the student parking lot, proclaiming to the world through twin exhaust pipes his angry frustration, venting his rage into the atmosphere as the engine revved and tires squealed.

Coach said, "That boy's a menace to society. He's got to be stopped." He stormed out, moving jerkily toward the office, leaving his students unattended in their nervous giggles and rising chatter.

A sheriff's deputy picked Ty up at Dorsey's a short time later and brought him back to the school. "We got a serious problem here, boy," the deputy announced in the patrol car. Coach Thompson's so pissed off, he's ready to file assault charges against you. Thinks you ought to be put away." Ty turned from the deputy, gritted his teeth, and stared out the window.

In the principal's office he was sullen, uncommunicative. Mr. Blakemon wanted to know why he attacked his teacher. Ty, sitting in front of the principal's big desk, replied through clenched teeth: "He shouldn't have poked me in the chest." The heavy, sallow-faced man soon grew impatient with the lack of cooperation and called in Coach Thompson.

With Coach seated to his right, Mr. Blakemon said, "Let me tell you something, young man. Attacking a teacher is not something we take lightly. Coach Thompson is considering filing assault charges against you, and I can't say that I blame him. I'd prefer resolving this another way, but that in part will depend on you—your attitude, I mean, and willingness to make things right. Do you have anything to say?"

Ty, in the big Naugahyde chair, locked his jaw and shook his head.

"You don't think you owe Coach Thompson an apology?" Mr. Blakemon asked.

"He owes me one."

"What? Owes you one?"

"See what I mean?" Coach Thompson interjected. "The boy's impossible."

The principal said, "You savagely attack a man for no other reason than because he's trying to encourage you, and you think he owes you an apology? When you refuse to do a legitimate assignment—a very good one, I might add—then Coach Thompson, any teacher, is obligated and expected to use reasonable means to motivate you to do your work. That's in your best interest."

"That ain't it," Ty answered.

"Well, then what is it? I would like to hear why you think Coach Thompson owes you an apology after you attacked him."

"He knows. Why don't you ask him?"

Mr. Blakemon furrowed his brow and glanced at his colleague, who expressed surprise and mock innocence.

"Is there something going on here I don't know about?" the principal asked.

Coach's voice came out high, indignant: "Well, yeah, there is. We've got a violence-prone kid trying to shift the blame for his behavior, that's what's going on."

Mr. Blakemon studied Coach Thompson, nervously bouncing his leg, then turned to Ty. He pushed back in his chair and tapped a pencil eraser on his desk-top calendar. His breathing was slow and audible, like an old tomcat trying to purr. He finally spoke with some abruptness: "Coach Thompson, let's step into the other room for a moment."

Coach's puzzled expression seemed exaggerated by his jerky movements in rising, while Mr. Blakemon rose with the weariness of an overweight cleaning woman. The two men passed through the door into the adjoining conference room, leaving Ty alone, grinding his teeth in the imposing office, struggling to keep the closet door in his mind shut. He was in the middle of a bitter contest, he realized. He looked around the room, amazed that the events of a normal day could turn so suddenly. He felt giddy as he played the game out in his mind. What chance did he have of winning?

On the wall behind the big oak desk hung the principal's framed diplomas along with a pair of color photographs of a slimmer, thicker-haired Mr. Blakemon and a boy about Ty's age. One was a posed picture of the father and son bird hunting in a golden meadow with sleek dogs on point while the boy made ready to shoot. Mr. Blakemon stood proudly by the boy with his gun un-breached over his arm. The other picture featured them resting in the grass on one knee with shotguns across their laps. The dogs, alert and erect, flanked them. In the foreground a dozen or so dead quail were fanned out in a neat semicircle. Father, son, and dogs all seemed very proud.

The men returned with more purpose in their bearing, as if they were ready to get this over with. "There are some things you've got to understand, young man," Mr. Blakemon said as he leaned forward, propping himself on his desk. "The first thing is that we want to do what's best for you and the school. The second thing is that you can't go through life attacking people, even when you think you've been treated unfairly. Now Coach Thompson here is willing to drop the charges against you—he's always had your best interest at heart—but neither of us is willing to drop this matter altogether. To let the kind of violence you've displayed here today go unpunished would be damaging to you and Prathersville High. You've got to learn that irresponsible actions bring unpleasant consequences."

Coach Thompson was standing, leaning forward against the chair back, nodding in agreement. Ty cocked his head as he watched Mr. Blakemon's mouth move. The man stopped talking and bent down to pull out the bottom desk drawer. He brought up a paddle cut from a one by six pine board, varnished, with a shaped handle on one end and rounded corners on the other. It was about two feet long with eight one-inch holes drilled two abreast in the middle portion. He held it in his right hand and looked directly at Ty.

"You've got to show that you're willing to make this right, so I'll expect a public apology to Coach Thompson tomorrow in class. And, of course, the harshness of your actions calls for physical punishment as well. It's only fitting, I believe, for the injured party to administer the discipline." He handed Coach Thompson the paddle. "Now, if you'll bend over with your hands against the desk here, we'll get this over with."

Ty said flatly, "I ain't taking no whuppin'."

"What?" Mr. Blakemon glared down at him. "You'll do what I say, young man! Now get up here and bend over."

Ty clamped his teeth together and shook his head. Coach held the paddle in front of him as a policeman would hold a nightstick. He smirked as he looked down at Ty through narrowed eyes. "Come on, Ragsdale," he said, "real men own their problems and face consequences."

"You go to hell."

"Young man! That language will not be tolerated. You're making your situation worse by not cooperating. I suggest you get up here and take your punishment!"

Ty's voice quavered. "I told you I ain't taking no whuppin'."

The adults looked at each other with dawning recognition. Mr. Blakemon spoke in low, measured tones. "Young man, if you refuse to cooperate and take the prescribed punishment, then I have no choice but to expel you. I'm going to tell you one more time: bend over this desk and take your paddling."

Ty didn't move.

"You are no longer a student at Prathersville High!" Mr. Blakemon blurted out. "I'll fill out the necessary papers and call your father to come and take you off our campus."

"He ain't home," Ty said as he stood and turned his back on the adults who watched silently as he stepped across the carpeted floor. With exaggerated softness, he eased the door shut behind him.

Chapter 9

Ty made up his mind to get a new job. Maybe now, since he didn't have school to waste his time, he could make some decent money. The prospect of having extra cash in his pocket excited him. He could still hang out with Toby and his old friends from school on weekends, and they would be impressed with his ability to pay for the beer and gas and hamburger steaks at the truck stop. He could get an eight-track player for the coupe and some new clothes.

The largest employer in the area had once been Jupiter Mills, but the textile industry was changing, and the plant had shut down its second and third shift operations. Different industries had set up on the other side of town in recent years in a new industrial complex. Of these, Weinraub Manufacturing—WM for short—was the largest and fastest growing. They made bright metal parts, aluminum and stainless, for the automobile industry. WM's business was booming and they needed young, strong guys like Ty who were eager and willing to work long hours feeding and controlling metal-forming machines that were greasy, dangerous, and deafening. Ty lied about his age and went to work there on the third shift a few days after being expelled from school.

A comfortable routine developed of work, sleep, and loafing. There were girls and women he could call on when he felt like it, along with other diversions: the pool hall, cruising around town or the back roads, working on the coupe, drinking beer, hunting and fishing. With his new job Ty became the primary sustainer of the household as the senior Ragsdale by degrees became a thinner shadow of himself.

★★★

At the beginning of spring the following year, when Ty was turning nineteen, the beer joint in town was taken over by new owners. The place had long been a staid, dingy hide-away where older guys went to unwind in the evenings before going home to their wives, but the new owners were savvy to demographic changes, including the dramatic rise of that segment of the population just reaching legal drinking age. This growing group became even larger when lawmakers lowered the drinking age to eighteen on the logic that if they're old enough to be drafted and die for their country, then they ought to be old enough to buy a beer.

Frankie and Johnny, the mod couple from Chicago who bought the old bar, decided to give the place a name. The old Pabst Blue Ribbon sign over the door came down in favor of one that featured a cartoonish portrait of a bull goat with unkempt beard, reprobate grin, winking eye, and long curved horns. The new name, *The Billy Goat Bar,* was proclaimed in bold letters curving around the top of the horns. The phrase, *est. 1972,* was centered below.

Frankie and Johnny, in an effort to keep the older customers happy, left the front room as it had been, but the back room—originally a segregated area for black customers—was opened up, enlarged, and updated. The jukebox was restocked with newer hits by groups like Three Dog Night, Creedence Clearwater Revival, and Deep Purple. The atmosphere was rustic and dimly lit, except over the pool table that occupied the center of the room. There were booths and tables, and along one end was a counter for leaning, talking, and watching the customers who came and went or ventured out onto the small dance floor in the corner. The menu was expanded to include pizza, "Chicago style," while retaining the popular burger baskets (with fries or onion rings), shrimp baskets, and hamburger steak platters. This back room, carefully planned to look as if it wasn't, soon began filling up with young people in the evenings and evolved into what the disapproving community referred to as a "pick-up spot."

Alcohol, youthful passion, and gambling combined in unpredictable ways at the Billy Goat Bar, and fights were a regular occurrence. Early one evening while Ty was winning a friendly game of eight ball, he noticed a stocky young man in the corner, drinking by himself and watching him. The man was one of those who goes bald early, and what hair he had was close-cropped and coarse. He wore the faded uniform—jeans, flannel shirt, and boots—of the outdoor building trades. By the looks of his hands and forearms he could have been a house framer or mason.

Ty had spent the previous Saturday night at another man's home, and now he was alert to the eyes of this stranger. The woman had told him about the separation and impending divorce, but while he enjoyed the pleasures of her bed, he was aware of a lingering male presence. He reveled in his intrusion, knowing that his gratification may come at a price.

As he chalked the end of his cue stick and pretended to survey the next shot, he watched peripherally the man approaching with balled fists and stride betraying his purpose. When he called out "Hey, Ragsdale," Ty was already turning to meet him. He shifted his grip on the cue stick so that both hands were on the small end, and he swung it like a baseball bat from an awkward, hurried stance. The advancing man took the blow under his left arm.

The cue seemed to find lodgment in the man's ribs. Actually, the cuckold's rage had sharpened his reflexes. He dropped his arm and grabbed the big end of the stick, gaining the advantage, which Ty was quick to realize. Rather than lose the pulling contest, he turned the shorter man's strength against him by stepping in with a hard elbow to the mouth. As the fingers loosened, Ty planted his feet and jerked back, regaining his weapon.

The next blow was an abbreviated punch. The fat handle struck the forehead sharply, making the sound of a popped cork. His head snapped back, but the husband managed to keep his balance and bring his fists up. Ty found the bridge of his nose with the stick, even though the blow was partially blocked by forearms. An arm-flailing counterattack followed—a paroxysm of pain and rage—but was stopped with a quick jab into his Adam's apple, bringing the man's hands to his throat as his tongue protruded from his red mouth. The next blow cracked against his cheekbone. As he reeled backwards, the head was an easy target, which Ty was quick to find.

A downward stroke brought the battered husband to his knees. A rapid succession of chopping blows followed. Ty swung the cue from a workman's stance as if hoeing out a drought-hardened corn row, striking shoulders, neck, arms, and hands as his defeated opponent tried in vain to protect himself. Ty kept swinging until the husband was face-down with his hands over his head, moaning and bleeding from his busted mouth and nose onto the gritty floor.

The manager, Todd Flemming, finally broke through the crowd and caught the stick as Ty was bringing it back for yet another blow. "Awright now," he said in Ty's ear. "He's beat. You got him. Lemme have the stick."

At the same instant someone else managed a hasty half-nelson, saying in a high, excited voice, "It's over, it's over," as he restrained Ty's left arm.

He bucked and strained against them for a few seconds before the world beyond came back into focus. He glanced jerkily from side to side, surveying the crowd who watched with gaping mouths; then he relented, releasing the stick without completely releasing his anger. They loosened their grip on him as he stopped straining. He blurted out, "What's wrong with that son of a bitch? What's his damn problem?" Then he broke free, stepped over the man he'd beaten, and walked out the back door.

It was a cooler than normal evening for early summer, but Ty didn't notice. He ripped out of the parking lot on his big Honda, the "Beast." He continued to ride hard past the town limits onto a familiar, curvy back road. He was searching for his rhythm of accelerating and backing off, leaning into the turns and concentrating on controlling the machine instead of what happened back there, when suddenly, as he came off a hill into a little hollow and began to lean into the next curve, the world turned ghostly white. He was in the middle of a dense patch of fog before he knew it, traveling at a high rate of speed into a curve that had disappeared.

There was no guiding line at the edge of the blacktop, and his eyes only vaguely discerned the shape of a rising bank to his right. He put out his left foot when his wheels dropped off the pavement. The rough shoulder hammered him, and the bike's suspension bounced him up onto the gas tank. Unidentified shapes rushed by. The bike dipped and rose violently as he crossed the ditch and started up the embankment. He was still upright somehow when the fog passed, revealing the gaping black hole of a fast-approaching metal culvert where the ditch ran under a gravel driveway. Farther up the embankment, the surface broke up into boulder-strewn gullies. It was all or nothing: at the limit of what he and the machine could do—left foot dragging the ground, bike leaning at an impossibly sharp, foot-peg-scraping angle—he passed just to the left of death's sharp edge.

Another bounce put him back on the pavement, able to see again. A wave of nausea coursed through him, forcing him to pull over and yank off his helmet. Trembling from the expenditure of effort—from his first swing of the cue stick until now as he tried not to vomit after seeing death's black void and struggling to steer the Beast away from it—Ty decided to slow down and to stay away from the Billy Goat Bar for a while.

Somehow, he was still alive and free. A sense of relief, borne on the cool night air, washed him as he rode. It was similar to a feeling he'd had once before at a high school dance when a pretty girl looked at him and soothed his anger, lifting him out of the demons' grasp. There would have been a fight that night had it not been for the girl and her peaceful aspect. He replayed those details from over a year ago and thought about her face as he rode.

Ty had approached the girl filled with his usual confidence. She'd been prancing about with some of her girlfriends, dancing to "In-A-Gadda-Da Vida," being cranked out by the local band, Sewer System. He'd picked her out of the group, noticing her thick hair and spirited movements, and when she looked, he offered a smile. She averted her eyes, redirecting her attention to her friends and the fun they were having. When the song ended Ty approached them in their laughter and said to the one he'd singled out, "I like the way you dance."

She looked away, then wrapped her arm around one of her girlfriends' shoulders. "Come on Becky, let's go get a Coke." They turned their backs and vanished into the crowd. Ty stood perplexed in a pocket of people he didn't know and for a moment felt a frantic need for security. He looked for his cousin Toby but couldn't locate him. The band launched into their next song, "Sunshine of Your Love." More bodies jammed onto the floor and began flailing about as they gave themselves over to the pounding rhythm. Ty, his tempo-keeping mechanism knocked off kilter, sought the safety of the sidelines, where the shy and clumsy sat in metal chairs or leaned against the wall.

He pulled a Winston from his shirt pocket, stuck it to his lower lip, and made his way around the perimeter of the room toward the door. He wanted to step outside to smoke and think about that girl and what to do next. As he cut across the corner to the exit, he felt an arm on his shoulder. He turned, expecting Toby or a friendly acquaintance; instead, he found himself looking into the hawkish visage of Coach Thompson. The man shouted over the racket, his face inches from Ty's, "You can't smoke in here, Ragsdale."

"It ain't lit," Ty shouted back.

"Well, if you go outside, you can't come back in."

"Why can't I? I paid my money like everybody else."

"Because that's the rule. Besides, you're not supposed to be here anyway. This dance is for students."

"Coulda fooled me—I thought it was for losers, like yourself."

"That's it, Ragsdale, you're outta here! We're not gonna put up with troublemakers."

Ty jerked away when Coach Thompson grabbed the back of his arm. "Get your damned hands off me." The kids around them stopped dancing, eager for excitement. Ty felt eyes upon him as he and Coach squared off. In the brief moment of reflection before fully committed action, he scanned the faces and locked for an instant on a pair of intense blue eyes, those of the girl with thick hair and spirited movements.

Coach said, "You'll do what I say, Ragsdale, or wish you had."

The dark creatures of Ty's mind began their tormenting distortion, but the girl's blue eyes shone through the swaying shadows like a beacon. Her light brought back the proper perspective. She looked at Ty for only a second, just long enough for him to return the gaze and notice the slight movement of her head from side to side saying earnestly to him alone, "No."

He turned back to the bristled little man before him and nodded. "Sure coach, I'll leave. I don't want to cause no trouble." Then he sought her face. Their eyes met for another instant, and he picked up the shy smile before she turned back to her friends. Ty left and drove home alone with his head full of sweet fantasies. He felt as if he'd been redeemed by the experience. Radiant vistas opened before him, making the grimy meanness of life's struggles seem trivial. As time passed, the girl's number in his wallet, procured through Toby's helpful detective efforts, became a seed of hope. Now as he rode the restrained beast reflectively through the darkness, these memories consoled him.

At work the next night, he learned that the man was okay. Several customers had lifted him, washed his face, and got him to his truck. He wasn't a regular, so no one knew what happened after, except that he'd been able to drive himself out of the parking lot. The fight was the main break-room topic for several nights, and Ty sensed the growing respect of the others, even the older men at the plant. He feigned indifference about the beaten man's condition or whereabouts and managed not to show that he was sick and worried inside.

Bowman, one of the young machine operators, a large-hipped boy who worked alongside Ty, was fascinated with the story. Like Ty, he ran a die press, but he lacked his counterpart's speed and grace in its operation. He wanted to know everything about that fight, and he kept pressing for details.

"So, you caught him right in the Adam's apple, huh? That's a pretty amazing shot with a cue stick! Was that the turning point in the fight, do you think? Was that when you knew you had him?"

"You know, it all happened so fast, I really don't remember."

"Some of the guys said he had a knife, that he came at you with a knife."

"Naa. He didn't have no knife."

"That's what they're saying, that he came at you from out of nowhere with a knife, and before he knew what was what, you was all over him with that cue stick, beating him like a yard dog."

He was just coming, that's all, ready to jump me. And I knew I had to do something."

Conversation usually took place in the break room. This particular night, however, Bowman's machine was down for repairs. He was supposed to be helping Ty with a set-up, changing dies and feeder settings on his machine for a new run of parts. He wasn't much help because of his incessant chatter, and the set-up was taking too long. Finally, Millwood, the foreman, came over. He was a tall, slender man in his forties, angular and slightly stooped. He watched, gauging progress. Bowman kept talking.

"Who was that guy anyway? Why do you think he wanted to jump you?"

"I don't know. I think he had me mixed up with somebody else."

"You sure about that, Ty?" Millwood interjected. "You think that man jumped you for no reason, 'cause he was crazy or something?"

"I don't know what his damn problem was, but I wasn't gon' stand there and wait for an explanation."

"So you attacked him with a stick."

"He was the one doing the attacking, I was just defending myself."

"Did he ever even hit you?"

"Hell, I didn't give him a chance. But he was coming at me, fists balled up, mad as hell 'bout something."

Bowman followed this exchange, eagerly hanging on every word as the older man continued: "You ever seen two tomcats fight, Ragsdale? They fight to protect their territory. They're very protective of what's theirs. Men are the same way, except there's an important difference. Men take their mates for life. It ain't no seasonal thing like with cats or other animals, and it's their duty to fight to keep some tomcat from taking what belongs to them. Marriage means something, boy. Didn't you know that?"

Ty looked down at the dismantled machinery. "She told me they was getting a divorce, that he wasn't around."

"She was a married woman, and that man you beat up with a stick—her husband—happens to be a good fella, a friend of mine. He ain't been able to work since it happened. He's hurting deep on the inside more than from all the bruises that stick left on the outside.

He's a man who tries to do what's right, and I ain't so sure it woulda turned out like it did if you hadn't had that stick."

Bowman's eyes twitched as he followed the conversation. Ty, unable to look at Millwood, studied the fit of the parts as the older man spoke. "You ain't gotta worry about me, Ragsdale. Everything's strictly business between us. I'm gonna treat you like everybody else, but I will say this: you better watch yourself. You better be careful where you go and what you mess around with. Now, if this machine ain't up and running in ten minutes, I'm gonna send both of you home. I don't want to hear no more talk about beating people with sticks and screwing their wives. I just ain't in the mood for it. Is that clear?"

Words of protest were forming on Ty's lips as he raised his face to answer, but when he saw the drawn brow of the foreman, he dropped his eyes. "Yessir."

Millwood left then and Bowman and Ty resumed their work, tapping the steel guides and dies into place and locking them down with their Allen wrenches. They worked without speaking, except for an occasional muttering from Bowman. After a while, Ty asked, "What did you say?"

"Oh, nothing. I just didn't know you'd been doing his wife."

Ty didn't feel like answering. In fact, he didn't feel as if he could continue working because of the sharp cramping in his gut. He waited long enough for Millwood to reach the other side of the plant, then left his post. The cramping was intense, causing him to step quickly. Something vile was boiling deep in his insides.

The lighting was different in the restroom where the stench and relative quiet signaled relief to his muscles. He was barely able to make it to the toilet before everything let go.

Relief came in convulsive waves as a hot brown river jetted from his insides. He expelled an inordinate amount of putrescent waste, and he wondered if his very organs had rotted and dissolved into the lumpy, stinking flood rising beneath him. Then it was over. Depleted, he trembled on the seat, alone in the stench of his bowels and the humming, flickering light. He rubbed his head, pushing the sweat on his brow back with the hair that had fallen across his face.

As he recovered, his eyes were drawn to the vulgar scrawls on the stall partition. The obscenities were piled on top of one another, and he read them half expecting to find his name written there. He saw that other name then, written in a smaller, neater script which made it stand apart from everything else. "Jesus loves you and can save you from your sins." It was a puzzling thought that lingered as he went back to work, feeling much better.

The remainder of his shift ran out smoothly, with no more talk of the fight. His head was empty except for a newly developed wariness as he walked out of the plant into the streaked orange effects of a lingering sunrise. He barely noticed the morning colors as he wiped the dew off the seat and gas tank of the Honda with the hand towel he kept in the tool compartment. Lazy clouds floated above the horizon. He supposed they looked like something, but he had no idea what. Their shapes represented nothing other than drifting, poorly defined smudges that were, for the moment, turned orange and glorified by the sun. The clouds remained before him on the horizon, holding their color as he rode eastward, toward home and much-needed rest.

He still had the blue-eyed girl's number in his wallet. For some reason, though, picking up the phone was difficult, like beginning a project without all the materials. It was easier not to start. But he still planned to call someday, and as he rode his mechanical beast into the morning, he thought about what he would say.

Chapter 10

He slept well into the early afternoon, and when he arose, the decision to make the call rose with him. There was no denying it. This was the day, and it would be better to just do it without thinking about it too much. He went to the phone with a sense of optimism, his mind still fresh from sleep. A woman's voice responded after two rings.

"Hello," Ty said, "Is Stacy there?"

There was a pause and then, "Why no, she isn't. She doesn't live here anymore. I'm her mother, can I help you with something?"

"Well, I was hoping I could get in touch with Stacy. I . . . haven't seen her in a long time."

"She decided to move out and get her own place a few months back. She still comes around a lot though. Usually every Sunday for dinner. Would you like for me to give her a message?"

"I guess not. I mean I ain't seen her in a long time, and she might not remember me.

"Hmm, I see. I'd be happy to give her a message, though, when I see her."

"No ma'am. That's awright. Maybe I'll run into her again one of these days."

"Well, okay then. You know, she thought she was old enough to be on her own, but she still comes around, especially on Sundays to eat dinner with her old momma and daddy."

"Yes ma'am."

"Both my babies done flew the coup. My boy left about a year ago for Atlanta, and I don't get to see him hardly at all. It's just me and Papa now, and I just can't get used to it. I always fix too much supper. But now it's working out better with the new hand. I send him a plate every evening. I'd a lot rather do that than let it go to waste. Before, I was having more leftovers than the dog could eat, and Papa would fuss at me for being so wasteful. But anyway, I'm thankful that Stacy still comes to visit. You know, we all got a lot to be thankful for."

"Yes ma'am."

Ty enjoyed hearing the nice lady talk. She was warm and motherly, and he tried to imagine those Sunday dinners. He hadn't had real home cooking in years. As the conversation was ending, Mrs. Stempton once again offered to give Stacy a message. "Okay," he said, "tell her that Ty called, the guy she . . . met—at the Valentine's dance a while back."

He hung up feeling oddly satisfied, even though he didn't get to speak to the girl or get a number where he could reach her. He had called, after all this time. Maybe Stacy would remember him and that special way they'd communicated. There was satisfaction in knowing that wheels were in motion, and there was a chance that he and Stacy would soon meet.

It happened within a few weeks, long enough for the conversation with Mrs. Stempton to begin receding and merging with more distant memories. The fight had slipped to the back of his mind too, along with the dread that came from thinking about it.

His first night back at the Goat had been awkward, with some of the customers staring and whispering and the manager glancing in his direction with a hint of challenge in his eyes, but the comfort level increased as nights rolled by. It was good to be able to drink, shoot pool, laugh with others, and watch the parade of eager young females who came through, available for his choosing. He was leaning back against the counter watching, drinking beer, and smoking when Stacy came in with a girlfriend.

It didn't register at first. Stacy Stempton, whose number he'd carried in his wallet for over a year, seemed out of place at the Billy Goat Bar, but there she was with her intense blue eyes and thick honey-blond hair, accompanied by a pretty, dark-haired friend. The girls took a booth near the back, laughing with nervous excitement. They seemed ready for some Friday-night fun. Ty watched them as they settled in and examined the menus the waitress brought. He didn't have to go into work that night, and he'd already finished his third beer. Stacy was turned towards him, and from his vantage point he could watch her changing, animated expressions and just barely detect the blue flash of her eyes.

He felt a little sad that she was here. Now something would have to happen that would change the way he'd thought about her all this time. He would have to approach her and start a conversation and it might not go well. He could discover that there had been no connection at the dance that night, that she wasn't interested in him then and still wasn't. Things could change, and probably would, but approaching her was unavoidable. Not trying would produce a question mark in his life and confirm what he already suspected but would never admit: that he was a coward at heart, that his outward confidence was only a mask covering the terror he felt inside—fear of the gaping hole at his core. Outwardly, through his actions, he could chink, putty, and fill the cracks, but always there was the fear of collapse from within. Soon he would walk over, but there was no hurry. The girls would order something and be there for a while.

Ty sipped his beer and tried not to stare. He noticed the other young people who were sitting at booths or milling about. There were more guys than girls, as always, but he hadn't noticed this lack of balance before. Guys were prowling through the room in tight jeans and rolled-up sleeves, their long hair parted just so and sprayed, their faces and necks shaved and splashed with cologne.

A big guy named Mikey Mitchum stopped at Stacy's booth and lingered, talking, gesturing, and smiling confidently. He wore a cowboy shirt with embroidery and shiny buttons, and tight flare-legged jeans over lizard-skin boots. Ty, watching from the other side of the room, was disturbed by his presence. After a few moments the interloper slipped into the booth beside the other girl. Ty could see the back of his head and Stacy looking at him, smiling and talking. The time had come.

All the booths and tables were occupied, and people milled about on the floor and around the pool table in the center of the room. Ty smiled and adopted the mood of the place, speaking to acquaintances as he strolled toward the booth where Stacy Stempton sat across from her friend and the big guy in the cowboy shirt.

He had known Mikey for years, so it was easy to speak to him first: "Mikey! What's goin' on man?"

The eager smile indicated that he'd walked up during an awkward moment and that Mikey was relieved at the prospect of adding Ty to the mix. He answered, "Hey man! Shoot, I'm just enjoying the company of these two fine ladies here. These girls are graduates from our old rival, Aaron County High. Used to be cheerleaders. Ain't they pretty?"

"Absolutely lovely! I noticed from way over there this whole place brightened up when they walked in."

The girls giggled and rolled their eyes. Stacy's response was pleasant but indicated no recognition. Mikey spoke up, over the edge of the subsiding giggles and rising awkwardness: "Girls, let me introduce this fella. He's Ty Ragsdale, famous around here for . . . um . . . several things we won't go into." More giggles, slightly nervous this time. "This is Becky Johnson and Tracy."

"Hi," Ty said politely, "nice to meet you."

"Stacy, Stacy Stempton," the blue-eyed girl said, "not Tracy."

"I know," Ty answered.

"Why don't you sit down and join us, Ty. I don't think the girls would mind."

"I'd like that, I mean if it's awright with you." Ty spoke to Stacy who gazed back with a puzzled look. She slid over to let him in beside her.

"You know my name," she reflected. "You called my momma, didn't you?"

"Guilty as charged. I remembered you from a school dance a while back. I'd hoped I would see you again."

"I didn't tell you my name then, at that dance."

"No, but I found out because I wanted to see you. You saved me that night, and I didn't get to thank you."

"So, you two know each other," Mikey blurted out.

"Um, sort of, I mean not really," Stacy answered. Ty said, "Yes" at the same time.

"Yeah, he looks kinda familiar to me too," said Becky. "I've seen you around somewhere."

"You were there too," answered Ty.

"Where?" asked Mikey.

The waitress arrived and placed three mugs and a sloppy pitcher of foaming draft heavily on the table.

"Awright! It's about time," Mikey said. "I'll pour." Then he called out to the harried waitress as she was leaving, "Bring us another mug, will you."

Ty answered, "I don't need one. Got a full bottle."

"You'll need it later. We've got to have some help with this pitcher."

"I was there too? Where?" Becky asked.

"At the dance, when I first saw Stacy."

"Well, there's been lots of dances, and you do look kind of familiar." She turned back to Mikey then as he handed her a mug.

"Speaking of dancing," Mikey said, "somebody needs to get that jukebox cranked up. Come on, let's me and you go over and pick out some tunes."

"Okay," Becky answered, and they disappeared into the crowd.

Stacy and Ty were sitting alone then, side by side in the dim light. Awkwardness rose like hot furnace air in a shut-up room. Ty, usually content to let others manufacture the small talk, felt uncomfortably warm in his neck and face. She was looking at him as if trying to figure something out. He wanted her to relax, to know that he was okay, a decent person. He decided to show his vulnerable side: "I'd almost given up on seeing you again, after your mom told me you didn't live there anymore."

"You really remembered me, after all this time?"

"Yep, since I first saw you."

"You said I saved you that night. How?"

"I was about to lose my temper and get in a mess," Ty answered. "When I looked at you, I felt different, and the anger went away. It's hard to explain. I've wondered about it a lot since then."

"I've thought about it too, that night I mean. I wondered why you came over to me in the first place and why you and that man seemed to hate each other so much. It was kind of scary. And I didn't want to see nobody get hurt."

"You were scared of me that night."

"Yeah, a little. I didn't know you, and you had that look in your eye."

"Look? What kind of look?"

"I don't know, a look of danger, I guess. Like you were somebody I shouldn't be messin' with, the kind momma told me to stay away from. Besides, I was scared of lots of things then."

"You're not scared of me now?"

"Naa," she teased, "I've learned about guys since then, that you're all really just little boys. Besides, you don't look scary anymore. I think maybe you're the one who's scared now."

"Well, the way you walked away from me like you did, it don't do much for a guy's confidence."

"I'm not walking away now, and besides, you had just a tad too much confidence that night. Everybody needs to eat a little humble pie from time to time."

Their hips were nearly touching. He gazed at her and nodded. "Hmm . . . I guess you're right." They were interrupted then by the returning Mikey and Becky and a sudden onslaught of loud rock and roll. A shrill, unfamiliar number blared from the speakers as the other couple, giggling, slid back into the booth. Conversation stopped while the four smiled, looked approvingly at each other, and bobbed their heads to the music.

After a few beats their attention was drawn to a skinny drunk boy making a spectacle of himself on the dance floor. He'd apparently worked out a routine to this particular song, and the fact that he seemed proud of his practiced moves added to the absurdity. He kept his hands in his pockets at first, limiting movement to his shoulders, head, and shuffling feet; then, as the song reached a shrill crescendo, he snatched his hands out and ceremoniously shook them as if flinging away fish guts or lard. His legs became infused with rhythm and he went into a high-stepping, thigh-slapping buck dance. As he continued these movements, resembling an idiot child desperate for attention, spectators throughout the room began clapping in time to show their support.

It was too much. Ty shook his head, chuckling. Guffaws erupted, the others joining him in gleeful, goofy laughter. As they regained control, they began to clap too. Becky, proud of her jukebox selection, looked at Ty and spoke over the noise: "This is a great song, ain't it? Have you heard it before?"

Ty shook his head "no."

"It's the new one by Humble Pie, 'Thirty Days in the Hole.'"

He glanced at Stacy. She elbowed him in the side, grinning, eyes flashing, and they laughed at this inside joke and their newfound intimacy.

Stacy saw something in him then that others did not—child-like longing and vulnerability. She decided at that moment to trust him with everything. Mysterious forces had been working all along at the center of things, pulling them together and spinning her soul's compass like a roulette wheel, clicking down now with the laughter to a stop, perfectly aligned with the magnetic pole of her deepest desire: the form and spirit of Ty Ragsdale, sitting next to her in the dimly lit booth of a rowdy beer joint. Her tummy hurt from laughing, but the pain was pleasant, radiating warmth throughout her young muscles.

As the evening wore on and the beer was poured, they were themselves poured, one into the other through deep-gazing eyes, shared secrets, and sensual finger games on the sticky table-top. They sat in the booth talking intimately while Becky and Mikey, dancing and mingling with others, came and went several times. The commotion around them faded into a softly humming patterned background, unobtrusive as elevator music. The entire world had become a backdrop to their unfolding drama.

Ty asked Stacy if she'd ever ridden a motorcycle. She answered, "Sure. Me and my brother had a Honda 50 when we was little."

"I got a little Honda outside. Would you like to take a ride with me?"

"I'd love to. Some fresh air would be real nice."

They left without bothering to tell the others. The air outside was a clean contrast to the smoke-filled environment inside the bar. The quietness added a crystalline quality to their conversation as they walked with their arms around each other's waist. Their words became a collection of blown-glass characters, placed carefully against the night's black velvet, while moonlight, filtered through the leaves of ancient oaks, caused the glass words to sparkle along with their eyes and teeth. Stacy's nostrils flared to imbibe the summer smells, a distillation of life's pure fragrances: plowed fields, meadows after rain, puppies—the smells of growing and striving toward ripeness and seed bearing, green life vibrating with energy and purpose. They walked across the cracked asphalt toward Ty's motorcycle, leaning on its stand beneath a giant oak tree, and their words meant nothing now, tinkling and clinking against the night, except as tiny gifts, tokens of this special time.

"It's so big!" Stacy commented as they approached the Beast. "You're not going to hurt me, are you?"

"Trust me and you'll be fine." Ty unstrapped the spare helmet from the seat rail and offered it to her.

"So, you always carry an extra helmet," she said. "How convenient."

"Well, a guy has to be prepared, you know."

Their eyes met for an instant as they each picked up the unintended implications. Ty managed a grin while Stacy blushed in the moonlight.

She tossed her head back and passed her fingers through her hair before trying to pull the helmet over it. "I don't know about you, Ty Ragsdale. I'm starting to think you're a rascal."

Ty replied, "You're right. I am, but I don't feel like one tonight."

"Good," she said, working the helmet over her thick hair, "because I do trust you. How do you fasten this thing?"

"I'll do it," he said, his face close to hers as he pulled the strap through the loops under her chin. "There. How does that feel?"

"Good! I like my new helmet."

Ty mounted the machine, started the engine and left it burbling while he showed her the passenger pegs. She threw her leg over without hesitation, settling her weight against him, and they rode off, intoxicated, into the night. The engine's heat made the air warmer and their bodies damp where they touched. Ty drove conservatively, making several passes through town and lazy, looping circuits through his favorite back roads. After a long time, a sense of destiny and an aching backside prompted Stacy to direct him into the mill village, to the apartment she shared with Becky. She pressed her chest into his back and, with her chin on his shoulder, talked into his helmet, guiding them toward their destination.

He showed his surprise when they arrived. "I can't believe you live here. Me and my dad live just a couple of blocks over. We're practically neighbors."

She pulled off the helmet and shook out her hair. "For real? Well I never. Come on in, I'll fix us something to drink."

Ty entered her world that night, a world that had been so close all along. Soon, he would bring most of his things with him, leaving only the rusty knives, broken lighters, spark plugs, and fishhooks inside the battered tin box of his childhood, forgotten in that run-down house he shared with his dissolute father. When the sun came up on them a few hours later, through the window of her tidy little room, it shone on a couple whose lives and fortunes were thoroughly combined.

Chapter 11

Plans were made in a new light that shone on them together. Much of their time was spent at the Billy Goat Bar, where they laughed and socialized with others their age who were searching for what they'd found. It was all very natural, even though events were unfolding at a dizzying pace. Within a week after their first night together, Stacy had quit her job as a receptionist in Dr. Loeb's dentist office to work as a waitress at the bar, where there were no forms to worry with, no fussy typing, filing, or glaring lights. It didn't seem like work at all, buzzing around tables of laughing people, tending to their simple needs. She enjoyed helping people have fun, and she could make more money and spend more time with Ty and her other new friends. He was nearly always there. During the week he had to leave for work before eleven, but a big chunk of evening embraced them in the confined space before they said goodnight. And morning came soon.

The period from after Ty left until she got off work around two a.m. became a zone of darkness, combining fascination with dread. She was tired by this time, and there was still much to do: helping to bus and wipe the vacated tables, putting up with the few remaining drunks, counting money and turning in her tickets. Sometimes she and the other waitresses, all young pretty girls, would adopt a shared attitude of zaniness as they worked to finish their duties and get out of there. The manager, a married man in his thirties with a hoot owl's face, flirted with them and teased in the manner of a lecherous boss who fancies himself witty, turning out innuendoes along with directives as he watched them work. The girls, since they valued their jobs, laughed along with him and flirted back just enough to keep things moving.

One night the manager, Todd Flemming, offended Stacy with his comments to the point where she considered telling Ty about it. She, the new girl, was bent over a booth, vigorously wiping the tabletop. The jukebox was blaring, so she didn't hear Todd as he approached her from the rear. His loud voice startled her: "I like the way you work, Stacy. Do you always put that much ass movement into rubbing things? Is it the work, the music, or thinking about your boyfriend that puts it into motion?"

Stacy's face flushed as she whirled to face him. "I'm just trying to do my job, and my ass ain't none of your business!"

"Whoa little lady," Todd chuckled. "I didn't mean no harm. Just admiring the view and trying to have a little fun, that's all. You keep up the good work!"

He slinked away then before she could think of anything to say. She finished out the night feeling violated by Todd's words, eyes, and thoughts, imagining what Ty would do to that creep in defense of her honor. She wanted to do something—to not just let it go—but the possible consequences presented themselves as looming cliffs, blocking her passage into the land of sweet revenge.

Telling Ty would be foolish. She knew about his anger, his sinew and quick reflexes. She only imagined Todd Flemming with a bloody nose or busted mouth. To take steps to make such punishment a reality would bring complicated problems and ruin everything. So she tried not to tell, but it came out anyway a couple of weeks later when they were spending Sunday afternoon at Eason's Mill, a favorite summer spot for young people.

Stacy had packed a picnic lunch and Ty had brought along a cooler full of beer. They swam for a while in the shady pond, laughing and splashing with a dozen or so others. Predicting who might show up at the mill was impossible. The place was secluded and often deserted, but it was also well known, drawing people from all over the county, especially on hot weekends. The waters of Hominy Creek were cool there, flowing out of the Appalachian foothills, and ancient oaks, hickories, poplars, and maples shaded the banks. The millpond, where the waters pooled before a mossy rock dam laid by mysterious ancestral hands, was partly shaded by overhanging limbs, the deep water blackened by the leaves' tannins.

There was a natural sandy beach beside the shallow waters below the dam. This was where Ty and Stacy spread out to relax and have lunch. They were in the sun, Stacy working on her tan. They sat

Indian style at the edge of their blanket in their frayed cut-offs. Ty was swigging from his fourth beer while Stacy sipped a Coke and brought out the fried chicken and potato salad she'd made herself.

The flowing water gurgled, and they could hear laughter above them. Across the creek a group of three guys and two girls were lolling about in the shade atop a smooth rock outcropping. Stacy was fascinated with them, having seen them before at the Goat. With their long straight hair parted in the middle, they were different from her usual group of acquaintances. One of the girls wore a beaded headband which kept her hair from falling into her face as she bent over something in her lap. They had not been in the water but seemed content in their sandals, halter tops, and loose shorts to sit quietly in the shade. After a time of eating and watching, Stacy asked, "Who are those people?"

"I don't know," Ty answered. "Just some hippies. Ain't you seen 'em around before?"

"Well, yeah, but it seems strange that we don't know who they are."

"Just some hippies. They'll probably be smoking dope over there in a minute, or else they're waiting for a drop-off."

"Drop-off?"

"Yeah. A lot of them come out here to make their dope deals. It's kind of a meeting place for 'em. Damn hippies, ought to get a job."

"Oh."

Stacy continued to observe them as she gathered up wrappers, empties, and leftovers. She became even more interested when she noticed another figure making his way through the trees on the bank, over the rocks to where the group was assembled. This person seemed heavier, older than the rest, and not dressed like a hippie at all. He wore khaki slacks, loafers, and a sport shirt. Ty noticed too, and he also noticed Stacy's reaction at realizing who the intruder was. She said under her breath, "Oh shit," and turned away as if she hadn't seen.

"What?" Ty said.

"Oh nothing. I just didn't expect to see him here."

Ty regarded her sternly for a second, then looked to the other side of the creek where Todd Flemming was kneeling with his back to them, showing something to the five hippies.

"It's just ol' Todd," Ty said quietly. "You didn't know he was a dealer?"

"No."

"Why should you care whether or not Todd's over there selling dope?" Ty asked, his voice taking on a slight edge.

"I don't. It's just that I feel . . . sort of uncomfortable around him."

"Uncomfortable? Why?"

"I don't want to talk about it."

"Well maybe dammit I do. What's going on between you and that son-of-a-bitch?"

"Nothing. He just . . . nothing."

There was a new noise then from Ty's mouth, and when she glanced up, she saw him moving toward her like a striking snake, his arm an uncoiling blur, slow-motion at first, but then fast like lightning in a summer storm. The heel of his open hand struck solid against the fair, delicate skin and cheekbone, splashing jagged light, leaving only darkness and a roaring vacuum.

She dropped to her knees in the sand, clutching her face, before rolling onto her side. She lay there with her face in her hands repeating softly, "Oh, oh. . . ."

The words spewing from his mouth had been, "Don't lie to me, bitch." Now, in the aftermath, with her lying on the sand, the hateful words and the thwack of the blow echoed in his head as he stood bewildered, looking about. What the hell had happened? The old shameful feeling of life dissolving weakened him, and he dropped to his knees beside her, as if he had also suffered a blow.

"Oh baby, I'm sorry, so sorry."

"Damn you, Ty Ragsdale," she sobbed. "I knew you were no good. Now everything's ruined, shot to hell."

"No, no. Ain't nothing ruined. I just snap sometimes when I think of somebody else. . . . It don't mean nothing. You know I love you."

"Does mean something. Means you're crazy and my face hurts like hell." Stacy sobbed through her hands as she lay on her side in the sand.

Ty squatted beside her, pleading, as if he could undo the deed through gentle entreaty. He reached with tentative hands. "Come on baby. Sit up now and let me take a look. I didn't mean it, I just. . .."

She rose partially, one hand pressed over the eye, and pushed herself back with her legs. "Get away from me."

No, no, please . . . it's gonna be okay, I promise. I'll make it up to you."

She sat up the rest of the way, knees in front, keeping one hand to her face. She scowled at him through her right eye, then pulled back when he reached out to her.

He said, "Baby, please," then reached again, moving cautiously.

"It hurts, dammit." She looked to the side then took her hand away.

He gently pushed her hair back and was unable to conceal his dismay. The eye was already swelling and turning dark. "It's gonna be okay," he said. "Maybe we can put some ice on it."

The ice didn't help. What was done was done, carrying its proclaiming banner into an unsure future. Ty was shamed. Everyone would know he did it. They would feel sorry for her and despise him, and the possibility of losing her after waiting so long to find her was real and sobering. He tended to her that afternoon at Eason's Mill, having her hold the ice wrapped in a dish towel to her face while he packed up their belongings. He didn't drink any more that day, and they rode back to town in awkward silence.

"What did you think," Stacy finally asked, "that I was fooling around with that creep Todd?"

"I didn't know—I mean, no. You were just acting funny, like you didn't want me to know about something. It's just that I love you so much, I can't stand the thought of losing you."

"There *was* something I didn't want you to know—about Todd, I mean. But it ain't nothing like what you was thinking. It hurts worse than your hitting me to think you don't trust me no more than that. I ain't got nothing for that jerk. I don't even like to be around him."

"Why? What's he done to you?"

She told him about Todd's comments and crude behavior. "But it don't matter," she insisted. "You've got to promise to let it go, to not make things worse for us."

"Okay, okay. But I'm gonna keep my eye on him, and I expect you to tell me if he tries anything."

"I expect something from you too, really two things. Wanna guess?"

Ty was driving Stacy's Valiant, looking back and forth from her to the road. He said, "I can be better, baby. I can be the man you want me to be." There was a catch in his throat and his head wobbled a bit.

"You can't hit me no more, Ty. That ain't right. You've got to learn to control your temper and to trust me, that is if you love me like you say you do."

She removed the ice from her eye, exposing the bruised, puffy flesh, and looked at him intently. The car swerved a little when he met her gaze and saw what he'd done. He quickly turned back to the road and looked straight ahead, searching for words. Finding something inside that felt real, he replied, "I won't do that no more. I don't know what happened. . . .. There's something comes over me sometimes, a kind of dark cloud, but I know it can pass. If I just look at you—your face, your eyes—I can get through it. I just got to remember to focus on you—us, I mean—and what we have. I promise I won't hit you no more. Can you forgive me this time?"

"I want to, but everything seems different now. We'll just have to take it one day at a time."

The days rolled on, with the black eye there between them, an ugly reminder of how things can suddenly turn dark and stay that way for a long time. It embarrassed Stacy, especially the first few days when the swelling was so bad. It was mid-week before she returned to work, wearing sunglasses to cover the purple streaks that, in her mind, transformed her face into a ruined piece of fruit. To her friends and acquaintances who asked, she offered the standard "walked into a door" response. Todd Flemming didn't ask but looked at her knowingly with a slight nod of satisfaction. The bruise was stubborn and lingered for days. It was faded somewhat by Friday evening, but she still didn't feel comfortable without the glasses. That was the night the stranger came in, a good-looking guy who talked with a Yankee accent.

When she took him home with her that night, she knew it was a big risk, but she also knew there was nothing wrong with it. Nothing was going to happen. She was just helping out a stranger who didn't know anyone and seemed to have no place to go. Ty didn't own her, and he didn't have to know everything. The stranger, Randy Walls from Pittsburgh, was obviously in no condition to be driving. He had sat there by himself and got drunk. She had been interested in him from the beginning, especially when she heard him talk, ordering that "reuben" sandwich. She'd never heard of such a thing. Where he came from must be really different from Prathersville.

During most of that evening, she'd not been able to show much interest in the stranger because Ty was there sipping his beer and observing things from his usual spot at the leaning counter. But he left for work at 10:45, just when everything was loosening up. Still over an hour until last call, time for almost anything to happen. He had talked to her in his awkward, endearing way before he left, trying to affirm their love and the promise to control his temper, but there was something, a tilt of the head or a cut of his eyes, that let Stacy know he had noticed the stranger in the booth drinking by himself and the fact that she seemed to be giving him especially good service. It wasn't a threat, but, in Ty and Stacy's evolving, non-verbal love language, it was close to it. Stacy said, "I love you too. I'll be waiting for you to wake me up in the morning."

★★★

She got word of the accident the next day when her mother, hysterical, called and told her to come home. "Something awful's happened," she sobbed. "It's your daddy. I need you." And that was all. Stacy didn't ask what the matter was—her mother wouldn't have been able to explain anyway—but she knew it was bad. Imagining the worst, she left Ty in bed and drove frantically to the only real home she'd ever known. Riding with her was the dark knowledge that life would be different from now on.

The big house seemed eerily empty. The sheriff had come and gone, after bringing the bad news and turning the body over to the undertaker. Stacy and her mom tried to comfort each other and, between sobs, make plans for the funeral. He would have to be put in the ground quickly. It was a freak thing, his getting cut nearly in two by the pulpwood truck's loader cable. Stacy noticed that the family car wasn't in the driveway and asked where it was. When Mrs. Stempton explained about the new hand who was living in Buena's old shack and helping her daddy, Stacy realized what she'd sensed the night before: that her life was to be somehow connected to that boy who'd come down here from Pittsburgh.

Aunts, uncles, and neighbors began to arrive, bringing pies, cakes, pot roasts, potato salad, and a variety of casseroles and side dishes. The rest of that evening through the funeral the next day went by in a blur. She was surprised that it was not altogether unpleasant. A numbness prevailed that allowed her to respond automatically to the people who thronged into the farmhouse to pay their respects. She drew little comfort from the old acquaintances but was bolstered the next day by a sense of stability when Randy arrived in her brother's blue suit. She felt as if a dear friend, or brother even, who'd been away for a long time had finally come home, and she hugged him from the center of her grief.

The graveside part seemed like a hollow exercise despite all that preaching. Her father, cut in two, was packed in a casket and lowered into the ground. The crowd of mourners—satisfied that customs and expectations were fulfilled—slowly dwindled until Stacy was alone in the big house with her momma and all that foil-wrapped food arranged tidily on kitchen shelves and counter tops. Some of the women offered to stay, but Mrs. Stempton dismissed them, insisting that she and Stacy would be just fine, that Timmy, Stacy's brother, would be here soon. While storm clouds were building outside, Stacy tried to relax with her mother in that house filled with memories, quiet now except for the phantom sounds of her childhood.

Mrs. Stempton had remarked as they were leaving the cemetery that God had blessed them by holding the storm back while they were putting Ben in the ground. But, after that time of stillness, nature's pent-up energy erupted in a squall that pounded the windows and tin roof with solid sheets of water. Protracted peals of thunder rattled the panes. The patterned lightning produced a strobe effect on the world beyond the window, making the trees and outbuildings dance. Stacy felt that the Almighty was paying tribute to her father, respecting his years of hard work and frugal living. The roaring and booming lasted only a few minutes as mother and daughter, awestruck, held hands across the kitchen table. When the clouds opened, a shaft of light made a square beside Stacy's feet on the green linoleum.

The world settled back into stillness both inside and out as the minutes passed. Stacy looked at the clock on the wall, a black and white plastic cat with numbers around its belly and a constantly swishing tail that served as a pendulum. Her mother had bought it to please her as a child, but as time passed Stacy had grown to hate its cartoonish appearance. Now, though, the regular swaying of the tail and the loud ticking produced a bittersweet comfort, a sense that some things remained.

Then a different sound reached her that, while coming from a distance, belonged to the unfaithful present. Ty's motorcycle was approaching, ripping up the dirt road. The sound changed as he eased off the throttle, riding respectfully as he drew near. With the feeling of insects in her stomach, she stepped out to the front porch, into steamy heat. A mist rose from the yard and the pastures surrounding the house. She watched Ty and the motorcycle grow larger, approaching slowly, weaving around the standing water that filled the potholes.

Her mother called out from inside, "Who's there? Is somebody coming?"

"It's just Ty on his motorcycle, come to check on us, I guess."

He eased into the yard, propped the bike on its stand. They each said, "Hi," as he walked up. They sat quietly in the porch rockers for only a short while before Ty grew restless. "I was thinking maybe you'd like to get away for a little while."

"Naa. I can't leave Momma by herself."

"So you're not coming back to the apartment?"

"Not now. I don't know how long I'll need to stay. We're thinking Timmy'll be here from Atlanta soon, and . . . I just don't know."

"Your brother? The one who's queer?"

"He's my brother, Ty."

"Sure, sure, I know. But . . . what about that other guy, the one in the blue suit who was at the Goat before?"

"He's not kin to us. Just works for Daddy."

"Oh."

Words condensed slowly on the surface of their thoughts and clung there, unable to enter the saturated air. Finally, Ty said, "I guess I'll be going." He stood, took a step, then stopped. "I love you."

"I love you too," she said. "I'll call you later."

His goodbye kiss was forceful and probing. Stacy didn't respond as she usually did, but pulled back, pressing against his chest with her palms. He gave her a lingering, brown-eyed look as he mounted up and fastened his helmet. He started the engine without revving it and eased off at just above idle. But the sound changed as he faded into the mist. The Beast began to roar, getting louder as the rear tire slipped on the slick road then caught. The pitch of the snarling engine modulated angrily as Ty snatched it through the gears at full throttle. She knew he was fishtailing, nearly out of control. She couldn't see through the fog, but she heard him for a long time. The crawling in her stomach persisted, and she wished—prayed—that he would slow down.

Ben Stempton's Boy

Part III—Randy and the Stemptons

Chapter 12

The heavy tears of a bereaved giant were dropping onto the steel barrel outside Stacy's window. Each tear made an echoing metallic *brrop* as it dropped, a rhythmic plop-dropping growing louder, the ripping pop-drop rhythm of giant tears like liquid popcorn popping in a big steel pan. Familiar yet unidentified, the sound of hard spurts on kettle drum heads tugged at her senses, becoming a song in her mind, a melodious rain without thunder, giant raindrops making a danceable Latin rhythm she knew from long ago. As the tempo picked up and the rhythm found itself, an aroma—mellow—slipped in easy like a fat tomcat. The nutty fragrance, earthy and round, suggested an open-air bazaar. Exotic Bogota: pictures from school came to mind. There was also bustling movement around her; things were getting done and she realized with a start that her participation was required. She sat up in bed, blinking and rubbing her eyes. As her nostrils expanded with the fresh-perked coffee smell, her mind filled with the knowledge that she was in her old bedroom and her daddy was dead.

Her momma was busy, talking to herself and Stacy at the same time, urging her to get up because there was much to do. "Stacy, baby, hop on up now and get dressed. The coffee's ready and I got an errand for you to run." Stacy knew well the tone of her momma's voice. There was no point in trying to resist. She threw back the sheet and padded into the kitchen, drawn there by the aroma and the sounds of her mother shuffling and working with utensils. Perplexed, she asked, "What are you doing, Momma?"

She was kneading a batch of biscuit dough. "I figure by the time you get back here with him, breakfast will be ready, and we can eat and talk about what we're gonna do now. I couldn't sleep last night for thinking about things. That boy, Randy, I feel bad about the way we dropped him off after the funeral like he was no more than a hired nigger—after he'd carried your poor daddy's casket. I want to talk to him and make things right. You ride on over to Buena's shack and get him. Breakfast will be ready when y'all get back."

"But Momma, I'm not ready to go out and see anybody. I look awful."

"Nobody expects you to look good the day after your daddy's funeral. I don't want to hold breakfast up on account of your primping. But . . . well, the oven ain't hardly had time to heat. I guess you could take a few minutes to brush your hair out. And I won't start the bacon and eggs till after you leave."

Stacy took a cup of coffee with her into the bathroom where she hurried to make herself presentable. It occurred to her that Randy had seen her when she first crawled out of bed once before, without makeup and still in her nightshirt, but this was different. This time she was going outside of the house, and she was supposed to pick him up and bring him back here, to the place that was her real home. After a few minutes her mother called out from the kitchen, "Hurry up, I'm putting the biscuits in right now."

She applied her lipstick in the car as she drove slowly over the dirt road in the direction of the shack. With her attention on her face in the rearview, she was slow to notice the hulking figure in the road ahead, someone walking toward her. She blinked the image into focus: Randy. She stopped the car, quickly kissed a napkin, and dropped it along with the lipstick tube into her purse. She wondered what he could be doing.

He was moving slowly, leaning forward like an old man, bearing his weight on a walking stick nearly as tall as he was. She knew it was him by his long dark hair falling across his forehead and the fact that no one else would be walking alone out here at this hour of the morning. With eyes downcast, he seemed to have not yet noticed her, stopped there in the Valiant watching him. She soon made out the reason for his leaning forward on the stick: he was laboring under the weight of a large backpack, and his brow indicated he was lost in thought. Finally, he looked up and paused for several seconds, contemplating. Stacy eased forward. Randy at last smiled as if he were coming back to himself from a pleasant daydream.

He leaned on his stick as Stacy pulled the car up alongside. "Where you headed, stranger, anyplace in particular?" she asked through the open window.

"Funny you should ask. Actually, no. I'm not—headed anyplace in particular. I just thought it was time to move on."

"Maybe you could use a good breakfast first, before you head out to wherever. Momma sent me over here to pick you up. She wants to talk to you."

"Hmm, I guess I could adjust my tight schedule to allow time for breakfast, especially if your mom's cooking." Randy leaned the walking stick against the fender of the car and began to hunch and twist his shoulders to remove the backpack.

"Nice stick," Stacy commented.

"Yeah, I like it too. Found it in the woods one day when I was working with . . . your dad. I trimmed it up and did some carving on it with a pocketknife he gave me."

Stacy looked at the stick, noticing its smooth surface and how straight and stout it was. She imagined Randy sitting on the porch of that old shack with a pocketknife, stripping the bark and whittling away the knots and rough places. At the passenger door, he struggled to get his gear over the forward-folded front seat into the rear of the car. He had to walk back around to get the stick. He seemed self-conscious as he passed in front. Stacy yielded to a childish impulse and blasted the horn, sending him into a spasmodic jerk as if he'd stepped on a live wire. His reaction—great movement compressed into an instant—sent him to Stacy's side of the car where he tried to recover, blinking, his mouth agape. She laughed impishly. "Sorry, I couldn't resist."

"It's okay," he said, beginning to grin. "I needed that. Now I feel really awake."

"Good! That was the idea. You don't want to be half asleep when you eat Momma's famous biscuits, do you? Grab your stick and let's go."

★★★

The ride back only took a couple of minutes. Randy appreciated the opportunity to spend time with Stacy, but he was thinking too hard about what to say, not knowing how sensitive she might be about her dad's death. As they pulled into the yard, she asked, "You weren't really going to leave without saying goodbye, were you?"

"Well, that's what I was thinking about before you picked me up just now, about how I should stop here at the house and say goodbye and everything."

Stacy switched off the engine and looked at him thoughtfully. "Come on, let's eat."

Moving toward the porch, he noticed the morning air and sky: there was something different, as if burying the old man had pushed the earth slightly closer to autumn. The smell of bacon and coffee beckoned as he followed Stacy through the screen door. This was the third time he'd entered the Stempton home. Yesterday before the funeral was the second time; the first had been just a few days ago when he'd been invited to supper. He hadn't even known Stacy then. Life-changing events had followed his coming here. The whole world seemed different now.

He followed Stacy into the hub of activity, the kitchen, where Mrs. Stempton was placing a circular baking pan filled with golden-brown biscuits on the center of the table. With artistic movements she managed to set the hot pan down on the same pot holder that she used to carry it. That done, she straightened her back at their approach. She wiped her hands on her apron then extended one. "Hello Randy. I'm proud you could join us this morning."

"Good morning. Thanks. I'm glad you asked me to come."

"Sit down right there. Everything's ready. I just need to put the grits in a bowl. Stacy, pour Randy some coffee."

"How do you take your coffee, Randy. Would you like cream and sugar?" Stacy asked.

"I've never had it any way but black. I didn't drink coffee until I came to Georgia. Mr. Stempton used to bring it to me in the mornings before we'd go to the woods."

Both women stopped for a moment at the mention of the dead man's name. "Well," Stacy said, clearing her throat, "you might like it with cream and sugar. Lots of people take it that way. It's not so bitter. I'll fix it and you can tell me what you think."

"Sure. I'd like to try that."

"I've got a big bowl of grits here Randy," Mrs. Stempton said. "Y'all ever eat grits up there where you're from?"

"Well, no. Not really. I mean some people do, but I never had them till I came down here."

Stacy placed a thick mug beside him, filled nearly to the brim with steaming coffee, creamed to a light caramel shade. "Here," she said, "this should be sweet and rich."

Randy sipped the steaming beverage and immediately fell in love, surprised by its smoothness. "Umm, that's good," he said, looking over the table at Stacy "It tastes entirely different the way you make it."

"My daddy was a plain and simple man. He didn't like nothing that was dolled-up or fancy, and he figured everybody else ought to be the same way. To him, black coffee was good enough. It probably never dawned on him that you might be a cream and sugar sort of person."

He nodded and took another sip as Mrs. Stempton placed a platter of sliced cantaloupe on the table in front of him. The aromas and female voices blended, making him feel slightly drunk. With his elbows on the table and eyes half shut he held the mug just under his chin so he could feel the rising steam.

"I think this one's good and ripe," Mrs. Stempton said. "You can always tell by the smell. You do like cantaloupe, don't you Randy?"

It took him a second to respond. "Oh, sure, I like cantaloupe just fine."

Mrs. Stempton began passing things. "Here Randy, have some grits," she said, holding the heavy bowl under his face. As he set the coffee mug down to take the hot grits, she said, "I didn't know how you like your eggs, so I just scrambled them. Most folks like them awright that way. We like ours a little on the soft side."

Stacy, having sliced open and buttered a couple of hot biscuits for herself, was ready to pass that platter around. Then came the eggs and bacon. He'd picked up his fork and was about to plunge in when Mrs. Stempton said, "My goodness, children, I almost forgot. We haven't returned thanks yet. Stacy, will you ask the blessing, please."

"Yes ma'am." She bowed her head and paused for only a second. "Dear Lord, thank you for this that we're about to receive and for all table comforts and for the blessings of this life. Bless us during these hard times, and bless Randy, so that he might feel at home and part of our family. In Jesus' name, Amen."

Mrs. Stempton answered, "Amen," and they lifted their heads. Stacy and her momma began to eat with purpose. Randy paused for a moment with the sound of his name and Stacy's prayer echoing in his mind. Being prayed for out loud was a new experience that made his scalp tingle, but he was too overwhelmed by the aromas of food to think about it for long. They were too busy eating to speak, but after a while they each paused to breathe. With the piles of eggs and grits on her plate reduced to about half of their original proportions, Mrs. Stempton said, "Well, Randy, I was wondering if you'd made any plans yet—about what you're going to do now."

He paused with a hunk of egg on his fork. "I don't have any definite plans, but I'd like to travel some—maybe go out west—and work along the way."

Mrs. Stempton nodded. "I guess that'd be okay. It just seems hard to me, moving around like that from place to place without having anywhere to call home. Why, I could count on one hand the nights I've slept somewhere besides under this roof since I married Stacy's daddy nearly thirty years ago."

"Yeah, we never went anywhere when I was a kid," Stacy said, "only down to Panama City a few times."

"That's not the point, honey. A person needs a home—a place where some roots can take hold, a roof overhead, some responsibilities, people who . . . care about 'em. Otherwise, they just don't ever—you know—bear fruit."

"Bear fruit? What kind of fruit? I don't get it, Momma. Can't a person go out into the world and experience what's out there without having to worry about fruit?"

"Yes, some people live that way, just thinking about themselves, but I don't think that's why the Lord put us here."

Randy slipped the cooling egg hunk in his mouth as his eyes went back and forth between Stacy and her mom.

"Well then, what did the Lord put us here for, Momma? To work all our lives just getting by, like Daddy, only to get cut in two in some freak accident? What kinda purpose is that?"

"The good Lord's plan is much bigger than us, child. Your daddy's hard work supported me, you, and your brother all these years. You wouldn't be here now if it weren't for him. That's purpose enough, I reckon."

Stacy looked down at her plate without answering. Randy did the same. Mrs. Stempton continued: "Now that your daddy's gone, things are different. We've got to find a way to carry on as a family without him. It takes money to live, you know, and we've got . . . obligations."

"What kind of obligations?" Stacy asked. "Ain't the house and everything paid for?"

"Yes, but we've got to eat. And there's upkeep to consider—you know that old well pump's about worn out—and the car's gonna need new tires pretty soon. The plumbing needs work, and winter's coming. It just goes on and on, and there ain't no savings. Your daddy's funeral took all that. I've got lots to worry over. Somebody's got to think about these things. It's your brother's rightful place, but he's too busy doing whatever he does over there in the city to come around, even to his father's funeral. So, it's up to us." She lifted a piece of bacon from her plate, then put it back down and continued speaking:

"That's why I wanted Randy to come over this morning. Your daddy had a contract to finish clearing the pulpwood off the Jenkins property over on Taylor's Gin Road—you know, Randy, it's where y'all started working last week. There was some advance payments made on that job that we ain't earned yet, money that's already spent." Her eyes moved back and forth between her plate, Stacy, and Randy. "There was to be another big payment when the job's finished. Plus what we get for the wood. Deal was that we—your daddy and Randy, I mean—were to clear off all the pine, pull up the stumps, and get rid of the brush. Mr. Jenkins and his partner are planning to put a subdivision or something in there."

"I didn't know about clearing the stumps and brush," Randy said. "I thought we were just cutting the pulpwood, as usual."

"This is a big job, Randy. And we were counting on it to help us get through the winter."

They thoughtfully resumed eating. Stacy wiped her mouth on a paper towel. "Momma, why don't you just sell the farm. We could get you an apartment in town. You wouldn't have to work so hard, and there wouldn't be nothing to worry about."

Mrs. Stempton didn't answer but turned her head away. Randy noticed her blinking eyes and the slight quiver of her lip. She got up, turning her broad back to them, went to the counter and started moving things around. After a moment she said, "Randy, would you like some syrup for your biscuits or more coffee? I can scramble up some more eggs if y'all will eat them. How about you, Stacy? Would you like more eggs?"

"No, I'm about full. We don't need nothing else, Momma. Just sit down here and rest. I'll clear the table."

"No, no, I'm fine. I'll clean up the kitchen. Why don't you and Randy go sit on the porch and talk about things young folks are interested in. Maybe you can persuade him to stay and help us finish that contract. There'd be some good money in it for him, too."

"Okay. Come on, Randy. You done eating yet?"

Randy looked back to Mrs. Stempton, who was putting things in the sink. Then he popped the last bite of thickened grits in his mouth along with a crisp rind of bacon and gulped the dregs of his coffee. "I am now."

Chapter 13

On the front porch they sat and rocked for a while, smoking and looking out across the road and the green hills beyond. Randy felt awkward. Then Stacy began to talk; her words trickled at first but soon gushed, like water through a thawing pipe. Randy, entranced by the drawling melody of her babbling, listened as she apologized for her momma's abrupt dropping of the "contract thing" in his lap. Then she explained her mother's behavior through reminiscences of their long and sometimes difficult relationship.

"I love her," Stacy said, "and she's been really good to me, her and Daddy both, but she always worries over things, like she's got to control everybody's life. That's why I had to leave, to get my own apartment."

Randy cocked his head, trying to imagine how that would be. "Your parents," he finally answered, "they're really good people. Seems to me that maybe somebody trying to control your life wouldn't be so bad. I never had that—well, except for the nuns and foster parents, but it wasn't like they really cared." This prompted the memory that always floated up, the one he hated most, but the man and woman in his mind evaporated when he turned back to Stacy. "Now that I'm on my own, half the time I don't know what to do next. . . ." She looked at him expectantly. Encouraged, he continued: "Just when I get a clear idea, something happens, and it all starts to shift again. I never feel like I know enough, and sometimes I'm afraid that whatever choice I make is gonna end up somehow killing me."

Stacy turned in her rocker and placed her hand on his knee. Looking into his face she whispered earnestly. "Well, you know what they say about life: you'll never get out of it alive. Might as well make the most of it while you can. At least, that's what I think."

From the blue sweep of her eyes and the lilt of her voice, Randy derived the pleasure of a shared pledge, a pact between him and this girl, that, somehow, they were in this together, and that together they would make the most of this confusing life. It was enough, and without speaking it yet, even to himself, a decision began to congeal in his heart. He was confident in his ability to finish out the contract. He could drive the truck, run the saw, and do whatever else was required. He would be willing to pit his muscles and skills against any obstacle to be near Stacy and contribute to her well-being. There was a shape and order to this, at least.

But he stumbled when he tried to imagine the job. The only work he'd done with the old man was cutting and loading pulpwood and driving the truck. He didn't understand the land-clearing part of the deal. Maybe Stacy would know about this aspect of the work; he could ask. The sense of comfort he felt with her had been there from the beginning, when she'd waited on him at the Billy Goat Bar. With yesterday's funeral in the past and their stomachs satisfied, the space between them seemed charged with warm currents. He lit another cigarette. "How was your father planning to clear that land? He didn't mention it to me, and I never worked at pulling up stumps before."

Stacy's chuckle pushed smoke through her flared nostrils. "You're such a city boy."

He smiled, looked down at his feet.

"Clearing land's a big part of what we do down here," She continued. "Most boys are experts at it by the time they're twelve or so. Of course, we start 'em out real young because it's kinda complicated."

"Yeah, sure. How complicated can pulling up stumps be?"

"You'd be surprised to know, being a city person and all, that stump-pulling requires huge amounts of planning and a careful strategy. But most of all it requires a tractor and a good chain, or at least a mule that knows how to gee-haw. Since the last mule Daddy owned died of old age when I was about six, I guess you'll have to use the tractor."

"Tractor? What tractor?"

"You mean Daddy never showed you? I'm surprised. That little Ford was his pride and joy. I think he loved it more than he did his kids. Come on, we'll go for a ride."

Adjacent to the house were several sheds and outbuildings. At the border of yard and fenced pasture stood a tin-roofed barn with a shuttered loft and sagging double doors closing off the central hallway. The steep roofline changed pitch just above head level on either side, forming two open sheds filled with old baskets, rolls of rusty barbwire, plows, ropes, straps, jars, and all manner of implements. To Randy's mind as he approached behind Stacy, who had left the porch at a trot, the scene presented a confusing array of junk. He quickened his step to close the gap between him and the girl.

A short length of rusty chain, looped through holes bored long ago, held the doors closed and secured them to each other. Stacy dragged the chain through the worn wood, then began to grapple with the door, tugging on an attached block which served as a handle. "Daddy always complained about these old sagging doors and how aggravating they were to open, but he never got around to fixing them. Here, help me lift up a little so they don't drag the ground."

He applied his strength alongside hers, and the doors swung on creaking hinges to uncloak an overwhelming aura. The smells of the old man's sweat and tobacco were mingled with the barn odors of moldy hay and manure, and there also was the smell of greasy tools, engines, and gasoline. Stacy entered the dim space first, reached up and pulled a string, bringing to glaring life a bulb hanging from the joists overhead.

The gray and red tractor, parked to allow walking room on each side, was bathed in the yellow glow like the centerpiece of a carefully designed arrangement. Everything else seemed to derive its reason for being from the machine: belts and radiator hoses hanging from the rough wall studs, old inner tubes, rusty hitch pins, oil cans, funnels, grimy spare parts on makeshift shelves, the mounted vise and workbench on one end, along with an array of wrenches, tools, and implements—all paid quiet homage.

Randy said, "Wow."

Stacy proceeded to the tractor's side. "I smell gas, don't you? Oh shit, I can't believe Daddy forgot to turn the valve off. The gasket's shot on the sediment bowl and it always drips a little. Daddy's usually real particular to turn it off when he gets finished, but it looks like he forgot."

Randy came around to examine the object of concern. The glass bowl, as big as half an egg, was mounted on the side of the engine and held in place from the bottom by a curved rod with a thumbwheel for tightening. Gravity was pulling the gasoline past the faulty gasket at the bowl's top, and its sides shimmered from the solvent's effect. Dripping fuel darkened the packed earth below. Stacy said, "Sometimes if you tighten this little wheel, it quits leaking." As she applied pressure to the bottom of the bowl, moving the wheel a bit, the frequency of the drips increased. "Shoot, that just made it worse. Guess we'll have to fix it. All we got to do is make a new gasket."

"Make a gasket? I thought you had to buy those."

"Well sure, we could, but that wouldn't be much of a challenge. Besides, we'd have to go into town to the tractor place and spend money and waste all that time. Daddy always figured out how to make things work." Stacy squinted, looking around at the shelves and back wall. "I've seen him make rubber gaskets out of old inner tubes, and one just happens to be hanging right there. We'll have it fixed in no time. Then we'll go for a ride."

"I'll admit, that'll be a new experience for me, but do we need to do it right now? Doesn't your mother need you?"

"She'll be okay as long as she's got work to do. She'll probably start in on fixing lunch soon as she gets those breakfast dishes cleaned up. Besides, if you're gonna stay and work out the rest of that contract, somebody's got to show you how to operate Li'l Trudy."

"'Li'l Trudy'?"

Stacy smiled and looked up from the tractor. "Yeah, that's what I named her when I was in seventh grade, after a girl in my class we called Big Trudy. I imagined if she lost about a hundred pounds, she'd look like this tractor here. Weird, I know. Something about this forward lean they both had. See, Trudy was real chesty"—Stacy hoisted imaginary melons in front of her breasts— "and all that hanging weight made her lean forward when she walked. Anyway, that's how the tractor got her name. Sometimes Daddy even used it. 'Guess I'd better fire up Li'l Trudy and go plow the garden,' he'd say."

Randy smiled and Stacy, after tossing her hair back, set herself to removing the fuel bowl. Randy was about to object, to assert his independence. He was thinking the words: Hey, wait a minute. I never said I was gonna stay . . . but as he noticed Stacy's eyes, intent on the task before her, and watched her busy hands, he decided to let the moment carry him wherever it would.

They were soon riding together in the morning sun, but as midday approached clouds of doubt began to gather. At one point, when they'd stopped the tractor on the other side of the pasture and Stacy was explaining the gears and hydraulic lift operation, Randy let her see his faltering confidence: "You know, I'm starting to think this may be more than I can handle. I want to help your mom and everything, but this is all so new, and it's so much—you know— *responsibility*. What if I can't get that place cleared off soon enough? What then? Maybe your mom should just hire someone who knows what he's doing."

Randy was sitting in the seat, Stacy leaning at his side against the tractor. When she looked directly into his face, he noticed the remaining hint of bruise under her left eye. She blinked and said softly, "Momma has full confidence in your being able to handle the job, and so do I. Shoot, I might even be able to help you some, before I go to work in the evenings. I've helped Daddy pull stumps plenty of times. It ain't no big deal. I know you're strong enough. I mean, look at you, all the way down here from Pittsburgh, on your own. I believe you can handle about anything, that is if you really want to. And the other thing is we trust you, Momma and me. You're the kind that does right by people, and that's hard to find." She paused, blinked, then added in a softer voice, "We really need you to stay, Randy. *I* need you to stay."

Her words blew across his doubts like a warm breeze, and he consented in the light of the sun, fully committing himself to something that could—at least part of him knew—be the most bruising task of his life. He made the official announcement to Mrs. Stempton at noontime when they gathered once again, as Stacy had predicted, around the table piled high with food.

Casseroles; sliced ham; a bowl of green beans; a platter of tomato, onion, and cucumber slices; and a basket filled with golden puffy rolls filled the table. Three sweating glasses of iced tea completed the place settings. Mrs. Stempton's forehead was also beaded with sweat. She used her forearm to pat the moisture back into her hair, which had started to fall. "Y'all got to help me here. There's so much food, can't let it go to waste. Wash up and sit down. I know you must be hungry."

Then, once again, the table became the focal point, an altar in a ritual Randy didn't understand. He and Stacy were relaxed in each other's company, but Mrs. Stempton seemed tired and tense, trying too hard to make them comfortable. When Randy commented that he wasn't really hungry after that huge breakfast, she replied, "Folks your age burn a lot of energy just buzzing around and being alive. You've got to eat to keep your strength up. Sit over here on this side, you'll get more of a breeze through the window. Here Stacy, take your usual place. There's some peach cobbler too, whenever y'all are ready. I figured it was too hot for coffee, but I'll make some if y'all will drink it. Some folks drink coffee all day long, winter and summer. I prefer a cold glass of tea myself, especially this time of year, and I like a lot of lemon. I think you got that from me, Stacy. You always did like lemons, even when you were a little thing. I remember you biting into 'em and making the funniest faces. . .."

She kept jabbering and patting her brow with her forearm as she moved things around and brought utensils to the table. Stacy looked at Randy and rolled her eyes.

When Mrs. Stempton bent to spoon some squash casserole into her plate, Stacy protested. "Momma, that's fine, really. I just want a piece of ham and a tomato slice and one of those rolls. We're not really that hungry. If you'll sit down and relax a minute, I think Randy's got something to say."

"Well, my goodness. If this young man wants to talk, then I'm ready to listen." She dabbed at her brow once more, then pulled out a chair.

Randy looked at Stacy first, then at the table. Expectant eyes were on him. He cleared his throat. "Stacy and I have talked, and I've thought about it, and I guess I could stay around a while longer and finish up that contract with Mr. Jenkins. That is, I'll try my best if you really want me to."

The tightly wound rubber band inside Mrs. Stempton relaxed incrementally as she looked from Randy to Stacy then back. She exhaled and took a long gulp of tea from her sweating glass.

Stacy finally spoke, "Well, say something, Momma. What do you think?"

"I think that's wonderful news, just wonderful. I feel like a tremendous load's been lifted. Randy, I don't know how to thank you, but I'll try to make sure you've got everything you need. I had faith all along that you wouldn't let us down. Now here, eat some of this casserole."

Randy sat quietly as she spooned the yellow mush into his plate. When he glanced over at Stacy, he thought she seemed pleased with him, and he felt the comfort that comes with doing the right thing.

There was much to talk about, the logistics of getting started on the big job. Details fell into place as if guided by fate. A mood of relaxed confidence permeated the discussion. Mrs. Stempton pointed out the particulars as Randy nodded in agreement. He would have to get the old flatbed truck out of the corn crib. He could use it for hauling brush and supplies and for getting around while the pulpwood truck was at the jobsite. It needed a battery and maybe a tire, but she could meet those expenses. Mr. Stempton had been planning to get the flatbed out anyway. It would be convenient for Randy to stop by the house each morning for coffee and a biscuit and pick up his lunch, which Stacy's mom would have ready for him. She would also feed him supper each night.

Stacy took over clearing the table and washing dishes as they made plans. She turned from the sink occasionally to offer suggestions, and Randy noticed that she always looked at him with that pleased expression. Mrs. Stempton smiled and nodded. At one point she said softly, "Thank you Lord, thank you Jesus." Then she got up and left the room. "Sit tight, you two. I'll be right back."

Stacy dried her hands and folded the dish towel. "Sounds like y'all about got things worked out."

Before Randy could answer, Mrs. Stempton reentered. "Here, take this for running money. You'll need things—gas, oil, and maybe a new chain for the saw. This should hold you for a while. Let me know when you need more."

Randy was surprised to see that she was offering a hundred-dollar bill. Stacy said, "Go on, take it. It's for operating expenses. Momma's always got a little extra put away back there."

Then the disappointment came, leaving an aftertaste like rancid butter on a biscuit. A nonchalant statement from Stacy turned the glow of wellbeing at Randy's center into a knot, similar to what he'd felt when the old man first brought him into the home. Reality had been misrepresented. But hadn't the distortion been in his own mind? He'd known all along about her boyfriend, Ty, and he should have known that nothing in that relationship had changed as a result of his agreeing to stay. This hard fact presented itself when she said that now, since her momma was feeling so relieved, she was going back to town—to the apartment she shared with Ty—and her job at the Billy Goat Bar.

On her way she dropped Randy off. "I'll see you later, and thanks, by the way, for making Momma feel a lot better. I appreciate it." While her expression toward him was the same, his feelings were different. The sun had disappeared again behind dark clouds of doubt. He replied, "Sure. See you later," as he wrestled his backpack from the car.

He approached the rickety porch steps knowing that Mrs. Stempton and Stacy expected him to get started in the morning. He tried to relax inside his shack, but the disappointment lingered throughout the evening and deep into the night as he squirmed on musty sheets, pressing the pillow around his head to muffle the mocking chorus of insects and night creatures.

Chapter 14

The bacon popped and splattered hot grease as Ty Ragsdale cursed the electric stove he wasn't used to. The skillet was too hot, and he couldn't get it to cool down quickly enough. At three in the afternoon he was making breakfast for himself. He had slept hard all day after working the night before, and now, with stinging splatter burns on his forearms, his aggravation was mounting over having to prepare his own food. He and Stacy had, over the last few weeks, developed a routine whereby she cooked in the afternoons—breakfast for him and supper for her—before she went to work at the Billy Goat Bar. Nothing seemed right with her away, and he felt large and awkward in the apartment without her.

Ty thought about how Stacy's old man getting cut in two had really messed things up. That and his hitting her in the face that day at the mill. He was still trying to work through that problem. He remembered her saying, "Now everything's ruined, shot to hell," as she lay sobbing on the sand. He had groped for a way to take it back, to rewind the tape and play it again with calmness and reason in control instead of those dark flapping things in his mind, but he latched on to nothing save the rush of hot air from a split balloon. He wanted to make things right, to show her that everything wasn't ruined, that he really could be a better person. But being a better person could be difficult, especially with an empty stomach and a pan full of smoking bacon.

Just as he was about to dump the whole mess into the trash, he recognized the sound of her car in the drive. Finally, he thought, we can get things straightened out around here. He switched off the eye and abandoned the smoke-filled kitchen to go meet her.

"Hey baby," he said as he pulled open the door. "Glad you're home."

"Me too. What's that smell?"

Instead of answering Ty pulled her to him, squeezed her back and butt, pressed his mouth to hers, and began probing with his tongue. She melted against him for a few seconds, then squirmed away.

"Wow!" she said. "Is that you smoking, or is the apartment on fire?"

"Oh that," he answered, releasing his grip. "I was trying to cook breakfast."

"You poor thing, waking up all by yourself with nobody to cook for you. You must be starving. Give me a second and I'll fix you something."

Ty looked her up and down. "Food ain't the only thing I need right now."

Stacy smiled. "Hmm, okay then. Maybe I can help you out in that department too."

"That's my girl," he said, opening his arms to her. She stepped into his embrace and they kissed, tenderly at first, then with mounting passion as their mouths became animated with desire. They slathered each other with affection in the front room of the apartment, their heads bathed in the smoke of burnt bacon. That and other matters became inconsequential as their bodies, attuned to each other, responded to the vigorous pressing.

She squirmed away and pulled him into the bedroom. He began to roughly undress her, yanking her shirttail out of her denim shorts. They each labored over the other's buttons and buckles, grunting and panting. Ty, surprised at Stacy's eagerness, decided to let her take the lead. Sitting back on the bed, he smiled as she pulled off his jeans and briefs in one stout pull. He quickly flipped his tee shirt over his head, then lay back with his ankles crossed, arms behind his neck.

Stacy wriggled out of her bra and panties, straddled his thighs, and bent to press her face against his smooth chest. She began to move up and over him so that her midsection, from breasts to navel, slid along the length of his erection, which throbbed against the changing contours. Ty wanted to drink it in slowly: the touch of her skin and the fragrance of her honey-thick hair, which he gathered in his fingers and pulled to his face.

He decided to remain passive while she set the pace. She began to whimper, and her sliding motion carried her farther up his body. Pushing against his shoulders, she raised her chest and arched her back. Her rump was over him. As she bumped and quivered, Ty, through closed eyes, rushing blood, and sensitized flesh comprehended her desire in merged images of vibrating orange.

She raised herself as he arched and pushed. She slipped back down and hit bottom. "Oh yes!" He kept his eyes closed while her butt made small squeezing rotations. His only movement was to tighten his buttocks to give himself fully to her. She rode slowly and deeply with a twitching pause at the top of each stroke as she gathered him in and released, tightening and relaxing in the rhythm of ocean swells.

A kaleidoscope swirled in his mind, bringing Florene Otwell's face into view, his first lover who had taken away his boyhood. But when he opened his eyes, Stacy's expression of hard-won pleasure was before him. Her hair was wild and fallen. He focused on her flaring nostrils and wet, open mouth. Reaching bottom again, she raised her head, revealing the flushed skin of her neck, and shook her hair back enough for him to see flashing blue eyes behind half-closed lids and the faded bruise he'd put there.

No longer able to remain passive, he pulled her down tight against him, arched his back, and pushed against the bed with his foot. Holding her against his chest, he flipped her over while preserving their intimate union. The pressure of his upper body against the backs of her legs folded her so that her heels bounced against his shoulder blades. Needing to reach places that had never been touched, he pushed his torso hard against her, using the footboard for leverage. With each thrust he plowed a deeper furrow.

Florene had taught him how to make it last, and he used this knowledge to possess Stacy fully, to fill, dominate, and control. His thrusts continued, hard, slow, and deep, while he concentrated on his boot with frayed laces, lying on the floor at the edge of the bed. The building of tingly sensations in his groin could be delayed for a while. His body worked as his mind detached itself.

Time stopped and the narrow bedroom expanded with his lungs as he pounded his hard body against Stacy, whose tiny whimpers and grunts marked the rhythm of his strokes. She tossed her head in an agony of submission, rubbing her tangled hair against his cheek. Her damp hair seemed to pass a current, and her nervous system became his own. The connection with the bootlace broke. He closed his eyes and let the nerve flow have its way as she strained and pushed against him, panting in hot, breathy bursts. The waves of pleasure crested higher into space beyond. The current concentrated in his groin, a high-tension electrical coil. The deep thrusts quickened and shortened into pelvic vibrations, fast as a drum roll; then, with the gathered energy of a summer storm, came the white-flashing release as Ty spent himself convulsively into Stacy, his girlfriend, his love.

The wind of desire slackened, leaving their bodies limp and wet as sails after a squall. He relaxed his arms and let his chest rest against hers as she slid her legs along his hips and thighs. She continued to squeeze him, cooing like a contented dove, as he softened inside her. When he started to roll off, she laughed, clamped him back down, and said, "Unh-uh. You've got to stay right here till I say you can go."

"Okay. I'm too weak to argue."

"I guess so, after that workout."

Ty laughed. "Umm-mm . . . I love you girl."

They kissed tenderly and lightly stroked each other's ticklish spots for a long time, changing positions but maintaining skin contact as reality crept back in. Finally, Stacy said, "I've got to get up and get ready for work."

Crawling over Ty, she patted his belly. "I need to hurry," she said. "I'm gonna jump in the shower. Oh shoot! I never did fix you anything to eat. I know you're starving. I guess I could go in a few minutes late."

Ty would have enjoyed lying back a while longer as she cooked for him, then stuffing himself with eggs, grits, and bacon. With her father's funeral only the day before, no one would fault her for not going to work, and he was about to tell her to take the night off and relax with him. He knew he could persuade her, but restlessness was creeping in, bringing the need to move, to be someplace else.

"That's okay, baby," he said at last as she stood, naked, waiting for his response. Her small breasts seemed alert and playful, eager to please. He answered with the sense that he was disappointing them. "Don't worry about it. I can grab something at Maggie's later, or make a sandwich."

"You sure? I mean, I'd be happy to fix you something." She bent to pick her panties up off the floor. "Won't take but a minute."

"Naa. I should get going myself. Need to run by the parts store before he closes and pick up a few things. The weather's gon' be getting cooler soon. I need to get the coupe back in shape so I can start driving it to work."

"Okay. But you'll be coming by the Goat tonight before you go in?"

"Sure babe. I'll see you there after I take care of some stuff."

Ty could hear the shower running as he pulled on his boots and grabbed his helmet. He left the apartment eager to unite with his mechanical soul mate, get some wind in his face, and push hard over his favorite stretches of back road.

Chapter 15

After Ty left on his motorcycle, Stacy realized she couldn't go into work that evening. She was overwhelmed by the events of the last few days and the reality of death. Dizzy, exhausted, and confused, she plopped down on the tattered sofa where Randy had slept only a few nights before, when he was still a stranger. She mustered the energy to call in and ask the night off, and she left messages for Ty. She would see him in the morning, but for now, she didn't know what to do. It occurred to her that she'd been behaving selfishly, and she began to worry about her mother.

With eyes closed she could still see her, there in the old kitchen, holding back the tears. Stacy should have known better than to suggest she sell the farm and move to town. Those few acres and that old house, along with her children, were everything to her now. She felt that she and Timmy had abandoned her in her time of greatest need. The more Stacy thought, the more miserable and empty she felt.

The emptiness radiated from her physical center. Making love with Ty had filled an immediate need. Now, alone in that little apartment, hastily furnished from the second-hand store, she felt hollow inside. Her father was gone—dead and buried—and here she was fucking a violence-prone high school dropout who really didn't give a damn, as if their satisfaction was the most important thing. Her mother was broken by death and disappointment, clinging to a thin vine of hope that a stranger, Randy Walls from Pittsburgh, could provide salvation from government housing and family breakdown. Stacy had abandoned her in that kitchen sanctuary with her cherished utensils, pots, and pans, all of which had become superfluous, like garden tools after an unexpected frost.

She imagined the repeating loop of worry that would be winding through her mother's mind: the urgent prayers for Timmy's salvation and safe homecoming; for Stacy's seeing the light and returning to the ways of her upbringing; for Randy's strength, stability, and confidence; for health and continued faithfulness for herself so she could continue to serve others; the needs of dozens of church and community members whom Stacy didn't know or care about, lifted up each Wednesday night at prayer meeting by her momma, while she served beer at the Billy Goat Bar. She trembled and sobbed, desiring more than anything to hug and be hugged by her mother and father and to breathe the earthy fragrance of their love and labor.

She would call to see how she was doing—to hear her voice—and then drive back over to spend the night. As she reached for the phone, it rang, scattering her thoughts. She took a deep breath and waited until it rang again before answering softly, "Hello."

"Hi Stace. It's me."

"Timmy! Where have you been? Why aren't you here?"

"Don't start in on me. I tried to come but I had car trouble and, well . . . it's a long story."

"You'd better have a good story, better than that 'car trouble' crap. You told me last time we talked that you had a brand-new Datsun."

"Well, I do, but my car's not the problem. Trent's battery went dead, and he had to borrow my car to get to work. Like I said, long story."

"You've missed your daddy's funeral. That's inexcusable. And you could have at least called. Mom's been worried sick. She's very disappointed."

"Yeah, so what else is new? I tried to get there, and when I realized I wasn't going to, I couldn't handle what I knew would come, all the sobbing and disappointment. This is all hard on me too. My life and everything. It's just not easy—"

"Yeah, tell me about it. It ain't easy here either. Mom's a mess. She needs us."

"What do you mean? How is she?"

Stacy answered as best she could, telling him about their mother's worrying over financial matters, her reluctance to give up the old home place, and how she had hired a drifter from Pittsburgh to finish out the wood-clearing contract their father made before the accident. "Well, he's not exactly a stranger. His name's Randy. Been here about a month working for Daddy. He's really a pretty nice guy. I think he'll do okay."

"Sounds like you've had time to get to know this guy and don't mind having him around."

"Well, yeah, that's true, but just as a friend. And to help Momma get the bills paid. I told you 'bout Ty, the guy that's sort of living here with me."

"The macho, motorcycle-riding, hunky guy?"

"That's him. Fact is, he's a little too macho sometimes, but he has a sweet side most people don't see. He just loves me. Things are going great with us. How about you?"

"I'm still with Trent. You know it's his apartment, and he pays most of the bills. He's got this great job with the phone company. He treats me good, except for when he's been drinking too much. Sometimes he gets a little rough. We party a lot. Living in Midtown's wild, Stacy, nothing like Prathersville. You wouldn't believe the weekends. You should come visit and bring Ty. I'm sure he'd be a big hit around here."

Stacy chuckled. "Believe me, Timmy, you don't want Ty Ragsdale at one of your parties in midtown Atlanta. It's all he can do to stay out of trouble in Prathersville."

"Well, you can leave Macho Man with the farm boys and just bring yourself. I've got *sooo* many friends I'd like you to meet. Come this weekend, you'll have a blast."

Stacy, ready to change the subject, twisted a strand of straw-colored hair around her index finger. "You know I can't. I work weekends, and it's like I said: Mom needs us. You should be here." She was still uncomfortable talking with her brother about his lifestyle. He had been away for a little over a year, and he seemed to be constantly exhilarated with his newfound freedom. He had changed so much; at times she felt as if she were talking to a stranger. When they were growing up, Timmy's being different was like a grain of sand inside an oyster, noticeable but unacknowledged, layered over under the idealized image of a boy on his way to becoming a man. Outside the shell was a kernel of hope that he would change as he grew up, but inside the calcification process continued. When their father tried to shape Timmy, he moved further away—first emotionally, then physically. Reentering the family now without producing open sores would be difficult, but for Stacy there remained a kernel of hope that they could at least have a comfortable relationship.

"I'm going back over to Momma's. I might stay a few days. I want you there. I'll come get you if I have to."

"I don't know if I can handle it, Stace. Is she gonna be crying and everything? And what about Aunt Ruth and the others? They'll ask me a million questions. I really don't want to deal with those people."

"Everybody's gone back home. It's just us. You've got to come. Daddy's gone, and we're all the family you've got left now."

Silence. Timmy finally answered in a soft, uninflected voice: "Daddy hated me, Stacy. You can't deny that."

"I don't know that he hated you. He just couldn't understand some things. It don't matter anyway. It's Momma who needs you now. And me. I need you too. I miss my big brother."

"I've never been much of a brother to you—"

"You're the only brother I've got, and I love you, so come home, *now!*"

The trailing edge of laughter broke the tension. "Okay, okay! I'll come, but if things get too weird, I'm outta there."

"*Yes!* I knew you'd do it. I knew you still loved us. Hurry up. If you leave now, you can be here before dark."

"Don't rush me. I'll try to make it tonight, but it may be tomorrow before I can work everything out. I mean, I do have to talk to Trent and my boss, and pack and stuff."

"Just hurry. I'll be at the house waiting."

Stacy ended the conversation with spirits brightened, as if a rope of sunshine had been pulled through her, but there were still a couple of dark corners where doubts about Timmy and their relationship resided. She hadn't seen him in months. One shadowy spot held the notion that he was not really her brother anymore and never would be, but the warmth of his agreeing to come cracked open that kernel of hope. As it sprouted in her mind, sending forth green tendrils, she tried to imagine their reunion.

★★★

Getting back to the house took longer than she'd anticipated; she had to pack a few things and straighten up the apartment. When she finally got there, Stacy was disappointed to find that more guests had arrived. A Buick sedan occupied the gravel area near the front porch where the Ford Galaxie usually sat. The Buick was angled into the space and pulled up too far, almost into the petunia bed. Stacy, wondering who it could be, parked on the parched grass alongside.

As she mounted the steps, she heard a familiar chirrup—the politely animated burble of older ladies engaged in conversation—a sound somehow menacing in its pleasantness, which she had often sat through as a child at church meetings and social events. The tone of these exchanges required a certain decorum, and deep inside Stacy's internal conduct scheme a switch was flipped. Reaching for the screen door, she hesitated.

She found herself consciously, carefully, using her hand as a shock absorber for the door to rest against as it closed behind her, instead of just letting its stretched spring slam it shut. Closing doors properly had been a hard lesson for her as a child, as she was always eager to move from one space to another. Her mom had often spanked her for not slowing down and following instructions, and the worst spankings always came after her impulsiveness drew the wrong kind of attention from those ladies who conversed in that particular tone. The spankings came later, when she was alone with her mom, who had been embarrassed by Stacy's acting like "some kind of wild thing who ain't had any raising." She learned that acceptable behavior was measured on a sliding scale, with the narrowest gauge applied in the presence of those syrupy-sweet, smiling ladies with thin red lips, white hair, and Sunday dresses.

She moved into the sitting room remembering the invisibility she had cloaked herself with as a child to let only certain parts show: the polite little girl who played with dolls, didn't get dirty, and always remembered her Bible and verse for Sunday school. The ladies, raising their neatly coifed and sprayed heads, turned toward Stacy as she entered the room. Two of them were seated on the settee, a third in a green upholstered armchair on the other side of the coffee table, and Mrs. Stempton sat in the matching armchair at the other corner. They had all been looking at something on the table, but when Stacy appeared, their attention was redirected.

"Why here she comes—Miss Stacy All-Grown-up! It's so hard getting used to seeing you this way. What a fine young lady you've become," said Mrs. Elmira Tuggle, the eldest of the group, from the armchair. "Come join us. I was just showing your momma some pictures."

"Hello Sweetpea," her momma said. "What are you doing home? I—um—thought you'd be having supper out this evening."

"Pull up a chair Stacy," said one of the women on the settee. "I believe you'll want to see this too, to know what a fine corpse your daddy laid."

"I took these myself with my Polaroid," said Mrs. Elmira. I knew your momma would want them for her scrapbook."

The realization that these old women were gathered in the parlor, with her mother, looking at photographs of her father's corpse was like a punch in the gut. She felt herself reeling backwards before something stiffened in her back. She looked at each of the women, then her momma. "I, I, think maybe I'll see them another time. I just came by to . . . um, get something from my room. Y'all excuse me please."

"Well don't go running off, hon," said her mother, reaching for the pictures. "We can put these away for now. I'm sure Mrs. Elmira, Novaline, and Iona would enjoy the chance to visit with you awhile."

Iona spoke up: "We sure would. I don't get to see near enough of you since you moved up out of my Sunday school class, hmm—let's see, how long's it been? Seven or eight years ago now. My, my, I can't get over how you've grown up. Don't let Elmira's pictures bother you, honey. You come on in and join us."

"Yes ma'am. It's just that—"

"I should have known it was too soon," said Mrs. Elmira. "Like your momma said, we can put them up for now, but there'll come a day when you'll be glad you've got them."

"It's just that . . . well, I've got a picture already in my head of how I want to remember Daddy. I don't want anything to interfere with that."

"I know exactly what you mean," said Novaline from the other end of the settee. When my Tom had his accident, I didn't want to see or think about anything but the way he had been when he was at his best—playing with the kids or taking us all on a Sunday ride. He always did enjoy a clean shirt and spending time with his family, bless his heart."

She was looking at Stacy so pleasantly now, as were the others, their faces upturned and smiling. The pictures were put away. Where were they? It didn't matter as long as they were out of sight. Perhaps now she could stay in the room with these ladies for a while. They were her mother's friends and mentors, and Stacy knew she should do what was expected of her in their presence.

She realized, with pictures put away, that she was the center of attention. The ladies were very interested in her life. They wanted to know about her job and plans, certain that the forthcoming information would affirm them and the righteous ways they'd worked so hard to impart while Stacy was growing up. Their main concern had always been the "upbuilding of His kingdom," and they were eager to hear of Stacy's contributions.

She didn't want to tell them about her job at the Billy Goat Bar, at least the part of her that had been so careful not to let the screen door slam, but there was another side the ladies didn't know about, a recently awakened part of Stacy whose switch their hands were not upon. She walked toward a straight-back chair on the other side of the room, next to the window. Reaching the chair required walking past the back of the settee then around Mrs. Elmira in the armchair. As she moved farther into the room, she could smell the ladies' face powder and perfume, the sweetened scent of decay. She passed close enough to Mrs. Elmira to see the fine fuzz that grew along her chin and jaw line and the tiny vertical lines around her mouth. Her red lips were shapeless, drawn with straight, bold marks. She was smiling up at Stacy and nodding, as were the other ladies.

Stacy sat down, her ears and cheeks hot. As the women used their best encouraging, mentoring voices in small talk, the pressure inside her remained high. She thought that the women probably knew how she'd been living. These women knew everything. But they might not know, and she was glad that the bruise around her eye was almost gone.

Iona began telling how it was when she lost her husband, Ernest. He had been sick for a long time. First it was the diabetes, then the stroke that left him paralyzed on one side. She was thankful that now, in heaven, he had a glorified body and didn't have to suffer because the suffering while he was here had been great. Stacy tried to appear sympathetic as she listened, but she realized she didn't care about these people. The things they spoke of were far removed from her, like dusty relics in a forgotten barn loft.

Iona said, "At least with your daddy, Stacy, you didn't have to watch him lingering for months, slowly wasting away. That cable slicing through him may have seemed like a freak accident, but everything happens for a reason. The Lord decided it was time to take him home, and He did it, just like that. It may not seem like it now, honey, but that's a blessing."

Stacy nodded and answered, "Yes ma'am," as she looked down at her hands folded in her lap. But something rising inside her was scoffing and incredulous. As the ladies droned on, she cocked her head and listened to an emerging voice: *How can it be a blessing to lose your daddy in a horrible accident? Look at these women, moldy old prunes. They've never been away from Aaron County. What do they know about the world and how to live? They've just sat here for years accepting each crappy thing as some great blessing and look at what it got them.*

But the ladies—Elmira, Iona, and Novaline—had been good to her, hadn't they? She had known them all her life. They had raised children of their own whom she'd known from church, although they had been much older and had long since married and moved away, leaving their mommas alone with their scrapbooks and empty rooms.

Now the same thing was happening to her mother. That was the real reason for the visit, she realized, tuning back into the ladies' conversation. Iona was saying, "We had our last meeting at Myra's Tea Room over in Stone Bottoms. She's got that place fixed up with real tablecloths and napkins and silk flowers and antiques everywhere. And it's buffet style—all you can eat. You should come with us, Bea, to our next meeting. It'll do you a world of good to get out and be with friends who've suffered the same kind of loss. We meet the other girls from Brother Abram's church over there, and we share how the Lord is working in our lives. That's how we came up with the name for our group, the Mourning Glories. Kind of catchy, don't you think?"

Oh, good Lord, said the voice in her head. *They're drafting Momma into their little group so they can all share what a great blessing it is to be miserable while they look at pictures of dead people. . ..*

Bea Stempton smiled and told them she appreciated their thinking of her. Mrs. Elmira turned back to Stacy. "Your momma really needs you now, honey. Fact is, you need each other, more than you ever did. I hope you'll remember that and stay close by. And you can call on us anytime. That's what church family is for, to hold each other up in times of weakness. Don't forget, we're here for you too. We've never stopped praying for you, ever since you quit attending regularly. Sometimes it takes a tragedy to bring the lost sheep back into the fold. You getting back in church like you ought to could be another of the Lord's blessings to come from this tragedy. Remember, His strength is made perfect in our weakness."

Stacy nodded back at Elmira while listening to the voice of her new self, scoffing: *What the hell does that mean? These people are nuts, always talking about blessings and weaknesses. They really seem to enjoy this stuff. This has got to be some kind of sickness to avoid. . ..*

Then she remembered a recent conversation with Ty. She'd asked him, halfheartedly, if he would like to come to church with her. He'd laughed and said, "Why would I want to do a thing like that?" Then he pointed out that he hadn't attended church since he was a kid and had done fine without it. Now, with her new way of seeing things, she knew it was true. All this church and Jesus stuff—her entire upbringing—was just a trick to keep people ignorant and close to home. Putting down roots, bearing fruit, the church family, strength in weakness—all part of a trap to keep everyone living the same old backwards way. With these thoughts came a feeling that she was smothering there in the parlor, that she needed to be outside, away from the heavy, stagnant air, redolent with the perfume and powder of old women and the smell of death. She scanned the room, looking briefly at each smiling, nodding face then, lastly, at her mother's.

Her momma was gazing back at her as if to measure the effect of Mrs. Elmira's words. Their eyes locked for a second, and Stacy felt like calling out to her, telling her not to listen to these walking corpses. There was still time to escape. Her mother didn't have to end up like them, if only she could see things differently and understand that sitting around waiting for God's will to be done and counting everything a blessing was not the only way to live. "Momma," she said, interrupting Novaline, who had started talking about another church lady whose husband had had a heart attack.

"What Sweetpea?"

"What are we doing? I mean, I don't understand what's going on here." The scoffing voice inside her was brazen, but when she spoke out, she faltered. She wished she could take the words back. They sounded silly after they came out.

All eyes turned to her; silence perched above them like a host of buzzards. Mrs. Elmira's eyes shifted back and forth from Stacy to her mother.

Mrs. Stempton answered, "Why honey, there's nothing going on here, besides a friendly visit. These ladies, our friends, came here out of decency and respect in our time of need. That's what's going on. Did you think it was something else?"

"No. I mean, I don't know. I guess I'm just a little confused right now . . . about certain things—God's will and stuff and how you can call having your daddy cut in two a blessing." There, she'd said it, and as soon as she had, she felt her face flush and a quickening of the pulse.

"Honey, there's a lot of things you don't—none of us—understand. God's plan is much too big. That's where faith comes in. Now you've been in church all your life. You know how we believe. Life is just a vapor. Our hearts should be set on eternal things, the things that rust and moths can't destroy. I know you miss your daddy now, but we can all look forward to the time when we're together again with the Lord in heaven."

"Does that mean Timmy too? Will Timmy be with us, and will we all be one happy family like we weren't here on earth?" Stacy's voice had picked up a powerful ironic edge. She felt herself growing larger, filling up the room. "Will Daddy still hate Timmy in heaven, or will my brother be left out altogether? I need to know, because if my brother's not gonna be there, I'm not so sure I wanna go."

Stacy's voice reverberated, and its effect was like leavening in a lump, swelling her up to fill the vacuum caused by the gasps of the speechless ladies. Mrs. Stempton, dumbfounded, stared at her, and Stacy noticed a slight tic under her mother's left eye. Seconds passed. When Mrs. Stempton looked away and began shaking her head, Novaline finally spoke: "Now see here, Missy. That's no way to talk to your mother, grieving as she is. She's done lost one child to the enemy and here you go talking like you're in league with him too. You're all she's got left now. Can't you see what this is doing to her?"

"Yes ma'am, I do," Stacy replied, her voice rising with her body as she got up from the chair. "I do see what all this nonsense about strength in weakness, and horrible senseless accidents being blessings is doing to her, not to mention telling her she's lost a child who's alive and well and just happens to be on his way here now. That's right, Momma. Timmy's coming. I talked to him earlier today. He should be here in a little while. I came to give you the good news."

Chapter 16

Ty Ragsdale made his way to the Billy Goat Bar at his usual time. After making love with Stacy at the apartment, he'd cruised around on the Beast until he got bored. Early evening—suppertime for folks who slept at night—had arrived when he pulled into the parking lot. He was ready for substantial food, regardless of what the meal was called. He still hadn't eaten after rising hungry and filling the apartment with smoke from the bacon he had tried to cook. There was plenty of time now to eat a cheeseburger and drink a couple of beers before his shift started.

He expected Stacy to be there waiting tables. He knew that with her influence the cheeseburger would be prepared just the way he liked: medium-rare with mushrooms, extra cheese and mustard, and she would slip him a large order of fried onion rings to go with it. There was a downside to Stacy's working at the Goat, though. With her there he couldn't talk to the other pretty waitresses in the free and easy way he had once enjoyed. He was always happy to see her, and even though his soul was buoyed up by their cresting romance— the first real love affair of his life—he missed being able to flirt openly with other girls. His sex appeal had served him well for years, and to bind it up and place it on the altar of fidelity was a sacrifice he was not able to make without remorse, especially when he was in the presence of Dawn Shumake, a trim-waisted brunette with long legs, who was smiling at him from behind the bar.

She had been trying to catch his eye since high school. Ty, in his nonverbal way, had let her know that he had noticed. On numerous occasions he'd looked at her, smiled, and nodded his approval. They had enjoyed the kind of flirtatious relationship where each signals desire to the other, waiting only for the right time and place. So far it hadn't happened. Dawn enjoyed the effect she had on men, and she loved to flirt, but she was generally faithful while involved with a guy, which was most of the time. She had even been married for a while right out of high school, and here she was recently divorced, working as a waitress at the Billy Goat Bar.

Ty felt her gaze from across the room. Her smile beckoned, and he was willing to let it pull him in, at least while Stacy was nowhere to be seen. There was one other person seated at the bar, a salesman type in his late thirties. He seemed disappointed at Ty's arrival and the prospect of having to share this pretty waitress. He muttered, "How ya doing," as Ty took a seat. Ty nodded and turned his attention to Dawn.

"What's up, big boy?" she asked as she set a frosted mug and a bottle of Michelob in front of her new customer.

"Nothing much, sweet thing. Just looking for a pretty face and a good meal." He held his head at a certain angle that he knew from experience accented his eyes. "Any chance for a guy to get something to eat around here?"

"Sure babe. you can have anything you want, anything at all. Need to see a menu?"

"Naa. I'll just have my usual. Say, where's Stacy anyway?"

"She called a little while ago. Said she needed to spend more time with her momma, that she was staying the night there." Dawn paused, dropped her chin to look at him through long lashes, then added softly, "She wanted me to tell you she'd see you sometime tomorrow afternoon."

Ty lifted his head, allowing his eyes to sweep over hers. She smiled back, giving the implications a chance to sink in. The salesman interjected, "Excuse me, can I get another beer please?"

A second passed. "Sure, honey, coming right up. What else can I get for you?"

Ty leaned back and watched her work. The bar doubled as a waitress station, and her job involved setting up the drink orders for the other girls who were taking care of the dozen or so customers spread out in the booths, eating burgers and pizza and taking advantage of the happy-hour beer prices. She was in the middle of a slight rush, but as she passed back and forth from tap to tap with glasses, mugs, and pitchers, Ty felt a tugging attachment, as if their bellies were connected by a stretchable telephone cord.

He sipped slowly from his mug while the wheels turned. This was a slack time at the plant. The third shift guys had been working for two weeks on degreasing machinery and painting everything to comply with the new OSHA regulations, a make-work situation. Millwood, the foreman, had been practically encouraging them to take time off. Ty, with money in his pocket, wasn't bothered by the prospect of his paycheck being eight hours short. He could call in, let them know he wasn't coming, and there would be no questions asked. These thoughts popped in randomly, but as he watched Dawn and her willowy movements, they began to cluster, connect, and solidify like viral, wart-producing seeds. He shook his head and tried to look away, to think about the new exhaust system he wanted to install on the coupe, but it was no use. He couldn't disconnect from the tightly coiled cord that continued to convey signals of shared desire.

If they played the cards right, Stacy would never know. He could spend the night with Dawn, then go to Stacy's apartment to sleep through the morning as if he'd been at work all night. He knew Dawn well enough to have confidence in her ability to keep a secret. She could be as devious as he could when the end justified the means. In their case, the promise of sexual release held the allure of nectar: they were as helpless as bees in a glade.

Dawn reached a moment in her routine where all the immediate needs were met. She turned to Ty and said, "You know, we're not all that busy. Even with Stacy out, the girls are taking care of everything just fine. They should be able to handle closing and cleaning up all right too. I'm thinking I might cut out about ten or ten-thirty. I could use some relaxation."

Ty glanced up from his beer and nodded. "Yep," he said, "we all need a little relaxing from time to time."

Dawn smiled. When she reached over to wipe the bar where his sweating mug had left a wet spot, the back of her hand brushed against his.

The salesman cleared his throat. "Yeah, I noticed it was sorta slow in here this evening. A little too quiet for me. I think I'll play something on the jukebox. I'm taking requests, sweetie. What would you like to hear?"

"I'm sorry. What do you need, hon?" Dawn replied, breaking her eye contact with Ty.

"I said I'm going to play some tunes. Anything you'd like to hear?"

"Oh, I dunno. Anything's fine—no wait—play that Humble Pie song, 'Thirty Days in the Hole.' That ought to liven this place up a little."

"What about you, sport. Got any requests?" he asked Ty as he rose from the barstool.

"Can't say that I do, chief. You go ahead, knock yourself out."

The man's eyes narrowed as he nodded. Then he swaggered off with shoulders thrown back in a way that accentuated his belly and knobby elbows.

Dawn turned back to Ty, rolled her eyes, and winked. She was about to say something when one of the waitresses approached from the side with an empty pitcher, drawing her back to her duties. Ty poured the rest of his beer directly into the mug. He enjoyed watching the foam rise and he liked the way it felt. He took a gulp, then wiped his upper lip with his tongue as he watched the fluid movement of Dawn's slender limbs. Soon, events would be put into motion. All he had to do was rise and make a phone call.

She glided back to him with another beer. He wanted to confirm it this time before she could get away again. With his head at the practiced angle he let the words ease out: "You know, what you said earlier about relaxing got me thinking. I've decided to take the night off. All I gotta do is call in, then I'm free. Maybe you and me could relax together."

She replied in an enigmatic feminine way, lips and eyes sparkling. "I'd like that." Then she was off again to fill another pitcher, her lilting voice echoing in his mind. He called after her, "Hey! I'm starving here. How 'bout checking on that cheeseburger!" Then he settled back on his stool as the speakers began to vibrate with the *a cappella* intro to "Thirty Days in the Hole," a song that had become familiar over the last few weeks. As the drums and guitars kicked in, he relaxed, settling into the rhythm.

★★★

The hours with Dawn passed swiftly. Afterwards Ty found himself astride his beloved mechanical beast, searching for a different rhythm. She had been supple and sweet, all he had imagined, but now he was riding hard over the back roads with his body full of energy and his mind filled with the familiar apprehension that always prompted him toward speed and rushing air. He was going both towards and away from a nebulous destination, a place where the ripped-out hole at his core could be mended. Stacy was his cure, the soul-patch he'd longed for since childhood. He needed to make the transition back to her world and bed, away from this distraction. More air, more speed, more movement, then rest and waking up with Stacy back at the apartment, everything returned to normal.

Dawn had fallen asleep in his arms in the early morning hours, but his body was on a different schedule. Wide awake with the girl nuzzled against him, he'd listened to the deep-sleep rhythms of her raspy breath while his mind bounced over a rough terrain of bad memories, bad choices, and potential problems. He extricated himself from her limbs and silken hair without waking her, quickly dressed, and made his way outside into the predawn stillness.

He mounted the Beast and coasted to the stop sign at the bottom of the hill before starting the engine. Then, weaving stealthily through the neighborhood, he passed the town limits and turned onto a familiar back road where he was in his element, comfortable enough to twist back the throttle, increasing the wind's velocity. The temperature had dropped into the fifties, and the air was like a cold shower as he sped through it, a ritual cleansing that washed the smell and taste of Dawn Shumake from his mind and body.

He thought of Stacy as he rode and how he'd made her love him, then how he'd almost ruined it by hitting her in the face that day. He went into the next curve a bit too fast. As he corrected the bike's path, he experienced the sense of riding on the edge, a familiar sensation that came without remorse. There was no intuition in Ty of human improvement or the possibility of altering his spiritual path, only the sense that a series of corrections could maintain balance. He knew he needed Stacy, and he was confident in his ability to keep her as a ballast in his life, the correction that kept him from the brink.

For several miles out of Prathersville, Taylor's Gin Road climbed and curved through rolling terrain, then plateaued and straightened before dropping into the Hominy Creek valley. He usually pushed for speed on this stretch—ninety miles per hour or more—then backed off just in time to lean into the next turn, but now, with open space around him, his attention was drawn to an orange glow in the sky. He released the throttle, trimming back to an old man's pace as he peered into the night. As he came off the plateau, a stand of hardwoods loomed, obscuring the light. He tried to peer over the treetops as the road carried him into a series of curves, then over the Hominy Creek Bridge. It was cool and damp in this low spot with woods all around, and the trees before him were silhouetted for an instant by an orange halo before the next curve pulled away to the right. A familiar road turned off to the left about a quarter of a mile ahead. As he slowed, a break in the trees opened the view, and Ty marveled at a sky filled with what appeared to be sparks flying off a colossal anvil.

A queasiness seized him. Whirling streaks of red pulsated through the orange background. He twisted the throttle, winding the machine up through the gears. Familiarity enabled him to handle the Beast through this pass at a high rate of speed. Florene Otwell lived on this road with her husband and son, and Ty knew what he would see before he got there. He was riding toward anguish, pain, misery, perhaps even death, and he felt the need to get there quickly. His head filled with the surging whine of the machine beneath him, or was that a siren?

He rounded the last curve and the scene burst into view, so bright he had to shield his eyes. He hurried, as if to hurl himself into the white-hot core, and almost dropped the bike at the edge of the yard as he slid to a stop. He struggled with the kickstand and dismounted awkwardly, his flesh recoiling from the heat. The red lights whirling against the orange glow and the wind-sucking roar of the flames overwhelmed his senses. Combatants, unwilling to retreat yet unable to advance, stumbled about, moving things and shouting commands. Four full-suited firemen—two per flank—pumped torrents of water into the orange monster from distended, sinuous hoses that seemed alive.

Ty peered into the glowing skeleton. The heat repelled, drying his eyes and burning his skin, but he couldn't turn away. He was bewitched, captive to a force that sucked the air around him into the roiling combustion. As the molecules of Florene Otwell's home and everything in it combined violently with oxygen, producing wondrous light and staggering heat, he felt the stirring between his navel and backbone of his soul seeking liberation. He shook it off and surveyed the surrounding scene.

Uniformed workers huddled beside the ambulance on the other side of the yard, a piece of equipment at their center—or maybe it was a wounded fireman or a member of the family. There were two broad backs and the profile of a smaller person. Moving closer he saw the stretcher, then another profile, a man raising himself as if to break away. The two male emergency workers were talking and pressing their hands against him, trying to keep him subdued as the young woman worked with rubber tubes attached to an apparatus. Ty moved closer, keeping his distance from the fire that boiled his insides.

Where was Florene? And her son, about his age, where was he? The man yanked the oxygen mask from his face, raised himself again, and began wailing and gesticulating.

The workers issued stern pleas: "Mr. Otwell, you've got to calm down. You did your best, and we're doing all we can."

"She's in there, she's in there!" he moaned, looking from face to face. "It's not too late—oh God! There's got to be a way. Let me up, let me go help my wife!"

The young woman said, "Sir, nobody can get near that house. It's in God's hands now. Anybody or anything that was in there is lost to this world. I'm sorry. You just need to relax. Put your mask back on. You've inhaled a lot of smoke. You'll get through this, and you still have your son to think about. Didn't you say he was away at college?"

"Yes, yes—Danny. Thank God he doesn't have to see this. I need to get to him. He needs to know I tried to save his momma. . . ." His voice trailed off into sobs and grunts. He struggled, jerking his head from side to side as if he would rush headlong into the fire.

So dramatic, Ty thought, as he drew closer into the circle. Can't he see that it's hopeless? Then the realization, which the husband seemed to be resisting, engulfed him: Florene was gone, along with everything in that house—devoured, existing now only as part of the billowing cloud that filled the atmosphere above the orange glow. He felt weak. Then, when Tom Otwell's eyes pegged his own and narrowed in recognition, Ty's knees nearly buckled. He saw reflected in those eyes the red orgy of flames, and also the truth: that it was all an act. He realized with sickening certainty that Tom Otwell had set the fire to put an end to his unfaithful wife.

This knowledge, instantly conveyed, was like oxygen blowing on the burning coals in his gut. He turned, reeling, barely able to stand on rubbery knees. He had to get away from the heat, acrid smoke, and Tom Otwell's demonic eyes.

In the guilty haste of a drunken pickpocket he re-crossed the yard to his motorcycle. Trembling, he straddled the Beast, yanked on his helmet, fumbled to get started. With back tire spinning, he blasted himself away—wobbling and fishtailing—from the scene of deceit, destruction, and death. The over-revving engine shrieked in protest; his spirit sought the natural order of night's dim comfort and the cooling rush of clean air, but the oppressive stench and vibrating orange glow seemed to stretch for miles. He rode dangerously hard back the way he'd come. Soon he was on Taylor's Gin Road heading toward Prathersville and the mill village, where he hoped to find what he'd left there safe and unaltered.

Chapter 17

Mrs. Elmira Tuggle and the other ladies excused themselves, after a period of silence and throat clearing, from the Stempton parlor following Stacy's uncharacteristic show of disrespect. Speech, mumbled and semi-coherent, finally returned as Stacy's former Sunday school teachers hugged her and Mrs. Stempton, assuring them they would be in their prayers. They rode away in Mrs. Elmira's Buick, leaving mother and daughter alone in a silent house filled with memories and regrets. Mrs. Stempton would not look at her daughter, and Stacy, hot blood still pumping, didn't feel like apologizing.

Minutes passed before she finally spoke: "Well, like I said, Timmy's coming. I guess I thought that would make you happy."

"It don't make me happy that he's showing up here a whole day after we put his daddy in the ground. And the way he's living don't make me happy neither. I can't help the way I feel, and what I know to be right and wrong, and I don't know the answer to your question about Timmy and heaven and all that. I can't understand the Lord's ways, but I do trust his promises. The Bible says it's not His will that any should perish. I just send that word back to the Lord in prayer over and over—that my children will be counted among his flock. That's been my prayer since you both was littl'uns." Mrs. Stempton abruptly rose then, without looking at her daughter, and trudged down the hall toward the kitchen.

"What are you doing?" Stacy asked the receding figure.

"You said he'll be here in a little while. I guess I better get something together for supper."

It was getting close to supper time, but Stacy wasn't the least bit hungry. She didn't know for sure when Timmy would arrive. He'd said that he would try to make it tonight, but it might be tomorrow. She was aware of the possibility that he may not come at all, but she hoped that this time he would. She didn't want her momma, who had retreated once again to her kitchen sanctuary, to be disappointed and worried anew, and she didn't want her working to prepare a meal that would count for nothing. Reluctantly, she followed to see if she could help.

Mrs. Stempton turned from the refrigerator with a casserole dish and clomped it down on the counter. Stacy reached inside for something to busy herself with. "Look, Mom," she said, pulling out a covered glass bowl. "Here's some of Aunt Ruth's cube steak and gravy. Timmy always loved that. And we can heat up these green beans. That's all we need. Let's don't go to a lot of trouble. I mean, let's just wait till he gets here. He may eat on the way or something, and it might be a while yet. He wasn't too sure about when he would get here."

"No, he wouldn't be. He never was one to commit himself, even if it meant saving worry for someone else. So, we're in the same place we were before you made your little announcement. We still don't know when Timmy's going to show up, or even if he will."

"He said he'd be here, Momma. Can't you have a little faith—in Timmy, I mean? He is your son."

Mrs. Stempton reached up into the cabinet to bring down some plates. She set them down deliberately, gently. "Yes. I know. I've never had any problem with that, but there was a time. . .." She stopped herself, cocking her head and squinting at something far away. "Well, there's no need to bring that up now."

Stacy was turning from the refrigerator with the dish of green beans when her mom's faltering comment brought her up short. "Bring what up now, Momma? What are you talking about?"

"Nothing. It's not important."

"You can't do that, start something, then just say 'it's not important.' Is there something about Timmy I don't know?"

"No, no. It's not really about him. I'm sorry I said anything. Let's just let it go."

"Momma. We were talking about Timmy. If it's not about him, then who? You? Daddy? You don't have to keep things from me anymore. I'm all grown up now."

"It just don't seem right, talking about him like that now that he's gone."

Stacy placed the bowl on the table and made her way to her mom, who had gone stiff with her back against the counter.

"Come on over here, Momma, and sit down," Stacy said, taking her hand. "I think we need to get this out in the open, don't you?"

Mrs. Stempton allowed herself to be led to a chair, shuffling and shaking her head slightly. "It don't matter now," she muttered.

"Let's don't have any secrets in this family, Momma. I want to know everything about Daddy, you, and Timmy."

The widow looked at her over the tabletop and blinked her wet eyes. "It was a passing remark your daddy made a long time ago. What you said just now made me think of it."

"What did Daddy say? Whatever he said hurt you, didn't it?"

"Yes, it did." Her eyes dropped. "He said he didn't believe Timmy was his son."

Stacy regarded her mother's face. "What? How could he think Timmy was not his son?"

Mrs. Stempton related the story, falteringly, of how she and Stacy's father had been separated for a few weeks about nine months before Timmy was born. Stacy was drawn into the mysterious world of her parents before she became part of their lives. She'd always had difficulty imagining them without her, when they were young and full of passion. Now as her mother began to confide in her at last— speaking to her as an adult—Stacy was disturbed but unable to turn away, as she'd been as a child when she watched their old cat eat her last litter of kittens.

"It was 1950," her mother said, "and it seemed like the whole country was full of energy and confidence. Your daddy had notions of moving away from here and making a lot of money at the Ford plant in Atlanta. He had a cousin working there who said he could get him on. Anyway, I didn't want to go and be that far away from my momma, so he got mad and left without me. Said he was going to check things out and would be back for me later. I told him there was no need to hurry hisself 'cause I was staying put no matter what. His parents were still alive then, so we were in that little rental house I told you about. He left me there by myself. We were both pretty mad."

"But Momma, he accused you of being unfaithful. Did he really think that, or was he just being spiteful?"

Mrs. Stempton shook her head. "Guess I never really knew much about what that man was thinking." She looked at her hands on the tabletop and picked at a cuticle. "I could drink a cup of coffee. What about you? Let's make a pot."

"Momma, wait a minute. I'm trying to understand this. Why would Daddy think that Timmy was not his son? Did he have any reason to think you were seeing somebody else? I mean, you of all people. You're like a saint."

"It was a long time ago, Sweetpea, and a hard time in our marriage. It was years later when he actually said it, when Timmy was nine years old. I remember because it was his birthday.

"When Timmy was nine, I would have been seven. I don't remember anything like that."

"No. You wouldn't. We kept our problems to ourselves when y'all was growing up."

"But what did you do when he said that? I still don't see why—"

"Timmy wasn't growing into what your daddy expected his son to be, and I guess he needed something to blame that on. He'd bought him a BB gun for his birthday, but Timmy didn't care nothing about it. Just wanted to stay inside with his coloring books. I could see it in your daddy's face, the frustration. It was just the two of us here in the kitchen when he said it. Then he stormed out and rode off in his truck. Neither one of us ever mentioned anything else about it. Till now."

Stacy struggled to recall old scenes and to imagine the conflicts she had been unaware of as a child. In the silence that followed, Mrs. Stempton rose and began preparing the stainless-steel percolator, rattling the parts as she arranged them on the counter. From the kitchen window Stacy could see that the leaves on the oak outside were beginning to turn and fall onto the parched grass. She had spent many carefree hours under that tree, and she remembered raking leaves as a girl and frolicking in the piles with her brother.

"So Timmy came along about nine months after y'all was separated?" she finally asked.

"Should I make a whole pot or just half?"

"Half, I guess. I don't know." She stumbled into the question she could not keep from asking. "I mean, was there . . . anybody else during that time?"

"Listen, I hear a car in the driveway." She dropped the little metal basket, wiped her hands on a dish towel, and crossed the room to the window while Stacy, pondering, remained seated at the table. "Look Sweetpea, it's one of them little Japanese cars, all shiny and orange. Your brother ain't driving one of them now, is he?"

"That's him!" Stacy answered, almost knocking over her chair as she rose. "I told you he'd come."

Then they were all on the front porch blurting out greetings and affirmations, hugging, crying, and laughing. The chatter was genial with no hint of reproach. "Y'all come in," Mrs. Stempton said. "I was about to put on a pot of coffee." Brother and sister, arms around each other's waist, followed their momma back to the kitchen, where she resumed making coffee and preparations for supper. The three of them settled around the table, comfortable for the moment and very much like a family.

As her mother patted Timmy's hand, Stacy marveled at her natural smile, the first one she'd shown in days. Outside the window, leaves swaying against a shockingly blue sky made her think of her father in the ground, the color of his eyes and the way they danced. It seemed that his burial had made a difference in the air, sky, and shadows, somehow moving the earth closer to autumn. Leaves would also be falling at the cemetery plot. Somebody should rake them off. She realized she could do that. She would be the one to rake the leaves off her father's grave, and she imagined the rake in her hands. She would do it by herself after Timmy left. The time now was for the three of them to drink coffee and talk in a language not concerned with immediate problems, future plans, or the past. She turned away from the window when the percolator made its first protracted sound, a gurgling burp like that of a contented infant.

Chapter 18

The next morning, the second day after the old man's funeral, Randy was up before daylight. He hadn't slept much the night before. Troubling thoughts about Stacy and what he had gotten himself into had kept him awake. One thing he hadn't thought about, though, during that long night, was what he would encounter when he got to the job site. He had been preoccupied with the idea of pulling stumps, but this morning, as he began to order things in his mind, he realized the wood must be cut and hauled first.

The pulpwood truck and saws would be where the old man had left them. He would have to begin where Ben Stempton ended to finish out the load. The thought of starting his workday at the scene of a grisly death was repugnant. He searched for a way to escape but weighing his options in the light of Stacy's smile and Mrs. Stempton's kindness produced the conclusion that he must do what he'd promised.

Mrs. Stempton handed him his day's sustenance, packed carefully inside a grocery sack rolled down tight, from the front porch steps. "Good morning. I'm pleased to see you out bright and early. I went ahead and got everything ready 'cause I knew you'd want to get started."

Randy was puzzled by the two cars parked in the yard. A boxy little Datsun sedan occupied the space in front of the petunia bed where the Ford usually sat. Parked alongside was Stacy's battered Valiant. He wondered what she could be doing here so early, but then he noticed that the windshields of both cars were covered with dew. Mrs. Stempton's manner in handing Randy the sack didn't invite conversation. Her overnight guests, as well as other family matters, were none of his business, and he already had too much to think about. If Mrs. Stempton shared any of his discomfort with where he was going and what had happened there, she didn't show it. Perhaps her mind was incapable of going into such dark places.

The Jenkins property was just outside of Prathersville on Taylor's Gin Road. He covered the six miles slowly, savoring his breakfast: a sausage biscuit as big as a cat's head with sweet creamed coffee from a thermos. He decided to try the radio, pressing each button, but found only country and gospel music amid the static. Using the tuning knob to explore between the presets, he stumbled upon Don McLean's "American Pie." He hadn't heard it since before he left Pittsburgh, when it was still at the top of the charts. Hearing it now rekindled his wanderlust.

He drove up to the rough access road with the lyrics in his head and noticed that the pulpwood truck was visible from the blacktop to anyone who happened to be looking. He turned in and stopped the Galaxie a short distance behind the truck, which was loaded with one layer of fat logs across its frame-mounted rack. He sat there trying to discern what he could from the car's insulated interior. With the truck positioned at an angle to the access road and the loader boom with its cable swung around to the far side, Randy could see nothing out of the ordinary. The rising sun made shadows, distorted images of leaves and limbs, sway and dance across the hood of the car. He told himself that it might not be that bad. Maybe the people who took the old man away had cleaned everything up. He was reaching for the door handle when he heard a vehicle approaching from behind.

He watched in the rearview the stately front end of a polished Lincoln making its way towards him, dipping and rebounding over the harsh bumps. He could make out two occupants, a man on the passenger side and what appeared to be a teenage boy behind the wheel. Randy grew apprehensive as the vehicle slowly pulled within a few feet of his back bumper. For a second, he cringed at the memory of the Prathersville cops who had pulled him over and handcuffed him.

The man got out and then the boy, who lagged behind, waiting for instructions. Randy stepped out of the old man's Ford. The approaching figure was slow and confident in baggy trousers, suspenders, and a white shirt. The stub of a wet, well-chewed cigar protruded from his slack mouth, and his receding gray hair was pushed straight back. As he drew closer, his rounded shoulders belied the initial impression of substance; Randy observed that his bulky midsection consisted entirely of soft flab.

He regarded Randy through narrowed eyes as he used his lips and tongue to shift the cigar. "Hello there, young man. You must be Ben Stempton's boy."

"Well, no. I just work for him. I'm supposed to pick up where he left off."

"You mean here, on this property?"

"Yessir. To finish out the job. That's what Mrs. Stempton and I decided."

"Y'all did, huh? That's fine that you got everything worked out, but you might've informed me since I own this piece of land. Name's Wayne Jenkins, and I'm the one who's already paid Ben Stempton to clear this place off. Who are you? When I made the deal with Ben, I figured Buena was still working for him. He didn't say nothing about no white boy."

"Randy Walls, from Pittsburgh."

The man appraised him as he worked the cigar around his mouth. "That sure was bad about Ben. Real bad. Who woulda thought it? Y'all must be kin."

"No. I just work for him. Met him about a month ago."

Mr. Jenkins looked down as if studying out a problem and Randy noticed his fancy cowboy boots. His young driver was leaning against the car door smoking a cigarette.

"An old lady found him, Miz Elmira Tuggle," the man said. "She was going to the grocery store and happened to look up this way. I imagine it was a real unnatural sight, ol' Ben squeezed up against them truck standards, hanging like a tater sack cinched in the middle. She called the deputies, and then I heard it on my scanner. They was getting him down when I got here. A real mess, damn shame too." He removed the wet stub from his mouth and examined it as if there were some mysterious connection between its ruined carcass and Ben Stempton's. A fleck of black tobacco was stuck to his tongue.

"You were here when they took . . . the body away?" Randy asked.

"Yep. I watched 'em load him up. And I'm here to tell you it's a miracle what Dougherty's funeral home was able to do. I never figured they'd open that casket at the service, but they did, and I know it was a comfort to Mrs. Stempton. Anyway, that's over and done with. The rest of us has got to keep going. Ain't that right?"

"Yessir, I believe so. That's what I'm trying to do."

"We've got to keep working and planning and making things happen, and what I'm trying to make happen is a small subdivision, twenty-five houses. They ought to sit real nice on this property, that is if I can get it cleared off so the builders can start putting in the footings. I need to get them houses dried-in before the weather turns cold and rainy, and time's getting short."

He examined both ends of the cigar stub, then flipped it to the ground. Randy waited for the point he seemed to be working towards, but instead of speaking he crossed his arms over his chest, shifted his weight, and began craning his neck, taking a slow visual sampling of each direction without looking directly at Randy, who finally recognized this as a cue for him to offer something.

"Mrs. Stempton and I have discussed everything. We're going to honor the deal you made with Mr. Stempton."

"I was thinking of paying Bea a visit to see where things stood, but I'd want to give her a few days, the funeral being so recent and all. I've been debating whether to go ahead and bring the big loggers and bulldozers in. I didn't figure she'd have any notions about finishing out the deal with Ben gone. Trouble is, that heavy equipment would tear this place up to where you wouldn't recognize it. I want to keep all these nice shade trees and preserve the natural beauty. Besides, bulldozers are too damn expensive. But on the other hand, there's this ticking clock. Always fighting time in the building business. There's a lot at stake here. I'm already committed—v*ery* committed—so I've got to make the best decisions. You following me?"

"Yessir. But I'm here this morning to get started, and I feel sure I can keep the schedule that you and Mr. Stempton agreed on."

Mr. Jenkins eyed Randy up and down, then motioned to the boy waiting back at the Lincoln. "Bring me a cigar, Lyle. They's some in the dash." The boy was soon at Mr. Jenkins' side, holding before him like a talisman a large brown blunt still in its cellophane.

Randy rested his weight against the back of the Ford as Mr. Jenkins tore off the wrapper and dropped it to the ground. He examined the cigar and worried over its closed end while Lyle fished in his pocket for a lighter. After nibbling off the stump and licking the cigar along its entire length, Mr. Jenkins was ready for his smoke. Lyle produced the lighter and held the flame at the glowing tip for several seconds while the man worked his cheeks, producing thick balls of aromatic smoke that hung about his head in an expanding festoon. The boy clanked shut the lighter, and Randy, sensing that he was looking at him, turned and shifted his gaze to the pulpwood truck.

Mr. Jenkins said through the dissipating cloud, "You know, the deputies sure were puzzled about what happened to Ben. They just couldn't see how he managed to get that cable wrapped around him thataway."

Randy worked a weed out from the ground with the toe of his boot. "I've thought about it—wondered, I mean. The old man, he could do anything. But the cable's stiff and it's got some kinks in it that get twisted up sometimes. It's freaky, but it could happen. Hooking the cable and working the loader is really a two-man job. I would have been here helping, but—"

"You're right, boy. Unexplainable things happen all the time. Best not to worry too much over 'em." He puffed on the cigar, as if pondering the wisdom of his words. Lyle looked at the man through the haze, then shifted his attention back to Randy, leaning uncomfortably against the trunk of the Ford.

"He said I could have a day off and I took it. I didn't know he was gonna...."

Mr. Jenkins withdrew the cigar from his cheek. "I got some real concerns here, young man. I don't mind telling you. I knew Ben Stempton—what he was capable of—and he always kept his word. He'd been doing this kind of work all his life. But you ... well, you seem like a fine young man, but I don't know if you're up the task. You know what they say: never send a boy to do a man's job. Can you clear off forty acres, haul out all the pine and brush and pull up the stumps by the end of October? That's what Ben and me agreed on. I can't afford to push it out no further."

"I wouldn't have taken the job if I didn't believe I could do it."

"Uh-huh. Well, at least you got confidence. You'll need it. I don't know what you and Mrs. Stempton worked out, but there's quite a bit more money in this deal, if it gets done on time. And y'all are getting all of whatever the pulpwood brings. Did she tell you that?"

"Yessir."

"Well awright then." He nodded before sticking the blunt back in his cheeks and puffing to bring the ember back to glowing life. "Looka here," he said, reaching around to find the bottom of his baggy trousers. He brought out a fat billfold, leafed through the bills, and picked a crisp hundred from the wad. "Here. Some good faith money. And I got a suggestion. When you finish this load, look and see if you can hire somebody to help you. I know there's usually some young bucks hanging around that pulpwood yard looking for work. Think about it: one sawing, one loading—another pair of hands to hook the cable around the logs and the chain around stumps. It'll go a lot faster. Besides, with a helper, you won't be all by yourself out here." He thrust the bill at him.

Randy felt Lyle watching to see what he would do. "I think I'd rather wait until I've actually earned some money."

Mr. Jenkins shook the bill closer to his face. "Don't be a jackass. You'll earn it soon enough out here in this heat. And, like I said, there's plenty more where this came from—that is, so long as I see progress. I don't mind paying some each week. This'll be your first payment, and you can use part of it to hire a helper."

The tone of his voice, his impatient shaking of the bill, and the smoke about his head combined to make an overwhelming force. Randy reached and took the money. Lyle looked on with a bland expression as if he were watching a TV sitcom.

"I'll stop by from time to time," Mr. Jenkins said, "to see how things are going. I'll give it a week before I decide anything about the big loggers and equipment." He rocked back on his heels and puffed in a satisfied way as he waited for Randy's response.

"I'll do my best."

"That's all that can be expected, young man, and I appreciate it. I've got a better feeling about this now. I believe you'll do awright." As he pulled at the cigar with his cheeks, he offered his hand. Grasping it, Randy was reminded of the cold and spongy slabs of bologna the old man used to buy at Ot Brown's store.

"Come on, Lyle. We got other fish to fry this morning. You take care, young man—Randy wasn't it? Don't get too hot. We'll be seeing you later."

And that was it. Mr. Jenkins, with Lyle bouncing alongside, turned back to his Lincoln, leaving Randy alone with the trees, vines, and briars, in the surrounds of the partially loaded pulpwood truck and culpable cable. The moment of facing what the old man left behind was at hand. Standing upright, he felt the crinkling bills in his pocket and realized he was in possession of more money than he'd ever had in his life.

He waited until the Lincoln was out of sight, then approached the other side of the truck circumspectly, hoping for the best, but the buzzing of flies presaged a disturbing reality. Dreading each step, he moved slowly until he was actually there, where the life had spilled. At first, he turned away gagging. The taunting chorus of dollars in his pocket reminded him that he didn't have to do this, that they and the old man's Ford could take him away from this place. But a softer, smaller voice persisted through the prattle, telling him he had to face it, a fact he accepted in his stomach where the churning was. Turning back was made bearable by a process he didn't understand, a knotting of something inside, accompanied by blue flashes in the outer realms of his consciousness—the bright morning sky glimpsed between swaying leaves, or the flickering glances of Stacy Stempton in his mind. As he faced the flies and the blood-soaked ground, spotted with chunks of dried and rotting organic matter, he was surprised at how easy it was. He told himself over and over, "This isn't so bad. It's not so bad. Not so bad. . .."

Then he was stepping over the spot of thickest clotting, where the flies, orgiastic, were loath to disperse. The cable was a mess, twisted up against the truck frame and kinked where Ben Stempton had died, smeared and stippled with daubs of flesh, tissue, and fabric. He opened the passenger door of the truck to reach in for one of the grease rags the old man always kept there. Before the cable could be rewound, it would have to be untangled and wiped down.

He set himself to the task, working the kinks out and rubbing the stiff metal cord. As he worked, time froze inside the hum of the flies. Finally, after starting the engine and winding the clean, straightened cable back onto its drum at the top of the standards, thought returned with urgency, telling him to move the truck away from that spot. The familiarity of the driver's seat, pedals, and gear lever brought relief.

He was able to move the rig only a hundred or so feet before he would have to clear out some brush and small pines, but at least he would be away from the stench and the flies. The truck seemed eager, unchanged by what had happened. As he engaged the clutch and began to roll over the rough terrain, he felt a loosening of the accident's hateful grip. The slow-rolling wheels pulled up a new scene with clean smells and sounds where Randy, through his muscles, could shape a different reality. He pushed the nagging thoughts of problems and expenses out of his mind, hopped down from the cab, and reached for the saw. Using his foot to keep it steady on the ground, he fingered the choke knob and yanked the cord.

Chapter 19

There was something about Stacy's eyes that seemed basic to life, and when Randy closed his he could see hers. The bruise was still there in his mind as he had first seen it, making her seem vulnerable and dear. The shimmering blue of her irises brought to him the picture and mood of an azure lagoon, pristine in its isolation, warm and surrounded by glistening sand and coral reefs. He remembered such a place from when he had been on vacation in Florida with his parents before the accident took them away. Or was he simply remembering a picture he had seen somewhere? He was sure about the water, though: it was translucent with special light-bending properties, teeming with exotic life. A ritual began that first day at the job site when the pain in his hands and back became unbearable from struggling with the logs and stumps. During such times, and there would be many, he would lay down his tools, lean back against a tree, and reach the place of restoration by slipping through those luminous blue orbs shimmering with life, portals to his personal azure lagoon. What was it about Stacy's eyes? He couldn't put his finger on it, but he thought of her in the worst parts of his agony.

The suffering began on the first day of work after he moved the truck away from the place of death. The saw started up, rattling and shrill, unaware of the recent shift in the universe. But after struggling halfway through the first small pine, Randy realized the chain was dull. The teeth did not bite and pull themselves into the wood, but resisted, causing undo strain on the engine and his arms. The chain would have to be sharpened. He'd watched the old man, bent over the saw in ritualistic concentration, perform the task many times, but he'd never done it himself.

It can't be that hard, he thought, rummaging around inside the truck's dashboard for the rat-tail file with a corn-cob handle. Digging through stubby pencils, broken wrenches, plastic forks, tattered papers, matches, and other neglected remnants from the old man's life, his fingers recognized the texture of the cob handle, and he brought out the file from its dark nest of debris.

Randy set the saw on a stump and went to work, filing the teeth the way he had seen it done. There were many teeth, and the process was tedious, made more so by biting flies and mosquitoes. Finally, he reached the last link and dragged the file across it until it shone like the others. Now, he thought, we can get something done.

He cranked the saw and worked the chain back into the original cut, eager for gratification. He expected wood chips to fly, but it cut even worse than before. He tried to force it, with engine screaming in protest and chain smoking. Grains of oily dust were pulled from the sapling's gash which slowly extended itself at a downward angle from the original cut. When he finally made it through, after six or eight minutes of near-frantic effort, he dropped the saw in disgust. Dammit! All morning to get one little tree down. At this rate, Randy thought, I'll die of old age before I finish the job.

He found a soft-matted, scooped-out spot on the ground between roots, leaned back against a shady oak, and rubbed his head with grease and rosin-smeared hands. He tried to think of convincing reasons for doing what he was doing. The money was in his pocket. The car was there waiting. Stacy was with her boyfriend. *Why not just leave this mess?* he wondered. Why am I so damn stupid? He sat that way until lunch—conflicted, tired, and lazy with frustration. But she was never that far away. Her eyes began to draw and soon he was at the Blue Lagoon in his mind with Stacy frolicking at his side. He ate his lunch slowly, then pulled the file back out and set himself to re-sharpening the chain.

He thought about the physics of what he was doing, examining each link before moving on. He began to see into the process and understand more of how the old man did it. The angle of the sharp edge was critical, and they needed to be sharpened consistently. He labored over each successive tooth until he could imagine it doing its work. His shoulders and back ached by the time he reached the final cutting edge, but at last he was ready for larger movement. He surveyed the woods around him for the next tree to cut.

He settled on a pine about ten inches in diameter, straight and tall. The tone of the engine was less shrill as the teeth bit their way in, but there was still some struggling to keep the cut straight. He let it eat about two-thirds of the way through, then worked the saw out and started a new cut angling down to where he had stopped the original line. This cut, when the lines met, would remove a wedge-shaped slab from the trunk, leaving a large notch. He had studied the tree and its surroundings before deciding where the notch should be. He knew that if he cut too far, it would begin to lean before he could remove the saw, and the blade would be hopelessly pinched. The cuts had to come together, but not too deeply. He stopped several times to remove the saw, examine the progress, and make necessary corrections. The muscles in his arms were weak and trembling when he finally brought the two cuts together. A light prying motion with the saw popped the sticky wedge out from the trunk, and Randy marveled at the small portion of wood still holding the tree upright.

It was as good as down. A short cut through the remaining wood from the back side of the notch would send it crashing into the clear spot where he wanted it to go, allowing easy access for cutting and loading. He gripped the handles and placed the saw just above the point of the notch. He was nervous, even though the placement was not so critical now. The tree would begin to fall with the removal of only a slight amount of material. The saw gurgled expectantly. His forefinger on the throttle made the command, and he watched the teeth eagerly chew through the soft bark into the sappy outer layers. He readied himself to yank it back out if he felt wood pinching the blade, a dangerous situation that meant the tree was falling wrong. He played it lightly, feathering the throttle, until at last he saw it begin—a pulling away from the blade so that further effort was unnecessary. He eased the saw out, gripping it in his left hand, as he watched and listened to the tearing of fibers and popping of limbs reaching a woody crescendo as the tree crashed gracefully into the predetermined spot.

He dropped the saw and pranced about, shouting. "Yes! That's the way! I *can* do this, dammit!" It was the first time he'd made the notch cut without the old man's help, and his pride burped inside him like fermenting fruit in a vat. The only thing lacking was someone to share his victory with. *If only Stacy were here,* he thought. *How proud she would be!* She would laugh and hug him, and they would dance together in the woods.

Chapter 20

It was the next day, the third day after the old man's funeral, around lunchtime, when Randy finally drove the loaded truck out of the woods. He idled the creaking rig over the undulating terrain in double-low gear until he reached the pavement of Taylor's Gin Road. He was ready to take the logs into the pulpwood yard to get unloaded and paid, and he was thinking about what Mr. Jenkins had said about hiring a helper. When he had gone in with the old man before, he had seen guys hanging around the yard who could have been in need of work. He had not thought about it then, but now he was concerned about how he would approach someone in that situation.

Anxious to get it over with, he decided to eat lunch on the road, but he underestimated the dexterity required to shift the gears and handle the old truck. There was half a revolution of free play in the worn-out steering mechanism, and no power assist. The gears were balky as well, with the cable shift for the two-speed rear-end requiring finessed coordination between the pull knob and clutch pedal. He sipped sweet tea from the Mason jar between gear shifts, and on the straight stretches of road he bit off chunks from his ham sandwich.

He was in control until a faded pickup pulled out of a side road directly into his path. The brakes, which tended to grab on the right front, caused the loaded rig to lurch toward the ditch as Randy stood on the pedal. Trying to correct with the unresponsive steering was more than he could do one-handed. He pumped the brakes and leaned on the wheel with his left arm while trying to find a place for the jar he'd been drinking from. The tailgate of the pickup was looming. The rig veered closer to the crumbling edge of the blacktop and the narrow shoulder as he slid the sloshing jar between his legs. He was going fast enough to drive the bumper of that pickup all the way up to its driver's ass and make an accordion out of the intervening metal. "Crazy old farmer," Randy muttered.

The pavement sliding by on his right was a jagged edge where it met the dirt shoulder. The drop-off spelled disaster for the top-heavy truck should the wheels slip over. Catastrophe loomed in front as the farmer crept along, unaware of the struggle going on behind him. Randy hunched forward, applying more pressure to the brakes. The tea jar tumbled onto the floorboard where it became a nuisance at his feet. When he pumped his leg to maintain the delicate balance, it rolled and wedged itself under the pedal.

The pedal wouldn't budge. He managed to downshift as he tried to worry the jar away with his toe. Looking up, he saw that impact was imminent. He stood on the brakes with all his might in a last-ditch effort. The jar shattered and the right front grabbed. The steering wheel slipped in his grip, and the truck veered toward the ditch. He twisted it back to the left and released the brake, correcting the truck's direction but not its center of gravity. The rear wheels, riding the edge of the blacktop, flirted with the washed-out shoulder. The rig began to teeter, elevating Randy. He saw a coil of barbed wire and a bag of feed inside the pickup bed, gaps in the wood of the floorboards.

He worked both arms against the loopy steering, making corrections on instinct while bracing for the worst. In his mind he saw the rig with him in it, rolling and smashing into the pickup. He must have blinked. Then he couldn't see for the thick cloud of blue smoke rolling over the windshield. A jolt to his lower back bounced him off the seat. He was still upright but where was the pickup? The billowing mass thinned as he rolled through it. Sight returned, revealing the source of the blue fog: the rusty backside of the pickup pulling away.

Randy applied controlled pressure to the brakes as he watched the farmer's head moving up and down, frantically checking his mirror. The old fool had looked up and gunned his engine just in time. The hunk of iron under his hood responded flatulently by blowing out a mass of petroleum by-products, the residue of which speckled the windshield that Randy peered through. He eased the truck over to the shoulder, shut it down, and sat there trembling.

He could still smell the oil smoke even though the pickup was out of sight. The lingering fumes convinced him that the episode had been real despite the dream-like quality it was taking on. It seemed that a violent accident was in the midst of happening, then stopped happening, erasing itself in a fraction of a second. There had been a gap in the flow of time. Then he was surrounded by smoke and everything was correcting itself—an amazing, mysterious reprieve that justified a few moments of quiet reflection.

He remembered how hungry he was and his half-eaten ham sandwich. Where was it? He'd left it wrapped on the seat beside him, but now the seat was empty. The driver's side floorboard was strewn with broken glass; the passenger floor was where he found the sandwich, to the right of the transmission hump. The bread slices were separated and lay mayonnaise side down in gritty filth. He smiled at what a minor inconvenience this was. He had money and could eat lunch in town. He deserved a treat after a hard morning's work and what had just happened.

When he opened the door and hopped down to clean up the mess, he noticed his pants were wet. At first, he thought he'd peed on himself—*that's just great!*—but then he remembered the tea jar: it had sloshed onto his crotch before tumbling to the floor. He chuckled. No big deal, but he hoped his pants would dry before he got into town.

Chapter 21

Randy's elevated mood gave way to one of apprehension as he approached the pulpwood yard. He had never driven the truck in by himself, and he didn't know what transpired between the people inside the tin-roofed office and the truck drivers. The yard was a busy place with a complicated protocol beyond his experience and understanding. The gravel entrance was dusty and cratered from the daily pounding of the heavy trucks in an endless procession from sun-up to dark, groaning in slowly with their logs and departing light, ready to repeat the process.

Randy knew enough to pull over to the side to wait his turn when he reached the center of this hive. Only one truck at a time was permitted to enter the unloading area, and there were two trucks ahead of him.

Diesel-powered tractors lumbered back and forth over their rutted paths. Heavily weighted with steel plates on the rear, they were rigged with front-mounted hydraulic booms and swinging cables which were hooked by the grimy operator around an entire rack of logs to lift them off the truck and stack them across rail cars lined up on a spur track. Loaded trucks either waited or jockeyed for position in the staging lane, their noisy engines reflecting the mood of the drivers as they idled or snarled impatiently. Mufflers were not necessary for hauling pulpwood out of the woods and were in fact nuisances, either cut off to get them out of the way or simply not replaced when they were snagged and ripped away by a stump.

The battered, lopsided appearance of the trucks attested to their utilitarian nature. They carried little in the way of comfort or safety features. The trappings of normal motoring, such as taillights, headlights, mirrors, and even window glass, were in scarce supply on these vehicles that resembled abandoned relics of war. Most of them, including the one Randy drove, had their cabs or front ends smashed from impact with trees that either took an unexpected twist when falling or stood too close to the logging road. The woods were thick, and the workers were usually in a hurry to make a load. Dents, dings, twisted sheet metal, stripped gears, broken belts, punctured tires and radiators, as well as calluses, bruises, and sprains, were all part of a day's work.

The men who owned the saws and trucks, if they were tough enough, resourceful, and willing to work through the cold winter rains and mud as well as summer's sickening oppression, could make a modest living from cutting and hauling pulpwood. A three and one-half cord load was worth over one-hundred and twenty dollars, and the old man and Randy had on several occasions hauled out two loads in one day. But that was under perfect conditions. Some days they didn't even finish one load, and there was fuel to buy and upkeep on the truck and saws. Acceptable stands of timber weren't always available, and, for the productive parcels, a substantial portion of the earnings went to purchase the logs from the landowners who had planted the seedlings twenty years before.

The helpers had to be paid as well—one man didn't have enough arms, strength, and energy to do it all—and good workers were hard to keep. The wages varied widely, with about ten dollars per day being the base rate for the most illiterate of the labor pool, usually haggard remnants of the old sharecropper system. Enterprising young men with driver's licenses, mechanical skills, and desire to learn were paid according to the owner's affection and the worker's ability to make himself indispensable. Randy, waiting on the outskirts of dust, noise and commotion, tried to imagine the type of person he could take on as a helper.

A stocky man with a clipboard walked up to the driver's window and shouted over the din of clanking metal and rumbling engines. "Caught me off guard, seeing this old rig pullin' up. I didn't expect to ever see it again after what happened to Ben. You buy out his equipment?"

"Uh, no. I, uh—"

"You ain't his boy, are you? I've seen you ride in here with him, but I didn't think his boy was around no more. Or if he was that he was suited to hauling pulpwood."

"No. I worked for Mr. Stempton. Still do, I guess. Or Mrs. Stempton, that is. I agreed to stay on and finish out a deal he made before the accident."

The man turned his head to spit, then looked at Randy. "Hmm. That must be over at the Jenkins property. Hear they're puttin' in a subdivision over there. Right smart of clearing to be done before the builders can come in. You planning on doing all that by yourself?"

"Well, I don't know." Randy cleared his throat. "I might . . . *hire* someone—"

"Yep. You might ought to." The man stepped back from the cab to scratch something onto his clipboard with a stubby pencil. He turned his head jerkily, eyeing the logs and squinting against the dust and glare. "That's a pretty good load you got there. We'll mark it as three-and-a-half. Come in the office soon as you get unloaded and get your money. Just be sure to pull over to the side so you don't block nobody." He spat again and cocked his close-cropped head to one side. "And you might want to look around while you're here. There was some boys hanging around a while ago looking for work."

Randy nodded as the man turned and walked to the next truck, indicating it was his turn to pull forward. Then the unloading rig approached, and he knew he should step out to acknowledge the worker and offer help. The operator nodded, then hopped from the tractor to the top of the stack to loop a thick cable around the logs. Two cables were required for each rack, so Randy climbed up to attach the second one. With hooks secured, the haggard and filthy worker swung himself back onto the tractor. He nodded again as he pulled the hydraulic levers. Randy stepped back. Soon the truck was unloaded.

He drove the empty rig across the lot and parked beside the office. A cluster of men seemed to be joking and laughing around the entrance to the tin-sided shack. Randy assumed they were laughing at him, and he climbed down from the cab with head and eyes averted. As he stepped clear, he noticed they were walking back to their own trucks, patting the fat billfolds on their hips.

On the shaded side of the building a cluster of black boys in their early teens sat in a circle on overturned buckets, slapping their thighs and hooting over some game that occupied the spot of dirt at their center. They looked up as Randy approached. One said, "Wha's happ'nin?" Randy smiled and replied, "Not much," wondering if he should say more.

Another young man sat at the corner of the building, just inside the line of shade. He was not part of the game but was instead drinking from a Mason jar—like the one Randy had recently broken—and eating from the grease-darkened paper bag which rested on his lap. He seemed more mature than the others, and he was further separated by the color of his skin. They were dark chocolate; he was soft caramel, and his hair, one shade darker than his skin, was not so tightly wound.

He looked up from his chewing, and Randy noticed in his almond-shaped eyes the soft metallic luster of burnished gold, flecked throughout with green and darker brown specks radiating from the pupils. The young man nodded and went back to his lunch.

The racket of the yard was muffled inside the office by the whoosh of dusty air through a window fan that seemed powerful enough to lift the structure off its footings. Randy couldn't make out where to go at first, his eyes being unaccustomed to the interior space. As he stood in the doorway blinking, the stocky man with the clipboard entered beside him. With his hands on Randy's shoulders he gently pushed him toward the corner of the room. "Miss Angie there'll take care of you."

The fat woman sat behind a wooden desk eating lunch from a Styrofoam tray. She mumbled from her stuffed cheeks, "Got you all ready to go. Just sign this copy and you can be on your way." She fumbled with a napkin, then slid a stack of bills and the paper across the desk. "Oh," she added, "Here's a pen."

Randy signed and pocketed the money. "Is that all I do?"

"Yep, till next time. I guess we'll be seeing more of you and Ben's old rig. Ray told me you was clearing off that Jenkins property back towards Prathersville."

As Randy was about to reply, the clipboard man interjected, "Yeah, he's got a job on his hands, for sure. Needs to take one of them boys out there back with him. I know that one on the corner, the one with light skin, is a good worker. Name's Buster. Some folks avoid him because of what he is, but I believe he'd make you a good hand."

Part IV—Thanksgiving

Chapter 22

A few withered leaves still clung stubbornly to the branches, protesting their fallen comrades' acquiescence to the advancing season. Because of the dry weather, early autumn had not produced the expected show of color, and by mid-November there was already the sense of impending winter, produced not so much by falling temperatures as by the drabness of the landscape. The climate had been cooperative, though, as Randy and Buster worked like brutes at the Jenkins property, clearing the land for the house builders. They managed to keep the grueling schedule that had been decided before the old man's death, before they even knew each other or had any notion of the ordeal before them.

Mr. Jenkins continued to check their progress every few days and slip Randy extra cash when he was pleased. October's end found them working on the last corner of the property as the foundations were going in on the tracts nearest the road, where Ben Stempton had died. Randy and Buster were finally able, during the first two weeks of November, to slow their pace and savor a foretaste of victory. This was a time of finishing up—hauling brush and a few light loads of easily accessible logs—and tending to some overdue maintenance on the equipment. They both appreciated that the old man had chosen to begin clearing at the roughest area of the property, where the slopes were steep, rocky, and covered with a thick tangle of briars and scrub. Their work had gotten easier as it progressed because of changes in terrain as well as their developing skills, stamina, and ability to work together.

Their relationship progressed smoothly from the first day at the pulpwood yard when Buster spoke first as Randy approached: "Hey man, you needing some help? 'Cause I'm for sure needing something to do."

Randy, relieved that he didn't have to be the initiator, stammered, "Well . . . actually, I do, and I was thinking of asking you. When can you start?"

"I was born ready, and I ain't got nothing going on for the rest of the week, or week after, for that matter. I guess you could say I'm seeking a long-term employment opportunity. What you got, anyway? And where you from? You don't sound like you from 'round here. Don't that truck you in belong to the man who got cut in two?"

Randy began his explanation as Buster rose from the overturned bucket and wadded up his lunch sack. Soon they were deep into a conversation that progressed in the truck as they rode back to the property. Their dialogue continued in the mornings, during lunch, and whenever the workload and noise level allowed. Now, after ten weeks together, they still hadn't run out of topics to discuss or observations to share. They'd overcome challenges that would sicken most men. They'd labored through the cusp of seasons and were now approaching another as the days grew shorter, the nights cooler.

Winter was not far away, and what remained of autumn—this blurred interval between two distinct states—was generally acknowledged as a time to count blessings and give thanks. Randy, for the first time in his life, felt pride in what he'd been able to accomplish and thankfulness for the way things had turned out— "God's providence," as Buster said. He also hoped that the upcoming holiday would provide the opportunity for him to spend some time with Stacy.

He hadn't seen her much during the weeks of struggling to finish the contract, but he had kept her close in his mind. Having Buster to talk to during the day magnified his evening loneliness, when he had no company except for the hounds and chickens. He would mumble to himself as he puttered around the shack, tried to read, or prepared for sleep. In bed he tossed on the sagging mattress, his body aching from fatigue, his soul longing for the comfort of someone to hold. When he slipped into sleep at last, it was by way of the blue lagoon in his mind, which he entered through the doorway of Stacy's eyes.

Whenever he bumped into her at the Stempton home, she was warm and friendly, as she'd been that night when they first met at the bar. She seemed glad to see him, and they would chat as much as their schedules allowed. After she and her mom had helped each other through their initial grief, she had gone back to her apartment. Randy didn't like to think about her there with that boyfriend, but he exulted in the moments they shared when circumstances brought them back to the home place—him on business, her to check on her momma. The first mentioning of Thanksgiving dinner and Randy's expected participation came when Stacy brought up the subject one Friday afternoon as the three of them chatted over coffee.

With a chill in the air and the blue sky visible through the freshly curtained window, there was a shared optimism, available to them for the first time since the accident. Randy had just gone over the financial details of the job, and Stacy, enjoying a couple of days off, was pleased with her redecorating efforts in the kitchen. The new eggshell paint and the colorful "country" accents—ducks, chickens, and old barns—had considerably "brightened this old place up," as Mrs. Stempton had said, her face looking ten years younger than on the day after her husband's funeral.

Stacy, from out of nowhere, said, "I can help, Momma, if you don't feel up to it. I'll even do everything if you'll let me!"

"Do what? Let you do what?" asked Mrs. Stempton.

"Put on a big Thanksgiving dinner for our family, including Randy of course, since he's the one who's given us reason to be thankful."

Stacy's mother blinked in bewilderment. "Why, Sweetpea, these things have to be planned in advance, and I ain't given it a bit of thought. Guess I've been too busy thinking about other things. Of course, we can have dinner here, but I don't know how big it'll be or who to invite. What do you have in mind?"

"I just meant us. Me and you and Randy, and I know Timmy would love to come out again. And Ty. You know he ain't got much family, and he needs some place to go. That's all. That wouldn't be too much, would it?"

"Well no, I guess not. And we ought to include your Aunt Ruth. She's been a real blessing to us, helping to take care of things and bringing food and such. We could show our gratitude to her, too. I don't guess that'd be too many. We'll just need about a twelve-pound bird and a ham, and you can help me make a big pan of dressing. And for dessert, maybe a pecan pie and some peach cobbler. We can go into town later and pick up some things—if you got time, that is."

"*Yes!* Of course I've got time. Oh Momma, I can't wait for us all to be together here at home with your good cooking! And you know—I'm just now realizing it—but we do have a lot to be thankful for." Smiling, she looked from her mother to Randy. "A couple of months ago everything seemed hopeless, but now. . . ."

"Amen. The Lord's been good to us, and we need to honor him and thank him for the way he's blessed us. 'All things work together for good to them that love God.' We've just got to remember to put him first in all we do."

"And we could make some ice cream too, Momma. Ty loves homemade ice cream, especially vanilla. Let's remember to get some vanilla extract and rock salt."

"Okay. We can make ice cream too. Maybe Randy'll feel up to cranking that handle. Him and Ty can take turns. That'd probably seem like pretty easy labor for you—wouldn't it, Randy? —after what you been through these last couple of months."

"Well, I guess so. I've never made ice cream before, but it can't be that hard."

Stacy laughed and said, "What a city boy!"

"He sure is," added Mrs. Stempton, "but he's coming around. Give him a little while, and you won't be able to drag Randy Walls back to Pittsburgh or any other big city for that matter."

Randy smiled. "I can see how living in the country could grow on a person. If I ever settle down, I might try some place like this where it's peaceful and quiet and . . . well, sort of stable. And working hard every day—I've never felt better, or stronger, now that I've gotten used to it."

"Hard work never killed nobody. That's what Ben used to say."

Randy, discomfited by the irony, was surprised that they didn't seem to notice. Mrs. Stempton continued good naturedly: "Working hard, eating right, and getting enough rest—that's what keeps people healthy. That and living by the Word. The good Lord blesses those who strive to do his will."

"Randy's certainly got the hard work part down, that and eating right with you cooking his meals. I still can't get over how he managed to get all that work done. Forty acres, that's a lot of land to clear."

"You got that right, Sweetpea, and what a mess we'd be in now if it weren't for his determination."

"I couldn't have done it if I hadn't found Buster. He worked every bit as hard as I did. Never once complained."

"You see, that's what I mean. The Lord knew you'd need some help—that we all needed help—and he placed Buster right where you'd be sure to find him. And I know having steady work's been a blessing to that boy and his family. They've had a right hard time. It was a real shame, what happened to his pa, and now his brother's gone too."

"He told me his daddy was dead, but that's all he said about it. What happened to Buster's father?"

"It was a sad thing all right, but you know he brought it on himself. Leon was always bad to drink. That's something a man trying to raise little ones can't afford to do, especially a colored man."

"But it wasn't right," Stacy said. "Ot didn't have to kill him, just because he came in his store drunk. If it had been a white man he killed like that, there would have been a big stink, and Ot would probably still be in jail."

"Well, we don't know that. Man's got a right to protect his property. Besides, Ot didn't mean to kill him. He just don't know his own strength."

Randy said, "You mean the black man Ot Brown hit with the bottle crate was Buster's father? Mr. Stempton told me the story, but I never connected it to Buster."

"Well, there's been some speculation about it," Mrs. Stempton said. "Leon was married to Buster's momma, but whether or not he was Buster's father is another matter. Leon was a dark-skinned man. Dorcas, his wife, is dark too. But Buster, well, he was the only one of them kids with such light skin. His father was probably a white man, much as I hate to say it. In those days, Dorcas was a loose woman. That's probably why her husband stayed drunk all the time."

"You know," Stacy said, "lots of men don't need much excuse to stay drunk. Ty's daddy drinks so much he can't even hold a job no more. If it weren't for Ty supporting him, ain't no telling what'd happen to him."

As Mrs. Stempton commented on what a shame it was, Randy remembered conversations he'd had with his friend and the many details Buster shared about his family—except for his father. Buster was the youngest child. He had told about his older sister Magdalene and how smart she was—even went to college in Atlanta for a couple of years. And there was a brother too. Buster said most folks called him Stinkum, but his real name was Voltaire. He got drafted in 1968 and died in Vietnam the following year.

There had been a period in Buster's childhood when "men came around." But, he'd been quick to point out, that was before his momma "got sanctified" and started taking them all to church. After the death of his father the family moved to town to live with an aunt who was a "righteous woman." Through her influence Buster's mother and sister, who would have been about fourteen, were "redeemed, washed in the Blood." Buster explained, "Me and Voltaire didn't have a chance after that. Them women had us scoured clean and in church every time the doors opened. It weren't long before we was singing praises and lifting up our hands to the Lord. And he's been blessing us ever since."

The conversation had begun, Randy remembered, when he'd commented on Buster's Tree Brand pocketknife, which was just like the one given to him by the old man. Buster had pulled it from his pocket to cut a fresh chew off a plug of tobacco. "Yep," Buster said, "This knife's the only thing I got left from them old dark days. A white man give it to me when I was about eight. All I remember about him is he told me he was my uncle. It was right after my daddy died and we was still living in that old shack. I don't reckon I'd ever get rid of this knife. Reminds me of how the Lord lifted me from darkness into the light."

Randy hadn't thought much of it then, but now his mind, sorting and sifting, pulled him away from the present. He was aware, though, that Stacy and her momma were continuing to develop Thanksgiving plans. Mrs. Stempton said, "I'd better check the pantry and make a list before we go. I know we'll need some cranberry sauce and maybe a jar of pickled peaches. Do you remember how your daddy loved those?"

"Lord yes," Stacy replied, "but he was the only one. Those things are disgusting."

"Well, it won't hurt to have some anyway. Randy might like 'em, and Ty." Mrs. Stempton got up from the table and began rummaging around in a drawer for a pencil and paper. "What do you like, Randy?" she asked. "What's your favorite Thanksgiving dish?"

The question, while bringing him back to the present conversation, dredged up memories. At St. Jude Home for Boys the holiday had been characterized by more institutionally prepared bad food, more prayers, and more scolding from the nuns for anyone who was unthankful enough to complain. He finally answered, "I don't guess there's any special one. I've liked everything you've cooked for me since I've been here."

"Oh, that's just because you're always hungry from working so hard. I could boil up shoe leather and you'd probably wolf that down too. But I want this to be special. I appreciate what you've done for us, and I'd like to show it by fixing your most favorite dish, as long as it ain't some Yankee food I don't know how to cook."

"Oh Momma, you can cook anything, Yankee food or not. Come on, Randy, tell us. Surely you've got a favorite dish, maybe something you ain't had in a long time."

Randy picked up his cup and looked into it as he swirled the cooling dregs around the bottom. The orphanage had closed in 1966, as he was entering the emotional jungle of adolescence. The shuffling afterwards from home to home prevented the establishment of traditions. The families all tried too hard, especially that last one, whose efforts to seem normal—*thankful* even, after what they'd done—made the holiday hollow. He had to reach back further for a pleasant memory.

"Well, there was this lady I lived with for a while that made something I liked. She called it mulligan stew. I don't know what she put in it, but it sure was good."

"I used to make brunswick stew sometimes—Stacy remembers."

"Momma, your brunswick stew is the best! We ain't had that in a long time. Make us a big pot, please. Randy'll love it."

"Well, we usually have that with barbecue pork, but I don't guess there's no law against brunswick stew for Thanksgiving, as a side dish. I could grind up some of the turkey scraps and use that. Better get some extra onions. I think we got enough canned tomatoes from the garden."

"Umm-um. I can't wait till Thanksgiving. Randy, you're gonna love Momma's stew. And dressing—hers is the best! Everybody says so. She's got some secret recipe or something. I hear folks up north don't eat dressing like we do. Y'all call it 'stuffing.' That's a shame, not to know about dressing and giblet gravy, especially momma's."

Bea Stempton set her empty cup down on the table. "Well, it's like I said: Randy's coming around to our way of living. This time next year, he'll be a true southerner, and I'll bet he don't ever go back. They usually don't, you know. Everybody I've ever known from up north who came down here ended up staying."

"That's the truth, like them Zelweigers from Wisconsin who joined the church a while back."

"Yep, them and a lot more just like 'em. And what gets me is how they come down here all high and mighty, ready to point out how ignorant and backwards we are, how bad our schools are, how we mistreat the colored, and so on. Then they end up building a big house and staying. Couldn't run 'em off with a stick. If things are so bad down here, then why the heck don't you go back to where you came from? That's what I feel like telling 'em sometimes. Not you, Randy, of course. I ain't talking about you. We're real glad you're here and we hope you'll stay. Ain't that right, Stacy?"

"We sure do, and I don't think we got much to worry about. Randy's part of our family now. You wouldn't leave us, would you?"

"Well, I haven't made any plans yet. But I have thought about traveling some and then starting college somewhere in a year or two. Of course, I'd have to work my way—"

"College?" Stacy said. "Why, we got a fine one over in Aaronville, less than thirty minutes away. You could drive back and forth to classes. That's what some of my friends are doing. I've thought about starting myself, but Ty thinks it's a waste of time. He says ain't nothing there but a bunch of hippies and weirdos. I know what you mean, though. Sometimes I feel like there's a whole lot more to see and know about than just what's here in Aaron County."

"That's fine I guess," Mrs. Stempton said, "but this part of the world's been good to us. It's our home, and a person needs some place to put down roots."

"Here we go again: Momma's favorite subject, putting down roots and bearing fruit. But that's what I'm saying. With the state college just over the hills, Randy can learn about the world and put down roots right here, all at the same time."

"You may be onto something, Sweetpea. Maybe y'all could ride over there one afternoon and let him see the campus. It's real nice, Randy. Lots of old brick buildings, big shade trees, pretty lawns . . . I believe you'd like it. Timmy was planning on going there to study art, but he changed his mind and went to Atlanta instead."

Stacy said, "We'll have to talk about it later, Randy. Now that y'all are about finished at the Jenkins property, you got time to take a holiday—speaking of which, we got a big one coming up! Momma, did you think of anything else we need?"

"Nope, reckon not. Got it all wrote down on my list."

"We better go on then before it gets too late."

"What's the rush, Sweetpea? Did you forget we got company?"

"Me and Ty's got plans for tonight. And Randy ain't company, he's family."

"It's okay," Randy said, sliding back from the table. "You two go ahead. I was just getting ready to leave myself."

"Awright, then. Since Stacy's so excited, I guess we'll go on. Let me get my coat and purse." She walked out of the kitchen, and the room grew quiet.

After a moment Stacy asked, "Randy, what are you doing this evening? You ought to get out more. Why don't you come by the Goat later? Me and Ty'll be there for a while. Then we're going over to Aaronville to a restaurant and to see that Burt Reynolds movie,

Deliverance. It's not very often I can talk him into doing something, and I usually have to work on Friday nights, so this is kinda special."

Randy nodded. She repeated, "You really should get out more."

Then Mrs. Stempton, purse in hand, reentered the room. "I don't look fit to go out," she said. "I ought to just let you go, Stacy."

"Momma, you're fine," Stacy answered, rising. "We need to do this together. I might get the wrong kind of turkey."

Randy stood and placed his cup on the counter, and the three of them walked out together.

Chapter 23

The half-joking comment Stacy had made at the beginning of Randy's crucial commitment proved to be true: "stump-pulling requires huge amounts of planning and a careful strategy." The dragging and hooking of chains; safely positioning the tractor; digging, prying, cutting; the possibility of flipping the machine over backwards as its rear tires bit into the loamy earth; hoping that nothing broke except roots; the constant entanglement of briars and vines; and countless other concerns about fuel, belts, hoses, not getting stuck, not puncturing the radiator, and not getting killed had all kept Randy's mind and body occupied.

He and Buster typically worked from sunup to sundown before parting ways. Then supper with Mrs. Stempton and tending to necessary details at the shack: a hot bath in the rust-stained tub, then refilling it to wash the clothes he'd worn that day; wringing them out and hanging them on a cord strung across the back stoop; cursing himself for being too stubborn to let Mrs. Stempton do his laundry in spite of her daily offers; then maybe, before collapsing on the sagging mattress, a few moments of mindless escape in front of the old black and white TV he'd picked up at the pawn shop. The cycle repeated itself each day except Sunday, which, Mrs. Stempton insisted, was a day of rest. Randy discovered, however, that rest didn't occur simply as a result of setting time aside for it.

Each morning throughout the week, he would grudgingly rise, consoling himself with the notion of sleeping late on Sunday, but when that day rolled around, his eyes would pop open before daylight. Going back to sleep was out of the question. The lumpy bed lacked the comfort to soothe his sore body, and his head would be already revving through a multitude of job-related details, along with the engrossing problem of how to construct a relationship with Stacy.

He was relieved that her mom had not been overly persistent in her invitations to attend church services, especially when he remembered that preacher at the old man's funeral and the puzzling way some in the crowd had responded. Worshipping with Mrs. Stempton and her neighbors would tighten the vine that bound them together and lead to a jumble of expectations. He felt affection for the woman, but he was wary of developments that would move him toward a brotherly relationship with Stacy.

As the evenings grew cooler, Sunday became simply a different kind of work day. A rusty box heater backed up to the rock fireplace in the main room was the only source of heat for the shack. The small stack of wood out back was soon depleted, requiring Randy to engage his tired muscles, if he was to keep warm, in additional labor: cutting, splitting, and stacking. An ancient blighted oak behind the cabin, having been felled but only partially cut up by previous tenants, provided plenty of fuel and additional exercise.

When the workload finally grew lighter, he had trouble adapting. On the Friday afternoon of the Thanksgiving plans, with the end of the land-clearing job in sight and the evening's fire laid in the heater, the sense of satisfaction he felt as he rested on the rickety porch was different from anything he'd ever known. He was close to being happy, but freedom from stress and exhaustion brought a keen awareness of his solitude. Stacy was right: he should get out more.

But where would he go and what would he do? He'd become acquainted with a few people—those he ran into at the pulpwood yard, Ot Brown's, and the hardware store—but they regarded him with detached amusement. There was never any invitation, implied or otherwise, for him to enter their world, and intruding was not part of his nature.

This wasn't the case, though, with Buster, who was always eager to open up like a well-worn pocketknife and present himself for service. He had the ability to cut through tangles and whittle away the rough spots in their work as well as life in general. He'd offered Randy advice about Stacy and other problems, and he'd invited Randy to his home and church.

Randy would have enjoyed sharing this evening with his friend, even if it meant attending revival services, but when he mentioned the idea to Stacy, as a response to her charge that he should get out more, she looked at him in disbelief. "Randy," she said, "coloreds and whites don't go to church together. That would be weird. Besides, who wants to go to church on Friday night?" Then she and her momma got in the car to go buy groceries. They drove away, leaving him in the yard with the flatbed truck.

He rode around the back roads for a while before returning to the shack. He thought about going to the Billy Goat Bar for a couple of beers but decided against it. Seeing Stacy and Ty together would be frustrating. He remembered that other evening he'd spent there, when he'd been sent by the old man, "to go out and have some fun." Randy had wondered since what his motives had been. Had he thought that having fun was simply a matter of showing up somewhere? That people Randy's age automatically entered the fun zone whenever they were together with beer and music? Would being near his daughter provide the key ingredient, or did he even know she would be there? He'd felt awkward that night, but Stacy had shown interest and tried to comfort him. They'd talked freely after he got drunk. They laughed and he spent the night at her apartment. Maybe it had been fun, or close to it. At least he'd forgotten himself for a while.

A puzzle piece fell into place as he reminisced on the porch: fun was an abandonment of self, freedom from worry and the fear of being misunderstood. And laughter—that was always a part of real fun. Other ingredients included sharing, companionship . . . love. *Yes!* Love had to be present, but this most important ingredient was also the most elusive. Without it no other combination could produce the kind of enjoyment—*fun*—that humans really need. A billboard on the highway of thought spelled it out. His mind played with the image, providing pictures of happy couples on the beach with children, sandcastles, and puppies. *Love: life's no fun without it!* Perhaps the old man had understood.

Randy smiled as he thought about Stacy and Mrs. Stempton in the supermarket buying groceries. They would be able to find the cranberry sauce, onions, turkey, and whatever else she had on her list because the aisles were clearly marked. You could go right to whatever you needed. But life was not a supermarket. His friend Buster, whom he'd grown to love as a brother, was on the other side of an imposed boundary; and he couldn't find his way to Stacy, whom he felt he had loved forever. As he rocked, watching the shadows lengthen in front of him, he was aware of the half-grown hounds curled up at his feet, and he was careful in his rocking not to mash a tail or paw.

As the sun dropped, the air grew chill. He went inside to spend another evening alone with the TV and his reading. He was still trying to get through *The Grapes of Wrath,* which he'd started as a high school assignment a couple of years ago. The book had been put aside when he was placed in that last home and a different school. He'd recently made up his mind to finish it, but he was usually too tired in the evenings for substantial reading. Maybe now he would be able to get back into it.

He left the TV on as he settled into his one comfortable chair, enjoying the bright voices, laughter, and music in the background. One of his favorite shows, "The Sonny and Cher Comedy Hour," would be on soon. Cher was so beautiful and cool. He'd read that she once suffered from paralyzing stage fright, but with Sonny's help she'd learned to overcome it. Their relationship seemed real, and Randy was interested in how they fit together, each one complementing the other. Last night he'd watched another of his favorite programs, "The Waltons." The show was a little too wholesome, but maybe families like that did exist. He imagined himself as the father of a house full of kids, with a strong, faithful, and loving wife. Together they would prevail over the challenges of life, their bond of love growing stronger with the passage of time.

He was positioned in ideal relationship to the TV and the light bulb hanging from the ceiling so that he could see both the printed page and the flickering screen. With commercial jingles blaring, he flipped through Steinbeck's thick novel, looking for his place. He remembered the part where the Joads had to bury Grampa on the side of the road because they didn't have enough money for an undertaker. They were displaced and destitute, looking for a better life, but Randy sensed that the family would face many more hardships on their journey. He wanted these gritty people to overcome their obstacles and realize their dreams. Surely there was hope.

The words on the page produced images that were incongruous with the pictures and sounds of the TV so that his mind was divided. Time passed, and after Sonny and Cher sang their theme song and the Joads threw in their lot with the Wilsons to continue their westward journey, Randy felt ready for sleep. He loaded the heater, set the dampers, and slid under the scratchy blanket, his mind drifting over tomorrow's possibilities. He and Buster had decided to take Saturday off. Maybe they could do something together. And Stacy—she would probably come back to her momma's house to talk about Thanksgiving. He could run into her there and they could all have fun. As the heater hissed and popped, he slipped into a hopeful dream filled with incongruous images that melded in his mind like warm Crayolas.

Chapter 24

Stacy woke up early Saturday morning in a sour mood. She lay there in her old bed at her momma's house thinking about what she should do and dreading the outcomes. Ty had once again acted a fool and messed everything up, getting drunk on the afternoon before they were to go out on their dinner and movie date. When she got to the apartment after grocery shopping with her momma, she found him there with his cousin Toby and a couple of their derelict pool hall friends, who had shown up at with a case of beer and a bottle of Jack Daniels. She heard them before she opened the door, laughing and talking loudly over the blaring stereo about things like drag racing and frog gigging. They seemed intent on a rowdy evening, trying to decide which type of ruckus would produce the most fun. When she opened the door, Ty appeared shocked at the sudden realization that he had a girlfriend who also lived there.

He became indignant when she reminded him they were to go out that night. "Hell," he replied, playing to his audience, "I can't remember every damn thing you're always planning for me to do. If it ain't one thing, it's another. More'n I can keep up with. We was just having a beer or two. No harm in that is there? But I can wait till some other time to hang out with my friends. If you want to go to a damn movie, then by God we'll go!"

She replied, "No, that's okay. Y'all go ahead and knock yourselves out. I'll seeya later." Then she went out the front door. At first she didn't know where she would go, but she had ended up at her childhood home with her momma, someone who really loved her and was reliable. Now it was morning and she would have to face the problem. She tried to convince herself that Ty was worth it, that his sweet side would eventually win out. He just needed lots of love. After all, he grew up without a mother and not much of a father. Guys like Ty, with his energy and magnetism, were hard to find, and she could imagine him becoming very successful one day, with her love to guide him. Going back to the apartment, though, after the scene last night, would not be pleasant. She wasn't ready to face him and what she would likely find there. She needed to collect herself first. She needed somebody to talk to, somebody with a level head.

Her momma was not the person she wanted to confide in. In fact, she'd told her a lie last night: "The schedule got mixed up, and Ty had to go in to work. We had to cancel our movie date, so I just decided to come spend the night with you." She didn't want her worrying over her affairs. She was a big girl now and could take care of herself. But it helped to have someone to talk to, and that was a problem since her best friend Becky worked Saturdays, and her other girlfriends from the Goat would still be in bed. There was someone, though, who would be glad to see her and would provide undivided attention. After a cup of coffee and a quick breakfast, she made up her mind to give Randy Walls from Pittsburgh a visit at that old shack.

It was mid-morning when she pulled her Valiant up into the yard and parked it under the nearly bare oak trees. She didn't see Randy on the porch and thought he might not be home, but the flatbed was sitting in the drive. Realizing he must be inside, she wondered what he did in there by himself. She mounted the steps and rapped on the door. She didn't wait long for a response but impulsively decided to announce herself: "Hey City Boy! You in there? Get your lazy butt out of bed. You got company!"

★★★

Stacy could not have realized the effect her calling out would have on Randy, bringing him through an amazing transition from dream to reality. He had slept late for the first time in weeks, and now, this lovely voice was pulling him into consciousness. He was startled and confused in the delighted way of a child who has been awakened by his parents on Christmas morning. "I'm coming," he called back. "Be right there." He scrambled out of bed and found a pair of jeans and an old army shirt. He thought he should go to the bathroom to splash his face and comb his hair, but Stacy called out again, "Hurry up! It's cold out here."

He didn't take time to put his boots on but pulled on the same pair of thick socks he'd worn yesterday. He greeted her in a rush of words. "Hey Stacy! Come in," he said, opening the door. Then he began apologizing: "It's cold in here too, at least till I get the heater going, and it's not very comfortable, but you can sit here. This chair's pretty good. And I can have the fire going in a few minutes. This place is kind of a wreck. I mean, it's fine for me, but I've never had company before, except Mr. Stempton. And Buster, he's been over a few times."

"Don't worry about it, Randy. I've been in this shack before with Daddy when I was a little girl."

"I'm glad to have it, really. Your dad made sure I had what I needed, but I've been too busy to go much beyond the basics."

"Wow! I remember that old heater! We had it in our house when I was little, before Daddy put gas heat in."

"It still works, but I'll have to admit, I've never had to make fire before to keep warm."

"Yeah, kinda primitive, ain't it? Especially for a city boy. I'm surprised you even knew what to do with it."

"It's not exactly rocket science," Randy replied, but when he knelt in front of the iron box and opened the door, a thick ball of smoke billowed out into the room. "Shit," he said. "I hate it when it does that."

"You opened the door too fast. Close it back and I'll show you." She knelt beside him in front of the heater, a bare knee poking through the frayed hole in her jeans, and opened the door just a crack. "Trick is," she said, "to let a little air in first, so the smoldering fire can come back to life. Once the flames start, the chimney will pull the smoke out." After a few seconds she said, "Look around the edge of the crack. See that little yellow flicker in there. She's waking up, hungry for more wood." Then she eased the door open to reveal the lazy flame dancing around the remaining charred wood chunks. This time the smoke followed its intended path out the back of the stove and up the chimney. "Load her up," Stacy said. "Let's get some heat in this place. It's colder in here than outside."

Soon they were cozy with their chairs pulled close to the heater as it popped and crackled with warmth. Randy switched on the TV set and cranked the dial until he found Saturday morning cartoons. Looney Tunes, they were the best. He and Stacy laughed as Wile E. Coyote hung the Acme Do-It-Yourself Pull-down Railroad Tunnel in front of the canyon's drop-off in another futile attempt to trick the Road Runner. The bird's scorching speed allowed him to defy physics, and poor Wile E. ended up temporarily flattened on the canyon floor, the hapless victim of his own sinister scheme. A commercial hawking the latest GI Joe figure provided the opportunity for more small talk.

Randy said, "The hard part about the heater is regulating it. It warms up fast once it gets going. I better close the dampers, that is if you're warm enough."

"I'm fine. Just needed something to take the chill off. You can probably let it burn out now. It's supposed to get up into the sixties today and only down into the fifties tonight."

"This weather seems strange to me. I mean, the afternoons feel almost like it's still summer. But at night it gets chilly. When does it get really cold?"

"It's hard to say." Stacy tilted her head thoughtfully. "I remember when I was little playing outside on Christmas day without a jacket. We'll have some cold days, though—a few freezing spells scattered through December, January, and maybe into February. A lot of our winter is just gray and dreary with misting rain—cold, but not freezing. Muddy and damp without much sun to dry things out, actually kind of depressing." Her tone changed as she turned her eyes to meet his. "Don't last long though. You can usually feel spring in the air by late February, early March. That's my favorite time of year, when everything begins to get green again with new buds, and the sky clears out nice and blue."

Randy loved the way she could put a smile in her voice like that. He agreed that spring was his favorite too, but then he stumbled, realizing the topic of weather was about exhausted. He wondered why she was there, but he had no skill in directing conversation. He was relieved when she asked, "You got any cigarettes? I left mine in the car."

"Sure, somewhere." He rummaged around in his pile of stuff on the floor until he came up with half a pack of Winstons. "Here," he said, tapping the package to produce one filtered end from the opening. She slid it out and Randy went to the hearth for matches. He lit hers, then one for himself.

"Thanks," she said, exhaling smoke.

"Sure." He slid his ladder-back chair closer to hers. "I just got this one ashtray. We'll have to share."

They puffed thoughtfully. Then Stacy suddenly turned her face to his and asked with a smoky mouth, "Randy, what are you gonna do today? I mean, what do you do when you're not working? Just sit around in here and watch cartoons?"

"Hardly," Randy chuckled. "I mainly just sleep here. I haven't had a lot of time lately for cartoons, remember?"

"Oh yeah, you did have those forty acres to clear." She pursed her lips, lifted her brows, and impersonated Vivian Leigh. "How silly of me." She batted her eyes twice before resuming her normal voice: "But now you're nearly done. You'll have some free time. What will you do for recreation and relaxation?"

"I like to read."

"Hmm, okay, but . . . shoot! Randy, it ain't right. I mean, look at you. You're a nice-looking guy and it seems like you don't ever have fun. It's like I said yesterday. You need to get out more." She motioned with her cigarette hand as if there was a world out there chock full of enjoyment just waiting for Randy's participation.

"Maybe I will. I've been thinking about it lately, having fun, that is." He paused to rub a tab of ash into the small metal tray resting on the floor between them. "I've also been thinking about what to do with my life."

She nodded. "Yeah, me too. I get to feeling sometimes that I'm missing something, that life's gonna pass me by if I don't reach out and grab hold at just the right time, kinda like jumping on a merry-go-round." She leaned forward, thrusting her face closer to his and into the mystery of life. "It's hard enough picking which horse you wanna ride but grabbing the pole and jumping on as it's going by— it's tricky. I don't wanna miss, and we never know how many chances we'll get." She settled back into her chair and looked at her cigarette. "Life can be kind of a short ride, I guess. At least it always seems short when you start looking back at things."

The commercial ended, and their attention was diverted by the zany antics of Bugs and Elmer on the snowy screen. After a moment Randy replied, "I know what you mean. Time seems to go faster now than when I was a kid in the orphanage. When I think back, it's like those years went by in a flash. But then—when it was happening—it seemed to go on forever." His voice trailed off until he realized Stacy was looking at him expectantly. "I didn't think I'd ever be finished with high school and out on my own. Here I am, though, and now I can feel time slipping by. Part of me wants it to move on to something better—the next phase of my life—and part of me wants to hold it back, to slow time down so I can figure things out."

"Ain't that the truth!" Stacy slapped the arm of the chair, causing ashes to fall. "How *are* we supposed to know what to do? We have to make choices that we know will affect us from now on, but it's so hard. What seems right today may be the very thing that screws up our lives. But being too careful—that's a choice too, ain't it?—that don't work. That's a sure way to miss out on everything. That's why I think it's best to trust your gut. Go with your feelings. There's really no way to do what you're trying to do—figure it all out—unless you can see the future." She made a sweeping gesture and looked around the bare little room. "And I know damn well you can't do that. Wouldn't be sitting here in this shack if you could. So I say try, try, try to have fun while you can. All the old people I know just sit around worrying and growing moss on their asses. I don't want to end up like that. I want to live. I want some *adventure*."

Randy tapped his cigarette over the ashtray. "I set out on an adventure back in July, and it brought me to this place. Then one thing led to another and I'm still here. I can't help thinking it was for a reason, that I was supposed to come here and go through all that I did. But now I don't know—if there's still a reason, I mean."

"Randy, Randy, please. That day when momma told you about the contract, I said then that we needed you, and we still do. You've become—I don't know how to say it—something, a part of our lives. And it's not just momma. It's me too. Please don't think about leaving."

Randy noticed the crack in her voice, and when he faced her, he saw her blinking wet eyes. She turned toward the bare wall, then back to him. Tears wet her cheeks as words began to flow from her contorted lips. Her face was flushed, and her red-rimmed eyes looked into his with a quivering intensity.

"Oh Randy," she said, "my life—it's sort of messed up now. I'm not really brave like I try to act." She sniffled and snuffed out her cigarette, then wiped her eyes on the sleeve of her sweatshirt. "Sometimes I feel like things just ain't gonna work out no matter what I do. The whole world seems fragile, ever since Daddy died. You being here's like the prop that's holding things up. I don't know what I'd do if you were to leave."

Randy's heart swelled in knowing that he meant so much to her, but he felt powerless about what to do in the presence of a crying female. Should he hug her, let her cry on his shoulder? The way the chairs were positioned made this an awkward proposition, and he was distracted by the subtle changes taking place in her face and voice. Finally, seeing the expectation in her eyes, he said, "It's okay, Stacy, I won't leave if you don't want me to. I don't have anywhere to go anyway."

She sniffled and smiled. "You promise?"

"Sure. I'll stay as long as you need me."

She sniffled again. "I do need you, right now, to get me some tissues."

Randy shook his head at his lack of social skills. "Sure," he said, rising from his chair. "I'll be right back." He passed between her and the TV into the kitchen and through the low makeshift doorway into the bathroom that had been tacked on some years earlier. He unrolled a wad of toilet paper and hurried back to Stacy, who'd risen from her chair. As he approached, she looked at him eagerly with her face changing again, like a child who's solved a riddle. He offered the paper as if it were a dish of pickles.

When Stacy reached for it, she held his hand. "I've got a great idea! Let's me and you go for a ride."

Chapter 25

Throughout the morning Ty lay in bed tenuously suspended between waking and sleep. When the strands of sleep slipped, the real world encroached by pounding through his eye sockets. If he turned and fixed the pillow just right, sleep could hold a bit longer, keeping the noise and harsh light outside. His thoughts, both conscious and dreaming, were of Stacy. His heavy arms groped about the mattress for her warm body. Disappointment that she wasn't there was bound up in the surging brightness that he would have to face upon waking. The protection of sleep's gauzy web was what he needed and clung to for as long as he could, but his field of vision behind fluttering lids continued to redden with each pulse. A burning thought brightened as if controlled by a rheostat, lighting up the inside of his skull and shouting him awake: *Where is she? Where has the little bitch been all night?*

He threw back the sheets and sat upright on the edge of the bed. Moving his head was painful, so he let his chin drop as he stretched his arms down between his naked thighs. His morning erection faced him, and he squeezed it between his forearms. As he stared at himself, he became aware that he was gritting his teeth. His body was tense, crying out for relief. This was not the way to wake up, without gentleness and love. Stacy provided a reprieve from this angry state, but she wasn't there, and her absence made everything worse. He didn't deserve this after the sacrifice he'd made in order to be with her.

★★★

He'd wanted to make things right, so he'd left his friends at the Goat and come back to the apartment early. He and the guys had shared a deep-dish pizza and more beer as a preliminary step to whatever adventures the night might offer. Toby and the others were keen on the possibility of hooking up with females. Ty, though, after stuffing himself, began to think of his girl and how he'd let her down. He got up from the booth as if going to the restroom and slipped out the back entrance. He didn't feel like explaining. They could chase whores without him tonight.

Funny what love can do to a man, he thought as he drove back to the apartment. He was drunk but not in a rowdy way. The pizza had stretched his gut, and his heart felt large and full as well. In this pleasant state he felt sure he could make things up to Stacy. She would probably be there when he arrived. If not, she would come along shortly and he would be waiting for her, ready to please, even willing to go to a movie if that's what it took. But she didn't come, and the generous mood yielded to feelings of increased frustration. Television provided mild distraction as he kept telling himself she would be along after a while, that she's probably visiting her mother or one of her girlfriends.

He was tired, but his mind wouldn't let him rest. His weekend routine was to stay up all day Friday after working the night before, and to wait till Friday night to crash. Then he was on the same sleep schedule as everyone else, at least until Sunday night at eleven p.m. when he had to go back to work. Friday evenings, without plenty of stimulation, could be tough to get through. He lay back on the tattered sofa and closed his eyes, thinking he could take a nap and wake up when Stacy got home. But thoughts about her possible whereabouts interfered, making relaxation impossible. The boys had left the bottle of Jack Daniels. As Ty tried to keep his eyelids still and look into nothingness, the whiskey beckoned to him from its place on the kitchen counter. He figured a couple of shots would help him relax.

One shot led to another as the evening drained away like sorghum syrup through a funnel. He was so tired. His nervous system, having been stretched repeatedly out of its normal shape since early morning, slumped into a trembling relaxation. The whiskey was finally having a sedative effect, although the nagging question of Stacy's whereabouts and who she could be with still flickered between his eyes like a candle flame diminishing as it consumes the last of its fuel.

The burning thought persisted as the late news announcers presented weather maps and reports of wrecks, break-ins, and school-board happenings in Atlanta. One more cigarette, then bed. The mound of butts grew in the ashtray, ashes spilled onto the tabletop. Another sip of Jack, lukewarm in a jelly jar glass. Commercial messages. Commentary about the election results. Summary of national news: Landslide . . . Nixon . . . what it means for investors .. . only her hairdresser knows for sure . . . according to Kissinger . . . peace is at hand . . . an agreement is in sight . . . continued troop withdrawals. . .. Then, as he was about to doze off, a voice that was familiar and welcome in its promise of comforting transport: *"Heeere's Johnny!"* Ty finished off the last quarter inch of whiskey in the glass and lit another cigarette.

Smiling and bleary-eyed, he forgot himself, carried away by Carson's disarming demeanor and risqué humor. He quipped about Burt Reynolds' centerfold and Joe Namath's knees and Kissinger's peace negotiations. And of course, the landslide, the biggest in history. Following the jokes took his mind off Stacy. Then, just as he was getting warmed up, Carson went into his phantom golf swing. Time for a commercial break and for Ty to hit the sack. As he peed into the avocado green toilet, the comedian-induced smile lingered along with the sense that the world was a funny place, nothing to get too upset over. He used his left hand to prop himself, a little wobbly, against the wall while he aimed with the other. Over the forceful plash of his urine, he heard a familiar slogan—*Building a better way to see the USA* —which set into motion a thought train about Fords, the better idea. His faithful coupe was waiting for him outside. He tried to count back to when he'd first started driving it. Just had turned fifteen—damn, that was fun! Sixteen, seventeen, eighteen, nineteen . . . hmm, that's a long time. . .. The ad placed an image in his mind of a Super Sport Chevelle. Beautiful. Then he pressed the toilet handle and became fascinated with the swirling water. As the gurgling whoosh diminished, he heard laughter from the TV.

He'd have to turn off the set anyway. Might as well check out the first guest. He recognized the face immediately: Goldie, the skinny blonde chick with big eyes who used to wear a bikini and dance on "Laugh In." She was talking with Johnny about her newest movie,

Something about butterflies and a blind guy. Carson kept getting her tickled. Her sexy giggle held Ty's attention for a moment, but he started to slip when they played a clip from the film. His eyes were so tired. He blinked and when he looked back Goldie was gone. A thin, wacky guy with an arrow through his head was on stage twisting up balloons into all kinds of shapes and playing a banjo, the stupidest act he'd ever seen.

He laughed out loud, alone there in the apartment. The sound of his own laughter, loud and hacking, was a reprimand. "Enough is enough," he said. "Time to crash." He stabbed the button and killed the zany comic, making him disappear into a white dot. Then he stripped naked and crawled into bed. He felt ready to drift off, but as he closed his eyes, the question of Stacy's absence persisted as an irritating pinpoint of light, a stubborn candle of anguish that continued to flicker throughout the night.

★★★

Now his stiff penis taunted him as he sat on the edge of the bed. The discomfort there and in his bladder compounded the throbbing in his head and queasiness of his gut. He moved to the toilet and relieved himself in the cramped, feminized space. Stacy's lotions, creams, conditioners, tampons, and shampoos were everywhere, producing an aroma of artificial sweetness. He needed to get out of there, to get some fresh air and something to eat. Then he could decide what to do about the bitch who'd caused him to be in this condition. After he splashed his face, he pulled on his jeans and boots and found his flannel shirt on the floor in the other room, stinking of stale beer and cigarettes. To hell with it, he thought, her and this place. Something fell off the wall when he slammed the door, but he didn't bother to see what it was.

Chapter 26

Randy was puzzled, then excited by Stacy's offer. The two of them alone in his personal living space, and she'd suggested they go for a ride. His fantasies had not prepared him for this moment. He stood there enjoying her smiling spontaneity, trying to board the same roller coaster. Finally, he stammered, "Sure. Why not? I don't have anything to do today and I'd love to go for a ride. With you, I mean. Is there some place in particular you want to go?"

"Aaronville, where the college is I told you about. There's lots of neat little shops and places to eat. And you can see the campus. It's a different kind of place from here, and it's not even that far away. We've got to start thinking about our future. Knowing there's a college with learning, books, and smart people just over the hills might give you reason enough to stay here, close to us." She tossed her head impatiently. "Come on, let's go! It'll be fun! And you can buy me lunch later."

Stacy's emotional state peaked shortly after they took to the road in her Valiant. She babbled at first about how great Aaron-Maslow State College was and the cool friends she had who went there, but a few miles out, as the road brought them down into the Hominy Creek Valley, her mood dropped to match the terrain. When Randy asked what was wrong, she shook her head. "Sometimes I just don't know if I can handle it."

"Handle what?" Randy asked.

"The uncertainty of everything. The future . . . and the present."

"It's gonna be okay. The contract's almost finished, and your mom's been able to pay the bills and save some money. Everything's more solid now. For me too. There were times when I didn't think we'd be able to do it, get all that land cleared off. Now, there's such a feeling of relief—"

"It's not that. You saved the day as far as Momma's situation is concerned, but there's other problems—my problems—that you don't know about." Her eyes darted to Randy then back to the road.

She drove with both hands on the wheel except for when she fiddled with the radio. Before he could think of anything to say, she pushed another button, changing to a clearer station. Mid-song, a jumble of notes, then the familiar lyrics brought structure to the melody: "... *it felt good to be out of the rain. 'Cause in the desert, you can remember your name, and there ain't no one for to give you no pain.* ..."

"Far out!" Stacy exclaimed. "I love this song." She reached over to turn up the volume.

"Problems?" Randy asked.

She was singing with the chorus and dancing with her head: "*La, la, la la la, la la la, la la* ..."

"Maybe I can help with those too," he said.

Stacy continued her sing-along, providing off-key vocalizations of the instrumental parts. Randy looked at her, saw her glance at him. He reached for the knob and turned down the volume. "Hey," she said. "That's my favorite song. Don't you appreciate good music?"

"Guess not. I've been out of the music scene lately. Haven't had much time to listen. There's something else I'm interested in right now, besides the top forty."

"Oh yeah? What's that?"

He gulped. "You. You said you had problems. I want to help if I can."

She reached over again, but not for the radio. She patted and squeezed his knee. "Oh Randy, you've been so good to me, to us. I don't deserve it."

"I haven't really been that good. I was working for myself too. I've made some money out of this deal, and I didn't have anywhere to go anyway. You and your family have helped me. I just want to return the favor. If it hadn't been for you giving me the ride that night from the bar, there's no telling what would've happened. I'd probably have killed myself or somebody trying to drive, drunk as I was. You were looking out for me, and I appreciate it."

Stacy laughed, placed her hand back on the wheel. "Yep, you were a sight that night. Nearly talked my ear off on the way back to my apartment. Then when we got there . . . you were funny and kinda sweet."

"Funny and sweet? I don't remember much of anything after leaving the bar."

Stacy smiled and looked at him for as long as she could before returning her eyes to the road. "It's okay. People say and do things they wouldn't ordinarily do when they've been drinking. I still think it was sweet."

"My God! What did I do?"

She giggled. "I'd tell you, but you might be embarrassed."

"Was it that bad?"

"No, no, not at all. So don't be embarrassed. Promise, if I tell you, you won't be?"

"I promise. Just tell me what I did that was so funny and *'sweet.'*"

"You tried to kiss me, there on the couch. Told me you loved me. That I was the 'girl of your dreams.' I didn't think much about it because I know how guys are when they're drunk and horny. I just laughed and pushed you away. I went to get you a sheet and a pillow. When I got back you were already out, curled up and sleeping peacefully."

Randy's face flushed. He looked straight ahead at the winding road for a moment. "I'm sorry, Stacy. I guess I wasn't much of a gentleman that night."

"You don't need to apologize. And you don't always need to be a gentleman."

They rode in silence, except for the radio, which Stacy turned back up to high volume. Randy tried to recall that night. He didn't remember trying to kiss her. But then he did remember something. When Stacy woke him the next morning, he had a sheet over him, and his pants lay folded on the coffee table. She must have undressed him and tucked him in. Oh great, he thought. She put me to bed like I was a toddler or something. How could I be such a weenie to pass out like that—

"By the way," Stacy said over a blaring car dealer ad, "I couldn't very well let you sleep in your boots and jeans. I've seen guys in their underpants before. It's not a big deal."

Randy shook his head in embarrassment. "That's easy for you to say. Now I feel like a little kid, having to be put to bed."

"That's silly. I'll always think of you as a man, especially after what you accomplished for us—you, Buster, and L'il Trudy the tractor."

"Aw shucks," he drawled in a poor John Wayne impersonation, "it was mainly Buster and the tractor that did all the work. I just showed up each day."

"Oh sure. I can tell by looking at those hands and arms of yours that all you've been doing is showing up."

"Yeah," Randy said as he raised and turned his knotty forearm. "I guess I have done some lifting, but it hasn't been so bad. I've enjoyed it, sort of. And you get some of the credit too. You played a big part in getting it all done."

"Oh, really? How's that?"

"The tractor, remember? You taught me how to drive it."

"Oh yeah! So that means I get half of the money, right?"

Randy laughed, his embarrassment gone. "Sure, why not. But you'll have to put it on my tab. Maybe buying you lunch today can count as the first payment."

"Deal!" Stacy replied, reaching for the radio. More blaring ads as she pressed each button in rapid succession. "Damn! Ain't that weird? Do these stations all follow the same schedule? Where's the music? My tape case is in the back seat. Reach back and get it, will you? Go ahead and pick us out something."

Randy hauled up the bulky vinyl-covered box and began browsing Stacy's eight-track collection. Bread, Three Dog Night, Creedence Clearwater Revival—he didn't really care, but he worried she would judge him by his choice. His fingers paused over each plastic case as he faltered. Stacy glanced over as he touched a tape labeled, "Chicago."

"That's great!" she said. "I see you've got good taste in music."

"This one? I mean, you like this one too?"

"*Yes!* I love Chicago. Go ahead, stick it in."

Randy complied, noticing as he removed the tape from its felt tray, the cover, which resembled weathered wood. Pushing it through the flap into the deck provided simple gratification. He felt the clunk and soft whir as the mechanism engaged. Then the speakers responded, blaring out a crescendo of horns, drums, and guitars.

They sampled several tapes from Stacy's collection during the twenty-mile ride, with Randy each time making the choice to her enthusiastic approval. When they reached Aaronville, though, the music faded into the background, playing only a supporting role to the visual medley presented by the bustling college town with its blend of old and new, provincial and avant-garde.

Aaronville was different from its neighboring communities in that it seemed to be pushing toward something rather than receding into the past, especially as they drew nearer to the campus. Here the shops with colorful psychedelic signs and clever names catered to the young and hip. Stacy parked in front of a freshly renovated storefront under a sign that read, "Epicurean's Delight." She said, "You've got to see this place. They've got about a million kinds of wine and cheese. Really cool."

There were things in there he'd never heard of, but Stacy seemed experienced and anxious to share her knowledge. Row after row of dark bottles with strange pictures and foreign words on the labels, and dozens of cheeses, wrapped in intriguing ways that made him wonder about ancestry. The short aisles in the center of the store were filled with dark, crusty breads and boxes of crackers with French and Italian names, along with exotic chocolates from far-away lands. Stacy examined the wine bottles along the walls.

The proprietor, who had been stocking shelves, noticed her and suddenly seemed eager to help. The young man's blonde goatee and mustache were thin, and his pale, blotchy skin gave him a sickly appearance. "Hi!" he said. "What sort of pleasure are you seeking today?"

Randy stepped out from the breads and crackers, puzzled by the unusual question. The man continued to gaze at Stacy through his wire-rimmed glasses. His eyes and lips were wet, glistening under the accent lights.

Stacy chuckled, looked at Randy then back at the man. "I'm not really sure. Just browsing, I guess."

"Take your time. I'll be happy to make recommendations or answer your questions. That's what I'm here for."

"Sure. Thanks!"

"Perhaps if I knew what you were leaning toward, white or red, sweet or dry, I could point out some of our best sellers."

"Hmm, now that you mention it, there is one wine I really like. It's called *Blue Nun.* You have that, don't you?"

The man stepped in closer. "Absolutely! Very popular right now, one of my favorites. You have excellent taste." Making his way to the end of the aisle, he brushed against her. "Here we are. How many bottles would you like today?"

She tossed her hair, glanced over her shoulder. "I don't know. Like I said, we're just looking. What do you think, Randy? Do you like Blue Nun?"

He cleared his throat, stepped over to join them. "Sure," he replied. "Yeah, it's my favorite."

"Excellent choice, my man," the wine guy said, pulling a bottle from the rack. "So, will you need one for lunch and another for dinner?"

Stacy giggled and shook her head. Randy answered for her, hoping to make a quick purchase—one that would please her—and get out of there. "No. One bottle's fine. For now."

Stacy turned away from the inquiring wine guy and leaned, smiling, against Randy. She said in a low voice, "Thanks! Do you really think we should? Maybe we could have some cheese or something to go with it, for lunch I mean."

"And what would you like to go with your wine?" asked the pale salesman. "We have some excellent Gouda that just came in from Holland. Goes really well with the Riesling."

"Yeah, sure. That sounds great. And some bread, too. Do you have Rye?"

"Absolutely! And once again let me compliment you on your taste. The heartiness of the rye and the sweet mildness of the Gouda make the perfect match. Combined with the dry, slightly tart wine you've chosen . . . well, it will be exquisite, to say the least. Makes me wish I could dine with you!"

"Yeah, well, maybe some other time," Randy said, reaching for his billfold. "How much do I owe you?"

Randy watched the pale man lick his lips and blink his eyes, which appeared weak and strained. He pushed buttons on the cash register. "Ten dollars and seventy-two cents. Would there be anything else? We have some fine imported chocolates."

"No thanks," Randy answered, handing over the cash. He forced a smile, as if he were pleased with his purchase and overall experience at "Epicurean's Delight." He took the sack and turned away from the counter. "You ready, Stacy?"

Soon they were rolling down Aaron Avenue, toward the heart of the campus, past fraternity houses, head shops, and boutiques. "This strip's not part of the college," Stacy pointed out, "but it might as well be. It's like a little village for the students. They hang out here, all kinds. Ty calls 'em hippies and weirdos. He hates this whole place. I don't know why. Before I started working Friday and Saturday nights, me and Becky used to cruise through here a lot. You know, just to look. Don't you think it's interesting, different kinds of people, I mean? I can't help wondering where they all came from and what brought them here." Her attention was suddenly diverted. "Look! Check out those Afros!"

Three guys about their age were conversing on the sidewalk. Their bell-bottom pants rode low on their hips, and their tie-dyed shirts vibrated with color. The leader's oval face was framed by a uniform cushion of tight curls, expanded miraculously to a height of several inches. "Wow," Randy said. I haven't seen 'fros like that since I left Pittsburgh."

Stacy giggled, stopping the car for a traffic light. "I know. Ain't it cool?" They watched the students milling around, laughing while the red light held. One of the black guys carried a rolled-up newspaper, and they all wore shiny platform shoes. They kept glancing expectantly at the storefront they stood before, one corner of a converted Victorian house. There was a sign over the door picturing a vivid yellow sun with eyes and benevolent smile. Swirly blue and red letters spelled out *Headquarters Boutique, established 1969.*

"Looks like they're getting ready to go in that head shop," Stacy said. "Probably to get some papers, or a bong, or something to get high with."

"What? They sell dope in there?"

"No. At least I don't think so. It's where hippies buy the stuff that goes with the dope. You know: rolling papers, pipes, incense, roach clips. I went in there once with Becky, just to look around."

The afro-sporting trio turned to face the shop door as it opened. Out stepped a brown girl, shapely in her tight hip-huggers and tie-dyed top, laughing and holding a package as she walked out into the late morning sun. Her mohair vest would provide little warmth, but by now the day was comfortable. The benevolent sun had chased away the chill. As she stepped off the porch, Randy caught a glimpse of chocolate-colored tummy between her jeans and short top. The light changed and the cars rolled out as joggers, pedestrians, and cyclists moved along the sidewalks, both with and against the traffic. The liveliness of the place caused him and Stacy to smile, but butterflies had begun to flutter above his groin.

"I'm gonna turn at the next light up there," Stacy said, "so you can see the old part of campus. The trees and buildings are really pretty."

Randy smiled, nodded, and tried to hide his nervousness, telling himself that he needed to learn to relax.

Chapter 27

After leaving Stacy's apartment, Ty's first stop was the house he sometimes shared with his father. Some of his stuff was still there, and he needed to eat a bite and check on a few things. In his pounding head the predominant thoughts were of his personal discomfort and how he would deal with Stacy, but twinges of concern for his dad were emerging. He hadn't seen him in several days. When he thought about his father, Ty became frustrated over his inability to stop the man's rapid decline. He was drinking himself to death, but Ty provided him with booze anyway because he couldn't bear his being sick and miserable without it. He figured it was the least he could do, to keep his old man comfortable at this point in his life. Ty's earnings covered most of their expenses. His father's income from a small disability payment and the occasional handy-man job was only supplementary.

When Ty stomped into the shaded den, Fletcher Ragsdale, wrapped in a blanket, was watching television from a lopsided recliner. "Whoa," he said. "Looks like somebody had a rough night."

"Rough ain't the damn word for it, but it's gonna get better, I can guarantee you that. We got anything to eat?"

"There ought to be something in there—beans, bacon, eggs. But why don't you tell your old man what the problem is first. Maybe I can help. You know, the voice of experience? I can see in your face that whatever's wrong has got something to do with that little Stempton gal you been shackin' up with. How come you and her ain't having breakfast together this morning?"

"'Cause I don't know where the little bitch is. She didn't come in last night. Why you sitting there, wrapped up in that blanket?"

Fletcher flipped the lever, raising the back of the chair, and coughed like a strangled tomcat. "I couldn't get the heat to come on. Guess the pilot light's gone out again. Where you reckon she is? Have you checked at her momma's house?"

"Hell, that's probably where she is awright." Ty plopped down on the sofa across from his dad, picked up the *TV Guide.* "I just ain't felt like calling. She wasn't real happy with me the last time I saw her. Damn! It is cold in here. Lemme see if I can get the furnace lit. What was you gon' do, sit here and shiver all day?"

"I knew it'd be warming up later and you'd be along some time or another. With my back like it is, I just can't crawl under there no more. Wouldn't be able to see what I was doing if I could."

Ty's rotten mood continued to fester as he fumbled around the foul-smelling kitchen for a flashlight, matches, and screwdriver. "Damn," he muttered, "getting to where he can't do nothing for himself, worse than an old woman." He finally found what he needed and went out the back door, letting the broken-down screen slam behind him. He moved some bricks and a rusty brake drum away from the termite-eaten plywood that covered the opening to the crawl space. A thick clot of frost-bitten weeds hindered his access. The weeds, cold and wet, stung his hands as he ripped them out of the ground. When he yanked away the plywood, a corner broke off. He flung it as far as he could.

So many problems. It was a shame his off day was going to be ruined because of stupid people, stubborn and helpless. He needed to relax his mind, especially with the way things were going at work. That lardass Bowman's brown-nosing had caused problems. Got himself moved into the front office and now a black guy was running his machine, or trying to. He had to be trained. Not fair, being expected to train this monkey, to sacrifice good production numbers for a nigger from the projects. Tommy Lee Chism was his name, lots of Chisms over there. Sorry as hell, too, every damn one of them.

His pounding head filled with curses as he crawled on hands and knees into the dark, musty space. He was about sick of this shit, trying to do the right thing and getting nothing but more headaches. Damn ol' man laid up in there watching cartoons. Stacy off running around somewhere—ungrateful as hell, both of them. He deserved more respect than this. Having to crawl around on his knees felt like living in a dungeon.

The space grew tighter near the furnace, and twice he scraped his backbone on the floor joists above him. As he lurched over the cold dirt, the flashlight's beams lurched also, exposing sweaty pipes, moldy rodent carcasses, and a dense community of meaty spiders clinging to the underside of the mildewed floor. He reached the furnace and struggled to position himself and the tools. He stretched out his leg in order to finger the matches out from his jeans pocket; this accomplished, he couldn't see well enough to find the access panel. A cover had to be removed to expose the gas valve and pilot light hole. He would have to prop the flashlight somehow, aimed in the right direction. His pounding head magnified the frustration.

He cast the beam about him. Almost within reach were two half-bricks and an old pressure cooker his mom had used years ago before the seal went bad. He scraped his back again dragging the cast-off items into place, but he managed to arrange them as a support to hold the light where it needed to be. Now maybe he could ignite the damn pilot and get out from under there.

He sat cross-legged and scooted over so that his face was near the panel. The rusty screws were resistant but yielded to his focused efforts with the screwdriver. The sulfurous smell of gas grew stronger as the panel came away, exposing the valve. He would have to turn the knob to the right position, then press the button in while he held the match. This part was a little scary. A tingling at the base of his spine accompanied an image of the house with him and his dad being suddenly engulfed in an expanding fireball. The image morphed and the tingle became a shudder: Florene, his old lover and patron, had gone up in flames. His face grew hot as he remembered gazing into the inferno and her husband's searing eyes. He struggled to suppress the urge to vomit. He blamed in on the Jack Daniels, acknowledging his need for food.

He dragged a match across the striker. It sputtered to life. He pressed and held the button with one hand, and with two fingers of the other reached into the hole with the burning match. The yellow flicker spawned a small blue flame, neatly conical, poised at the base of the rusty iron burner. He would have to hold the button down for about a minute to heat up the thermocouple; otherwise, the flame would go out when he let go. Seconds dragged. When he finally released the button, the pilot remained lit, bringing the tingle back to his spine.

He turned the knob. There was a click inside the mechanism, then an uncertain pause that allowed him to move his face away before the thumping whoosh occurred, introducing a symphony of blue flame from the burner, dozens of dancing cones, controlled and joined together for the purpose of providing comfort. Ty exhaled. He finished up and crawled out, wondering why that damn thing always made him so nervous.

He reentered the house, letting the screen slam again, then pushed hard against the main door to seat it properly against the cold. "All right, Pop, now you can get out from under that blanket."

Fletcher hacked again from his recliner. "I heard her come on. Good job, son. It'll be warming up in here now. Why don't you sit down and tell me about your girl problems?"

"I'd rather get me something to eat. Besides, there really ain't much to tell. She's probably over at her momma's, like you said."

"There ought to be five or six eggs in there. How 'bout scrambling 'em up for us? One thing I know for sure: you can't never take no shit off a woman. You gotta keep 'em in their place, let 'em know who's boss. There's plenty more out there, just remember that. All of 'em's looking for a damn man too. I ain't found one yet that could be trusted. They're just like us you know. They get horny and want some strange sometimes."

"I ain't wanting to hear that kind of talk, Pop. Stacy ain't like that. She just got ticked off at me because I forgot we was supposed to go to a movie last night."

"Yeah, I know. That's the way it is, always wanting you to take 'em some damn where and spend money. Then getting mad over the least little thing. I don't know how it is between you and this gal, but if you ask me, you're better off without her. A man's got to be the captain of his own fate. That's what I say. Can't let some little . . . umm, *female*, plan out his life for him."

Ty had turned back into the kitchen to find the eggs and a clean skillet. He recognized the irony: his father, of all people, trying to give advice on managing relationships and controlling fate. He resented his comparing Stacy to all the other sluts out there, but maybe there was a grain of truth in the old man's words.

He hurriedly consumed his portion of the slapdash meal before his father could finish the pork and beans. He stacked the dirty dishes in the sink, thinking about where he could go. He'd developed an itch for a new car. The coupe had become a nostalgia piece. He didn't feel he could ever part with it, but it no longer suited his maturing personality. It was a teenager's car, a makeshift hotrod that was out of place in this new world of sleek muscle cars. Super Sport Chevelles, GTO's, Roadrunners, Chargers, Mach I's—these were the chariots of young men who controlled their own destinies. He could afford one and he was ready to go shopping.

Aaronville would be the place if he wanted to look at cars. The dealerships had been advertising year-end "inventory reduction" sales. He could check out the deals, and while he was there, he might as well check out some of those hot college chicks who were always strolling up and down Aaron Avenue or riding their bikes around campus—"pedaling pussy," as Toby had commented back in the spring when they were cruising around on a Friday afternoon. Ty chuckled at the recollection. Maybe this day was salvageable after all.

He strode towards the front door. "See ya, Pop. Got some things to check on today."

He didn't wait for his father's reply, but stepped out into the sun, pulling the door closed behind him.

Chapter 28

The oaks, elms, and maples along Front Campus Drive still held most of their leaves, their color more prominent than elsewhere in the region. The buildings, dating back to the 1890's, represented an assortment of architectural styles: Antebellum, Victorian, and Colonial, with a touch of Greek Revival. The window frames, doorways, and columns shone white against the weathered brickwork, which was accented in places by manicured green ivy. The surrounding grounds comprised undulating, grass-covered mounds, shrubs, and cobblestone walkways with low seat walls and concrete benches. Some of the bushes were in bloom, and everything bore the stamp of meticulous care.

"Let's park and get out," Stacy said. "We can follow the walkways past these old trees and buildings all the way down to the quad—that's where most of the classes are held. Then we can cross over in front of the student center and go through this little patch of woods down to Love Valley. There's a pond down there. We can relax, watch the ducks, and have our picnic!"

"You're the tour guide." Randy replied.

"A while back me and Momma and Timmy actually took a campus tour when Timmy was thinking about coming here to study art. I don't know why he changed his mind."

Two squirrels, plump and bushy-tailed, began to dart along the canopy of branches spreading over the path. They led the way, providing amusement, as Stacy and Randy began their stroll. The squirrels, as if playing a game designed to impress humans, skittered and leaped across the lawns from tree to tree, over branches, and up and down trunks.

"I've never seen such fat squirrels," Randy said.

Stacy laughed. "They sure are having a good time. I guess this weather agrees with them."

"I wonder what they think they're doing. I mean, what's going through their little brains right now?"

"My guess is, not much. Except maybe, 'Let's show these people what we can do. Let's see if we can make 'em laugh!' I think their whole purpose is to entertain us, just like everything else about this day: the trees, the pretty blue sky, these old buildings, the hippies on Aaron Avenue, even that weird wine guy. This day was made to order, just for me and you. At least it seems that way, don't you think? Don't you get the feeling sometimes that God brought everything together in a special way and put you right in the center? I know it's weird. I can't really explain it."

Stacy stopped walking and placed her hand on Randy's arm as she waited for a reply. He felt himself teetering. Words and images from the past began to swirl inside his head as Stacy's eyes probed, searching for shared feelings. Many steps had led to his being here. A vortex of memories formed, pulling him into a new reality, and he understood what she was saying. "Yes. I know what you mean. I've felt it before myself, but I can't explain it either. I just know I'm glad—to be here with you."

They walked quietly as the squirrels continued their play. They passed a bustle of activity on a lawn adjacent to an old dormitory building. Three girls and two guys were having an animated discussion, but they were too far away for their words to register. The tallest girl, in the center of the group, was trying to interpret some thing or sentiment through her gestures and bodily contortions. The others found this funny, stomping their feet and shaking their heads, as the tall girl swayed and undulated with her hands pressed together above her head. Stacy and Randy glanced at each other, smiling. "Yep," Stacy said. "Them too. They're here to amuse us."

"Looks like they're doing a pretty good job of amusing themselves," Randy said. Stacy smiled back and their leisurely walk continued. Soon they reached the spot Stacy had referred to as "Love Valley."

"Ain't this great?" she asked. "Don't you like it?"

"Perfect. And that picnic table over there is in the sun. That'll be a nice, warm spot."

The neatly mowed lawn leveled out around the boundaries of a small kidney-shaped pond. The sun, nearing its apex, cast shadows of the trees that cradled the grassy glen. Lines were sharply defined as they moved nearer the water and the picnic table that waited only a few yards from the tranquil edge. The smooth surface of the pond held before them an inverted image of trees and sky as they sat and spread the contents of their lunch sack.

Across the pond another couple shared a table that was less exposed than Randy and Stacy's. They were shaded from behind by a large oak, and Randy didn't notice them at first, as he busied himself with unpacking the bread, wine, and cheese. When his eye caught movement on the other side, he looked up and saw they were waving. Stacy, seeing them at the same time, smiled and returned their peace sign.

"You know them?" Randy asked.

"Naa. They're just being friendly. Most of the young folks here are like that, always waving at everybody with that peace sign. Look: they're getting high over there, and they don't even care that we can see what they're doing."

Randy paused in his unwrapping. "Wow. Seems like these college students smoke a lot of dope."

"Yeah, that stuff's everywhere these days. Have you ever tried it?"

"Not really—well, there was this one time, at my last foster home. One of the boys there was pretty wild. Julian was his name." He gazed into space as the memories came, blinking away those of Jack and Emma's bedroom. "He was a little older. I guess he'd tried about everything, seemed sort of bored with life. He pulled out a joint once when we were supposed to be trimming the shrubs in the back yard. I took a couple of puffs just to show him I wasn't afraid, but it didn't do anything except make me cough."

Stacy smiled. "Yeah. It affects some people like that. Sometimes you have to smoke it two or three times before you feel it. At least that's what Becky told me."

"So you've tried it?"

"Yeah, but it was like you said. Nothing happened, except me coughing. Of course, that's just between you and me. Ty would get real pissed if he knew I'd been fooling around with that stuff. He hates hippies and pot heads almost as much as he hates black folks."

Randy didn't reply, but at the mention of that other name he cringed and turned back to the cheese and bread. It was ridiculous of Stacy to think he would ever discuss anything with that boyfriend of hers. She must have felt it also because she reached for the bread as if to remove an unsightly blemish. "Here," she said, "let me help."

Then the realization that they were ill-prepared for a picnic hit them. "Look at us," she exclaimed. "We don't have any cups, plates, napkins, or anything!"

Randy laughed. "I guess it won't hurt us to eat with our hands. We can tear open this sack to make a table cloth, and . . . oh yeah— at least I've got a way to slice the cheese!" He reached in his pocket and pulled out his knife. "It's good and sharp too."

"Great! And I guess we don't need cups. We can just swig out of the bottle."

They began reaching at the same time, their hands meeting at the center of the table. Stacy said, "Go ahead and open the wine. I'm thirsty."

He puzzled over the neck looking for the cap. She took it from him to show how to peel off the foil. "Shoot," she said. "We ain't got no corkscrew."

"Lemme see it. Maybe I can get it with the knife."

"Yeah, that'll work. I've seen that done before." Under Stacy's direction he worked with the sharp blade, cutting out little chunks until the cork was loose in the bottle. "Now," she said, "we still can't pull it out, but you can press it on through and let the sucker float in there while we drink. It ain't likely we'll want to close it up again anyway. I expect we'll drink all of it while we're sitting here."

They passed the bottle back and forth as they nibbled. Randy used the knife to slice the bread and cheese. The slices disappeared into their mouths, and conversation was replaced with chewing and swigging. After a while Stacy commented, "That's the knife my daddy gave you, ain't it?"

"Yep, sure is. And it's a fine one too, a Tree Brand. Really holds a good edge. Your dad told me they were the best kind to have. He liked them even better than Case knives."

"Well, Daddy would know. He took a lot of pride in his tools. The fact that he gave you that knife shows how much he thought of you."

"I appreciate that more now than when he gave it to me. I'd never part with it."

"I'm glad you've got that knife. I hope it'll always remind you of my daddy, and us." They looked at one another. Then she added, "You know, as long as someone remains in the memories of others, it's like they go on living in a way. I believe my daddy'll be here with us for a long time."

Randy smiled and went back to his slicing. Two neat stacks of bread and cheese rested on the flattened-out sack in the center of the table. The bottle was half empty.

"Umm-mm, I'm enjoying our lunch. How about you? Do you like the wine?" Stacy asked, reaching for another swig.

"I do. It goes down really well with the bread and cheese."

"Yep. And this bread—what kind did you say it was?"

"It's rye bread. Have you never had it before?"

"Nope. Don't think so. I grew up on plain old white bread, biscuits, and cornbread. And yeast rolls on special occasions, like Thanksgiving. I like this rye though, it's different."

Randy smiled and nodded as they ate. Soon only crumbs and a few sips of wine remained. The ruined cork bobbing near the bottom of the bottle indicated how much they'd drunk. Stacy said, "I feel so comfortable now. The sun is warming me up all the way to my bones."

Randy pulled his cigarette pack from his shirt pocket, shook out two. Stacy took hers and waited for a light. As he reached with a match, he noticed her gaze moving to the couple across the pond. He glanced in that direction and caught a whiff of marijuana smoke, carried over the water on a gentle breeze. He leaned back, moving the match to his cigarette.

"Randy," Stacy said, "we can try something—if you want to." He looked beyond the small flame to her face, then shook out the match. She continued: "I just remembered. I think it's in here." She pulled a wallet from her jacket pocket and began to probe inside. "Got it. Becky wanted me to have this. Said I might have an opportunity to try again soon and she wouldn't want me to miss it." Between her thumb and forefinger, she held a tightly rolled joint. "How 'bout it? Wanna smoke some weed?"

He looked around nervously. The couple across the pond were moving, getting ready to leave. "It's awright," she said. "Nobody'll see us out here, and no one really cares anyway. Let's try it, just to see what happens."

He put his cigarette down and pulled out another match. "Give it here."

Chapter 29

Randy lit the joint as he would a cigarette, drawing in only a small puff of paper and sulfur smoke. "Yuck. Tastes awful." He squinted and crinkled his nose then brought it back to his lips to try again, but the joint had gone out.

"Sit over here by me," she said, "and I'll hold the match while you take another toke." He moved to her side of the table and straddled the bench. "This time," Stacy said, "keep pulling on it as long as you can. You've got to hold it down deep in your lungs."

She struck the match and he, pulling in air, watched the flame bite through the paper into the weed. His lungs expanded with the smoke. "That's it," she said. "Now hold it in." He felt his eyes bulging after a few seconds as he tried to suppress the urge to cough. The pent-up gases erupted spasmodically, despite his efforts, and he hacked and snorted smoke as he tried to regain composure.

Stacy laughed. "Good job! You actually got some that time. How does it feel?"

"Rough," he answered, trying to control the spasms. "Like a blast furnace in my throat."

"You're tough, you can take it."

He regarded her smile through watery eyes. "Sure, I'll be fine. Now it's your turn." He passed the joint to her, but it had gone out again. He readied a match. "Now remember," in a mocking tone, "keep pulling for as long as you can and hold it down deep."

The joint, held slightly apart from her lips with the flame at its tip, crackled as she inhaled. She waved Randy and the match away and continued to draw slowly, sucking in air along with the smoke. She gulped to lock it in and passed him the joint. "Hurry," she whispered. "It ought to stay lit now." Her eyelids drooped languidly as she croaked out the words.

He worked at it slowly as he had seen her do, and she nodded her approval. His toke continued as her coughing spell began. She squinted, wrinkled her nose, and puffed out her cheeks, trying to curb the impulse. She at last surrendered, the barking from her lungs softer than Randy's had been. Her eyes watered, but soon she was ready for another turn.

They continued this way until the joint was nothing more than a short brown roach. When she couldn't hold it without burning her fingers, Stacy set it down. "Well," she said, "I guess that's it. You feel any different?"

"How do you mean? What's this stuff supposed to do to you, anyway?"

"Get you messed up, like you are now."

"I'm not messed up. I feel normal."

"Sure you do."

As Randy was about to reply, he became fascinated with Stacy's teeth and the contour of her lips. It seemed that her smile was consuming space and time, replacing the elemental constituents of existence. Her lips were moist, teeth white and glistening. The normal time flow halted, as if the conductor had stopped the train to allow him the luxury of basking in her beauty. He had been about to reply that he did feel normal, but the smile forming on his face made it difficult to speak. The sun was so warm, and the humming inside his head was connected to that warmth, as was Stacy's smile. He realized then, with a sudden joy, that things weren't normal, and he was about to share these new perceptions with her when a harsh quacking sound behind him drew his attention away from her mouth.

He looked around to discover that three large domestic ducks had joined them. The apparatus inside the throat of each strained to produce the racket as their bills opened and closed repeatedly. These ducks were intent on attracting attention to themselves, quacking insistently at the picnic table, under the bench, and at their feet. They reminded Randy of the hungry hounds back at the shack, always wriggling around at his feet, but by their plumpness the ducks shouldn't be so hungry. They seemed already stuffed. Duck droppings littered the ground as their quacking grew louder and more insistent.

"Damn," Randy said. "Those are the fattest ducks I've ever seen."

Stacy laughed. "That's what you said about the squirrels."

"They act like they're starving."

"Let's see," she said, reaching, "we've got a few crumbs of bread left."

She tossed a piece of crust to her right and the ducks immediately waddled off in that direction, quacking while competing for that one small piece. They seemed full of purpose with their constant quacking, waddling, jockeying for position, and dropping of droppings. Stacy and Randy began to laugh, but soon the ducks were back at the table around their legs, imploring with their bills and throats, seeking more bread. Randy tossed another small piece farther away in the opposite direction. Laughing he said, "Go on ducks, leave us in peace."

But they kept coming back and soon the crumbs were all gone, leaving no means for sending them away, no relief from their obnoxious quacking. The most aggressive duck, in its impatience, became more demanding by using its bill to tug jerkily on the legs of Randy's jeans. Aggravation mounting, he suddenly kicked his leg upward— "Go on, dammit!"— sending the duck flapping backwards.

The others scurried away to regroup and quack it over. Randy's outburst left him feeling small and inadequate. When he glanced over, Stacy's look of dismay reflected his unease before her face began to color and change. Her eyebrows lifted, her head tilted to one side, and she made a sound of suppressed laughter. She grinned as a small giggle escaped. "Being kinda hard on the poor creatures ain't you? After all, they're just looking for something to eat."

"Well, they can look someplace else. I've about had it with their damn quacking. And I'm not about to let them eat my blue jeans!"

Her laughter erupted and the effect was contagious, even though Randy still sat in a pool of puzzlement. It all seemed so strange. Then, as the ducks began to waddle back, quacking louder than ever, the absurdity of the situation settled over him like a heavy net, the cords of which were made from strings of silliness. There was no escape from these zany, aggressive, seemingly starving, incessantly quacking ducks. Laughter bubbled up like Jell-O injected with helium.

The ducks, laborious at their feet, continued to quack as Randy and Stacy leaned into each other, shaking the table with their laughter. Between snorts and guffaws, he managed to say, "These ducks should be arrested and carried off to a zoo somewhere."

Stacy, laughing just as hard, replied, "Yeah, charge them with cruelty to humans."

"That's them, all right—the cruel ducks. They're making my stomach hurt with their cruelty!"

She exclaimed in mock anguish, "We must escape! We've got to get away from the cruel ducks!" Then she scooped the empty wine bottle and sack up off the table, dumped the trash in a nearby receptacle, and fled the scene, scurrying up the grassy hill in the direction from which they'd come. Randy, clutching his stomach, struggled to speak. "Wait, wait! Don't leave me here alone with the cruel ducks!" Then he set out, stretching into long clumsy strides, to catch up.

They both collapsed under the first tree they came to, safely away from the ducks, who were still scrounging beneath the picnic table. They looked at each other expectantly as their chuckles subsided and their breathing returned to normal. After a quiet moment in hilarity's afterglow, she said, "That was about the funniest thing I ever saw, you kicking that poor duck."

"Yeah, I could tell you thought that was pretty funny, but I bet you'd have done the same thing if it'd been your leg it was pulling on."

"Sure I would, that or wrung its damn neck. I guess it's good we left when we did, or there'd probably be three dead ducks beside that pond, and feathers everywhere."

Randy chuckled. "Those cruel ducks were treading on some pretty thin ice. And just think, they don't even realize how lucky they are. Look at them down there, still searching for bread crumbs."

"Yep, like the only thing that matters is stuffing their gullets, and the only purpose for humans is to provide them food."

Randy lifted an eyebrow and looked at the sky. "That reminds me of what you said earlier—how God brought everything together just so he could put us in the center. 'It's all here for our amusement,' you said. I guess those stupid ducks must feel like everything's made especially for them, that God put them at the center of creation. . . ."

His voice trailed off as he reached his conclusion, as if it were too profound for the normal conversational tone. He had the feeling that he might be rambling. She answered, "Wow," and they sat quietly on the hillside, looking down on the ducks from a distance. They basked in the sun's warmth and the pleasantness of shared speculation. For Randy there was a sense of harmony that had been unknown before. On that hillside with Stacy there were no promptings in his mind that he'd better get moving in order to accomplish some task.

He was following the slow procession of wispy clouds across the blue sky when she asked from a place far removed, "Whatcha wanna do now?"

"Nothing. I'm fine right here."

"I know. It is nice, but time's passing. At least I think it is. If you want, we can go back to the car and drive over to the other side of campus. You can see the ball fields, and all the new buildings."

"Sounds good. I'm just along for the ride, remember?"

Soon they were between the old brick buildings, heading toward Front Campus Drive. When they reached the section with the oak trees and fat squirrels, Randy felt a twinge of apprehension. He hoped the playful squirrel couple wouldn't become aggressive as the ducks had been. When they appeared, running along the branches in front of him, he realized how unfounded his concern had been. These were normal squirrels, if a bit oversized, accustomed to humans but skittish nevertheless. He felt sure they wouldn't get close enough to nibble his pants leg. He and Stacy had not spoken since they left the hillside, and he was uncomfortable with these thoughts. The trees seemed grotesque now, and the shadows had taken on a menacing quality.

The sprinkling of color from blooming shrubs along the path encouraged him in his need to communicate: "The squirrels aren't quite as active as they were before lunch. They're still having fun, though. I sure am glad they can find acorns on their own without relying on us to feed them."

"Oh, I dunno. I was just thinking how funny it'd be if one of them rascals started chewing on your jeans—if those sweet little squirrels, all of a sudden, turned into . . . the *Cruel Squirrels!*"

Stacy was grinning impishly, her face upturned, blue eyes flashing. Her aspect was sufficient to bring back the levity. Randy chuckled. Waving his hands about his head, he said, "Oh God, No! Anything but the cruel squirrels with their sharp little teeth!"

She laughed and leaned against him as they continued their walk, oblivious now to the surroundings. Their giggles erased the menacing edges, and there was nothing worrisome on the path before them. Stacy's Valiant waited in front of the Administration Building, a short distance away.

As they approached Front Campus Drive, Randy's eyes were drawn to a little island at the intersection of the walkways. Low shrubs with deep blue blossoms occupied the center of this space. An oak tree and two stately maples defined the corners. Benches were positioned along two of the sides, with the front of the triangle facing the quiet street. It seemed a good place to sit and watch the sluggish traffic and playful squirrels. Suddenly Stacy's voice, high and tense, shattered the calm: "Oh shit!" She tugged on his arm as if to yank him away from a dangerous precipice. "Get down, quick!" she said in a tense whisper.

Randy, baffled, allowed her to pull him into the lower side of the shrub island. She squatted behind the maple tree, placing the bushes and blue blooms between them and the avenue beyond. "It's him," she said, her voice still tense. "That's Ty's car. He'd have a fit if he knew I was here with you."

Randy heard the rumbling exhaust note of the coupe, and he glimpsed a flicker of red between the green leaves and blue blossoms as the car cruised past.

"We can't let him see us," Stacy said.

Randy didn't answer. A breeze caused the blooms to sway, as if wagging their heads at him. He looked from them to Stacy and noticed that the blue of her eyes, faintly outlined in red, was nearly the same shade as the flowers and the sky.

The engine sound changed as it dropped into a lumpy idle. "Shit," she said. "He's noticed my car, and he's stopped beside it, wondering what I'm doing here."

His impulse was to stand and pull her up with him—to carry on with their business regardless of Ty—but her hot palm pressing down on his thigh said no.

He squatted beside her, looking from her flashing eyes to the blue blooms, which swayed mockingly in the breeze.

★★★

It didn't occur to Stacy that Randy might be uncomfortable squatting there behind the bushes. She just wanted to be sure that Ty didn't see them. That would ruin everything. By now her anger over Ty's behavior from the night before had abated. Sure, he could be a jerk sometimes, but she knew there was good in him, and he loved her, even if he didn't always show it. In an ideal world there was room for both Ty and Randy, but in the current context they couldn't coexist, and she was willing to resort to desperate measures to keep them separate. Randy's docility was a comfort to her now. He would do anything to please her. All that was needed to keep him in place was a little downward pressure.

They remained there hiding for what seemed a long time while the red coupe, burbling, was stopped beside her car. Ty finally stabbed the accelerator, making a snarling noise, before jerking the coupe into gear and pulling away. Stacy could see him in her mind—his narrowed eyes, knitted brow, and tight grip on the gearshift knob. She knew he was mad and suspecting the worst about her, but she was sure she could convince him of the innocence of the day trip, that she'd been here with Becky or one of her other friends. As her mind worked out the details of the story, she also imagined making up with him later, back at the apartment. She would get there first and have everything cleaned up before he returned.

As Ty pulled away, she eased her palm pressure on Randy's thigh. She turned to him and noticed in his hazel eyes the disappointment and confusion, but she saw something else there: resolution and a type of courage she knew Ty lacked. A childhood memory fluttered up of her father teaching her to ride a big gelding named Gus. She hadn't been afraid of the horse, and everything was fine until Gus became impatient with her lack of skill and the mixed signals she sent through the reins. He quickly turned his massive head and glared back at her. She realized then the power of the beast and the potential for disaster if he ceased his willing submission. She had whimpered and cried in her vulnerability until her father lifted her from the saddle.

She learned to ride the horse by shaking off feelings of insecurity and proceeding as if she had total control. It was a lie that worked, if you acted resolutely within it. She had handled Gus, and she could handle this situation too. She held Randy's gaze and smiled. "Sorry 'bout that. He just wouldn't understand—us here together, I mean. He's got this temper, you know."

"So do I," Randy answered, standing. "So does everybody. But I believe real men learn to control their temper. At least they shouldn't hit girls, and you shouldn't have a boyfriend you're afraid of."

Stacy looked away. This truth was useless because life could never be that simple. The problem was that nobody understood her—not Randy, not Ty, not her mother, brother, nor any of her friends. She guessed nobody really understood anybody, and she wondered why life had to be so damn complicated. "Come on," she said. "We need to get out of here. We can go back out the way we came and maybe we won't run into him."

Back in the car, Stacy's mind began working out the details of spending her afternoon with Ty. An excuse for being on campus was easy to concoct: Becky's cousin lives in one of the dorms, and they went to have lunch with her. "After all," she could say, "I didn't know where you'd gotten off to. What were you doing on campus anyway? Trying to pick up college girls?" This simple line should suffice, especially since it was Ty who'd ruined their plans the night before. He was the one in the doghouse, not her, and she knew that he too would be eager to make up. As she drove, she looked forward to tidying their apartment and what would follow later in the evening.

A dull ache developing behind her eyeballs dampened her optimism, as did Randy, sitting there beside her looking out the window. Maybe stopping at his place had been a bad idea. But getting high and clowning around had been fun. She wished they had another bottle of Blue Nun and a joint to go with it, but she realized that wouldn't work. She couldn't get high and mess around with Randy and make things right with Ty in the same afternoon. In fact, she couldn't bring the two together in any imaginable scenario. But there had to be a way. Her happiness depended on both of these guys being in her life. She glanced at Randy's hand on the seat beside her and noticed the scraped knuckles and mashed, blackened thumbnail. This prompted a glow inside, something like affection.

"Hey dude," she said, "you awright?"

"Yeah. Just feeling a little rough. Getting a headache from that wine."

"Yeah, me too. It was fun, though, wasn't it?"

Randy looked at her for the first time since getting in the car. "Yes. The most fun I've had in I don't know how long."

"It's too bad we've got to get back. I've got some stuff to do at the apartment, and I'm scheduled to work this evening."

"I know. I need to get back myself."

"Really? You got stuff to do?"

"Yeah. A couple of things: number one is to swallow about four aspirin, and number two is lie down and take a long nap."

She smiled. "Sounds like a plan."

She turned on the radio and left it on the same station, even through the ads. She was mostly absent from Randy and their shared interior space, having projected herself into the evening she would spend with Ty. But she was aware of him beside her, and fond thoughts popped into her mind. She hoped that life would be good to him. She realized he was disappointed in their afternoon being cut short and in the way she'd acted. With this came the desire for correction, to make Randy think better of her and to help him in any way she could. She imagined him alone on the porch of that broken-down shack, whittling on a stick. But what could she do? He was strong and good and dedicated to worthy causes, and she was. . . .

Well, there was no way to make everybody happy. A person could only do so much. She was determined to keep Ty, aware of the huge void his absence would leave, but she couldn't imagine being without Randy either, his goodness and consistency. Her imagination, struggling to reconcile life's disparities, leaped at the remembrance of her Thanksgiving plans, and she found hope that the guys she loved best—Ty, Randy, and Timmy—*could* coexist in her life, around her momma's table. Yes! She thought. I can make this happen. She looked at Randy, smiled, and aimed her Valiant towards home.

Chapter 30

The weekend soon ended, and Randy found himself back at the Jenkins property working with Buster. It would be a short week, and they were both excited about having four days off in a row. Randy was looking forward to spending Thanksgiving with the Stemptons, although he was apprehensive about Ty's presence there. After all this time, he still hadn't met Stacy's boyfriend face to face. There was no doubt, however, of his dislike for this person, someone who'd hurt Stacy and who stood between him and her. He imagined the unpleasantness that might exist between them, but he assured himself that any friction would be smoothed out by Mrs. Stempton and Aunt Ruth. At least he would be near Stacy, and he was looking forward to meeting Timmy, her brother whose suit he'd worn on the day he carried their father's body to the grave.

Randy's options for where to spend Thanksgiving had been limited: the Stempton home, alone in his shack, or with Buster's family. He had initially considered his friend's invitation, but when he remembered what Stacy had said about coloreds and whites not going to church together, he said, "I appreciate it, but I think Mrs. Stempton's expecting me. She's going to a lot of trouble to cook some special dishes, so I don't want to let her down."

"Okay, but I don't know how you gon' act, being there with Stacy and that sorry boyfriend of hers. Y'all ain't gon' never be buddies, not as long as there's one Stacy and two of you."

As Buster climbed up the truck's iron standards to work the loader, Randy replied thoughtfully: "You're right about that. From what I know about him, I don't want to be his friend. But I can't just not show up." So the matter was dropped, and Buster and Randy made their separate plans as the holiday drew near.

On Wednesday they pushed hard to finish a load and get it to the yard before closing time. Their anticipation mounted along with the stacked logs. Having extra cash on hand padded their basket of possibilities: stores would be open on Friday and Saturday, and there would be things to do and places to go.

They'd hooked the cable around a heavy log, and the rig was straining to drag it uphill through a tangle of underbrush. The truck engine was near to stalling, so Randy reached inside the cab and pulled out the knob to give it more throttle. Buster was at the top of the standards with the boom and levers. After the log cleared, Randy would guide it up the stack from the ground. Buster would swing the boom around and shift the winch levers at the right moment. They had performed this task together countless times, their eyes, hands, and bodies working together automatically, as if folding a bedspread.

This log, though, because of its gnarled shape, required additional effort. Randy had to climb onto the stack to push its butt end, breaking the grip of the protruding knots that caught on the sticky sawed ends of the stacked logs. He pushed and pried, and Buster wrestled the boom around. The moment came, and he shifted the lever into reverse, dropping the log into place at the top of the stack, another obstacle overcome. The friends, satisfied, grinned at each other. Randy said, "That one tried to put up a little fight, didn't it?"

"Sho' did, but its fighting days is about over, now that it's on its way to the paper mill. Won't be nothing but toilet paper before long. Then it can fight dingleberries."

"Serves it right," Randy laughed, "to end up in somebody's septic tank being eaten by bacteria. That's what it gets for messing with us."

"That's right! And speaking of which, don't you think it's about time to get this bunch of logs started in that direction? We 'bout got a load here, ain't we?"

Randy, hopping down from the truck, smiled. "Sure. Close enough, anyway. Let's go."

★★★

The next morning Randy tried to sleep late, but his internal clock and habitual sense of urgency wouldn't let him. After spending an hour or so wrapping and unwrapping himself in the sheets, he arose at around seven inside a chilly cabin. He threw on some clothes and his jacket and shivered in front of the old heater, worrying over kindling, paper, and matches. Soon he was warm, but the heat radiating from the crackling stove provided little comfort. He ate a bowl of corn flakes and tidied up the place. He bathed, shaved, and worried about what to wear. But it was too early to get ready. The chunk of time before the appointed noon hour afforded ample opportunity for imagining a variety of worst-case scenarios. He wondered what he would do if Ty were to become abusive toward Stacy. How would he handle such a situation? How would her homosexual brother, Timmy, fit into the picture?

He needed to quit worrying about it, to stop wasting energy. He remembered what Stacy had said a few days earlier about old people who "just sit around worrying and growing moss on their asses." She said the best way to live was to grab hold and try to have as much fun as possible. He guessed she was right, but it was hard not to worry, to simply act.

There was nothing on TV. He picked up *The Grapes of Wrath* and found his place. The Joads had made a difficult decision. After burying Grampa on the side of the road, they'd hooked up with the Wilsons and continued their westward journey, traveling along Route 66 past diners, truck stops, and sprawling America. Now, with a bad connecting rod bearing on the Wilson's touring car, they were faced with another hard choice: whether or not to split up the family. Randy contemplated Ma's decisive act, how she'd grabbed a jack handle and defied first her husband then the entire family for the sake of keeping them all together. It was a risky thing to do, but Ma reached her decision without much deliberation.

Randy committed himself, as he read, to an emerging philosophical goal: to act decisively from his best instincts. He grew comfortable with these thoughts, the morning slipping by like a leaf floating down a lazy creek. He laid the book aside and rose from his chair. Before leaving, he polished his boots and put on his best jeans and a red flannel shirt.

★★★

While Randy was reading and thinking, the Stempton kitchen was filling with an assortment of blending aromas: hot grease for the okra, melting butter, the yeasty smell of dough for the homemade rolls, roast turkey, simmering beans, peppery brunswick stew, onions, sage, and a hint of pungency from the cloves in the baked ham. Aunt Ruth had arrived early to help, certain her sister-in-law Bea would not be able to prepare such a meal properly, although Bea Stempton had been cooking for family and church functions for years.

Such was the nature of their relationship. Ruth—a couple of years younger than her deceased brother Ben and two years older than Bea—was a "know-it-all." The fact that she'd managed a successful career as a single woman conferred special status, at least in her mind. She had gotten out of Aaron County and made a lot of money from her stock in Coca-Cola, having had the foresight early on to invest a substantial portion of her earnings from Rich's, the downtown Atlanta department store. She had worked there for thirty years and was now enjoying early retirement back in Aaron County, living in a mortgage-free brick home in a subdivision on the other side of Prathersville. While at Rich's she had worked her way up and learned about the world. Now she was eager to share her knowledge of all things with those less-fortunate folk who had been relegated to the simple rural life. Ruth Stempton, though childless, felt that her rightful place now was as matriarch of what remained of the family.

"I want us to have everything ready at the same time," she explained to her sister-in-law. "I hate having to keep one dish warm while another is cooking. I learned in business that through strict attention several activities can be managed at once. Even the pots and pans and utensils—I like to keep them washed up as I go, so there won't be such a mess to clean up afterward." She spoke as she shuffled about, from counter to table to stove to sink, running water, lifting things and putting them back down. She was a short, heavy woman and her bulk threatened to displace Bea Stempton from her own kitchen.

But Bea was firmly entrenched. "I know what you mean. I learned years ago when the kids were little how to manage my meal preparation. Ben used to say he didn't see how I did it, got everything ready—a meat and three or four vegetables, bread—without a bunch of pots and pans piled up everywhere. Every once and a while he'd try to cook to give me a break, breakfast on a Saturday morning or supper on Saturday night, and he'd make the biggest mess. Ended up being more work for me, having to clean up after him. He finally decided to leave the kitchen—the whole inside of the house, really—to me, just as I left the farming, logging, vehicles, and everything else to him. We developed an understanding about things. Worked together pretty well as a team over the years."

"I'll say you did, and I know you miss him, bless your heart. He was a good, simple man. I guess that's the best kind to have."

"I still need that onion chopped, when you get a chance, for the dressing. It's about time to put it on," Bea said while wondering what on earth Ruth could know about sharing a life with a man, keeping a household together, and raising kids. She was mixing the dressing—crumbled cornbread, biscuits, and turkey giblets—in a large glass bowl.

"Where'd that chopping knife go?" Ruth said. "I can't seem to find anything in this kitchen. Besides, isn't it too early to put the dressing in? What time will the guests be arriving?"

"I told the kids we'd eat at noon. If we put the dressing in now, it'll have time to cool down a little before we serve it. Should be just right, like you said: everything'll be ready at the same time. The beans and the stew are fine for now, the longer they simmer the better."

"Brunswick stew for Thanksgiving dinner," Ruth snorted as she began to chop a large yellow onion. "I never heard of that."

"I hadn't either. That was Stacy's idea. She thought Randy would like it, and I didn't see no harm in trying to please that young man, after all he's done for us."

"Where is Stacy, anyway? Shouldn't she be here helping, especially since it was her idea?"

"She was planning on helping but ended up having to work late last night. I told her to come when she could, that we'd make out awright." Bea had moved to another bowl, working sliced okra into the flour, cornmeal, and salt and pepper mixture that would provide its crispy texture when fried in the waiting hot grease.

Thanksgiving dinner took shape. The awkwardness between the women was balanced with congeniality as they worked together to make things nice for the young folks, who were making preparations of their own.

★★★

A short drive away, at her apartment in town, Stacy was in the preliminary phases of a mounting sense of urgency. She had been in bed all morning with Ty, since he'd come in from work keyed up and ready to get his weekend off to a good start by making love, long and hard, to his girl, who was eager to oblige. She adored him in the mornings, the way he woke her smelling of machinery, cigarettes, and the expenditure of masculine energy after working all night at the plant. And this was the fifth morning in a row, since their making up on the evening after she'd gone to Aaronville with Randy. That day had ended up exactly as she'd planned, and now she was beginning to think about this new day, a day that she felt could also be shaped by her desire and ingenuity. But her participation was required.

Ty was relaxed beside her, smoking. Her body, having pulled vitality from his, was ready to stir about and get busy. Her role in preparing the meal was greatly diminished from her original proposition, when she'd offered to do all the cooking. She would've been willing, but things had worked out differently with her job keeping her up late and Ty occupying her mornings. She'd told her mother that she still wanted to do something, and they agreed on her fixing one special dish.

She'd learned the recipe a few years earlier as part of her momma's instruction on how to be a good homemaker and wife someday. The dish, a perpetual favorite at church socials and family dinners, seemed simple enough but, as Stacy had learned, required a precise list of ingredients, measurements, and a careful execution. The result was an exalted macaroni and cheese, elevated to main course status through its surprising combination of textures and flavors. She'd gathered the ingredients the day before: sharp cheddar, paprika, whole milk, flour, salt and pepper, butter, and a fresh bunch of scallions. Now, as Ty lounged naked in the bedroom, she set herself to the task, rattling pots and pans, chopping, measuring, and grating. Her version may not be quite as good as Momma's, but it'd be close. She'd do her best, and compliments would be sure to follow. She imagined the faces of the guys with satisfied smiles, and even Aunt Ruth nodding her approval.

★★★

Fifty miles away, in the middle of Atlanta, Timmy Stempton's alarm was jangling, urging him awake and into the light of a cool fall morning. After indulging in another wild night, he battled with himself there in bed with Trent and this other guy they'd just met. They began to squirm, arms and legs intertwined, smacking their sleepy mouths and turning to escape the blaring alarm. There was a stench of spent sexual energy and morning breath, rank with alcohol fumes. But Timmy found comfort in this kind of intimacy, something his sister and the others back home couldn't understand.

The colors of the night—soft pastels, reds and blues, warm greens and browns—pulsed rhythmically behind his closed lids. He shut off the alarm and slipped back into sensuality, letting it claim him as the beach tide claims cigarette butts and worn-out flip-flops, grinding them and pulling them out to the salty depths. Opening his eyes would bring pain: harsh light and the expectation of being somewhere at a certain time. He could surrender to the tide and forget about this day with family. After a few more hours of sleep the three of them (what was family, anyway?) could wake together, and who knows what might happen. Their breathing began to drop again into the slow steady rhythm. He pushed his back against Trent's abdomen and felt his moist breath on his neck.

But his eyelids seemed to have strings attached, with Stacy at the other ends, tugging hard. He could hear her saying, "You're the only brother I've got, and I love you, so come home, *now!*" When he'd done her bidding after their father's funeral, he'd surprised himself by returning to his Atlanta life reluctantly, with a refreshed feeling about home and family. It all seemed different now that his daddy was dead. Part of him had wanted to stay in Prathersville, away from the stench of his manic lifestyle, a sucking vortex that was pulling him down. Blood ties were stronger than he'd thought. The subconscious knowledge that he needed his sister more than she needed him finally pulled his eyes open, and so the battle, this time, was decided.

Chapter 31

Randy turned the flatbed into the Stempton drive at exactly twelve noon and noticed that Stacy's Valiant was already there. He parked on the far side of the yard, out of the way, and mounted the porch steps. He paused at the front door, wondering if he should knock or just go in. He was lifting his hand when the door opened. There was Stacy, facing him with a broad grin and dancing eyes. "Yay! It's Randy. Come on in." Then, taking his arm and pressing against him, she said in a softer voice, "Hi sweetie, I'm glad you're here."

She led him down the hall, calling out to all present, "Hey y'all, look who I've got—our guest of honor!"

A reply from the kitchen: "Good. That's everybody, except Timmy. We can eat as soon as he gets here." Randy noticed an unfamiliar edge in Mrs. Stempton's voice.

Aunt Ruth, turned from the sink, drying her hands on a dish towel. "Do you think he'll show up? I'm not sure he can find his way back here from Atlanta anymore." She greeted Randy with a smile. "Hello, young man. It's good to see you again."

"Hello. Thanks—"

"Oh, he'll be here awright," Stacy said. "He loves us and misses us. I've got faith in my brother, and I can't wait for him to meet Randy and Ty."

Randy, marveling at Stacy's perkiness, hoped she wouldn't be disappointed. Stacy turned to him. "Ty's in the den trying to find something on TV besides that stupid parade." She called out, "Ty, come in the kitchen, baby, and meet Randy." They all stood awkwardly for a moment looking at the table, piled high with food. Randy was wondering where they would sit when Stacy added, "Y'all excuse Ty. He's been up all night. Works the graveyard shift, you know." Then he sauntered in, reluctantly becoming part of the group.

Stacy said, "This is Randy Walls from Pittsburgh, the one who's been working so hard to help Momma get the bills paid."

"What's happening, chief?" Ty said, offering his hand. "I've heard a lot about you."

Randy took the hand, returned the firm grip. "Oh, not much. Just glad to be here. I've heard a lot about you too."

Mrs. Stempton was looking around for a place to set a bowl of green beans. "I can't believe y'all are just now meeting after all this time. I'd think you'd have lots to talk about. Randy needs to meet more people his age. We want him to make friends here and be happy. I've been telling him Aaron County's a good place to put down roots. He's done some traveling, you know. Used to live up north."

"That's what I hear," Ty replied. "Pittsburgh, wasn't it?"

"That's right."

"Well, how do you like it? How does living way down here in a sharecropper shack compare to life in a big city?"

Randy looked at Ty's face, trying to uncover his intent. Mrs. Stempton jumped in: "Everybody's gotta start somewhere, ain't that right Randy? That old shack's just temporary. There's bigger and better things in your future, as hard a worker as you are. Living where he is helps him save money. Won't be long and he'll be able to buy his own place. I might even be willing to work out something with him on the shack and some of the acreage around it. With time and effort, a few improvements here and there, that place could be turned into something real nice. That is if he decides this is where the Lord wants him."

He cleared his throat. "Well, I don't know—"

"Don't worry 'bout it, Randy. You know how Momma is, always wanting people to 'put down roots' and 'bear fruit.' You gotta do what your heart tells you. But I hope you will stay around here for a while. Momma's done got attached to you. I don't know what she'd do if you decided to pull up stakes. She'd probably try to drive that pulpwood truck herself!"

A few nervous giggles as Randy considered Stacy's words. He knew she had to be watchful of how she said things, but this was confusing. He felt his face flush.

Ty cleared his throat. "I think I'll go back to the den and put down roots in front of the TV, until we're ready to eat. It's a little stuffy in here."

"Sure, y'all do that," Mrs. Stempton replied. "It may be a few minutes yet. We'll fix our plates, then go to the dining room. Y'all just relax for a while. I'll need both of you strong boys later, though, to turn the handle on the ice cream freezer. Don't that sound good? Homemade ice cream, it was Stacy's idea."

"Umm-mm, can't wait," Ty said with a hint of sarcasm.

Then the three of them were together in the den, where Randy had sat last summer, watching a Braves game with the old man just before the accident. The TV flickered warmly, as it had then, but this time Ty was occupying the place that had been Mr. Stempton's, a sagging recliner covered in brown vinyl. On its right stood a spindly end table and a lamp with a dented shade. Stacy settled into an armchair in matching brown beside the table. A loveseat against the perpendicular wall was available to Randy. He took the end nearest Stacy, for the best angle to the TV.

"There's got to be a football game on," Ty said, getting up to turn the dial.

"I think it starts later this afternoon," Stacy said. "Should be a *TV Guide* around here somewhere."

Ty cranked the dial with nothing coming up but the Macy's parade and local newscasts.

"Shoot, baby," Stacy said, "that's good. Just leave it on the parade. We're gonna eat in a minute anyway. Randy might enjoy watching some of the floats and stuff."

"I'm fine with whatever you guys want to watch."

"Ha! I love it! Ain't it great, Ty, the way he says 'you guys'? I'm sorry, Randy, it's just that we don't hear that around here very often."

"Don't worry about it, chief," Ty replied. "I'll bet Stacy would get lots of laughs up in Pittsburgh with the way she talks. That *is* cool though— 'you guys'—I might try it on the boys at the plant."

"Wouldn't be the same coming from you, baby. You sound more like a hick than I do."

They laughed as Ty's face registered mock offense. Randy said, "I think it's cool too, the way *y'all* talk. You'd have people where I come from lining up just to hear you."

Chuckles followed, slightly forced; then the crunching sound of gravel from outside and the drone of an approaching engine interrupted the settling awkwardness.

"That's him!" Stacy exclaimed, jumping up from the armchair. "That's my brother." The nearest window was behind the loveseat where Randy sat. She plopped down with knees in the cushion, craning her neck to see. The way she squirmed for the right angle placed her against Randy, her arm pressing his shoulder, hair brushing his cheek. "It's him awright! He's driving his little orange shoebox." Her excitement reverberated in his ears.

Then she suddenly hopped back up and reached for her boyfriend. "You've got to see his car, Ty. It's one of them little Datsuns."

Randy felt appraising eyes for an instant before his rival answered: "Yeah, my boss at the plant drives one of 'em. Says it don't burn hardly no gas, and it'll run rings around a Volkswagen."

Stacy bounded out of the room.

"Wouldn't have one of the damn things myself," Ty added, turning back to Randy. "Ain't enough room or power. Japanese are little short people, used to being all bunched up. Besides, all that junk they keep sending over here's knocking American workers out of their jobs. That's what my old man says, and he reads the newspapers a lot."

Randy nodded. "I'm thinking of buying myself a car pretty soon. Not a new one, just a used car in decent shape."

"Look at 'em," Ty said, pointing out the window at the animated greetings of Stacy and her brother. "Kinda sickening, ain't it? Did you know he's a queer?"

"I remember Stacy mentioning it," Randy replied, wondering if this personal knowledge would arouse Ty's jealousy. But then he didn't care. After all, he was his rival. No sense in trying to see it in any other light. Buster's words came back to him: *Y'all ain't gon' never be buddies, not as long as there's one Stacy and two o' you.*

The screen door slammed shut as giggling chatter and footsteps proceeded down the hall. Stacy, adopting cheerleader mode, exclaimed, "Look who's here everybody, the prodigal son. Time to start the feast!"

Randy and Ty stepped into the hallway for whatever was going to happen next.

"It's all ready and waiting, child," Mrs. Stempton said, coming out of the kitchen to embrace her son. After a long squeeze, she held him at arm's length. "I'm glad you made it, and on time too! The Lord is faithful. I been praying that he'd bring you home."

Aunt Ruth stepped up to take her turn. She wiped her hands on her apron, took hold of Timmy's face, and looked into it. "I'm glad to see you, young fella! We miss you around here, and your momma needs you. Haven't you had enough of the big city yet?"

He exhaled, blinked coyly. "Well, it is good to be home. I miss you guys too."

"Oh no! Did you hear that? My own brother saying, 'you guys.' Now we got two of them. Have aliens taken over your body, or what?"

"No, no. It's just that the people I'm around all the time don't have country accents. I guess it's rubbing off on me."

"I know what you mean," Aunt Ruth said, still looking into his face. "All those years I spent working in Atlanta had that effect on me. People in the city don't talk like we do out here. But I found myself, after I moved back home, dropping right back into the old ways I grew up with. It's hard to escape your roots." She moved her hands over his cheeks, patted his shoulders and chest.

Mrs. Stempton nodded in agreement. "That's what I've been trying to get Stacy to understand. Roots are a person's family and upbringing, their connection to the world, where they draw their strength from. I know in my heart that Timmy's roots are strong, and

I'm still praying for him to come back home. Scripture says 'Raise a child up in the way he should go—'"

"Don't start in on him with that stuff, Momma. He just got here. Let me introduce everybody. Hmm, let's see. Randy, this is my brother Timmy Stempton. Timmy, Randy Walls from Pittsburgh. I believe you've heard me speak of him. And this fella is Ty Ragsdale. You've heard me speak of him too."

Randy immediately offered his hand. Timmy took it with what seemed to be an exaggerated firmness, eager to convey that he was steadfast and trustworthy. Ty, keeping his hands in his pockets, simply nodded and said, "What's happening?"

"Well," said Mrs. Stempton, "I guess everybody's here, unless Stacy invited some folks I don't know about."

"Nope. That's it."

"With all this food I wish she had," said Aunt Ruth. "I feel like we fixed way too much."

"It'll be awright. We'll eat as much as we can today, then enjoy leftovers for a week."

"That's right, Momma. We all love turkey and ham sandwiches. You might be surprised, though, at how little is left over. These boys can eat."

"I hope they're good and hungry. We've got quite a variety, so there should be something for everybody. Timmy, I made that sweet potato soufflé you like."

"Umm–mm! Thanks, Ma."

Mrs. Stempton added, "But before we fix our plates, we need to remember what this day is set aside for."

A groan escaped from Ty. Stacy shot him a quick scowl.

Mrs. Stempton untied her apron and began to fold it as she spoke. "Let's step into the kitchen, where all the food is. I want each of us to have a chance to say something." The young people shuffled obediently into the mother's sanctuary, replete with meats, vegetables, casseroles, side dishes, and desserts. Aromas mingled. Randy and the others began to position themselves around the table.

"Let's form a circle," Mrs. Stempton said, "and join hands."

Randy's placement suddenly became important. He would have rather been between Stacy and her mom, but he stood between Ty and Timmy. He didn't want to hold hands with these guys, but he knew not complying would produce even more awkwardness. He watched Mrs. Stempton, Stacy, and Ruth latch on, and he sensed Timmy's hand on his left being offered. He took it and extended his other hand toward his rival. Nothing there. Glancing over he saw that while Ty had grasped Stacy's hand, his left remained in his pocket. Randy lowered his hand, hoping Stacy's mom wouldn't notice.

Aunt Ruth cleared her throat. Mrs. Stempton said, "Shoot, I almost forgot. There's something else we've got to do before we eat. We need to partake of a different bread, not just for our bodies, but for our souls." A collective sigh as hands were released. She turned her head about, searching. "Where'd that little box go?"

"It was right here on the counter," Ruth answered, moving bowls and dishes around. "Here it is. Almost got lost in all the food." She produced a sturdy cardboard box with a snug fitting lid. As she handed it to Mrs. Stempton, Randy could see the words printed on top: "Our Daily Bread: Reflections and Meditations from God's Word."

Mrs. Stempton, trembling slightly, removed the lid. "Timmy and Stacy, y'all might remember this. It was a tradition for a while, when your Maw-Maw and Paw-Paw Hart were still with us. Any time we got together for a meal, your grandmother would always have devotion first. Started using these when I was a teenager. Kept it up for a long time after y'all came along, but then your grandparents got sick; first one thing then another. Anyway, I think the tradition needs to be reestablished, especially in light of all that's happened in the last few months."

"I remember those little cards," Timmy said in his airy voice. "We'd each take one and read it out before we sat down to eat. I didn't want to do it, but Paw-Paw helped me with the big words and made it okay."

"That's right, it was okay, wasn't it? I was proud of you that day. We all were."

Timmy blushed and looked away. Mrs. Stempton seemed to forget herself, until Stacy spoke up: "Well go ahead. Pass them around. Everybody's hungry."

Her mother smiled. "Okay. We'll each take one, then share what the Lord has for us." She fumbled to extract one small card from the pack; then she passed the box to Ruth. It went around the circle with each person drawing.

Mrs. Stempton said, "Now, as y'all see, there's a scripture verse on each card and, on the other side, a thought to meditate on. When Momma was alive, she'd have us each read till we'd gone all the way around. Then we'd ask God to bless the food. I'll start us off." She raised the card and squinted, extended her arms, opened her eyes wider, brought it closer to her face. "Shoot, I can't see to read without my glasses. Where'd I put 'em?"

Ty moaned. Timmy shook his head. Stacy said, "Jeez, Momma, this is gonna take all day. The food's getting cold."

"Now just hold on. I set those glasses down in here somewhere when it started getting steamy." She moved her head from side to side, trying to remember.

Aunt Ruth turned and peered up and down the counter, patting the surface and moving dishes around. At last she said, "Here they are. Got pushed all the way to the back, behind the tea pitcher."

"Thank goodness," Stacy said.

Mrs. Stempton put on her glasses, cleared her throat. "Okay. Mine's from Proverbs, chapter eighteen, verse ten: 'The name of the Lord is a strong tower: the righteous runneth into it and is safe.' And the reflection says, 'Those who live by God's word have nothing to fear, knowing that earthly trials are only temporary. God will never forsake His children. Do you find assurance in your relationship with the Heavenly Father? Do you know where you will spend eternity?'" She lowered the card and looked over her glasses at each face. It seemed to Randy that she looked longest at him. Then she said, "Your turn, Ruth."

"Hmm, let's see. Mine is from Psalm ninety-two, verses thirteen and fourteen. 'Those that be planted in the house of the Lord shall flourish in the courts of our God. They shall still bring forth fruit in old age; they shall be fat and flourishing.'"

Stacy suppressed a giggled. Aunt Ruth smiled, blushing. "I don't know about bringing forth fruit, but the fat part certainly applies. Go ahead, Timmy. Your turn."

Timmy looked up at his mother. She nodded. "Go ahead, son."

He cleared his throat and began to read. Randy marveled at the similarity between him and Stacy, their mouths and cheekbones and the shape of their faces. Timmy's lips moved in that familiar feminine way. "'Professing themselves to be wise, they became fools, and changed the glory of the uncorruptible God into an image made like to corruptible man, and to birds, and four-footed beasts, and creeping things.' That's Romans, chapter one, verses twenty-two and twenty-three."

"Read the reflection," his mother said. "What else does it say?"

Timmy rolled his eyes. *"Okaay*, Momma." Then he read in the voice of a bored high school student, 'God is the sovereign creator of the universe. Does He occupy His rightful place on the throne of your life?' That's all."

Mrs. Stempton nodded and smiled. "Thank you, Son. Now, Randy, what does your card say?"

Randy cleared his throat; Stacy looked at the floor. His voice in his ears sounded stronger than he expected: "'For ye have not received the spirit of bondage again to fear; but ye have received the Spirit of adoption, whereby we cry, Abba, Father.'" He looked up at Mrs. Stempton.

Nodding, she said, "That's from Romans, isn't it? Chapter eight?"

"Yes. Verse fifteen. The other side says, 'Those who have been reborn into the family of God no longer live in bondage to sin and the fear of death, but face life boldly, secure in their father's loving protection. Are you ready to claim your heavenly inheritance?'" As the words settled, Randy felt a tingling up his neck and at the top of his head, as if his hair was being tousled by a strong, loving hand. A sensation followed of being in the center of creation, similar to what he'd felt on his picnic with Stacy. He smiled at Mrs. Stempton.

"Okay, my turn," Stacy said. "Wouldn't you know it, mine's about putting down roots and bearing fruit. Just kidding. It's from Second Peter, chapter one, verse four: 'Whereby are given unto us exceeding great and precious promises: that by these ye might be partakers of the divine nature, having escaped the corruption that is in the world through lust.' Okie dokie. Oh wait, I'm supposed to read the little thought for the day too." Her mother looked at her sternly. Stacy flipped the card and read in a mocking schoolteacher voice: "'God's children have access to the power that created the universe, and through that power are capable of leading virtuous and meaningful lives in this temporary world and in the eternal world to come. Are you ready to claim God's promises and live the life for which you were created?' That's it. Okay, big guy, your turn." Grinning, she elbowed Ty in the ribs.

He replied, "But teacher, I don't like to read. Do I have to?"

"You sure do, that is if you want to eat. Momma said so, it's a family tradition."

"In that case . . . let's see. It's the number one, then some big *C* word." He held the card so Stacy could see.

"That's First Corinthians, chapter one, verse eighteen. Read this part and then flip it over."

He read in a deliberate monotone, enunciating each word: 'For the preaching of the cross is to them that perish, foolishness; but unto us which are saved it is the power of God.' And the other part says, 'The cross with its message of Christ's sacrificial death is the central image of Christianity. It is the means by which God redeems sinful mankind to Himself. Unfortunately, this message is often misunderstood in a dying world. What does the cross mean to you?'" He lowered the card, retaining the hint of a smirk.

Mrs. Stempton looked over her glasses from face to face. At last she said, "Well, that was good. I appreciate y'all doing that, and I hope you'll think about what we've heard. The Bible says God's word shall not return void. I trust we've each received the message he intends. Now, I reckon we can eat, after we give thanks. Let's join hands."

Another collective sigh. Randy, this time, offered his hand to Timmy only.

Mrs. Stempton seemed confused, squinting and darting her eyes around the group. Timmy and Stacy bowed their heads. Wasn't someone supposed to pray now? Who would say the words? Randy assumed it would be Mrs. Stempton. He closed his eyes to the faint beginning of a daydream, remembering the time he'd ridden on the tractor with Stacy. Mrs. Stempton cleared her throat. Another pause, then he heard his name. "Randy, would you ask God's blessings on that which we are about to receive?"

Chapter 32

Conversation didn't begin to flow again until after the plates were fixed and they were all seated around the big dining room table, where they retained the same positions: Randy between Timmy and Ty, with Stacy farther down, to his right. He began to eat without any sense of how he'd gotten there, the words he'd prayed still bouncing around in his mind. He wanted to remember what he'd said to know he hadn't made a fool of himself.

He'd never been asked to pray out loud before; when Mrs. Stempton called his name, he felt as if a whiplash had cracked across his shoulders. He almost said no, but he realized the embarrassment from this response would be worse than praying. With his eyes closed he felt he was being tested, as he had on that other occasion when the old man sent him to town to "have some fun."

He searched for a way to free himself from this chain, wondering how many more tests would be required of him. The pressure of the moment produced a flash: Maybe this isn't linked to the old man's schemes at all, but sent directly from God, the beginning of a new series of events. Words formed. It wasn't that hard, really, to speak, and he'd heard people pray blessings before. So, he talked to God and the others there around the table. He expressed thanks for the family, for friendships, the food, and he asked blessings upon those who had prepared the feast. He'd said more, but as he cut into a slab of turkey breast, he couldn't remember. Oh well, it was done. People were eating, smiling, talking. Everything seemed okay. Anxiety dripped away, then drained in a gurgling rush when he looked up and caught a winking grin from Stacy. He smiled back as he chewed, realizing the turkey was delicious.

"Randy, have you tasted the brunswick stew?" she asked. "I gotta know what you think of it. But wait. Daddy always liked to doctor his up with some hot sauce. You might like it that way. Momma, you didn't put the Tabasco out. Where is it?"

"It's in the fridge, but he might not need it. At least let him taste it first, it's pretty spicy."

"That's right, Stacy," Aunt Ruth said, "Most people don't like as much hot pepper in their food as Ben did. If you ask me, it's plenty hot enough."

"I guess I'll try it both ways." Randy dipped his spoon into the thick bowl filled nearly to the brim. He savored the mouthful, then nodded. "Umm, delicious."

Stacy said, "I'll get the Tabasco. Does anyone else . . . now wait a minute. Randy, I see something that ain't right. You don't have any macaroni and cheese on your plate, and that's the dish I fixed. It's Momma's special recipe, but I made it myself. You've got to try it. Anybody else need anything?"

"You can pour me some more tea, and put some ice in the glass," Ty answered.

Timmy said, "I'm fine."

Randy bragged on Stacy's macaroni and cheese, as did the others, and they ate and ate and ate. The Stempton women beamed with pride as the compliments went around the table. Stacy seemed to enjoy this special day, taking interest in the others and seeing that they had everything they needed.

Aunt Ruth took charge of the conversation by asking the young people about their lives, work, and plans for the future. Ty, though, seemed reluctant to elaborate, his clipped answers barely within the boundaries of politeness. When she asked him about his work in a "manufacturing plant," he replied, "It's just a factory. I run a machine making metal parts. Ain't much to it."

Stacy tried to smooth the edge of his answer: "He makes really good money, and it takes a lot of skill to run those machines. I know for a fact he's the best operator they got. Ty's so good, they use him to train the new guys they bring in. Ain't that right, Baby?"

"Well, yeah, 'cept right now it's a hopeless task. They're expecting me to train a . . . *negro* to do what I do, as if that was possible."

Randy thought about Buster and how quickly he had mastered the details of their work.

"Well, I'm sure you'll do your best," Ruth said. "Sounds like your employer has a lot of confidence in you."

"There's even been talk of them sending him to the trade school—what is it they want you to study, baby?"

"Industrial mechanics."

"Yeah, that's it. *Industrial mechanics*. They're grooming him up for a supervisor job. Then he can get on day shift, ain't that right, baby?"

"Yeah, maybe. In about ten years."

"And it's a really good company. He gets paid vacation, health insurance. . . ."

"Well! That sounds very promising, Ty. When I entered the work force, we didn't have opportunities like that out here. That's why I went to Atlanta. And I found a company that treated me well, offered benefits, and I stayed with them. Paid off too, in the long run. I remember when I was your age thinking I wasn't getting anywhere, but things kept opening up as time went by." She spoke as if making a speech. "There's a lot to be said for being consistent, showing up each day and doing your best. A good company will recognize that and reward you for it."

Ty nodded. Stacy said, "That's exactly what I been telling him! I'm glad he's hearing it from you."

When Aunt Ruth turned to Timmy, she found common ground, a platform from which to give advice. Timmy worked in retail, an upscale boutique in the trendy Buckhead area. Ruth was impressed. Unlike Ty, Timmy seemed to harbor high hopes for his future with this company. "My dream is to work my way up to buyer, not just for the store, but the entire chain. Right now, though, I mainly just tend the racks and dress the windows. You know, keep it all looking pretty."

Ty glanced at Stacy in disbelief, rolling his eyes. Ruth gushed, "That's exactly how I started out at Rich's. And it wasn't long before I moved up into buying. Did that for about fifteen years, before they put me in employee relations. Buying was always my passion, though.

Felt like I was putting part of me—my personality—out there for everyone to see."

The jiggling cranberry sauce threatened to slide off Timmy's fork as he waved it emphatically. "I know! I love it too, at least what I know about it. I even like what I do now, especially the windows. It gives me a creative outlet, something I *desperately* need."

"Well, we all need to find something to do in life that we love, that provides—as you say—an outlet for our talents, whatever they may be." Aunt Ruth kept her hands in her lap as she spoke, looking around the table into each of the young faces. "Once you find that special place, just keep working at it, and you'll achieve your dreams. That's been my motto, and I believe I've proven it to be true."

Stacy asked, "What about art school, Timmy. Don't you still want to study art?"

"Sure, I do. But it's so hard to get accepted. My portfolio's nowhere near what it should be, and I'd have to make higher on that stupid entrance exam. And it's so expensive. In the meantime, there's my job, which I love. I can always do art in my spare time. I'm gonna keep trying though. Maybe by next fall, I'll be ready to get in. And Trent said he would help me with tuition. I'm keeping all my options open." He glanced toward Aunt Ruth, seeking her approval.

Randy noticed that Mrs. Stempton's face seemed drained of color. Her head trembled as she looked down at her plate.

Timmy picked up his fork and began to pat and fiddle in a dab of sweet potato soufflé. Randy tilted the bowl and scooped out the last bit of stew. Stacy let out a little moan. "My, my. I'm afraid I overdid it. I feel as stuffed as one of them Yankee turkeys Randy used to eat before he came down here."

Everyone moaned in agreement. It was time to move away from the table, to do something else with this Thanksgiving Day, but no one seemed willing to take the initiative. Finally, Mrs. Stempton said, "Let's don't quit. There's still a ton of food. Y'all ain't had your third helpings yet. What about you, Randy? You've been sitting there mighty quiet. Wouldn't you like some more turkey or stew? What about a little more dressing?"

The young people, prompted by the women, returned from the kitchen with smaller portions this time. While the eating seemed forced, the conversation flowed easier. Aunt Ruth no longer directed but sat quietly next to her sister-in-law as the others chatted. The talk shifted to Randy: how he needed to get out more, meet people, have fun, especially now that the contract was nearly finished.

"You should come to Atlanta," Timmy offered. "There's always something happening—concerts, clubs, shops, parties, you name it. I could show you around and introduce you to some people."

Ty snickered, then tried to cover by clearing his throat. "Yeah, that big city lifestyle's probably closer to what you're used to, coming from Pittsburgh and all."

Randy, no longer able to imagine any redeeming qualities in this redneck, saw into his hatefulness and tried to ignore it.

"It's amazing," Timmy said, "the variety of people you run into. Sometimes you even meet folks from around here who go to the city to escape the boredom. Oh! That reminds me. I ran into somebody the other night, Stacy, that we went to school with, but you probably wouldn't recognize him now."

Stacy looked up. "Oh really? Who?"

"He was sort of pudgy and quiet when we were in school. Stayed to himself a lot."

"Who, Timmy? What's his name?"

"You remember that Otwell kid? Danny?"

"Yeah, I think so. Lived off Taylor's Gin Road in a subdivision."

"That's him, but you should see him now. He's lost his baby fat and turned into a freak. He was at Richard's when we went there to see Iggy Pop and the Stooges the other night—"

"Hold on a minute. Richard's? Iggy what?"

"Richard's. It's a rock club in Atlanta. The Stooges are a punk rock band. Iggy Pop fronts them. Anyway, there's always a bunch of freaks in the place, but this one guy kept looking at me. He seemed familiar, but I had no idea. I finally asked him, 'Do I know you?' He said, 'Name's Dan'—that's what he goes by now— 'Dan Otwell. And you're Timmy Stempton. We used to ride the same school bus.' Then

I recognized him when I saw past the beard and long hair. It's weird how people change."

"You mean chubby little Danny Otwell's a hippie now?"

Randy noticed the small rhythmic movement of Mrs. Stempton's head as she looked down at her plate. Aunt Ruth wore a puzzled expression. Ty slid his chair back.

Timmy answered, "Well, I guess you could say that. He's something different, anyway. Seems he's been through a lot. Started college in Atlanta, then while he was away, his house burned down with his momma in it."

"That's right! I remember now. Their house burned slap to the ground couple months ago. Mr. Otwell got out, but his wife—what was her name?"

"Florene," answered Mrs. Stempton, her voice coming from a distance. "We had the family on the prayer list for a while. I ain't heard no more about them lately."

"Yep, Florene Otwell," Stacy said. "Didn't find enough of her to bury, even. I heard they just scooped up some ashes and put them in a bag for Mr. Otwell. Same as cremation, I guess."

"It was bad," Timmy pointed out. "Bad enough to freak Danny out. He was way out there the night I saw him, doing acid or something. It got weird just talking to him. We finally moved to another table."

Stacy furrowed her brows and made a slight motion with her head to remind Timmy they were in the presence of older ladies who didn't understand such things.

Ty's voice sounded garbled: "I'm going out to the porch for a cigarette." Touching Stacy's arm, he added, "Why don't you join me?"

"You can smoke in here, baby. Daddy always did."

"That's okay. I need to get up and stretch a little." Then he was gone, noisily pushing back the chair and clomping in his boots across the hardwood floor.

Stacy followed him with her eyes then turned back to Timmy. "I just can't get over it. Danny Otwell . . . his momma burns up, and he turns freak."

"Yep. I guess that's the way it goes," Timmy said. "But anyway, Randy, you really should come to the big city for a weekend. Bring Stacy with you. I could take you to some great clubs and restaurants."

"Thanks for the offer," Randy answered. "Maybe later. I've still got a good bit of work to finish up at the Jenkins property."

"Aw come on, Randy," Stacy said. "Don't make excuses. You know—"

"Well, Bea," Aunt Ruth interrupted, "I guess we should start straightening up while the guests are chatting." She placed her napkin on the table and turned to Randy. "Y'all are fine. We can have dessert later, after our dinner settles a little."

Mrs. Stempton looked at her as if waking from a dream. "Yes. Let's go back to the kitchen and leave these young folks to talk about things they're interested in. Randy, feel free to help yourself if you want more turkey or anything."

The table, without the ladies, was a wasteland with the wadded napkins, depleted plates, and soiled cloth. Randy was looking for an escape route, a way to move to another room, when Stacy said, "I don't know about Randy going to Atlanta, now that I think about it. He might like it and decide to move away. Actually, he's been exploring his options around here. Ain't that right, Randy? He's been checking out Aaronville and the college. We've been talking about it, starting college, I mean. We were over there last Saturday, looking around." She lowered her voice, leaned over the table. "That's just between us, though. Ty don't know about it. He wouldn't understand."

"What's not to understand?" Timmy asked. "I think your boyfriend's a little too narrow-minded. Maybe you should consider trading him in."

"You hush up! He has his sweet side. Speaking of which, I'd better go check on him. Don't want him getting lonesome out there. See y'all in a few minutes. Don't go anywhere, Randy. I'll show you how to make homemade ice cream afterwhile."

Then she was gone, and Timmy said, lips moving like Stacy's, "Well, here we are, Thanksgiving in Aaron County. Ain't it great?"

Randy answered, "Yes, it is. Your family, I mean."

Timmy's expression turned thoughtful before his voice went breathy. "It has its good points. But warts, too, like all families I guess."

Randy realized that by "warts" Timmy meant his relationship with his father, who'd pushed Timmy away from the family and brought Randy into it, giving him work, a place to stay, and "a chance at some fun." This reality echoed as he remembered wearing Timmy's blue suit at the old man's funeral.

Randy sensed a building resentment. He didn't know what to say. He felt like telling Timmy that what he'd received had not been much, neither love nor warmth, that he'd been treated more like a pack animal than a son. But he only said, "Well, family . . . it is nice, though—important, I mean. That stuff your mother says about roots and all. I think maybe there's something to that."

"What does she know? She's never been away from this place, never known anything but this kind of life. Besides, if family and roots are so important, what are you doing way down here away from your own family?"

Randy, incredulous, looked into Timmy's face, noticing that while the lines were like Stacy's, the eyes were different. His were soft brown like his mother's instead of the luminous blue that Stacy had inherited from her father. Timmy needed to know the truth. "I don't have a family. My parents were killed in an automobile accident when I was three. I came down here to find my only living relative, a great uncle, but he died before I met him. Mr. Stempton gave me a job and a place to stay. I guess you know the rest of the story."

Timmy shook his head. "I'm sorry. I didn't know. Stacy never said anything about that, just that you were down here from Pittsburgh, working for Daddy. Your background, it's not at all what I imagined."

"It's okay. I guess a lot of things aren't what we imagine them to be."

"Stacy should have told me."

"I assumed you knew." Randy pushed his plate away. "But it doesn't matter. I mean here we are—however we got here—all of us together in this place at this time. That must be what's really important."

Timmy smiled. "And you're a philosopher too. You're just full of surprises."

Randy, catching the lighter mood, recognized an opportunity to move. "I sure could use a cigarette."

"Me too. Let's go out on the porch."

Randy, realizing he would rather not be near Stacy and Ty as they exchanged intimacies, scowled without meaning to.

Timmy said, "Oh, the love birds. . . .. It's okay. Four rocking chairs out there, room for us too."

Chapter 33

To Randy's surprise, they found the front porch unoccupied. "I guess they went for a walk," Timmy said, "even though it's sorta cold for that."

"I know. I'm surprised at how the weather's turned the last week or so," Randy said as he drew a pack of Winstons from his shirt pocket. "Hasn't warmed up much since this morning." He handed Timmy a cigarette. As they smoked and rocked, Randy was mindful of a morning back in September when he'd sat in the same spot with Stacy, being drawn into her confidence. Now, Timmy rocked where Stacy had been, the day was colder, and there didn't seem to be much to talk about. "I guess it's time for it, though. The cold weather," he said.

"Yeah, Thanksgiving sorta marks the beginning of it for us. That's when Daddy always checked the antifreeze in the vehicles and started winterizing everything, wrapping the pipes and covering the windows with clear plastic." Timmy drew his lip up and wrinkled his nose, as if someone had vomited on his shoe. "I always hated this house in winter with that plastic stapled up all over it. It made it seem dead somehow, like leftovers, wrapped up and pushed to the back of the refrigerator. You don't see plastic on the windows of the newer houses in town, just the old farmhouses and shacks out here in the sticks. It was embarrassing."

"Hmm, that's interesting. People don't put plastic over their windows where I come from, and it's much colder up there."

"I think people up north are better prepared for winter. The houses are better insulated. At least, that's what I've heard."

"Yes. I think that's true."

"I wonder where the love birds went," Timmy said.

Randy shook his head. "Who knows?"

Timmy drew lightly on his cigarette, holding it between his thumb and first two fingers. He inhaled, then blew out a tiny puff. "She may ask you to do it, you know."

"Do what?"

"Put the plastic up on the windows, since there's no one else now. It's a yearly ritual. Mom will go nuts if it doesn't get done. She's probably in there worrying about it now."

Randy nodded and tried to imagine what the job would entail. "I'd be happy to do that for her. I could bring Buster over to help."

"That's nice of you, but you're going to have to break away at some point, that is if you want to have a life. She'll keep you doing odd jobs around here forever if you let her."

Timmy had stopped rocking. Randy looked toward the barn. Finally, he replied, "Well, if she needs help, I don't mind. At least for a while. She's been good to me."

"My momma's good to everybody, but that doesn't mean you owe her your life. You seem like too sharp of a guy to settle in Aaron County. I can't help but wonder what's really keeping you here."

Randy extended his gaze across the gravel drive and beyond. Timmy said, "My sister's kinda crazy, you know. I mean, she's a good girl—always stayed out of trouble—but she has a wild side that most people don't see. It was there even when we were kids. She was always braver than me, willing to climb higher in the trees, all the way to the skinny branches. And she was the one who always wanted to slap the wasp nest with a broom, then run away, daring them to sting us."

Randy, fascinated, took a drag from his cigarette as Timmy continued: "We had a motorbike, a little Honda 50. It's probably still out there in the barn somewhere. We'd go off on that thing and she'd always want to drive. Scared the crap out of me riding on back, the way she'd push it just as fast as it would go. There's a part of her that's attracted to danger. I'm a thrill-seeker too, but in a different sort of way, as you might have guessed. It's in our blood somehow, but I don't know where it came from. Our parents are so, so . . . I don't know—*dependable.*"

Randy nodded. "Yes, they're both very hard working, reliable people." He wondered if Timmy's shivering was caused by the cold or rising emotion.

"Sure, you know about Dad and Mom. But Stacy and me are different. We missed that responsibility gene and got rebelliousness instead." He sat up straight and gestured with his cigarette hand. "All of Mom's Bible quoting and talk of glorifying God, doing unto others, bearing fruit, and stuff—not to mention making us go to church all the time—just made it worse." He sat back and took a drag. "At least I know it did for me, and now I see it in Stacy. You remember what she said earlier when she was planning your future for you?"

Randy thought back to the conversation before dinner. Stacy had said to him, *You gotta do what your heart tells you.* Yes, he remembered.

"She's following that advice herself," Timmy said, "and you and I both see where it's taking her—down the dangerous road. That's the way she's always chosen." Timmy took another little puff from the cigarette then flipped it away. "Damn, it's too chilly out here. Gonna have to go back inside. Care to join me? Maybe we can find something on TV."

Randy followed Stacy's brother back into the house, past the parlor and down the hall to the kitchen, where his mother and aunt chatted among the clutter and leftovers, stacking dishes and putting things away. The table was being prepared to receive the desserts. Mrs. Stempton said, "Randy, would you prefer peach cobbler or pecan pie? You can have a piece now and a dish of ice cream later."

Randy replied that he was still too full for dessert. Timmy commented that it hadn't warmed up much outside.

Aunt Ruth smiled pleasantly. "As for myself, I enjoy the cool temperatures, especially this time between now and Christmas. That feeling of anticipation that makes each day special. I guess it has something to do with the years I spent in retail, Timmy. The shopping season, it's what the rest of the year leads up to, the icing on the cake. And I used to love decorating for Christmas—the store, I mean. I never did much with my apartment, but now that I have a larger place and so much time on my hands, I'm planning to go all out. Maybe you could help me with some ideas."

Timmy brightened. "I'm *so* bored with all the red and green. Some people just have no imagination. I mean, *use other colors,* for Christ's sake." He went on to elaborate on the virtues of silver and gold and how much he loved those little white twinkly lights.

Mrs. Stempton, seated at the corner of the table, followed the conversation in a detached way. "I can feel it in here, the chill," she said thoughtfully. "And these windows are still uncovered. I sure would like to get that plastic up, before it turns really cold." She looked at Randy, who was leaning against the counter, then back to Timmy who was describing some kind of ornament to Aunt Ruth. "I think I'll put on a pot of coffee. Might help take the chill off. You'll have some with me, won't you, Randy?"

Time passed with coffee and conversation between the generations. Aunt Ruth and Timmy focused on retail and decorating, while Randy and Mrs. Stempton discussed sealing the windows. The gas heater emitted a soft blue glow with its barely audible hiss.

Randy was talking about putting new chains on the saws and spark plugs in the truck when Mrs. Stempton changed the subject. "Where is Stacy? Where did she and that Ty get off to? Do y'all think they're awright?"

"I'm sure they're fine," Timmy answered. "They'll be back in a little while, ready for dessert."

She rubbed her hands together, opening and closing the fingers. She glanced with a puzzled expression from Timmy to Randy then back. "What did you say?"

"I said they'll be here in a little while. Don't fret so much over everything."

"Mrs. Stempton said, "Why don't y'all go find 'em. Tell them we're ready to serve dessert, and the pleasure of their company is requested."

Randy wanted to ease her mind, and he would have liked to be near Stacy, but he had no desire to go searching for her while she was with her boyfriend. He looked across the table to Timmy. "Where do you think they could be?"

"They're fine," Timmy answered, picking up his coffee cup. "They're just walking around or something. The car's still out there. Let's give them a few more minutes."

Mrs. Stempton said, "But it's cold, and they've been gone for nearly an hour. What could they be doing? What if they need help? Stacy might have stepped on a snake."

"Momma, there are no snakes out now, it's too cold. You know that. If they're not here in ten minutes, we'll go look for them. Let's have another cup."

"Well," aunt Ruth said, rising to get the pot, "I think it's a shame. It was Stacy's idea for us all to be together, and she goes waltzing off with that Ragsdale boy. What do we know about him, anyway, Bea?"

"He's from a rough background. But he holds down a job and seems to think the world of Stacy."

Aunt Ruth clucked disapprovingly as she poured the coffee.

Randy remembered Stacy's black eye. She must have convinced her mother it was an accident. Mrs. Stempton would have wanted to believe that, to think the new boyfriend was okay, but she must have had doubts. Now the anxiety was evident. He marveled at the depth of her eye sockets and the thin veined lids, gray and fragile as tissue paper. The skin of her brows and cheekbones seemed drawn by some powerful suction on the inside of her skull.

She rubbed her fingers, opening and closing her left hand. She looked up at Randy. Then she turned to Aunt Ruth as if to speak, but there was some delay, a glitch in the working of her mouth. Timmy asked, "Mother, are you all right?" Then they were distracted by the sound of the front door opening and closing and footsteps in the hallway.

"They're back," Timmy said. "See, I told you they'd be here in a few minutes."

Aunt Ruth said, "Thank heavens! I was getting worried myself."

A slow smile came to Mrs. Stempton. "Yes. They're here, now we can have dessert."

Randy exhaled, relieved that finally they could make progress toward finishing up this exercise. He felt more fatigued than if he'd worked all day in the woods.

The couple stood in the doorway smiling like culprits. Randy didn't want to look at either of them, but he couldn't help himself. Stacy's eyes beckoned, and he felt Ty staring at him. Stacy said through her grin, "Feels good in here. It's a little chilly outside."

Ty pulled her close and rubbed the small of her back. As Stacy looked from face to face, Randy noticed a stub of straw stuck in her hair.

"It's about time you got here," Timmy said. "Momma's ready to serve dessert."

"Sorry 'bout that. We've been kinda busy. I mean . . . well, we've got an announcement to make." Leaning against Ty, she cut her eyes up to his face. "Don't we, baby?"

Ty, smirking, nodded and looked from her to each person. Expectation filled the room. All eyes were on Stacy as she grinned and pressed against her muscular boyfriend.

"Well, out with it!" Timmy said.

Stacy, realizing the moment had arrived, blurted, "We're getting married, y'all!"

The air in the room seemed to rush and whirl, slinging images into Randy's mind: the old man's face, then that of his tenth-grade science teacher saying, "Nature hates a vacuum." Then came the noise of chair legs scraping. Mrs. Stempton was getting up. No, something slipped. Her mouth went slack, glistening at the bottom corner.

Stacy said, "Momma—"

Mrs. Stempton slumped, her bosom pressing the table. The chair slid out from under her. She fell to her left, toward Randy, and with the impact of her side against the linoleum, gas escaped from her body. Her limp arm couldn't break the fall. Her head struck hard, a hollow knock, the last sound Randy heard before Stacy's protracted wailing. She erected a wall of sound with those cries, damming the river of time. Randy reached out stupidly from his chair. His ankles felt shackled, and, during that dream-like moment, he didn't know if he would ever be able to move.

Part V—Homegoing

Chapter 34

The sensible thing, in the aftermath of her mother's stroke, would have been to postpone the wedding, but Stacy stubbornly clung to the original plan as conceived on Thanksgiving Day. They wanted to begin the new year as husband and wife, but December was just too busy, with Mrs. Stempton requiring extended hospitalization and frequent follow-up visits. They brought her home just before Christmas, without any attempt to decorate or prepare for the holiday. There were too many other considerations regarding the needs of the patient, now quite debilitated, especially on her left side. Thankfully, Aunt Ruth took the lead, leaving Stacy a measure of time and energy to plan her wedding, which took place on the sixth of January, the first Saturday of the new year.

It was a hastily conducted affair. The ladies responsible for church decoration were confused by the prospect of a wedding so soon after Christmas. Thinking that appropriate flowers may be hard to get this time of year, they left most of the poinsettias in the church and removed only the Christmas wreaths, bells, and ornaments. Against this background of red, white, and green, Stacy splashed some pink and yellow—bunches of snapdragons spaced along the center aisle. Her corsage consisted of white gardenias and babies' breath. The men wore small red rosebuds in the lapels of their dark suits. Spindly candelabra flanked either side of the altar.

Stacy wore a diaphanous white gown, sleeved, with a cinched waist and low neckline trimmed in lace. Her plain, shoulder-length veil, attached to a pearlescent comb, fanned out in a single misty layer around the back and sides of her head, accenting her glorious honey-colored hair, which hung below the veil in heavy ringlets. Her face beamed as she stepped eagerly down the aisle, slightly ahead of the music.

Those in attendance smiled at her lack of affectation, her enthusiasm, natural beauty, and the incongruity of the scene. The prevailing mood was that somehow this could all work out, a sentiment supported by the preacher as he quoted from Philippians 4:13: "I can do all things through Christ which strengtheneth me." He encouraged the couple to keep the Lord at the center of their relationship to guide them through the storms of life. Ty and Stacy gazed into each other's eyes, seemingly pleased with his words.

Mrs. Stempton, sitting at the front of the sanctuary in her wheelchair, was emotional throughout the service. She continually daubed at her eyes and the slack corner of her mouth with a wadded handkerchief. Randy, seated behind her, could see her shoulders shaking with silent sobs. Getting her in the church had been difficult, requiring him and Aunt Ruth to lift her and the chair up the steps at the rear entrance. The pastor tried to help, his neck veins bulging from the effort, but he was too fat to be of much assistance. He said, "I reckon we'll have to put a ramp in, and maybe widen that door frame. I'll get the deacons on it right away." Then he was off to make last-minute preparations.

As he spoke before the wedding guests, Reverend Bledsoe's brow perspired as it had back in September during the funeral, but on this occasion, amid the flowers and flickering candles, his tone was brighter. Where his cadence before had been syncopated, like a bowling ball rolling over rain-warped hardwood, now the words lilted like an ice dancer, skating to an up-tempo beat. His eyes, reflecting the glint of the candles, shone with optimism and love for the young couple and his faith in a bountiful future.

Randy saw things in a different light. He listened as the preacher shared passages of scripture, knowing the words were as lost on Stacy and Ty as they were on him. *I can do all things through Christ. . .. Yeah, right.* He wondered if they even heard what the preacher said, the way they stood there gazing at each other. Ty wore a smirk, as he had when they'd announced their wedding plans. That was the first time in Randy's life he'd experienced such hatred, raw and gaping, like a wound from a snarling chainsaw. But there hadn't been time to examine or bind it up: Mrs. Stempton's collapse came only seconds later. Everything changed that day beginning with Ty's smirk, and there it was before him again. He couldn't see a way to fix things or any point in trying, but there was Stacy's mom to consider.

He and Aunt Ruth had discussed the situation. Lurking beneath the physical demands of caring for the invalid were the financial problems brought on by medical expenses. Mrs. Stempton's being widowed qualified her for disability payments, but the paperwork was staggering. Aunt Ruth discovered through her inquiries at the government office that it could take as long as two years to get everything cleared. She was willing to tend to those matters, having knowledge of business and the way things worked, but there were immediate needs. Without a stream of money flowing into the household for utilities, groceries, and general upkeep, Mrs. Stempton's meager savings would soon be depleted. "It would be a great blessing to this family," Aunt Ruth had said, "if you could stay on a while longer, working the same arrangement you had with Bea before her stroke. Otherwise, I just don't see how we can continue, how we can make it through this."

Of course, he *could* stay. He had already talked with Mr. Jenkins about additional jobs, parcels of land to clear and pulpwood to cut and haul. There was enough to keep him and Buster busy for quite a while. Mr. Jenkins, pleased with their work, was interested in keeping the pair committed to him. Randy, by slow degrees, had come to enjoy the arrangement, especially the time spent with Buster, who also benefited from the regular paydays. Randy's cut of the earnings, after meeting expenses and settling up with Mrs. Stempton, was enough to buy new clothes and a few pieces of furniture. He'd started a savings account, and he enjoyed a steak dinner in town whenever he felt like it. It was a good set-up, but without the prospect of Stacy in his future, it all seemed hollow.

★★★

Stacy, aware of Randy's disappointment, began to struggle with her own after only a few months of marriage. Ty's jealousy and lack of trust grew worse during this period. As if that weren't enough, she also suspected him of being unfaithful. She could sense it whenever she was around Dawn Shumake, and her work schedule often placed them together. Stacy had thought, not long ago, that she and Dawn were becoming friends. They had chatted easily and worked well together during those early weeks of Stacy's employment at the Goat. Then, for no apparent reason, Dawn's manner toward her changed, becoming not unfriendly but stiffer, more formal. The spontaneity was gone, and Stacy noticed that when Ty came in, Dawn seemed to avoid them both, allowing her work to take her in the opposite direction.

Ty and Dawn also behaved differently toward each other. The eye contact and flirtatious banter became restrained pleasantries, stiff and unnatural, arousing in Stacy a deep jealousy in place of minor irritation. Stacy could see the effort in Ty's face of not watching Dawn's butt as she walked away. He'd watched before, and he still looked at the other girls without trying to disguise his eyes' wanderings. Stacy was sure that something had happened, and she suspected it was continuing to happen right under her nose.

Since the wedding, Ty seemed to find more reasons to be away: going into work early, having to work later, or needing to go see some man about something. The time they did share was not intimate and fulfilling as Stacy had imagined, but fraught with tension. Asking him where he'd been or where he was going would likely trigger an irritable response: "I already told you, dammit, we was working twelve-hour shifts this week. You need to quit worrying 'bout my business and tend to things around here. This damn place looks like a dump. I'm ashamed to bring my friends over."

Despite the purported longer work hours, they were constantly low on funds. She never saw his paychecks, and when she needed to buy groceries or pay a bill, she had to ask for the money. Every cent of her earnings went into their domestic life, but she didn't make enough to turn the place into a real home. Ty earned twice what she did, but he'd become miserly, except where his wants were concerned. His contributions were offered resentfully, a twenty tossed on the table as he glared, irritated, at the TV.

On weekdays they would eat an afternoon meal together, tuna or macaroni and cheese or occasionally cube steak with niblet corn out of a can. Then Ty would be off in his brand new, metallic blue GTO to work or wherever. Most days she would leave for her job at the same time. Once there her mind would be occupied, but on her off days the situation was frustrating. What was she supposed to do with herself, sit there all evening watching TV? He would leave her with some directive—to clean the bathroom or hang those new curtains they'd ordered from the Sears catalog—but Stacy didn't like being alone and she didn't like taking orders, even from the man she loved.

She could jump in her Valiant and drive over to visit her mother but being there with her the way she was now—barely able to walk or carry on a coherent conversation—was so depressing that Stacy found excuses not to go. Then she felt guilty over not spending time with her sick momma and got more depressed. Her relationship with Becky was strained beyond repair, ever since Ty moved into the apartment. Becky had been getting involved herself since it all began, with Mikey Mitchum, and she was now living with him and some other guy in a rental house at the edge of town. She was no longer available to chat or get high with, and Stacy was lonely on those evenings when Ty left her with nothing but doubt, worry, and fear of the future.

On these evenings suspicion magnified the urge to get out. Once she thought about calling the plant to check if he was there, but she knew that would only make him angry. She decided to ride by and look in the parking lot, knowing that his car being there didn't mean he was. He could drop it off and leave with someone else. Not seeing his car wouldn't prove anything either. He may have parked on the far side of the lot which wasn't visible unless you turned in and drove past the guard shack. She could ride by the plant anyway. Maybe she would see the car and that would count for something. Not seeing the GTO would be another step toward confirming what she suspected.

The evening air was cool enough for her to run the heater as she drove through Prathersville. By the time she reached the industrial complex on the other side of town, the car was cozy, but she would have preferred riding with windows down, basking in warm outside air. She was ready for spring with its promise of new beginnings. This winter had been long and cold. Even her wedding, which should have brought joy and hope, existed in her memory as the first in a tragic series of events, the result of an ill-advised, selfish decision. Her lack of judgment was underscored each time she rode past that parking lot, looking over the sterile, brightly lit space for Ty's car and not finding it.

The wind was gusting and howling past the Valiant's rattling windows. A rumpled Tastee-Freez sack blew across the hood on her last pass up Industrial Avenue. She was sure he wasn't there but knew he would have some excuse if she confronted him. Oh hell, probably best not to say anything this time. It would be better to wait until she had more concrete evidence.

Unresolved, though, was the question of what to do with the remainder of the evening. Here she was, a married woman riding aimlessly in a car by herself. She thought of going by the Goat for a beer with friends. Everyone there would be laughing, drinking, and having fun. Sometimes, though, being around those single people, flirting and trying to partner up for the evening, made her uncomfortable. Her priorities had shifted, and with her daddy gone and mother the way she was, there seemed to be a dark cloud over her. Appearing happy would require great effort; she'd almost decided against going there, until she thought of Dawn Shumake. Finding Dawn at the Goat would mean she wasn't with Ty.

She turned into the parking lot to find the coveted places near the back entrance empty. A slow night. She slid the Valiant under the giant oak, into the same space Ty's motorcycle had occupied on the night they first got together. She killed the engine and looked up through the limbs. A few shriveled brown leaves from last year clung to the branches which were everywhere popping out with tiny green buds. Soon the tree would be covered in new leaves, but now it seemed suspended between life and death. It felt right parking under this tree, although other spots were available. She sat there for a while before going in.

Chapter 35

Randy was comfortable inside the shack despite the howling wind. He'd laid a few sticks of split oak atop a glowing bed of coals in the heater, and the clear plastic stapled over the windows kept the drafts to a minimum. Cool air infiltrated, though, especially on windy nights like this one. He was glad spring was coming: letting the fire go out meant one less thing to tend to.

He'd had his hands full throughout the long winter. Whenever the weather permitted, he and Buster worked to keep the truck loaded and the money rolling in. When he wasn't cutting and hauling, the myriad needs of Mrs. Stempton required his time and energy. Aunt Ruth needed periodic relief from her sitting duties, and the women found plenty of projects for him around the house: stapling plastic over the windows, wrapping the pipes, and building a ramp over the front steps for the wheelchair. At first he didn't mind, during the early weeks after the stroke, but since Stacy's wedding he'd tended to these chores with growing resentment. On this particular evening, as he listened to the wind slapping the screen door and whistling against the chimney, he contemplated his future without Stacy and thought about going out for a beer. He considered getting drunk, even though he wasn't much of a drinker. His friend Buster, being sanctified, didn't partake of alcohol, and Randy was hesitant about going to the Billy Goat Bar because of the likelihood of running into Ty or Stacy. He had no drinking buddies. He did have a six-pack in his fridge, though, so he decided to have a few by himself and spend the evening at the shack working on his scrapbook.

He'd begun reading the local newspapers, *The Prathersville Patriot* and *The Aaron County Times,* shortly after his arrival in the area. Since the old man's death, Randy had been cutting out articles of interest and taping them into a leatherette binder he'd bought at the variety store. The practice helped him make sense of the place and get through the lonely evenings. The scrapbook included stories of fires, car wrecks, robberies, deaths, weddings, and local political scandals. The more articles he collected, the more connections he was able to make between people and events. It had become something of a game, a kind of solitaire without cards. A couple of recent issues he hadn't yet gone through, thick with sales inserts from the Piggly Wiggly, rested on top of the stack in the corner. He moved them to the table and set himself to work, scissors at hand, perusing the front pages.

When he tilted his head back for a swig of beer, he saw an unusual sweep of light across the opposite wall. He hadn't heard anything as the wind and the droning of the TV muted all other sounds. Setting his beer down, he cocked his head to a short series of muffled barks from one of the hounds under the porch. Must have been a vehicle passing by, but the angle of light had been unusual. Puzzling. He wasn't expecting anyone, and if a car had turned into his drive, there would be someone at the door any second now. He was sitting there by himself, drinking beer and working on a scrapbook of old newspaper stories. He would feel a little silly if someone had come to visit.

Seconds passed. The dog stopped barking, and there was no sound at the door. It must have been a passing car, but he still felt uncomfortable. He went to the window to have a look. What he saw caused a weakness in his legs. Stacy Stempton Ragsdale was sitting in her car with the interior light on, looking at her face in the rearview mirror, applying lipstick and fiddling with her hair. Randy turned from the window, hurried back to the table, and began to gather things up. He threw the papers back on the stack and picked up the scissors and scrapbook. He didn't want Stacy to see it, so he dropped it to the floor in front of his recliner. Just as he was sliding it under with his foot, he heard the knock at the door and Stacy's voice, a bit unsteady: "Hey City Boy, you in there?"

He tried to take a calming breath before stepping across the room. As he placed his hand on the knob, she knocked again. "Randy? Come on, it's cold out here."

He pulled the door open.

She stepped in, brushing past him in the doorway. They were inside the shack together, standing in the middle of the room. Stacy held a six-pack of Miller High Life under her arm. She looked at Randy's right hand, still holding the scissors. "Whatcha doing?" she asked.

"I was just. ..." He cast about for an answer. His open beer sat on the table along with some cut newspaper remnants. "I don't know. Just doing stuff to kill time."

"With scissors?"

"Well, yeah. Maybe I should ask what you're doing." Randy looked at the beer cradled in her left arm, hand and wedding ring visible.

"I don't know. I just got lonely. Thought you might have a beer with me."

"Well sure. Anytime. It's just that you surprised me. I wasn't expecting anyone, especially you."

Stacy cleared her throat, smiled, tossed her head to flick back her bangs. "I guess that just goes to show: you never know who might turn up at your door. Life's full of surprises, ain't it?"

Randy smiled as he moved to lift a stack of laundry from the chair beside his recliner. He dropped the scissors onto a battered end table. "Come on in. Sit down. Let me take the beer to the fridge. I was just having one myself. You came at a good time." He fumbled around with the laundry and Stacy's six-pack while she sat down.

He returned with his beer and one for her and settled into the recliner. He didn't know what to say. He rose, went to the TV, and cranked the dial to another channel, then another. The screen went from a sitcom to *Sonny and Cher* to *Adam-12.* There were no more channels, and nothing seemed appropriate. Stacy said, "Randy, relax. Why don't you turn that thing off so we can talk for a while?"

He killed the TV, then turned up his beer and drained it. "I need another one. I'll be right back." In the other room he tried to collect himself. He'd spent time with Stacy before, but this was different. He didn't know why he felt such apprehension over her being there. He still loved her, though. That was certain. A queasiness fluttered through him as he opened the refrigerator. He closed the door and leaned against it.

"Randy, you okay in there?"

"Uh, yeah. Just thinking."

"Thinking? Well, can't you think in here, with me?"

"Sure, I mean I was thinking about . . . supper. I'm kinda hungry. What about you? Want something to eat? I could make us sandwiches or something."

"Food, wow! I ain't had a bite since lunch myself. I guess I am hungry, now that you mention it. Let's see what you got."

She joined him at the refrigerator, elbowing him out of the way to open the door. "Hmm, let's see . . . bologna and hoop cheese—you must buy your groceries at Ot Brown's, 'cause that's about all he keeps. Wait a minute, what's this?" She withdrew a chipped plate which held a large, tinfoil-wrapped mass, oozing red liquid at the creases.

"Oh that. It's a pound of ground beef. Just bought it yesterday. I stopped by the Piggly-Wiggly and picked up some things."

Stacy smiled as she handed him the plate. "And what were you going to do with a pound of ground beef?"

Randy shrugged. "I don't know. Eat hamburgers, I guess."

Stacy teased, "And what do you eat with those hamburgers? You know too much red meat's bad for you. You need fruits and vegetables, too. Let's see what else we've got."

She opened the bottom bin. "Perfect! I'm glad you bought groceries." She pulled out a head of lettuce as she continued rummaging around. "This meal's starting to take shape: hamburger steak cooked with onion and bell pepper, and salad so far. But we still need something else, a side dish. What you got in here?" She reached up to the ice-encrusted freezer compartment, opened the door, and withdrew a foiled-wrapped package the size of a small loaf of bread. "Hmm, this looks interesting."

"Oh yeah, I'd forgotten about that. It's corn-on-the-cob your mother sent me. Came out of their garden, I think."

Stacy looked at the package. "Wow. My daddy planted this corn and tended to the plants before. . . ." She blinked and looked up at the ceiling.

"Yep. I guess so," Randy replied softly.

"Well! I think we got all we need now. Here, set this stuff over there, and run some warm water in the sink so we can get the ice off this corn. It'll finish thawing as it cooks."

Randy's kitchen area was sparsely equipped: a plywood sideboard and primitive upright cupboard occupied the spaces on either side of the sink, and there were two sagging shelves above. The sideboard and sink cabinet seemed to have been part of a set; they were both finished in chipped white enamel. The refrigerator rested against the other wall to the left of the sink. He set the vegetables on the sideboard.

She handed him two bell peppers as she closed the refrigerator with her hip. "Well, what are you waiting for? You do have a kitchen knife, some bowls and stuff, don't you? What about a skillet? We need a big frying pan."

Then they were both busy, moving around the small space, bumping into each other. Randy produced a heavy iron skillet, and soon it was full of meat, chopped peppers, and onions, sizzling atop the antiquated electric stove. As she tried to adjust the temperature, Stacy said, "I can't believe this old thing still works." She informed Randy that the relic had been her Momma's years before when she and Timmy were little. It was old even then, purchased before the war by her grandparents. "Momma always fussed about it," she said, "how hard it was to regulate. She used to burn about half of everything she cooked when we were kids." She sprinkled salt and pepper into the skillet, then doused the meat with Worcestershire sauce. "That ought to do it," she said, turning the knob one more click. "It needs to cook kinda slow, so the flavors can have a chance to mingle."

As the sizzling skillet filled the room with appetite-stirring aromas, Randy stood at the sideboard with a big kitchen knife, cutting carrots for the salad. Stacy said, "We need to get the corn boiling. You got a big pan?"

Randy turned and pointed with his knife. "In the bottom of the stove." But then he remembered something: "But wait, that's not gonna do us any good. You've got the hamburger cooking on the only eye that works." He leaned back in his puzzlement against the sideboard, the big knife pointed at the floor.

Stacy put her hands on her hips, wrinkled her nose, patted her foot. "Shoot! I had my taste buds set on some hot-buttered corn-on-the-cob. Wait! I got an idea. You got some tin foil?"

"Around here somewhere. What you gonna do with that?"

"Just get it. You'll see."

He dug around inside the cupboard until he came up with a flattened box of Reynolds Wrap. Then Stacy took over, laying the corn in the center of a big sheet of foil. Next, she topped them with three or four pats of butter each, sprinkled them with salt and pepper, and wrapped them snugly in the foil. "Now," she said, "take 'em over there to the heater. Open it up and use the poker to scoop out a place underneath the hot coals. Push the corn up under there and cover it good with ashes and coals. It'll be ready by the time everything else is."

"Amazing. I would have never thought of that."

She winked. "It's a good thing you got me to teach you things, City Boy. There's a lot to learn besides what you get in books." He smiled and carried the bundled corn to the heater, worked it under the coals, and went back to preparing the salad. There wasn't much else to do. Stacy sat at the table with her beer and began to wad up the little paper slivers that were left over from Randy's scrapbook activities. She watched him working on the salad. Finally, she said, "You're a strange bird, Randy Walls, but I sure am glad you're here."

She hadn't tarried long at the Goat prior to visiting Randy. She'd chatted over beers with a few of the regulars while she surveyed the establishment in hopes of finding Dawn Shumake. The suspicions that flooded her after she confirmed Dawn was elsewhere made it impossible for her to drink and talk as if nothing was wrong. She made up an excuse about having to pick up something for supper and walked out, having no idea what she would do.

In the car, she rummaged in her purse for a tissue to daub her eyes as she backed out from under the oak tree. She cursed and pounded the steering wheel. "Dammit, dammit, dammit!" Why couldn't things work out like they were supposed to? Why did people have to get cut in two, or have strokes, or be unfaithful? She needed around her the arms of someone who cared and who could understand what she was going through, and she urgently needed something to take the edge off the pain.

So, after a few aimless passes through town, she'd ended up at Randy's shack with a six-pack of Miller. She'd felt uneasy about going to the door, but after sitting for a moment in the car and doing what she could to repair her face, the feeling passed. After all, nothing was going to happen. She was just visiting a friend.

Now, basking in the blending aromas, she was glad she'd come. There was something about the shack, changeless throughout the seasons, and Randy's presence in it that brought comfort. She watched him there at the counter slicing carrots. His hands were large and awkward, but capable. His seriousness in performing the simple task highlighted the importance he attached to her being there. She knew her presence had a certain effect on him, but a subtle change had occurred: her power over the relationship had diminished. Control had shifted mysteriously from her to him and resided in those calloused hands.

He replied, "I'm glad you're here too."

Soon everything was ready. Randy produced chipped dishes from the shelf and Stacy opened two fresh beers. "I'll fix the plates," she said, "while you get the corn out."

"Do you think it's been in there long enough?"

"It'll be fine. Don't need to cook much. I'm sure it was tender when Daddy pulled it."

Randy had trouble retrieving the foil-wrapped ears. With the door open, the flames flared before he could expose a corner to grab with a potholder. "Shoot! It's hot in there." He finally came up with the bundle, gingerly switching it from hand to hand.

"Bring it over here," Stacy said as she arranged the plates, salad bowls, and condiments on the table. "You didn't burn yourself, did you?"

"Nah. I'm fine. Just singed the hairs on my arm a little."

"Well, that's a small sacrifice for this fine meal," she said, smiling.

As they began to eat, she took pleasure in knowing she'd been right about the corn. The salty-sweet kernels, when they popped, were hot and juicy on her tongue.

"Umm-umm, corn's good, ain't it?" she said, wiping her mouth with a paper towel.

Chapter 36

Stacy had been only partially correct in her estimation of Ty's unfaithfulness. He had been lying about the long work shifts and where he'd been, but those hours weren't being spent with Dawn Shumake. Throughout the winter Ty had been venturing deeper into uncharted territory, the darker world of a co-worker who had taken over the operation of the die press machine next to his. Tommy Lee Chism, Tomcat to those who knew him, began working at WM just before Thanksgiving, and Ty had been charged with training him. At first he resented the assignment; it was bad enough having to share space with him, much less trying to teach him skills that were beyond his capabilities. Ty had rolled his eyes in exasperation when Millwood introduced the new employee. The young men nodded and grunted, barely acknowledging each other. Ty motioned with his head for the foreman to step aside. Ty, with his face at Millwood's ear, spoke over the banging din of the plant: "Shit, Boss. It's gon' take weeks to teach this dumb nigger how to run that machine. What about my pay? I won't be able to keep up my own production. You know I got the highest numbers in the plant."

Millwood lifted an eyebrow and pointed his chin at Ty. "I'm well aware of your numbers. That's why we want you to train him. Don't worry about your pay. While you're training Tommy Lee, you'll be earning the average of your highest weeks of production. Just teach him to do what you do." Millwood's Adam's apple shot up, then settled back into its corded nest.

Ty grinned. "I don't know if that's possible, but I guess I can try."

Millwood's eyebrows came together. "I expect you to do your best and to keep an open mind. He may be capable of more than you think."

Millwood's prediction soon proved accurate. By the end of their second week together, Tomcat's production numbers were rising. He was strong and graceful in the handling of the equipment, and he caught on to the technicalities of the job much faster than Ty had imagined he would. A rivalry developed between them through which Ty's spirit took a generous turn. He didn't withhold knowledge but revealed more as his pupil progressed, keeping him at the top of his learning curve.

Neither of the young men at the beginning could have expected such a productive outcome. It was largely a result of Tomcat's easy, disarming smile and Ty's puzzlement over someone of that race performing at a level approaching his own. Ty had grown up convinced that blacks were inferior to whites in all endeavors, with the possible exception of sports that required speed and agility. He'd clung to this notion stubbornly. The seed of bitterness that sprouted years ago when Stinkum humiliated him in the hay field was now a thick-stalked vine of hatred. It had been easy over the years to rationalize Stinkum's superior skill at tire mounting and hay stacking. After all, he'd been older, bigger and stronger. Ty was sure, though, that now—if Stinkum hadn't gotten himself killed in Vietnam— things would be different. He was stupid, plodding, and conniving, like all niggers. If presented with a real challenge, like the die press machine, he would've had to rely on a white man to sort it out for him into manageable tasks, the way his race had always done.

But Tomcat was different. Perhaps there were other possibilities, exceptions to the rules. Tomcat was amiable, despite a brooding quality that mirrored his own moodiness at times, and Ty found himself, during set-ups and breaks, talking to him about life outside of work. They each boasted of sexual exploits, fights, and other masculine adventures, and Ty developed an interest in the cultural threads woven into Tomcat's tales. It seemed that the expectations and opportunities for young men were different where he came from.

A place known for miles around as the Crack existed across the railroad tracks on the northeast side of Prathersville. Replete with prostitutes, drug dealers, winos, and unemployed derelicts—along with the shootings and knife fights common to such environments— this setting was home to many blacks. No whites lived there, and very few ventured across the tracks, especially after dark. The area comprised a range of housing from the modest, single-family homes bordering the white neighborhoods, to the low-roofed, government-funded apartments characterized by concrete stoops, iron-framed crank-open windows, and uninspired brickwork. This section of government housing, the core of the Crack, appeared derelict and institutional, like a correctional facility abandoned by its warders. When Tommy Lee Chism arrived—about a year before he met Ty— after dropping out of school and teetering along the edges of the juvenile courts and correctional system in Atlanta, he'd already developed the skills necessary for success in such a place.

Pool hustling was his specialty. When he commented that there was only one man in the Crack whom he couldn't easily win money from and began to describe this person as the brooding, jet-black, one-handed Willie, Ty's face lit up. "I know Willie!" he exclaimed, raising himself from the side of the machine he'd been leaning against, lazily supervising the set-up. "Everybody knows him. He's famous. Used to shoot sometimes over at Fred's pool hall on front street."

"That's right," Tomcat answered, tapping a die into its slot. "I heard him talk about that place and how Fred was 'bout the best around at nine ball."

"Yeah—him and Willie, that is. I've watched them two play nine ball for hours. They'd usually play for a dollar a game, while everybody else placed bets on the side. Those matches were something. They ended up about even most of the time. Whoever broke would usually win that game, you know, just run the table."

Tomcat laughed. "That Willie a pool-playing fool! You let him get the break, you might as well sit down a while!"

"That's right, and I love watching him too, the way he holds the stick with that hook where his hand used to be—"

"I know, weird, ain't it? They's an old guy live on the back side of the Crack, got a little woodworking shop behind his house. He the one fixed up Willie's sticks for him that way, with that hole in the handle for the hook to fit through. It's gotta be just right, you know, else Willie won't have it."

Several years had passed since Ty had seen Willie shoot nine ball. He had been one of the few blacks who visited Fred's on front street, back when Ty was first venturing out in the coupe with Toby. The boys had been fascinated by the men who frequented the place, their crude jokes and swagger. The nine ball matches between Fred and

Willie were major events, day-long tournaments between living legends, played out before a ring of spectators speaking in hushed tones of awe while nodding their heads and placing bets.

Willie's face was unforgettable as he lined up each shot with smooth, preliminary strokes of his custom-made stick. His slack mouth, holding the stub of a cigar, made tiny movements, tightening and relaxing in time with the stick's pumping, and his jowls quivered as if extracting pot liquor from a wad of turnip greens. The tongue occasionally flicked out between the lips to moisten them and adjust the cigar stub, black in its wetness. His lips were almost black, the same hue as the bottom of a pile of wet leaves in February. The skin of his cheeks, etched with deep lines and pockmarks, rode high over the bone structure, supported by a layer of subcutaneous fat that seemed to ooze from the pores. Willie's entire head was emotive in its impassivity: large, round, and continually twitching and gesturing in subtle movement while maintaining the expression of one grown tired and wise.

Ty was lost in his memories for a few moments. He had not been in Fred's pool hall for some time, having relocated his pool-shooting to the Billy Goat Bar. As Tomcat elaborated over Willie's skills and the intensity of the matches at Lamar's Place in the Crack, Ty became nostalgic. He missed that kind of competition. Most of the pool he played now consisted of friendly games of eight ball. He didn't share the fact that these games were all he could get because he was known among his peers as the best pool player in Aaron County. He had reached the point, before he stopped hanging out at Fred's, where he was consistently beating the master, Fred himself, on his own table. That had been a while back when he was at the top of his form, but he believed the skills were still there and could be brought out again if the opportunity arose.

"So, you've spent some time around a pool table too?" Tomcat asked as he tightened down a die.

"Yeah, a little." Ty watched Tomcat's hand gripping the Allen wrench.

Tomcat looked up from his work and grinned. "Hell, you ought to come hang with me in my neighborhood some time. We could shoot pool at Lamar's. Willie be there, and you could see how me and my people live."

Chapter 37

Stacy was pleased that Randy was enjoying the meal. "It's all delicious," he said, "everything." He smiled as their eyes met. With the several beers she'd drunk, his approval added to her feeling of contentment. This, along with her need for someone to confide in, began to get the best of her sense of propriety.

"Randy," she said thoughtfully, "we've been through a lot together, haven't we?"

With mouth full he replied, "Uh-huh." He was gnawing along a yellow ear of corn; when he lowered it, a mashed kernel clung to his lower lip.

"I don't know what I'd have done without you being here through all the stuff that's happened—first Daddy, then this, this . . . situation with Momma." She looked at his face to gauge the effect of her words.

Randy cut a chunk of meat with his fork, speared it along with some slivers of cooked pepper and onion. "I know," he said finally. "It's been rough all right, on all of us." He slipped the forkful into his mouth and resumed chewing, methodically.

"I know—Lord, Lord, I know—it's been really hard on you, but you never let on, never complain. I look at you now and see—I don't know. It's just hard. . . .." She stabbed her fork into the salad bowl, making a clinking noise.

"It's okay, Stacy. A man's gotta make a living somewhere. I didn't have any place else to go, remember?"

"Yes, you did. That's just it: you could've gone anywhere you wanted, but you didn't. You stayed here." She sat for a moment looking at his hands. He stopped chewing, elbows on the table, the corn inches from his mouth. She felt her voice shaking as she continued: "You stayed here and worked like a dog for us, me and momma, and look at what it's got you. When I see those scraped-up knuckles and callouses and think about what you've been through—

still go through each day—and then look at myself, my pitiful, selfish life, it's . . . depressing as hell. You spend more time than I do seeing after Momma, even. Seems all I'm good for is serving beer at that stinking bar and moping around worrying about the mess I've got myself into." She set her fork down and finished her beer in a gulp. She burped, swiped her lips with a paper towel. Unable to meet his gaze or to inject energy into the bleakness of her voice, she said, "I wanted life to be better, but I'm beginning to think it ain't ever gonna be, that all we're ever gonna get is work and suffering and disappointment."

Randy pushed his plate back and swigged down the rest of his beer. "I thought things were getting better for you. I thought you were happy. After all, you got what you wanted."

Stacy felt as if she'd been slapped, but she knew he didn't mean for his words to be hurtful, or did he? Failing again to hold his gaze, she sniffled and looked away. Fuck it. She turned back with an explosion of words: "Dammit Randy! I didn't get what I wanted. Don't you see that? I didn't get anything like what I wanted. If I did, I wouldn't be here—"Tears leaked onto her burning cheeks, and the wetness triggered a response in her throat. Such a relief to let the erupting sobs go! Shaking, she relinquished control of her body and face. Better to get it all out. He'd either understand or not.

He sat there with a blank expression. Then he came around the table toward her as she was sliding her chair back. That's when everything started changing. His arms were reaching and there was something in his face she didn't recognize. Then he was touching her.

His hands, rough but gentle, wiped the tears from her cheeks, brushing the moisture over her ears and into her hair. She grasped his forearms and returned his gaze. He pulled her to him, bringing a mixture of comfort and excitement. His face was in her hair, then against hers. Moisture. Was his cheek wet from her tears, or was he crying too? He kissed her eyes and mouth with salty, wet lips. He exuded a masculine heat, fueled by genuine love, that she couldn't resist. Feeling him against her, she left the confines of the shack and entered a dimension without walls, bathed in the light of the cosmos. When she wobbled, Randy picked her up and cradled her like a child in his arms. Her surroundings became kaleidoscopic until she found herself on his bed, the center of a radiating pattern.

His chest was a source of warmth. As he kissed her, she reached under his shirttail and pressed her palms against his skin. The warmth was there also in his belly, and farther down too. There was something inside him that her insides craved. He kissed her as he stroked her cheeks and neck with the tips of his fingers.

While tenderly stroking, kissing, and softly moaning, they wriggled free of their clothes. The warmth was everywhere as they strained toward a balance of passion. Stacy stretched herself under him, desiring as much contact as possible, a precious forbidden touching. When he pushed against her, she lifted her hips and pulled with her palms against the small of his back. The warmth now was centered in her pelvis, and they were both engulfed in the spreading glow as the separate flames became one.

He seemed more concerned with her pleasure than his own. He entered her gently, continuing to kiss her lips and eyes. She felt his arms under her shoulders, cradling her head in his hands, as he pushed slowly in as far as he could go. The perception that her face, mind, and body were precious to him coaxed murmurs from her throat. She felt him trembling against her as she returned the kisses, drawing his tongue into her mouth. He broke free of her lips, raising his upper body on his elbows. She opened her eyes and saw on his face an expression of exquisite anguish. He grunted eight or ten times in a rapid series timed to shuddering pelvic strokes. There was a moment of rigidity, then one more shudder before his body slackened against hers. His face was in her hair, breath against her neck. Warmth was exchanged all along their points of touching, and Stacy sought to preserve the aura. When he began to soften and pull away, she wrapped her legs around him and squeezed.

They lay that way for a while, drifting in the reverberations of their lovemaking. Randy at last moved to her side and Stacy turned so that her back was against his chest. With his arm around her, pressing her ribs and breast, he tried to speak. "Stacy, I, I—"

"Shhh, it's okay. You don't have to say anything."

"I love you. I just want you to know that."

"I know. I love you too."

He nuzzled her hair, the back of her neck, and cupped her breast with his hand. "There's more I want to say, but—"

"Shhh, let's just relax and be quiet for a minute."

Stacy's contentment was short lived. The realization that serious complications were sure to follow negated the comfort of his affection, and his emotional state was irksome. She was unwilling to accept responsibility for the level of happiness in Randy's life. Why had he chosen her, anyway, as the object of all his desires? She didn't deserve or want that kind of attention. Or did she? His warmth, strength, and trustworthiness were desirable and comforting, but she couldn't accept them in a way that was worthy of his love and sacrifice. And now he would have different expectations. What mattered most in her life was essentially unchanged, but her relationship with Randy would be different. This new condition emerged as a galling infection that had been festering under the skin for some time. As she lay there in growing discomfort, his arm heavy around her, she struggled mentally with how to put things back the way they were.

She did love him. She'd spoken truthfully moments ago, although now she wished she hadn't said those words. This love would be better left unsaid because the way she loved him was not what he wanted. She would have liked for her feelings to be different, but there was a cold, hard fact looming like an iceberg that Randy's warmth could never melt: she loved Ty more. The multiple facets of this truth remained beneath the surface of her understanding. She lay there on the sagging bed listening to the wind howling outside. Randy's arm was heavy and hot, his breath moist on her neck. Her foot tapped to an internal rhythm and her restless legs felt tingly. Soon she would move. She just needed to think a bit, and it was nice being with someone who loved her unselfishly, who was thoughtful and kind. Randy Walls from Pittsburgh, so sweet, so caring. Who would have ever thought? When she got up to go to the bathroom, she didn't know if she would get dressed and leave or if she would return to his side. But the cold floor and toilet seat prompted her back toward warmth, to indulge in this freighted moment.

Nestled in, she soon felt him stirring beside her—first his face in her hair, nuzzling her neck, then his arm and thigh moving softly, catlike, over the contours of her body. His fingertips tickled under her breasts, along her ribs, over hip and thigh. The tickling movements at first barely interfered with her thoughts, but the circles of sensation grew wider, persistent manifestations of his growing need. He nudged her hips and the hot hinge of her thighs with a stiff column of flesh that seemed foreign, an alien thing that had attached itself to him. When he rolled her shoulder back against the mattress and positioned himself over her, a surge of adrenalin made her tremble.

His tongue went into her mouth while his hands continued their tickling motions. His pelvis pressed against hers. He began to explore other sensitive parts of her body. Her nipples then her entire breasts, each in turn, were pulled into his mouth, hot and persistent, as his fingers probed everywhere. My goodness! She wasn't expecting this. Part of her wanted to escape Randy's probing and sucking, but that little cool chip was melting. Moaning in resignation, she began to offer her tingling flesh. This process of love moved deeper into her secret parts, and the problems of life ceased to exist as Stacy surrendered to rolling waves of pleasure.

He retraced his journey, moving upward over sensitized expanses of flesh—stomach, breasts, neck and face—kissing tenderly along the way. When his mouth reached hers, she kissed him back, tasting herself on his lips and tongue. Then, in a slick instant he was deep inside her. The foreign thing possessed them both, and she rejoiced internally at its presence. Surprise rippled through waves of pleasure, breaking the peaks into foaming whitecaps. She couldn't believe the person doing this to her was Randy. Where had he learned to love this way? She wondered if she really knew him at all. It didn't matter. She kneaded his back, pushed against him, fell into a pelvic rhythm— the very rhythm of life—returning his love stroke for stroke until their individual bodies melted together, transmitting heat into the cool cabin, and there was nothing left of either of them apart from the other.

Afterwards they lay together in sticky silence, Randy enfolding her, and she slept for a little while as the wind outside whipped and howled.

Chapter 38

Yes, it had happened. She was gone, but the stains on the sheet testified to her having been there, along with the dinner plates and beer bottles that remained on the table where they'd left them. It had really happened, and now everything was different. But why had she left without saying goodbye? She had to get back to her husband. But surely, this time, it would be temporary. She couldn't possibly want to be with Ty now—to live with him and sleep with him—after what happened last night. She'd professed her love to Randy and now he was sure that things were turning in his favor, but God! He needed confirmation.

He found his underwear, jeans, and socks in various locations around the bed and pulled them on. "Damn, it's cold in here," he muttered, flipping the rumpled covers back to look for his shirt. There it was at the foot of the bed, wadded up in the sheet. Before he could get it buttoned up, he started shivering, partly from cold and partly from euphoric anxiety.

Shit! The fire was completely out. He began wadding newspapers in a frenzy and throwing the paper balls into the cold iron box. He would have heat in a few minutes; then maybe he could quit shivering. Then maybe he could think of what to do. Stacy! Her absence made him ache. The pain radiated outward like radio waves from a broadcasting tower. He fumbled with the kindling, barely aware of what he was doing.

What day was it, anyway? Shoot! Thursday, a workday. He had to get going. Buster would be waiting for him. But how could he go to work as if this were a normal day? Something of major importance had occurred, and he knew he would never be the same. But certain facts of his existence were the same: here he was alone in a cold, empty shack getting ready for another grueling day of manual labor. Here he was thinking about Stacy, who was somewhere else. Here he was not knowing what to do next, beyond tending to the basic necessities of survival. Damn! Stacy's fragrance was in the room, in his head, but she was not there. Worse still was the slow-dawning realization of his limited options.

He couldn't call her or pay a visit because she was married to a violence-prone redneck. Randy imagined himself knocking Ty's teeth down his throat, turning that smirk into a ragged, bleeding hole. This fantasy disclosed a new kind of helplessness: Randy's inability to contain the hatred he felt for the person who stood between him and what was now rightfully his. He was not afraid of Ty, but he was afraid of his own anger and its possible consequences. He was fearful of what Ty might do to Stacy if he found out his wife had been unfaithful.

His head reeled as he dashed about the shack trying to prepare himself. The circumstances of work gathered reluctantly in his mind like underexposed images. He sat down and rubbed his face, trying to bring the fuzzy pictures into focus. Buster, truck, saws, woods. Okay. They were working this week on a steep tract, accessed through a gravel road that crossed a creek. He was supposed to pick Buster up at his house because it was sort of on the way. Sure, he could pick Buster up. No problem. But the clock reminded him he was running late, and Buster would be waiting.

Since Mrs. Stempton's stroke, Randy had been making his own breakfast and lunch before leaving the shack in the mornings, but today there wouldn't be time. He was hungry and in need of a bath, but when he went to the bathroom to splash his face, he was smiling just the same. Something wonderful that had existed before only in his dreams had become real, and he felt like telling the world. He squeezed out some toothpaste and began to brush vigorously. His mouth filled with foam and minty freshness, but when he spat the blue froth into the basin and rinsed it away, he realized he couldn't tell anyone about his newfound joy. Damn! Having to hide happiness was almost as bad as being unhappy. He wasn't sure he could act normal, especially around Buster. Emotions intertwined like fighting cats, but when he looked in the mirror, he saw a grin of satisfaction in himself as a man.

He needed to get his mind on what he was doing. His attempts at building a fire had failed. The iron box was still cold, but it didn't matter. The truck would provide heat on the way to Buster's. After pulling on his boots and jacket, he dumped last night's supper scraps along with a couple of scoops of dry chow into metal pans for the hounds, who eagerly greeted him at the corner of the porch. He scratched and patted their heads.

The morning was crisp and clear. He was surprised at how bright the day had already become. The sun, peeking over the hills, greeted him, as if his life had become a commercial for breakfast cereal. His steps to the truck were infused with snap, crackle, and pop. He was anxious to face this day knowing it really was the first day of the rest of his life, his real life, the one he'd anticipated all the other days leading up to this moment. Stacy's whereabouts and Ty's jealousy, whether or not to tell Buster about what had happened, the state of the equipment, and the problems related to hauling logs off a mountain—details that had previously goaded like biting flies—were trifles now in the changed light of early spring.

The sun was in the truck with him as he covered the fifteen miles to Buster's house. He arrived there almost magically, as if by some fluid means of transport that required no effort other than the desire to move. Turning onto Buster's block near the outer boundary of the Crack, Randy glanced at his watch. He was only a few minutes late.

Buster's house, a well-kept bungalow with asphalt siding and brown trim, sat at the end of the street, and his friend was there waiting, rocking on the porch. As Randy stepped out of the truck, Buster stood, waved, then turned and disappeared inside the house. He reappeared in the doorway a moment later with a brown paper sack in his hand and his slender, apron-clad momma at his elbow. She waved to Randy. "Good morning. I sure do 'preciate you coming this way to pick up Buster. Saves me a lotta time and gas."

"Well, sure," Randy replied, leaning against the truck. "I'd be coming almost by here anyway."

"That's right. Well, I 'preciate it just the same. Y'all be careful and don't work too hard." Buster was moving toward Randy and the truck when she stepped out of the doorway and grabbed hold of his arm. "Now you wait jest a minute. Don't I get a hug?" He turned and wrapped his arms around her so that Randy could only see her slender brown hands kneading the muscles of her son's broad back. After their embrace, as Buster was stepping off the porch, she waved her willowy arm again. "Bye-bye. You take good care o' my boy now, Randy Walls, and yourself too."

"Yes ma'am," Randy answered.

He became aware of Buster's scrutinizing eye on him as he backed out of the driveway. He felt it still as they headed out toward the main road. "What?" he asked.

"I dunno. You tell me. You the one who's late and grinning like a possum."

Randy tried to control his face. "Nothing. Just overslept."

"Yeah, right. Like I believe that. Oversleeping ain't gonna put that kind of grin on yo' face. You been up to something, probably some kind of foolishness. Scripture say, "For vain man would be wise, though man be born like a wild ass's colt." I get the feeling you been acting like a wild ass and might need some praying over. Better come on out with it and tell me what happened."

Randy turned onto the avenue that led out of the Crack and regarded his friend. Sometimes it was hard to tell when Buster was being serious. He was at least half-serious now, and he'd sensed that something important had happened. Was it that obvious? Randy groped for an evasive strategy but only found a way to repeat himself: "Nothing. I just sat up too late reading and I forgot to set the alarm."

Buster glanced sideways at Randy, puckering his cheek in disbelief. "Okay then. I see how it's gon' be. You gon' keep secrets from your friend. If you can't tell me, then you shouldn't have done it, and if you done something you shouldn't have, that's all the more reason to tell me. We done learned how to work together, to help each other out. Figured you knew that by now. You think you can't trust me?"

"No, that's not it." Randy felt his grin evaporating. "Maybe there's some things a man's gotta work through by himself."

"Uh-huh. Well, I see that while you been working through this whatever it is, you done forgot your lunch. You probably ain't even had breakfast. Might as well turn this truck around and go back to the house so Momma can fix you up something to eat. You ain't gon' be no good to me on the job without some nourishment in your belly."

Randy realized his friend was right—Damn! he was perceptive—and he felt the grin returning despite his efforts to subdue it. "You win." He stopped the truck and backed around into a driveway. He shifted the gear lever down from reverse to low gear, but before he could pull back out into the street, he had to wait for a vehicle approaching from the right. With Buster's words reverberating in his head, recognition was slow. The approaching car was a shiny, metallic blue GTO. Just prior to actually seeing his face, Randy realized who it was. Then he was there in front of him, Ty Ragsdale, driving into the Crack with a passenger, a black guy with an Afro. There was a moment of mutual recognition as Ty turned to look at Randy, sitting there looking at him. The moment rolled by.

The blue car passed and turned onto a street that led deeper into the Crack, toward the projects. Randy sat there blinking until he felt Buster's eyes peering into him. He raised his foot to engage the clutch; the truck shuddered, and they rolled back out the way they'd come.

Buster continued to examine him, shaking his head in disbelief. "Yep," he said, "That was him awright. Ty Ragsdale, the crazy redneck whose wife you been messing with."

Chapter 39

Stacy didn't sleep much beside Randy on the small, lumpy mattress. It had been difficult finding a warm spot under the covers, and there was much to think about. She'd dozed for a while, just after the lovemaking, encircled in passion's afterglow. Her eyelids, though, had popped open after midnight. Randy was snoring beside her with his arm still over her, a suffocating dead weight. She sought comfort there for another hour, trying again and again to reposition herself and Randy without waking him. He was sleeping like a child after a day of frenetic pursuits. She knew his dreams had reached the symbolic level, and that she was there at the center, the object of all his desire and striving. This realization came not in words but as a fluttering of butterflies in her belly, and she remembered again her fear of Gus, the big horse, when she'd mounted him for the first time.

She turned on her side, propping on her elbow. She examined his face, lightly fingering the stubble of his chin. The whiskers were dark there and along his jaw line. There was hair also on his chest, curly and soft. She pressed her palm against it, then lifted the covers to look. Moonlight through the window and the light from the other room revealed the details. He stirred for a moment under her gaze but didn't emerge from his dream. Her eyes followed the contours of his body, not quite as lean as Ty's, but firm and muscular. The hair was interesting. Ty's body, except for armpits and pubic area, was smooth, but Randy's dark curls formed a line down the middle of his trunk, fanned around his navel, then narrowed and flared into a black triangle at his groin. His penis emerged white and erect from this dark tangle. She wondered what it was like to sleep that way, and she imagined herself dancing through his mind. She smiled to think that at some level she'd made him happy.

She allowed her hand to slide from his chest down his abdomen, playing along the line of hair. Below his navel the texture changed. Her fingers moved gently through the thick coils and the back of her hand rubbed against the stiff penis. His pelvis seemed to swell toward her at this touch and a note of pleasure passed through his lips with his rhythmic breathing. Desire stirred inside Stacy, urging her to straddle him and love him into consciousness, but something restrained her. This ain't right, she thought. She replaced the covers and rolled over to her other side as if to extricate herself from his dream.

Before easing out of bed, she turned to look at him once more. She kissed his cheek and whispered, "Bye Randy. I didn't mean to do all this. I do love you, but I can't stay here. Sweet dreams." She pulled her clothes on as quickly and quietly as possible and let herself out through the creaking front door. From underneath, one of the hounds made a throaty snuffling sound, a muffled half-bark, as she crossed the porch. She paused at the steps, hoping the dog wouldn't make a ruckus and wake Randy, but it really didn't matter. She was leaving anyway and would be gone before he could get out of bed. The hound settled itself. Stacy got in her car and drove away, straight to the apartment she shared with her husband.

Once there, she became conscious and ashamed of the untidy condition of the place. Dishes were piled in the sink, the trashcan was full, ashtrays were dirty. She hadn't even made the bed. In the bathroom the toilet and sink needed scrubbing and that trashcan was full too. Damn. What kind of wife was she, anyhow? No wonder Ty didn't like to stay home. He liked things neat, and this place was a pigsty. She set in to making it right, beginning with the kitchen sink—washing, drying, putting dishes and utensils in their place. Over the next hour and a half, she scrubbed and tidied the entire apartment, even mopped the floors. Surfaces gleamed and the place smelled of Pine-Sol. Her husband would be pleased. She took a quick shower, then lay down, exhausted.

He'd be getting off in a couple of hours if he was working his normal shift. She tried to relax as she lay there waiting. Her eyes burned. When she closed them, she still saw Randy—his shack, his face during sexual release and in peaceful repose, his body in the moonlight, stretched out beside her. She replayed their evening: fixing supper, eating corn-on-the-cob, talking. She marveled at how Randy had found himself, taken control, made love to her. He would be disappointed when he woke up and realized she was gone.

Well, that's just the way things were. He was a man, after all. He'd just have to get over it. Ty was her husband and that wasn't likely to change. She was committed now more than ever to making the marriage work. She loved Ty, and she could be a good wife to him, if only he'd come home and love her the way he had in the beginning, before they were married, before her father's death and mother's stroke.

Images swirled and thoughts collided, but she finally sank below the choppy surface, sleeping for a while until finally awakened by a clanging bell, some kind of alarm. God, what a racket! Where was it coming from? Telephone! It must have rung a dozen times before she could get to it, there on the kitchen wall.

"Hello."

"Hello, Stacy. Are you okay?"

"Yes. I'm fine, Aunt Ruth. How are you?" She tried to make her voice sound as if she hadn't just then been awakened.

"Well, we're okay, I guess. Haven't heard from you in a couple of days. Your mother was getting concerned."

Stacy blinked her eyes, tried to get her bearings. The clock on the wall told her it was nearly lunchtime. "Oh. Sorry I didn't call. Been kinda busy."

"You don't sound like yourself. You sure you're not sick?"

"No. I'm fine. I was just in the middle of some housecleaning."

"Me too. It's amazing how this place stays in such a mess with just the two of us. Anyway, your mother would like to see you. She's been feeling down lately. You always seem to cheer her up. And I could use a little help with the laundry."

"Okay. Sure. I'll stop by in a little while, before I go to work."

"That would be nice. Maybe we can all have supper together."

"Well, maybe. That sort of depends on Ty's schedule. He's been working crazy hours lately."

"Yes. Of course. Well, you just come when you can."

"I will. And tell Momma I love her."

Stacy felt a surge of brightness as they said their goodbyes. The clean apartment and being fully awake on a brand-new day contributed to the lighter mood. She looked at the clock again. Ty would be here soon. Or not, she never knew anymore. Shoot! There it was again, reality. But he would be here at some point, and when he came through the door, he would be pleased with her and she with him.

She washed her face in the bathroom, brushed her hair, and brushed her teeth. Then she stepped into the living room and turned on the TV. *Days of Our Lives*—she could watch to see how the Bradys and Hortons were handling their various crises as she waited for her husband. She was hungry, but she'd rather wait and eat with him. Then she began to think about what she could fix. She went back to the kitchen to check the refrigerator. That's when the trembling began. The bright light and cool air inside the fridge prompted a giddy feeling like the dropping of an elevator. No, that wasn't it. She'd heard it as she was pulling the handle, the sound of the GTO in the driveway. Her husband was home. She pushed the door closed and leaned against it.

This would be weird, awkward, but she couldn't let it seem that way. He mustn't know that anything was different, except the apartment, and he would be pleased with its cleanliness and with her. That was it. Smile. Act normal. She turned away from the fridge and went to the door to meet him.

"Hi, Sweetie. I'm glad you're home."

"Hey, Baby. What's happening?" Ty pushed the door closed behind him, then paused to take off his jacket and hang it on a peg. When he turned back to Stacy, she noticed a slight flaring of his nostrils and his eyes scanning the room. "Well," he said. "I see somebody's been busy."

"Yeah. I had a little time on my hands, and this place was overdue for a good cleaning. I'm sorry I let it get in such a mess."

"Hell, don't worry 'bout it." He paused to look at her face, then moved his eyes to a far corner. "I—I know you've had a lot on you lately. And I ain't been much help around here, working so much and all."

"That's okay. You can't help those crazy hours they put you on. Maybe things'll get back to normal soon. You hungry?"

"A little."

They moved together toward the kitchen. Stacy felt the brightness returning. This was going to be all right. "I'm hungry myself. What do you feel like, breakfast, lunch, or supper? I never know with you and these hours you keep."

"I know that's right. I don't know myself, whether I'm coming or going half the time."

She put her hand on his back, as they walked together toward the kitchen table, and guided him toward his chair.

"Sit down, baby, and take a load off. I'll fix whatever you want. If you plan on staying up a while, I'll make some coffee."

Ty took his place at the table and surveyed the clean floor and counters. Stacy went back to the refrigerator and peered inside. "I could fry up some bacon and eggs or fix you a hamburger."

"You know, come to think of it, I'm not really that hungry. I think I'd rather lay down for a little while, then eat when I get up, before I go to work."

She closed the refrigerator and turned to face him. Her eyes were drawn to his as he continued: "But I'm not really that sleepy either. Maybe it's something else I need."

She winked, leaning back against the refrigerator to latch the door. "I wonder what that might be."

He blinked lazily and grinned.

She pushed herself forward and took a seat next to him at the wobbly little dinette table. "I've missed you lately."

"Me too."

She took his right hand in both of hers and began to massage it. "These fingernails of yours always got grease under 'em. The only time I ever saw them clean was our wedding day."

"Had to do a set-up last night. Guess I always got my hands in something black and greasy."

"Ain't it the truth. But that's gon' change before long. When you get that supervisor's job, somebody else can do the dirty work."

He nodded as she rubbed his hand. When she looked at his face again, his eyes were closed. She pressed her knee against his and rubbed up his forearm, kneading the muscle. "You're tired, ain't you, baby?"

"A little, but not too tired." He lifted his lids in that slow way and looked into her eyes. She placed his hand softly on the tabletop

"I think it'd be great if you could get on day shift, then you wouldn't be so tired and gone all hours of the night."

"Like I said, I ain't too tired." He moved his hand, placing it over hers, then shifted around to face her. With his foot he turned her chair so that her knees were between his.

"I'm glad, 'cause I ain't too tired either." There was an awkwardness there between them that she wasn't accustomed to, and she sought to dispel it. "So, what'll it be? Did you decide yet?"

"Decide what?"

"Bacon and eggs, hamburger, coffee . . . or *me*?"

"Oh, I done decided that. I was working on a different question entirely."

"Really? What might that be?"

"Whether to take you into the bedroom or fuck you right here on top of this table."

Stacy checked her laughter after a few chuckles escaped. She looked at the table, shook it with her hand. "I don't think it'd hold us," she replied, smiling.

"Well, I guess that settles it." Ty stood and pulled her up with him. Both chairs slid backwards. He squeezed her tight against him, one hand against the small of her back, the other pressing between her shoulders. She watched those lids drop again, then looked at his lips before they met hers. He kissed her hard on the mouth, probing in the familiar way. Familiar also was his smell: cigarettes, machinery, and something else, a masculine musk that was simply Ty, a part of him she loved.

When they broke apart, he looked at her and said, "You're my girl, ain't you?"

She replied, "You betcha." Then Ty, bumping chairs out of the way, picked her up and carried her into the bedroom.

Chapter 40

Randy made a point of being at Mrs. Stempton's house as often as possible in hopes of running into Stacy, but it seemed she'd always just left or should be there soon, according to the ladies. He hadn't seen her in weeks. He made himself useful to Mrs. Stempton and Aunt Ruth, and there was always plenty to do to keep the household running. With spring's arrival and the threat of frost finally past, Mrs. Stempton insisted on a garden. "Ben always planted before now," she said, her slurred speech making her sound like a drunk. She raised her good arm to point at the big oak outside the kitchen window. "Look at the new leaves. When they're big as a squirrel's ear, it's time to plant. Them leaves are big as a squirrel's whole head. Each day that passes is time lost." When she spoke, spittle accumulated in the slack folds on the left side of her mouth. Her eyes were often moist also, tearing up at the slightest provocation. References to family and her husband—what he did or would have done, what she would do if she were able, and Stacy's not being there—always brought her to the point of tears. No one mentioned Timmy.

Ruth agreed, between sips of coffee, that a garden would be just the thing. "Having fresh vegetables keeps the grocery bill down. And we can fill up the freezer and pantry for the winter months. We're still enjoying corn and field peas that Ben grew last year, but there's not much left. I don't know what we'll do if we have to start paying for all our vegetables."

A sob escaped from Mrs. Stempton, sitting in her wheelchair. She scooted herself around with her right arm on the wheel and her right leg on the floor, as if she would escape the situation by leaving Randy and Ruth at the table, but she stopped after lining herself up with the kitchen sink. She sat there and gazed out the window, dabbing her eyes with the handkerchief she kept in her lap. Randy took a sip of coffee, looked up at Aunt Ruth and Mrs. Stempton's back. "Sure, we can plant a garden. I'll get started right away, but someone will have to show me how deep and far apart to put the seeds, and that kind of stuff. I don't even know what kind of seeds to buy—"

"Already got 'em. In the drawer of the pie safe," Mrs. Stempton said, mumbling into her handkerchief.

Ruth shuffled across the linoleum to the cupboard and slid open the shallow drawer underneath the tin-paneled doors. "Sure enough," she exclaimed, "there's a whole bunch in here, all we need." She flipped through the colorful packets one by one. "Trucker's Delight corn, yellow squash, cantaloupe, cucumbers, pole beans, okra, crowder peas, watermelon, banana peppers—my Lord, where'd all these come from?"

"Ben ordered 'em," Mrs. Stempton said between sobs, "from one of his catalogs, just before. . .." Her voice trailed off as her head and shoulders shook.

"She gets like this a lot lately," Ruth said, turning to face Randy. "Lord, I don't know what we're gon' do with her." She dropped the packets back into the drawer and moved to Bea's side, placed her arm around her shoulders. "There, there, sweetie. It's all right. Randy's here and he's gonna plant those seeds, and we'll have more vegetables than we can eat. Me and you'll can some and fill up the freezer, just the way y'all used to every year."

"Okay. Ben loved his garden, you know that."

"I know. We'll do one for him that would make him proud." Ruth rubbed between her sister-in-law's shoulders as Bea sniffled and nodded her head.

"Okay."

Randy thought about what he'd gotten himself into as he sipped his coffee—that he'd just committed himself to more backbreaking labor—but he was encouraged by the hope that Stacy would soon accept her rightful place beside him. There was always the chance that she might stop by in the afternoons or on Saturday when he would be working on the garden. He imagined conversing with her about the tractor and plows, how to lay off the rows, and how deep to plant the seeds. He knew she'd be full of advice and would laugh at his inexperience, calling him "City Boy." He also imagined talking about their life together. If he could just talk to her, to get an idea where things stood. Surely she felt the same way after what had happened. But she was bound by her work schedule and circumstances. He would see her soon, though, especially with this garden as an added reason for his being at the home place. He told the ladies he would come the next Saturday, the last one in April, to do the plowing.

The first step was getting the tractor serviced and rigged for the task. Li'l Trudy had been ensconced in the barn all winter, since they'd finished with the stump pulling. Randy dragged open the sagging doors. The smell of gasoline, mingled with grease, sweat, and tobacco was as prevalent as it had been when he and Stacy first opened those doors last September. He'd been particular about putting things back whenever he needed to use the old man's tools or find a spare part. The enclosed space had become a shrine to Ben Stempton and his equipment, to the enduring bond between man and machine.

Randy had himself forged a rewarding relationship with the tractor. During the property clearing time, he'd learned to indulge her few eccentricities in exchange for the satisfaction of overcoming obstacles. Distinctive squeaks, especially from the clutch pedal linkage and front end, let him know it was time for grease. On hot afternoons, she would signal her need to rest with a metallic pinging from the engine accompanied by a faint wheezing and reluctance to pull. On those glaring days of high humidity and still air, he usually felt weak himself at about the same time, so he was willing to steer into the shade and shut down for a few minutes. These breaks provided opportunities for him and Buster to drink deeply from their iced tea jars and discuss the progress they were making in work and life in general. After a twenty-minute cool-down the trio would eagerly reengage the stubborn stump, confident of the victory that would follow. The tractor sounded stronger, Randy's vision and reflexes became sharp once again, and Buster's handling of the chain became lively and masterful.

Now, at the beginning of a new season, Randy checked the tractor over carefully and realized that a full servicing was in order. The oil was black; the fan belt was loose and frayed; and the battery terminals were covered with heavy corrosion, a crystallized froth resembling a lime-flavored confection. He spent Saturday morning tending to these needs before he was ready to attach the turning plow, which, the ladies informed him, would be the first implement to use on the hardened soil.

Pulling stumps hadn't required familiarity with the three-point hitch system, the drawbar being the only implement used, and this lack of experience led to confusion in attaching the plow. Randy's initial impression was that the thing simply wouldn't fit. Each time he got one of the side arms in place, the other would be a half-inch shy of clearing the hitch pin. The plow's weight made for a difficult wrestling match and trying to inch the tractor backward or forward resulted in throwing the whole arrangement out of alignment. Through experimentation with raising and lowering the hydraulic lift, he finally got the side arms over the pins and the cotters in place. But the top link was still way off.

This bar could be lengthened or shortened by turning its middle portion, a threaded sleeve. The rusty threads required oil and considerable effort applied through a large pipe wrench. The bar's resistance to turning indicated it had long maintained its current length, but the damn thing was too short. Finally, after wrenching till his arm ached, the holes lined up. He shoved the pin and cotter in place, then stepped back to survey his work.

He started the engine and fingered the lift lever, raising and lowering the plow. Something was out of whack. The angle of the implement to the ground appeared unworkable; the plow point was pitched too far up. Randy scratched his head, lit a cigarette. Even though he was outside of the ladies' view from the kitchen window, he felt their eyes were on him. They would be wondering what was taking so long. He took a deep drag and slowly exhaled. As the smoke left his lungs, he recognized the problem: Damn! The top link's way too long now. The old man had it where it needed to be to plow properly. It would have to be wrenched back to where it was.

Turning the sleeve was easier this time. Each revolution produced a subtle change, bringing the top of the implement in closer while angling the plow point back, and he was soon able to return the bar to its former position. Now he could get started.

He was surprised at how enjoyable working the earth could be. With Li'l Trudy singing a contented note, the plow was pulled under the crusty, weed-covered surface. The point dug in and the blade sliced through. Its broad, curved surface turned everything over, exposing roots to the withering power of the sun, whose dual role Randy pondered: destroyer first, then life-giver, after the desired seeds were planted.

Looking backwards, he steered with his left hand and placed his right hand against the fender for balance as he watched the plow do its work. In yielding to the iron blade, the earth seemed almost fluid, rolling and cresting like ocean waves. Unlike water, though, the soil held its shape after the plow's passing, forming ridges and troughs. The ringing hiss of the blade slicing the soil reached his ears as both a sigh of anticipation and a dying shriek of protest.

The earth was the house of death, where all living things ended up, and Randy breathed in the fragrance of decay as the soil was turned. Life and death together, one yielding to the other in a continuous process—like in that poem he'd studied in eleventh grade. What was it? An old poem about viewing or seeing death, written by a teenager. Death in life, life in death. As the plow did its work Randy decided to focus on the promise of new life contained within the musty ground waiting for seed. He thought of Stacy and the pleasure of her receptive flesh. Damn! Where was that girl?

Chapter 41

Stacy didn't come that Saturday, and as the sun dropped behind the hills, Randy thought about his next opportunity. Tomorrow was Sunday, a day set aside for family and a big meal after church. He knew he would be welcome for Sunday dinner at the Stempton home, but he had to be careful. Now that Stacy was married, the women's interest concerning him and her had changed. Mrs. Stempton seemed to avoid mentioning Stacy in Randy's presence now, whereas before she had been eager to provide opportunities for them to be together. It seemed that she and Aunt Ruth were complicit in trying to keep him away from Stacy. The marriage had occurred, and vows were made before God. Even though the women may not have approved prior to the actual wedding, and would have preferred having him in Ty's place, they would recognize and protect the union as something sacred. Randy's position was untenable. So he spent Sunday alone—thinking, reading, watching TV, and trying to rest.

The work week began with rain, forcing Randy and Buster out of the woods just after lunchtime. They decided to drive the flatbed into town to pick up supplies at the hardware store. Driving through a steady drizzle, the friends laughed at the vacuum-operated windshield wipers on the old truck, the way they sped up going downhill and nearly stopped going up. Randy said, "It's a good thing Prathersville's located in a valley. If it was on top of the mountain, we'd never see to get there."

"I know that's right. We'll have a hard time getting back up the side of that hill we was working on, if it keeps on raining."

"I figure we might as well call it a day. Looks like this rain has set in for the afternoon."

Buster nodded and looked out the window. There was a lull in the conversation as they negotiated an inclined stretch of road. On the other side of the crest, their talking picked up with the speed of the wipers. Buster said, "Might be too wet to work tomorrow, if this keeps up. We don't wanna get the truck stuck, it half-loaded."

"Nope." Randy swabbed with a dirty rag at the condensation forming on the inside of the windshield. "I was planning on taking the afternoon off today or tomorrow anyway, but with this rain I don't know. I need to get back over to Mrs. Stempton's to get her garden planted."

"Gon' be too wet for that now."

"Maybe by the end of the week, if it dries out enough."

"You seem to be in a hurry 'bout that garden."

"Yeah. I've already done the plowing. I'm anxious to get the seed in and see what happens. I've never tried to grow anything before."

"You got to fertilize it too, you know."

"Fertilize?"

Buster shook his head. "Unh, unh, unh. You sure got a knack for getting into things you don't know nothing about."

"Well, I . . ." Randy glanced at his friend who was still looking at him in mock exasperation. "Yeah, I guess you're right. Seems like everything I start ends up being five times more trouble than I bargained for."

"You in for a lot more trouble—maybe more'n you can handle— if you don't leave that girl alone."

Buster knew that Randy had slept with Stacy and had expressed his concern that day when they'd run into Ty Ragsdale driving into the Crack as they were heading out. Randy had not denied it or tried to make excuses; there was no need. Buster figured it all out from his behavior that morning and disapproved on biblical grounds. "Thou shalt not commit adultery. Look at what happened to King David for taking another man's wife. Scripture say God will judge whoremongers and adulterers."

Randy had been quick to reply, "Stacy's not a whore."

"I didn't say she was. I'm just giving you some friendly advice based on God's word."

Randy spoke harshly for the first time to his friend that day: "That's not the kind of advice I need. You don't understand the situation, and it's none of your business anyway."

"It's the Lord's business and his word will not return void. You might ought to think about that."

Now the touchy subject had come up again, and Buster was forcing Randy to look at something he didn't want to see: the moral implications and potential dangers of continuing to pursue Stacy Stempton Ragsdale. Randy turned his face away, cranked his window down a notch for air, and squinted, trying to see the road in front of him. He finally said, "I haven't seen her since that night."

"That's good, but it ain't because you didn't want to. You still got it on your mind. I can see that."

Exasperation elevated Randy's voice: "Well, what am I supposed to do? Sure, I want to see her and be with her, more than anything. I can't help it."

"Man, I can't tell you what to do. All I can say is what I already said, and you don't wanna hear that. Just be careful. And be prepared for some rough sailing if you don't change the course you're on."

"She's not happy in her marriage. She told me she loves me. I believe she'll leave him, that she's trying to find a way."

Buster looked out his window, wiped it with his sleeve. "They's a time for sowing and a time for reaping, a season for everything under the sun."

"What's that supposed to mean?"

"It means wait, knowing that all things work together for good to them that love the Lord. You'll see his hand in things, working it all out for you—on his schedule, not yours—once you get yo' heart right."

"I'm afraid my heart's about as right as it's gonna get."

The wipers slowed again then came to a halt as they started up a long hill just before the final descent into town. "Damn," Randy said. I wish I could see where I'm going."

Buster replied in a voice that merged with the rain and the swish of the tires, "I know that's right. I'll be praying 'bout it, that God'll keep you safe and grant you the desires of your heart."

★★★

Prathersville Hardware and Supply provided goods to cover a wide variety of needs related to the maintenance and operation of home and farm. Building materials, gardening supplies, tractor implements, lawn equipment, hand tools, ammunition, nuts, bolts, plumbing parts, glue, caulk, rubber hoses, drive belts, boots, overalls, gloves, and hats all contributed to the dizzying array of merchandise housed within its evolving configuration of shelves, corners, crannies, and stalls. Randy had, over time, become familiar with the establishment and the people who operated it, but he still felt like an outsider whenever he walked through those old-fashioned, glass-paned doors.

The store, under its current proprietorship, had begun in the late 1940's when Clarence Waldrop, fresh from the army, used his savings and good name to buy out old Horace Dewberry, whose struggles in the hardware business could be traced back nearly to Prathersville's beginnings. The transaction proved lucrative beyond Clarence's hopes as Prathersville grew, during the decades following the war, into the second largest town in Aaron County, its population leveling out by the end of the sixties at about half that of Aaronville, the county seat.

The two towns, always rivals, developed along different paths. Both were served by the railway, and by the late nineteenth century each had become a center for the collection and distribution of cotton. Political interests, though, in 1907 provided a more progressive path for Aaronville. The Georgia legislature mandated the establishment in each congressional district of A&M schools to provide the state's youth with the agricultural and mechanical training necessary for successful farm life. Aaronville, through political machinations, was chosen as the site for the district's new school. Aaronville A&M operated until 1933, when Georgia broadened its support of higher education and formed the state university system from the old agricultural schools. Aaron-Maslow State College flourished from the beginning, offering degree programs in the arts and sciences, business, and education.

Other developments concurred with the expansion of the college. In the late 1930s, a civic-minded doctor named Elijah Taylor, seeing the need for more comprehensive medical services, established a hospital that would become the largest in West Georgia. The town's leaders, intent on rivaling even Atlanta in the scope and quality of service, poured investment dollars into the facility. Support for Taylor Medical Center also came from unexpected sources. Around 1950, Darlene Masterson, a prominent film actress, bought a large farm just outside of the Aaronville city limits. She loved the pastoral setting but was fearful of being without adequate medical care during her sojourns to the area. She was obsessed with her health and that of her husband, a wealthy businessman a decade her senior. The couple poured thousands into the medical center and into making her farm a showplace of agricultural elegance. They raised thoroughbred horses, Polled Hereford cows, and peacocks. To serve her spiritual needs, the actress built a Catholic church, which remains to this day the only one in the area.

At about that time Rayford Robinson, a self-reliant tinkerer, stumbled upon an opportunity during the construction of a new chicken house. He was intending to raise chickens using the newest methods, which required long, low houses equipped with automated systems to feed and water the chicks. With the aid of his fifteen-year-old son and an unreliable helper, a young man named Fletcher Ragsdale, Robinson had the entire structure framed and roofed within a couple of weeks. When he started the wiring and plumbing, though, he ran into problems. The post-war building boom had created a huge demand for materials, and Robinson was unable to procure enough galvanized pipe and copper tubing to finish the job. Necessity and his improvisational nature prompted him to explore the possibilities of manufacturing these products locally.

The structure he'd erected never housed a chicken but proved suitable for his early experiments in pipe making. Toward the end of 1950, the refitted chicken house became the operational base of Southern Pipe and Tube. The People's Bank of Aaronville loaned him money, and Robinson soon had in his employ six local people, among them Fletcher Ragsdale, who was fired after a few months for being chronically absent on Monday mornings. By the end of the decade, the manufacturing facility had eclipsed all the area textile mills combined in the number of people employed. Robinson provided good pay, benefits, and a stable future unrelated to farming. Families poured into Aaronville for the opportunities offered by Southern Pipe and Tube.

Aaronville grew on the speculations and aspirations of people with ideas, people interested in the future. Prathersville, on the other side of the county, grew as does an old house being continually remodeled—an embodiment of incongruity—with rooms and hallways preposterously tacked on to an original structure, cherished despite its crumbling foundations. By the early seventies, Aaronville had become a town comprising a dynamic blend of doctors, lawyers, college professors, blue-collar workers, college students, social workers, and hippies. Prathersville, twenty minutes away, was populated mainly with the same merchants and families who had long controlled the old business district, along with mill workers, sporadically employed construction workers, elderly farmers who had sold out and retired to the projects, and a smattering of professional people. Both towns were growing and changing, but Prathersville had more trouble lifting itself out of its history of sharecropping and segregation. The natives didn't like being thought of as rednecks, and feelings of inferiority spawned resentment toward the "snobs" of Aaronville and educated, upwardly mobile people in general, especially those with northern accents.

The hardware store was situated in the middle of the old part of town, taking up a block of storefronts and the lots behind them. By this time Clarence Waldrop's two sons were playing a major role in the store's operation. Johnny and Joe, born a year apart, had grown up in the hardware business and knew it inside out. They had also grown up having better toys and clothes and a nicer house to live in than the bulk of Prathersville's kids. They each had an eye for fashion, dressing for work in authentic Hush Puppies shoes, the latest jeans or khaki slacks, and colorful Izod shirts.

Johnny and Joe didn't load or unload trucks, cut pipe, stack lumber, or even sweep the floors. Two other employees—gray, stooped men who had been with Mr. Waldrop since the beginning— took care of those details while the owner's sons handled "sales and purchasing," duties that entailed talking to reps and customers, shaking hands, smiling, joking, and saying, "We appreciate it!" Pleasant boys for the most part, especially with the regular customers, they were handy with their smiles, winks, and inside jokes, and often gave away printed promotional items: ballpoint pens, carpenter pencils, matches, and, for their better customers, cloth nail aprons and caps. They looked remarkably alike, except that Johnny, the elder, was slightly darker and leaner, with curly hair. Each young man had a nice Roman nose and a small cleft in his chin.

Johnny and Joe were about the same age as Randy, who now was swabbing the condensation inside the truck cab and squinting through the balky wipers as he and Buster made their way into town. There wasn't much traffic because of the rain, and they found a parking spot right in front. The large window underneath the awning featured a display of gardening equipment and supplies: a gas-powered walk-behind tiller, hoes, a small planter with a wheel in front, a tightly coiled green garden hose, and baskets of various shapes and sizes. Randy killed the engine. "Come inside with me. You can help me remember what we're supposed to get."

"Naa. I'll just wait in the truck."

"Come on, it's depressing sitting here in the rain. You might find something you need in there. They got lots of stuff."

"I been in hardware stores before."

"Yeah, I know, but I need you to look at the bush axes to help me decide. They got two different ones."

"Unh, unh, unh." Buster shook his head as he got out of the truck.

At the entrance Randy hesitated for a second before pushing the door open. Attached to a metal bracket on the inside was a little brass bell whose metallic tinkling signaled the arrival of a new customer each time the door was opened. The bell usually rang so often no one paid attention to it, but on this day the rain was keeping customers away. Randy, when he pushed on the door, announced his and Buster's arrival.

They entered, and everyone looked up from what he had been doing, which was nothing much. The first person Randy saw was a gray-haired white man called Mr. Tom, kneeling in the aisle beside a box of pipe fittings, methodically restocking the shelves. Mr. Waldrop, the owner, was visible through the window of his office, a small room in the back corner. He'd been reading a newspaper with his feet propped on his desk. Johnny was sitting behind the checkout counter with a magazine opened before him, while his brother, beside him on a stool, ate his lunch from a Styrofoam tray. Near the back wall old Lucius, brown and weathered, was propped against his push broom.

With five sets of eyes on Randy and Buster and no other customers in the store, seconds passed before someone finally spoke. Johnny set the magazine aside and said, "What can I help you boys with today?"

Randy cleared his throat. "We want to look at the bush axes, and we need new chains for the saws." Randy looked back to see if Buster had anything to add and found him languishing near the doorway, looking at the floor.

"Well, for the chains, I need to know the size, pitch, and how many links. There's several different kinds, you know."

"Poulan S80's, two of 'em. One with an eighteen-inch bar, the other one twenty-two."

"It'd help if you had your old ones to match up with."

"Buster—" When Randy turned, he saw his friend was already passing back out the door to fetch the old chains from the truck. "Yeah, he's going to get 'em."

Johnny nodded in agreement, smiled.

Randy stepped up to the counter, turning his head as if surveying the aisles.

"What else y'all need?" Johnny asked.

The younger brother, Joe, with a gravy-drenched piece of cube steak speared on his fork, looked up in anticipation.

"We need some new files. Half a dozen."

"Okay." Johnny began scribbling on the receipt pad. "What else?"

"Uh—" Before Randy could answer, the bell tinkled, and Buster came in holding the oily chains. He approached the counter with his eyes averted and set the chains down, fussing with them to keep the links untangled.

Johnny picked them up with a faded shop rag. "Here you go, Mr. Tom," he called out. "Go cut these fellas some new chain."

The old man stood from his spot in the plumbing aisle, wincing slightly, and shuffled over in an air of humility. He nodded at Randy and smiled as he took the chains, then faded away through a doorway behind the counter. Johnny folded the rag, dropped it. "He'll cut that chain for you. Meanwhile, bush axes are down that aisle, all the way to the far wall. Was there anything else?"

Randy glanced at Joe, who had gone back to his cube steak, then turned to Buster. "What else do we need? You said something about fertilizer."

Buster's eyes held a hint of reproach. Before he could answer, Johnny said, "Fertilizer. Well, we got plenty of that. Whole shipment next door in the warehouse. What is it you're trying to grow?" Joe paused again in his chewing, a look of amusement on his face.

Randy glanced at Buster and found him miserably examining the countertop. Randy answered, "Well . . . beans, corn, squash, you know, that kind of stuff."

Johnny smiled. "Most folks use 10-10-10 on their gardens. I'd be happy to get Tom and Lucius to load you up with all you need. There's one problem, though."

"Oh yeah? What's that?"

Johnny nodded toward the front windows and the rain-drenched world beyond. "You wouldn't have nothing but a truck load of mush by the time you got back with it."

Both boys, smiling from their places behind the counter, looked expectantly at Randy, who finally answered, "Well, sure, I guess we can come back and get that later, when it quits raining."

"Okay then. Like I said, bush axes are on the far wall."

Buster stepped away from the counter, in the direction Johnny indicated. Randy stood there a moment longer, then joined Buster at the end of the aisle.

"Which one you like best?" Buster asked, hefting an ax and rubbing its smooth handle.

"I don't like either damn one of them."

"I was talking 'bout the axes, not the Waldrop boys. I don't like them either."

Randy focused on the axes. One was longer with a thicker handle and wider blade, made for heavy-duty use. He called out, "How much are they?"

Johnny answered from the counter, "It'll be $12.95, if you want to go with the best. The other one is $8.50. I'd recommend the heavy one for the kind of work you fellas do. Your boy there looks like he's stout enough to swing it without much trouble."

Randy felt his face flush, noting Buster's pained expression. "*Boy?* He's not my boy, he's my friend. We're the same age."

Johnny replied, still smiling, "Oh. Well *excuse* me. I didn't realize you two were such close . . . *friends.*"

Randy was ready to get out of there. He grabbed the heavier ax and said to Buster, "Come on, let's go." But they couldn't leave as quickly as he wanted to. There was a delay at the counter. Mr. Tom had not yet returned with the new chains, and Johnny had to put the files in a sack and total everything up. While Randy waited, Buster stepped over to the next aisle and examined the work gloves.

The old man finally emerged with the chains.

"Okay," Johnny said. "Let's put their old ones in a separate bag." He and Mr. Tom sacked up the chains while Joe got off his stool and stuffed the empty Styrofoam tray into the trash can.

"How much?" Randy asked.

Johnny calculated the numbers. "Comes to forty-four dollars and seventy-six cents. That's including those gloves your *friend* bought."

Buster spoke up: "I didn't buy no gloves. I was just trying on a pair. They too little anyhow."

Johnny, smiling pleasantly, said, "Well, after you've had your hands in 'em—stretching them all out—we can't rightly sell them to somebody else. That's our policy with gloves: you put 'em on, you buy 'em."

Hot blood pulsed into Randy's cheeks and there was a rush in his ears. He was still gripping the bush ax handle, and, for a second, he felt like swinging it. He breathed, collected himself enough to speak. "That's an interesting policy. Does it apply to everybody, or just colored people?"

"Well, you know how it is. Policy's policy."

"I see," Randy said, releasing his grip on the ax handle and leaning it against the counter. "But I got my own policy: to not do business with people like you. So, you can take your ax, chains, files—and gloves—and stuff 'em up your ass. Come on, Buster. Let's get out of here."

Buster stopped in front of the counter, Nodded his head. "That's right. He got his own policy." Randy walked to the door and yanked it open. Then he shook it back and forth several times, loudly agitating the tinkling brass bell. He held it open so Buster could pass through first. The Waldrop boys' faces registered mild surprise and amusement, as if a child had played a practical joke. In the doorway, Buster went through the motions of shaking something off his shoes before he stepped outside.

Back in the truck, Randy asked, "What was that all about?"

Buster looked puzzled. "You ought to know. You the one who threw the fit in there."

"No. I mean that little thing you did with your feet before you stepped out the door."

"That's what Jesus told his disciples to do whenever they left any place that didn't welcome them or show the right kind of respect for the word they be bringing. See, I was shaking the dust of that place off my feet so I wouldn't be contaminated by their unrighteousness. I'm done with 'em. Now it's up to God to judge as he sees fit."

"Johnny didn't know it, but he came pretty close to having his judgment day today. I was so mad there for a second, I felt like swinging that bush ax."

Buster laughed. "Lord, don't I know it! I seen the grip you had on the handle. I was glad when you let go of it. Wouldn't do to go taking things into your own hands thataway. We gotta leave that kind of judgment to the Lord."

"Suits me," Randy replied, grinning. He noticed the wipers were moving back and forth over a dry windshield. The rain had stopped. He reached up and turned the knob on the dashboard. "I'm like you, though. I'm done with them. I'll drive all the way to Aaronville from now on."

Chapter 42

The skies cleared and stayed blue for several days, allowing the garden time to dry. Randy and Buster took advantage of this by getting the truck loaded early, so they could knock off at lunchtime. Buster also needed the afternoon off, to run errands for his mother. So, by the time the sun, brilliantly white, had reached its apex, Randy was driving the tractor, pulling an iron implement through the soil.

The lay-off plow was much lighter than the turning plow, with two points instead of one. It was designed to make rows only a few inches deep to receive the seed. The women decided to watch the proceedings from the edge of the yard, where grass met plowed earth. They were also there to give the novice gardener instructions, Mrs. Stempton remembering the way Ben had always done it and Aunt Ruth remembering the way her father had done it when she was growing up.

They disagreed about the fertilizer. Aunt Ruth believed it needed to be worked in throughout the soil prior to laying off the rows. She said that the ground needed to be broken up finer anyway and that Randy should go back through the entire plot with the walk-behind tiller. Mrs. Stempton replied, her voice slurred and choppy, "That's too much work. We're running late with this garden as it is. He can lay off the rows, then put a little fertilizer in each one, before he drops the seed in. Just doing that's gon' take the rest of the afternoon."

Bea, arguing from her wheelchair, prevailed. It was her garden anyway—the same spot she and Ben had planted every year while Ruth was still in Atlanta, so it was right for her to have the last say. Once in agreement, both ladies began giving instructions on spacing the rows and how deep they should be. They also debated which seeds should go in each row. That's when they realized they didn't have any tomato plants.

"Shoot!" Bea exclaimed. "We was thinking so much about those seed packs and getting the rows laid off, we forgot all about tomatoes. Me and Ben never grew them from seed. He always bought little plants from the hardware store, in cups so you can just set out the whole thing. They don't cost much and that's the easiest way."

Randy said, "I can get some plants later, maybe Saturday, and we can plant them then. We can go ahead and plant what we got today."

Ruth agreed, but Bea snuffled and whimpered at the idea of putting off any aspect of the garden. With her eyes teary and her voice quavering, she said, "No! It needs to be today. Today is the day for planting, and it may be too late already. Randy'll just have to ride into town and get some tomato plants."

Randy surprised the ladies and himself. "I'll pick up some plants Saturday morning and plant them then. I'm gonna finish the rows and planting the seeds this afternoon, while there's enough light." He noticed the look of disbelief on Mrs. Stempton's face—that he would assert himself that way—but he didn't wait for further discussion. He was climbing back onto the tractor when Aunt Ruth declared, "Well, Bea, I think he's right. Let's leave him to keep working while you and me ride to the hardware store. That way, we might can get it all done this afternoon. I can put the tomato plants in myself, if you show me where you want them. I won't have time to fix supper, but we can open a can of soup or make sandwiches."

Mrs. Stempton's lip quivered. "Okay."

Randy breathed a sigh of relief as he started the tractor. Ruth, taking hold of Bea's wheelchair, called out over the engine, "We'll be back in a little while, with some tomato plants. This way she can pick out the prettiest ones." Randy nodded from the seat, engaged the clutch, and shifted his attention to steering a straight path through the soil.

The women left him with a sense of relief over dodging a sensitive issue. He would not go back to that Prathersville store, but he didn't want to explain himself to the women. They didn't need to know everything. But wait: they would find out what happened when they went in for the plants. Everyone in town understood his relationship to the Stempton women, and those Waldrop boys would probably tell them their side of the story. Too bad. It couldn't be helped. If the ladies confronted him with it, he would simply explain what had happened. He had done nothing wrong, and he would not be sorry for standing up for his friend.

As he worked, Randy's thoughts turned to Stacy and the fact that he'd not seen her for what seemed like forever. A month had elapsed since their night together, and the new season, only a promise then, had now reached its height. His memories of that night were more vivid than his recollection of yesterday's activities, but they'd become a source of despondency.

Laying off the rows was going smoothly. Realizing he'd be finished before the ladies returned, he notched the throttle lever down to make the job last longer. Without the women there he wouldn't know how much fertilizer to put in each row. He guessed, as he was nearing the end of his last pass, that he could go back through the plot with a hoe or his hands and break up clumps until they returned. He wanted to make this garden a good one. Then, as he was about to shut off the engine, he saw her.

From where he sat on the tractor, a stretch of road beyond the gravel drive was visible through the trees. Stacy's Valiant was approaching, slowing to turn in. He caught a glimpse of her in the driver's seat. Butterflies surged from his groin all the way to the top of his head, making his scalp tingle. She'd come finally, and he would be able to talk to her without the squelching effect of the disapproving ladies. He steered out of the garden, killed the engine, and stepped off the tractor.

His hands were dirty, but he couldn't find anything to wipe them on. His jeans would have to do. Then he ran his fingers through his long hair, pushing it back from his forehead. He leaned against the tractor and waited for the familiar sound of gravel crunching in the drive. But the sound didn't come. Where had Stacy gone? Maybe she stopped at the mailbox, but that wouldn't take long. He stilled his breathing and listened. Through the midday sounds of insects and chirping birds he heard it: the receding drone of her car moving away. She'd passed up the driveway of her home place, but why? Why had she been on that road to begin with if she wasn't going to stop and visit her mother?

The answer, when it hit, jolted him like a body block in a vacant-lot football game. He stood there tasting dirt after the sudden impact: Stacy was avoiding him, had been avoiding him ever since that night when he'd made love to her.

This couldn't be. She'd responded to him, loved him back and told him so. Why would she drive away now at the sight of him? But she may not have seen him at all. She could have gone by for any number of reasons, and as Randy looked for plausible ones there came the sound he'd been seeking, of car tires on gravel. Had she turned the Valiant around? No. The ladies were back from Prathersville Hardware and Supply with tomato plants for him to put in the ground. Now he would have to respond to them and all their directives and conflicting opinions.

The remainder of the afternoon was miserable, made more so by the women's attempt to reprimand him for his behavior at the hardware store. They were placing the tomato plants and their little cups into the loose soil after he'd methodically planted the seeds and covered the rows according to their directions. Ruth, actually helping with this part of the task, remarked offhandedly that they had heard about his "little incident" at the store. He looked up and saw her pursed mouth and Mrs. Stempton's lowered head shaking back and forth, denouncing his unfortunate lapse in judgment. Randy, on his knees, looked back down and continued to press dirt gently around a tender new plant.

"In a rural community like this, we have to be very careful in our dealings with others," Ruth pointed out.

Mrs. Stempton sniffed and haltingly said, "We have . . . our . . . reputations—"

"That's right," Ruth offered. "People are judged sometimes by their . . . *associations*, and the behavior of those around them."

"I ain't got nothing against the colored," Mrs. Stempton blurted out, suddenly finding her voice, "as long as they keep their place. But I don't want folks thinking I'm a nigger-lover. You've got to remember that boy—Buster—is a niggra. Worse than that: he's a high-yellow."

Randy stood. "Buster is—no matter what you think of him—my friend . . . my best and only friend. And you should know that if it weren't for him, the contract with Mr. Jenkins would never have been finished. Buster contributes just as much as I do to this . . . *household*. I won't have him insulted by rude, spoiled boys, and I won't be sorry for what I did." He looked from one face to the other as the women dropped their eyes. A second passed before Ruth lifted her gaze to respond. Randy cut her off: "That's all I got to say, and all I want to hear about it."

He left as soon as the job was done. Ruth half-heartedly offered to fix him a sandwich, but he declined, saying, "Naa, thanks anyway. I've got some leftovers in the fridge."

He didn't go straight to the shack but rode around the back roads for a while. As the sun was setting, he found himself crossing the Hominy Creek bridge at Eason's Mill. He pulled the truck over and killed the engine. He sat there watching the sky turn pink and orange, listening to water gurgling over smooth stones and the crickets and tree frogs tuning their instruments. Time was flowing like the water, a lapping, rushing flow carrying life and death, life in death . . . love. Was there such a thing? Or was this life simply a matter of fulfilling biological urges, like crickets singing before death, a mindless mating song? Perhaps it was that simple: urges and desire were nothing more than components of the reproductive cycle. No need to be so damn emotional about it.

But he was emotional. Tears pooled and threatened to spill as he puzzled over his place in the natural order. He blinked, patted his wet eyes with his sleeve. The sky slowly darkened as the creek gurgled, and stars appeared in the gloaming. He got out of the cab and hopped up on the back of the flat bed. He sat there with his legs dangling, looking up as the voices of more and more creatures joined in nature's symphony. The sounds were not altogether soothing. The chirpings and croaking were accusatory and angry, with an undercurrent of grief. The whippoorwill's song was one of loneliness, and the owl, instead of pouring wisdom from its throat, produced only an off-key monotony. Canines in the distance—dogs or coyotes—in trying to boast, revealed fear and suspicion. Competition and strife pervaded the animal kingdom. The stars seemed cold in their distance, surgical in their precision. Only the water and air, inanimate yet containing and transporting life, offered comfort. The cool breeze pressed his cheek and dried his eyes, while the creek's gurgling held the promise of renewal, hope, and clear flowing purpose.

His head began to hum, and he felt he was falling under the spell of an irresistible influence, like the marijuana he'd smoked with Stacy. The trees around him gave up their individuality to the darkness, merged, and marched inward. He thought about how reality shifted under the weight of changing circumstances. Each creature around him generated waves and patterns from the center of its universe, selfishly influencing others. He felt a fresh kinship with them, along with the people he knew, all trying to make sense of their own little worlds. He, Stacy, Buster, and even Ty, were part of this constant humming—needing, seeking, trying to get. Good and evil merged in his mind, a connected string of selfish actions. A memory came of that last foster home and the time he'd spent with Jack and Emma. They'd taken him in, along with other boys, having established their purpose beforehand. His legs began to ache from the edge they were dangling over. He looked up again at the stars and saw them as tiny, white holes—flaws in the fabric of darkness.

He slid down from his seat. Tired, hungry, and lonelier than before, he got back in the truck and drove to the shack. He ate a bologna sandwich, watched television, sat on the porch and smoked, drank a beer, fed the dogs, took a bath, flipped stations on the TV, turned off the TV, and stared at the dark patterns in the grain of the pine-planked walls. Finally, he got out his scrapbook, thick with clippings, and began to flip through the pages. He barely looked as he turned them. He'd read all the articles several times, and now they were dead to him. School board and city council meetings, ongoing work on the new sewer system, car wrecks, and house fires all seemed insignificant. He moved quickly to the last item, Stacy's wedding announcement, dated nearly four months ago. He looked at the grainy picture of Stacy in her wedding gown. The caption read, "Mrs. Stacy Stempton Ragsdale." He slapped the book shut and tossed it on top of the growing newspaper stack in the corner, then opened a beer, facing the prospect of another evening alone.

But this night was different. A new, terrible knowledge was growing inside him of the necessity of selfish action. He could no longer grow moss on his back while the river of life flowed past. Decisive movement was the sculptor of reality, and he felt the power of creation coursing throughout his body. He couldn't build his life on hope and pure chance. Driven by these feelings, Randy decided to go see Stacy at her apartment. He imagined himself knocking on her door and looking into her eyes when she opened it. He would ask her why she'd been avoiding him. And he would let her know that all his future plans included her, that he couldn't go on without her, that he would do whatever it took to have her at his side.

There was no hurry, though. He decided to wait until after midnight to leave. This should be a work night for Ty. If he didn't see the blue GTO when he pulled up to the drive, he would know his nemesis was away for the night. Under those circumstances—face to face with Stacy, Ty gone—who knew what might happen? Something. That much was certain. He opened another beer and tried to relax, indulging himself in luxurious recollections of times spent with her. That time when they'd gone to Aaronville and picnicked at the college had been the best. He laughed, thinking about getting stoned and those crazy, aggressive ducks—the "cruel ducks." He should have kissed Stacy that day. He realized now that he could have, but he'd let the moments slip by until they were on Front Campus Drive looking at the back of Ty's car. He didn't like to think about that part, squatting there in that bush, hiding. He moved to other times with Stacy, trying to piece together the history of their relationship, searching for hidden meanings in words and gestures. It was all there—his destiny—and tonight he was going to claim it.

Midnight finally arrived. He opened another beer for the road and headed out into the darkness. Except for where his headlights shone, the moonless night was black around him. Even the stars were obscured by cloud cover. There was no one awake in the few occupied houses along the dirt road, no artificial lights from late-night TV watchers to suggest a sense of companionship, only the baying of hounds as he passed the home of a coon hunter, a man who raised dogs; the canine sounds made him feel more alone, like the only human on earth. He'd been lonely inside his shack, but the world outside was even lonelier, too dark and quiet. He decided to take the Prathersville Highway into town rather than the back way. Along the highway there'd be lights and opportunity for interaction with other motorists through the ritual of headlight dimming.

Rolling along that ten-mile stretch, his sense of connection was reestablished. He met several cars and at least a dozen tractor-trailer rigs. Clicking and re-clicking the floorboard switch was a friendly activity, like a casual wave or nod. Each person he met was wrapped up in his own desires, but dipping the lights acknowledged they were in this together, vibrating instruments within a swelling symphony.

At the edge of town, he passed the truck stop, lighted and bustling. The parking area in back was full of tractor-trailers, and several cars and pickups were parked in the spaces in front of the all-night restaurant. Randy felt a sudden urge to go in and have a cheeseburger, coffee, and maybe some conversation, but he shook it off. The empty feeling in his stomach was appropriate to the task before him. So he kept driving into the lighted sections of town, where there were storefronts, side streets, and neighborhoods.

The red lights at this hour were set to caution mode. He barely slowed as he drove through them. Soon he was on the avenue that passed Jupiter Mills. He knew well the street that would take him into the mill village, although he'd avoided Stacy's neighborhood since that night when he'd first met her and slept on her couch. Ty, even though he hadn't been there, had loomed in the background then, and he was looming now. He would be at work, though, Randy felt sure, but still. . ... Best to keep eyes peeled for that blue car.

The side streets lay quiet in the soft glow of streetlights. The tenants of the mill houses, weary from their workdays, had long ago lain down to sleep. But Stacy would still be up. She may have had to work this evening at the Billy Goat Bar. If that were the case, she would probably be getting home about now. If she wasn't there, she would be soon. He could circle the neighborhood until he found her car in the drive. That might not be a good idea, he realized. A paranoid resident could notice his behavior and call the police. It had happened before. But tonight was different.

The faded red pickup was still on blocks in the same cluttered yard. When he'd passed it that other time, he'd been younger and confused. Almost there, only one more turn. As he approached Stacy's apartment, he saw her Valiant by itself in the driveway. A quick fluttering in his belly raised goosebumps. He turned in, killed the engine, and took a deep breath. Small voices in his mind murmured their doubts and fears, but he knew better than to listen. He pulled up on the clamped pair of Vice Grip pliers that served as the door handle and stepped out.

He rapped softly on the front door, listening for signs of life. Nothing. He knocked again, harder. The faint sound of water running. A sudden breeze kissed him gently with the odor of jonquils. One more time—he would knock one more time and if she didn't come, he would leave. That would be enough. At least he would have tried. He knocked again with his knuckles: three firm, evenly spaced raps. As if switched by that third blow, the porch light suddenly illuminated the vicinity in sickly white. The door opened, and there she stood, blinking, looking sleepy and confused.

"Randy. What are you doing?"

"I came to see you. I want to talk."

Standing in the doorway, she leaned forward, looking up and down the street. "What about?" She wore a man's faded flannel shirt, red and green plaid, which hung to her knees. She held the fabric closed above the top button, covering her neck.

"Stacy. You know what. I want to talk about us and why you've been avoiding me."

"It's late. You shouldn't be here. I was in bed." She leaned back inside, one hand holding the door.

Her posture was not what he'd expected. The words he thought he would say were no longer available. "Are you just gonna stand there like that," he finally asked, "after everything that's happened between us? Don't you know who I am? Don't you remember?"

"A lot has happened, Randy. That's what life is, a bunch of stuff happening. Some of it maybe shouldn't happen—wouldn't happen if people didn't make mistakes."

"No. It's not a mistake. My loving you is not a mistake, neither is my being here. I want us to be together." He reached out to touch her hair. She pulled back, then released the fabric at her neck to take his hand.

"Randy, listen. I never meant to hurt you. You're wonderful, and I can never repay all you did for us. But fact is, I'm a married woman. What happened at your place that night shouldn't have happened. It was my fault. Don't blame yourself—"

"There's no blame. I don't regret what happened. I still believe in us, that we should be together, whether you're married or not. You can leave him. You know what he is—"

"He's my husband, Randy. You don't know him." She let go of his hand. "And there's something else you don't know about." Her hands went to her tummy, the fingers tracing light circles on the flannel. She looked down and said in a hushed tone of reverence, "Me and Ty's gonna have a baby."

Gravity pulled hard then, and it was all Randy could do to remain standing. He tried to find her eyes, but they were averted. She pushed gently against his shoulder. "I'm sorry, Randy, but I can't see you no more. You'd better go now." Then she withdrew, pushing the door closed against him. The bolt, turned from inside, clicked into place.

Chapter 43

Ty Ragsdale was struggling with ways to convince his wife of his faithfulness and himself of hers as he shifted the GTO through the gears. He slipped apprehensively through the side streets of the Crack, quiet at this early hour, back toward the main part of town. He was wary of his surroundings as well as the circumstances of his marriage. Something had not been right that day when he'd come home to a freshly scrubbed apartment to find his wife so sweet and eager to please, as if she was trying to make up for something. Making love to her had felt different, like returning to a vacated house that had been occupied and redecorated in his absence.

A changed relationship began that day. He responded in kind as she seemed eager to reclaim the marriage, to show love, passion, and common courtesy. But Ty couldn't help wondering if there'd been an event that triggered Stacy's increased devotion. In the days leading up to Morning of the Clean Apartment, he had felt her beginning to pull away, asserting herself more, questioning him about his work hours and whereabouts, letting things go at the apartment as if to challenge his authority. Then something slipped. He'd left for work one evening and come home the next day to a different wife and home. And now, since he'd learned she was pregnant, his feelings swung wildly between joy, anger, and despair.

He was tormented by what might have happened in his absence. Sometimes he thought the worst; other times he was able to convince himself—temporarily, at least—that Stacy wasn't that way. She wasn't the kind of girl who cheated, and he was certain of her love for him. After the way he had loved her, she couldn't possibly want anyone else. But he'd been away an awful lot. Loneliness can drive people to all sorts of things. He remembered the words of advice from his father who'd said from his recliner, between smoky coughs and sips of whisky, *Women are just like us, son. They want it all the time too. They just don't go about getting their strange in quite the same way.*

*Most of them won't turn down a good opportunity, though. You can
bet on that.*

He hated to admit it, but, from his own experience, Ty knew his
father's words were true. And there were those evenings when he'd
left her alone while he, after lying about his work hours, experienced
life in another sphere, the Crack, with his new friend, Tommy Lee
Chism. He'd lied to her repeatedly while playing recklessly with their
marriage. He realized, after the recent turn in their relationship, that
she was capable of similar behavior, but that's where the comparison
ended. He did what he did as a man; he felt no guilt over the fact that
he was slipping away, under cover of predawn darkness, from the bed
of a young black woman whose man was away in Aaronville, working
the third shift at Southern Pipe and Tube.

Ty had not actually lied about going into work. He had worked
for a couple of hours to make sure Tommy Lee's machine was
properly set up and he'd be able to handle their only pending order,
a small run of Buick hubcap insignias. Tomcat winked when Ty left
to clock out because he was privy to the arrangement and had acted
as liaison. Ty had been at the plant long enough for his clothes to
absorb the oily machine odors of the place. Now it was time, the
wink seemed to say, to take care of some different business, the
business of sowing seed, of getting some strange, of being young and
full of spunk.

It had been easy setting things up with the girl, Belinda. She had
shown interest the first time he met her at Lamar's Place. Ty had been
there shooting nine ball with Tomcat one evening before work, doing
a little friendly wagering while Willie and several other men watched
and placed bets on the side. They were playing for a dollar a game,
and Ty was careful to make the match seem competitive. He didn't
want the men to know how good he was and how easy it would be
for him to win. He wanted things to come out about even, so he
could enjoy playing there for a while before he walked away with
everyone's money. That could happen at some point in the future;
there was no hurry.

He was startled by the appearance of a sexy female in this
masculine world. She had come in to announce to her uncle Willie

that his wife needed him at home to fix a drainpipe. Her manner was nonchalant. She'd obviously been in before and felt comfortable around these men who were old friends and acquaintances or relatives. She seemed to welcome their appraising glances when everyone, even the four guys at the back table, turned to look at her. She was chocolate brown with a short afro and darting black eyes. Her lips were plump as ripe figs, red along their outer edges, shading to pink where they parted to reveal straight white teeth and a pink tongue. She paused between the first two tables, looked at each man in turn. She placed her hands on her hips and leaned forward. "Uncle Willie, you better get home now. Aunt Mavis getting pretty upset. Drain done come loose on the kitchen sink again and she trying to wash up the dishes. Water running everywhere."

Ty, who had been lining up a shot when she came in, raised himself from the table. He kept watching her, even after she stopped talking. She smiled, and her eyes glistened in that instant when they met his, leaving the imprint of desire in his mind. She turned back to Willie, who slowly eased his bulk down from a stool, shook his head, pulled the wet stub of a cigar from his mouth and pressed it with his good hand into the crunchy litter of a dented metal receptacle. "Damn. Always one damn thing or another. Man can't get no peace."

The girl smiled, "Aw hell, Uncle, you be getting plenty of peace, if that's what you call hanging out at this pool hall. You here from the time Lamar opens till he closes every night. How much peace you need?"

The guys laughed, and Willie shook his head as he shuffled toward the door. His right arm was bent at the elbow, and the hook where his hand should be repeatedly reached into space a jerk ahead of each step. The girl's eyes met Ty's again as she was turning to leave. He smiled despite himself, then watched the movement of her round rump in tight hip-hugger jeans. At the door she called out, "You boys take it easy now, and don't get too much peace."

Laughter circulated before Ty noticed Tomcat looking at him. Tomcat raised his chin and grinned. "It's your shot, man," he said as the chuckles subsided.

"I know." Ty leaned over the table and placed his bridge hand on the felt. He sensed that Tomcat and the other men were watching him now, as if they'd noticed those looks between him and the young woman and were wondering what he would do next, if he'd be ballsy enough to make some comment acknowledging his interest in the sexy black girl. His mind had followed her out the door, but he didn't want to give anything away. He lowered his chin and sighted along the stick. The shot was long but nearly straight in, the eight-ball. He could make it easily, then the money ball, which was situated on the rail near the pocket at the other end of the table. The game was practically over, and he would be expected to take this one. He pumped the stick twice, then made his shot with top English on the cue ball to provide shape for the next shot. The eight-ball rolled toward the corner but hit the side rail at the pocket and wallowed out.

Ty said, "Shit."

Tomcat shook his head as he leaned over to finish the game. "Looks like somebody lost his concentration."

Ty shrugged and managed a grin. Tomcat dispatched the last two balls, and Ty handed over a dollar. He checked his watch. "Looks like you got me this time. We'll have to pick up where we left off later. 'Bout time to be heading on in to work." They placed their sticks in the rack. At the door Ty waved to the guys. "See y'all later."

Lamar answered, as he racked balls at the end table, "Yeah man, later." The other men, absorbed in their games, grunted or nodded.

As Ty steered them out of the Crack toward WM, Tomcat said, "You know, nine ball's a fast game. Can't afford to lose concentration and make mistakes like you did back there. Seemed like you weren't paying attention."

"Yeah, well, it happens. Sometimes a man gets distracted."

Tomcat smiled. "Your distraction's got a name, Belinda. Willie her uncle. She stay just one block over from my place with this older man, Bodie. He gone a lot, though. Works graveyard, like us, all the way over in Aaronville." He leaned forward in his seat, looked Ty in the face, lowered his voice: "Word is she be having some extracurricular activities, but folks don't discuss it. You interested in getting distracted some more? I can talk to her. Something might could be worked out."

"Sure, why not?" Ty grinned as he shifted the GTO into fourth gear on the main avenue. He pressed the gas, kicking in the four-barrel. He reveled in the force that pushed him against the seat and the bass note of the engine's insatiable suction. He wanted Tomcat to feel it also.

Tomcat answered, "Man, this bitch'll damn sure fly!"

Now, slipping out of the Crack, Ty smiled. He was trying to decide if the stories he'd heard as a boy were true, that black women were hotter. She'd been plenty hot, that was for sure. He eased along in third gear, barely above idle, trying not to attract attention. He was on his way home to his pregnant wife, and he would arrive there at the expected time, a little after seven. He had some time to kill, though, because he needed to get out of the Crack before daylight, when folks started stirring. It wasn't even six yet. He could stop by the truck stop and grab a bite. Being seen there wouldn't matter. He could always say he'd just gotten off a little early, had left things with Tomcat, which was true. Everything seemed to work out, if you kept a clear head and paid attention. Paying attention was the key, and with that thought his mind turned back to his wife and the way she'd been behaving.

Chapter 44

After his brief visit with Stacy, Randy drove back to the shack, sick, angry, and intent on leaving. He threw some things into a duffel bag, but just before dawn he unpacked almost as hastily. He'd been seeing over and over a replay of Stacy's fingers circling her belly through the flannel of Ty's shirt. There was a baby in there, and it occurred to him, as the sky was beginning to lighten, that it might not be Ty's. Stacy could just as easily be carrying his child. He dumped his belongings back onto the bed: jeans, socks, underwear, work shirts, boots, his extra belt, a couple of books. At first, he'd only entertained the possibility; then it crystallized into probability. By the next afternoon he'd convinced himself that the baby was his, and this knowledge made it impossible for him to leave.

He sat on the porch and rocked. The hounds, hoping for food, a kind word, or a pat on the head came sidling up, wriggling their hindquarters, but they soon sensed their master's mood and slinked, tails tucked, back down the warped steps to their usual places underneath the porch. Randy rocked and stared into space, thinking about the garden he'd planted a couple of days earlier and how he didn't give a damn if it came up or not. Mrs. Stempton and Aunt Ruth probably had a list of chores for him, but he wasn't going over there today. He just didn't feel like it. He wondered what Buster was doing, but he didn't want to see him either, with all his perceptiveness, pat answers, and Bible verses. What could he do with this Saturday and the days to follow? If he gathered his things and left, his baby would grow up with that fool Ty for a father. Randy, with a blank spot in his memories where a father should be, couldn't allow his child to be raised by that smirking, violence-prone, redneck. Cutting off a hand would be easier.

But staying and watching from the sidelines while the real family lived what was real life would be unbearable also: his child being raised by a man he hated, the man who had also claimed his woman, the love he felt he'd rightfully earned. He was unable to imagine any acceptable scenarios. Mrs. Stempton, with her mounting medical expenses; Aunt Ruth, with her need to be in charge; Stacy, with her mixed-up needs; Buster, with financial burdens; and now a brand-new person, his child, with a batch of unforeseen needs—all seemed to be grabbing at him at once, either shouting directions, crying, or quoting the Bible. He needed them to hush. Maybe by staring past the trees, fields, and rolling hills on the horizon, into the blank sky for long enough he could think of a way to survive this hell.

He sat there for a long time, rousing himself only for necessities. The hounds respected his solitude and stayed under the porch, occasionally scratching or snuffling to one another. They were lazy dogs. Randy envied their ability to exist in a state of untroubled inactivity, with no expectations or desires beyond their basic needs—unless something came along and tempted them, a raccoon, rabbit, or another dog. As long as they had some chow, a place to lie down, and an occasional scratch behind the ears, they were content. Randy knew that he could be also, that it wouldn't take much. Why, though, were the few things he needed always just out of reach? He imagined himself as a dog, not a lazy porch hound but a greyhound chasing a mechanical rabbit. He could run himself to death and never get what he wanted. Having a life meant finding a way to get off the track.

But nothing came. He finally realized he was hungry and was contemplating how much trouble it would be to get up and fix a sandwich when he heard the sound of tires on the dirt road. The vehicle was approaching from a distance, but cars hardly ever came by. Could someone be coming to see him? He trembled in anticipation. Should he rise and freshen himself up?

But of course, it wasn't her. It was Buster in his momma's Chevrolet. He parked the car in slow, deliberate movements next to the flatbed and got out while Randy watched from his rocker. Neither spoke as Buster walked toward the steps. He paused at the sight of his friend sitting in a porch rocker on a perfectly good Saturday afternoon and threw up his hand in mock enthusiasm. "What's happening, bro? Thought I'd come by and check on you, since you didn't show up for work yesterday. You awright?"

"Nothing's happening, man. I'm just not feeling well. Sorry about yesterday. I should have called."

"Ain't no big thing. You the boss, remember? You can take off work whenever you want to."

"No. I should've called. I'd expect you to let me know if you weren't coming to work. I don't know why I didn't. I've just got so much on my mind."

Buster mounted the steps and took the rocker next to Randy's. "Now you mention it, I do need to be off Monday. I've got to take Momma back to the doctor."

"Back to the doctor? I didn't know she'd been seeing a doctor. What's wrong?"

"Well, that's just it. I took her last week—that day we knocked off early so you could go plant Mrs. Stempton's garden—and they want me to bring her back for more tests. She been having lots of problems lately, female problems, and hurting too."

Randy looked at his friend, saw the strain in his face. "I'm sorry to hear that. I'm sure they'll get her fixed up. You take all the time you need and let me know if I can help with anything."

Buster nodded, looked at his shoes, stopped rocking. "I can't stand seeing my momma suffer. She try not to show it, but I can tell when she hurting, and it makes me hurt, just looking at her."

Randy nodded.

One of the hounds decided to be friendly. She wiggled her way up one step at a time, tongue out, sloppy mouth in a smile. Buster said, "Come on up, Belle, come on girl."

"*Belle?*"

"Yeah. Don't you know your own dog's name?"

"Hell no. Didn't even know she had a name. Where did you get that?"

"It just come to me. I guess 'cause of the way she was shaking her back end coming up the steps, kinda ringing her bell. Naming things, that's another of my many talents." Buster scratched the dog's head. She sat at his feet.

"Naming dogs is certainly a useful talent. Maybe you can name the other two while you're at it."

"Naa. Can't force it. I got to be inspired. And I'd need to actually see 'em doing something besides laying under the porch licking themselves."

"I guess they'll go nameless then, since that's about all they do. I haven't done a very good job with these dogs, have I?"

"Well, most folks do name their pets."

"I've always got so much on my mind, and now . . . I can't even see straight. Maybe I should give the hounds away. There's a man out the road here, a hunter, who offered to take them. He took the pups when . . . *Belle* had her litter. You remember, before you explained to me what that pen out back was for. What do you think? Should I let the man take them?"

"One less thing to worry about, and you'd know they'd have a good home."

They rocked in a silence that was soothing, like a warm bath after a grueling day.

Randy said, "I'm getting kinda hungry. What about you? Had lunch yet?"

The comfortable quiet followed them into the kitchen, where they devoured peanut butter sandwiches, potato chips, and a half-gallon of milk.

Buster turned up his glass, finished it off, and wiped his mouth. "That gal done made you miserable, ain't she?"

Randy shook his head. "Way past miserable. I'm at hopeless and desperate now."

"I know you're in love and all, but can't you just give up and move on, find another girl, one who ain't married?"

Randy fingered the last corner of his sandwich into his mouth and chewed thoughtfully. When he spoke, his voice reverberated in his ears: "She's pregnant."

"Oh hell! You thinking that baby might be yours?"

"I believe it is. But she won't talk to me, doesn't want to see me anymore. Says she wants to stay married to Ty, the guy who hits her and runs around on her."

Well, shoot. I mean there ain't nothing. . .. What you think you gon' do, anyway?"

"That's why I been sitting here for two days. I don't know what to do. But you don't need to worry over my problems. You got enough of your own."

"Bible says not to worry. 'Be anxious for nothing.' Know what we're supposed to do in times like these?"

"I give up, what?"

"We're supposed to pray for each other. Hold each other up before the Lord."

"I'm not much for praying. You know that. Don't feel like I even know how."

"Maybe it's time you learned, bro. You facing some serious shit here, more'n you can handle alone."

Randy wiped the crumbs off the table into his hand, carried the glasses to the sink, and placed the milk jug back inside the fridge.

Buster said, "All you gotta do is trust the Lord and call on him. He'll be there for you."

Randy wasn't sure about God being there for him, but he sensed that Buster would be. He was glad his friend had come over. "Tell me again about your mother. What do the doctors think is wrong?"

Chapter 45

Buster's momma was admitted to the hospital on Monday for overnight observation. The details of admission, release, doctors' instructions, and medication would keep Buster busy until Wednesday. With his friend occupied, there wasn't much for Randy to do at the job site. They had already cut enough big logs to finish out a load. Getting them winched up onto the truck was a two-man operation. Randy used the time off mainly for moping and deliberation, but by Tuesday his attitude had mellowed, and he decided to go check on the Stempton ladies.

He realized when he pulled in that he needed to cut the grass, and there would be other chores waiting for him. Somebody had to do it. Maybe working through the day would help him get his mind off things, help the time pass. Aunt Ruth greeted him on the porch. "Praise the Lord, the prodigal has returned. Where you been, son? We were beginning to think you'd abandoned us."

He heard Bea whoop from inside, "Whooee!" Then Ruth hugged him, pressing her bosom against him. She led him into the kitchen for "brunch"—bacon, lettuce, and tomato sandwiches, cantaloupe, and chocolate cake.

Before he left late that afternoon, the yard was cut and trimmed, the furniture in the parlor was rearranged to allow more room for Bea's wheelchair, and the new garden was watered. The day passed easier than he'd expected, and with mid-week approaching, Randy felt eager to get back to the woods, truck, and saws and to spend time with Buster.

He drove into the Crack the next morning to find his friend waiting for him in his rocker at the appointed time. But something was different. Buster didn't smile and wave as he usually did, and the front door remained closed. From inside the truck Randy sensed new problems; when Buster sat down beside him, he saw the flesh around his friend's right eye was purple and swollen, leaving only a narrow slit for the golden iris to peek through.

Randy said, "Shit, man. What happened?"

"Let's don't make no big deal out of this."

"Big deal out of what? Who you been fighting?"

Buster didn't want to talk about it, but Randy wouldn't start the truck until he knew what had happened. Buster's insistence that it was "just a little accident and a misunderstanding" served only to elevate Randy's curiosity.

"What kind of accident?"

"Routine thing, fender-bender I guess you'd call it."

Bit by bit Randy gathered that Buster, in his Momma's Chevrolet, had been rear-ended driving out of the Crack. He had been on his way back to the hospital on the morning of his mother's admittance to deliver her gown, slippers, and other necessary items for the overnight stay.

"What caused it," Buster said, "was ol' Miss Mercedine pulling out in front of me, on her way to the grocery store. I had to slam on brakes to keep from hitting her. Then from out of nowhere came a banging against my rear end, hard enough to snap my head back."

"I can see you getting a sore neck from the impact, but that doesn't explain the black eye."

"Like I said, a misunderstanding."

"Damn! You're a pain in the ass sometimes. Why don't you just tell me what happened? Obviously you got in a fight with the person who rammed you. But that's not like you. You're gonna have to give me the details."

Randy pieced together most of what happened through his own imagination, as Buster kept a tight grip on the facts. Getting the name out of him was the most difficult. Randy, considering Buster's possible motives for concealing, was near to figuring it out when Buster finally gave up and told who the other driver was. Who else but Ty Ragsdale? Damn! That son-of-a-bitch again.

And there had been someone with him, a black guy called Tomcat who'd moved in a while back from Atlanta. So, it was two against one, that's how Buster came out on the short end. Buster had simply been trying to do the right thing by calling the police and filing a report.

He'd not been at fault, and his car was damaged—bent bumper and broken taillight lens. But Ty didn't want to hang around.

No. He wouldn't, since he and his friend both smelled of booze at ten in the morning. And he would want to avoid having a police report filed placing him in the Crack at that time. He wouldn't want Stacy to know he'd been hanging out there instead of working. So, when Buster insisted that he stay at the scene and wait for the police, things got rough.

Despite Buster's reluctance to tell the story, Randy's imagining of it was accurate. As Ty was about to leave the scene, Buster had said "What about my car? We're supposed to get the police to come out and look at what happened."

Ty answered, "Look man, I ain't got time to hang around and wait for the cops. But you can trust me for the damages. Send me a bill. You know me. I'm in the book."

When he turned to get back in his GTO, Buster grabbed his arm. "Wait. You can't leave the scene of an accident—"

Ty spun around and knocked Buster's arm away. "I told you dammit, I ain't got time to hang around here. Keep your damn yellow hands off me before you get hurt."

With mounting anger Buster stepped in to grab him again. Ty stopped him with a quick, well-aimed left jab. Buster was shocked for an instant.

Ty said, "I warned you dammit. Now back off Yellow Boy."

Tomcat thought this was funny. "Hell yes, he fast and crazy too! You better get the hell back on your little momma's boy errand 'fore things get worse."

Suddenly furious, Buster started swinging, catching Ty with a couple of shots to the chest and ribs. Then his arms quit working when Tomcat slipped in from behind and wrapped him up in a full nelson. Ty's face registered the familiar smirk as he took aim at the easy target. He slammed a straight right into Buster's gut, doubling him over. Tomcat let go and Buster collapsed onto the street.

Ty said, "You don't hit near as hard as that dumb-ass brother of yours that got killed in Nam—Stinkum. He was a real genius, but maybe you're smarter. Smart enough to know who not to mess with."

Tomcat said, "Les go, man."

Buster, struggling for breath, tried to rise. The doors slammed shut on the GTO. Ty started it up, revved the engine, barked the tires as he backed up to maneuver around Buster and the Chevy. He called out as they pulled away, "Like I said, send me a bill, and don't work too hard with your queer boss-man from Pittsburgh."

When he had gotten all he could out of Buster, Randy said, "We can't let this go. Something's got to be done."

"Now hold on. Remember, we got to leave judgment to the Lord."

"I'm not talking about judgment, just making things right. That bastard banged up your mother's car and attacked you."

"They's a time for sowing and a time for reaping, a season for everything under the sun. They'll come a time for making things right. But for now, we got to concentrate on our other problems."

They were still sitting in Buster's driveway, in the flatbed with the windows down. Randy brought the side of his fist down like a hammer on the metal dashboard. "Damn!" He gritted his teeth and looked out the window.

Buster said, "Come on, les move. We got a half-loaded truck waiting for us on the side of a mountain."

"Yeah, yeah. Okay. But I'm not letting this go."

"Like I said, my Momma's sick, you got . . . *personal* problems, and we got logs to haul. I ain't worrying over Ty Ragsdale right now."

"Maybe you're not, but I am. That son-of-a-bitch needs to die."

Chapter 46

Randy and Buster's routine of cutting, loading, and hauling logs reestablished itself with the inclusion of daily admonishments from Buster about harboring anger and the importance of "leaving judgment to the Lord." Spring gave way to summer, the sun resumed its role as punisher, and the garden grew, with the help of the occasional thunder shower and Randy's regular tending.

Stacy's stomach was also beginning to grow. As summer ripened, Randy found his path crossing hers more often, even though he'd given up on trying to make that happen. She'd begun stopping by more regularly now, with visible tummy bulge, to visit her mother. The inevitable meetings grew less awkward as summer wore on, and he was encouraged that she'd at least stopped trying to avoid him.

There was a different kind of feeling when he was around her now, a soft glow, but it only lasted while they were together at the home place. When she left to go back to Ty, those other feelings returned: bitterness, hatred, anger.

Sometimes she tried to recapture their old way of being together, joking and calling him "City Boy," but it wasn't the same. Things could never be as they were before. Even though Stacy's eyes were as beautiful as ever, they darted away whenever he tried to latch on. Randy saw much in those skittish eyes: fear, pain, and the need for someone to step in and rescue her from a life she never wanted.

An array of human needs, along with Stacy's, echoed between them whenever they were all at the house together: Bea, widowed and afflicted; Ruth, forced into the uncomfortable role of caregiver; and Randy, seeking a way to cast off these burdens and to live his own life. By August the combined level of discomfort was approaching crisis point.

Late in the month, on a sticky Saturday morning, the women were on the porch drinking iced tea and fanning themselves when Randy drove up. Ruth stood as soon as he got out of the truck. "Finally . . . praise the Lord! We got a serious problem. We need a man's help."

This was nothing out of the ordinary. On most Saturdays when Randy came over to check on things, the ladies were having some sort of emergency. He had recently tended to a frayed power cord on the attic fan, leaking faucets in the kitchen, and a flat tire on Ruth's Oldsmobile. He had driven over this morning expecting chores, but hoping, at least, for routine mindless work. These hopes evaporated into the summer sky when he heard the exasperation in Ruth's voice.

"What is it this time?" he said, stepping onto the porch. "I was looking forward to a normal day around here."

Stacy shook her head. "No such luck, City Boy. You ought to know by now nothing's ever normal around here."

"Yeah, right. But, you know, a guy can always hope."

"You ain't gonna like today's emergency," Stacy said. "It's a little worse than usual."

"It's bad, Randy," Ruth said, wringing her hands. "I hate for you to go back there, but something's got to be done."

Bea said, "It's a mess!"

Randy forced a smile. "After living here for a year, I'm used to messes. Might as well get at it."

Ruth led the way down the hall toward the back of the house. The smell of the place was worse than usual, different from the normal musty scent of old women and sickness. This odor was more like the sewers of Pittsburgh. Ruth stopped and pointed at the bathroom door. "It won't flush, backed up something awful. Plunger don't help. It's done overflowed twice, and I had to get down on my hands and knees and clean it up. Now I don't know what to do."

Stacy, pushing her momma in the wheelchair, joined them in the hallway. The four of them stared at the door. Randy finally said, "Okay, let's take a look."

When he opened the door, the stench rolled out. Stacy said, "Damn. That's nasty."

Her momma said from the wheelchair, "Watch your language, young lady." Then she added, "Whooee, that stinks!"

Randy didn't say anything, but his mind reeled back to the time nearly a year ago when he had had to clean up the rotten aftermath of the old man's death. This couldn't be that bad. Before stepping inside, he said, "Let's get the box fan out of the kitchen and put it in the window. That'll make it a little easier to work in there."

Ruth turned to go get the fan. "Good idea. I'll be right back."

After Randy got the fan set up, Stacy leaned into the doorway and asked, "What you gonna do? You think you can fix it?"

"I dunno. May have to pull up the toilet and run a plumber's snake through the drainpipe. There's one hanging up in the barn."

"That's right. Daddy had some other plumbing stuff out there too, in that back stall. I'll go see what I can find."

"Yeah, I don't blame you. I mean, sure, that's a good idea. Might as well bring that snake."

"Okay." Stacy went out the back door. The ladies waited in the hall. Bea said, "That fan's helping some."

"Yep. It's not so bad." Randy stood gazing into the toilet bowl at the putrid brown sludge. He didn't know what to do. They'd already tried the plunger, and he didn't want to risk another overflow. Lifting the bowl off the floor would result in the leakage of more filth, and he would have to work with his face right in the mouth of the thing in order to get the fasteners and fittings loose. He mumbled, "Well, shit."

Ruth asked, "Do what?"

"Oh, nothing. Just thinking out loud."

"I guess you'll have to take the toilet up."

"Yeah. Guess so." Then the screen door slammed at the back of the house. Stacy called out from the kitchen, "Randy, I found something. Don't do anything yet."

She hurried past the ladies and stepped into the bathroom. She carried the plumber's snake coiled around her shoulder, and in her left hand a gallon jug. "Take a look at this." She leaned the coil against the wall. "I remember Daddy saying this was some good stuff."

"Yeah, okay. Let me check it out. But you don't need to be in here. You know, with all the germs." He glanced at her belly then back at her face as he took the jug.

"Guess you're right."

Randy read the label:

INDUSTRIAL STRENGTH CLOG-B-GONE

Quick Acting Acid Solution for Blasting Through Tough Drain Clogs

(To be used only by qualified professionals)

Directions: Pour no more than one cup of Clog-B-Gone directly into clogged drain. Powerful solution works through standing water and sludge. Allow ten minutes for the unique compounds to bust through and blast the blockage, then gently plunge. That's it! Flush your problems away. If blockage persists, mechanical augering or drain excavation may be required.

There was another paragraph of warnings he didn't bother to read. He was ready to flush his problems away. He turned the jug up and poured about half its contents into the toilet.

A hissing froth rose inside the bowl, accompanied by a sudden issue of acrid fumes. "Damn," Randy said, blinking and muttering.

Ruth asked, "What did you say?"

"Oh nothing. Just that this stuff seems to be working. We're supposed to give it a few minutes. Let's go back to the porch."

Outside the day was heating up. The garden was by now petered out, so there wasn't much to talk about. In his rocker, Randy pulled out his pack of Winstons. Stacy did the same. He looked at her middle, then her face. "You think you should be doing that?"

She met his gaze, then looked down at her stomach. "I'm trying to cut back, but quitting's hard."

Randy nodded, lit up, reached over and lit hers.

Ruth said, "So, you think that stuff might work?"

"Sure hope so."

"Ben tried it before," Bea said. "Didn't work. Had to dig up the line to the septic tank."

"Well, maybe it'll work this time, Momma. Let's try to be optimistic."

They rocked and made small talk about the weather and when it might rain. Ruth fixed Randy a glass of tea. After a while she asked, "Do you think it's been long enough yet?"

"Yeah, I think so."

They made their way back down the hall and congregated at the bathroom door.

Randy looked at Stacy and said, "Wish me luck."

"I got my fingers crossed."

Bea was praying audibly, "Please Lord, help us get through this mess."

Randy stepped inside and saw that the level of sludge in the toilet was lower than before. There were rings of green froth inside the bowl up to where the level had previously been. Despite the fan, the sharp chemical fumes remained in the room, underlined now with the smell of rotten eggs. He positioned the plunger's rubber lips in the opening of the toilet's throat. One stout push was followed by a deep thrumping sound. The surface of the sludge quivered and seemed to drop a bit. Good signs. The Clog-B-Gone was doing its job.

He called out to the women, "Looks good, better I mean. I think the stuff's working."

Stacy said, "It's gon' work, it's just got to. I got full confidence. Go ahead and send that crud to the septic tank."

"Okay. Here goes." Randy pressed the lever. Cold water spiraled into the bowl, swirling down as it was supposed to. A vortex began to form, but the swirling suddenly stopped. The water level began to rise. Randy said, "Oh crap."

"What's that?" Ruth asked.

"I dunno yet. Water's starting to—oh shit!"

The women, hearing Randy's exclamation and a roaring noise, crowded into the doorway in time to witness an artesian well of dark brown foam, spewing like a shook-up bottle of Coca-Cola from the toilet. Shit was flowing freely over the sides of the bowl onto the floor, and copious amounts had literally hit the fan in the initial gush. Randy, recoiling in disgust, had fallen backwards into the bathtub. Bea shouted, "Oh shit! Oh my!"

Ruth cried, "Oh Lord, make it stop!"

The spewing and gurgling slowly subsided.

Randy's voice echoed from the tub: "I can't believe this. My whole life's turned to shit!"

Then Stacy started to giggle. Randy raised himself on his elbows, feet dangling over the edge. His face and shirt were splattered. Stacy's giggles became howls of laughter. Everyone looked at her as she doubled over with her arms under her belly.

Randy said, "I don't see the humor."

Ruth said, "Stacy, Randy's splattered with . . . and you're . . . oh my—"Then she turned away, trying to control her own laughter.

Bea, who'd managed to push herself up from her chair, said, "Lordy, lordy, we've had a doo-doo explosion!"

This set them all to laughing, even Randy as he tried to pull himself out of the tub. Through her laughter, Stacy managed to put her hand up and say, "No, no. Just stay in there, shower yourself off, clothes and all!"

Randy surprised the women and himself by following her suggestion. He drew the curtain and turned on the hot water. He let it flow over him as hot as he could stand, steaming up the enclosure. He stayed in there for a long time, washing his face, hands, arms, and clothes with a bar of soap. He smiled at how good it felt, then began to laugh again at the absurdity of the scene, the "doo-doo explosion." That was definitely a first. With the hot water stinging his face, he knew he would find a way to work through the problem, even if "augering and excavation" were required. One thing was certain, he wouldn't try Clog-B-Gone again.

When he turned off the water and opened the curtain, he saw that the women had been busy. Ruth and Stacy were wringing sponges into soapy buckets of water and wiping down the walls. A wet mop leaned in the corner; the floor was clean. Stacy turned to face him, and he felt silly, standing there wringing wet with his clothes clinging to him. She said, "I was only joking about showering with your clothes on, but I guess it was a pretty good idea."

"I'd say so. I feel much better now."

She smiled. "That's good. We found something for you to put on." She nodded toward a folded pile on top of the toilet tank. "Some of Timmy's old stuff. We'll step out and let you get changed. Those towels hanging up are clean."

After going back to his shack to get some properly fitting work clothes and dry boots, Randy returned to the Stempton bathroom with Buster at his side. The explosion convinced Randy that the drain problem was going to be an ordeal, but the women had to have a flushing toilet, and that was that.

Pulling it up wasn't so bad since most of the muck had been blown out. They augered the plumber's snake through the drain several times as far as it would go, but it seemed to be working through a near-solid obstruction.

Oh well. What next? Bea answered from her wheelchair, "Go out back behind the house and look for a wet spot. . . .." She opened and closed her mouth to provide more explanation but couldn't get the words to form. She shook her head in frustration, lifted her right arm and pointed. "Septic. Drain line."

Stacy said with a note of sympathy, "That's right, I remember now. Daddy had to dig it up a while back."

They found it easily enough, the wet spot, a swampy area out back with mosquitoes swarming. Randy had noticed the lush grass before, but the last time he'd mowed, the lawn wasn't wet. Buster said, "Drainpipe done got busted somehow."

Randy looked up through the afternoon glare to see Ruth pushing Mrs. Stempton in the wheelchair across the yard. They stopped at the margin of wetness and Bea began to point at a pair of nearby plum trees. She said, "Dry weather. Them trees'll do anything to get water. Roots done got in the pipe again. I . . . I . . .," she shook her head, "told Ben to cut 'em down last time."

Randy and Buster understood. They spent the rest of that day with shovels, digging through the wet grass and topsoil, then through a foot of gravel before getting to the clogged and collapsed pipe. The roots—a knotted mass of thin white tentacles, blind and determined—had completely strangled it.

It took them several days to finish the job. A section of pipe had to be replaced, gravel had to be hauled, and this time Bea insisted that those trees be cut down. Stacy was there throughout most of the ordeal. Walking across the yard with the beginnings of a pregnant woman's waddle, she brought them iced tea in quart jars, and every hour or so she checked to see if they were ready for more.

Chapter 47

Buster sat on the front porch of the little house in the Crack, enjoying a few moments of quiet reflection as he waited for Randy to pick him up for work. The last few days had been filled with challenges and surprises. After three days of struggling with Mrs. Stempton's drain problem, he was ready to get back to cutting and hauling pulpwood, familiar work on dry ground in the pine-scented woods. Hauling logs provided a sense of movement and rhythm that had been lacking from the work on the septic line. And, even though he stank at the end of a day in the woods, the odor was from his own sweat, not something else. The saws and sap, bugs and briers, lifting and straining would be a definite improvement, not to mention the fact that hauling logs actually brought in money.

Of course, Randy would try to pay him for those hours spent fixing the drain, and Lord knows he needed all the pay he could get these days, with his momma's growing medical expenses. But he wouldn't take money from Randy that wasn't earned through their business of hauling pulpwood. The drain line work had to be done for the women, and Buster was glad to help. Working with Randy over the past year had been a blessing to Buster and his family, part of God's providence. Now Buster's desire was to support his friend in any way he could.

Being a blessing to others could be complicated, though, especially when they didn't know what was good for them. Randy was stubborn about that girl, and he insisted on doing things his way, not recognizing the Lord's workings, seeing the signs, or heeding warnings. Keeping him away from Ty Ragsdale had been a matter of prayer and persuasion. Buster knew that no good could come from a confrontation. The roots of Randy's hatred ran deeper than Buster's black eye and Randy's desire to honor their friendship. This was really about Stacy—Ty's wife—and Randy's wanting what he couldn't have.

Keeping them apart had required Buster to do something he tried to never do. A few days after the fight, Buster lied to Randy that Ty had sent a note in the mail apologizing, along with two-hundred dollars to cover expenses. It was a risky move, and he remembered Randy's puzzled expression as he struggled with information that cut across the grain of his hatred. He didn't believe it, but then Buster said, "You ought to know me better'n that by now. I always tell the truth." Randy was reluctantly satisfied, and they were able to get back to their work.

Buster had prayed over the situation and told the lie in good faith, knowing that the Lord would somehow cover it. So, the letter in the mailbox he received weeks later had not really been a surprise, but a confirmation. It was amazing, though, that God had brought to pass exactly what Buster had spoken. He read the note a couple of times before throwing it away. He could still see the words:

Buster,

I'm sorry about what happened. I just couldn't wait around that day. I meant what I said about sending me a bill, but you never did. So here is some money that should be enough to cover it. I hope there is no hard feelings.

Ty Ragsdale

And the timing was perfect. Now he would be able to pay the bills this week without taking payment for helping out at the Stempton place.

Randy needed money too, if he was to ever get away from Aaron County and make something better of his life. Buster knew the day of Randy's leaving must come sooner or later. It bothered him, though, not knowing what role he would play in Randy's future. They had spent so much time together, laughing amid their struggles. It was hard imagining life without his friend. But his faith reassured him that the future would be worked out, all in God's time, even the issue of the child Stacy was carrying.

That girl was all right, just blown about like a sparrow in the storm of her own mixed-up desires. But not a single sparrow falls, the Bible says, without the Father's knowledge. God loved her, and now Buster did too. He had begun to see her in a different light as she waddled across the Stempton yard carrying those iced-tea jars. She had been nice to him, asked him if he was hungry and if he needed more tea. And she was a precious vessel now, with a baby growing inside. Somebody's baby. Too bad she'd chosen Ty Ragsdale for a husband. Buster feared there would be more suffering ahead for Stacy. He remembered Randy telling about her black eye when he'd first met her. Buster smiled at the thought that he too had carried a black eye from the same hand. Amazing, how God controls events in mysterious ways, beyond human understanding. Buster decided to add Stacy to his growing prayer list, that she and the new life inside her would be safe in the coming storms of life.

A familiar sound interrupted his thoughts. A Chevy six with a glass-packed muffler was slowing down to turn onto his road. That would be Randy in the flatbed, Ben Stempton's old truck, a vehicle that for years had been a familiar sight around town. It sure was familiar, but different now with Randy driving it. An image flashed in his mind of old Ben at the wheel, arm out the window, gray hair blown back by the wind. He had known Ben Stempton, but not really. That image of him in the truck was a fixture of his memories all the way back to his childhood and the packed clay yard of the sharecropper shack where he'd grown up. Those were the days when men came around, before he and his family moved in with Aunt Esther. Days he had tried to forget, but smudged pictures lingered in the back of his mind. He couldn't bring them into focus and had long since stopped trying. There had been too many men and fights and shouting before his daddy got killed. Now they were redeemed, washed in the blood. The Lord had cast his momma's past into the sea of forgetfulness; he should try to do the same.

Sometimes, though, fragments of that old life came back—white men with blurry faces, gestures, words—but it didn't matter. "Sufficient unto the day is the evil thereof." No need to worry about the past, or the future either. There was work to be done today, plenty to keep them occupied, thank God. Then the flatbed was coming toward him with Randy at the wheel. Buster lifted his arm and waved as his friend turned in.

The morning passed with familiar ease. Buster dropped into the rhythm of the work: dragging the brush, hooking the cable, running the saw, lifting the logs. His muscles sang, swelled, and ached with the joy and effort of doing what they were made to do. Randy seemed content also, moving to the same beat. By noon the truck was over halfway loaded. Randy dropped another big log onto the top of the stack with the loader, climbed down, and switched off the engine. "Let's eat," he called out.

Buster killed the saw, set it down on a stump, and pulled off his gloves. "Sounds good."

They walked over to the shade where the flatbed was parked and pulled their lunch sacks from inside. Looking back, Buster said, "I like being able to see the fruit of our labor and thinking about the good money it's gon' bring."

"Yep, we should be able to get out of here with a full load in a couple more hours. Maybe we can knock off a little early."

Buster nodded as he unwrapped his bologna sandwich. He looked at Randy's face to gauge his mood and was relieved to see little evidence of strain. The morning's work in the woods had been good for him. He hoped they could pass the rest of the day without mentioning or dwelling on their problems, just working side by side. This would be how they would survive, doing what they were supposed to do and leaving everything else to the Lord.

Randy pulled a can of Vienna sausages out of his sack and began opening it with the little twist-off metal key. The metal tab would not pull away from the seam, though, and when it broke off, Randy said, "Damn." He held the stubby can away from him, looking at it as if it contained all the world's evil.

Buster saw what Randy was about to do: reach back and throw the aggravating thing away from him. "Wait! Lemme see it. I'll open it for you. Ain't nothing to it." Buster took it, reached into his jeans, and pulled out his pocketknife. Working carefully with the point of the blade, he soon had the can open. "There you go," he said.

"Thanks. I guess I coulda done that. I got my knife too."

"Sometimes it pays to be patient."

Randy nodded. "Yep. I guess my patience has been wearing a little thin lately." He used his fingers to wiggle out the tightly squeezed first sausage, then offered the rest to Buster. "Go ahead. Eat as many as you want. I got another can."

Chapter 48

The prevailing color of late summer—drab, dusty green—had withered to a yellowish brown by mid-October. It was almost time to prepare for another winter, which for Randy meant checking the wraps on the pipes at the Stempton home as well as his shack, stapling up the clear plastic sheeting, and splitting and stacking firewood. He still had no plan for getting away, so he kept on working, doing the things he knew needed to be done. And he continued to watch Stacy from afar, her growing belly and darting eyes.

With little rain and cooler temperatures this was a good time for work, and Mr. Jenkins kept Randy and Buster busy. The most recent run of jobs involved cutting and hauling out the pulpwood from a series of small parcels around the county. They could clear the logs off each of these tracts within a few days and be ready to move on to the next one. This provided for changing scenery and the rapid passing of days.

Before Randy had a chance to realize it, another Thanksgiving season was upon him. Buster reminded him one afternoon on their way home from work: "Hey man, you given any thought to next week?"

Randy scanned his mental lists and found nothing there but routine work. He took his eyes off the road to look at his friend. "No . . . should I?"

"Well, yeah. Next Thursday is Thanksgiving."

"Oh, great."

Buster cocked his head, scrutinizing his friend.

Randy said, "What? Can I help it if I don't like holidays, especially Thanksgiving? I try not to think about things like that."

"Not thinking about it don't make it go away. Maybe, since you're the boss, you can force yourself to consider it and tell me what you come up with. That way I'll know what kind of plans to make."

Randy's eyes moved back and forth between Buster and the light traffic. "Well, I guess we can take a four-day weekend. That suit you? Working through Wednesday should about finish up this job anyway. We can put off starting on that Eason's Hollow tract until the next Monday."

"That works for me."

Randy turned onto the street that crossed the tracks and led into the Crack. "You making big plans?"

"Naw, just us. My sister's coming out from Atlanta, and there'll be Aunt Esther, Momma, and me. We ain't gon' try to do too much with Momma sick as she is. What about you?"

"Like I said—"

"Yeah, I know. You try not to think about holidays. You can come spend the day with us, though. You're always welcome at our house."

Randy didn't answer, just nodded.

Buster continued: "I can tell Aunt Esther to set another place. She the one be doing all the cooking, and that woman can cook, too. You might want to think about it pretty hard. Ain't often you get a chance to feast on the kind of soul food she be serving up."

Randy nodded again, trying to suppress the rising uneasiness that always accompanied being invited into someone's home. He didn't want to feel this way with Buster. The situation was ironic considering their friendship. He'd worked with him for over a year and still hadn't set foot inside his house. He had met his momma and aunt, and they'd exchanged greetings, with them standing on the porch while he waited by the truck for Buster. They would smile, wave, and call out to him, as he and Buster backed out of the drive: "Y'all be careful now and don't work too hard," or "God bless you, Randy Walls. We 'preciate you taking care of our boy. Bring him home safe."

Sometimes when he would drop Buster off in the evenings, they would invite him to stay for supper. Randy always replied, "Thanks, but I need to get back and check on things at the house." In the past, stepping into the homes of others had brought shifting circumstances and relationships followed by disappointment or tragedy. His years of not having a real home had made him a permanent outsider filled with longing and trepidation. He couldn't go rushing in even when that was his strongest desire, to be absorbed and become part of something larger, a spinning universe held together by love. The years of wanting to belong had magnified his not belonging. He hated himself, his foreignness, and he responded by turning inward, away from others. A photographic negative of a real person, that's what he'd become, and in this state he guarded himself from the disappointment of feeling too much, of having hopes and expectations.

There was, though, this matter of passing time. Another Thanksgiving already. Rolling into the Crack with Buster beside him, he imagined himself after the passing of many years still sitting in that rocker on the front porch, accompanied only by lazy, nameless hounds, crickets, and tree frogs, living what was not life. He thought about that dumb-ass Thoreau again. He had it all backwards. People, family, love, laughter, touching and being touched—these qualities made up the marrow of real life.

Buster's voice brought back the sounds and colors of reality. "It ain't like you got a whole bunch of other options. I know you ain't already booked Thanksgiving, since you didn't even know what day it was."

Randy tried to focus on his friend's face. "No. I don't. It's just that Thanksgiving is kind of depressing to me, especially after last year. Me being at your house might bring everybody down."

"Man. You take yourself way too serious. Things ain't exactly joyous around my house either, with Momma being like she is. But we gon' make the best of it. We still got a lot to be thankful for. And that's what we gon' do, give thanks to the Lord and have a big meal together. And you're invited."

Randy steered the flatbed into Buster's driveway and eased the gear lever into neutral. Buster, hand on the door handle, said, "Think about it and let me know."

"I don't need to."

"What?"

"Think about it. I can come for Thanksgiving. I'd like that." His eyes moved from Buster's face to the dashboard. "I, uh . . . appreciate your thinking about me."

Buster pushed the door open and stepped down. "Ain't no big thing. I'll tell Momma and Aunt Esther. I know they'll be happy to add you to our table."

★★★

On Thanksgiving Day, Randy was met at the door by Buster's aunt, who greeted him with a big hug. The day was cool and clear outside, but inside the air was steamy, redolent with the aromas of a large meal. Buster approached him from the back of the small house, wiping his hands on a dish towel. "Hey, bro! Come on in. Dinner's almost ready."

They stood in the living room for a moment: Randy, Aunt Esther, Buster, and a young woman who stepped toward Randy, offering her hand. "Hello. I'm Magdalene, Buster's sister." She wore a colorful flower-print dress with a green sweater. Her skin was half a shade lighter than milk chocolate. Her jet-black hair was shiny and carefully swept across one side of her forehead. It poofed slightly on top like black meringue behind a green hair band, then curled at her neck. "I've heard a lot about you."

She was a pretty young woman with a fresh appearance and wholesome demeanor. He took her hand. "Hi. Pleased to meet you." Then he realized he was underdressed in his best pair of jeans and button-down shirt. Buster and his family looked as if they were going to church.

Aunt Esther stepped over to Randy and put her arm around his shoulder. "Yes, we have heard lots of good things about you, Randy, and we're glad you could join us today. The steady work you've provided for Buster has been a blessing to us all. It ain't easy . . . well, we just thankful you came along when you did." She was a large woman, wearing an apron over a dark blue pleated dress. She was nearly as tall as Randy and heavy in a tightly packed way. "And speaking of being thankful, we might as well go ahead and say grace while we all gathered, that is if you'll go get your momma, Buster. Tell her it's time."

Buster disappeared down a narrow hallway. There was a moment of silence that Randy felt the need to fill: "Buster's been a great help to me. I couldn't do without him."

"Well, we mighty proud of him. He's always been a good boy, and a good worker. He just needed an opportunity to show what he could do."

Then came the sound of a door closing and movement in the hallway. Buster was coming back into the living room with a withered brown woman leaning against him. Her arm was over his shoulder and his arm was around her waist. They moved slowly, her slippered feet shuffling along the floor.

Randy was shocked at her shrunken appearance. He remembered her being thin, but now, with hollow cheeks and bulging yellow eyes, she couldn't have weighed more than sixty pounds. Her head bobbed as they walked, as if she were searching for something.

Aunt Esther said, "This is my sister, Dorcas Dobbs, Buster's momma."

Randy answered softly, "Yes ma'am. We've met."

"Why sure you have. Don't know what I was thinking. I'm getting to where I forget things sometimes."

Mrs. Dobbs raised her bobbing head and focused on Randy. Her voice came out in a hoarse whisper: "God bless you, Randy Walls. I'm thankful you could be here. Please excuse my appearance. Ain't been feeling well lately."

Randy said, "Yes ma'am."

Esther said, "How you feeling, sister? Were you able to rest any?"

"Much better, thank you."

Randy looked at Magdalene standing next to him. Her eyes were on the carpet, a faded orange shag. The room was small, and they were grouped close together. Esther, on his other side, took his hand and squeezed. She said, "We a praying family, Randy. I hope you don't mind joining us in thanking God for our blessings."

"No ma'am."

"Go ahead, Buster."

Buster said solemnly, in his deepest voice, "Let us pray." Randy closed his eyes and bowed his head with the others. With the intoning of the opening words, "Our dear, most gracious and loving heavenly Father," his mind freed itself. His eyes popped open, scanning the faces and the room beyond. The colors were warm and muted, greens and browns with a splash of orange here and there. The coffee table pressing the back of his leg wobbled at the slightest shifting of his weight. Matching slipcovers snuggly wrapped the sofa and chairs. Across from him an old portable TV sat atop an end table with spindly legs. A small shelf held an encyclopedia set and a few pictures in gold-tone metal frames. The dominant one featured Buster's brother, a proud young man in military uniform, flanked by his family. Buster looked like a little kid in the picture, and Magdalene was still a teenager. Mrs. Dobbs seemed healthy and proud of her family, what they had been through. At that moment when the shutter snapped, she had not known what was ahead. No one ever does, but it was strange looking at a picture of a dead person while being with the others who were pictured with him. Randy thought about a snapshot of today and how it might look in the future. Then he noticed that Buster's voice had become livelier.

The prayer seemed to be growing wings and lifting itself. He heard his name: ". . . and thank you Lord for Randy Walls and what he's meant to our family. Bless him and keep him and provide the desires of his heart according to your will, precious Father. . .." Randy closed his eyes. Then another voice, Aunt Esther's, proclaimed, "Yes, yes, thank you, Jesus!"

Buster, encouraged, continued with a more pronounced cadence as the others interjected expressions such as, "Hallelujah!" and "Praise Jesus!" The prayer went on for some time, circling their heads, engulfing them. Randy could feel the women swaying with the music of the words, and he felt himself getting dizzy.

Buster thanked God for the good weather, the bountiful table, good health, the ending of the war, friends, family, and many other things including the very breath of life; and then he asked God to bless his mother, those families who had lost loved ones in Vietnam, and the Stempton women in their time of hardship. Finally, he was done: "All these things we ask in the name of Jesus, Amen." That last word echoed around the room and Randy felt both his hands being squeezed, then released. He opened his eyes.

They were all looking at him and smiling. Buster said, "Let's eat!"

The kitchen was a much lighter room—mostly white, trimmed in blue—made brighter by the oversized fluorescent light mounted on the ceiling. The table was not large enough for the place settings and all the serving bowls, but Aunt Esther had a buffet system worked out. She insisted that Randy be served first. "Start here," she said, "with the turkey and ham. That's right, serve yourself, but better get more'n that." Randy placed several thick slabs of meat on his plate. "That's it," Esther continued. "Now then, dressing, rolls, and Hoppin' John on the stove. Collard greens and sweet potatoes on the table. Here, let me help you with that dressing. It may be stuck to the pan a little."

Magdalene fell in behind Randy. Buster helped his momma to the table, then got behind his sister with his own plate. As Randy spooned peas and rice into his bowl, he heard Buster say, "Come on, sister. I'm gon' starve to death waiting on you to pick out a little piece of turkey."

"You hush up."

"Y'all come on around children," Esther said. "Go ahead and start when you get to the table. Don't wait on me."

Randy, holding his plate, didn't know where to sit. Esther gently nudged his elbow and pointed with her head. "Right here, Randy. We gon' put you at the head of the table."

Soon they were all eating heartily, except Buster's momma, who had nothing in front of her but a bowl of broth. It was an effort for her to lift the tiny spoonfuls to her lips. Buster encouraged her. "Come on, Momma. You need to eat all that. It'll give you strength." She nodded, or seemed to. When Randy looked at her, she turned her eyes to him and smiled.

They began to talk about their work: Magdalene's state job in Atlanta and her recent promotion, Esther's job in the school cafeteria and how trying those children could be sometimes, and how Dorcas had had to give up her work cleaning white folks' houses because of her health. Esther wanted to know about the work Randy and Buster had lined up, if they thought they would have enough to carry them through the winter.

"Mr. Jenkins keeps coming up with jobs," Randy said. "Soon as we finish one, he's got another for us to start on. I think we can count on plenty for a while. And we can work most days during the winter, as long as it doesn't get too muddy."

"Got to be careful," Buster said. "Getting the truck stuck can cost us a lot of time. Don't want that."

Esther nodded. "I know that's right. Well, I guess Mr. Jenkins is happy to keep y'all busy 'cause he making lots of money off y'all's labor. That's the way rich folks do it. They just get richer off the work other people do for them. That's okay, though. If he don't make nothing, then he can't pay y'all."

"He pays us pretty well."

"I know, I know, thank the Lord."

Dorcas followed the conversation with her eyes, occasionally lifting the spoon to her lips, but she couldn't make it through the meal. Randy had eaten about half of his turkey and dressing and a few bites of Hoppin' John when she let out a soft moan. Her head had begun to bob in that searching way. She said softly to Buster, "That's 'bout all I can do, Son. You gon' have to help me get back yonder now."

"Okay, Momma."

With her place empty, the conversation dwindled. Esther finally said, "Lord, Lord, it's a shame, being struck down like that at the prime of life. But the Lord is just in his dealings with us. He gon' hold us up through this." She looked around the table at each face, pausing at Randy's. "All we can do is keep praying. And we gon' keep you in our prayers too, Randy."

He felt their eyes, a comfortable sensation. A loving strength was being communicated toward him, and he enjoyed being at the center of their warm attention.

He ended up staying through the afternoon, watching football with Buster on the small black and white set. Esther and Magdalene joined them in the living room occasionally. At other times they were out of sight, probably tending to various sickroom needs. He wondered what it must be like back there, but he pushed those thoughts away. To think too much about the burden of those women—the odors and ugliness of it—violated their dignity. He knew they wanted him to feel comfortable; realizing that he did came as a pleasant surprise.

Chapter 49

Buster's momma died two weeks later. The ceremonies associated with her "passing" went on for days. Randy, participating from the periphery, was expecting this death to be handled as the old man's had been, and he was confused by the extended period of mourning and the level of emotion woven throughout. When Randy arrived at the wake to pay his respects, the driveway and curbside were filled with cars. He managed to wedge the flatbed into a tight space at the edge of the cul-de-sac. The house and porch were crowded with people sitting in folding chairs. Flowers and food were in abundance. The visitors laughed, cried, prayed, and sang to mourn the death of Dorcas Dobbs while celebrating her life and "homegoing." Randy left after muttering condolences to Magdalene and hugging Buster and Aunt Esther; he learned later that the closest friends and family members stayed at the house all night, "sitting up" with the deceased.

The body was moved the next morning to McKay's Mortuary in the heart of the Crack, where the immediate family would receive visitors each day. The funeral services were scheduled to take place on Friday, five days after the death. Randy stopped by on Thursday to see how Buster was doing and to find out the details of the funeral, since he, for the second time in his life, had been asked to be a pall bearer. He and Buster walked out to the parking lot to smoke and talk in private.

"What time should I be here tomorrow?" Randy asked.

"Early, about eight, dressed and ready to go. You do have a suit, don't you?"

"Sure, I do. What do you think I am, some kind of loser who lives in a shack or something? In case you've forgotten, I'm a successful businessman, got a closet full of suits."

"Well, okay then. Just be sure you wearing one in the morning. Everything else ought to take care of itself."

Randy rose early, at his usual work-day time, and began dressing in the new suit he'd purchased the afternoon before in Aaronville. This time his funeral suit would fit properly; he'd made sure of that. He'd been surprised by the price, but it didn't matter. He wanted to look his best for this occasion, and he imagined that the relatives and other mourners would all be decked out in their best attire. Being a pall bearer, and white, would make him highly visible. For the sake of his friend, his appearance needed to be just right.

With the help of a stooped little sales lady in a lime-green pants suit, he'd finally decided on a charcoal three-piece with pinstripes. He'd also tried on a half-dozen pairs of shoes before choosing shiny oxblood wingtips. The lady assured him that his selections would be perfect for a funeral or any other occasion that required a suit. He arranged his purchases neatly beside him on the seat of the truck before heading back to the shack.

The next morning, though, the suit didn't seem as right as it had in the store. He worried over the tie, the size of the knot and getting the length right. Four tries and it still wasn't perfect. Finally he gave up, accepting what was barely good enough. Next came the vest. It was a snug fit when buttoned, and with the tie knotted at his throat, he felt pressure against his chest when he breathed.

He couldn't be late. He carried some chow out to the hounds, wiped his hands, and shut the door. Waiting for him in the driveway was the old man's Galaxie. It hadn't been driven much lately. Yesterday he'd pumped up the tires and left the battery charging while he drove the truck to Aaronville. The Stempton women, once they understood the situation, had insisted that driving the flatbed in a Negro funeral would be unacceptable.

Sitting in the Ford brought conflicting emotions, but the seat was comfortable, and the old car looked decent after the wash job he'd given it. This was gonna be okay, over soon, and he and Buster could get back to their familiar routine. But the day proved difficult. Before it was over, he felt as if he'd been pressed against the bosom of every black woman in Prathersville. The services began at the funeral home, with the body on display at the front of the chapel. There were preachers to bring the word, singers to sing Dorcas's favorite hymns, and family members to testify.

At the cemetery Randy took his place at the graveside for another round of preaching. The minister, a man of about thirty, was tall, straight, and impeccably dressed in a black suit with a yellow rose in the lapel. He wore his hair in a short Afro. His deep voice ebbed and flowed, lifting the mourners toward heaven, then gently setting them back on earth. He rolled off long passages of scripture from memory. His closing words stuck in Randy's mind: "Precious in the sight of the Lord is the death of his saints."

The minister paused. Was it over? The family members stood. Then he spoke again: "Dearly Beloved, let us now join hands and go to the throne of grace, beseeching our Lord to comfort this family in their time of grief and to go with us throughout the remainder of our days. . . ." The prayer this time was short, closing with something about being thankful for the food and joyous fellowship. Randy's mood brightened on the hope that soon he could get out of that suit and tie. Then, as people began to move about and hug one another, he felt a heavy arm around his shoulders. Aunt Esther said in his ear, "You come on now and stay with us. We going to the fellowship hall to celebrate. Can't let you go home hungry."

Food, laughter, hugging, singing. Despite his fatigue, Randy found comfort in the relaxed, festive mood. After stuffing himself with barbecued ribs, cabbage, red beans, and chocolate cake, he unbuttoned his vest and loosened the tie. Buster sat beside him and asked how he was doing.

"Okay. How about you?"

"I'm good, proud we sent Momma off so fine."

"I'm sure she'd be pleased."

"She ain't got to suffer no more."

"Nope."

"Come on. Let's step outside for a minute."

Just beyond the back door was a strip of lawn with a long concrete table and benches for eating outside. The December sun was low in the clear sky and the air was growing chill. They sat on the concrete, lit up, and chatted easily, blowing smoke into the breeze. Buster said, "That sure was pretty when Sister Louise sang 'Get Away Jordan.' She got such a sweet voice. That was Momma's favorite."

"Yes. That was nice."

"She the preacher's wife, you know. They sure been a blessing to our community. Always there in times of trouble."

Randy nodded, trying to ignore the pain in his feet from the new shoes.

Buster said, "I like your suit. You clean up pretty good."

"Thanks. You don't look too bad yourself."

"We appreciate you, being here for us and all."

"It's no big deal, the least I could do, really."

"Still . . . I don't guess you ever been to this kind of funeral, have you?"

"Nope. I only been to one other funeral, Mr. Stempton's. It wasn't like this."

"White folks don't know how to celebrate. Make everything too serious. Death is sad—I'm gon' miss my momma—but joyous too. She gone to a better place. And after somebody dies, guess what? The Lord sends a brand-new person into the world. Birth always follows death. That's the way of things, and reason to celebrate."

Randy nodded, looking across the parking lot. He felt Buster studying him.

"I shoulda thought about that, though."

"What?"

"That you ain't used to this kinda thing. All these people, preaching, singing, hugging. I'll bet you about ready to get out of here, ain't you?"

Buster was perceptive, as usual. Randy was near the limit of his endurance. "Well," he said, "it has been a long day."

"Look, man. You ain't gotta stay. You go ahead on. I'll tell Aunt Esther you had to check on Mrs. Stempton."

"You sure?"

"Yeah. You done enough for one day."

Chapter 50

Stacy gave birth on the day after Christmas, and Randy visited the hospital the following day. As he drove into the parking lot, his face got hot. He hoped that Ty wouldn't be there, holding the baby. He wasn't sure if he could stand that. Parking the car, he remembered Buster's words about leaving judgment to the Lord. Buster had said there would be a time for making things right.

In the lobby Randy walked to the front desk, past the artificial Christmas tree. The volunteer lady looked up the room number in a smiling way and pointed out the direction. He found it easily enough: straight down a long, beige hallway, through the double doors marked "Maternity," second room on the right.

Stacy answered when he knocked, "Come in." She was propped up in bed watching "Days of Our Lives" on the wall-mounted TV. Aunt Ruth was in the reclining chair; Stacy's momma sat in the straight-back with her aluminum walking stick beside her. Stacy said, "Randy."

Mrs. Stempton smiled. Ruth said, "Hello there! Thought you were working today."

"We worked this morning. Got the truck loaded and nearly another load on the ground. That was about all we could do. Yard's closed till after the first."

Ruth said, "WM's running tonight. Ty had to go home and get some rest. He just left."

Mrs. Stempton lifted her good arm and said, "Come here."

Randy walked to her and pressed his face against hers as she patted his back. Her cheek was wet. He straightened and looked around, his face reheating. He turned toward Stacy and said, "So . . . you okay?"

"Much better, thank you."

Bea said, "She had a little trouble, but it's okay now."

Ruth said, "I'll say. It was a long day."

Stacy said, "Sit down, Randy. There's another chair over here."

"I can't stay. Just wanted to come by."

"I'm glad you did. Come sit down." Her eyes met his then skittered away.

As he was moving to the designated chair, Ruth spoke up over the TV. "She did a good job, Randy, her and Ty. Made a fine baby boy, seven pounds, three ounces."

Bea said, "God made it, not them, and, and. . . ."

"Well, they certainly had a part in it. You know what I mean."

Stacy rolled her eyes.

Ruth spoke up again: "You can go see him in the nursery down the hall. I think they got the curtains pulled back."

"Well, I would like to see the baby." He looked at Stacy and noticed her eyes were wet.

She said, "Come here."

He moved to the side of the bed. She reached up to him, hugged him, held his face in her hands; then she fastened her eyes on his for a moment, long enough to whisper, "He's beautiful, Randy. Beautiful." The shadow of a sad smile passed over her face before she let him go.

"There's a couple of other babies in there," Ruth said, "but you'll know little Benjamin. He's the prettiest one."

Randy felt his chest tightening; he could hardly draw a breath. "Okay. I'll go take a look."

He stepped out into the hallway, trying to breathe normally. After pulling the door closed, he paused for a moment, leaning back against the wall. He walked past a large bulletin board filled with pictures of babies, along with nurses, doctors, and mommies holding babies. He made his way to the viewing window and saw through the open curtains a nurse bent over one of the tiny plastic bassinets. Randy scanned the area, searching. A garland of red and green tinsel hung along the walls. Fat red and green letters spelling "Merry Christmas" were stuck over a doorway in back. There was a picture of Santa in his sleigh taped to the big picture window, and the bottom corners were frosted with spray-on snow.

He steadied himself against the handrail. He had never experienced such nauseating excitement. There was a baby in there—his son, but he couldn't find him. The nurse, a young black woman, short and chubby, looked up and smiled. She approached the window and asked through the glass, "Find the one you're looking for?"

Randy shrugged, shook his head no.

She held up a finger to say, "Hold on," then disappeared through the doorway under the Merry Christmas letters. After a minute she returned carrying a blue-wrapped bundle. She stepped over to the glass and held up the baby, folding the blanket back from around his face.

He was sleeping. The little cheeks were puffy and dark—ruddy, like those of an English gentleman on a fox hunt. And there was a wisp of hair at the front of the baby's head, peeking out from under a tiny knit cap. The nurse smiled, then turned to place the baby in the nearest bassinet. With her back to Randy she worked with the blanket, getting it just right. She reached into the pocket of her smock, brought out a white card, and slipped it into a plastic holder. She stood then, smiled at Randy, and moved on to her other duties.

There he was: a baby, child, person—his son, the product of love. Randy was a father now, but not really. He didn't know what to feel. Something was surging inside. He looked at the face again and noticed the fine dark eyebrows. The nurse had left a pacifier in his mouth, but in his contentment, he'd let it fall away. The pink tip of his tongue protruded slightly. A little spasm passed over the sleeping infant, a tiny shaking of his head. His arm moved, and the fingers tightened and relaxed. He seemed to drop back into deep sleep then. Dreaming, but of what? His only experiences were of a dark, watery world. Maybe he was dreaming of the future.

Randy's conflicting emotions were for a moment supplanted by hope and joy. It was, after all, Christmas, and a new baby had come into the world. He remembered Buster talking about death being followed by birth. If there ever was a reason to celebrate, this was it.

He lingered at the window, absorbing every detail. He focused on the card at the front of the bassinet and read these neatly printed words:

Benjamin Tyler Ragsdale
December 26, 1973
Seven pounds, three ounces

Reality brought a rush of saliva, hard to swallow. There he was again, in his mind's eye, Ty—the son-of-a-bitch—with that smirk on his face. He blinked, shook his head, and looked at the baby, the peaceful, precious child. He had to turn away, but he didn't know which way to go. One thing was certain: he couldn't be with Stacy right now, or those women. He walked down the hall in the opposite direction from her room. The hallway was long, with an exit at the end.

Outside the air was crisp. He gulped it in as he looked about. Coming out a different exit had put him on unfamiliar ground. He faced a looping drive that provided access to the emergency room. Beyond that was the back parking lot. He needed to figure out how to get back to the front without going through the building. He walked past some holly bushes, wrought iron benches, and the emergency room entrance. A side street took him past a small clinic and a pharmacy.

He found the front parking lot as he turned the corner; then he heard someone calling his name: "Randy! Hey man, is that you?" He looked up and saw a young couple approaching. The guy was waving and hurrying toward him. "Hey, Dude. Long time, no see. How are they? Have you seen them? Oh, this is my friend, Dot. Dot, Randy. He works for my mom, practically part of the family. He and Stacy are good friends." The girl was a step behind, smiling. She extended her hand and Randy took it, noticing the firm grip.

"Pleased to meet you," he said.

"Yeah. Me too."

The two looked alike with similar hairstyles and clothes, as if they'd dressed to complement each other. Their hair was cropped short on top and stood up off their heads. The sides were cut in layers that covered their ears and hung over their contrasting turtlenecks, his white and hers black. They both wore hip-hugging bell bottoms with wide belts.

Timmy asked, "What does he look like, my new nephew?"

"He looks . . . great. Dark hair and eyebrows. Good color. He was sleeping just now."

"Far out! I can't wait to see him. You wanna come back in with us? We'll make it a party. At least a short one. We probably won't stay long. I thought I'd ride Dot around and show her this godforsaken place where I grew up. You should join us."

"No thanks. I need to be getting back."

"Oh come on, Randy, loosen up." Timmy winked as he held his thumb and forefinger to his lips and made a rapid series of tiny air sips. "I got some really good stuff." He turned to Dot. "Randy's cool. Gets high with my sister all the time, at least when Macho Man isn't around."

Randy was dumfounded. "That's not true. I never even see Stacy anymore, except at her mother's."

Timmy giggled, winked at Dot. "Stacy and I talk, you know. I hear there's some pretty aggressive ducks over at the college."

Randy groped for words. "Well, there was that one time. I can't believe she told you."

"It's okay, dude. Stacy and I have always shared everything. I don't blame you for wanting to hang out with her. She's lots of fun. I can't wait for Dot to meet her. Come on, let's go inside."

"Naa. Really got to get back. You guys go ahead."

"Okay. Later, then. Good seeing you."

Dot smiled politely, revealing an overbite and a gap between her front teeth. "Nice meeting you."

Randy watched them walk away, swinging their arms and laughing. He couldn't believe Stacy had told her brother about their getting stoned that day on the college campus. He wondered what else she'd told him. Had she told that silly boy about their special night together? Had they laughed about it and the foolish way he'd acted afterwards?

His cheeks flushed, but the blood quickly cooled. He realized he didn't care if Timmy, or anybody else, knew what had happened. Part of him wanted the world to know he loved Stacy, that he wanted her to leave Ty, that the baby in there was his. These truths resided at his core and could not be denied.

Chapter 51

As it turned out, Stacy didn't have to leave Ty; he left instead, in a way nobody could have predicted. The following story ran under a banner headline on the front page of *The Prathersville Patriot:*

LOCAL MAN FOUND DEAD ON RAILROAD TRACKS

By Rusty Roberts, *Staff Writer*

Local police, along with the Aaron County Sheriff's department, are investigating the death of 20-year-old Tyler Ragsdale of Prathersville.

Ragsdale's decapitated body was discovered around 4:00 a.m. on Friday morning, February 15. The body was lying beside the railroad tracks, just east of the crossing at McKay Avenue.

The head was found about 100 yards farther east underneath the train. Railway workers saw Ragsdale on the tracks but were unable to stop in time. It is not clear whether Ragsdale was dead or alive when the train struck him.

A similar incident occurred in the same area less than a month ago. In January, the body of 24-year-old Sanford Strozier was found along the tracks, also decapitated.

At first authorities suspected that Strozier had fallen asleep on the track and was run over by a train. Now, after Ragsdale's death, they are not sure.

Police Chief Chester Bidwell has not ruled out the possibility of foul play. "It doesn't seem right, two deaths less than a month apart with similar circumstances in that part of town. We won't leave a stone unturned in getting to the bottom of this," Bidwell said.

Chief Bidwell also pointed out that the Georgia Bureau of Investigation (GBI) has joined the investigation. "These deaths may be drug-related," he said.

Bidwell added that his department has been looking into the "high level of drug activity" in that part of town. "We're not really equipped for this sort of thing. We're understaffed. But we'll do whatever it takes," he said.

Ragsdale leaves behind an infant son and his wife, Stacy Stempton Ragsdale. His father, Fletcher Ragsdale, resides in Prathersville.

When asked if he knew how his son could have gotten on those railroad tracks, the elder Ragsdale replied, "That boy was always bad to get into things and go places where he wasn't supposed to be. He was a good boy, though. I don't know what I'll do now. He was the one who looked after me and made sure I had what I needed."

Fletcher Ragsdale, 54, lives alone and has been in poor health for some time.

Funeral arrangements have not yet been announced. According to Chief Bidwell, an autopsy will be performed in the near future. He said, "These boys may have been already dead before the trains ran over them. Their time of death is what we've got to determine."

An autopsy was not performed on Strozier, but Bidwell said his body could possibly be exhumed for further examination. "It just depends on what those GBI boys want to do, and how far we need to go with this thing."

Ragsdale was employed on the night shift at WM manufacturing. His supervisor, Rayford Millwood, verified that Ragsdale had been scheduled to work on the night of his death but had called in sick.

Millwood added, "Ty Ragsdale was the best die press operator I had. He was fast and did good work. He will be missed."

Randy clipped the article and pasted it into his scrapbook, then read it again to let it sink in. His feelings, now that this had come to pass, were puzzling. Ty Ragsdale had been the one person on earth he hated; now that he was gone Randy felt—in place of happiness or a sense of victory—only an emptiness and a dull throbbing in the back of his head. Randy's realization that Ty was, after all, a fellow human being brought an unexpected sense of loss. He wished he had not allowed himself to hate him so much.

★★★

Stacy had gone straight to her old home place with the baby the same day Ty's body was found, and she had hardly come out of her room since. She had been a child there, when life was safe, and even though the safety was gone now, at least there was the memory of those times when things were permanent, before her father's death and mother's stroke.

She left her apartment, the one she had shared with her now dead husband, longing for a loving, restorative hug from her mother. Frantic and bleary eyed, Stacy maintained a vision of her momma as she drove, the image of a whole Bea Stempton, before the stroke had diminished her empathy and ability to respond, along with the use of her left side.

"Momma!" Stacy cried, bursting through the door with Benji on her hip. She found her at the kitchen table in her wheelchair, drinking coffee with Aunt Ruth. "Momma...." Stacy stood speechless, looking from one woman to the other.

Mrs. Stempton stared back at her, making small movements with her tongue and mouth.

Ruth finally said, "What is it, child? What's wrong?"

Ruth seemed expectant, eager to empathize, but Stacy sensed that the depth of understanding would be shallow from this woman who'd never married or had children. She felt Ruth studying her like a scrupulous accountant going over a ledger. Stacy didn't want scrutiny; she needed love, unconditional, the love of a mother for her child.

She moved toward Ruth awkwardly, paused, and handed her the baby. Then she made her way to her mother and bent to her. It was a lopsided, one-armed hug, made more awkward by the wheels and footrests of the wheelchair. Her momma's cheek was wet, as usual. Stacy slumped to the floor, convulsing with sobs.

After a time she made it to her room, but that was as far as she could go. The future had never been terrifying before, but now huge chunks of meaning had been ripped from the text of her life. She couldn't turn pages for fear of finding more holes.

Randy sensed that in her solitary grief, she would want to see him least of all. His hatred of Ty made him unfit company at the time she needed him most. He went to the Stempton home on Saturday morning, the day after Ty's body was discovered, not knowing what to expect. Aunt Ruth met him on the porch. "It's bad, Randy, real bad. She's been in her room crying since yesterday. Says she don't want to talk to anybody." She placed her hands on the railing and leaned against it, shaking her head.

He stood there at the steps looking up at her. He finally said, "Well, is there anything I can do? Any of you need anything?"

"No. No, there's nothing. We'll let you know if . . . well—"

"Sure. I understand."

As he turned, he heard a car coming up the drive. It was that boxy orange Datsun—Timmy, and he had that girl with him, Dot. Randy acknowledged them with a nod as he was getting in the flatbed to leave. He didn't feel like talking to anybody either.

★★★

The coroner's office moved quickly on the case, but they were unable to pinpoint the exact time of death and therefore unable to determine if Ty was killed by the train or something else. There had been problems with the investigation from the beginning, most of which involved the passing of time coupled with human error. The railway workers, after realizing what had happened, couldn't agree on protocol. They radioed their trainmaster and discussed the situation. Several minutes passed before they called the police, who, shorthanded as usual, were unable to get an officer out there immediately. Minutes ticked away. Finally, Chief Bidwell was called at home, roused from his warm bed just before daylight. Ty's body, uncovered and drained of blood, was cooling rapidly.

Bidwell's first act was to call the coroner; then he questioned the workers. He concluded the guys must have been half-asleep when it happened because the switchman, conductor, and engineer all saw it differently. The engineer thought he saw a person, upright and

389

moving, at the edge of the tracks just before the switchman signaled him to stop. The conductor claimed to have seen the headless body rolling away from the track after impact. The switchman said he saw something lying on the track prior to impact, but he wasn't sure if it was the victim or not. Must have been, he guessed.

By the time the coroner arrived, the sun was burning off the fog and a crowd was gathering. Most of Prathersville's police department was there by then, detouring traffic around the blocked crossing and controlling the crowd. Onlookers began to piece together bits of information—headless body, stopped train, police everywhere—and saw in the circumstances a heinous act of police brutality whereby one of theirs had been slain. Chief Bidwell had his hands full, as reporters were gathering as well.

The mood of the crowd shifted from accusatory to scoffing after he explained that the victim was a white male, and that what had happened was probably an accident, that he had probably gotten drunk and stumbled onto the tracks.

A contemptuous response echoed through the crowd: "Accident hell! Damn fool ought to know better than to be messin' around over here in the middle of the night. White folks got no business in here, unless they looking for something they can't find on they own side of the tracks. Shoulda stayed his ass where he belong."

Amazingly to Bidwell, the onlookers figured out who the victim was. A slender man dressed in work boots and denim jacket said, "Hell, I'll bet my paycheck it's that Ragsdale dude. Everybody know he sorry as hell, slipping through here at all hours in that blue Pontiac. I seen his car last night parked over behind Lamar's Place."

A chorus of agreement: "Uh huh. That's right." When reporters began questioning the onlookers, Bidwell realized that concealing the identity was pointless, and he'd better go ahead and contact the next of kin. There was also the problem of the blocked crossing. He needed to get the crowd dispersed and traffic moving again.

He talked things over with the coroner, Taylor Blige, a pudgy man of about thirty, balding on top. Blige, newly elected and inexperienced, agreed that the scene needed to be cleared. Ty's remains were gathered up and transported to the morgue. Blige had neglected to take the temperature of the corpse, which was by this time quite cool. After a couple of weeks, autopsy complete, the body was released to J. Dougherty and Son Funeral Home, as the family had requested. The only thing the coroner had determined with certainty was that Ty had died with a high level of alcohol in his blood.

★★★

Reverend Bledsoe conducted the funeral services before a small crowd inside the same church where he had married Stacy and Ty. It was the first time Randy had seen the minister since the wedding, and he was amazed that he had grown even fatter. The fabric of his suit was strained across his middle, and when he gestured with his arms, which seemed too small for the rest of him, Randy feared that a button would pop. Even though it was drafty inside the old church, Reverend Bledsoe kept his handkerchief in his hand and used it frequently to mop his sweaty brow.

The minister's sadness seemed genuine. He spoke haltingly, laboring over the words. Twice, when he looked at Stacy in the front pew, he shook his head and dabbed his eyes with the handkerchief. Even though the crowd was sparse, Randy had chosen to sit with Buster near the back of the small sanctuary. He could see the preacher's face clearly, and he tried to attend to the words, curious as to what ray of hope the minister would be able to bring.

As Reverend Bledsoe groped about in his storehouse of verses, phrases, and mannerisms, Randy's mind wandered back to a few days earlier, after the funeral arrangements had finally been made, when he and Buster had discussed the situation. They had gone to the shack for lunch, since they were working only a short distance away. Sitting at the kitchen table Randy had explained to his friend how awkward he felt, mainly because of his fervent hatred for Ty, and that he didn't want to attend the funeral.

Buster said, "That ain't got nothing to do with it. Past feelings don't matter. Funerals are a time for healing, for making things right."

"How come you always understand these things?"

"Just another one of my talents, I guess. I understand something else too, that we probably ought to be getting back to work, if we gon' get anything done today."

"You know, I just don't feel up to it. I need to think—sort things out—and you can help me. Sit tight while I make some coffee."

As Randy banged around in the kitchen, Buster stirred up the coals in the heater and added several sticks of split hickory. They settled into an afternoon of discussion instead of going back to the woods. Buster explained the importance of finding respect for a person when death comes, even though he may have been an enemy in life. The fact that their lives had touched obligated them to offer a decent farewell, even though they'd both struggled with Ty. Then he said, "And you gotta go to this funeral for Stacy, to show your respect and support. Me too. That girl's been kind to me. I want her to know she can count on me as a friend."

"She doesn't want to see me."

"You don't know that. You ain't no mind reader."

"I haven't even spoke to her since it happened. When I went over there, Ruth didn't invite me in. She told me Stacy didn't want to see anybody."

"There ain't nothing personal in that. She just grieving. She'll talk to you when the time comes, but she needs to see you there. How you think she gon' feel later on, knowing you didn't even come to her husband's funeral?"

Randy cringed at the word "husband" and the prospect of having to attend another funeral, but he realized Buster was right.

Now, as the preacher spoke, Randy surveyed the size of the crowd. He realized that with so few in attendance, every person mattered. And he felt the satisfaction of doing something for Stacy. He believed what Buster had said, that she would talk to him when the time came. There had been a brief recognition before the service began when he and Buster were coming in. She was being led to her seat in front when she saw them. Something like a smile darted across her face. Then, confronted with that closed casket, she crumpled into the pew, her momma and Ruth on one side, Dot and Timmy on the other.

Randy looked at the back of her head and listened to the message. The words gained intensity as Reverend Bledsoe moved toward his main point: the need for assurance of where our souls would spend eternity. He pointed out that this security came from belief in Jesus Christ, followed by a public statement of faith and believer's baptism. Unfortunately, in the case of Ty Ragsdale, there had been no public acknowledgement of a relationship with Christ. Those he left behind could, though, cling to the hope that he had, at some point in his life and inside the privacy of his own heart, accepted Jesus as Lord and Savior. This hope was bolstered by the fact that for a time during his childhood, Ty had attended church. "But oh!" the preacher said, "how much lighter the burden for a minister of the gospel when he can perform the funeral service in the blessed assurance that the deceased had known and loved the Lord, as demonstrated by words, deeds, and church attendance; blessed assurance that our loved one is at this moment with the Lord, worshipping and singing praises, and that soon—in the blink of an eye—we too will be with Him. Oh, brothers and sisters, there is still hope! God is merciful and just. . .."

The preacher had found his cadence, and Randy became rolled up in it. There was something fascinating about these notions of heaven, hell, eternity, and salvation. The words thundered from the man's barrel-shaped chest and whirled through Randy's insides, urging him to action. The preacher stepped out of the pulpit and moved to the front of the center aisle, beside the casket. His old Bible was limp in his hand like a shaken rag doll. "Brothers and sisters," he said softly, "There may be, even now, souls among us who don't have this blessed assurance of where they will spend eternity. Now is the time to change that, to turn this sad occasion into a time of rejoicing."

He called for the musicians to take their places for the hymn of invitation, "Blessed Assurance." Then, speaking in a voice like gentle waves on the sand, he called on the congregation to stand. "As we all sing softly this precious hymn, let God work in your heart. If you are heavily burdened, come forward so that I may pray with you. Today is the day. Your life could be taken at any moment, unexpectedly, as was this young man's. Let God have his way as we sing. . . ."

A lightness inside Randy almost lifted him out of his seat, but his backbone stiffened, and he stayed put. He wondered, though, what it might be like to walk down in front of everyone, if he would know that he was loved and would live forever in heaven. He wondered how Mrs. Stempton and Stacy would respond. Would they hug him? Would they be proud of him? Then the song was over, and it was time to move outside to the grave.

Chapter 52

Buster's rationale for funerals being a time of celebration brought a measure of joy to Ty's final event, but the promise seemed hollow now. For Randy the only thing born after Ty's death had been more disappointment over Stacy's protracted mourning. No new life there. Then, within a few weeks, just as the trees were beginning to produce buds, Mrs. Stempton died.

According to the doctor, she had continued to have "mini strokes" after the first big one, and after a time her damaged brain could no longer manage the body's complex systems. She had been sick with one cold after another throughout the winter, and, after being chilled at the graveside on the day of Ty's funeral, she came down with pneumonia. In the hospital, they loaded her up with antibiotics, but after a few days her kidneys began to fail. Then everything else. The doctor said she seemed to be giving up, that she was ready to go.

During her hospitalization, Randy made frequent visits, but he didn't usually stay long. Reverend Bledsoe and groups from the church were often there, along with Timmy and his friend Dot. Stacy was there too with the baby, but she seemed to reside in a solitary cell guarded by invisible sentries.

When Mrs. Stempton was moved into intensive care, Randy was excluded. The nurse said, "I'm sorry sir. Only immediate family members are allowed in ICU. If you'd like to leave a card or gift, I'll be sure she gets it." He noticed, though, that on more than one occasion Dot had been allowed to go in with Timmy. But it didn't matter because it was over soon enough.

The funeral came and went in a blur, and Aunt Ruth's frustration surfaced immediately afterwards. The mourners were gone, and she and Randy were standing in the Stempton kitchen, once again filled with food brought by friends and church members. The pressures of the funeral had taken their toll, and Ruth seemed frazzled even before they heard the whimpers coming from Stacy's old room.

"Benji's crying," she said, trying to find room in the fridge for a platter of sliced ham. "I thought he was with his mother. Where is Stacy, anyway?" When they stepped across the hall to check on the baby, Randy discovered, along with the fact that his diaper needed changing, a note attached to the crib:

Randy, I know I can count on you. I have to go away for a while and try to get better so I can face things. I'm not strong like you. I hope you will understand. I believe Aunt Ruth will help you. She's a good woman who never had children of her own. He's not much trouble.

Love, Stacy

Randy read the note, then announced, "Stacy's gone away for a while. I guess we'll have to take care of Benji."

"What! Let me see that!" Ruth yanked the note out of his hands, then stood there shaking her head in disbelief. She looked at Randy as if it was his fault. "What in the world has gotten into that girl? How could she just leave her baby? People don't do that. At least not in our family."

"She's been through a lot," Randy said. "She'll probably be back in a day or so. She just needs a little space, a little time away." He found the diapers, bottles, formula, and other baby items at the foot of the crib and attended to the task. Ruth stood there watching, muttering and grumbling.

With Benji in a fresh diaper, they moved back to the kitchen. Ruth said, "This is just too much. There's no way we can take care of this baby. You have to work every day, and I . . . I don't even like kids! I've lived this long without taking care of babies; now I'm too old. I don't have the patience. And besides, I'm tired after all this."

"Well, somebody's got to take care of him, and his mother isn't here." The infant seemed content in Randy's arms, sucking on a pacifier. "I've been around babies before. I know what to do."

"So do I—feed, bathe, rock, change—around the clock attention. But knowing what to do isn't the same as wanting to. There's other things I'd rather do with my life. I've worked hard to get where I am, and I plan to enjoy my retirement."

"It's only for a few days," Randy said, jiggling the infant. "Stacy'll be back soon. If you'll watch him during the day while I'm working, I'll take care of the rest."

Ruth shook her head stubbornly. "Neither of us is equipped for this—you know that as well as I do—and there are people, *agencies*, who are. I think that would be the best thing, to just go ahead and call Family and Children Services now—"

"No! That would be wrong! This baby has a family, a mother and . . . others who love him. Once he's placed in that system . . . well, kids get lost in there, shuffled around from place to place, and Stacy, when she comes home, would have a hard time getting him back. She's trusting me to take care of him. If you won't help, then I'll find another way."

Ruth retaliated. "Just you hold on a minute. I don't see that you have the final say here. I'm this baby's aunt, and you're . . . you're just a family friend, not really part of this. With his father dead and his mother gone, I'm the only real family this child has, and I'll be the one to decide—"

"Not part of this? That's funny, 'cause I was sure I was these last two years—since your brother got killed—every day as I worked— cutting, hauling, and clearing land—as I worked to bring in money to keep things going around here. I could have sworn I was part of it. Stacy thought so too, I guess. That's why she addressed the note to me."

Ruth's head dropped. Then she looked at the baby's face, his eyes half-closed in contentment, chubby cheeks pulling hard at the pacifier. She shook her head. Took in a breath and exhaled. "Well . . . I'm sorry. I shouldn't have said that. I'll do what I can to help, as long as you and I both understand this is a temporary arrangement. You can drop him off in the mornings on your way to work and pick him up each evening. And in the meantime, maybe we can find Stacy and talk some sense into her."

Randy and Ruth conducted investigations into her whereabouts, making phone calls and a trip to Atlanta. Timmy was not much help and seemed to be covering for her. The only information he provided was that she was "with Dot now, and they go out a lot."

Dot had attended Mrs. Stempton's funeral with Timmy. Randy had regarded her closely that day: her compact, athletic build, muscular shoulders, and unisex shag haircut. He also noticed the inordinate amount of attention she was affording Stacy. She had hugged her at the cemetery and run her hands through Stacy's thick hair. Dot. Now Stacy was "with" her. In fact, she'd left with her that very day, turning her back on him, her son, and everything else. Randy convinced himself it was only temporary, that, as the note said, Stacy was trying to get better so she could "face things." After all, she'd been through a lot.

Yes. She would be back soon, and they could make out till then. In a way these new circumstances were exciting. Even though Stacy wasn't there, taking care of their baby made Randy feel more closely connected to her. He felt like a husband and father whose wife was off on a short trip for the sake of her health.

The fact that Ty was listed on the birth certificate as the father was made easier to accept by the way the baby's name had evolved from the original *Benjamin Tyler Ragsdale* to Benji, in honor of the old man. Randy remembered a comment Stacy had made when she'd brought the baby to the home place a few days before her husband's death. She'd said Ty didn't like the name, that he thought it sounded "faggy." But it was beyond his control now. Benji he would be, and he was indeed beautiful—strong with good lungs, clear blue eyes, and a head full of hair the color of pecan hulls.

★★★

A routine established itself. With Bea Stempton gone, Aunt Ruth resumed full-time residence at her house in town. They decided Randy could stay at the home place with the baby, at least until Stacy returned. After all, Benji's crib and something of a nursery were already set up there, and the house, unlike Randy's shack, had a proper kitchen, bathroom, and washer and dryer. In the mornings it was convenient for Randy to drop the baby off at Ruth's on his way to Buster's house. After quitting time, he would swing by and pick Benji up to go back to the farmhouse with him.

Buster took a strong interest in the baby from the beginning. One evening in the early phases of the new arrangement, he insisted that Randy, instead of taking him straight home, drive by Ruth's house first to pick up Benji. "I want Aunt Esther to see my nephew," he said. "Besides, it's on the way."

Inside the truck, Buster held him in his lap, squeezing his little hands and talking baby talk. Benji smiled up at him. Randy said, "I guess I should have known: taking care of babies is another one of your many talents."

Buster grinned. "Well, not really. At least not just any baby, but this little fellow . . . me and this guy's gon' be *tight*."

At his house, Buster was like a child who had picked up a stray puppy. He was out of the truck and carrying Benji up the steps before Randy got the engine switched off. Buster and Benji disappeared through the front door, leaving it open for Randy, who followed several steps behind.

The baby brought a ray of light into the dreary little den. Esther cradled him tight against her bosom. Buster's fingers were in his hair. "Sho' is soft," he said.

Esther replied, "This here's the prettiest little blue-eyed baby I ever did see." Grinning, she looked at Randy. "You a good boy to try and take care of this child by yourself, but it's too big of a job with you working every day. You gon' need some help."

"I'm not really doing it by myself. Stacy's aunt Ruth is keeping him during the day. He's already bathed and everything when I pick him up in the evenings."

"I know, but still. He's got to be fed and put to bed, and then fed again during the night, and you got your own supper to fix. Y'all just come by here each day after work and we'll eat supper together. How about that?"

Buster said, "Yeah, bro. That'll be one less thing you'll have to deal with, and Aunt Esther'll get to hold this child every day. She loves babies more'n anything."

"Well okay, I mean if it's not too much trouble."

"No trouble at all. I got plenty of time in the afternoons now. I come home from work as soon as we get the cafeteria cleaned up, usually around two-thirty. In fact, I could go by on my way and pick up little Benji, have him already here for you. I bet Ruth wouldn't mind having a few extra hours to herself."

"I'm sure that would be okay with Ruth, but—"

"I got plenty of time for this pretty child and to help you out a little, after all you done for us. With Buster and Magdalene grown and Dorcas and Voltaire gone, I need somebody to take care of. Me and this baby, we gon' hit it off just fine. I can tell already."

Chapter 53

Randy, with the help of Buster and two mature ladies with time on their hands, was able to meet Benji's needs while continuing his business arrangement with Mr. Jenkins. Weeks passed, and spring proved to be a pleasant, productive time for them all, especially Benji, who became a fat, gurgling, happy baby, thriving on love, Similac, and pureed vegetables from little glass jars. There was no word from Stacy, even though Randy continued trying to reach her through Timmy. After a while even that tenuous connection failed. One evening in late April when he called to leave word that Benji was gaining weight and eating solid food, he got only a recorded message saying the number had been disconnected.

What the hell could that mean? He kept trying over the next several days but always got the same response. He became a little frantic each evening as he prepared Benji for bedtime, just the two of them there in the Stempton home place. Where could Stacy be? He decided action was necessary and convinced Buster to go to Atlanta with him on the first Saturday in May. Timmy had mentioned some bars and clubs, and Randy had visited Timmy's apartment in Midtown earlier with Ruth, right after Stacy disappeared. Maybe he and Buster could find Timmy or Dot or someone who could help them locate Stacy.

Aunt Esther agreed to keep Benji for the day. As soon as they were underway, rolling out of the Crack, Randy noticed an uncharacteristic wariness in his friend. Buster seemed to be eyeing all the side streets and driveways of his neighborhood, looking for something and hoping not to find it. Randy said, "Man, you seem nervous this morning. What's the matter? You trying to dodge an old girlfriend, or a jealous husband?"

"Naa, you know better than that. I had an unexpected visitor last night. I was looking to see if he might be around this morning."

"Sounds like you're not too crazy about seeing this person again."

"Black man ain't never eager to see the police."

Randy, easing the Galaxie over the railroad crossing two blocks from where Ty was decapitated, gave Buster a puzzled look. "Police?"

"Yeah. Scared the shit out of me, that old white man who claim to be chief, pulling up in my driveway. I watched him get out of the patrol car, real slow, looking around like he expecting somebody to jump out from behind the shrubbery and ambush him."

"What did he want?"

"He's all full of questions about Ty Ragsdale. Seems to think I know something."

The light turned green. Randy pulled out onto the highway in the direction of the interstate ramp. "That's weird. Why would he think that?"

"Somebody been giving him information. He asked me about the little tussle we had in the street that day. Wanted to know why I didn't report it. I tried to explain that there weren't nothing to report, that I decided to let it go. But he just nodded his head and looked at me funny, like he thought my story was real amusing."

"How could he know about that? I thought nobody even saw the accident."

"As far as I know, nobody did see it, except that Tomcat dude. He was there. He know exactly what happened."

"So, he must have told him. Police have probably been talking to him."

"Yeah, and that ain't all. Chief asked me about "bad blood" between me and Ragsdale. He even knows that him and my brother hated each other, that Voltaire busted his nose in a hay field. Funny ain't it?"

"What?"

"When that Strozier dude got killed on the tracks, police hardly even looked at it, said it was an accident. Now, let a white person get killed in the Crack, and they all over the place, talking to old ladies and everything. Before this happened, they hardly even come in, let all kinds of stuff go on, like it was our own problem, but now they everywhere you look."

"Old ladies? They been talking to your aunt too?"

"No, not yet. I was just saying."

"I see what you mean. But maybe it's the fact that the same thing happened that makes it not look like an accident, not so much that Ty's white. I mean if the second victim had been black—"

"Whatever. All I know is I don't like him looking at me the way he was."

Randy reached up to turn the radio on but left it off instead. "Is that all he said? What else did he ask you?"

"I told you, he was full of questions. Your name came up too. Don't be surprised if he shows up at your place next."

"He asked about me?"

"Yeah. He knows I work for you and that you work for the Stemptons. He even asked if I knew Stacy, and. . . ." Buster's voice trailed off as he turned to look out his window.

"What? What about Stacy?"

"He wanted to know what kind of 'relationship' you had with her."

"Shit! You're kidding. How could he know anything about me and Stacy?"

"Don't ask me, man. Like I said, somebody's been giving him information."

"What did you tell him?"

"I had to tell that white man a lie, bro. Told him I didn't know nothing 'bout your personal business."

Randy's mind spun like a whirligig in a storm. When he first read the newspaper article about Ty's death, he'd recognized the name; now it came back to him. Bidwell was the cop who'd questioned him at length nearly two years ago, after he got arrested for prowling around in Stacy's neighborhood. Even though he hadn't had any run-ins with the law since, Randy imagined that the policeman might remember, that he probably still had the entire episode on file in some back room. He remembered also Bidwell's quote in the article: "We're not going to leave a stone unturned in getting to the bottom of this."

Buster said, "Old Bidwell's a real thoughtful man. I could see him thinking while we talked, like he's putting together a big jigsaw puzzle, trying out each piece before he goes to the next one."

"Well, he'll be disappointed if he talks to me. He can't make this piece fit into his picture."

★★★

Getting into Atlanta didn't take long, the interstate being open for most of the way. Navigating inside the city, though, was a different story. There were confusing exits and many lanes of traffic. Randy took a wrong turn and they spent most of the morning trying to get back to Peachtree Street. There were several roads named "Peachtree," and nothing looked familiar. One-way streets kept taking them away from the direction Randy felt was right, and the traffic grew heavier as the morning wore on.

They rode past historic-looking brick storefronts and churches, glittering skyscrapers, downtown jewelry stores and dress shops, then through neighborhoods of small bungalows sitting right against the street, cracked concrete walls holding back their truncated yards. From a distance they could see an elaborate marble building that stood out, even though it was surrounded by larger downtown structures. Its gold dome flashed in the sunlight. Buster explained that it was the Georgia Capitol. On top of the golden dome stood a statue of a woman holding a torch. Railroad tracks, brick warehouses with broken windows, body shops, machine shops, factories and liquor stores, black folks, white folks, bus stops. They passed a cemetery with a red brick wall around it that went on for blocks, tombstones lined up like white dominoes. Buster said, "This city must have more dead folks than live ones."

"Judging by this traffic, I'd say there's quite a few live ones too," Randy said. "It was easy before, when I rode over here with Ruth. His apartment is near Piedmont Park. I remember that."

"Piedmont Park can't be hard to find. It's famous. All we gotta do is ask somebody."

"I guess you're right. And I'm getting hungry anyway. Maybe we can find a place to eat and get directions too."

They were passing through a neighborhood with painted houses and neat yards nearly large enough for a game of catch. They turned onto a main thoroughfare and chanced upon a retail district covering several blocks in each direction. Randy was reminded of the bustling "village" which bordered the college in Aaronville. Here also was the feeling of looking forward rather than the resigned acceptance of decay he'd felt in other parts of the city. The people on the sidewalks were youthful, smiling, and engaged in conversation.

"This area seems kinda nice," Randy said, braking for a stoplight.

"Maybe a little too nice for me. These folks might not like to associate with the colored."

As Buster spoke a striking couple stepped out from a boutique. He was tall and black with a three-inch afro and platform shoes. She was nearly as tall, with the figure of a fashion model and long blond hair draping over her shoulders all the way to her tailbone. She wore a halter top and hip-hugger jeans with studs up the sides. Buster said, "Wow. Maybe these folks do all get along. That brother got him something fine."

"I'll say."

As they rolled past, Buster turned his head, following the couple down the sidewalk. Randy said, "Hey, you're not supposed to be doing that."

"What?"

"Lusting after women, since you're practically a preacher."

"They's a difference between looking and lusting. I'm just enjoying God's creation."

"There seems to be a lot more of it to enjoy, just ahead."

A cluster of people, holding drinks, smoking, and laughing, were gathered on a patio in front of a shop. A half-dozen of them were young females, trim and sexy in tight jeans, revealing tops, and high platform shoes. The diverse group also contained guys and older couples. As they drew closer, Randy noticed a voluptuous girl with rich brown skin and a short, jet-black afro. She wore chunky beads and earrings of orange, brown, and green that matched the bold pattern of her short, woven vest. She projected pride in her African heritage and elegance in her bearing. Randy looked at Buster and nodded. "Check that out."

"Wow! God's creation is good, ain't it?"

"Amen, Brother."

The small group had gathered for a sidewalk show in front of an art gallery. Buster said, "Man, they all looking at cartoon pictures of naked women with cat faces. Pointy boobs and straight legs, like a little kid drew 'em. Sure is lots of strange stuff to see in the city."

"I'll say. They'll probably spend big bucks for those ugly things and hang them in their fancy apartments. Maybe I should buy some paintings for the shack. Add a little class to the place."

"Only thing that would add class to that place is a gallon of kerosene and a match, or maybe a bulldozer. It's about time you started thinking beyond that old shack. I feel a change coming, drifting in on these fine spring breezes."

"Yeah, me too. It's been weird, staying in the big house with Benji. I like it in a way. I mean, it's a lot more comfortable, but it's not home. I feel like an intruder there."

"Gets sorta creepy, don't it? That big old house with all of Mr. and Mrs. Stempton's stuff still in there."

"Yeah. But I try not to think about it."

"I mean, all them little items—the things they touched and used every day—are still there, waiting. But they both gone and ain't coming back."

"Like I said, I try not to think about it."

"That place ain't haunted, is it?"

"No, man, you know I don't believe in that stuff. It's just a house, a place for sleeping and taking care of Benji. Besides, I'm too busy and tired in the evenings to even notice whether it's haunted or not. Don't have time for it."

"I know. You a busy man awright. That's something else that needs changing. It's time for you to get some kind of life for yourself. You're young and single, remember? Ought to be having some fun."

"Single? I don't really feel single. I still don't know—"

"You are single, whether you feel like it or not. A single man with a baby on his hands. Hey, that place looks interesting."

Randy looked ahead, then flipped the blinker when he read the sign: Miss Anita's Southern Café, *best fried chicken in Atlanta*. "That'll work," he said.

Chapter 54

The restaurant, a converted folk Victorian-style house with a wraparound porch, was a busy place. With the lot in back full, the nearest parking spot was across the street, behind a record shop. As they were walking over, Buster said, "Must really be the best chicken in Atlanta, all these folks here eating. Hope it don't cost too much."

"Don't worry about it. Lunch is on me today. I got us covered."

"Oh yeah, I keep forgetting about you being such a successful businessman and all."

Randy smiled. "That's right. I've been so successful I'm thinking about spreading out, 'diversifying,' as they say."

"Really? Gon' get you another truck and helper?"

"Naa, that's too much work. I'm thinking about getting into another line altogether, like buying an old house and going into the restaurant business. These folks seem to have the right idea."

"I know that's right. And you can get Aunt Esther to cook for you."

"That's it! Then we could say, 'Best fried chicken in Prathersville.'"

When they reached the restaurant, they found people relaxing, eating, and talking on the porch. Inside, the place was filled with the odors of southern-fried food, loud voices, busy waitresses, and the clinking of silverware. They joined others in the lobby to wait for a table. Soon they were having a conversation with a smartly dressed middle-age couple.

When Randy asked for directions, the man smiled patiently and lowered his head to look through the top portion of his bifocals. "Well, that's easy enough. Piedmont Park's just a few blocks over. You'll want to take Virginia Avenue out here. It'll run you almost into the park. It's a pretty big area."

***

As they left Miss Anita's, Buster said, "I can't believe that's the best fried chicken in Atlanta. It was pretty good, but Aunt Esther's got it beat by a mile."

Randy agreed, "Yep. That's all the more reason to start that restaurant. But I think we ought to put it in Aaronville instead of Prathersville. Near the college. I believe those people would appreciate good home cooking."

"Yeah, and some real soul food. We'd have 'em lined up for blocks, waiting to get in. We should do it."

Something about the day—the mild temperature and being in the city—made thinking about the future exciting. Planning a business venture with Buster was fun, even though Randy doubted they would ever open a restaurant together. But they might do something. There were other possibilities, lots of them. Buster's words echoed in his mind: *I feel a change coming on, drifting in on these fine spring breezes,* and Randy felt it too.

Soon they were in the Piedmont Park area. Randy turned on Thirteenth street and recognized the old two-story brick building with a terra cotta roof. "That's it. It's on the second floor." They parked and went up the dusty stairs only to find Timmy's apartment vacated, empty except for a dark-haired man walking around on metal stilts, repairing the water-damaged ceiling. He didn't seem happy about being interrupted in his work. When Randy asked if he knew where the guys were who used to live there, he answered, "Hell no. You expect me to keep up with all the queers in Atlanta?"

"What we gon' do, bro?" Buster asked on their way back to the car. "How we gon' find Stacy now?"

Randy tried to display optimism. "I don't know, but I think she's probably here, right under our noses." He waved his hand in a circle. "This area is where they all hang out. We'll cruise around, talk to people, see what we can find. They couldn't have just vanished."

They covered the perimeter of the park, then drove through the winding roads inside the gates where there was mostly foot traffic: people walking dogs, gay and straight couples, and hippie families with small children. There were grassy areas, picnic tables, pavilions, tennis courts, and a lake with ducks. Couples were spread out on blankets eating or simply lolling about, rubbing each other with lotion.

"I been hearing about Piedmont Park all my life," Buster said, "but I didn't know it was this kind of place."

"What kind?"

"You know, where folks just go around flaunting their unrighteousness. I ain't never seen nothing like it."

"Yep," Randy said. "It's something else, all right. I'm gonna park the car so we can walk around and get a better look."

Outside of the Ford, the sun warmed their faces. Without a cloud in the sky, the day had become an early harbinger of summer's heat. Braless hippie girls wore midriff halters and hip-hugging cut-offs with a fringe of frayed denim encircling their thighs at the crotch. The guys wore cut-offs and tee shirts or no shirts at all. They were running and laughing, throwing and catching frisbees over the gentle green slopes.

It almost felt right to Randy, this entire scene, as if he belonged. But there was also something wrong with it: the fun, laughter, and spontaneity seemed too easy to be trusted. This much enjoyment must come with a steep price. What would be the cost later for the pleasures of today? He looked at Buster and found the expression of a playful child trying to figure out some new game.

Then his attention was diverted by a wave of young people rushing with purpose over a grassy rise. They were excited, shouting things like, "Yeah, man—at the bandstand, this way," and "Come on, hurry, so we can get in front!" The crowd swelled, and Randy and Buster were caught up in it.

Buster asked, "What's going on?"

Randy tapped a guy on the shoulder, wearing patched jeans, sandals, and long, straight hair parted in the exact center of his head. "Where's everybody going?" Randy asked.

"It's a happening, man. Free concert. Great band, 'The Unisex Love Cycle.' They're setting up now. Hurry, and you can get close to the stage."

"Come on," Randy said to Buster. "Timmy likes to go to concerts. Maybe we'll find them there."

They managed to stay near the front of the crowd as people thronged around the bandstand. At first there wasn't much to see, except a slender guy riding a unicycle around the stage. He wore only black platform shoes, a black Speedo, and a large gold medallion around his neck. His bright red hair was cut in a long shag. He rode about, maneuvering around the equipment in an expert manner, but he didn't speak or engage the audience.

"That's it," someone said. "The love cycle. They'll be out any minute now."

The unicycle guy continued his antics alone for several more minutes. It didn't matter; the crowd seemed content. The smell of marijuana was strong. Randy smoked a Winston as he scanned the throng for Stacy.

Buster said, "This is some pretty weird shit, bro. I don't understand what this is about."

"I don't think it's about anything. Like the guy said, it's a 'happening.'"

"Don't look like much of a happening to me, some naked fool on a unicycle, and a bunch of fools getting high on weed."

"Be patient. I think this is gonna get interesting pretty soon."

The rider dismounted, letting the unicycle fall to the stage floor. He leaned against one of the speaker cabinets, looking out into the audience and nodding his head.

People began to respond in sporadic bursts of clapping and chanting, then in a rising chorus with everyone finding the same tempo. The chant consisted of four clapped beats and three distinct syllables repeated over and over: *u–ni–sex, u–ni–sex, u–ni–sex. . . .* The syllables rode on the first three claps; the fourth clap provided an exclamation mark. The unicycle rider seemed to approve, with a nod of the head timed to each clap. The chanting and clapping grew louder.

Another figure appeared onstage, taking his place behind the drum kit. He also wore a shag haircut, and a psychedelic, high-collared shirt, opened to expose his chest. He kept his arms crossed as he pedaled the bass drum, in time with the second and fourth claps. This small offering seemed to excite the crowd, and the chanting grew louder. Randy and Buster watched, glancing at each other, shrugging their shoulders.

The crowd's enthusiasm began to wane after a few minutes. The decline in volume seemed to be the cue for additional movement on stage. Two hefty men in jeans and tee shirts began carrying on furniture. They set up on one side a wooden dinette table with two matching chairs. Dishes were placed on the table, along with a jug of milk and box of cereal. On the other side they placed a small sofa and TV set. The television was arranged facing the audience and turned on. It displayed nothing but snowy static.

A girl came out dressed in a plaid miniskirt, saddle oxfords, bobby socks, and blue sweater. Her thick blond hair flowed over her shoulders. She sat at the table and began to eat a bowl of cereal. A quiet tension surged through the crowd. Someone shouted, "Far out!" and people began to clap. The unisex chant started up again but died when the men reappeared on stage carrying large panels of plexiglass mounted in wooden frames with sturdy bases. Painted across the top of one clear sheet, in swirly psychedelic letters, was the prefix *Uni*. The word *Sex* was painted in a similar fashion on the other. Both panels were carefully moved into place between the audience and the flickering TV.

The audience grew quiet once again. The guy on Randy's right mumbled, "Holy shit! This is gonna be weird." Randy answered to no one in particular, "Already is."

The girl continued to eat her cereal, seemingly oblivious to the conservatively dressed, overweight man who was moving a stand and microphone to the front of the sofa. When he had it arranged just so, he sat down and began speaking slowly and deliberately into the mic. His voice boomed from the speakers with a reverb effect. He read from a heavy book about the need for adequate ventilation when spraying pesticides.

As he read and the girl ate, another person appeared in a space suit, or it could have been a deep-sea diver's suit. He nonchalantly pulled a chain saw from a box and cranked it up. He revved it shrilly eight or ten times before he began to move zombie-like toward the girl eating cereal. The man on the sofa was reciting the sexual and reproductive consequences of continued exposure to DDT.

The girl continued to eat her cereal until the space-suit chain saw man was nearly on her with the snarling saw. Then she jumped up and frantically began undressing. She ripped off her skirt and top and threw them into the crowd, along with the wig that had been her beautiful blond hair. Underneath the wig the hair was bright red and shaggy. Underneath her skirt she wore tight, black panties—no, a Speedo. Underneath her top was a bony, hairy chest and gold medallion: the unicycle guy! He leaped away from the table just before the chain saw bit into it. The guy in the space suit, with excessive revving, cut the table and chair up into kindling. He faced the rapt audience for a moment, brandishing the saw; then lots of things started happening all at once.

The unicycle guy strapped on a guitar and moved to center stage. He used his instrument to produce screeching airplane sounds, explosions, and machine gun bursts, while chainsaw wielder, having abandoned his zombie movement, was high-stepping about, revving the saw. They faced each other to play an angry, high-pitched duet. The guitar player's arm spun like a propeller, and space-suit man, head thrown back in ecstasy, made phallic thrusts with the screaming saw as the drummer pounded out a rapid, staccato rhythm.

The earsplitting racket was even louder, Randy thought, than the pulpwood yard. The band reached a crescendo with the drummer working the cymbals to hair-raising effect. The chainsaw dropped into idle as the guitar eased into a mournful, tremolo-laden melody. During this interlude of relieved tension, the crowd cheered and clapped. Randy, without thinking, clapped also, but stopped when he remembered himself and Buster beside him.

The conservative guy stood up from the sofa and started swaying to the music. He loosened his tie, then removed it. As the melody grew punchier and louder, becoming an electronic march, he jerked his shirt out of his trousers and ripped it open. He began prancing about, chanting with deep monotony: "Love—love is one. We are united in love—love is sex. There is one love and one sex. Unisex. We are united in sex-love fusion over the planet, becoming one skin, one stretched tight condom over the world of unisex—Toxins are bound up in our embrace as we purge ourselves in the one love. . .."

The guy with the chain saw was marching toward the television behind the plexiglass panels. The music began to build in tempo and volume, and the recitation became faster, the words slurring together in a higher pitch. The crowd was clapping, stomping, and bouncing up and down in time with the music.

Randy understood now the purpose of the clear panels. The space suit protected the destroyer while the plexiglass protected the audience. The guitar screamed an elaborate run of electronically embellished high notes; the saw screamed destruction as it ate into the plastic cabinet. When it reached glass and metal, the sound was agonizing: a series of pops and explosions, smoke and sparks, glass flying all over the saw wielder and the stage floor. The entire television and the table it rested on were soon nothing but a pile of debris.

People in the audience began to shout, "Cut it up, cut it up. . .." Chain Saw Man, encouraged, turned his attention to the sofa, cutting through it, sending bits of stuffing and upholstery into the air. The music abruptly stopped while he continued to cut the sofa into several pieces. The drummer stood and froze as if at attention. The guy with the saw methodically demolished the sofa, then disappeared off stage.

Several guys appeared with brooms and began to move the debris into a pile, sweeping the smaller stuff into a circle and throwing the larger pieces on top. The chain saw was placed near the front of the stage, while the drummer stood at attention. Everything was quiet. The audience was hushed, passions temporarily sated. But the afterglow faded quickly. Was that all? What were they gonna do next? Randy stared at the scene of destruction and at the drummer, who remained rigidly standing, staring into space.

He glanced at Buster and saw on his face the former look of bemused puzzlement transformed into the expression of a worried parent, and there was pain there also, emanating from behind his golden eyes. This spectacle was hurting Buster, disappointing him in some profound way. Randy thought that maybe they should leave—at least move away from the stage—and resume their search back through the crowd. It was hard for him, though, to turn away. How long would the drummer stand there like that? What would they do next? Finally, he turned to his friend, "Let's go, man. We need to look for Stacy, and besides, I've had about enough of this."

They moved deeper into the crowd, searching, but not leaving until "The Unisex Love Cycle" had played their last crashing note. Randy continued to follow the performance as he and Buster weaved their way through the audience. After their initial chain-saw antics, the band took up more conventional instruments. The guy in the Speedo, continuing to play guitar, was joined by another guitarist, the space suit guy, still wearing the baggy silver pants minus the helmet and gloves. One of the furniture movers picked up a bass guitar, the other one played keyboard, and the conservatively dressed orator continued as lead vocalist, singing and hitting raspy, piercing high notes.

The drummer came out of his trance to establish complex, shifting rhythms. At times, the band members each seemed to be playing to a different beat or melody, but then the parts would find one another, and a breathtaking harmony would be achieved. When the songs finally ended, they did so in a sustained crescendo involving thrilling runs from the instruments, interlaced like musical vines of ivy. The word *arabesque* came to Randy's mind, although he couldn't quite remember what it meant. He didn't know much about music, but he recognized the complexity of the compositions and the skill of the musicians. He began to appreciate what they were trying to do: push the limits, reach, discover.

He didn't find Stacy that day but discovered instead an emerging awe over the flood of life's possibilities—so many ways of being, the consideration of which made his small existence seem less restrictive. Here was an ebullient flow of people inventing new ways to have *fun*. Stacy had plunged herself into this river to escape sorrow and had been washed away. Another life, the promise of variety and rich experiences: they had talked about these things before. Now he understood her feelings and knew he could communicate with her about them. His belief that he could provide what she sought and needed was confirmed. If he could only find her.

Chapter 55

Satisfied that she wasn't at Piedmont Park, Randy and Buster got back in the car and began searching up and down Peachtree Street, the section from Tenth to Fourteenth known as "The Strip." They stopped at a Krystal restaurant and ate about ten tiny cheeseburgers each, with fries and milkshakes. The placed seemed dirty, occupied by a variety of street people: strung-out hippies, drug dealers, winos. In the restroom, a derelict-looking man with lint in his hair was sitting on the floor by the sink, his back against the wall. There was no privacy panel at the urinal, and Randy felt the man watching him as he tried to pee. His body tightened despite his efforts, and he was forced to zip up and leave in frustration, trying not to look at the man on the floor with half-shut eyes and slack, wet lips.

As he drove, Randy took in as much as he could. They passed head shops, boutiques, and record stores intermingled with older businesses. The traffic was heavy. From the curb, hawkers peddled tabloid papers titled *The Great Speckled Bird*. Others were selling pornographic magazines. As the sun began to set, people filled the sidewalks. Randy wondered where they were all coming from.

Buster said, "I ain't never seen so many lost souls in one place. I ought to talk to Brother Moncrief, see if he want to start a ministry over here. He been preaching about outreach a lot lately."

"That's a good idea. Maybe you could be a street preacher, get you a sign that says, 'Repent! The end is near.'"

"Very funny. The Lord *is* coming back one day soon. Somebody needs to tell these folks so they can get ready."

"Maybe they are ready. A lot of hippies are Jesus freaks. Didn't you know that?"

"Yeah, I heard of 'em. But I ain't seeing much Jesus in these freaks. You still think we gon' find Stacy over here in the middle of all this?"

"Yeah, I do. She's got to be here somewhere, with Timmy and his friends."

They found a place to park near Fourteenth Street behind a business with a garish purple front, whose sign read, "Strangelove Adult Book Store: Peep Shows, Toys, Magazines." Randy had seen a couple of guys go inside who seemed gay. Timmy could be in there, or maybe someone would know him. It couldn't hurt to ask.

Buster walked to the front of the shop with him but declined to go inside. "I'll just wait out here, bro. Try not to be too long."

Randy pushed the door open and stepped into a dense atmosphere, pulsating with heavy rock music. He blinked and looked around. The walls and shelves presented rows of lurid images of every imaginable sex act: men with women, men with men and boys, women with women, even pictures of sex with dogs and donkeys. Dildos, rubber vaginas, suction pumps, and inflatable dolls were hanging everywhere. Fascination and revulsion flip-flapped inside him. A little paddle wheel of memories began to spin: that last foster home—Jack, naked, watching from his chair, then in the bed with them. Fear. Desire to please. Pleasure. Shame. Desire in the shape of Stacy; he remembered her eyes, breasts, and the tastes of her body. Then he envisioned her yielding to Dot, pushing herself against her, as she had strained against him.

He blinked the images away and focused on a flimsy partition across the room that supported a bank of closely spaced doors. He watched as they randomly opened and closed, men going in and out, singly and in pairs. He didn't recognize anyone.

He uneasily approached the counter. The pale, fleshy young man behind it, regarding Randy closely, tossed back his oily hair and leaned forward on his stool. He blinked his eyes against the smoke of an incense burner. "Is it true what they say about guys with big feet?"

"Big feet?"

"Yeah, and long fingers too. I just happened to notice."

"I don't know anything about that. I'm looking for somebody."

"Aren't we all?"

"Yeah, sure, but I'm talking about a specific person. Timmy Stempton's his name. About my size, sandy hair cut in a shag, brown eyes."

"The name's not familiar, and the description . . . well, sounds like about half the boys who come in here. You got a picture?"

"No. No picture."

"You're not a cop, are you?"

"No. Like I said, just looking for somebody."

The guy shrugged and blinked his wet eyes. "Wish I could help. Maybe you'd like to hang for a while, check out the peeps." He motioned with his head toward the wall of doors.

Smoke from the incense was curling around the young man's face, wafting through the heavy air to stick in Randy's nostrils. The fragrance was sickeningly sweet, a berry smell with a hint of cloves. It was all suddenly too much, nauseating. "That's okay. Thanks."

The outside air, though filled with exhaust fumes, was refreshing. Finding his friend there waiting provided additional relief.

Buster looked Randy in the face, studied him. "Man, you got a different kind of smell about you, coming out of that place. What did they do in there, spray you with something?"

"Incense. They were burning incense. Come on, let's get away from here."

"Suits me. I done had three guys come up and try to sell me some dope."

"Really? What did you say to them?"

"Told them Jesus loved them and I'd be praying for them."

"Far out."

The Strip held many nooks teeming with young people, and Randy kept picturing Stacy in their midst. The streets, sidewalks, and storefronts vibrated with music, laughter, and honking car horns. They walked up and down Peachtree, then branched out to cover the adjacent blocks, checking out the shops, diners, and joints. They saw hippies, gay couples, prostitutes, and dope dealers in every direction, but no sign of Stacy, Timmy, or Dot.

After circling around to Peachtree and Tenth, their feet were tired. They stopped in an area where several clubs were bustling. People were gathering around a place off the corner that looked as if it could have been a drugstore twenty or thirty years before, a brick building

with a fake frieze and cornice and little concrete keystones over the
blacked-out windows. An adjacent lot had been incorporated,
providing space for a patio with tables. Young guys were clustered in
groups drinking bottled beer, and there was a stream of people
moving in and out of the main doorway under a sign which read, in
fat, backwards-leaning letters, "Plumb Pudding." Randy suggested
they go in to look around and get something to drink.

"I don't know, bro," Buster said, "That don't look like my kind of
place."

"It's not mine either, but I'm thirsty, and it does look like Timmy's
kind of place."

Inside the music was loud, and guys were packing themselves onto
a small dance floor, gyrating and thrusting their pelvises against each
other. They seemed carefully dressed and practiced in their moves.
Some sat at the bar, leaning in close to converse over the music.
Randy and Buster edged through the crowd and found barstools at
the end farthest from the dance floor. Randy ordered a Pabst Blue
Ribbon, Buster a Seven-Up.

The bartender was a muscular guy with a blond crew cut. He
wore a white shirt with short sleeves rolled up over his biceps. He
made his work a performance as he opened bottles and mixed drinks,
swaying and dancing to the pounding rhythm. Obviously proud of
his body, he seemed to relish attention. He projected, in that over-
sexed atmosphere, the attitude that he was the focal point of "Plumb
Pudding," itself the center of the universe.

He held his arms up, a bottle in each hand—moving them just
enough to suggest maracas being shaken—accenting every other beat
with his shoulders and torso as he brought Randy and Buster their
drinks. He set the bottles in front of them, looked at Buster, then
Randy. "I love this song. It's Bowie's latest. What do you think?"

Randy pretended to analyze the music, nodding his head
rhythmically as he listened:

Rebel Rebel, you've torn your dress
Rebel Rebel, your face is a mess
Rebel Rebel, how could they know?

Hot tramp, I love you so!

"Yeah. That's good. Nice beat, easy to dance to."

"Oh, so you like to dance?" the bartender asked.

"No, not really. It just seems like it would be easy to dance to, judging by the crowd on the floor."

"What about your friend? He looks like a dancer."

Buster shook his head. "Naw, man. I ain't no dancer, especially with other guys."

The bartender smiled and shrugged his shoulders. Then he put his hands on the bar and leaned toward them. "Listen. You boys should relax and have some fun. I mean, you must be interested. Something brought you in here. And with your looks—you both must work out a lot—you could get plenty of action." He bit his lower lip, started swaying. His eyelids drooped languidly as he slipped back into the music.

"*You've got your mother in a whirl cause she's*

Not sure if you're a boy or a girl. . .."

He turned to move away, but Randy stopped him. "Wait. Actually, we're looking for somebody. Maybe you could help."

He shrugged his shoulders again. "We're all looking, Sweetie."

"No. You don't understand. It's important that we find this person. His name's Timmy Stempton."

"Unh-unh. It doesn't work that way. People who come in here wanna be found, but not by their straight relatives. I'm afraid I don't know him." He turned his back to them and, finding the beat, danced his way to the other end of the bar.

Randy said, "Well shit."

Buster said, "I don't think I can stand it in here much longer, bro. I'm gon' have to go back outside. You coming or what?"

On their way out of Plumb Pudding and midtown Atlanta, Randy persisted in looking for Stacy, but to no avail. The trip had accomplished nothing of their original purpose; he had succeeded only in disappointing his friend, darkening his ordinarily cheerful outlook. And there was Benji to consider. It was late, time to get back to the real world. He was, as Buster had pointed out, "a single man with a baby on his hands," a fact he would have to accept, at least for now.

Chapter 56

After the Atlanta trip, the routine of work and caring for Benji continued. The arrangement with Esther and Ruth could go on indefinitely, but Randy, with Buster's prediction of change reverberating, knew that it wouldn't. This premonition did little to prepare him for what he faced one evening a week or so later when he turned into the Stempton driveway with the baby. Two cars were in front of the house. One was from the sheriff's department; the other was a Prathersville police car. He parked the Galaxie anxiously, scooped Benji up out of the seat and got out.

Two uniformed men were rocking on the porch. He recognized one of them immediately: Chief Bidwell. His uniform was blue and gray. The other man's was brown.

Chief Bidwell threw up his hand and waved from the porch as Randy approached. "Hello there, young man—Randy isn't it? Don't be alarmed. We're just here to talk to Stacy Ragsdale—you know—about her husband."

Randy greeted them with a nod and mounted the steps. The men both stood. Chief Bidwell continued: "This here's Sheriff Tucker. We're both still investigating that case—really a shame what happened to that young man—and we had a few questions for his widow. We couldn't find her in town. We were told she was staying out here now."

Randy stood on the porch nodding, holding Benji.

"Is that right?" Chief Bidwell asked. "Does Stacy live here now? I mean that seems kinda strange, just her and the baby in this big house with her momma gone. Poor Mrs. Stempton, she was a sweet lady."

"Well, yes. Stacy does live here, but she's not here right now."

Sheriff Tucker, a lanky man except for a paunch below his belt buckle, reached over to rub his finger against Benji's cheek. "Fine looking baby. He belong to you?"

Randy felt their suspicion spreading like spilled black ink, then a prickly sensation at the back of his neck. "Uh, no. Not my baby."

The men looked at him, waiting for an explanation. He took a breath. "Belongs to Stacy. She's visiting her brother in Atlanta. I'm keeping him for her till she gets back."

Chief Bidwell made a throat-clearing sound. "I see. Y'all must be pretty close for her to trust you with her baby . . . the son of her dead husband."

"I'd say so," Sheriff Tucker said. "I wonder how close they were before Ragsdale's death."

Bidwell smiled, looked at Randy. "And since she's not here and you are, you must be expecting her any minute. Guess we can stick around till she gets here."

The prickly sensation at his neck turned hot. "I don't know what you're suggesting, but—yes—Stacy and I are close friends. I've been close to this whole family. They took me in, gave me a job and a place to live."

In a patient, kind voice Bidwell said, "Then Mr. Stempton gets cut in two shortly after. And now, here you are driving his Ford, and, it would appear, living in the big house with his recently widowed daughter."

"I'm not living with Stacy. I told you she wasn't here."

"And when do you expect her?"

Randy looked to the sky, shook his head in frustration. "Let me explain. . . .." He unfolded the whole story, trying to maintain his composure: Stacy's inability to handle the pain and stress of recent events, Timmy and Dot in Atlanta, and how he was standing in temporarily until Stacy could get better.

"So," Bidwell said, "you don't know where she is—the mother of this child—or when she's coming back, or even if she's coming back at all." He glanced at the sheriff, who shook his head to underscore how unfortunate the situation was.

"She'll be back. I know it." Both men looked at Benji, who was starting to squirm and make raspberry noises. Randy gently jiggled the baby. "It's time for his feeding."

Sheriff Tucker said, "Babies sure do need lots of attention. Must be hard on you. How long did you say she's been gone, the mother?"

Randy shrugged. "Not that long, really."

Bidwell asked, "How long, son, has this been going on? A few days, a week, several weeks?"

Randy sighed, "About eight weeks, I guess. Since the day of her mother's funeral. But I don't take care of him by myself. Stacy's aunt Ruth and Buster's aunt Esther help out during the day."

"Buster?" Sheriff Tucker said. "Ain't he the boy that works for you?"

"Yes. We work together. But he's not a boy."

The sheriff made a squint-eyed, puckery face. "Do tell."

Chief Bidwell looked thoughtful for a moment, then released a measured flow of words: "This is not a good situation. Very unusual for a young single man to take such an interest in a *friend's* baby. You don't have to do this, you know. We have systems in place—"

"It's the least I can do, really. Like I said, this family's been good to me. And we don't need a system, we've got a system. Look at him. He's fine."

The thoughtful look returned to Bidwell's face, a squinting of the deep-set gray eyes with a tiny twitch underneath. He studied Randy for a moment, then shifted his attention to Benji. "I see. Well, we shouldn't keep you any longer from tending to this child. I imagine you're both ready for your supper. But we'd still like to talk to Stacy. You'll let her know, won't you? When, you see her, I mean. And we expect you to be available also. It wouldn't be a good idea to do any traveling right now, while this investigation's going on. That wouldn't look good at all, would it? I mean with things the way they are."

"No sir. I mean, I guess not. I don't plan on going anywhere."

At that moment he was telling the truth, but plans of leaving began to form as soon as the men drove away with their suspicions and information he had not wanted them to have. He imagined the official ways they had of dealing with these cases and tried to guess how long it would be before he got a visit from the Department of Family and Children Services. And their investigation now had a focus. Randy had had a taste of Prathersville justice, and he had read in the newspapers many stories about arrests and convictions. The unkempt faces of the felons in the pictures always carried the same expression—dazed and sullen—like prisoners of war who had been beaten and held in solitary confinement. The legal system here, if it could be called that, was a blunt instrument.

He plodded through the evening routine, trying to devise an escape, but Benji kept distracting him with his gurgling noises and repetitive "baa-baa" sounds. He had recently begun flapping his arms about and reaching for things. And some of his expressions . . . hilarious, and beautiful. His personality was changing daily, taking shape. He could sit up now, although Randy was always there for support, and in the tub he'd developed the habit of splashing and giggling. This time of day was exhausting, but also the time Randy loved best.

He got Benji settled in his crib and fixed himself a sandwich. A stack of mail was there on the table. Tired of daily disappointment, he'd gradually stopped hoping for a letter from Stacy. There was never anything for him, so he'd let the envelopes and cards accumulate. As he ate, he absently began sorting, making one pile for trash and another for items that required either payment or Aunt Ruth's attention. About a third of the way into the stack he was jarred by the sight of his name, handwritten on an envelope.

He pushed his milk glass and sandwich aside and ripped it open, a letter from Stacy:

Hello Randy,

I know I have disappointed you, but I can't help it. I had to take some time to make sense of all that has happened. Getting away has been good for me, and I appreciate you giving me the opportunity to find myself. I understand now what I need to be happy. Dot has been a great support through these hard times. We love each other, and we are ready now to give Benji a home. He needs his mother, and he is all I need to make my life complete. We are coming soon to take him off your hands. You've carried our burdens long enough. Now you need to make a life for yourself.

We also need to settle Momma's affairs. Timmy and I decided to have an auction. We both know that we could never live there again. I know this isn't what you wanted, but believe me, you are better off this way. There is someone out there for you. Your perfect mate. Just keep looking.

I don't know exactly what day we are coming because of Timmy's and Dot's work schedules. Probably the next week or so.

Thanks for everything,
Stacy

He set the letter down and took a bite of his sandwich. The stale bread and rubbery bologna felt huge in his mouth. He washed it down with a swig of milk and waited for the emotional wallop. Not what he expected, really, the way it made him feel: somehow lighter, like walking the first few unburdened steps after carrying a heavy log uphill then dropping it onto the truck. Fact was he didn't feel anything new, just a touch of relief and his usual nagging sense that there were things he needed to do.

He picked up the telephone and dialed. As soon as Buster answered, Randy said, "Pack your bags, man, we're leaving."

"Leaving? What you talkin' about?"

"Me, you, and Benji. It's time to get out of here."

"Hold on bro! Leaving? I ain't been studying about that."

"Well you should be. Just what is it that's keeping you here? The lack of opportunity? Not being trusted? Looked down on by whites and blacks alike? Face it, Prathersville and Aaron County aren't exactly the land of opportunity for somebody like you."

Chapter 57

As the windshield wipers flapped ineffectually back and forth, Randy realized they probably hadn't been replaced since before the old man's death nearly two years ago, and here he was driving the Galaxie through the heaviest rain he'd seen in months. He squinted through the downpour and chuckled, thinking of what the old man would have called this rain—a "gully washer," or a "turd floater." He'd also heard Buster use those expressions. People in the South sure had a peculiar way of talking. He guessed he might miss that, but at least he had Buster with him, asleep in the backseat, as an ongoing reminder.

Benji had also fallen asleep, thank God. Randy had driven for miles listening to his whimpering, sniveling, and crying as Buster cooed and cajoled, trying to get him pacified. Now there was quiet inside the car—well, not really. The rain produced a constant roar along with the tires' slicing through water, and booming thunder vibrated the windows. But these sounds didn't distract thinking the way human sounds did. He was enjoying relative quiet for the first time since they'd rolled out over five hours ago. Concentration was required to see through the rain and keep the car on the road, but a part of his mind managed to engage the larger circumstances.

He was driving toward Pittsburgh, but they probably wouldn't stay there. That would be the first place they'd look, if they came looking. He somehow doubted they would. He knew Stacy, and even though she was a different person now from the waitress he'd first met and fallen for at the Billy Goat Bar, she still had some sense of justice along with respect for his judgment. She would just need a little time to think things over. Randy was convinced of the rightness of his actions and he knew that, with time, she would be too.

Sure, he was breaking the law, but he wasn't taking anything that wasn't rightfully his. The car was free and clear; Mrs. Stempton had signed the title over to him. And the baby was his too. He and Stacy both knew it, even though the fact had not been openly acknowledged.

Lord knows two years was long enough to stay in Aaron County. During this entire time Randy had been in the process of leaving or planning to leave, but before the opportunity could be realized, some hope, need, or tragedy—like the paw of an invisible cat toying with its prey—had always slapped him back into that old shack. Over and over he'd found himself turning his weary body atop that sagging mattress or sitting alone in the battered recliner, trying to read or watch TV, thinking about what he would do with his life. Now, by God, he was finally doing it—something. Moving. At least he'd made a start.

But he couldn't move very fast in this rain. The plan had been to drive all night and arrive in Pittsburgh the next morning, but now he thought they'd better stop somewhere. He was already tired from the strain of it all: convincing Buster to come, Benji's fussiness, and trying to see through panels of rain, swaying fitfully before the headlight beams.

The wipers' rhythmic slapping of the water back and forth stirred his mind, evoking memories that played out against the curtains of rain. He remembered Stacy in the hospital after Benji's birth, someone who would make a good mother, he'd thought. But a person could only take so much. It was understandable that she broke the way she did, and Randy thought no less of her. Something might still be worked out someday, but Benji's needs were immediate.

He needed what all kids need, something Randy never had: a permanent, real father. His son would not be absorbed by the children's welfare system, nor would he be raised fatherless in midtown Atlanta. He was determined to fill that role, and Buster— he should start calling him "Uncle Buster"—would also be a permanent part of Benji's life. That's as far as he could go with it, and he didn't try to imagine the details of their future. What he had was enough, a foundation to build on. His eyes burned and he was tired of thinking and driving, but he had never felt stronger.

★★★

Buster had slept for only a few minutes. He dozed off soon after Benji got settled but was awakened when he felt the car swerve. It was okay. Randy was keeping it between the lines, but it was a bad night. Buster tracked Randy's driving while he remained still in the dark of the big backseat, not wanting to wake Benji. The quiet was nice, and he, like his friend, had lots on his mind.

He thought about the way Randy had put things when he asked him what there was about Prathersville that made him want to stay. Randy had said that Aaron County had nothing for somebody like him, to which he'd answered, "I know that's right." Yes, he knew what Randy had meant: that he was a "high yellow," a breed that, while accepted in other parts of the country, was shunned in the deep South. Yet Randy had treated him as an equal from their first meeting, given him work and responsibility, and become his friend, proving that a better life was possible.

Buster's concerns about leaving had been easily addressed. He knew Aunt Esther would be fine without him, that she had a job and church activities to keep her busy and no one to take care of but herself. He had a little money saved up, and he believed Randy's promise that they'd be able to find work easily up north. No one in Prathersville depended on him now. But he knew that Randy and Benji would have a tough time on their own. They would need physical help and someone to pray for them. God had lined things up this way to provide a clear choice. The decision had been easy, easier than he had let on. Buster chuckled to himself. It had been fun making Randy work for it, listening to him build his case for leaving while he pretended to resist.

His musings were interrupted when he felt the tires running onto the shoulder. Randy, suddenly roused, overreacted. Buster cried out. They were fishtailing from one side of the rain-soaked highway to the other. He reached over and restrained Benji, keeping him in the seat. The skidding seemed to go on for a long time; then finally, miraculously, their path was corrected. The baby had not been disturbed, but Buster and Randy were both wide awake.

Randy spoke first, meekly: "Sorry 'bout that. Everybody okay back there?"

"Yeah man, we good. Benji still 'sleep. We should be too. Let's find us a place to stay for the night. I believe we done gone far enough for one day."

★★★

Morning found them in the Mountain View Inn just outside Roanoke, Virginia, sharing a queen-size bed. Randy woke first, eager to get back on the road, out of the South, and farther away from Chief Bidwell and Sheriff Tucker. Something internal had been set into motion with last night's departure from the Stempton place and was still moving in spite of the brief rest. He would've slept for a few more minutes, but his eyes wouldn't stay shut. He longed to see Pittsburgh again—where he'd always lived before getting himself entangled—now that he'd become someone who could control things, someone who owned a car and had two thousand dollars in his wallet.

And he had something else now: a family, "roots," although he wasn't putting them down but pulling them up instead. If plants can be transplanted, Randy concluded, people can be too. He rolled out of bed, went to the bathroom, and splashed his face.

"Hey Buster," he called out, "let's go, man. Rise and shine. Time to hit the road."

Buster mumbled and pulled a pillow over his head. Randy lifted the sleeping Benji and cradled him against his shoulder. The little fists curled. He pushed and squirmed, lifted his head, opened his eyes and blinked. He made quirpy, complaining noises. "I know," Randy said. "You're hungry and wet. Let's take care of it."

Randy bathed Benji in the motel tub, which seemed sanitary compared to the old chipped and stained tub at the Stempton home. Benji was happy, as usual, in the water, fascinated with the new surroundings and colors, the gold and blue of the tiles, the toilet in matching gold, the shiny chrome frame of the mirror, and the fluorescent light flickering from the low ceiling. He pulled at the

431

plastic shower curtain with its red and green pictures of frolicking dolphins. He splashed and made yelping noises: yeow, yeow, yeow.

After getting him fitted in a disposable diaper and a onesie outfit, Randy cast about for a feeding method. He had formula and bottles with little disposable plastic liners. He could use the chest-of-drawers to set things up. He placed Benji, squirming and burbling, back on the bed, on his stomach next to Buster, who pulled the pillow away from his head and turned to face the infant. He smiled and said, "Hey, Buddy, what you doing?"

Randy said, "We're done in the bathroom if you want to get in there."

"Might as well take a shower, since they ain't no chance of sleeping with you two stirring about."

Soon everyone was dressed and ready. Benji gurgled and cooed contentedly; Buster looked at Randy with a hopeful gleam in his eyes, but concerns gathered on the surface of their easy morning banter. "Just where are we, anyway?" Buster asked. "I ain't never seen so many mountains."

"Look here," Randy said, spreading a road map across the bed. "Roanoke, Virginia, and right up here's where we're going. Pittsburgh. Almost due north, on the other side of all these mountains."

"But you ain't planning on staying there, right? 'Cause Stacy, and the Sheriff, and Chief Bidwell, and everybody else know you from there. When they come looking, that'll be the first place."

"Oh, I dunno. It may seem so obvious that they wouldn't look there, thinking we'd know better. Besides, I doubt they're that interested in finding us anyway. It's about all Bidwell and Tucker can do to take care of their own business. And Stacy . . . well, she's being pulled in a lot of different directions. Probably won't be able to muster the energy to come looking. And there's one more thing." Randy lifted and started folding the map.

Buster, sitting on the edge of the bed, asked, "Oh yeah? What's that?"

"Pittsburgh's a big city. I think we'll be able to get lost there, for a few days at least, until we can figure out something else."

Buster stood up and scratched his head. He paced the couple of steps to the chest of drawers, then turned back. There was a tightness in his forehead and the corners of his mouth. Randy said, "What?"

"One thing still bothering me, bro. I'll spell it for you: G-B-I. Them boys are investigating Ragsdale's death too, and they don't play. Bidwell sic 'em on us, it'll be over. And leaving like we did gonna seem mighty suspicious. Just look at us. We ain't that hard to spot— me, you, and a baby in that old Ford that can be traced right back to you."

Randy smiled. "You're exactly right. That's why we're gonna do a little shopping this morning."

"Shopping? For what?"

"A different car. Driving that old Ford's getting kinda depressing anyway. Lots of car lots in a town this size. Let's get out of here and see what we can find."

Chapter 58

Randy had first gotten the idea of seeing Virginia's Natural Bridge, "One of the Seven Natural Wonders of the World," from a travel brochure as he was checking out of the motel. Since Route Eleven carried them north out of town and crossed the Natural Bridge, he and Buster agreed it would be a shame to miss it. "How much further?" Buster wanted to know, after they'd gotten past the Roanoke suburbs.

Randy replied, "The way this baby runs, we'll be there in a few minutes." They were riding now in a 1969 metallic green Chevelle Malibu, a good-looking two-door hardtop powered by a 350 V8. The dual exhaust pipes exuded a throaty bass rumble as they rolled northward along the ancient valley trail, flanked by mountains on either side.

Buster sat in the front, on the green vinyl bench seat, holding Benji in his lap. "Yep. She runs good awright. Sounds good too. Five-hundred dollars boot, though, I don't know 'bout that. I pray we don't run out of money before we find work and a place to stay."

"We'll be all right. I'm a successful businessman, remember?"

"That was before you left. I don't know what you are now."

"I'm not sure either, but the billfold's still pretty fat."

The road carried them through green pastures, small towns and farming communities. Soon they were there. Billboards along the way had promised a spectacular sight "just ahead," but they didn't realize how close they were to Natural Bridge until they were literally on top of it, and then the view was blocked by a high fence on the roadsides put there for that purpose. Signs pointed them to parking lots, trails, and the gift shop.

"What a rip-off," Randy said when he realized they would have to pay admission to actually see anything.

"Yeah," Buster agreed, "six bucks to see something that's supposed to be natural don't seem natural to me. But then again, Natural Man's always greedy."

"Well, this natural man's gonna keep his six dollars. We could buy a good meal for the same money."

"Suits me. I'm satisfied with just riding over the thing. At least I can say I been there."

The highway carried them northward through the Shenandoah Valley. They turned left onto Route 250 and began their climb over the highest peaks they'd yet encountered into West Virginia. The Chevelle proved hardy against the forces of gravity and inertia, but Randy began to tire. He pressed on through the switchbacks, curves, and steep slopes. Finally, he agreed to let Buster take the wheel just south of Philippi, where the mountains smoothed out to rolling hills. When he pulled onto the shoulder, they took a moment to stretch.

Benji began to squirm and whimper as Randy cradled him against his shoulder. It was past his feeding time. "Might as well fix his bottle while we're stopped."

Buster replied, "Yeah, it's past lunchtime for all of us. I'll pull in the next little store we come to and get us a cold drink and some Beanee Weenees, Moon Pies, or something."

"Good idea. Maybe a snack will tide us over till we get to the next town. Here, hold him while I fix his bottle."

Randy's hands shook as he dug around in the trunk for the formula and bottle components. Tearing off the plastic liner and inserting it properly was difficult. He methodically attended to the details, pressing forward against mounting aggravation over not having a flat surface to rest things on. Finally, he was ready. He climbed into the back seat with Benji and the bottle, reclining in the corner as much as possible, positioning Benji against his stomach. Buster settled himself into the driver's seat and they were off.

It took Buster a few miles to get the feel of the car. The Chevelle reminded him of his momma's Impala, but lighter, nimbler, and faster. The eagerness of it comforted him, even though he had to work to keep it under the speed limit. It was a good feeling, being at the helm, controlling much more power than was needed. The rolling green countryside took his mind off his hunger, and the wind blowing through the open windows refreshed as it spoke promises of the new life to come.

He tried the radio, turning the knob across the AM dial. Nothing but static and country music. He clicked it off. The wind and the engine's humming were music enough. He called out, "Hey guys, how y'all doing back there?" No answer. He found Randy's face in the rearview and saw that his eyes were closed. Benji was also asleep, lying cuddled against him. Buster smiled, pleased that his friend trusted him to keep them safe, and with the Lord's help he would do just that: drive as far as he could, safely, while they rested.

Buster enjoyed peaceful thoughts until he glanced up to check the rearview. An approaching car—a big car, coming fast—shattered his reverie. Then lights. Flashing lights that made him shake with adrenalin. Oh shit, the man! he thought. This is it. The car was very close. He could see the patrolmen's faces. Nothing to do but pull over. He flipped the blinker and slowed, hands trembling on the wheel. To his amazement, the patrol car sped past. He stopped the Chevelle on the shoulder and watched the ominous vehicle as it pulled away into the distance, lights still whirling. Blood rushing in his ears, he took a deep breath and began a prayer of thanksgiving: "Oh Lord, oh God, thank you Jesus—"

"What? What's happening?" Randy, not quite awake, mumbled from the backseat.

"Uh, nothing, bro. It's all good. I just thought I saw something. But it's gone now. I think it was a deer, but it's done run off." He pulled the car back onto the road. "Everything's okay. You can go back to sleep."

Randy mumbled again. Buster looked in the mirror and saw that his friend had settled back, still cradling Benji. He eased the Chevelle back up to speed, praying for protection.

They passed Earl's Crossroads Grocery at a little community called Bethel, but Buster decided not to stop. He didn't want to disturb his sleeping passengers. Soon they were entering the outskirts of the next town. Paved roads branched off the main highway, and houses appeared in clusters. He saw fire hydrants and streetlights mounted high on poles. He was interested in this town, Philippi. The name brought to mind the biblical city and one of his favorite passages, Philippians 4:6-7. Buster had memorized these verses that encouraged believers not to worry "but in everything by prayer and supplication with thanksgiving let your requests be made known unto God. And the peace of God, which passeth all understanding, shall keep your hearts and minds through Christ Jesus."

Buster often felt this kind of peace. He was prayed up, and he had a thankful heart before the Lord. He was being led out of bondage into a new promised land, but he wouldn't be afraid like the Israelites. He would march into that valley ready to face the giants, in whatever form they may take. He needed to set a strong example for Randy and Benji. They were his people and he, like Moses, was their leader. Randy was the boss in the things of this world, but not in matters of the spirit.

Inside the city limits, Buster began looking for places to eat. He sure was hungry, but he hated to stop while they were asleep. He decided to keep going, straight on through Philippi. They could eat later, and Randy would be pleased with how much progress they'd made, but then he saw something that changed his mind.

The road ahead disappeared into a long, covered bridge, unlike anything Buster had ever seen. It was wooden, with two arched openings, serving both lanes of the highway, a relic from the horse and buggy days that now carried modern cars and trucks over an expanse of flowing water. There was a small park with a historic marker on the banks of the river next to the bridge. The cars in front had slowed before entering the structure, allowing Buster to get a sense of it before going through. He knew Randy would want to see this. There were parking spaces provided and even a walkway with a hand railing down one outside wall of the bridge.

"Randy," Buster called out, "wake up, man. You gotta see this!"

Buster's voice and the changed sound of the car rolling into the parking lot startled Randy awake. His eyes popped open and he sat up quickly, holding Benji against him. "What? Where are we? What's going on?"

Buster pointed with a nod of his head. "The bridge, man. Check it out."

Randy turned to see, then froze for several seconds. He finally answered, "We gotta get a closer look at this."

The historic marker informed them that the bridge was built in 1852 and was the only remaining "double-barreled" construction of its type, as well as the only covered bridge still in use as part of a federal highway. It was considered a masterpiece, constructed of yellow poplar and utilizing "the famous Burr Arch Truss." Buster was also amazed to learn that "no iron was used in the construction, other than the bolts that held it together," and that the bridge had played a role in the first land battle of the Civil War.

"Man, just think about it," he said, "troops from the North and South was fighting over this bridge, right in this very spot, a hundred and . . . something years ago."

"Yep," Randy answered. "and the North came out on top. You remember what they were fighting over, don't you?"

"Yeah. I learned a few things in school. That's one of the lessons I couldn't forget even if I wanted to."

★★★

They drove into Pittsburgh late that evening, exhausted from a hectic day of changing scenery and circumstances. Randy longed to see more, to revisit the places of his youth and to share them with Buster. But additional sightseeing would have to wait. They stayed the night at the first budget motel they came to, an Econo Travel, with its smiling mascot pictured on the sign, a girl in a scotch plaid skirt and tam. It was all they needed and nothing more: a cheap place to crash.

They rolled out early the next morning with a lengthy agenda. Coming in from the suburbs on the Washington Road, Randy was flooded with memories. He wanted Buster to understand his past. He couldn't decide whether to take the Liberty Tunnel into downtown or go through South Side and over the hills for the view of the rivers and famous skyline.

There was also that house in the Allentown neighborhood. He'd tried to push those thoughts away as they were making the trip up, but now that they were in these old surrounds, images persistent and unprincipled as carnival hawkers displaced the memories he would have liked to entertain. A bloodsucking thing from his past was being resuscitated.

It was a clear, sunny morning. Maybe, if the smog wasn't too bad, there would be other things to see and think about. They could park and ride the incline down the mountain. But the tunnel was also amazing. They'd have to see that. And he wanted to go through all the old neighborhoods and to check out the orphanage where he'd spent his childhood, St. Jude Home for Boys, even though it wasn't an orphanage anymore. He realized he was talking fast, trying to say too much. Buster sat in the front seat holding Benji on his lap, cooing and chatting baby talk. He looked and nodded as Randy pointed out the various sights.

Benji had been fussy since leaving the motel. He seemed tired of the car, of moving and of being held, yet he insisted on being held. Randy hoped he would settle down and be a good baby today, as he had been for all of the trip so far.

The morning passed quickly. Most of it was spent winding through the streets of South Side, back and forth over Carson and up and down Mount Washington. They rode through Allentown, but Randy drove past the street that would have carried them to the house where he'd lived with Jack and Emma. This thing from his past had now risen, fully formed—memories solid as a wall. The house, near the corner of Climax Street and Vincent, had looked like all the others: square, two-story, German-built with a stubby front porch and squat brick columns. About eight feet of lawn in front surrounded by a broken fence, a little more yard in back, wider than the other lots and reaching all the way to the hedges at the edge of the alley. He had lived there for a year.

When he drove past the street for the third time, Buster said, "What is it about this place, man? Something here's got a hold on you."

"Naa. Just trying to get my bearings. Things seem different from when I was last here."

"Some things be changing, some things stay the same as time rolls on. And sometimes it's us that's got to do the changing."

"Is that in the Bible?"

"Naw, man. Just some shit I made up."

"That figures. Sounds good, though. You should write that one down."

They drove through Allentown to the top of Mount Washington and parked the car, then rode the Mon Incline down to the station and back up several times. At first Benji cried the whole way, but he recovered enough at the bottom for them to try going up. He soon became fascinated with the process and began making his yelping, gurgling noises to the delight of the few tourists riding with them.

Back in the car, Benji started whimpering. Randy knew he was hungry. His schedule had gotten all messed up, and he and Buster hadn't eaten either. Randy's favorite sandwich shop, Reuben's Corner, was only a couple of miles away, near the Birmingham Bridge. Benji could take his bottle there and maybe a little cereal. Randy would order for himself and Buster the greatest sandwich in the world along with curly fries and cheese. He knew Buster had never had food like this.

But his friend so far had not shared Randy's enthusiasm with Pittsburgh. Randy knew Buster sensed something wasn't right. The tightness had returned to his brow and the corners of his mouth, and he didn't have much to say about the places Randy pointed out, although he was impressed with the Victorian houses and the old shops and storefronts of South Side. In the light Saturday morning traffic, Buster commented on the variety of people who occupied the area.

"That's right," Randy explained. "All kinds of people settled here to work in the steel mills: Germans, Russians, and Italians, and lots of

Blacks migrated up from the South. People blend more here. It's not so divided—so black and white—like in Prathersville."

They got a corner table at the sandwich shop, which was beginning to fill. Randy recognized the guy behind the counter, Bernie, but didn't speak, didn't think he'd remember him. He'd eaten lunch here only occasionally during his last year of high school, before reporting to his part-time job on the loading docks, back when he was just a kid. The girl who took their order didn't look familiar.

To Randy's frustration, neither Buster nor Benji enjoyed their lunch. He had to admit the densely packed Reuben, heavy with an almost rancid taste, wasn't as good as he remembered. Buster, after working through half of his, set it down to focus on the fries.

"You don't like it, do you?" Randy asked, jostling Benji on his knee and trying to get him to take a spoonful of cereal.

"It ain't like nothing I ever had before. I guess it takes some getting used to. I like these fries, though. I wonder how they get 'em to wind up like that."

"Just cut them in a spiral. Simple. Come on, we might as well go."

"Where we going now?"

"You haven't seen downtown. We need to cross the river."

As they traveled west on Carson an understanding settled. He felt it on his skin and breathed it in with the smog. This was not the place; they couldn't stay here for even a few days. The past was the problem. Randy's rotten past was not Buster's, even though his had been rotten too. They and the baby needed someplace new. But there was one more thing he wanted Buster to see, one of Pittsburgh's many bridges.

They crossed the Monongahela on the Smithfield Bridge, then continued north for a few blocks to Fifth Avenue. The closeness of the buildings, the intersections, and the frequent stops had a calming effect on Benji, who sat wide-eyed in Buster's lap sucking his pacifier. Buster's eyes widened also as they approached the Allegheny Courthouse and Jail, a massive medieval-looking structure built of stone. They parked and walked around the city block that the fortress, with its domed spires and arched openings, occupied. Then they were face to face with it: a covered stone archway that spanned the street connecting two parts of the castle. "This is it," Randy said. "It's called the Bridge of Sighs."

Buster was speechless. He handed the baby to Randy so that he could take it in. "Lordy mercy," he finally said. "I ain't never seen such. And to think we didn't even have to pay to see it, like at that bridge they call "natural" back in Virginia. How old is this thing and how come they give it such a sad name?"

"It's not really that old—a hundred and something years—they just made it to look like it's from the Middle Ages. Modeled after one in Italy, I think. Prisoners have to walk over it, on their way from the courthouse to the jail."

"I hope and pray we won't never have to make that kind of walk."

They stood looking for a few minutes, then passed under it. They looked at the other side, and up and down the streets. "Well," Randy said, "I guess that's it."

"Where we going now?"

"Not sure, but I'm ready to leave Pittsburgh—after one more stop, that is."

"Amen, Brother. We need to leave the past behind. This place seem kinda dirty to me anyhow. But where else can we go?"

"Lots of places. Pennsylvania's a big state. I haven't seen most of it myself."

Buster's face brightened. "What about Philadelphia?"

"Never been, but I've always wanted to go."

"How far?"

"Hmm. It's a long way, but we could probably be there by a little after dark."

"Let's do it, bro. I've always wanted to see that Liberty Bell. Here, give him back to me. I'll hold him for a while."

Benji was craning his head, trying to look at things, sucking on his pacifier.

Before passing him over, Randy lifted the baby and held his face close to his own. "What do you think, Buddy? You want to go see the Liberty Bell?"

Benji, suddenly amused, pushed the pacifier out of his mouth and smiled.

Randy chuckled. "Well then, I guess it's unanimous. Let's go."

"What about that 'one more stop'? You goin' back through that neighborhood, ain't you? That place you keep circling by."

"Yep."

"What you gon' do? Nothing foolish, I hope."

"I'm not sure, just got a feeling—I guess you'd call it belief—that I'll know what to do when I get there."

The End

About the Author

Ron Yates has been learning to write for most of his life. He produced good essays in high school, but his adolescent energies were largely devoted to drag racing, drinking beer, and trying to stay out of trouble.

Although encouraged by his English teachers to pursue higher education, Yates, after graduating high school in lackluster fashion, spent time languishing in factory jobs. An aching back, the remembered encouragement of former teachers, and the urgings of caring friends prompted him to explore other options.

His enduring love of reading and nascent knack for writing guided him to a degree in English and a career teaching high school. He went on to earn an MA in English from the University of West Georgia and, years later, an MFA in creative writing from Queens University of Charlotte.

Yates lives near Mt. Cheaha, on the shore of beautiful Lake Wedowee in Alabama. He has published stories in a variety of journals including *Wilderness House Literary Review, Hemingway Shorts, KYSO Flash, Still: the Journal, The Writing Disorder, The Oddville Press,* and *Prime Number Magazine.* He has a son and daughter and is married to his sweetheart, Carol Yates.

About the Press

Unsolicited Press is a small press in Portland, Oregon. The team produces outstanding fiction, creative nonfiction, and poetry.

Learn more at www.unsolicitedpress.com.